The Advent‹

ANDE**RS**

Gregory Mackay

ALLEN&UNWIN
SYDNEY • MELBOURNE • AUCKLAND • LONDON

For the inquisitive

Australian Government

Anders and the Comet *was assisted by the Australia Council for the Arts Children's Picture Book Illustrators' initiative, managed by the Australian Society of Authors.*

First published by Allen & Unwin in 2019

Anders and the Comet originally published in black-and-white by Allen & Unwin in 2015
Anders and the Volcano originally published in black-and-white by Allen & Unwin in 2016

Allen & Unwin
83 Alexander Street
Crows Nest NSW 2065
Australia
Phone: (61 2) 8425 0100
Email: info@allenandunwin.com
Web: www.allenandunwin.com

 A catalogue record for this
book is available from the
NATIONAL
LIBRARY National Library of Australia
OF AUSTRALIA

ISBN 978 1 76063 207 6

For teaching resources, explore www.allenandunwin.com/resources/for-teachers

Colouring by the author and Charlotte Watson
Illustration technique: drawn by hand, with digital colour
Cover and text design by Gregory Mackay and Sandra Nobes
Set in 13 pt Anders Gothic, created by Gregory Mackay from his handwriting
Printed in China by C&C Offset Printing Co., Ltd.

1 3 5 7 9 10 8 6 4 2

anderscomics.com

MIX
Paper from
responsible sources
FSC® C008047

Contents

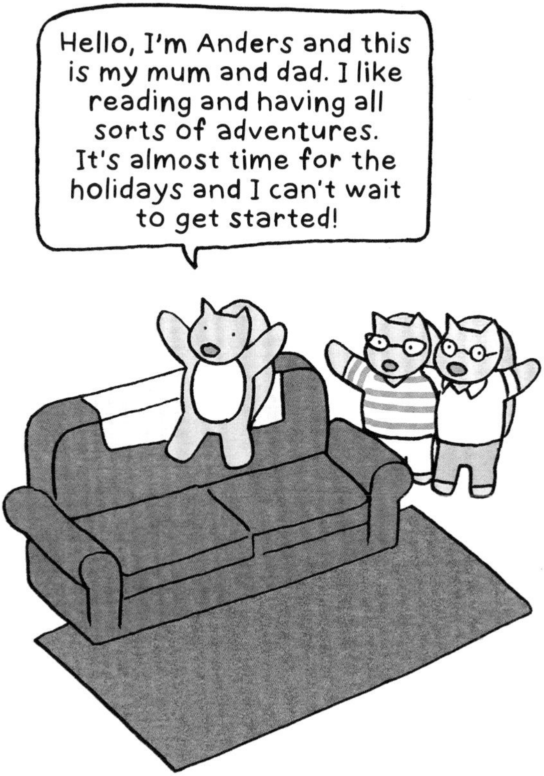
Hello, I'm Anders and this is my mum and dad. I like reading and having all sorts of adventures. It's almost time for the holidays and I can't wait to get started!

ANDERS

and the

COMET

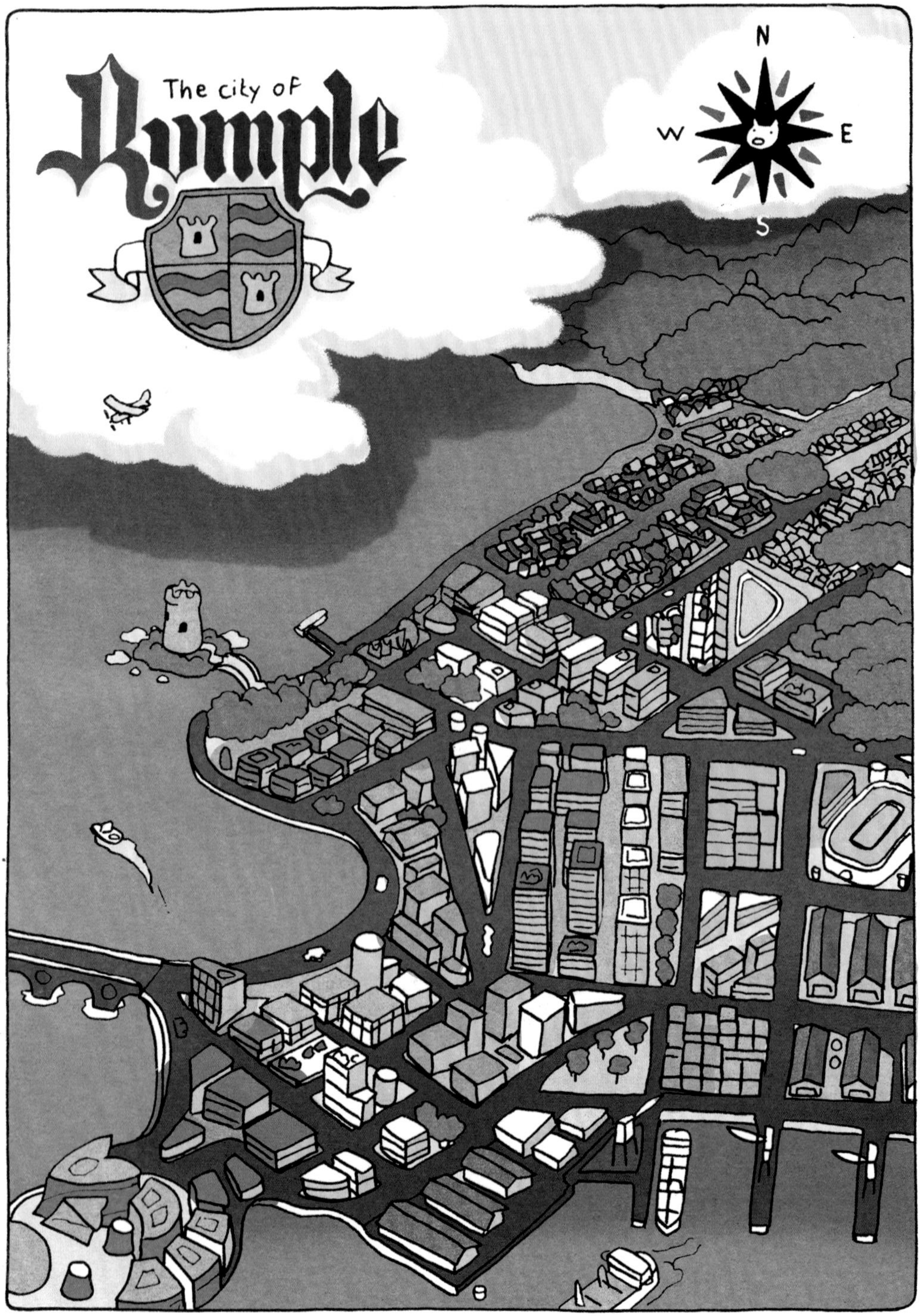
The city of
Rumple
N
W
E
S

Chapter 1

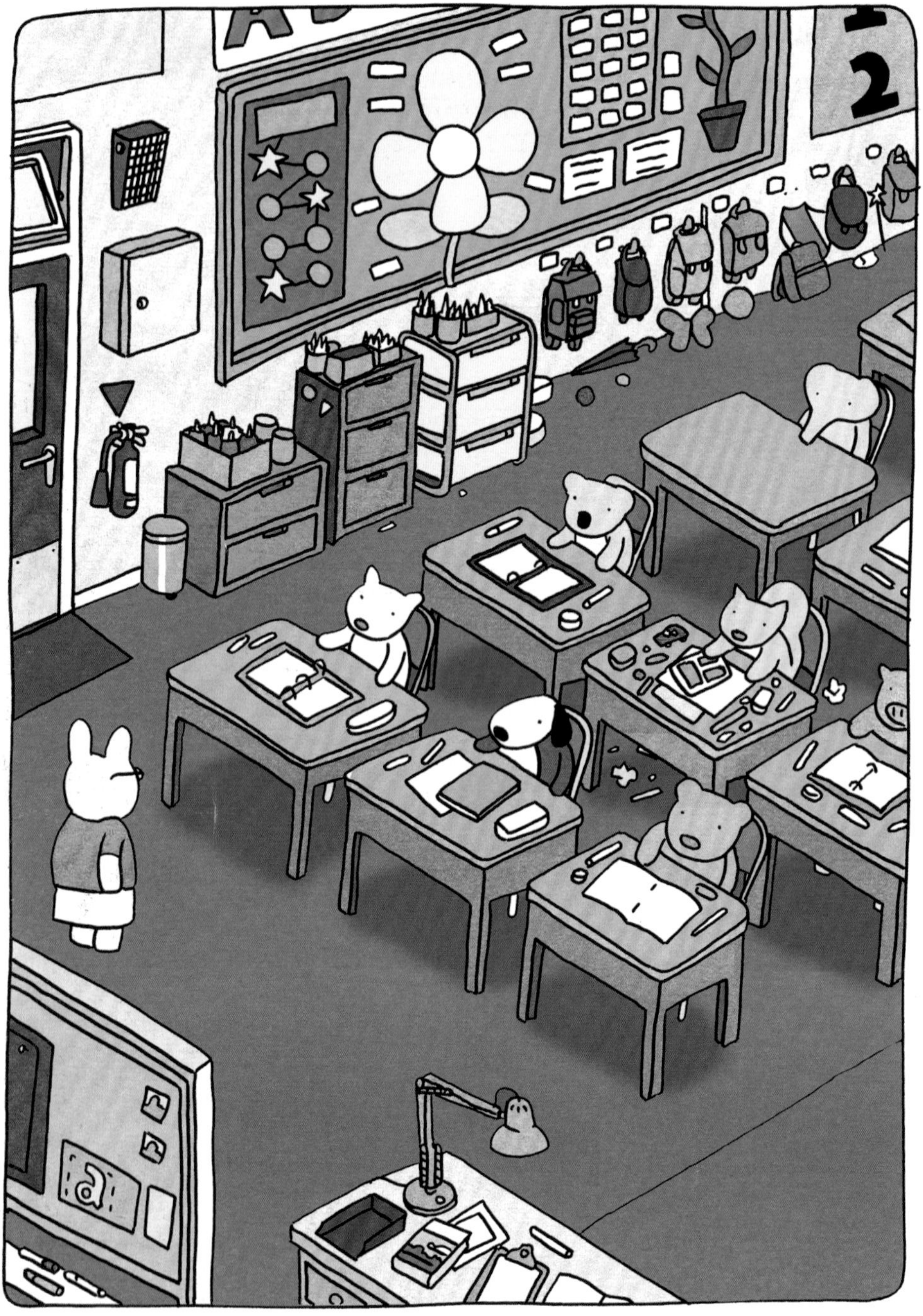

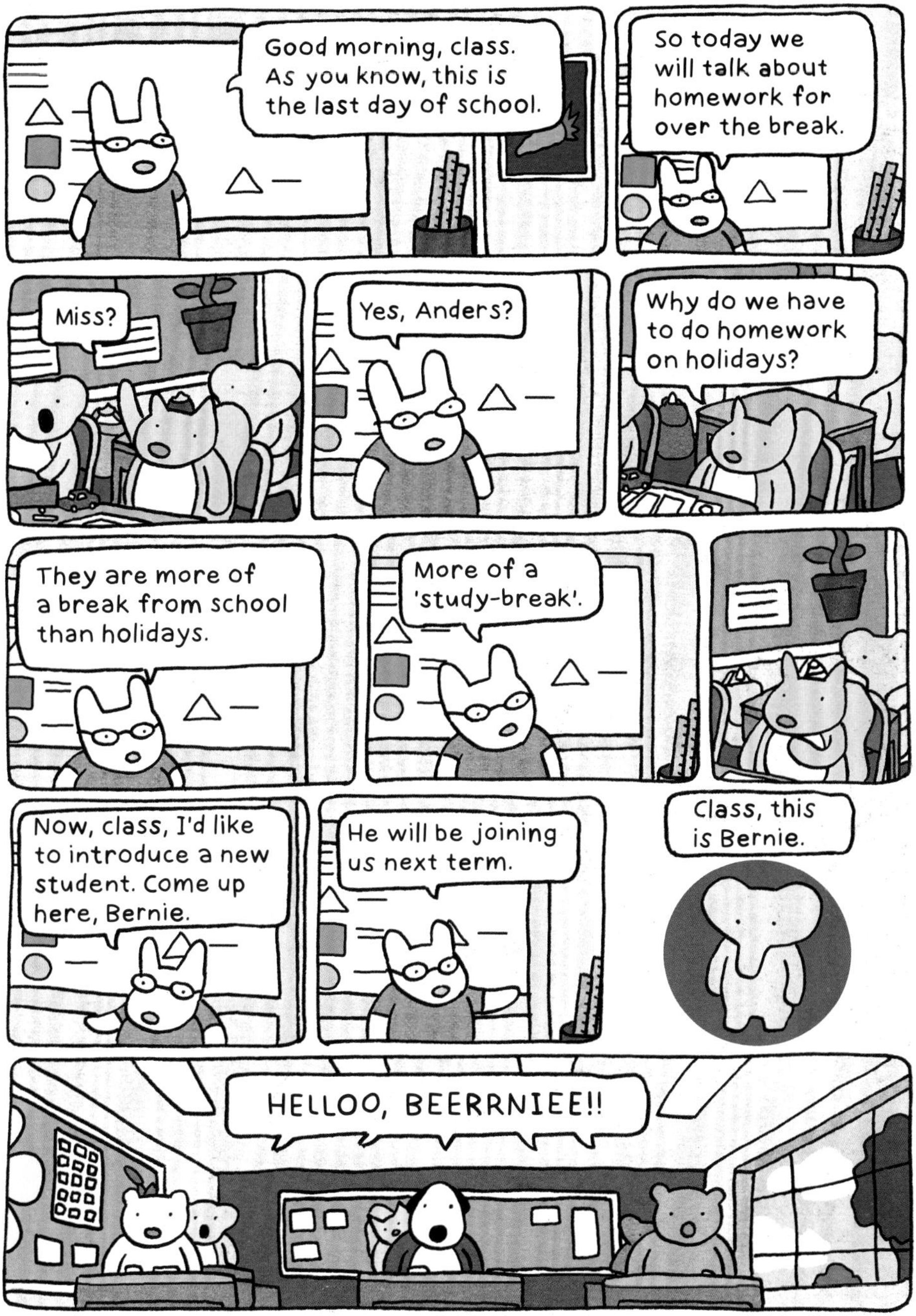

Good morning, class. As you know, this is the last day of school.
So today we will talk about homework for over the break.
Miss?
Yes, Anders?
Why do we have to do homework on holidays?
They are more of a break from school than holidays.
More of a 'study-break'.
Now, class, I'd like to introduce a new student. Come up here, Bernie.
He will be joining us next term.
Class, this is Bernie.
HELLOO, BEERRNIEE!!

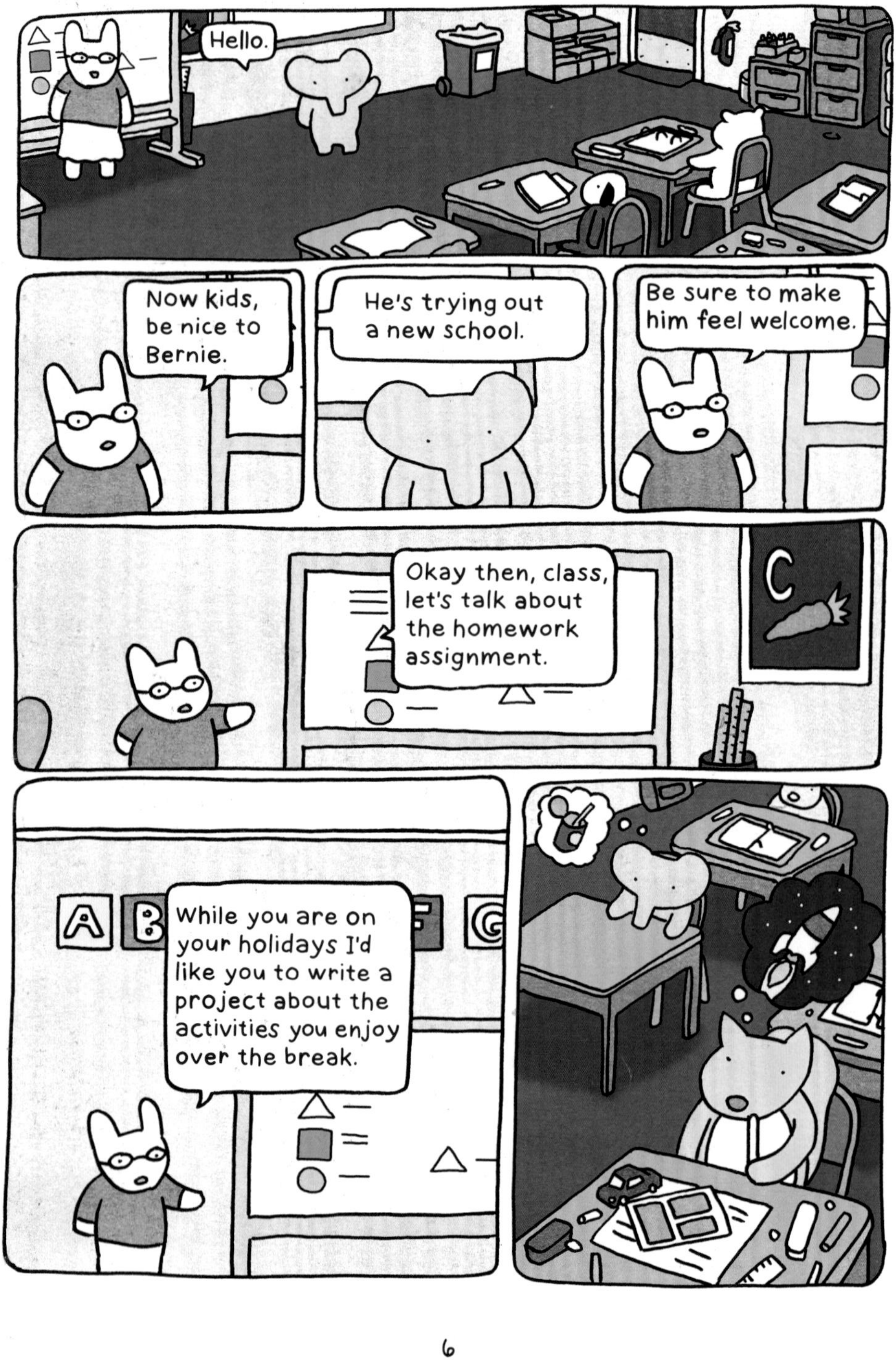
Hello.
Now kids, be nice to Bernie.
He's trying out a new school.
Be sure to make him feel welcome.
C
Okay then, class, let's talk about the homework assignment.
A
B
G
While you are on your holidays I'd like you to write a project about the activities you enjoy over the break.

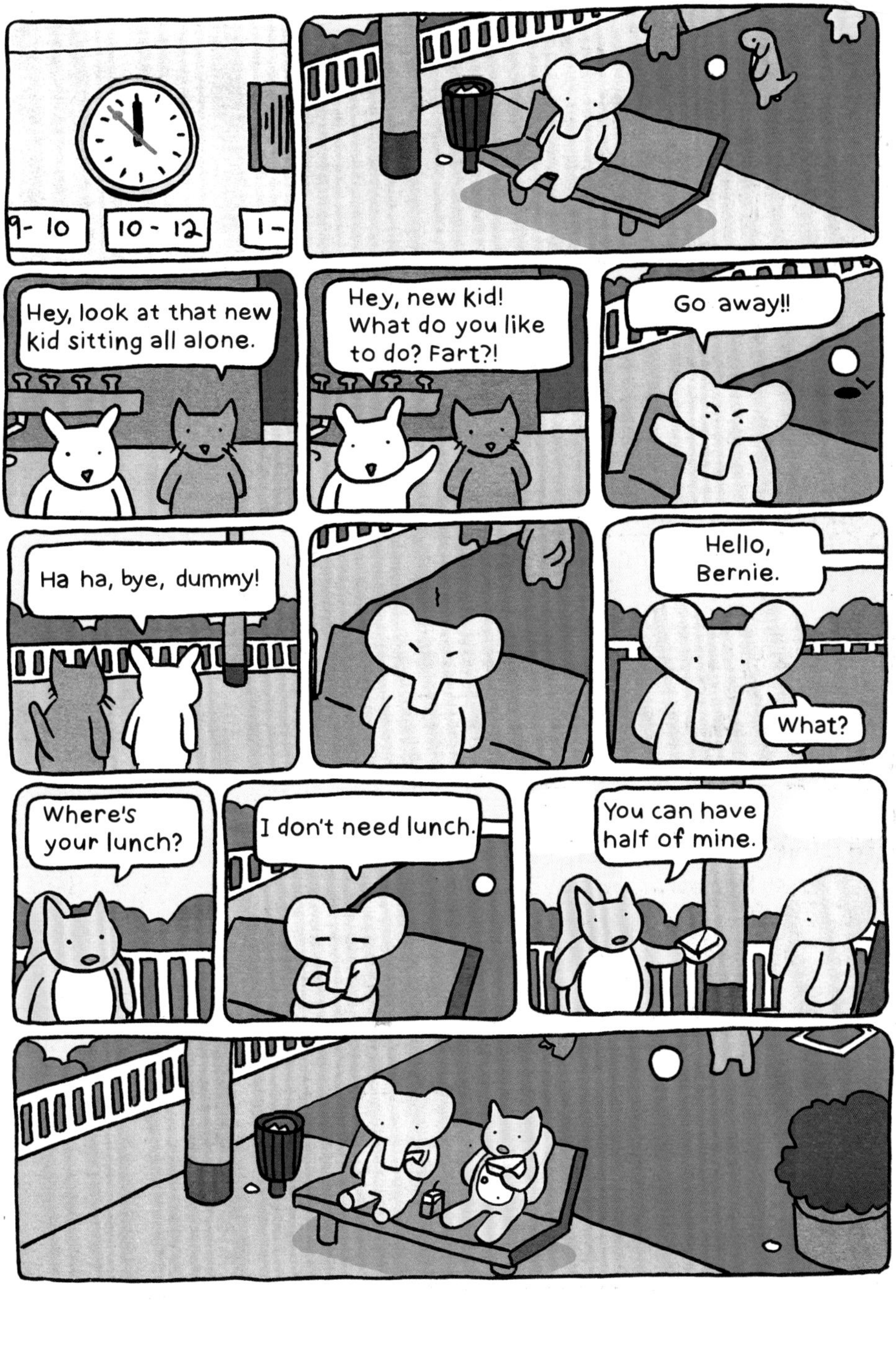
9- 10
10 - 12
1-
Hey, look at that new kid sitting all alone.
Hey, new kid! What do you like to do? Fart?!
Go away!!
Ha ha, bye, dummy!
Hello, Bernie.
What?
Where's your lunch?
I don't need lunch.
You can have half of mine.

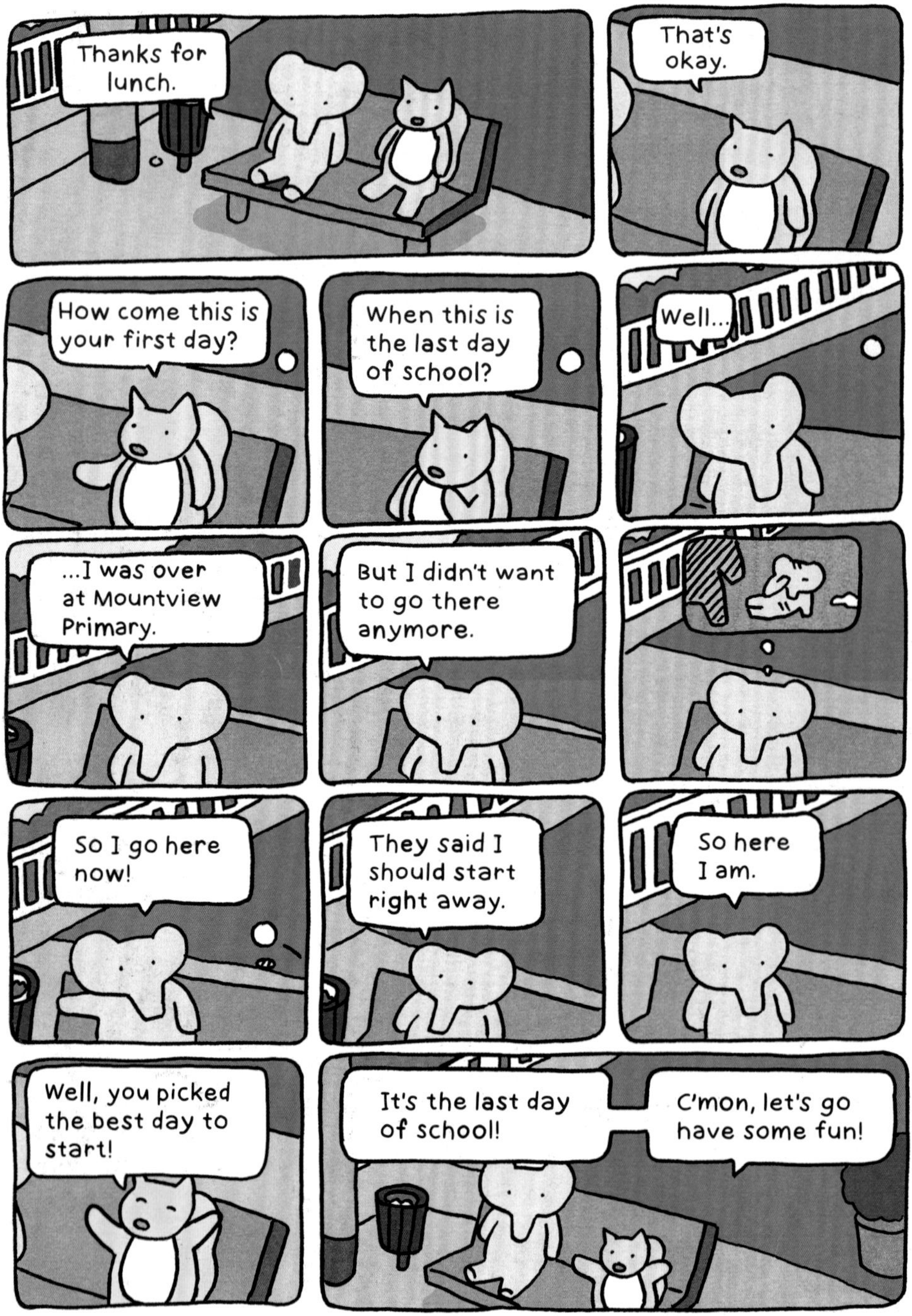
Thanks for lunch.
That's okay.
How come this is your first day?
When this is the last day of school?
Well...
...I was over at Mountview Primary.
But I didn't want to go there anymore.
So I go here now!
They said I should start right away.
So here I am.
Well, you picked the best day to start!
It's the last day of school!
C'mon, let's go have some fun!

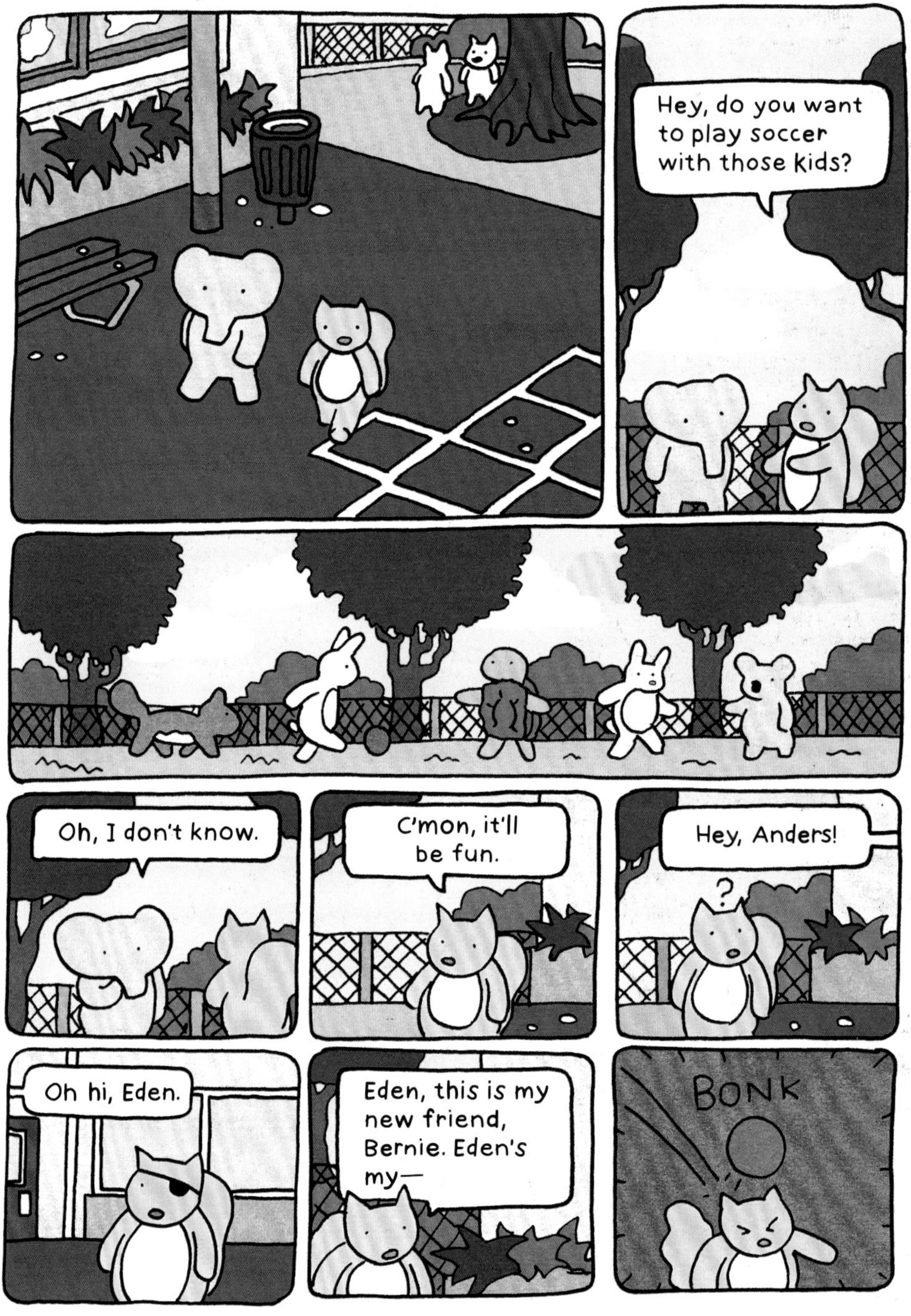
Hey, do you want to play soccer with those kids?
Oh, I don't know.
C'mon, it'll be fun.
Hey, Anders!
?
Oh hi, Eden.
Eden, this is my new friend, Bernie. Eden's my—
BONK

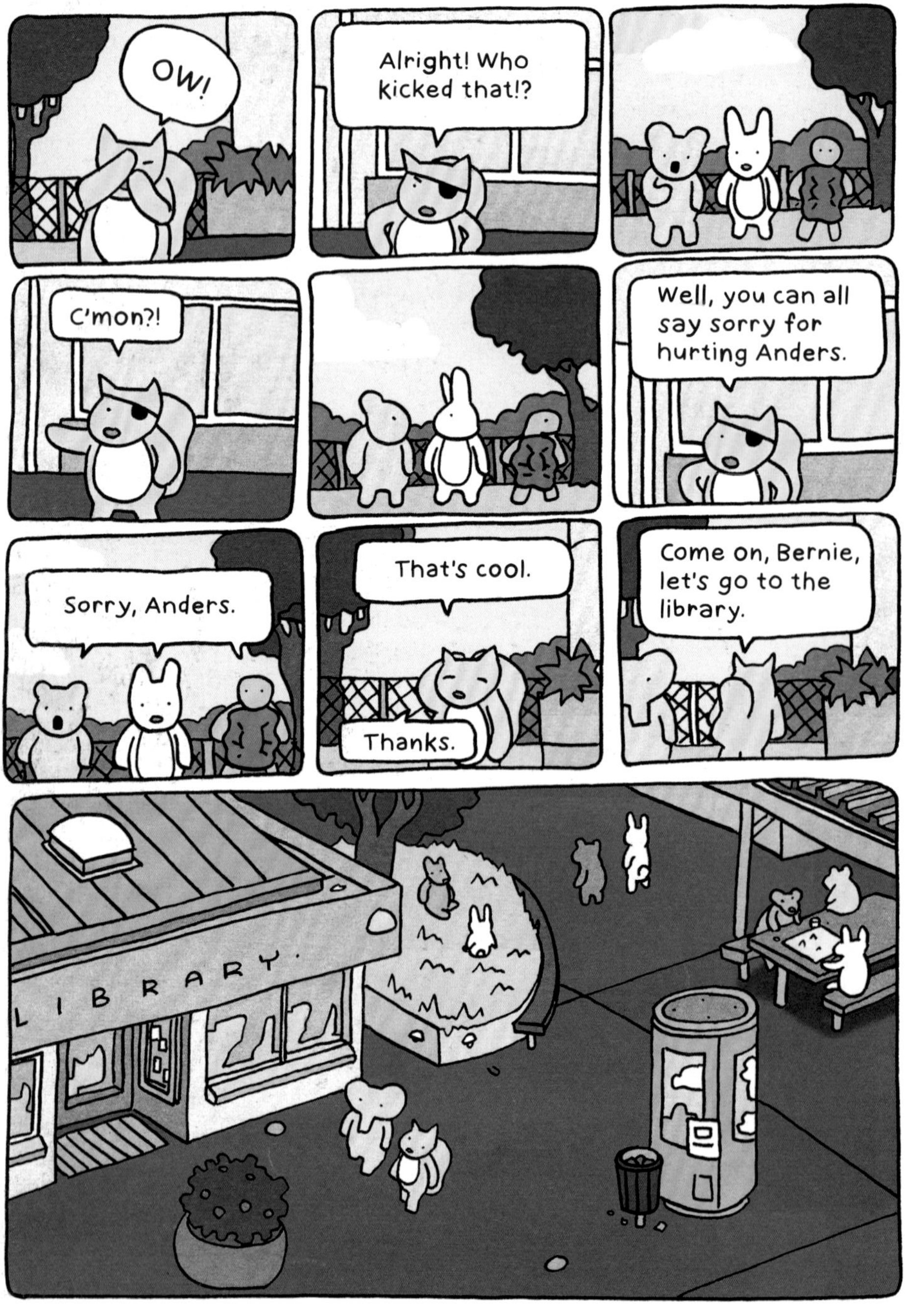
OW!
Alright! Who kicked that!?
C'mon?!
Well, you can all say sorry for hurting Anders.
Sorry, Anders.
That's cool.
Thanks.
Come on, Bernie, let's go to the library.
LIBRARY.

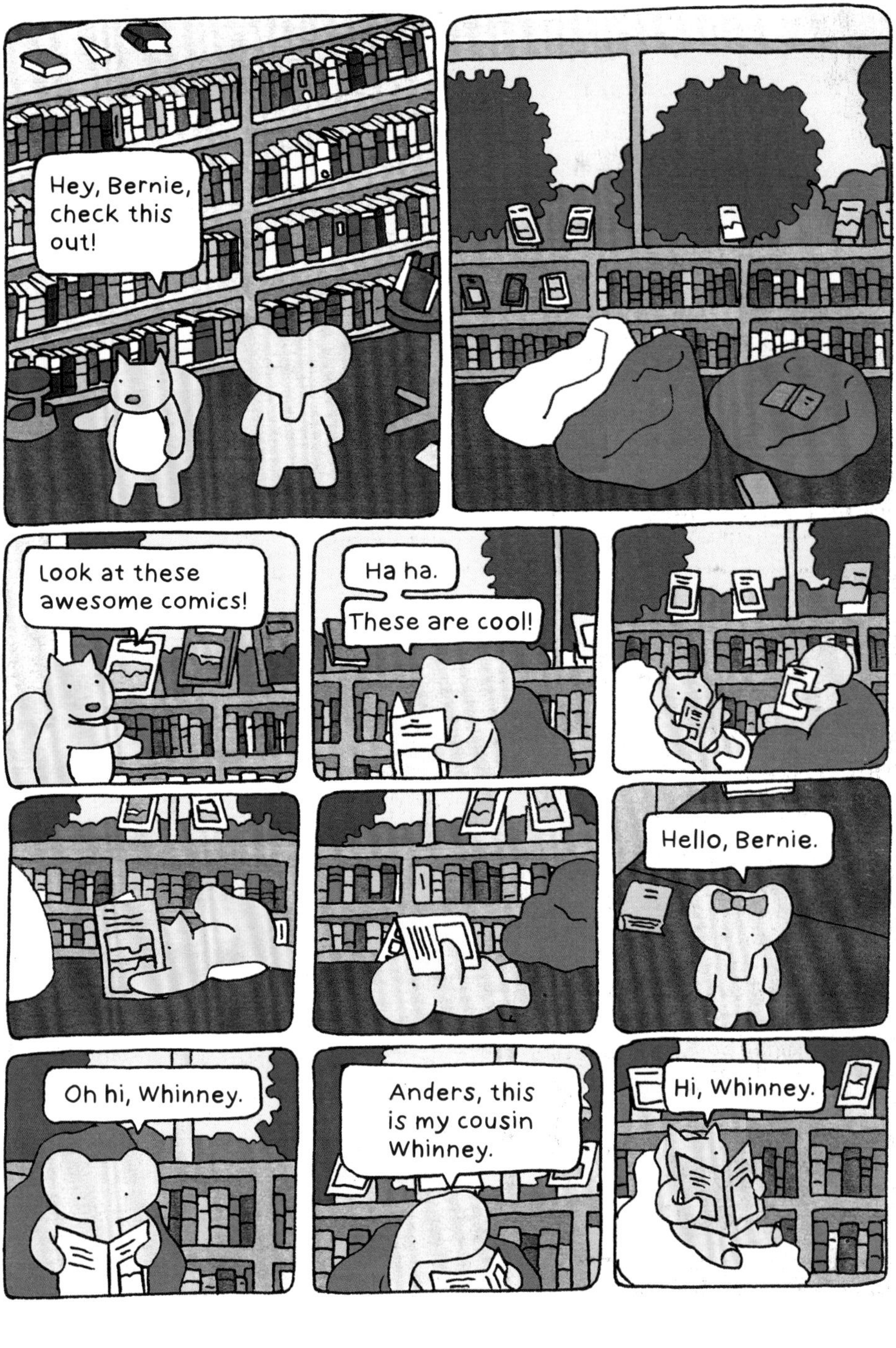
Hey, Bernie, check this out!
Look at these awesome comics!
Ha ha.
These are cool!
Hello, Bernie.
Oh hi, Whinney.
Anders, this is my cousin Whinney.
Hi, Whinney.

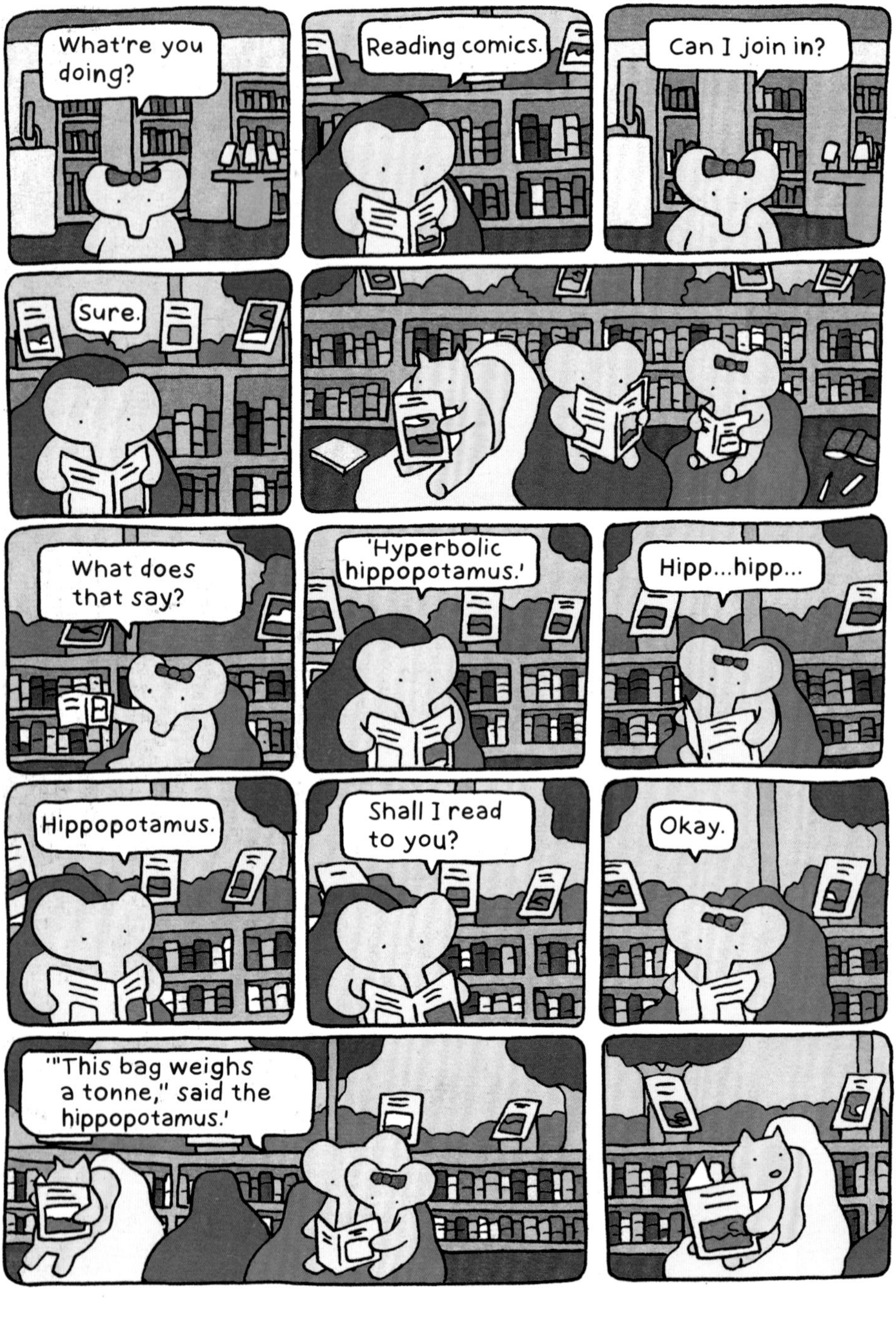
What're you doing?
Reading comics.
Can I join in?
Sure.
What does that say?
'Hyperbolic hippopotamus.'
Hipp...hipp...
Hippopotamus.
Shall I read to you?
Okay.
'"This bag weighs a tonne," said the hippopotamus.'

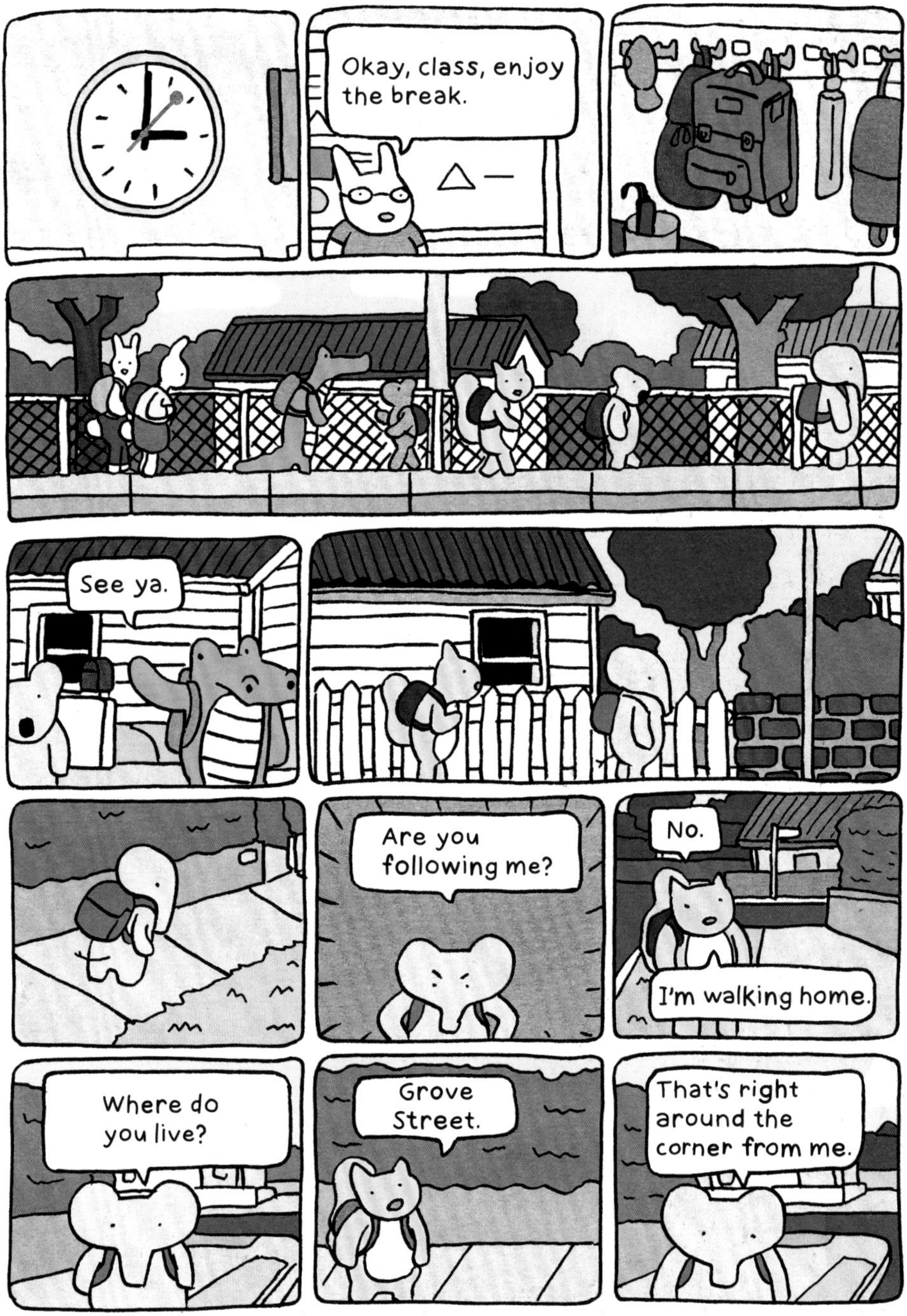

Okay, class, enjoy the break.
See ya.
Are you following me?
No.
I'm walking home.
Where do you live?
Grove Street.
That's right around the corner from me.

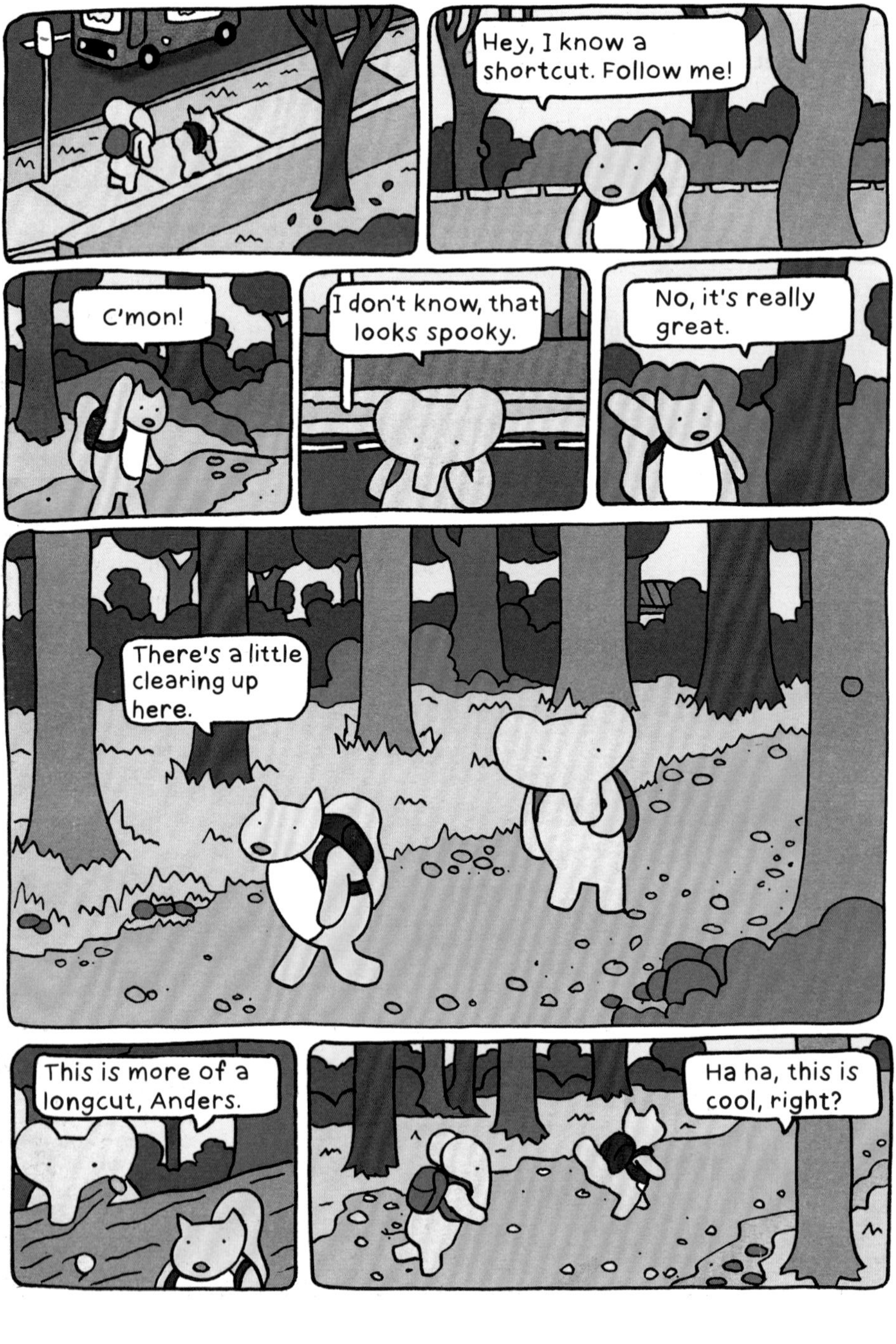
Hey, I know a shortcut. Follow me!
C'mon!
I don't know, that looks spooky.
No, it's really great.
There's a little clearing up here.
This is more of a longcut, Anders.
Ha ha, this is cool, right?

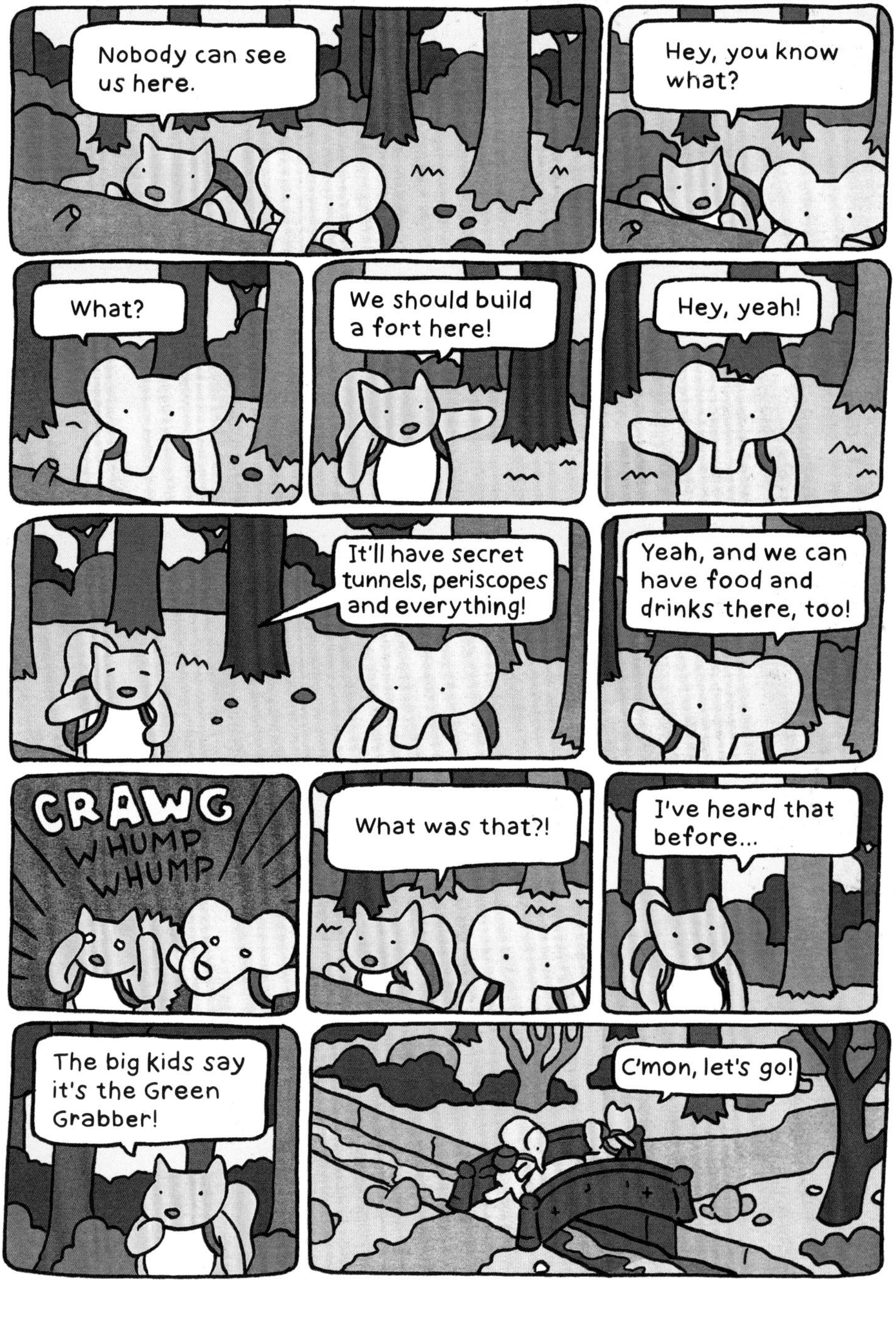
Nobody can see us here.
Hey, you know what?
What?
We should build a fort here!
Hey, yeah!
It'll have secret tunnels, periscopes and everything!
Yeah, and we can have food and drinks there, too!
CRAWG
WHUMP
WHUMP
What was that?!
I've heard that before...
The big kids say it's the Green Grabber!
C'mon, let's go!

Nearby.

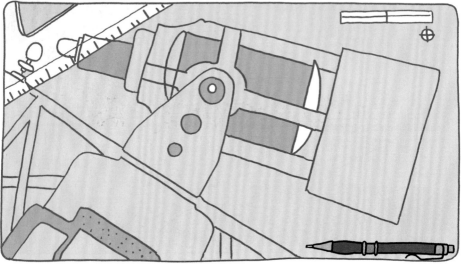

Chapter 2

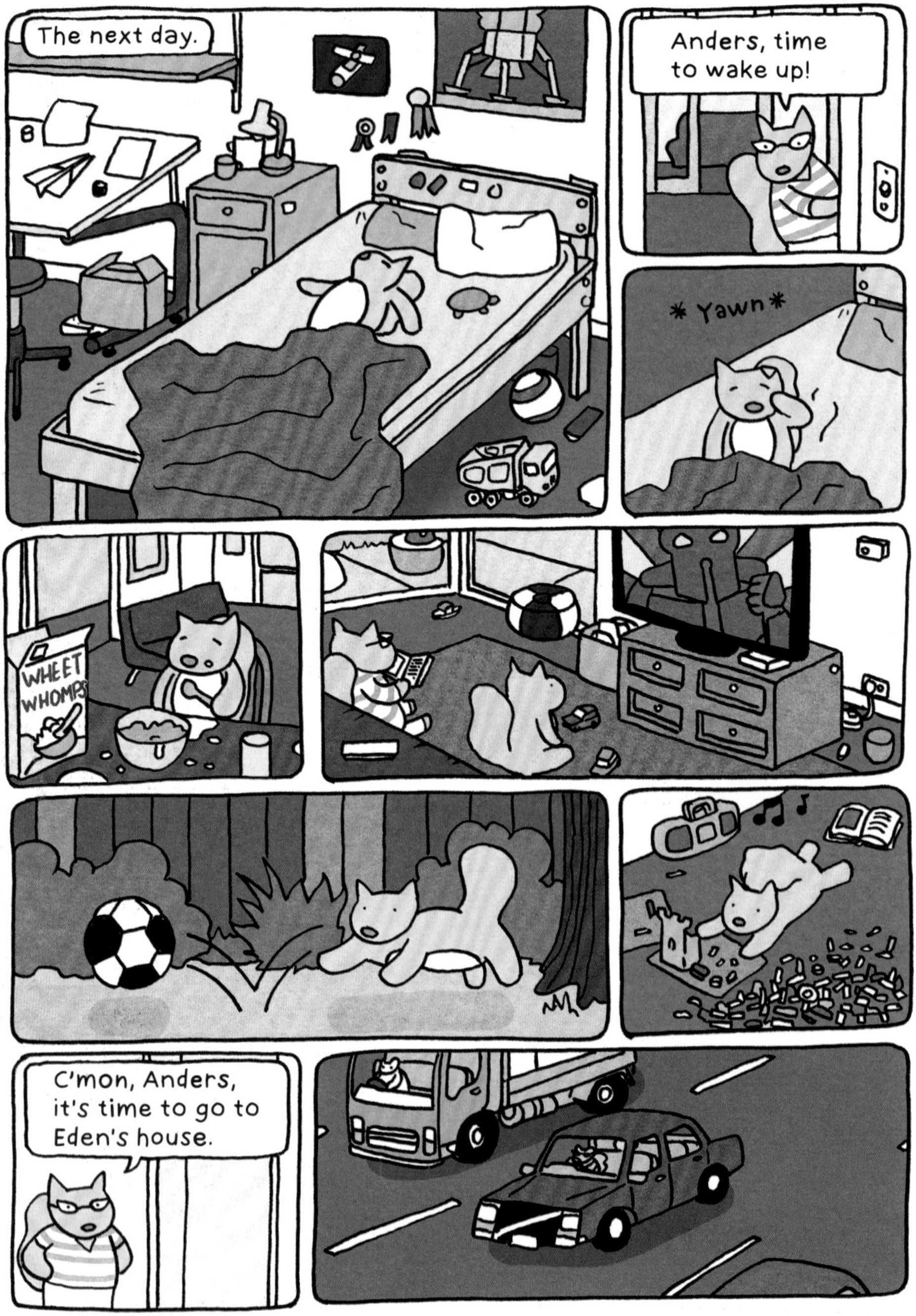
The next day.
Anders, time to wake up!
* Yawn *
WHEET WHOMPS
C'mon, Anders, it's time to go to Eden's house.

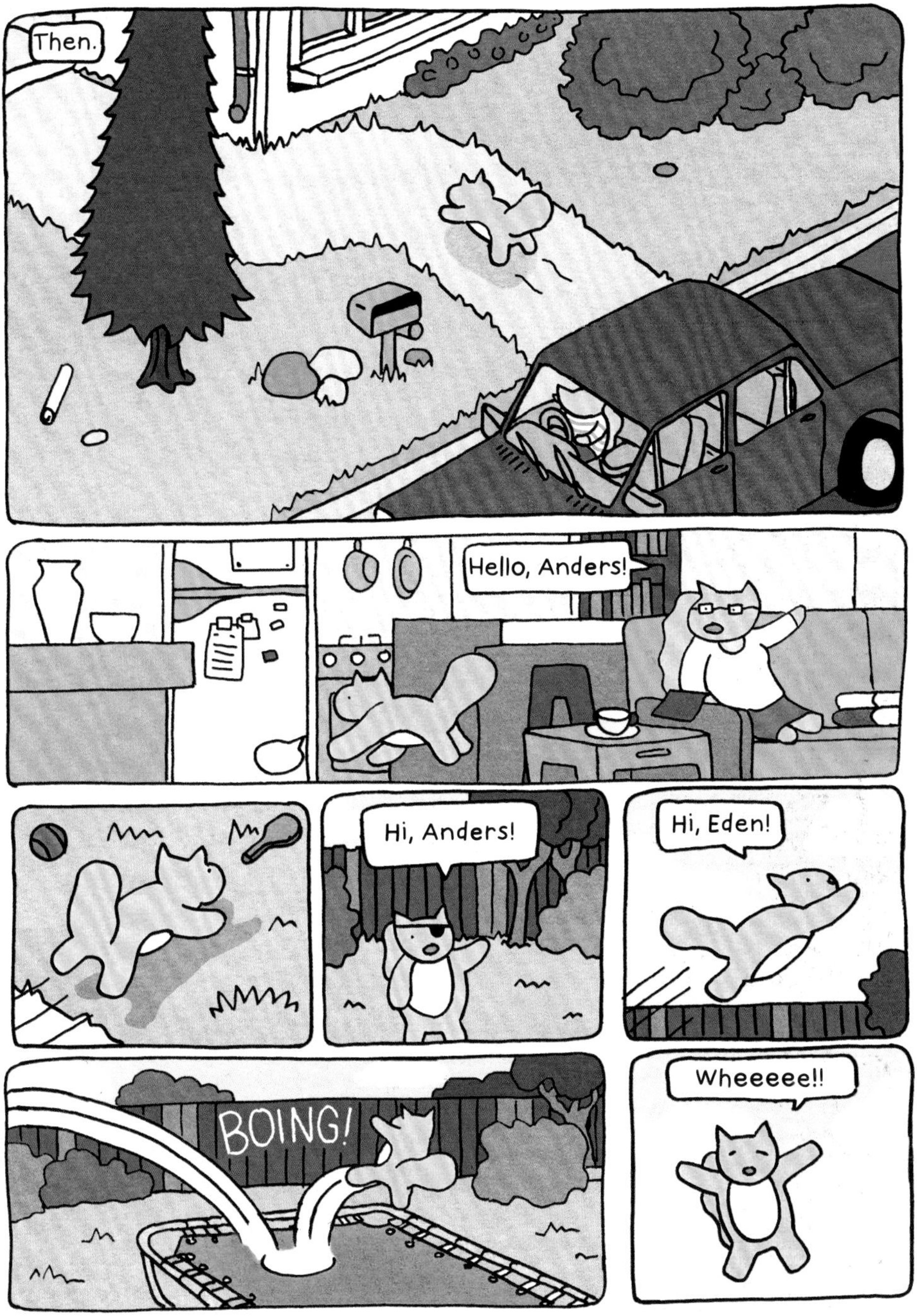
Then.
Hello, Anders!
Hi, Anders!
Hi, Eden!
BOING!
Wheeeee!!

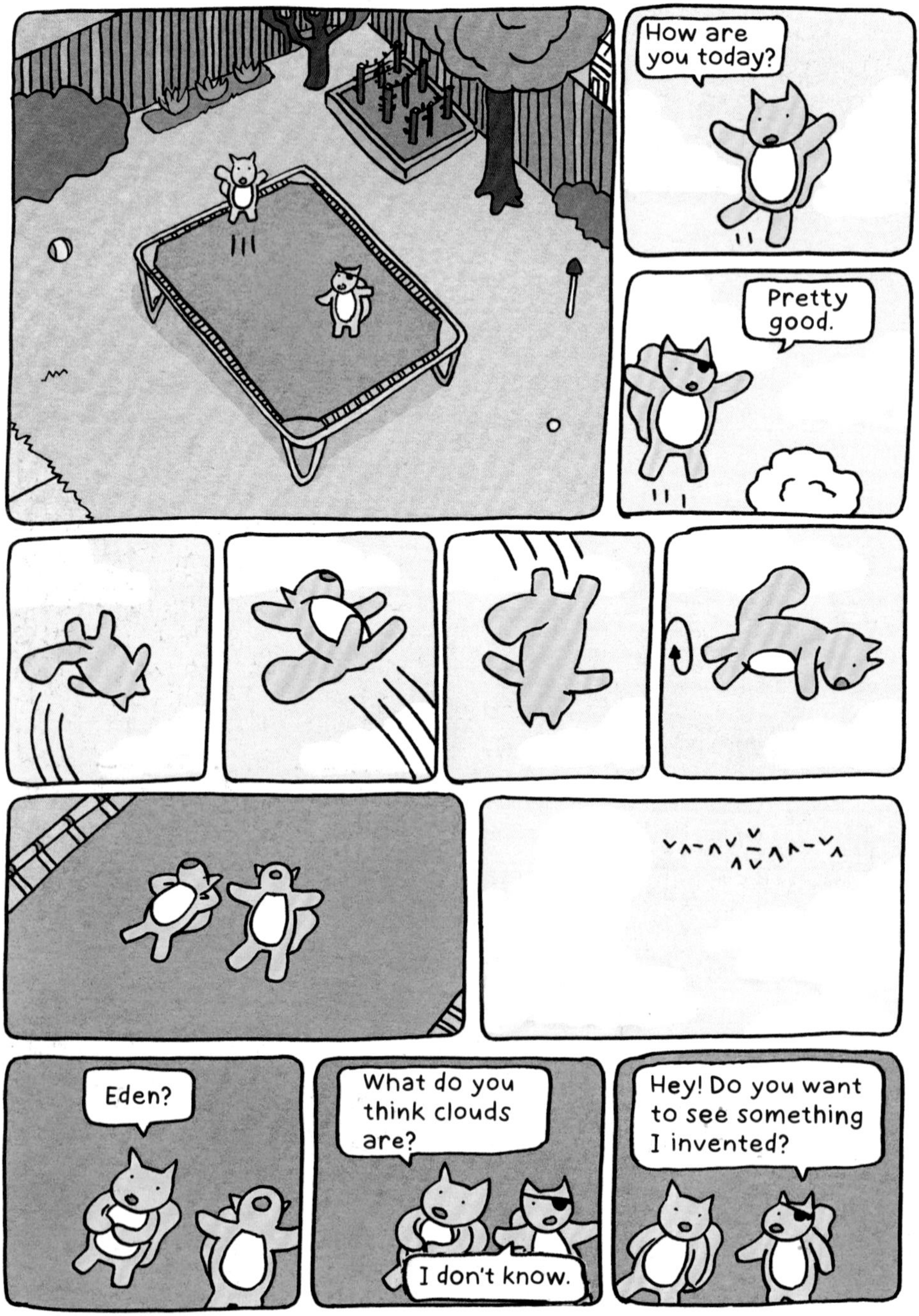
How are you today?
Pretty good.
Eden?
What do you think clouds are?
I don't know.
Hey! Do you want to see something I invented?

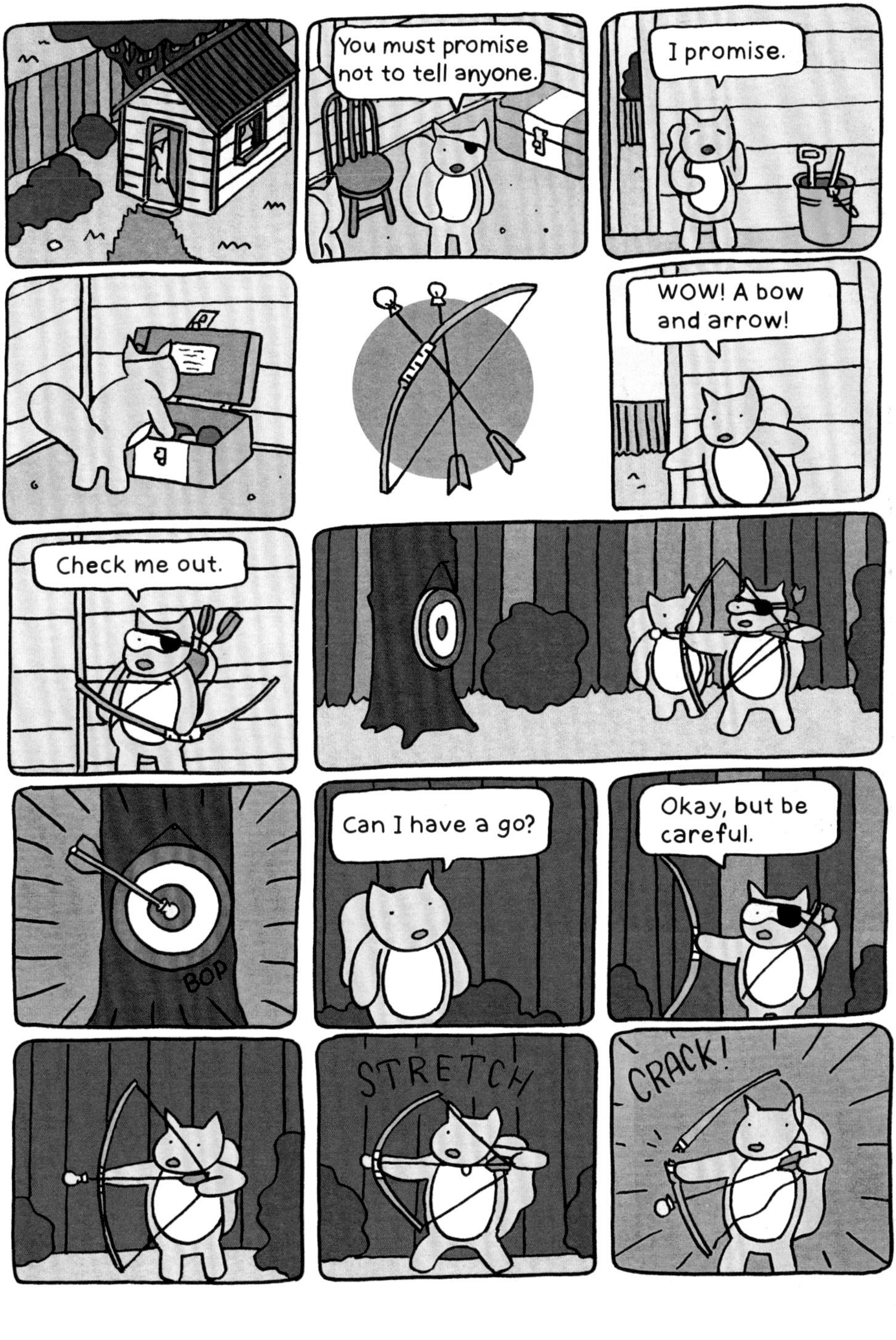
You must promise not to tell anyone.
I promise.
WOW! A bow and arrow!
Check me out.
BOP
Can I have a go?
Okay, but be careful.
STRETCH
CRACK!

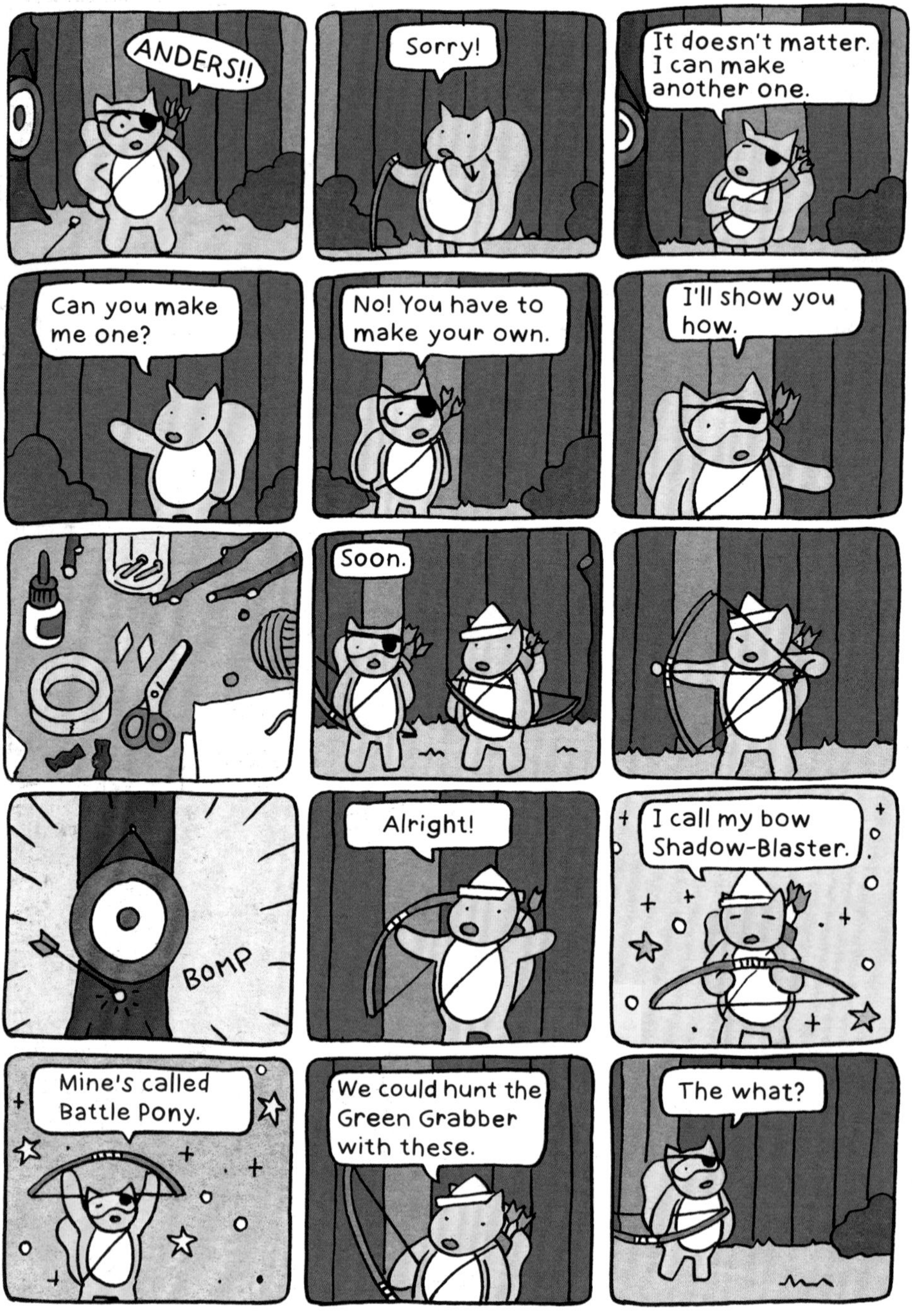

ANDERS!!
Sorry!
It doesn't matter. I can make another one.
Can you make me one?
No! You have to make your own.
I'll show you how.
Soon.
BOMP
Alright!
I call my bow Shadow-Blaster.
Mine's called Battle Pony.
We could hunt the Green Grabber with these.
The what?

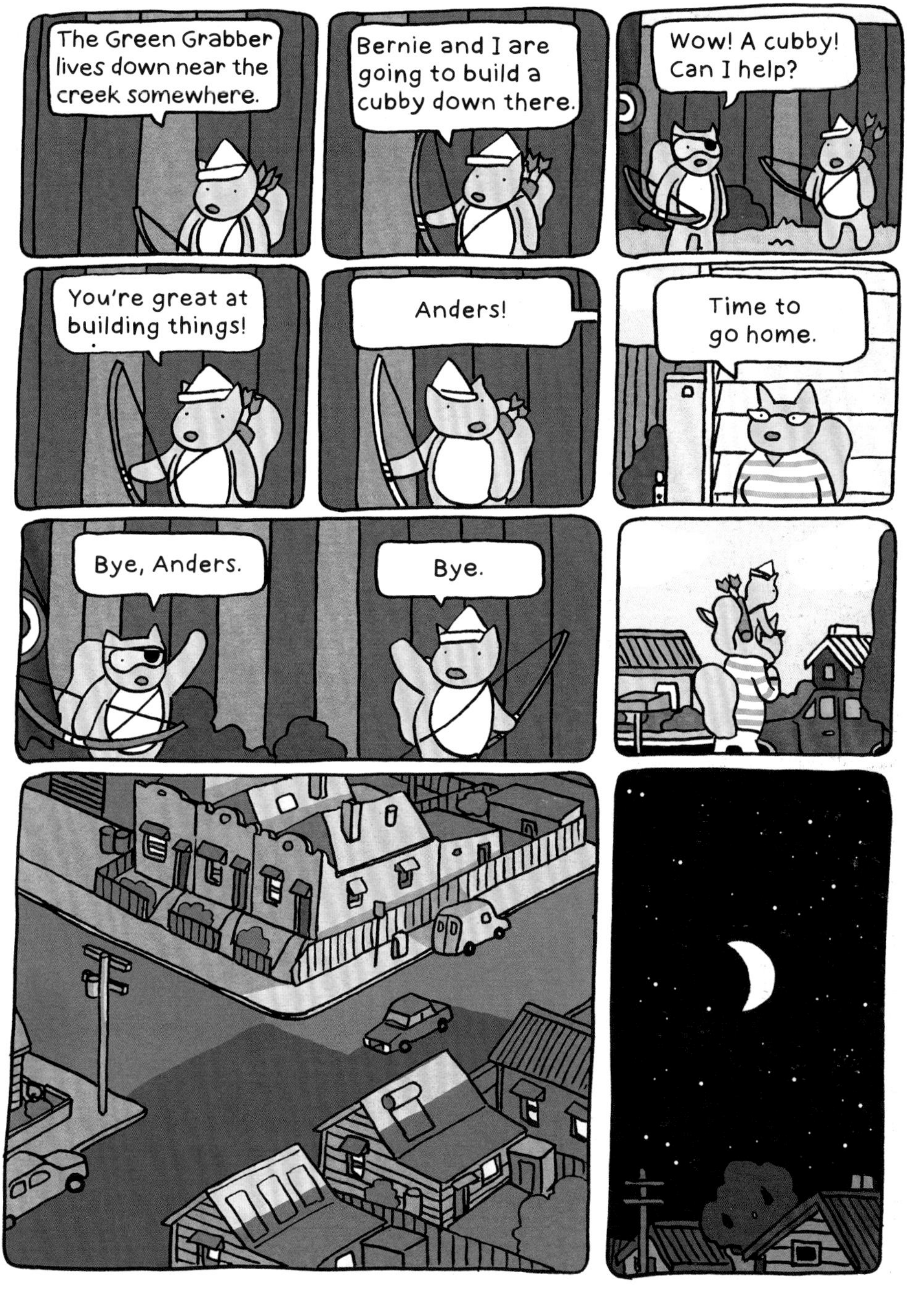
The Green Grabber lives down near the creek somewhere.
Bernie and I are going to build a cubby down there.
Wow! A cubby! Can I help?
You're great at building things!
Anders!
Time to go home.
Bye, Anders.
Bye.

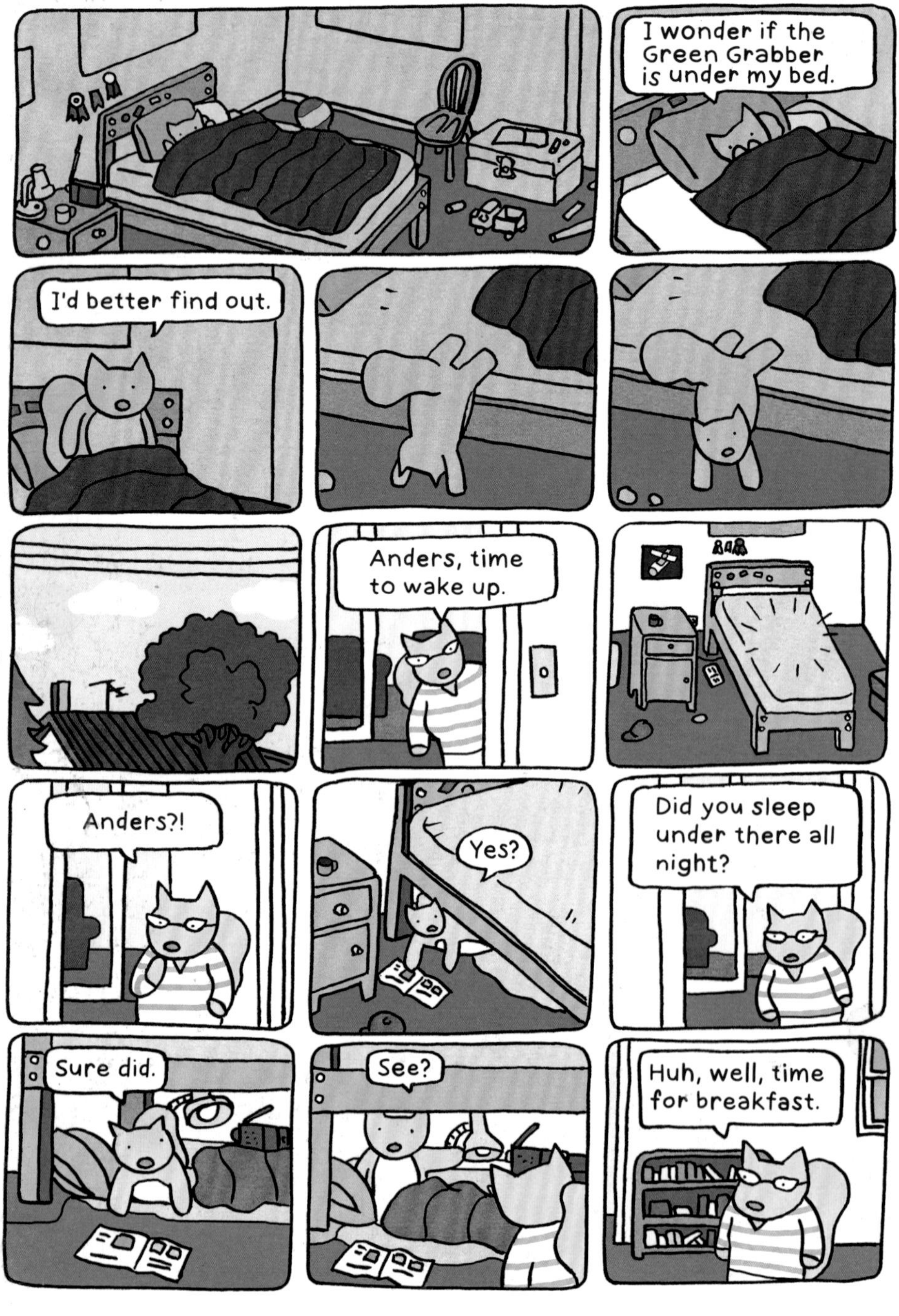

I wonder if the Green Grabber is under my bed.
I'd better find out.
Anders, time to wake up.
Anders?!
Yes?
Did you sleep under there all night?
Sure did.
See?
Huh, well, time for breakfast.

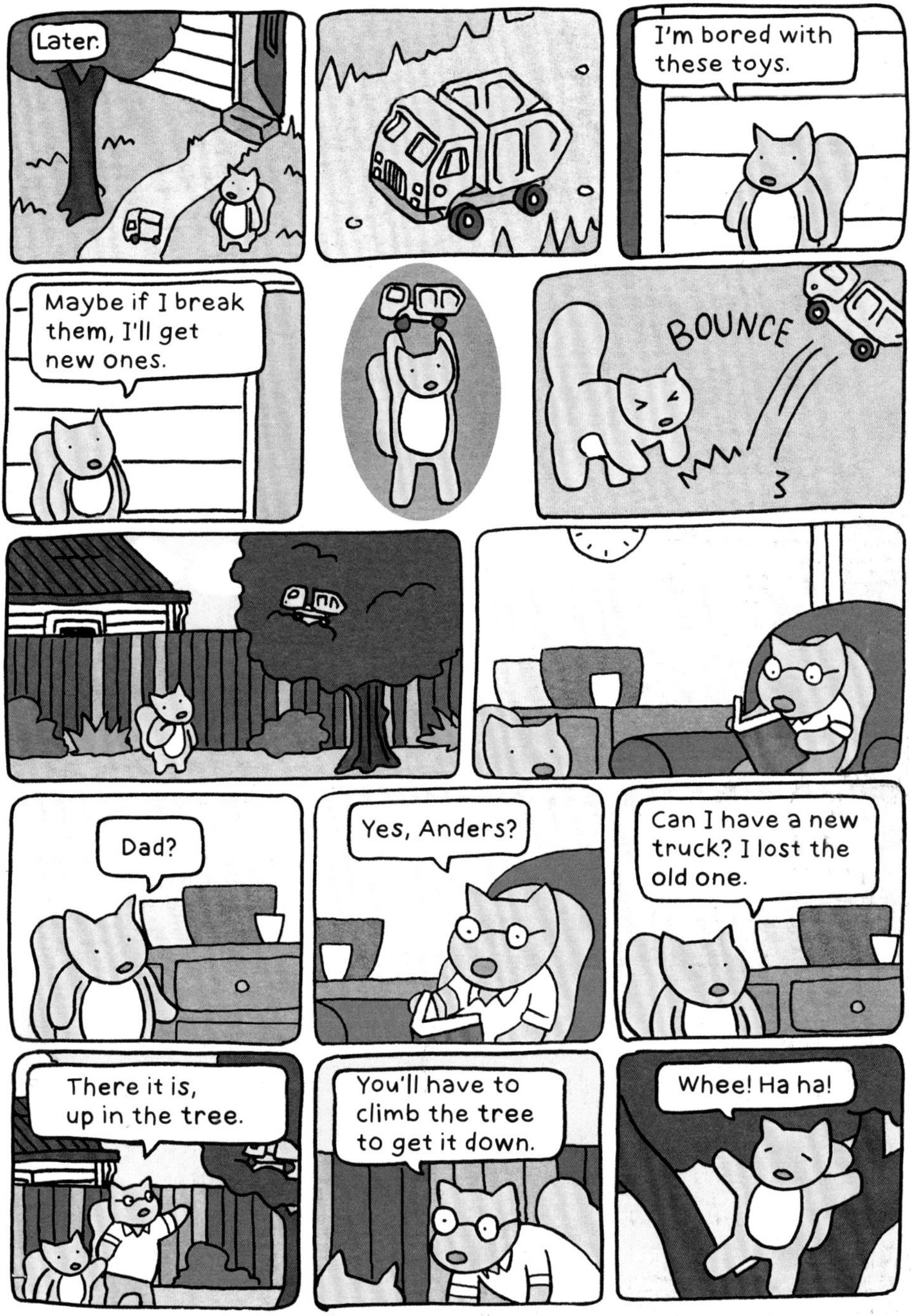
Later.
I'm bored with these toys.
Maybe if I break them, I'll get new ones.
BOUNCE
Dad?
Yes, Anders?
Can I have a new truck? I lost the old one.
There it is, up in the tree.
You'll have to climb the tree to get it down.
Whee! Ha ha!

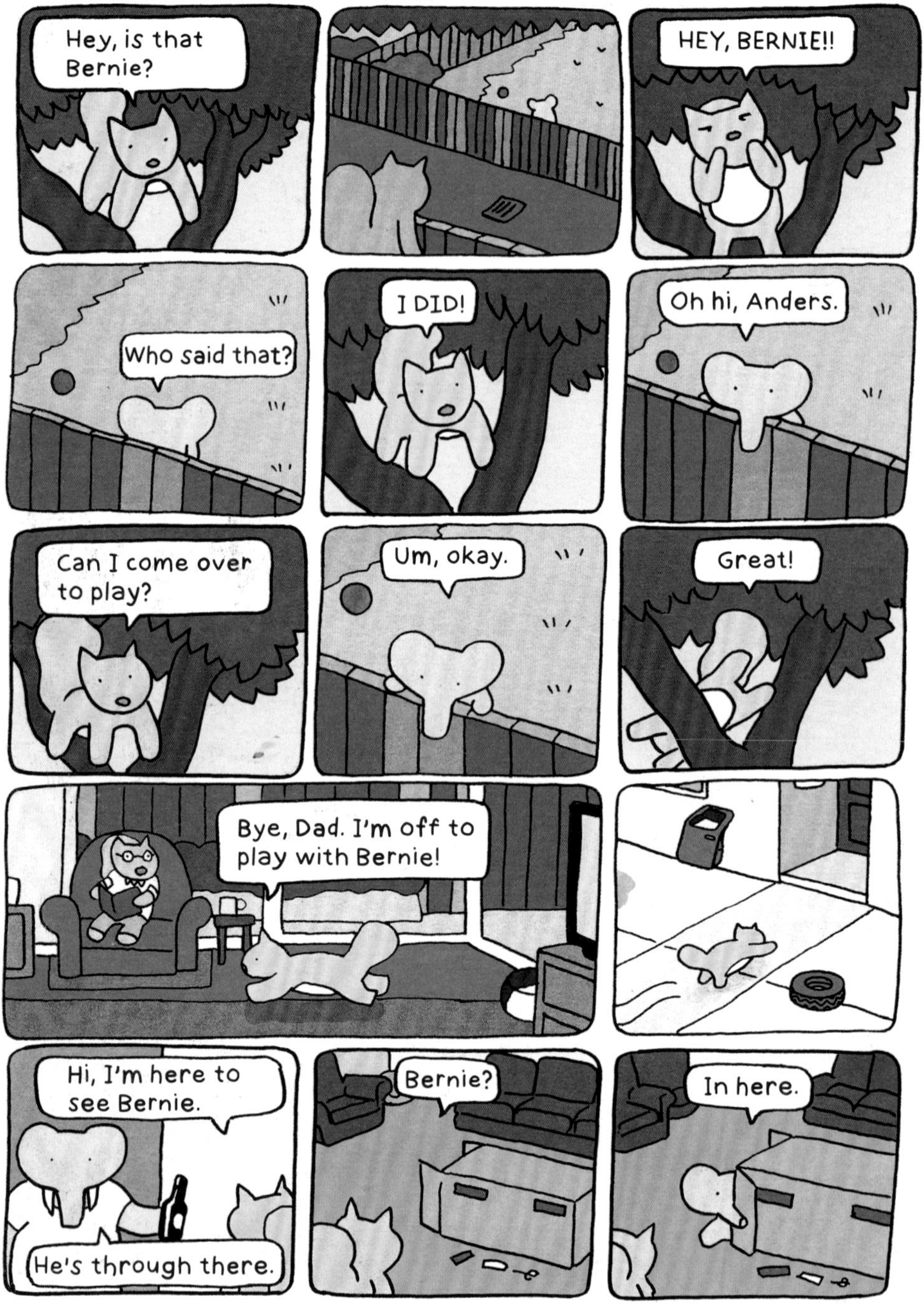
Hey, is that Bernie?
HEY, BERNIE!!
Who said that?
I DID!
Oh hi, Anders.
Can I come over to play?
Um, okay.
Great!
Bye, Dad. I'm off to play with Bernie!
Hi, I'm here to see Bernie.
He's through there.
Bernie?
In here.

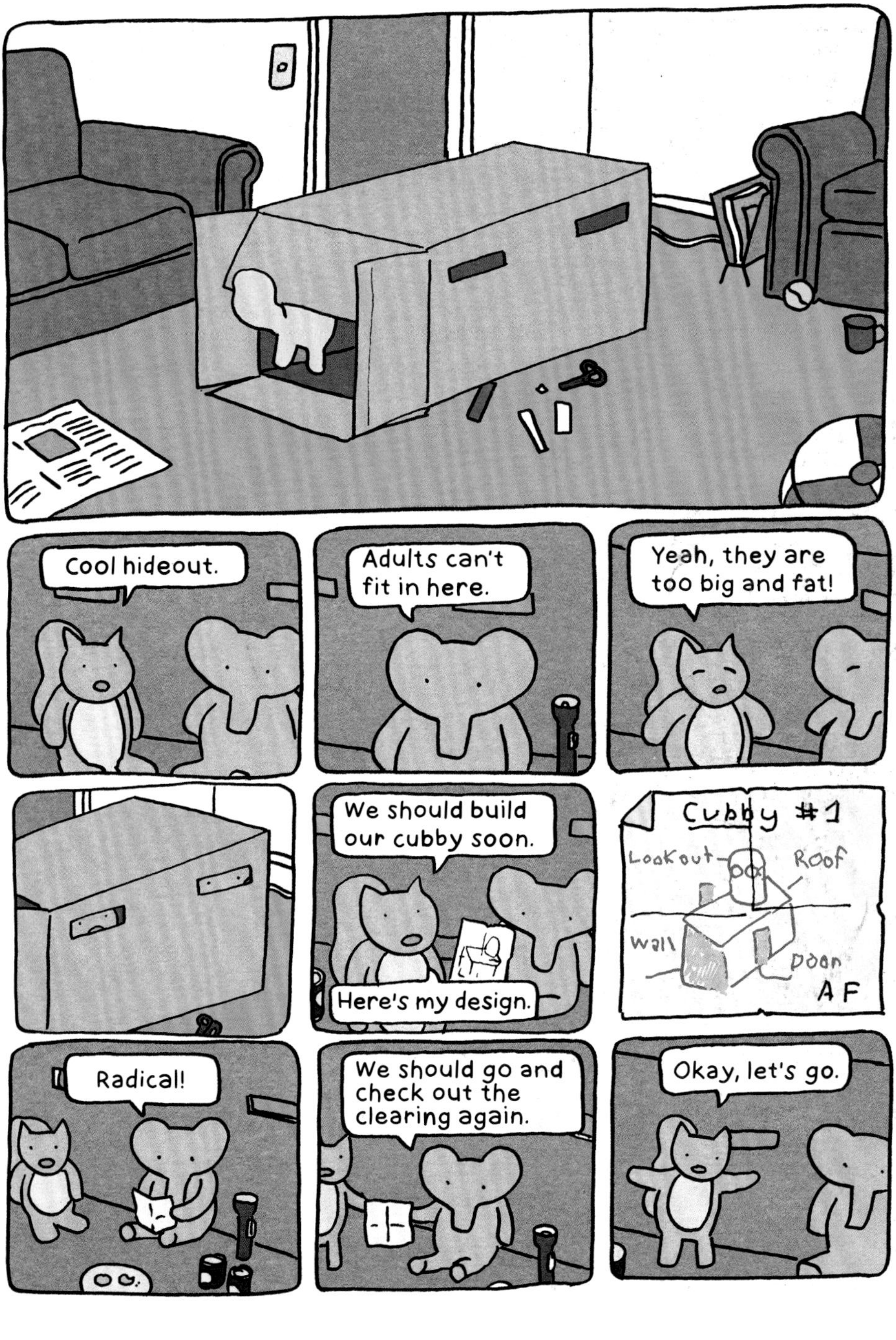
Cool hideout.
Adults can't fit in here.
Yeah, they are too big and fat!
We should build our cubby soon.
Here's my design.
Cubby #1
Lookout
Roof
Wall
Door
AF
Radical!
We should go and check out the clearing again.
Okay, let's go.

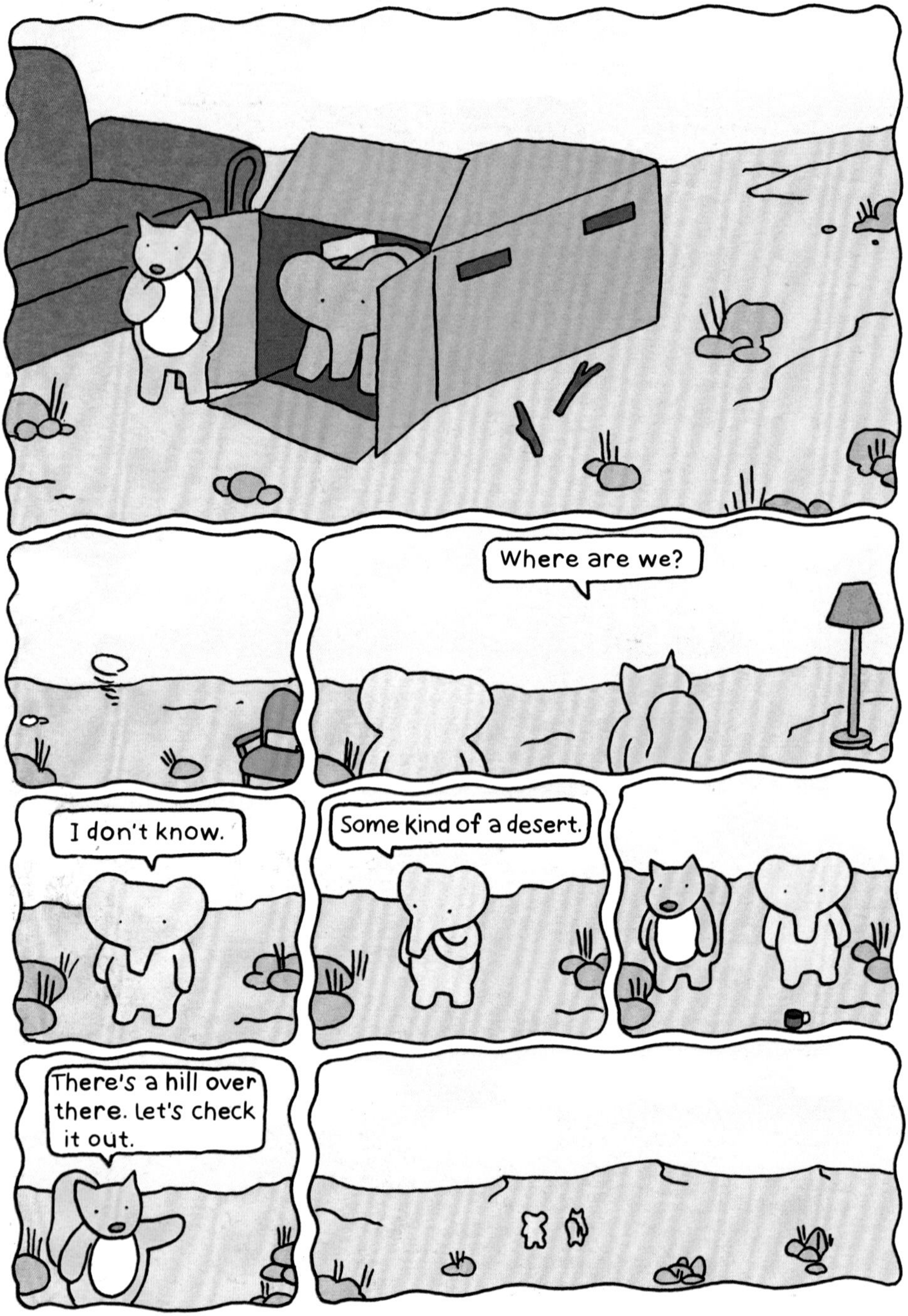
Where are we?
I don't know.
Some kind of a desert.
There's a hill over there. Let's check it out.

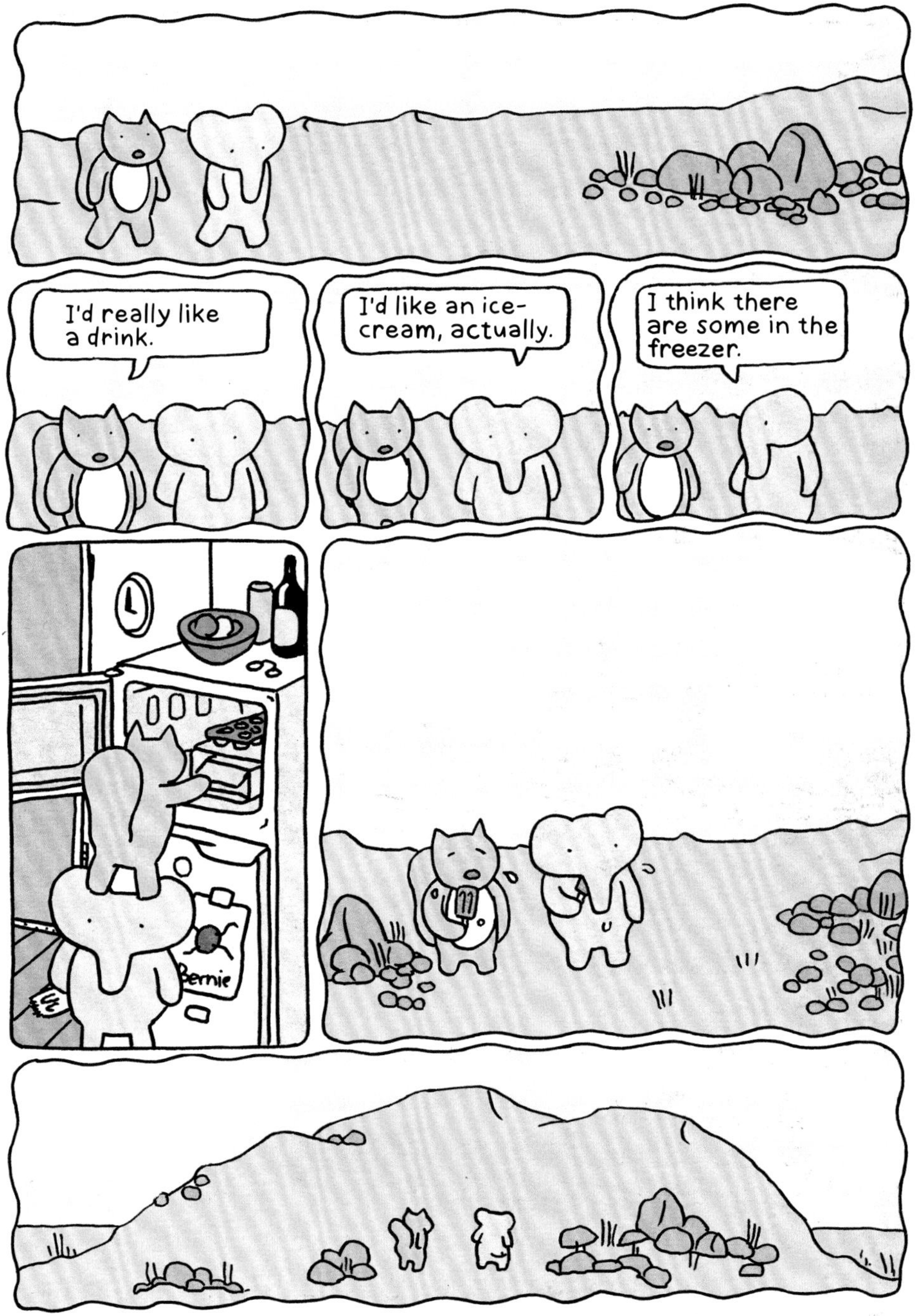
I'd really like a drink.
I'd like an ice-cream, actually.
I think there are some in the freezer.
Bernie

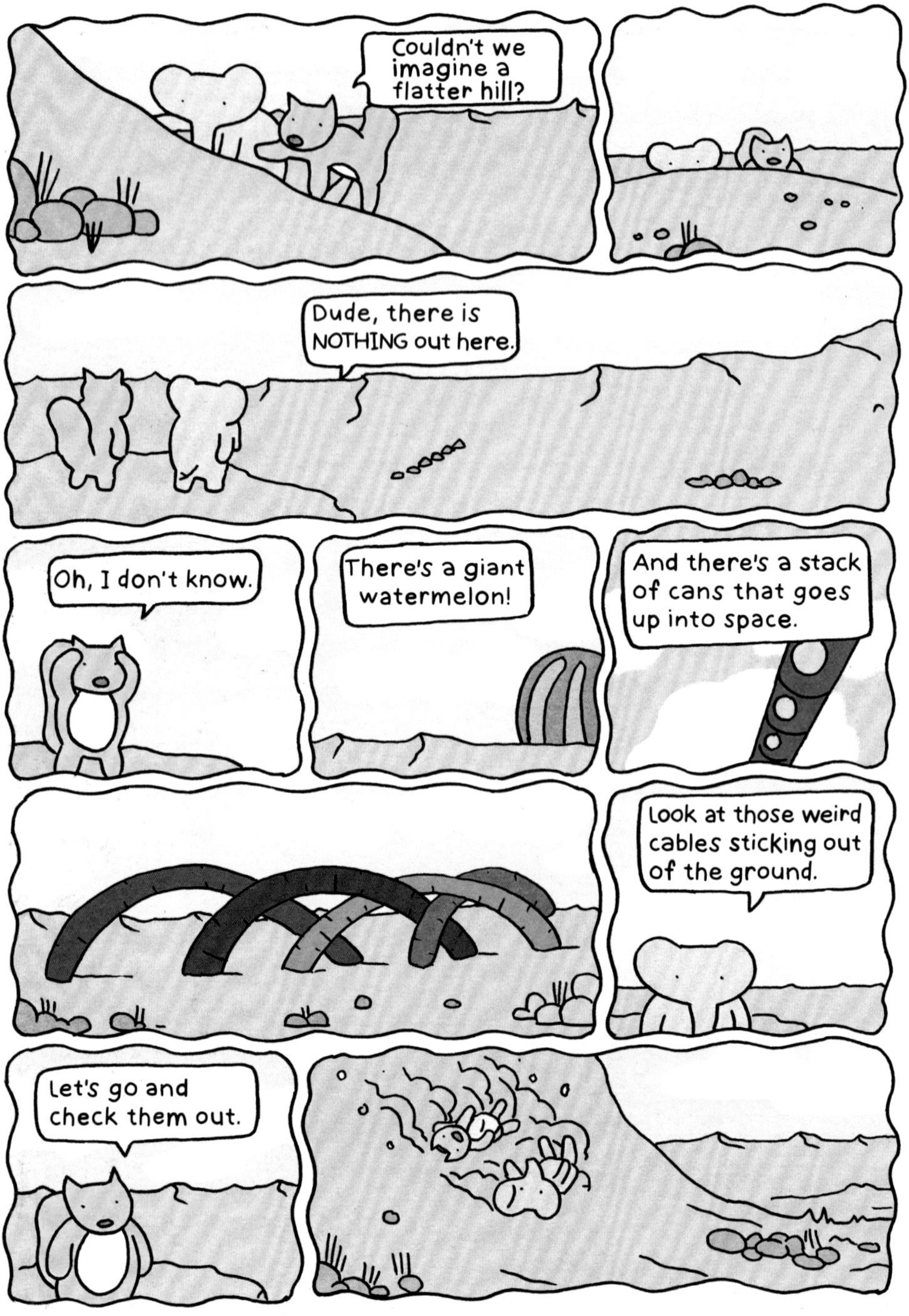
Couldn't we imagine a flatter hill?
Dude, there is NOTHING out here.
Oh, I don't know.
There's a giant watermelon!
And there's a stack of cans that goes up into space.
Look at those weird cables sticking out of the ground.
Let's go and check them out.

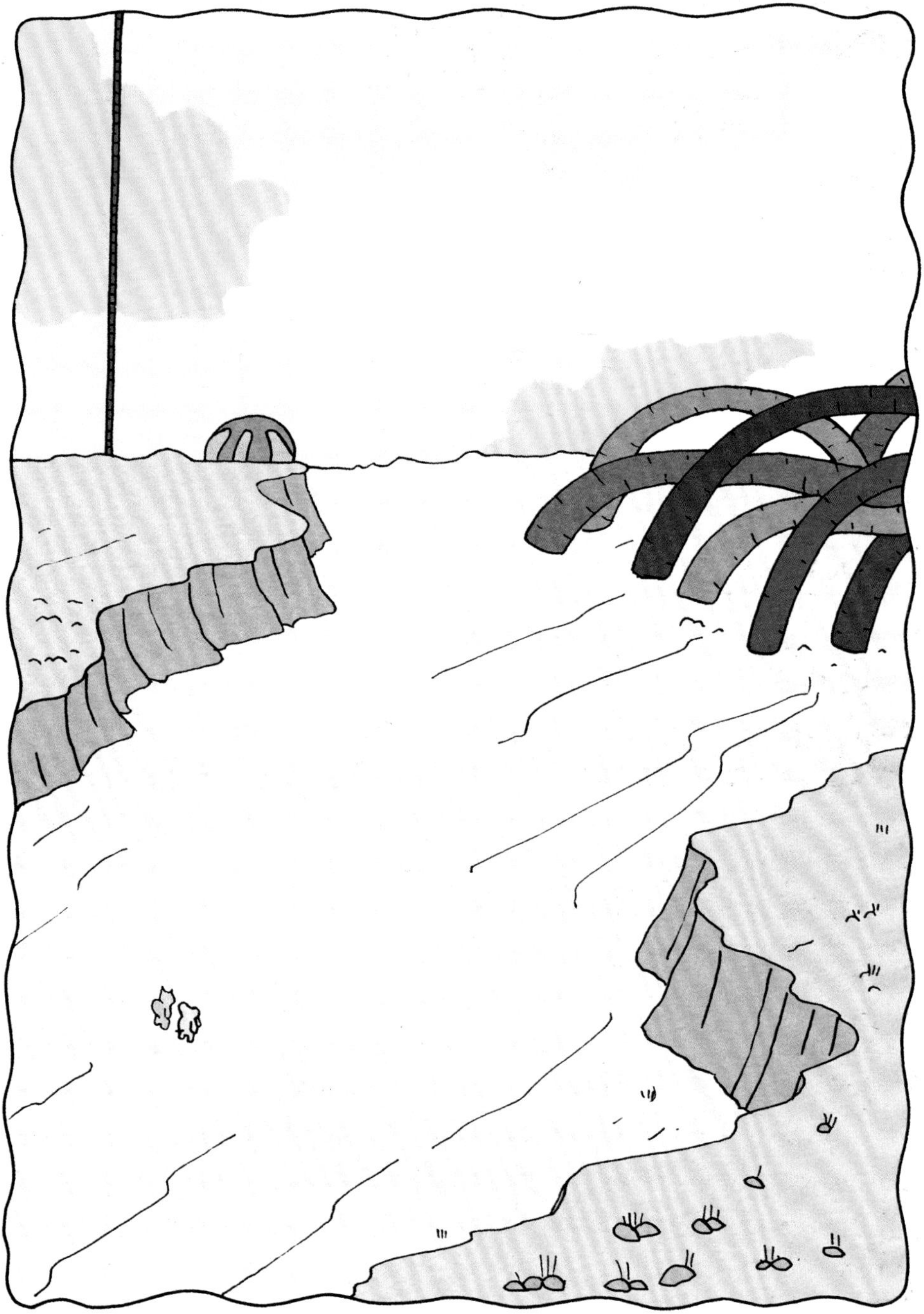

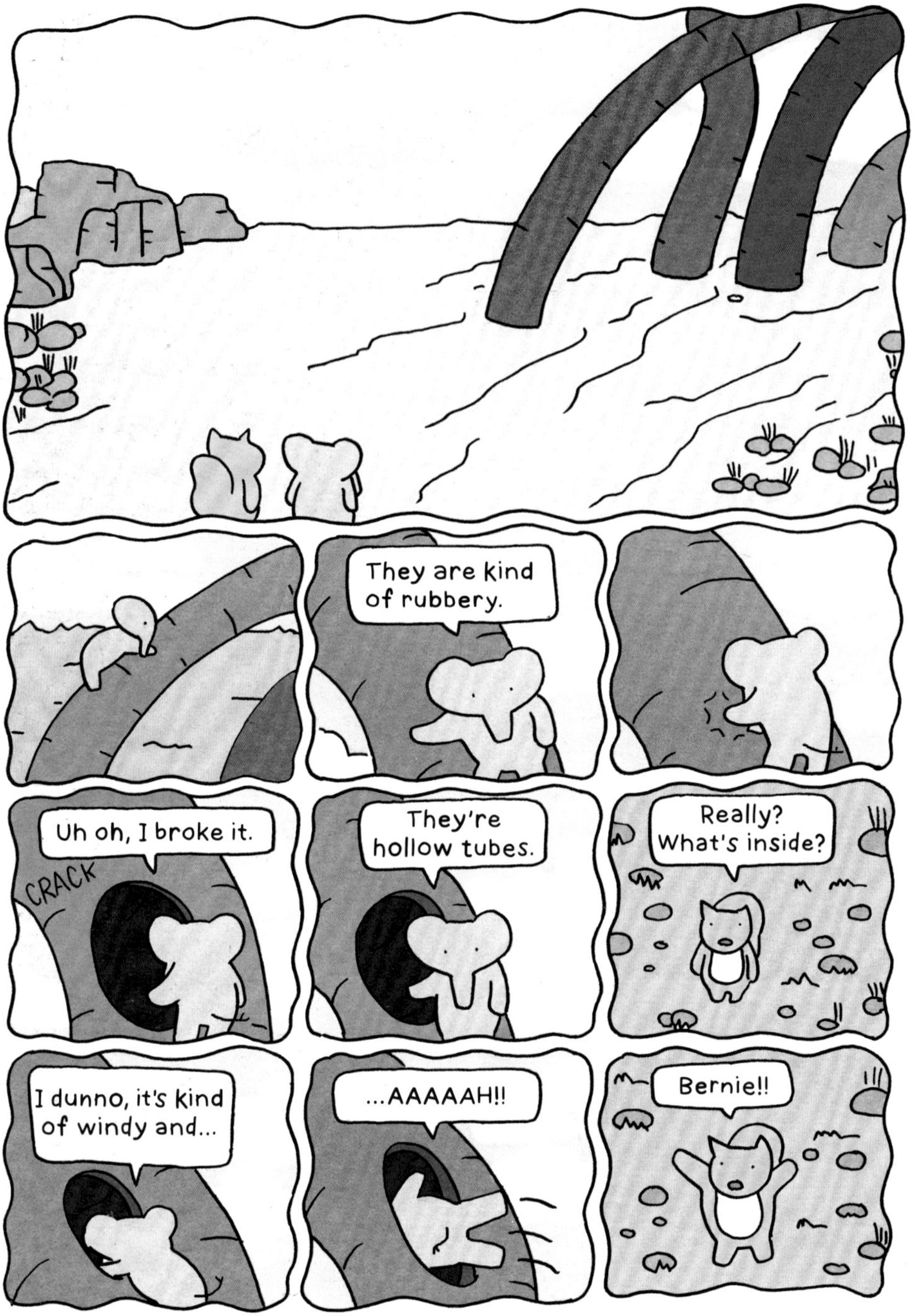
They are kind of rubbery.
Uh oh, I broke it.
CRACK
They're hollow tubes.
Really? What's inside?
I dunno, it's kind of windy and...
...AAAAAH!!
Bernie!!

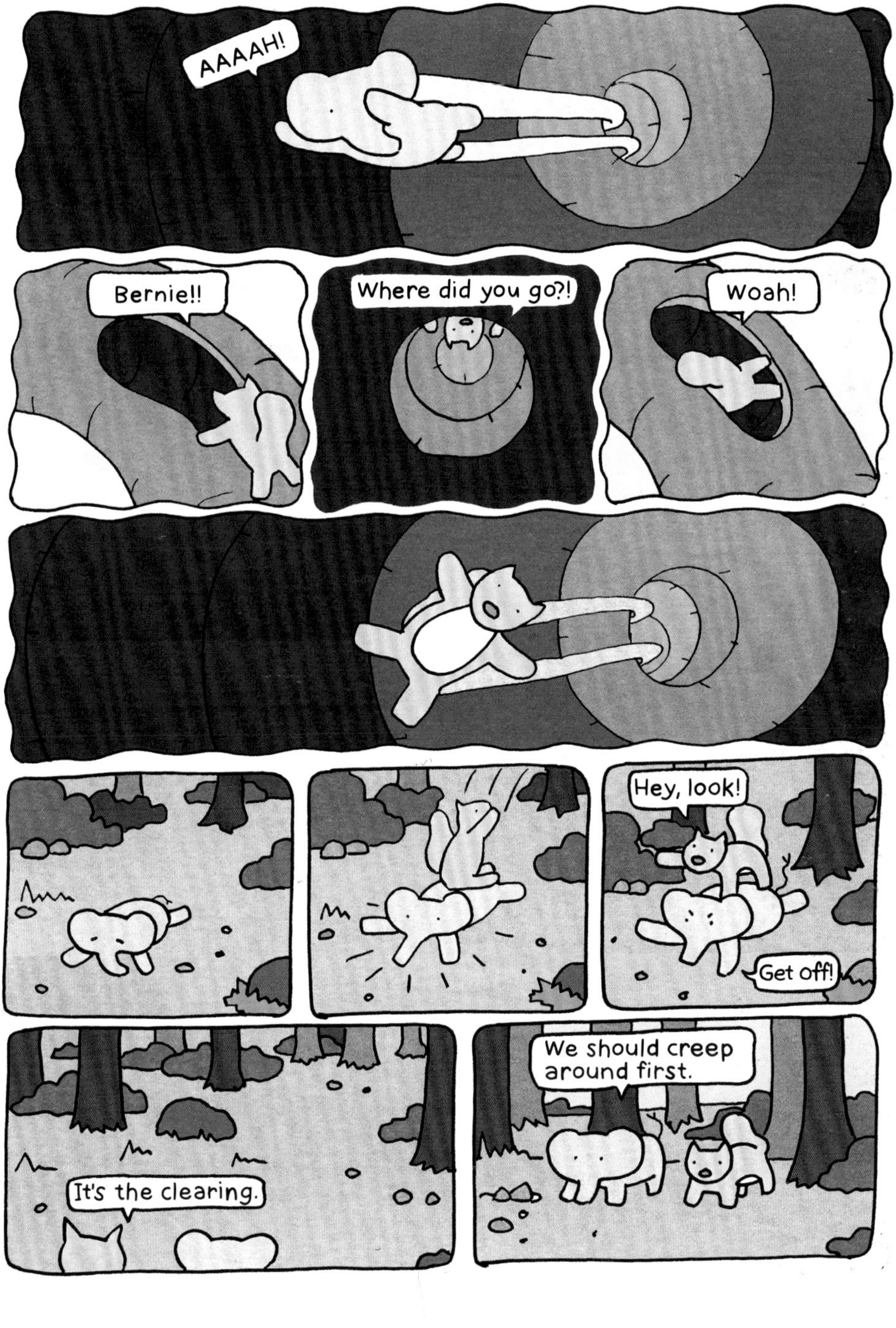
AAAAH!
Bernie!!
Where did you go?!
Woah!
Hey, look!
Get off!
It's the clearing.
We should creep around first.

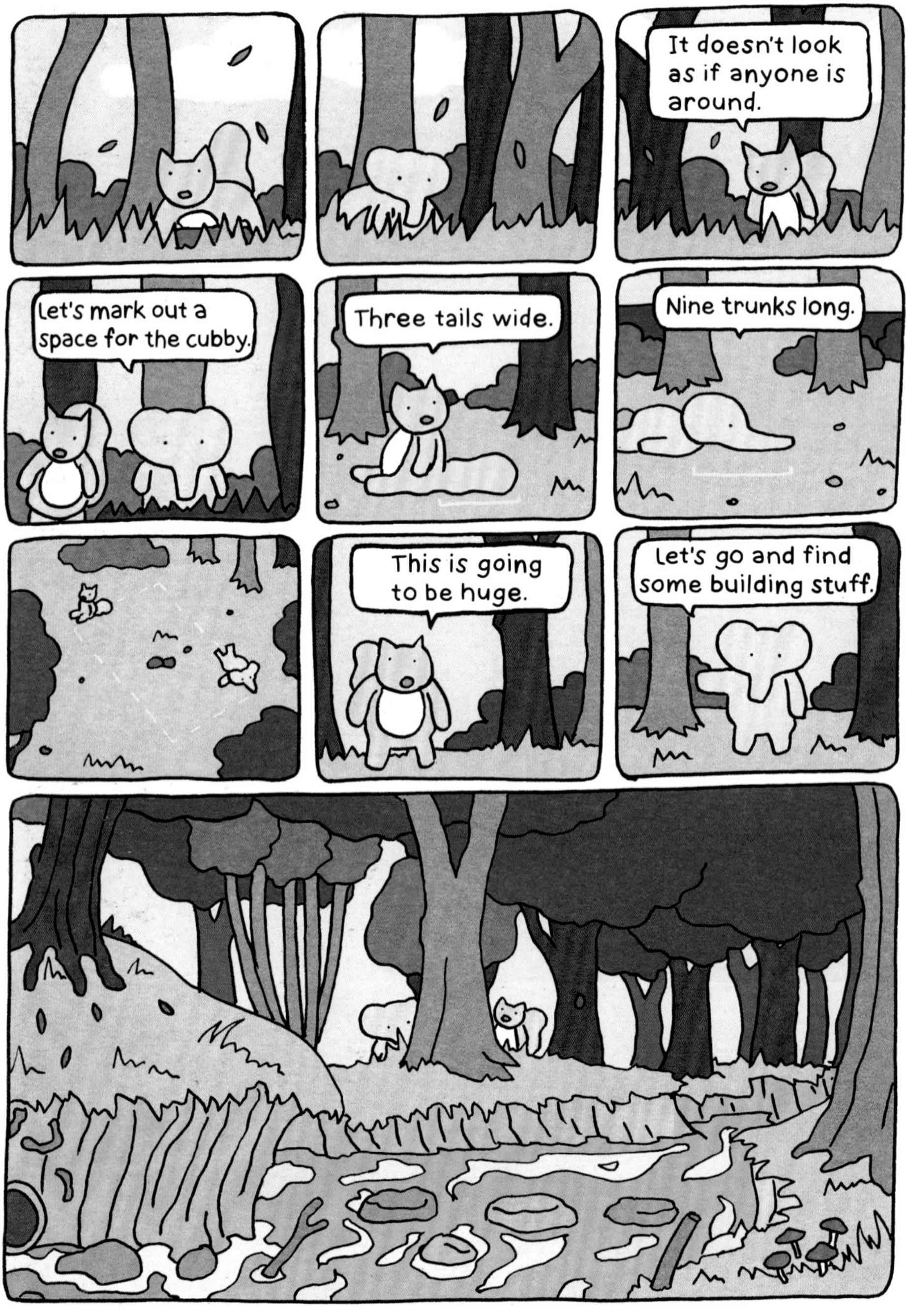
It doesn't look as if anyone is around.
Let's mark out a space for the cubby.
Three tails wide.
Nine trunks long.
This is going to be huge.
Let's go and find some building stuff.

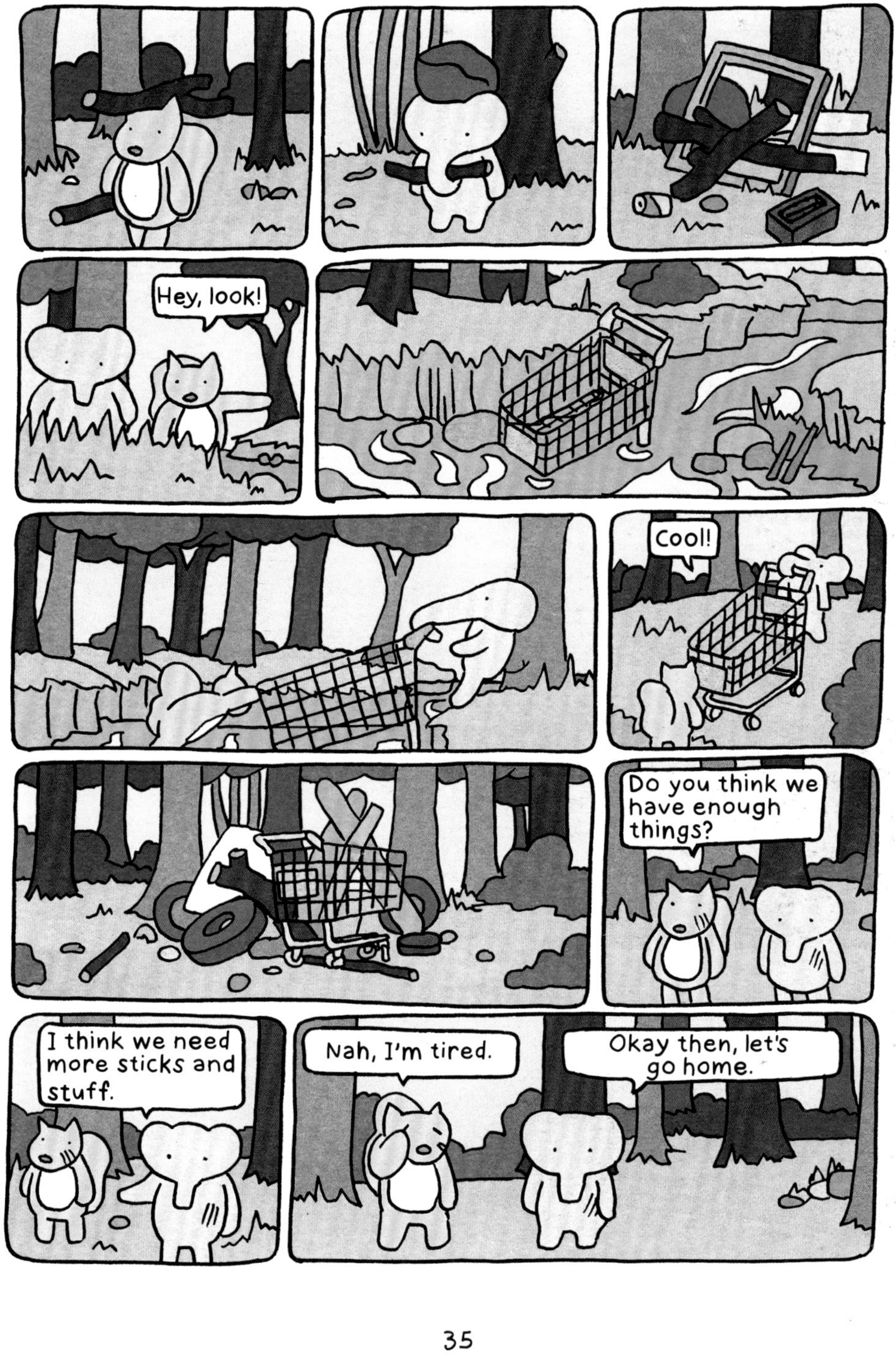
Hey, look!
Cool!
Do you think we have enough things?
I think we need more sticks and stuff.
Nah, I'm tired.
Okay then, let's go home.

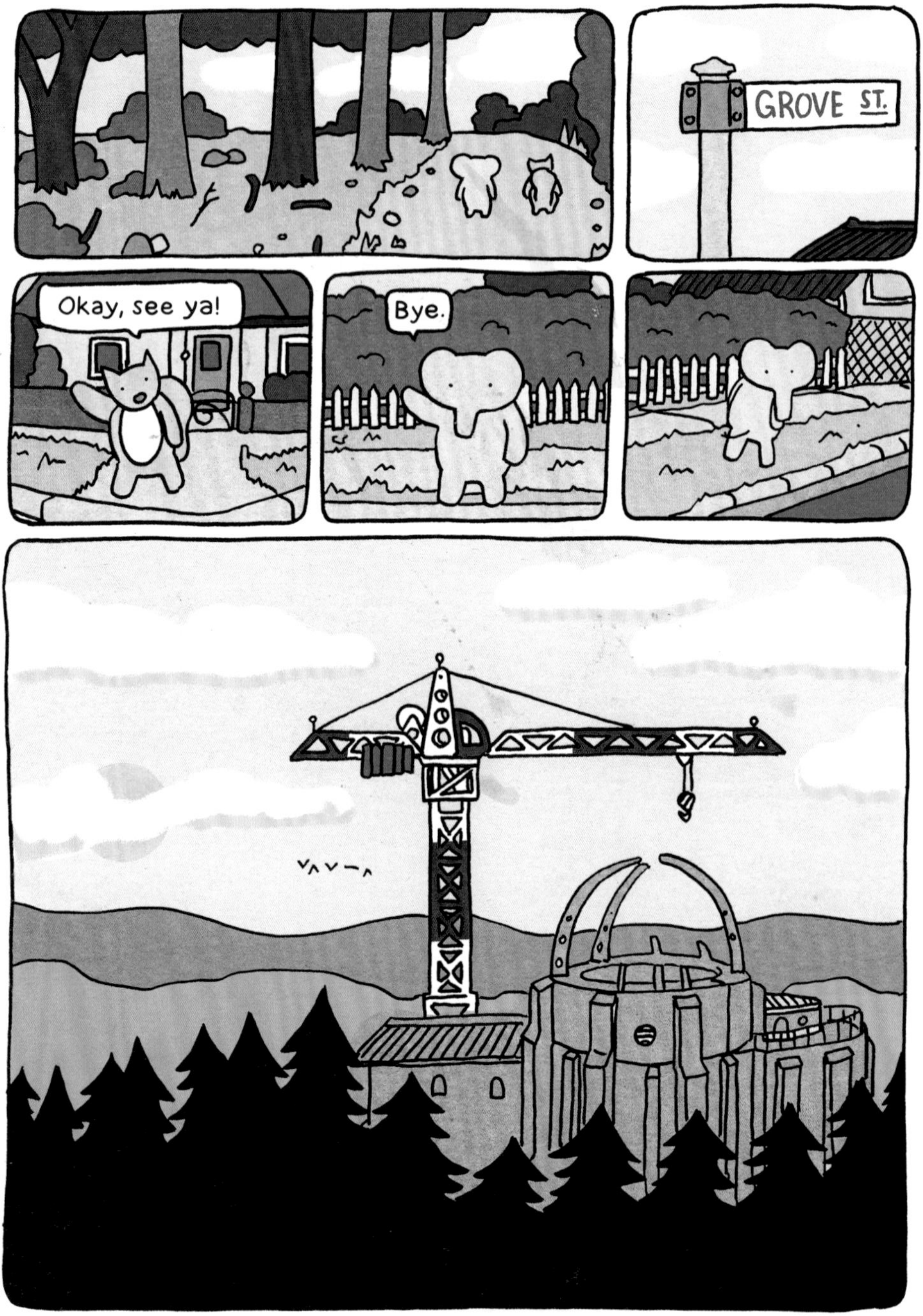
GROVE ST.
Okay, see ya!
Bye.

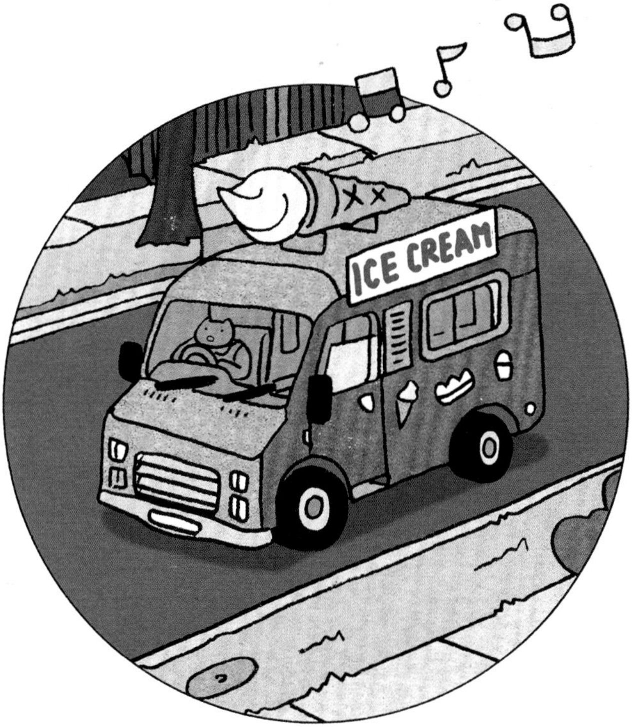
ICE CREAM

Chapter 3

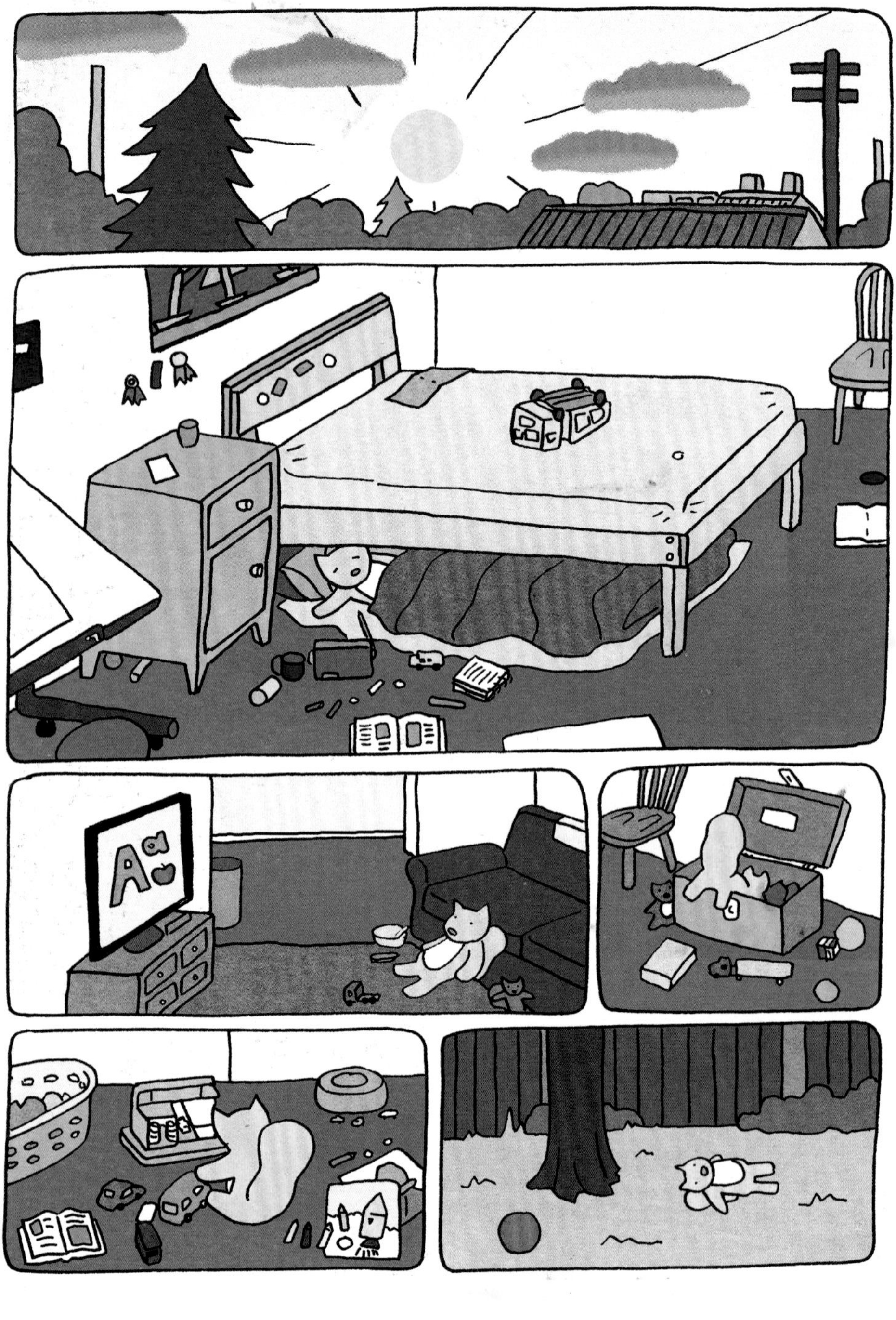
A

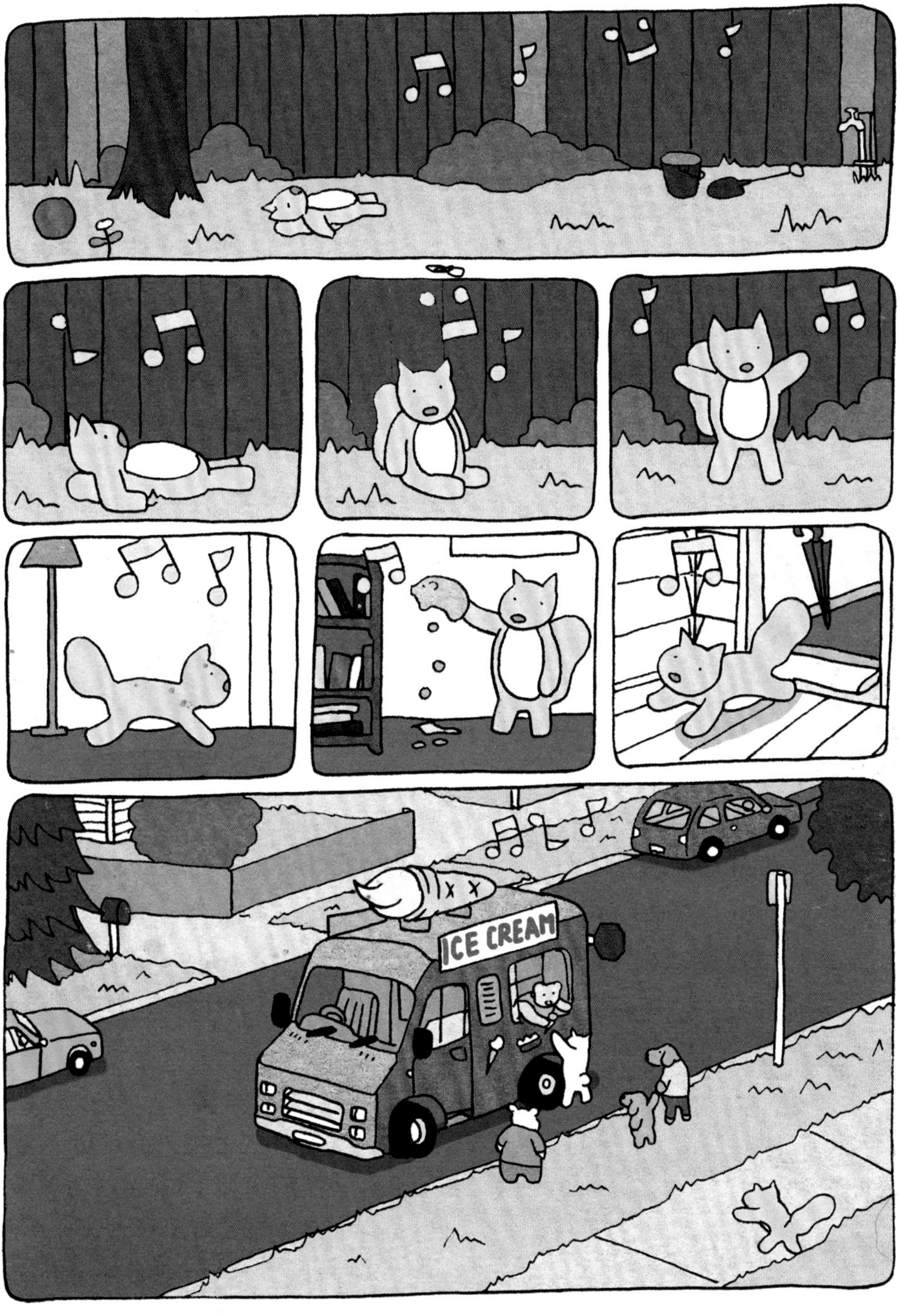
ICE CREAM

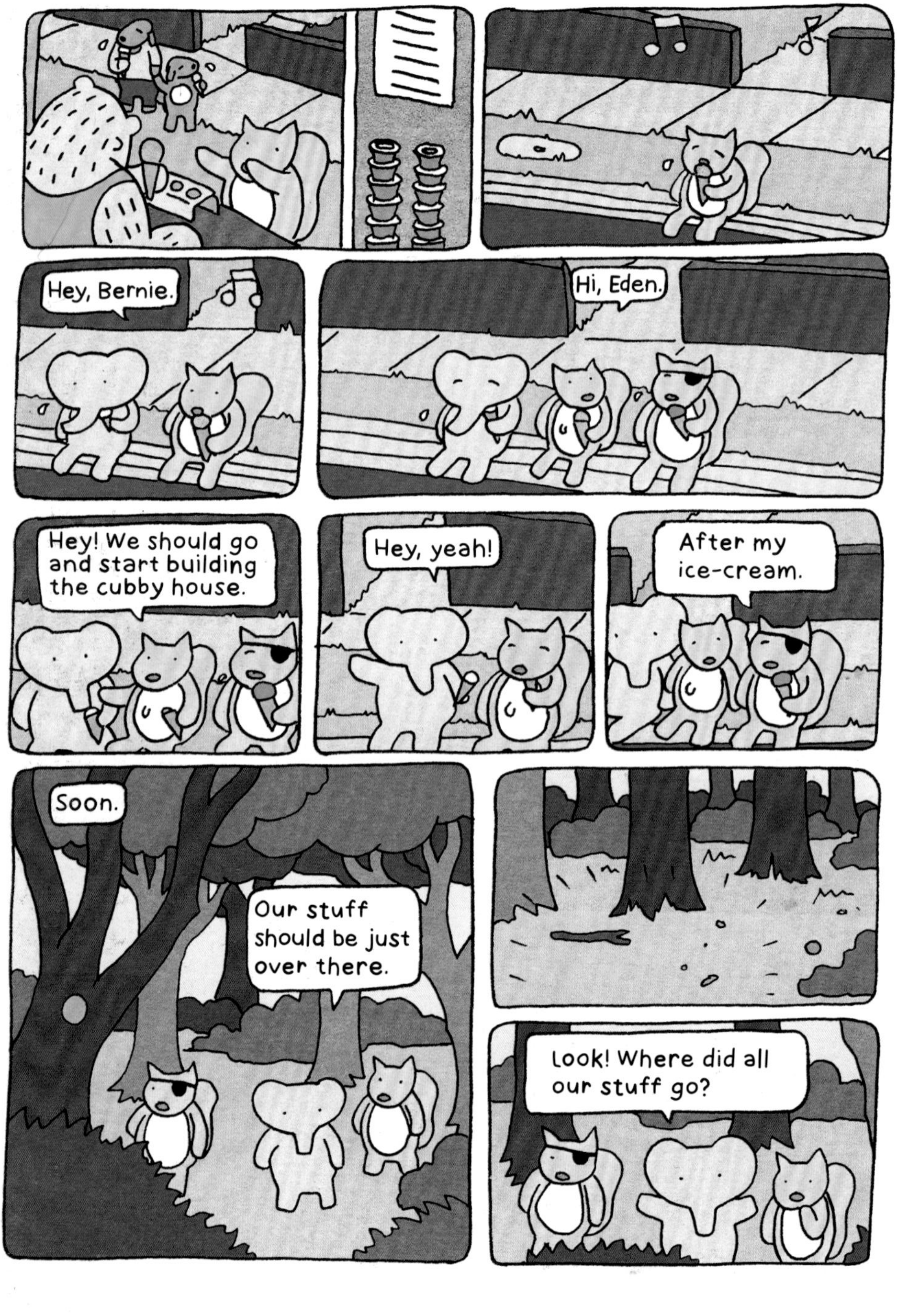
Hey, Bernie.
Hi, Eden.
Hey! We should go and start building the cubby house.
Hey, yeah!
After my ice-cream.
Soon.
Our stuff should be just over there.
Look! Where did all our stuff go?

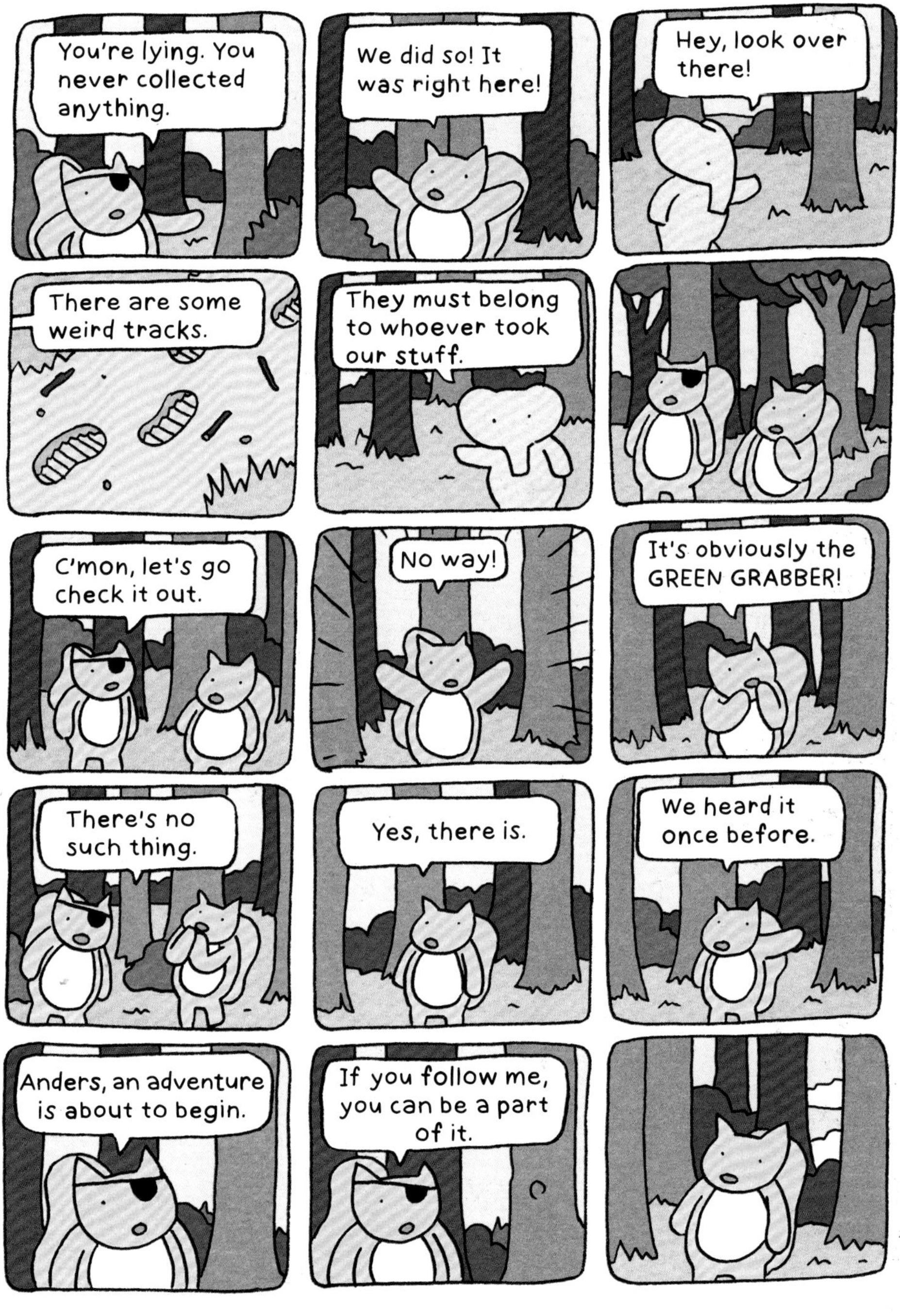
You're lying. You never collected anything.
We did so! It was right here!
Hey, look over there!
There are some weird tracks.
They must belong to whoever took our stuff.
C'mon, let's go check it out.
No way!
It's obviously the GREEN GRABBER!
There's no such thing.
Yes, there is.
We heard it once before.
Anders, an adventure is about to begin.
If you follow me, you can be a part of it.

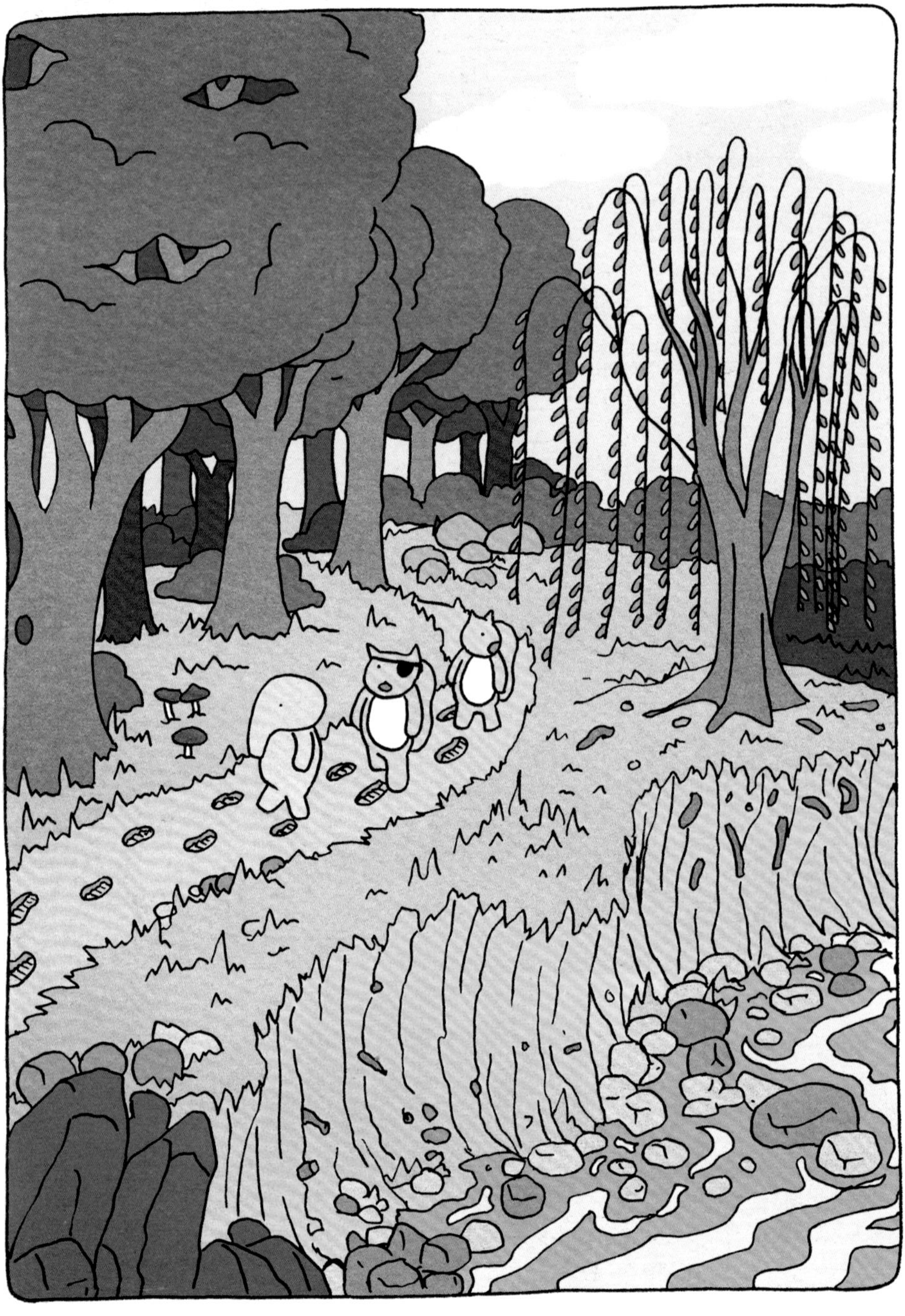

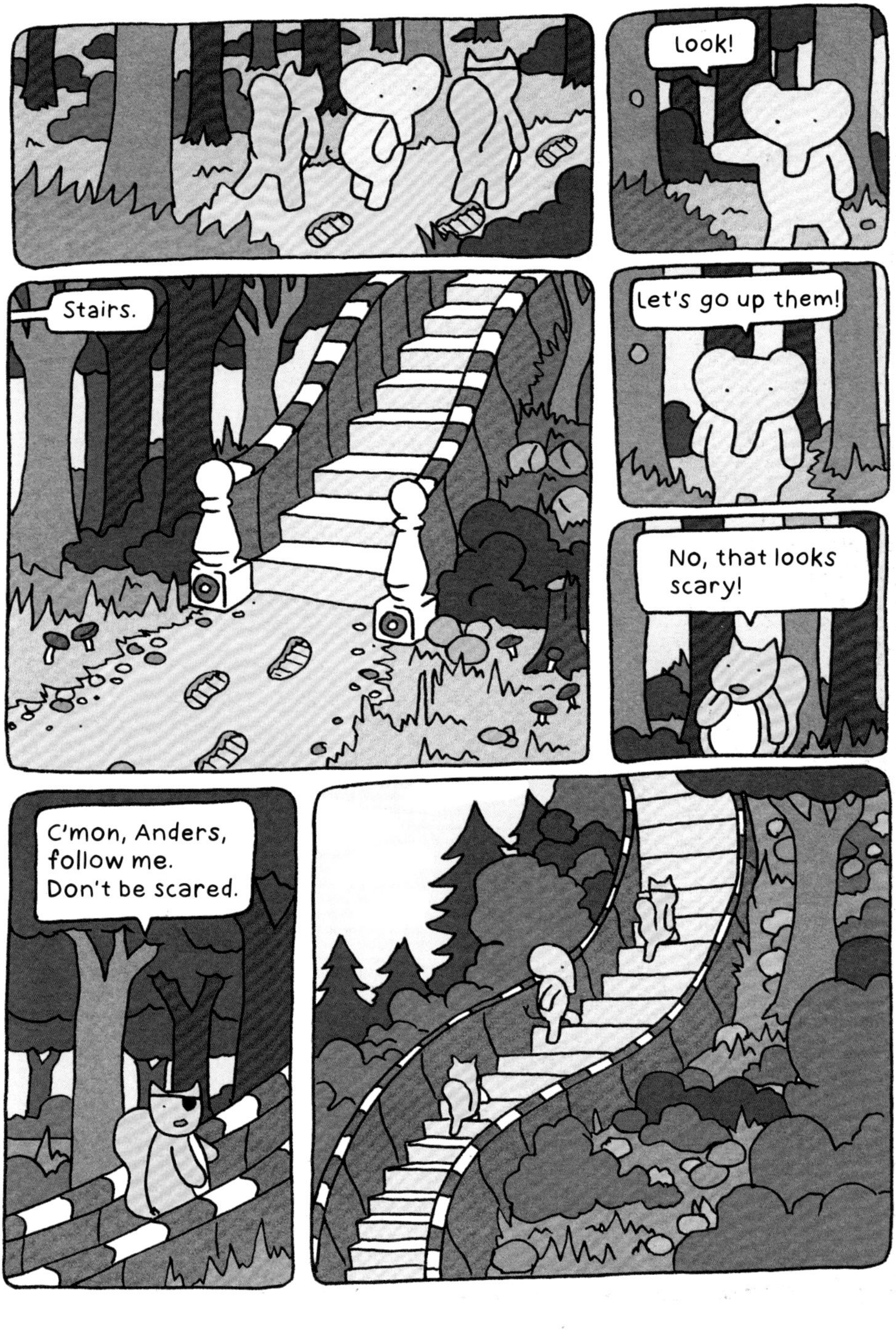
Look!
Stairs.
Let's go up them!
No, that looks scary!
C'mon, Anders, follow me. Don't be scared.

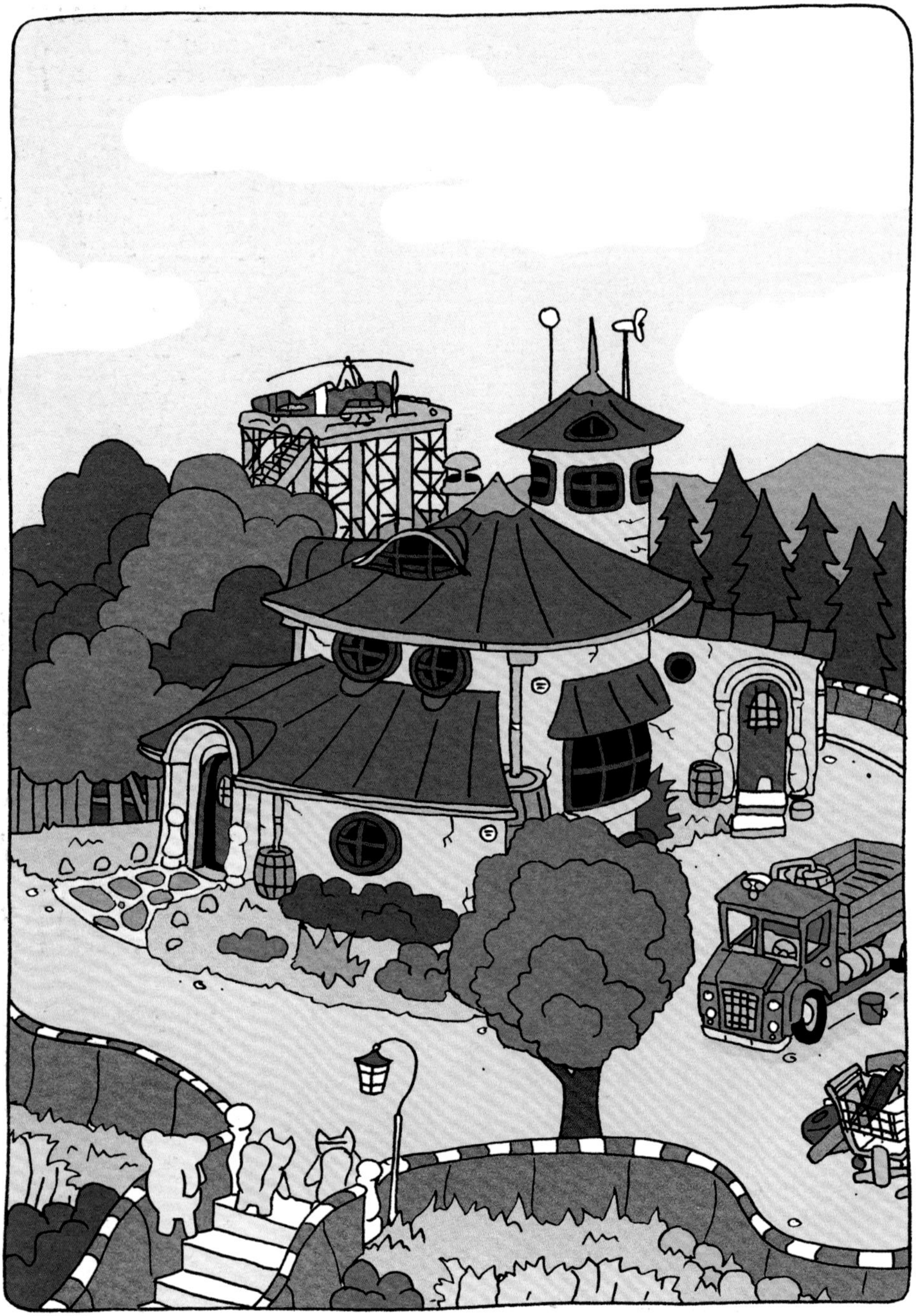

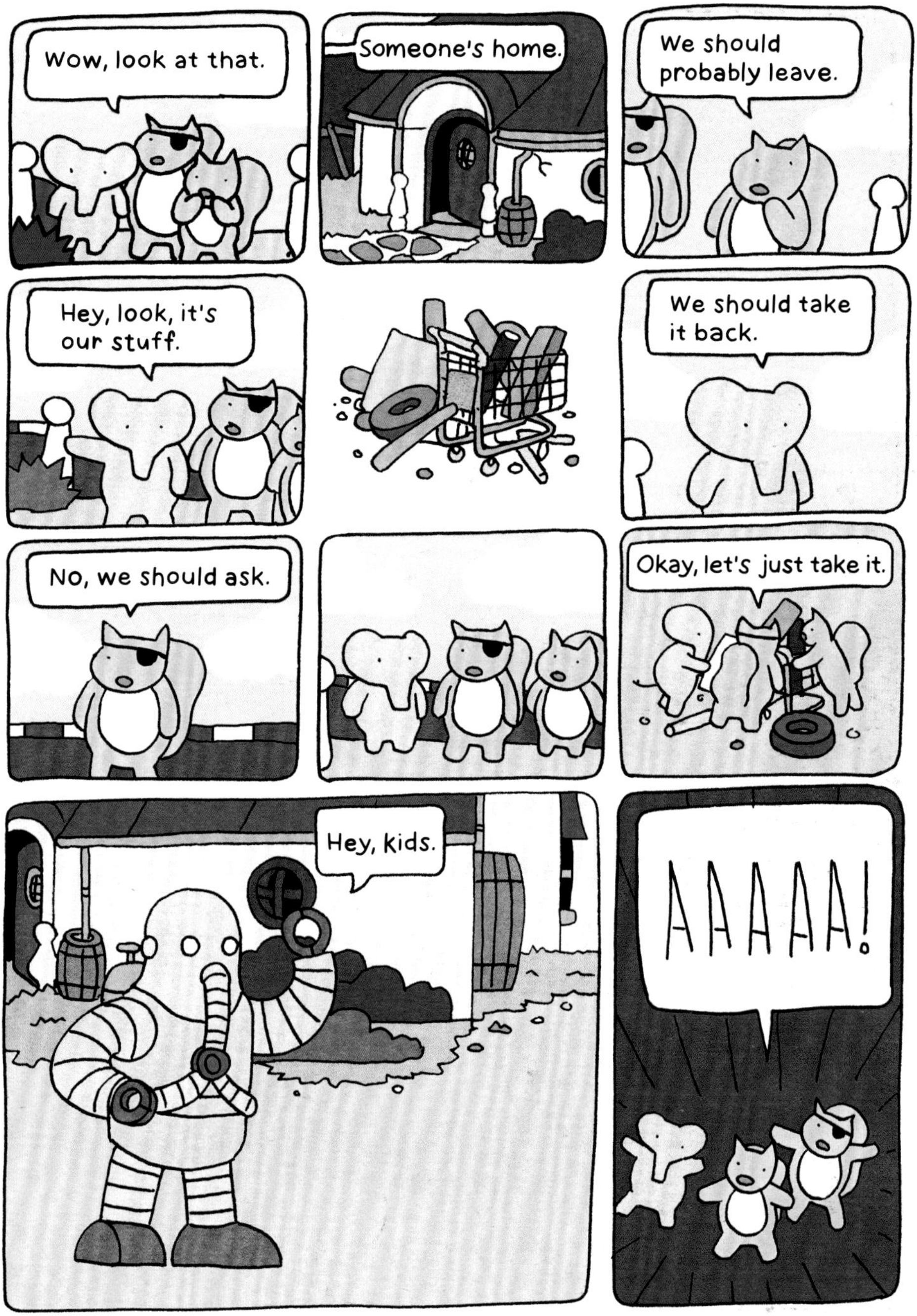
Wow, look at that.
Someone's home.
We should probably leave.
Hey, look, it's our stuff.
We should take it back.
No, we should ask.
Okay, let's just take it.
Hey, kids.
AAAAA!

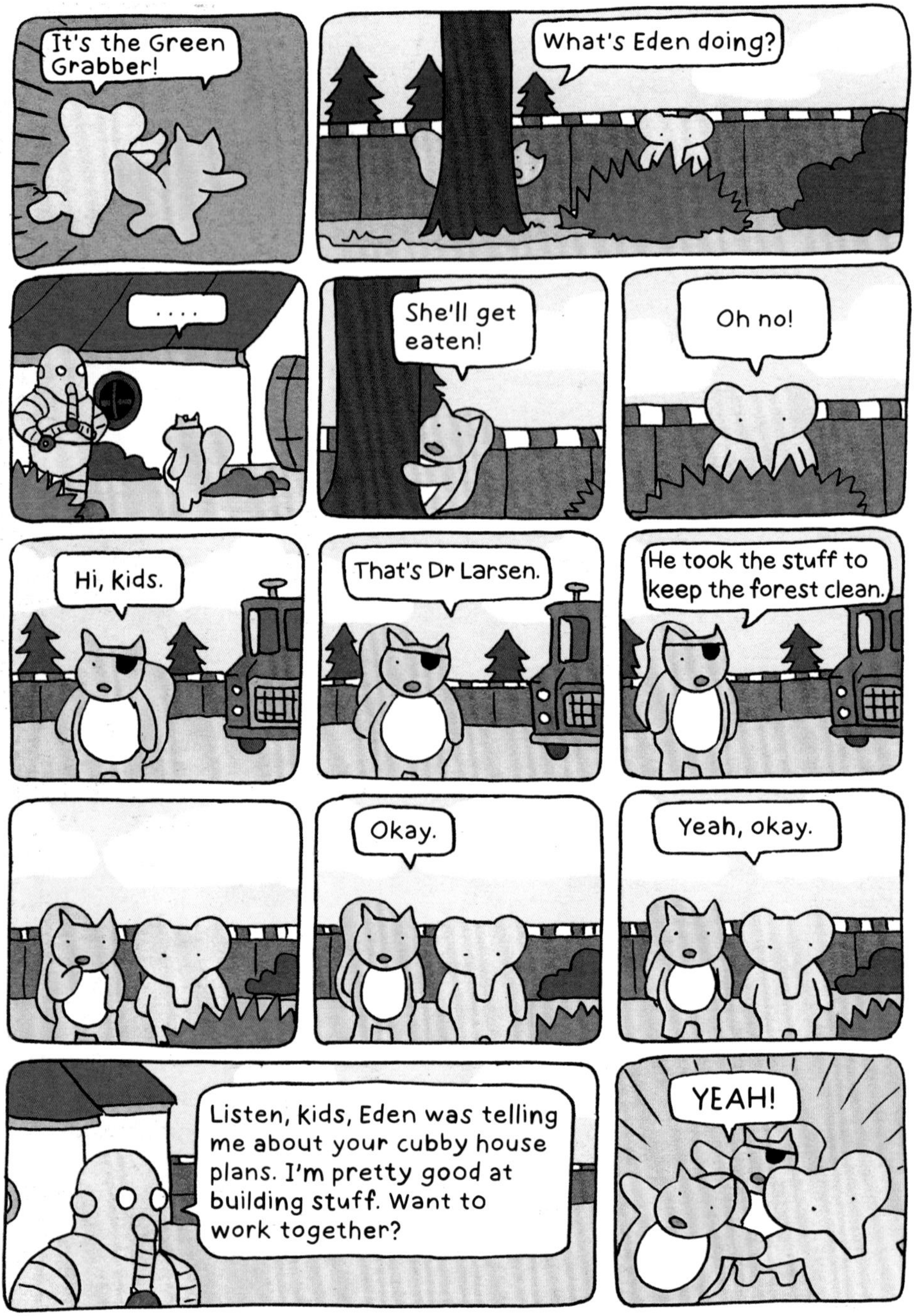
It's the Green Grabber!
What's Eden doing?
....
She'll get eaten!
Oh no!
Hi, kids.
That's Dr Larsen.
He took the stuff to keep the forest clean.
Okay.
Yeah, okay.
Listen, kids, Eden was telling me about your cubby house plans. I'm pretty good at building stuff. Want to work together?
YEAH!

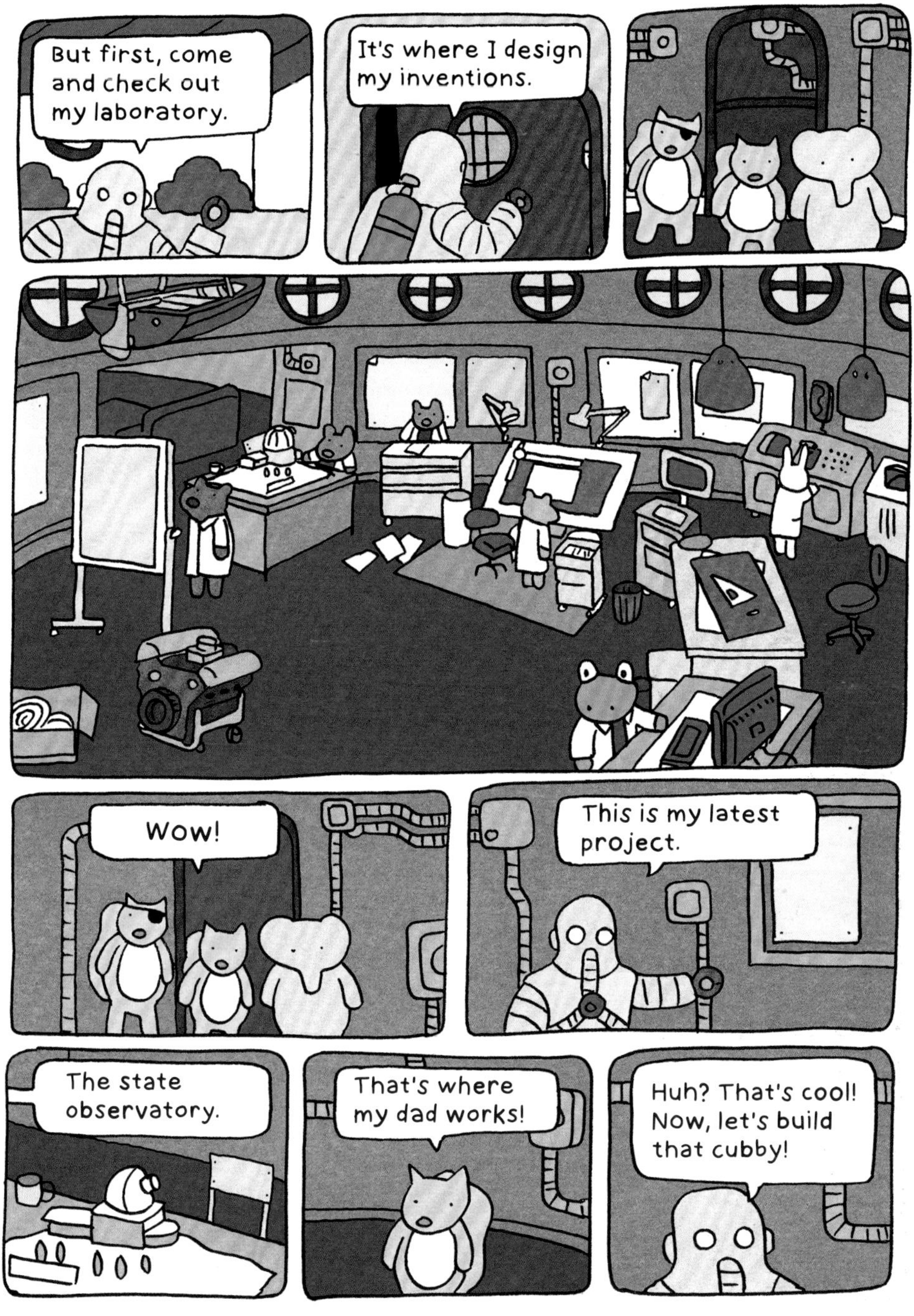

But first, come and check out my laboratory.
It's where I design my inventions.
Wow!
This is my latest project.
The state observatory.
That's where my dad works!
Huh? That's cool! Now, let's build that cubby!

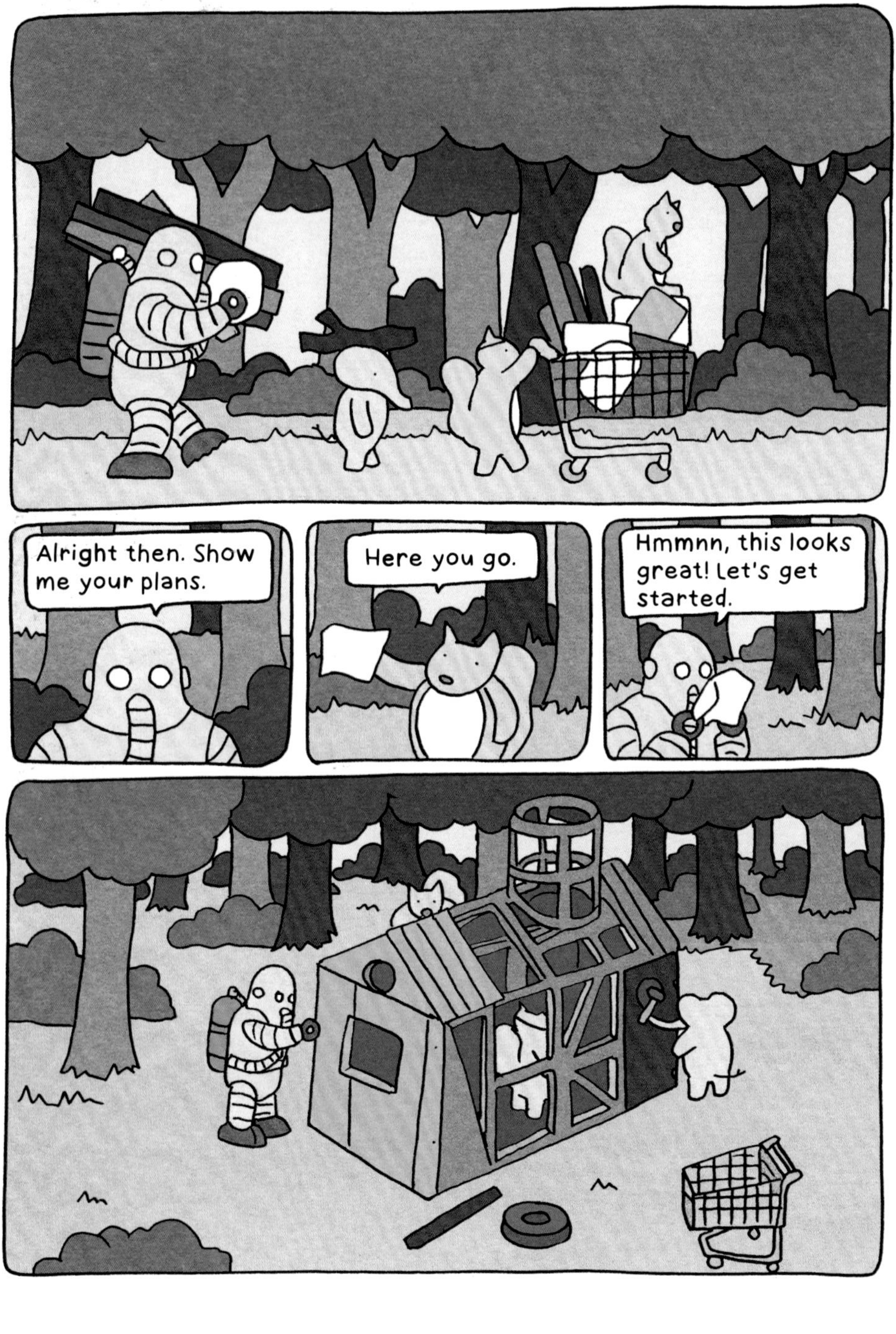
Alright then. Show me your plans.
Here you go.
Hmmnn, this looks great! Let's get started.

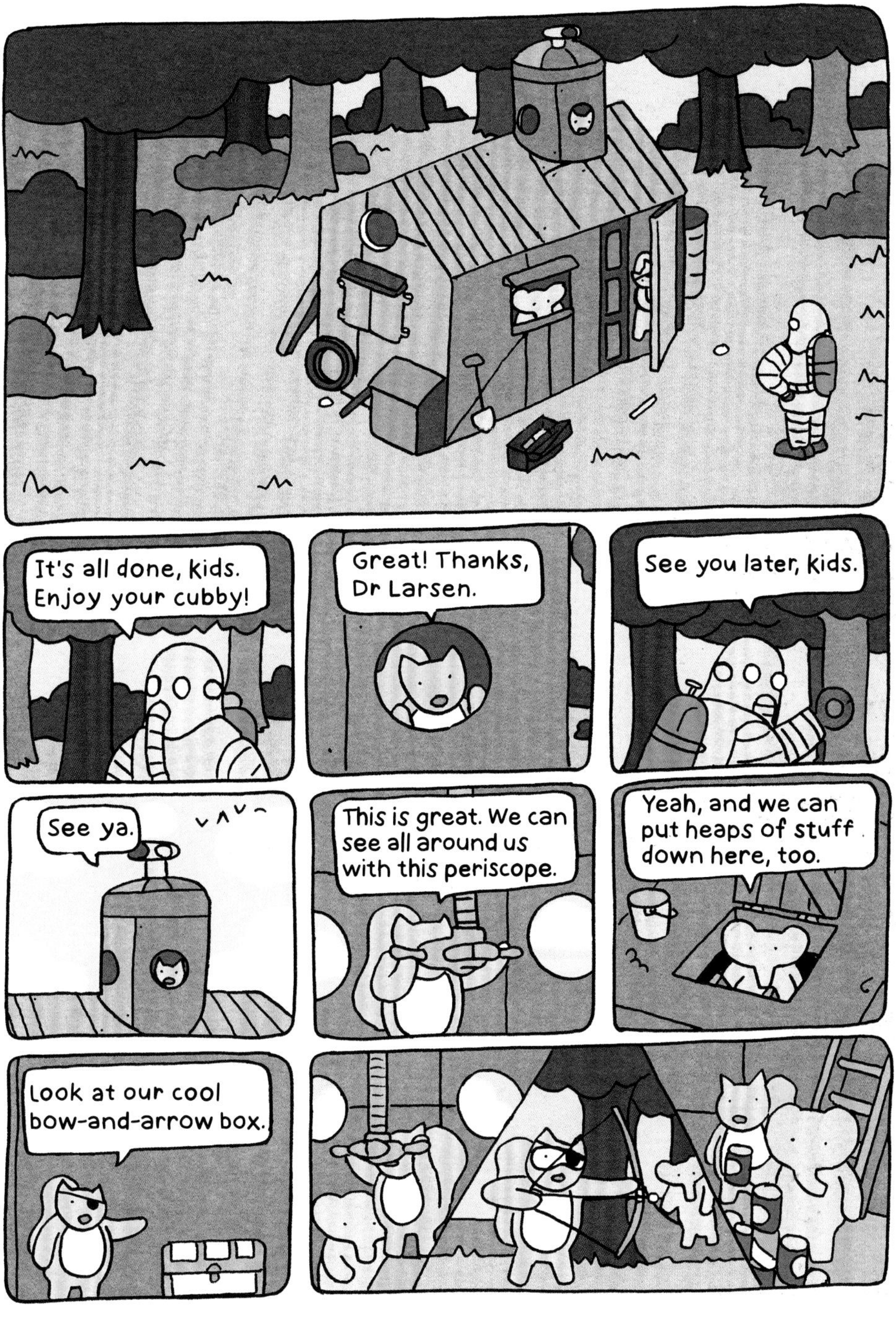
It's all done, kids. Enjoy your cubby!
Great! Thanks, Dr Larsen.
See you later, kids.
See ya.
This is great. We can see all around us with this periscope.
Yeah, and we can put heaps of stuff down here, too.
Look at our cool bow-and-arrow box.

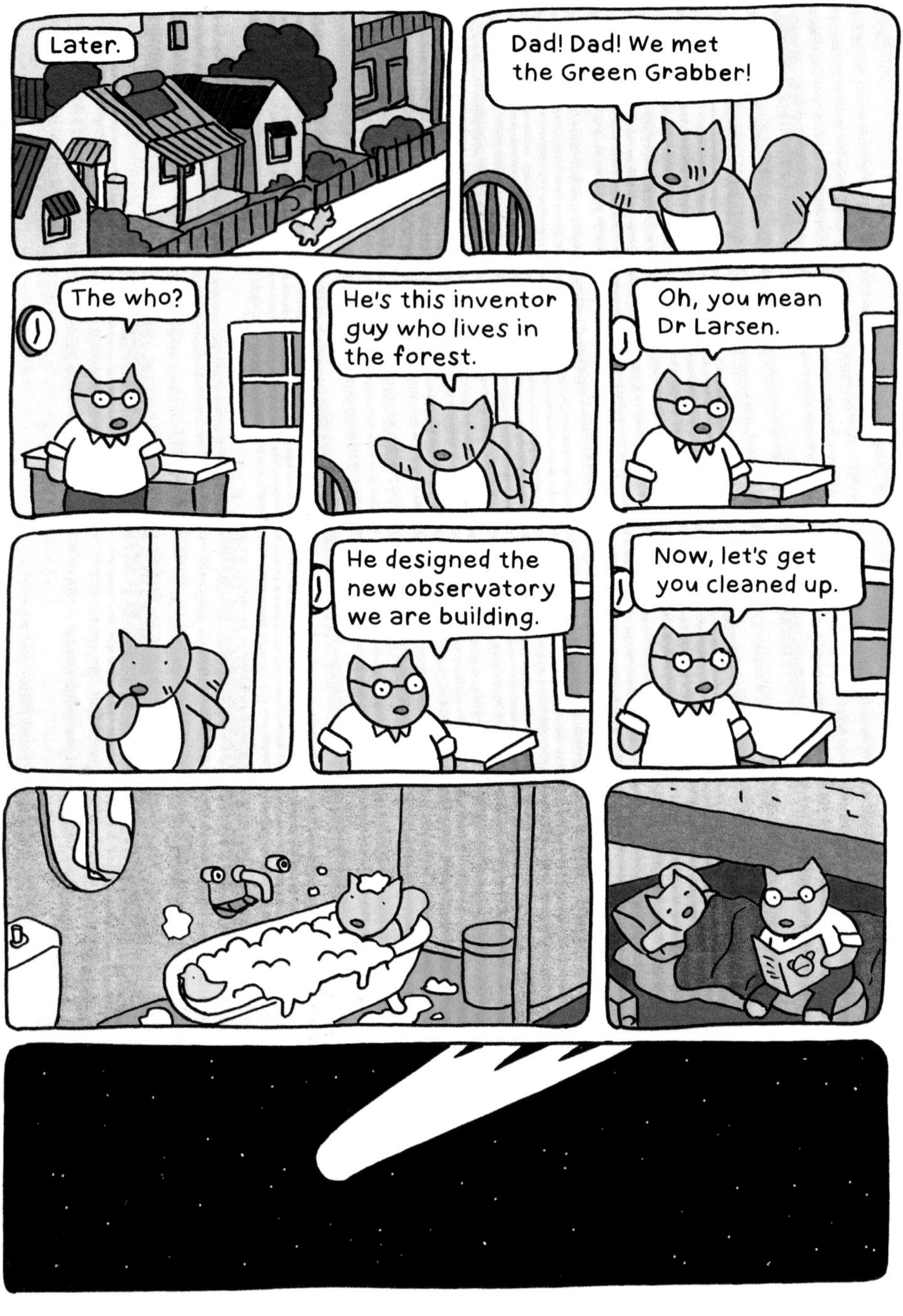

Later.
Dad! Dad! We met the Green Grabber!
The who?
He's this inventor guy who lives in the forest.
Oh, you mean Dr Larsen.
He designed the new observatory we are building.
Now, let's get you cleaned up.

Chapter 4

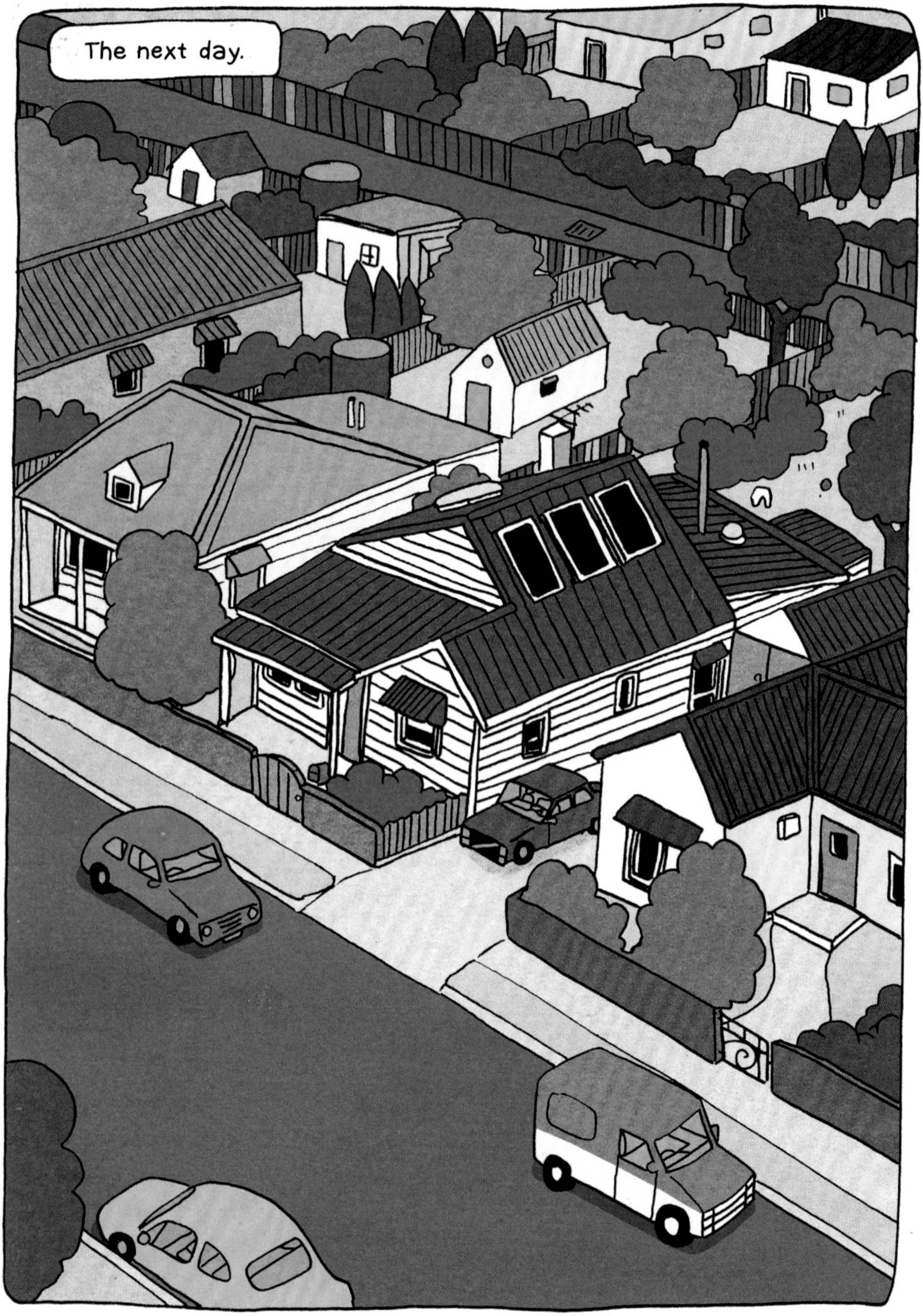
The next day.

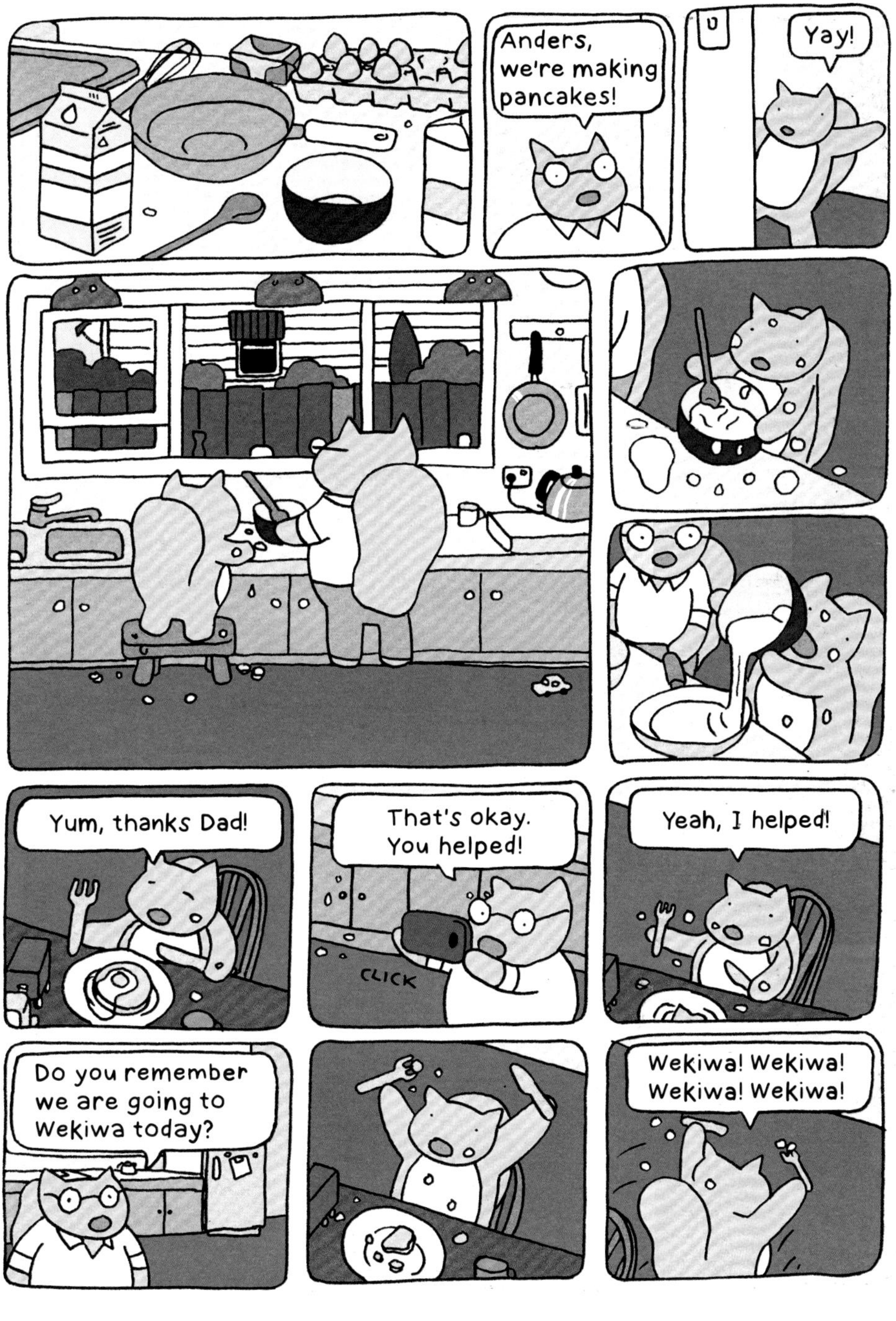
Anders, we're making pancakes!
Yay!
Yum, thanks Dad!
That's okay. You helped!
CLICK
Yeah, I helped!
Do you remember we are going to Wekiwa today?
Wekiwa! Wekiwa! Wekiwa! Wekiwa!

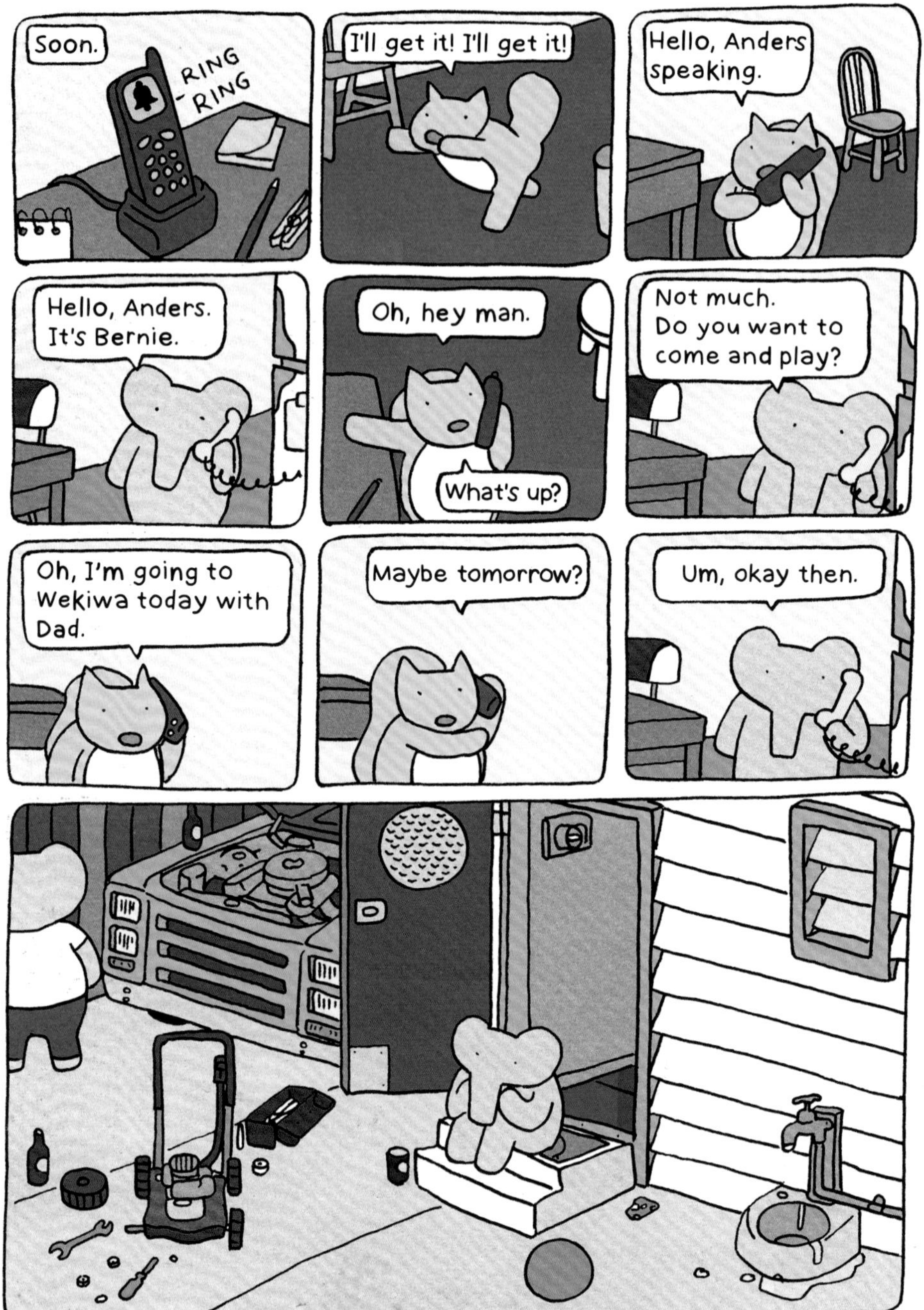
Soon.
RING RING
I'll get it! I'll get it!
Hello, Anders speaking.
Hello, Anders. It's Bernie.
Oh, hey man.
What's up?
Not much. Do you want to come and play?
Oh, I'm going to Wekiwa today with Dad.
Maybe tomorrow?
Um, okay then.

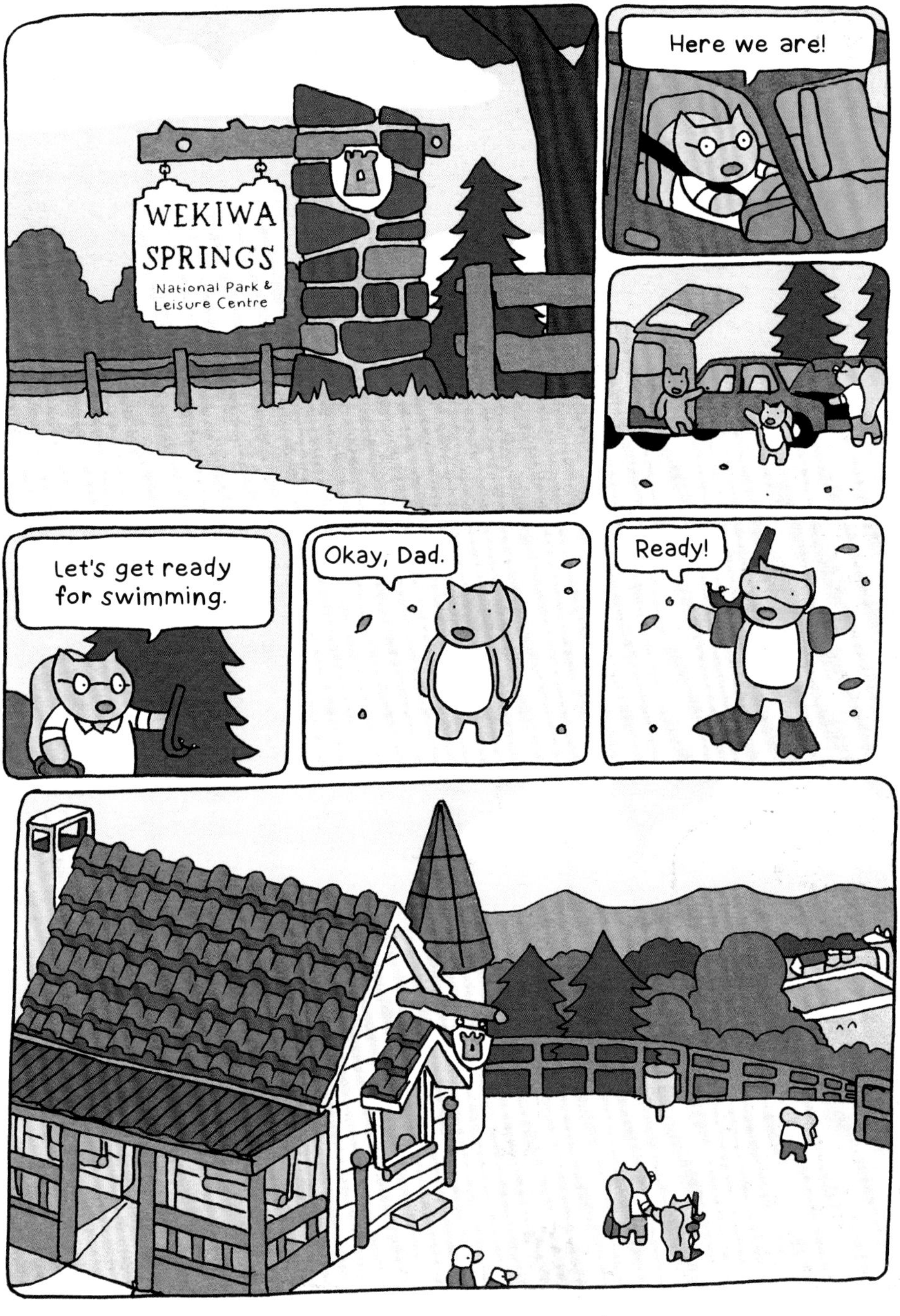
WEKIWA SPRINGS
National Park & Leisure Centre
Here we are!
Let's get ready for swimming.
Okay, Dad.
Ready!

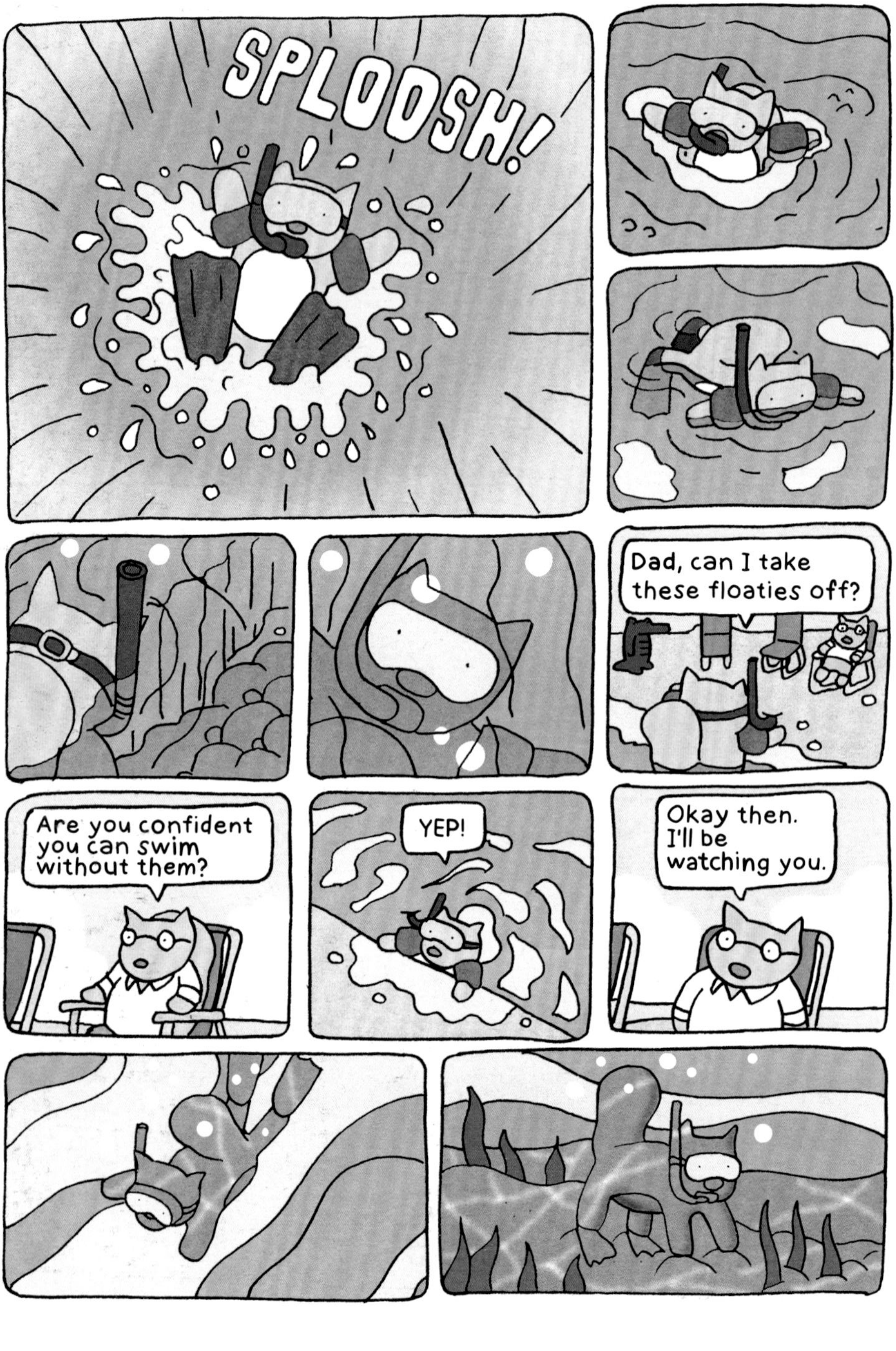
SPLOOSH!
Dad, can I take these floaties off?
Are you confident you can swim without them?
YEP!
Okay then. I'll be watching you.

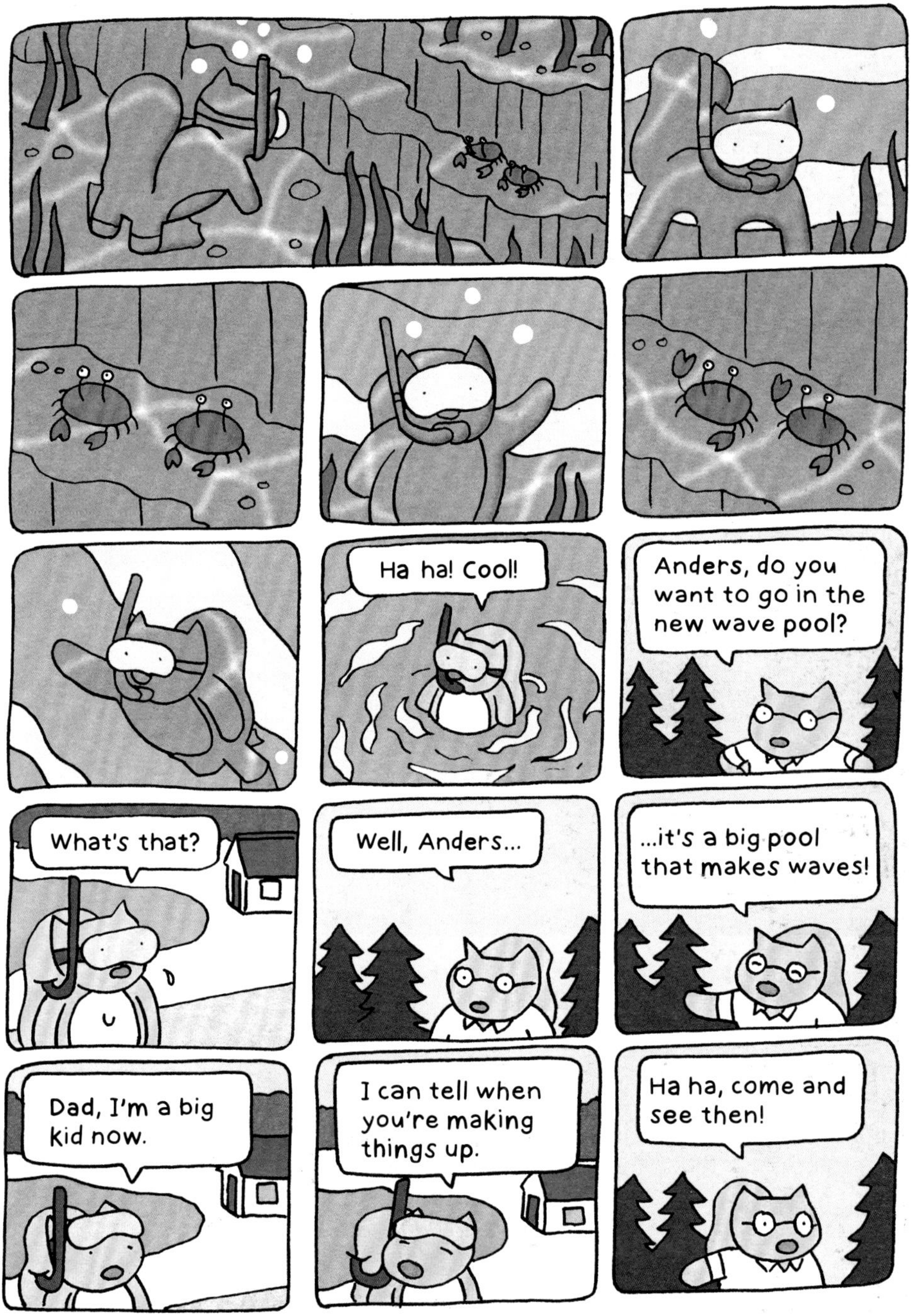
Ha ha! Cool!
Anders, do you want to go in the new wave pool?
What's that?
Well, Anders...
...it's a big pool that makes waves!
Dad, I'm a big kid now.
I can tell when you're making things up.
Ha ha, come and see then!

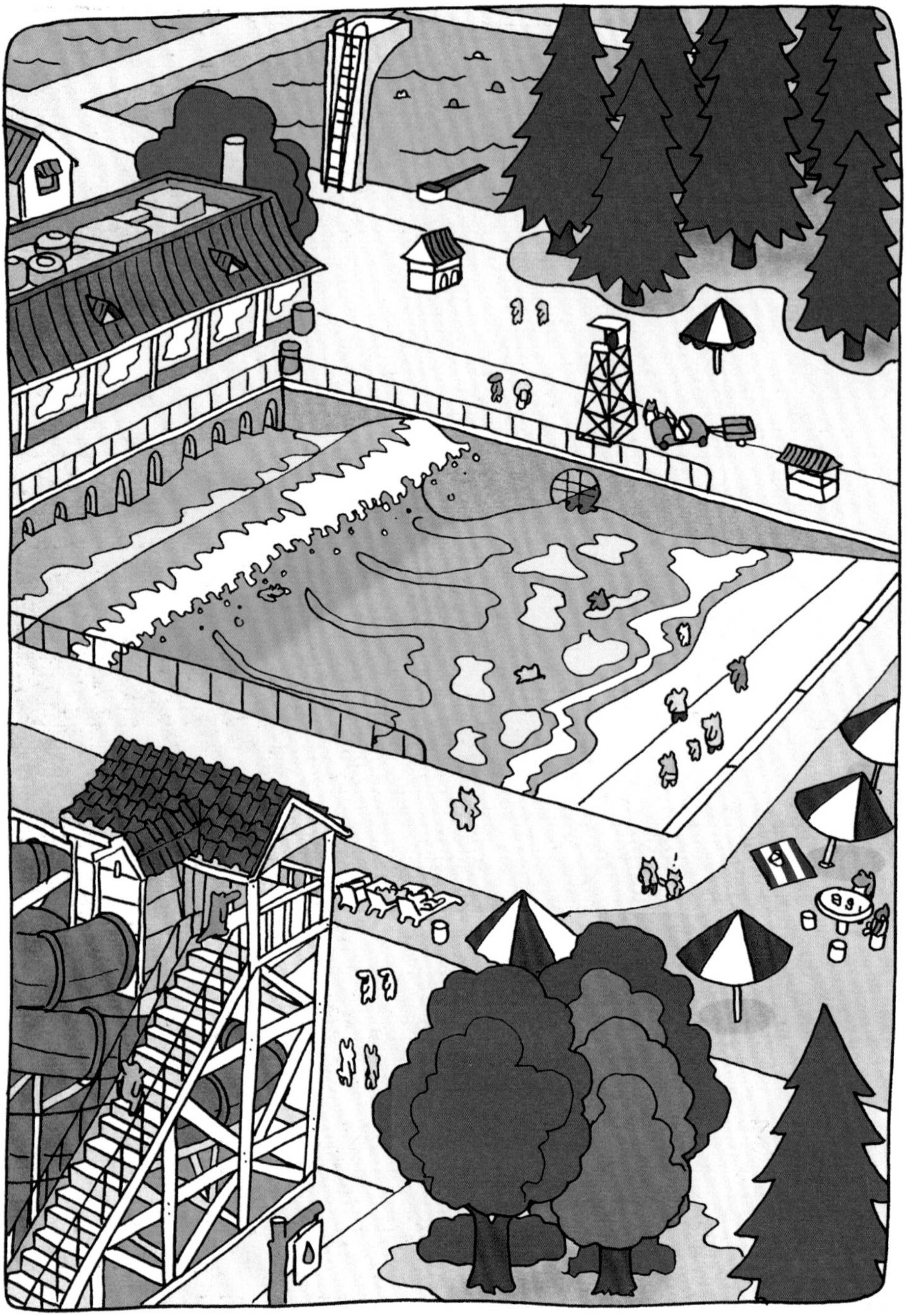

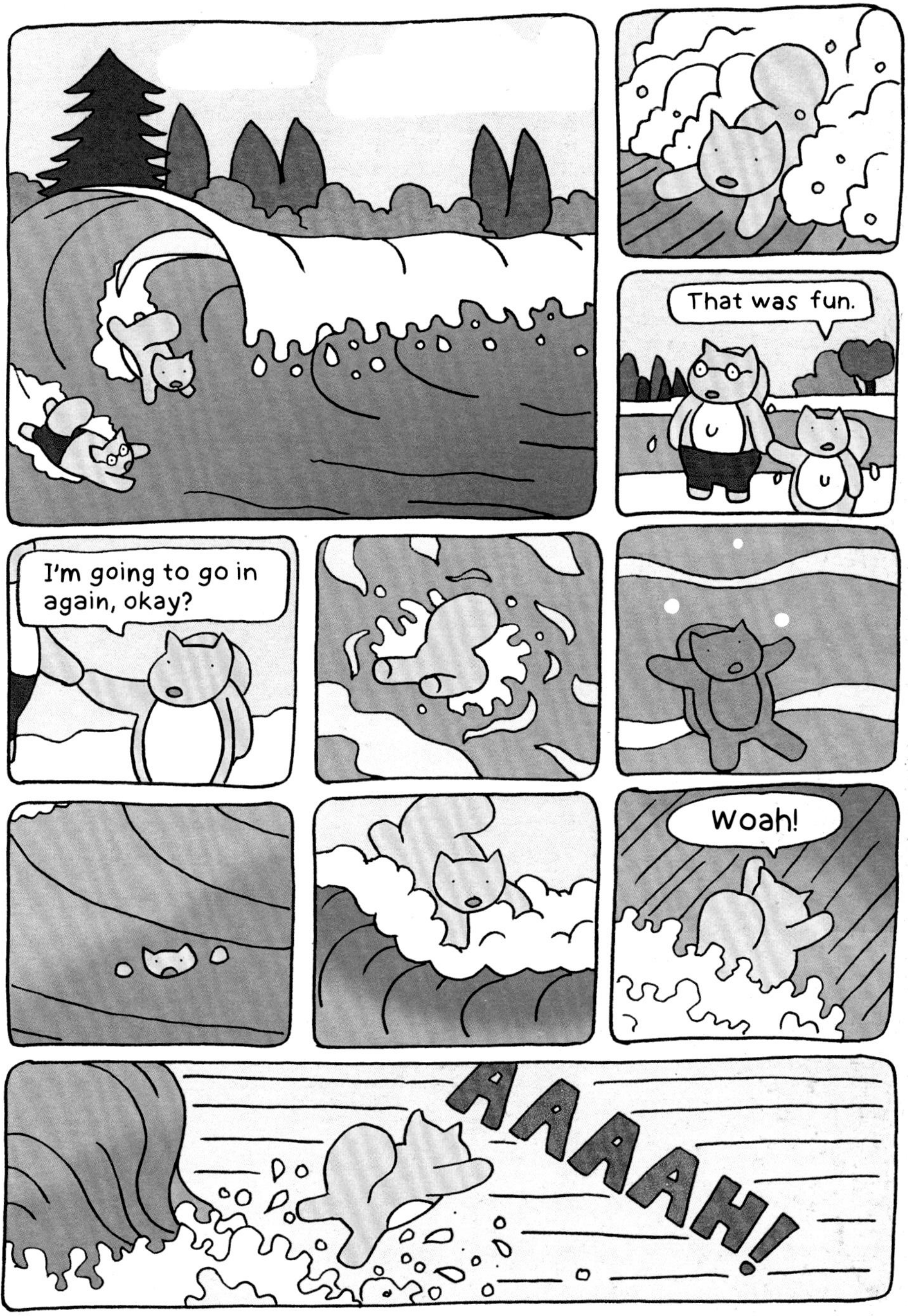
That was fun.
I'm going to go in again, okay?
Woah!
AAAAAH!

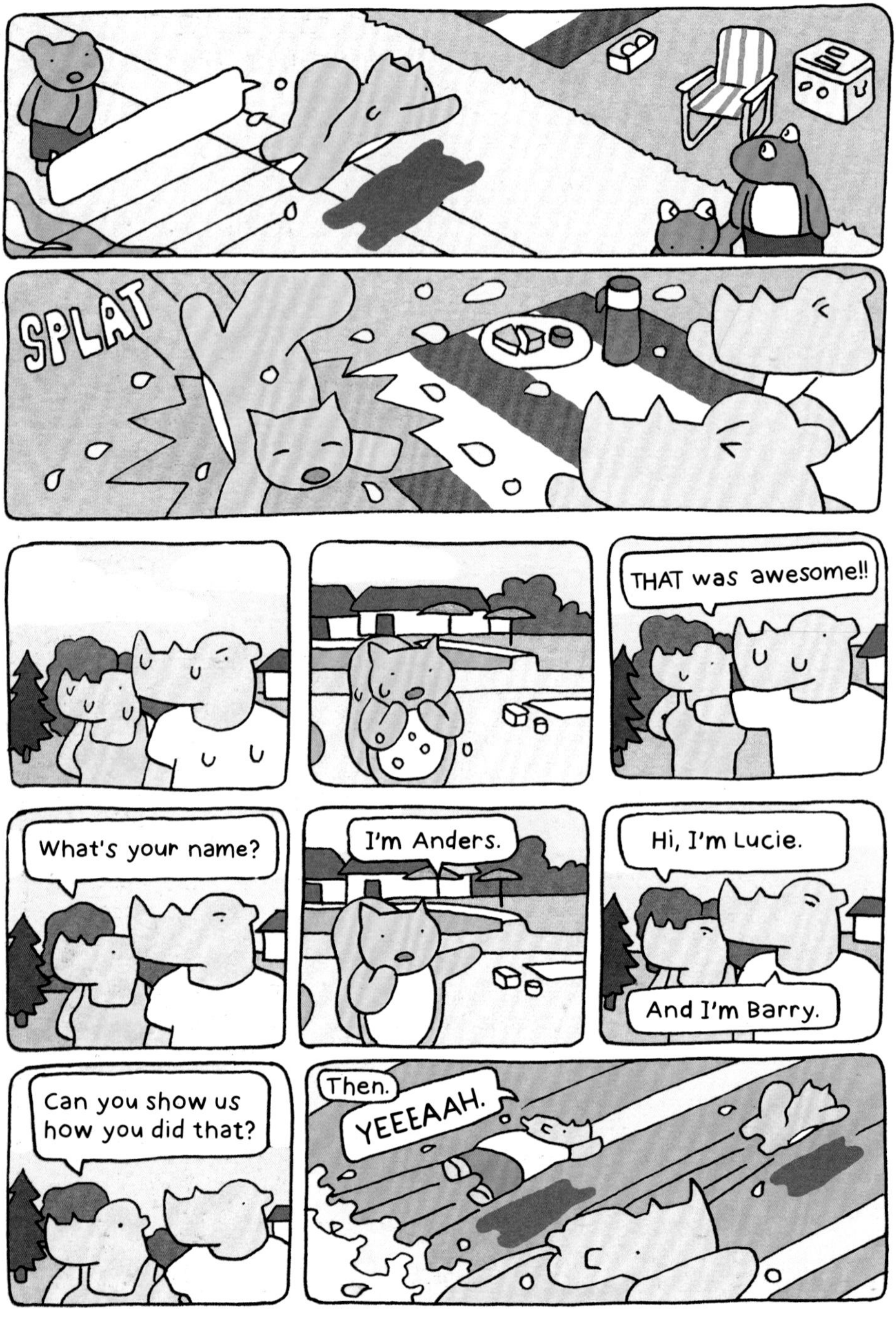
SPLAT
THAT was awesome!!
What's your name?
I'm Anders.
Hi, I'm Lucie.
And I'm Barry.
Can you show us how you did that?
Then.
YEEEAAH.

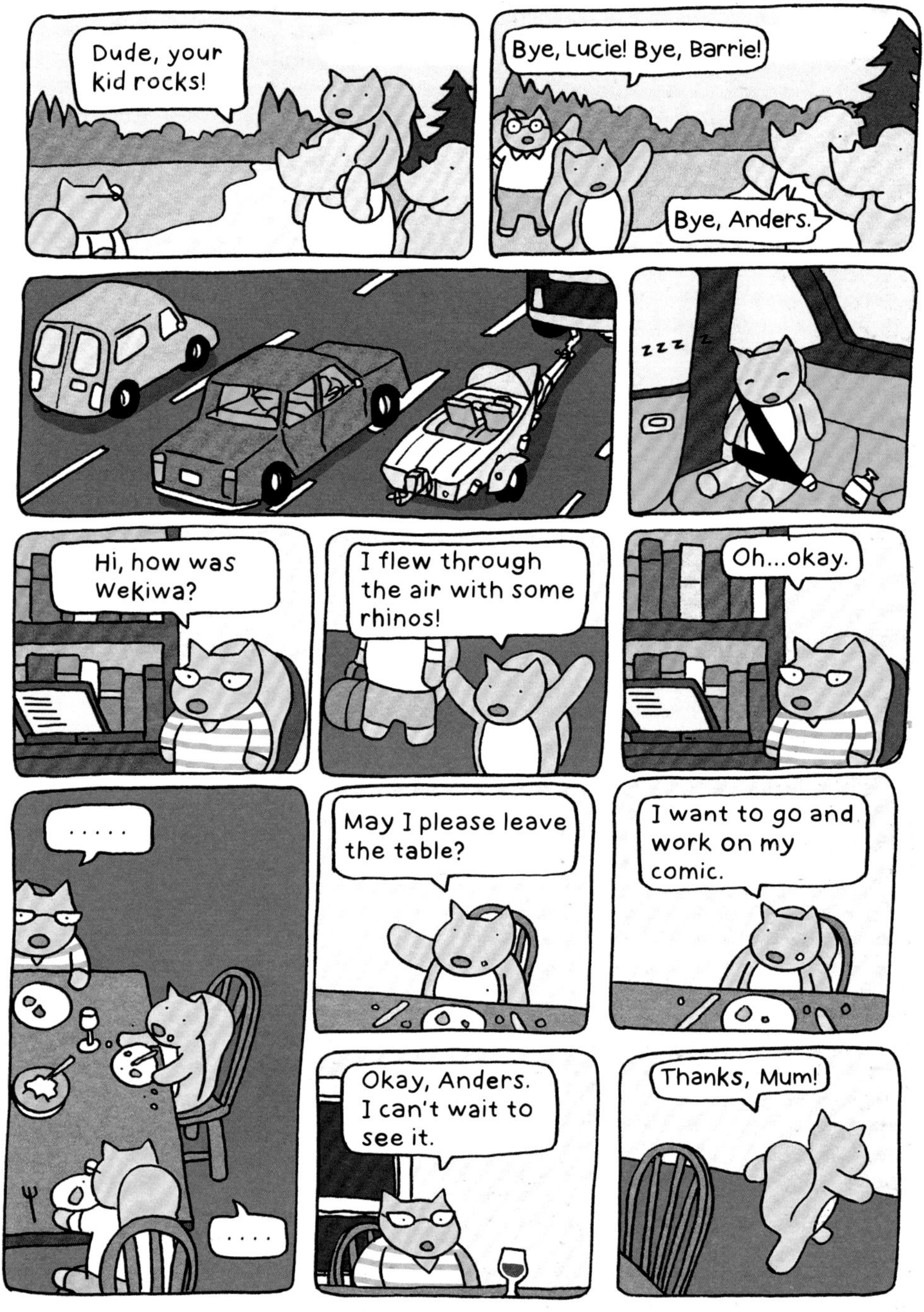
Dude, your kid rocks!
Bye, Lucie! Bye, Barrie!
Bye, Anders.
ZZZ Z
Hi, how was Wekiwa?
I flew through the air with some rhinos!
Oh...okay.
.....
....
May I please leave the table?
I want to go and work on my comic.
Okay, Anders. I can't wait to see it.
Thanks, Mum!

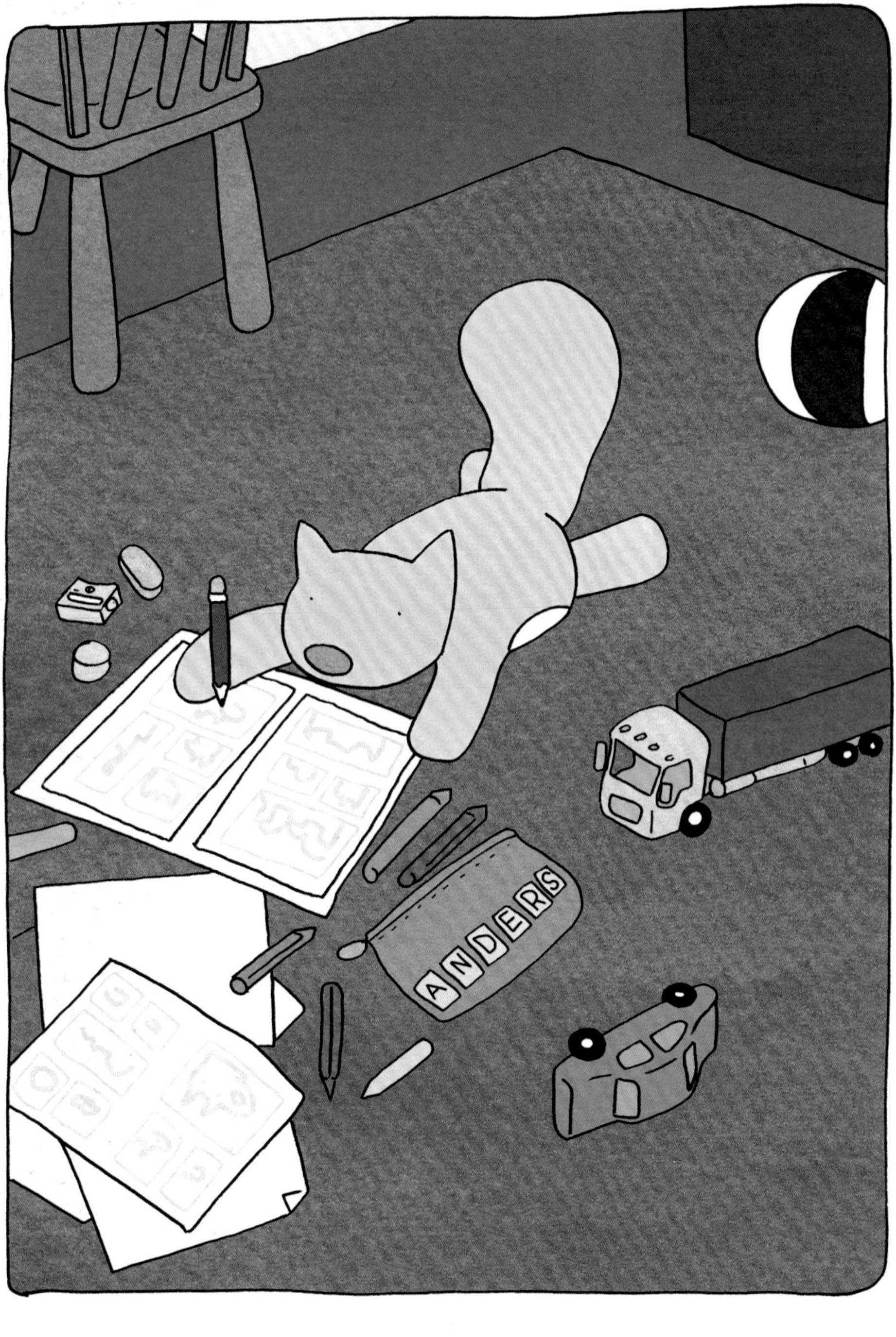
ANDERS

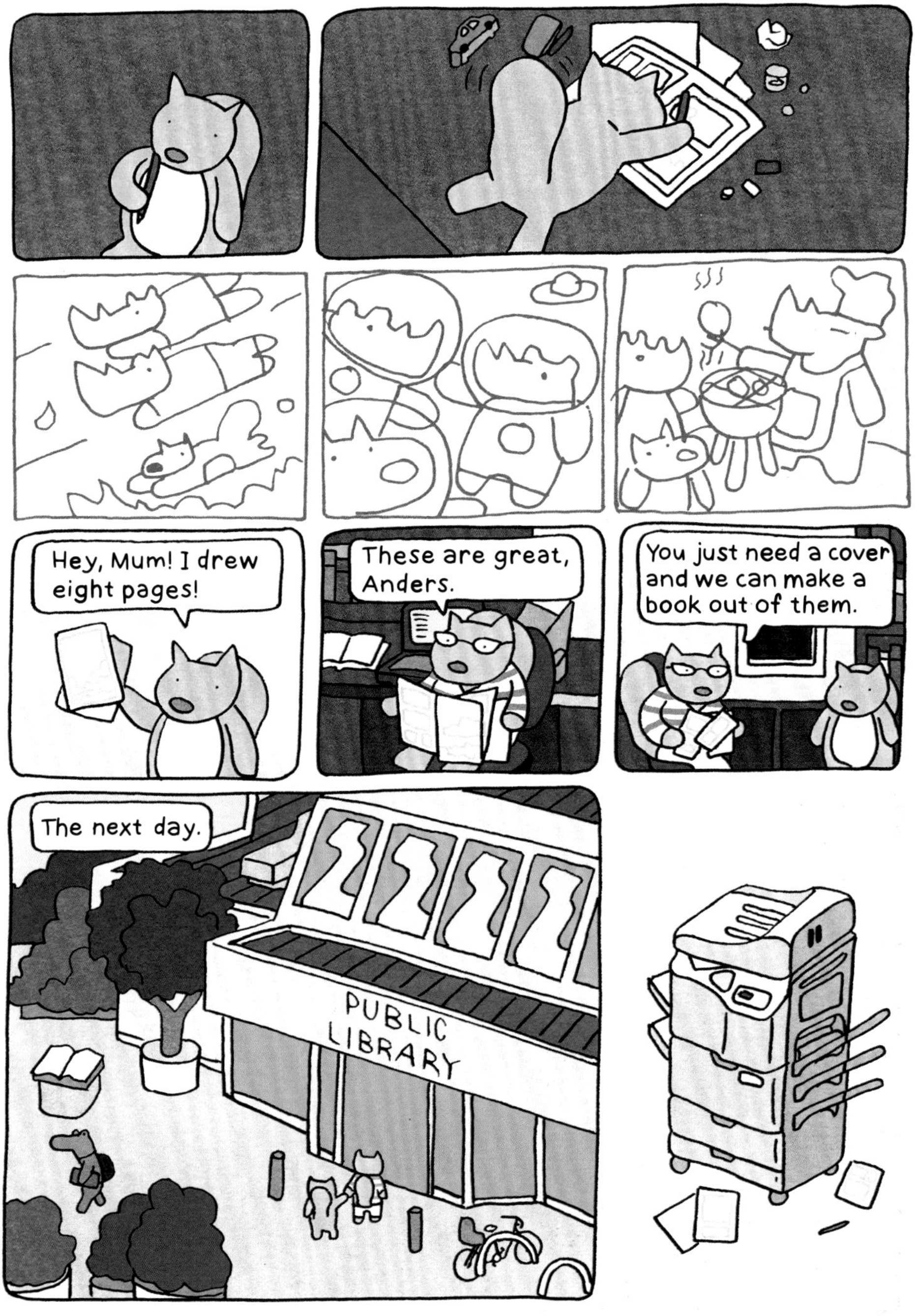
Hey, Mum! I drew eight pages!
These are great, Anders.
You just need a cover and we can make a book out of them.
The next day.
PUBLIC LIBRARY

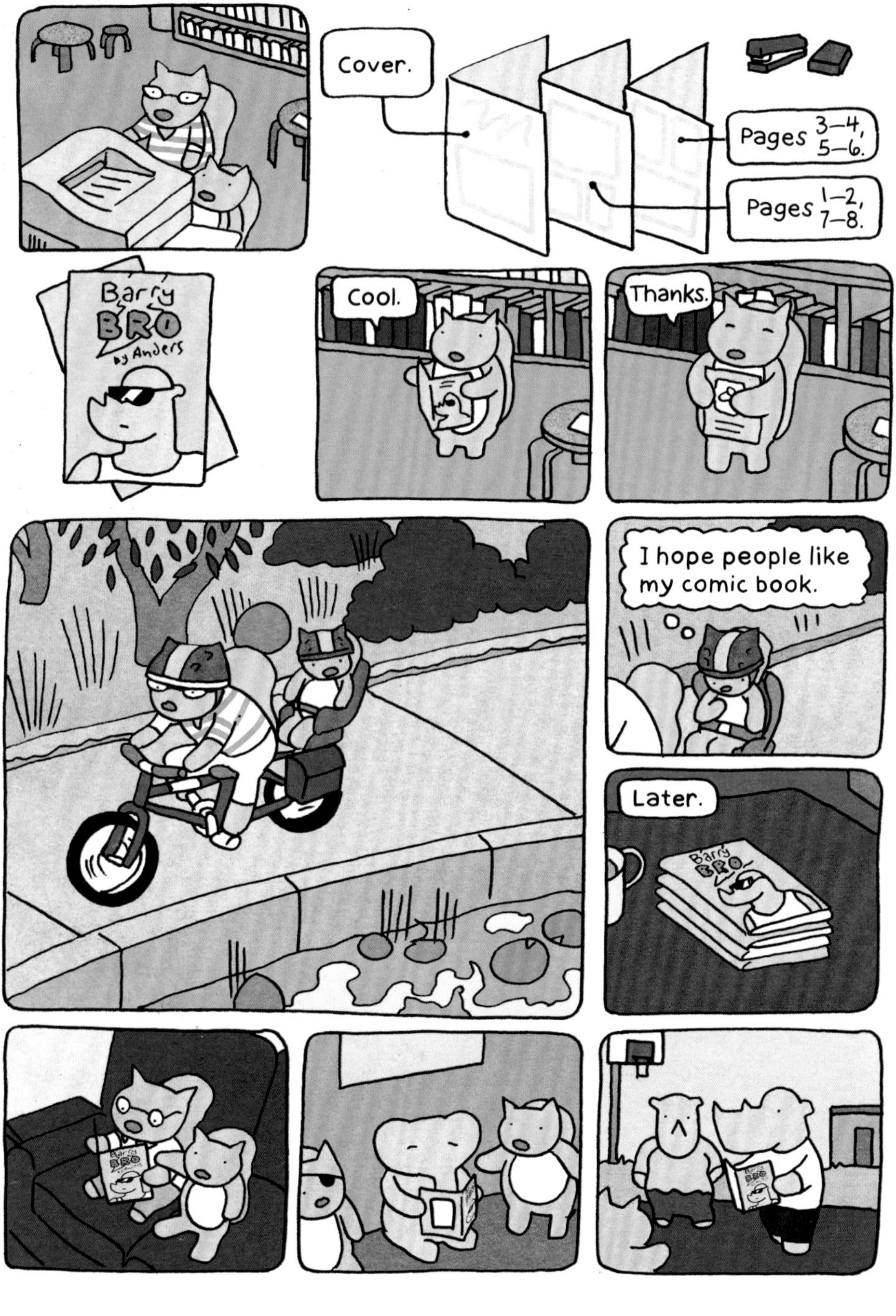
Cover.
Pages 3–4, 5–6.
Pages 1–2, 7–8.
Barry BRO by Anders
Cool.
Thanks.
I hope people like my comic book.
Later.

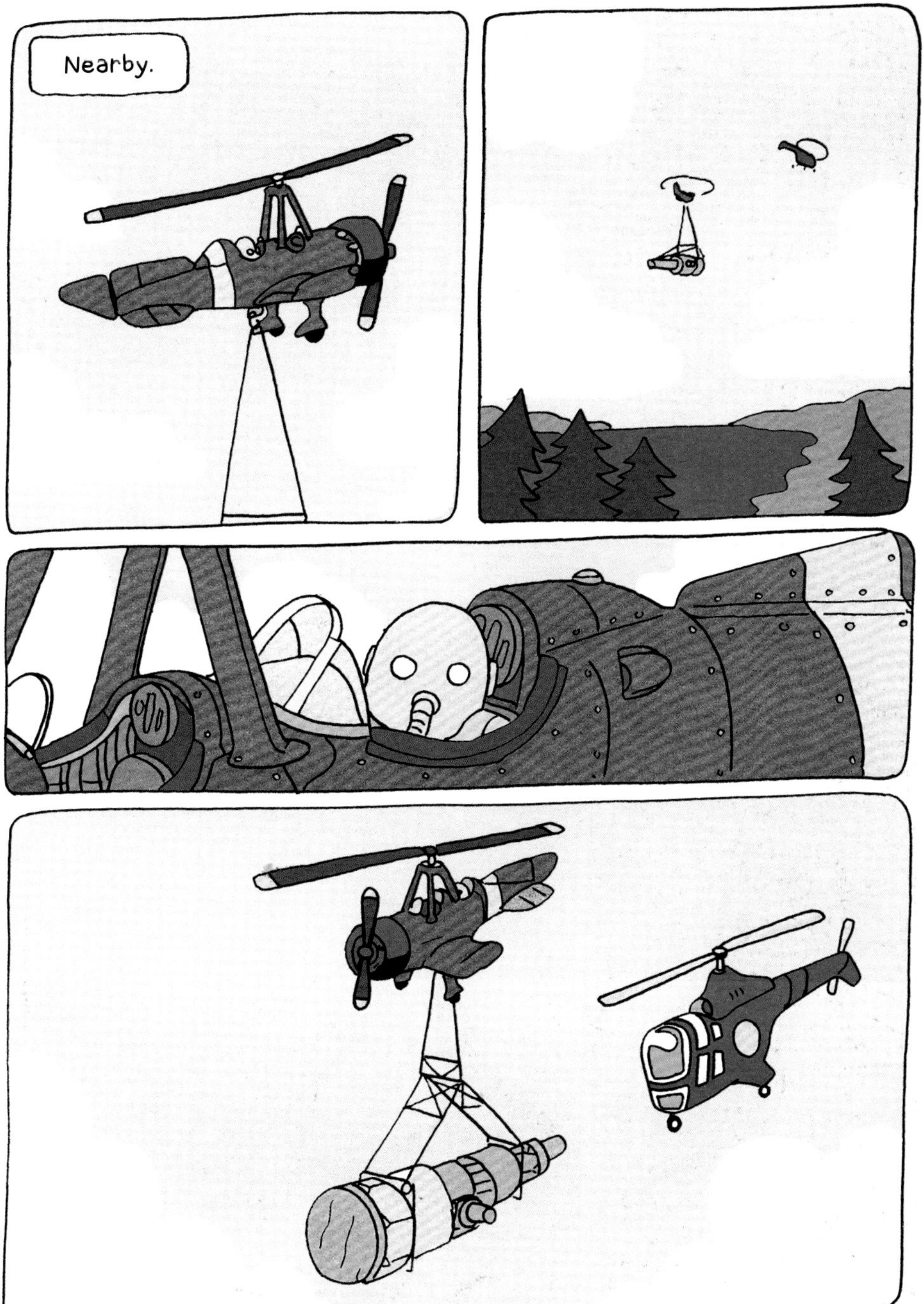
Nearby.

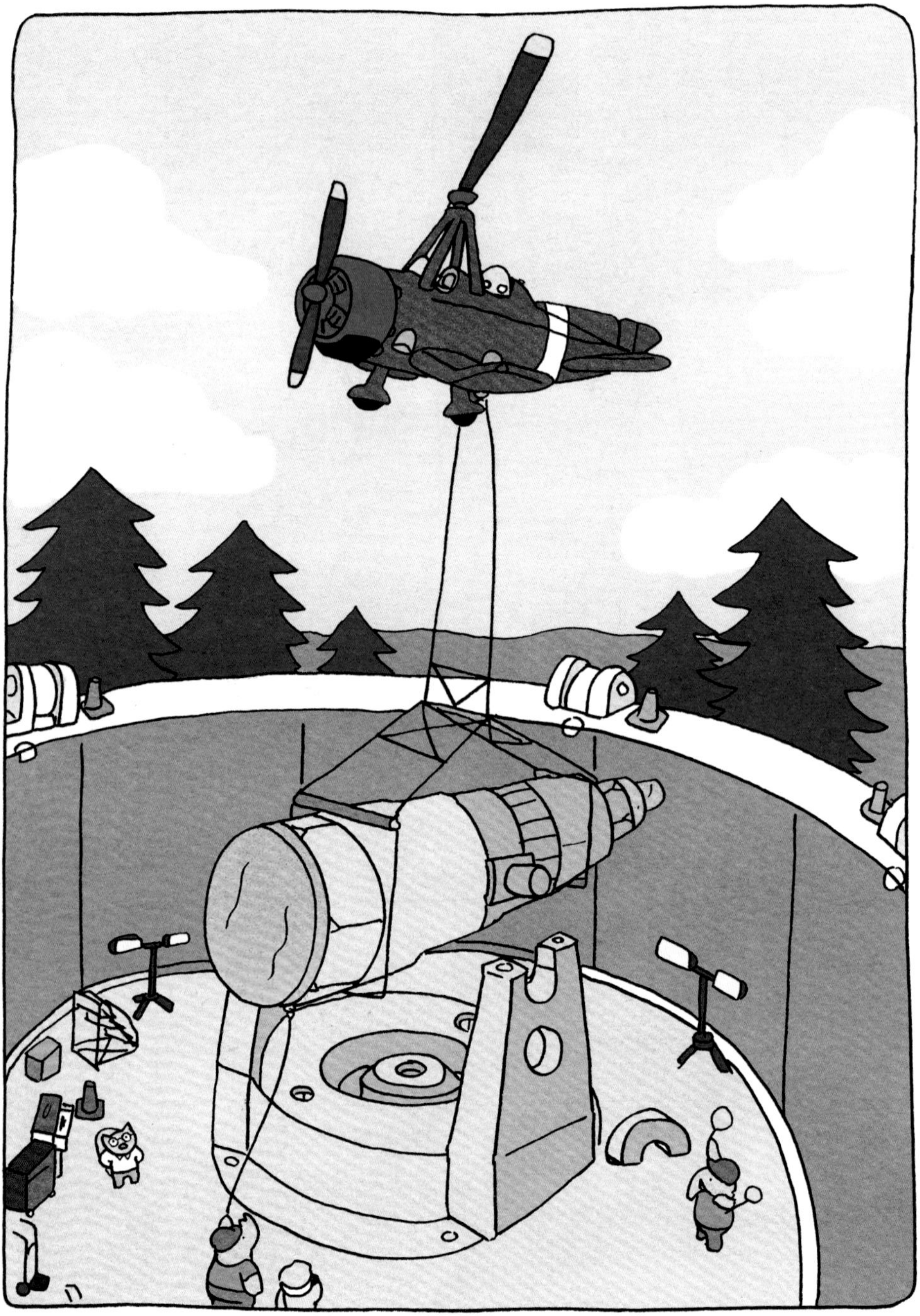

Chapter 5

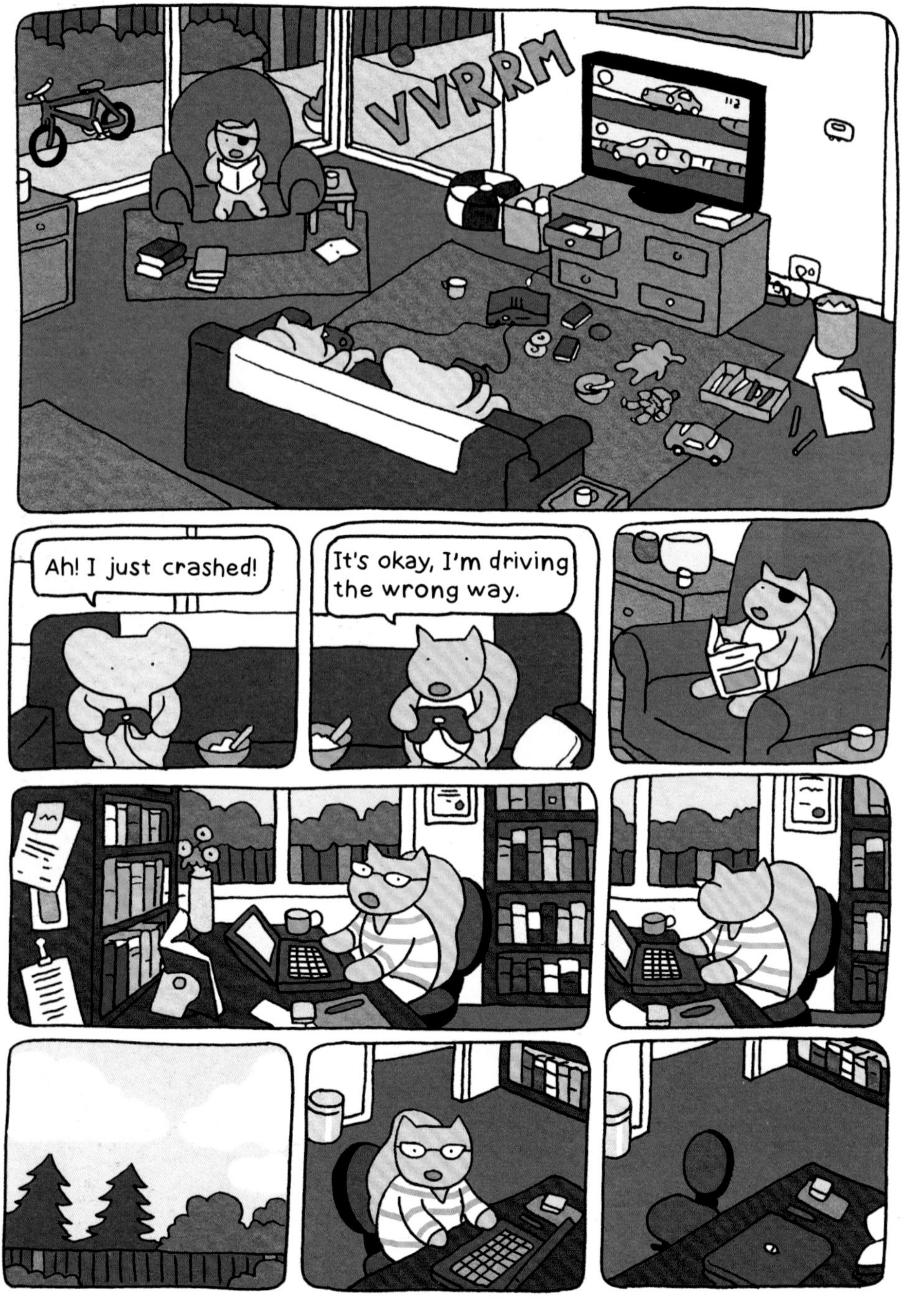
VVRRM
Ah! I just crashed!
It's okay, I'm driving the wrong way.

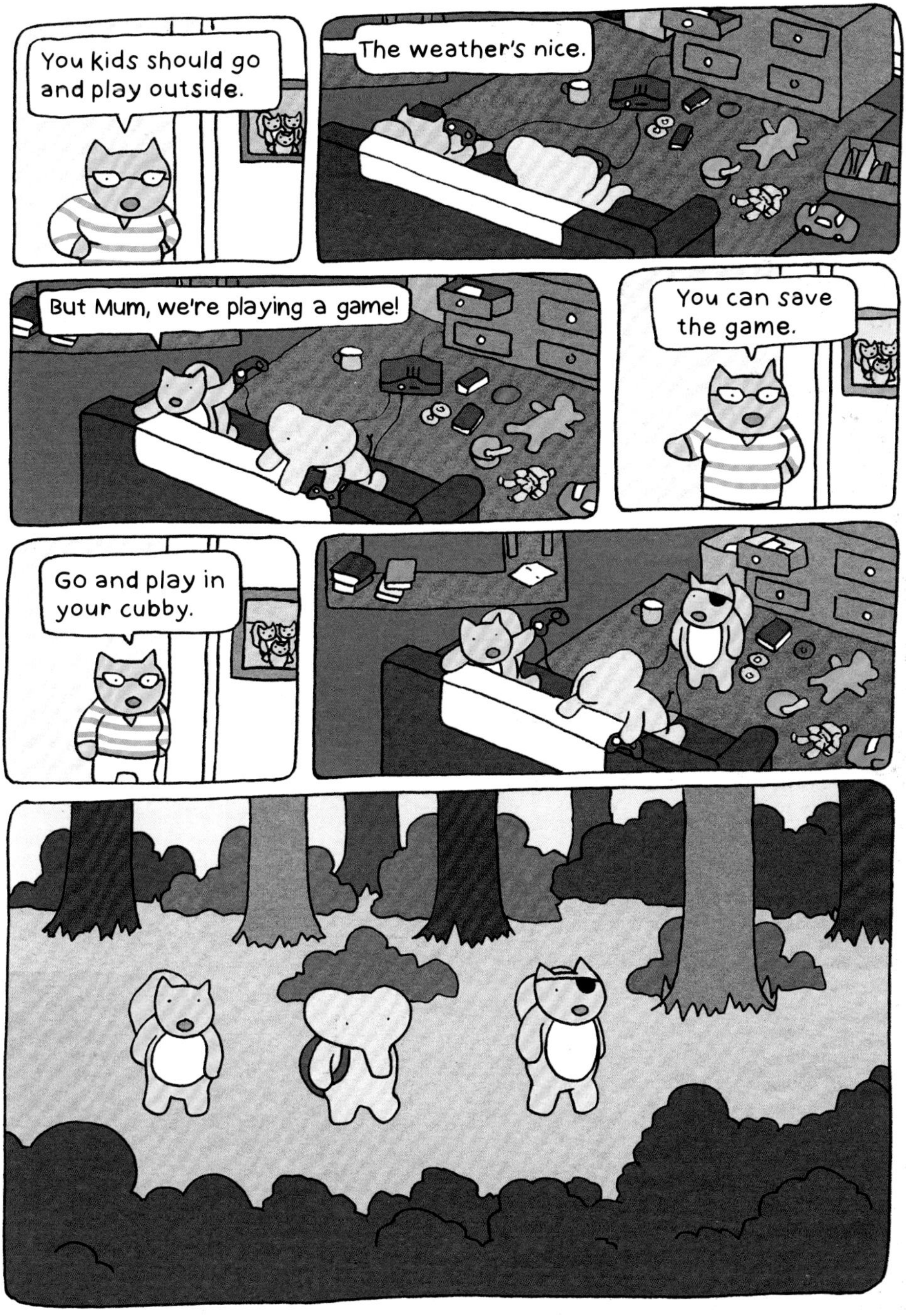
You kids should go and play outside.
The weather's nice.
But Mum, we're playing a game!
You can save the game.
Go and play in your cubby.

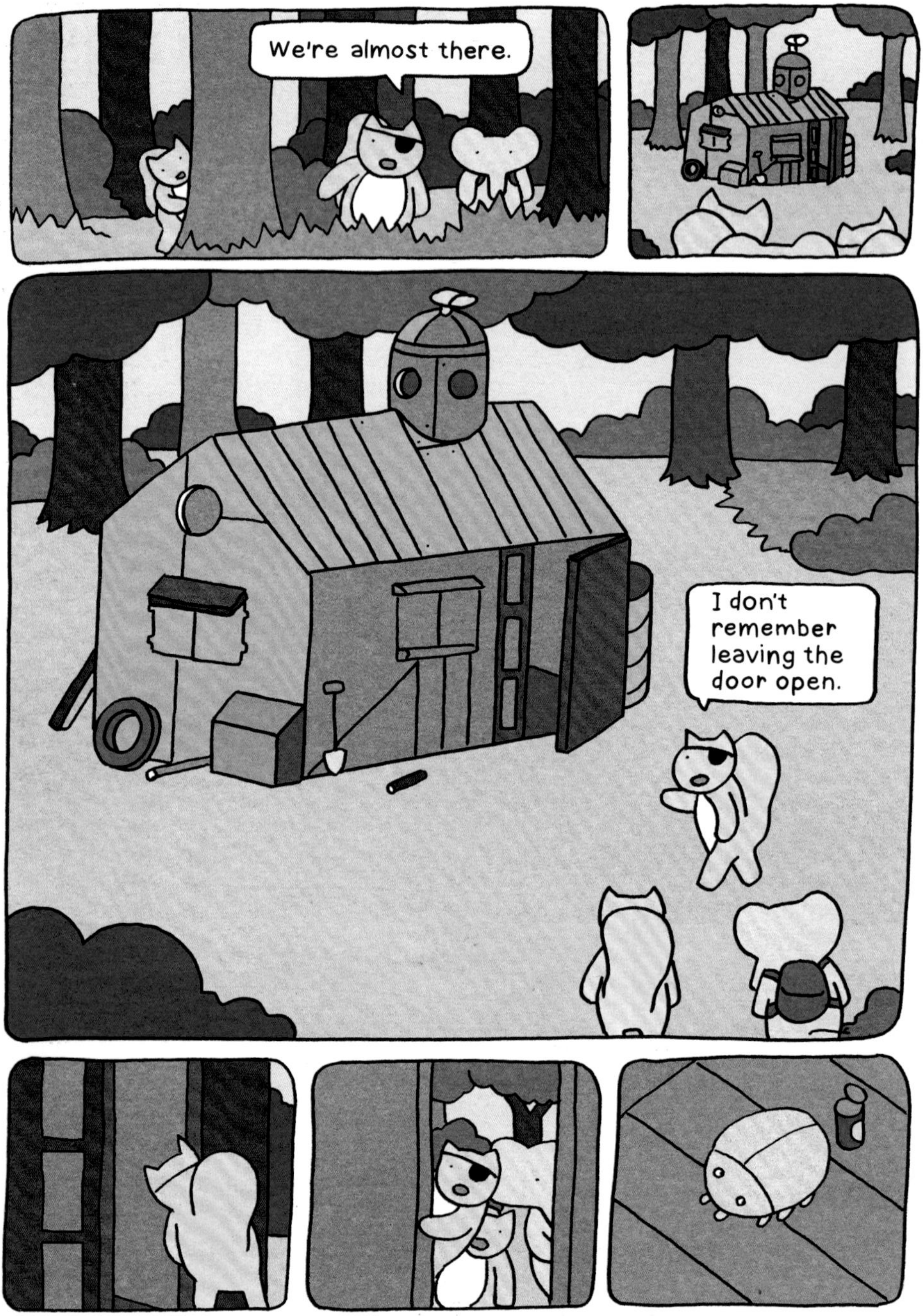
We're almost there.
I don't remember leaving the door open.

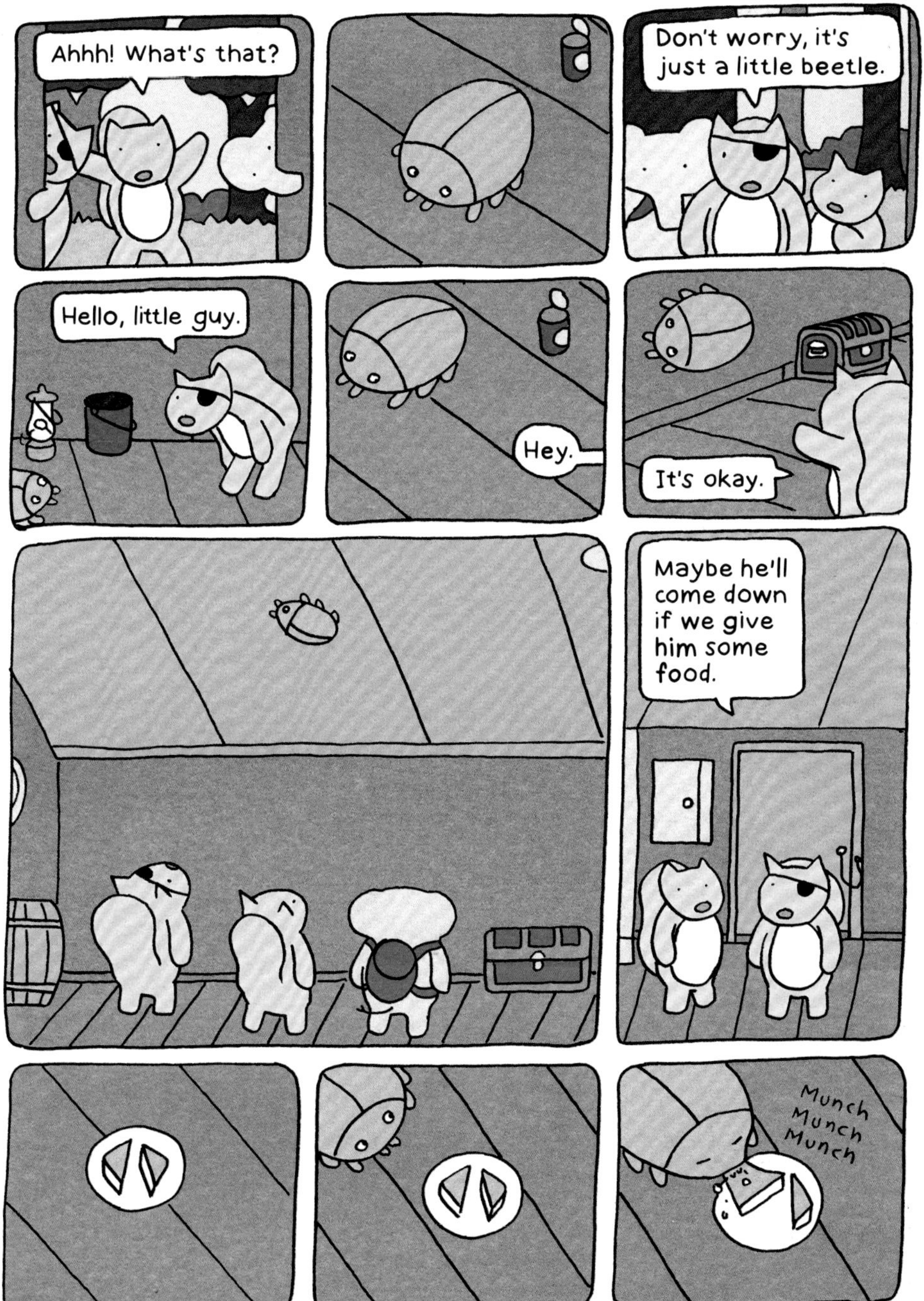
Ahhh! What's that?
Don't worry, it's just a little beetle.
Hello, little guy.
Hey.
It's okay.
Maybe he'll come down if we give him some food.
Munch Munch Munch

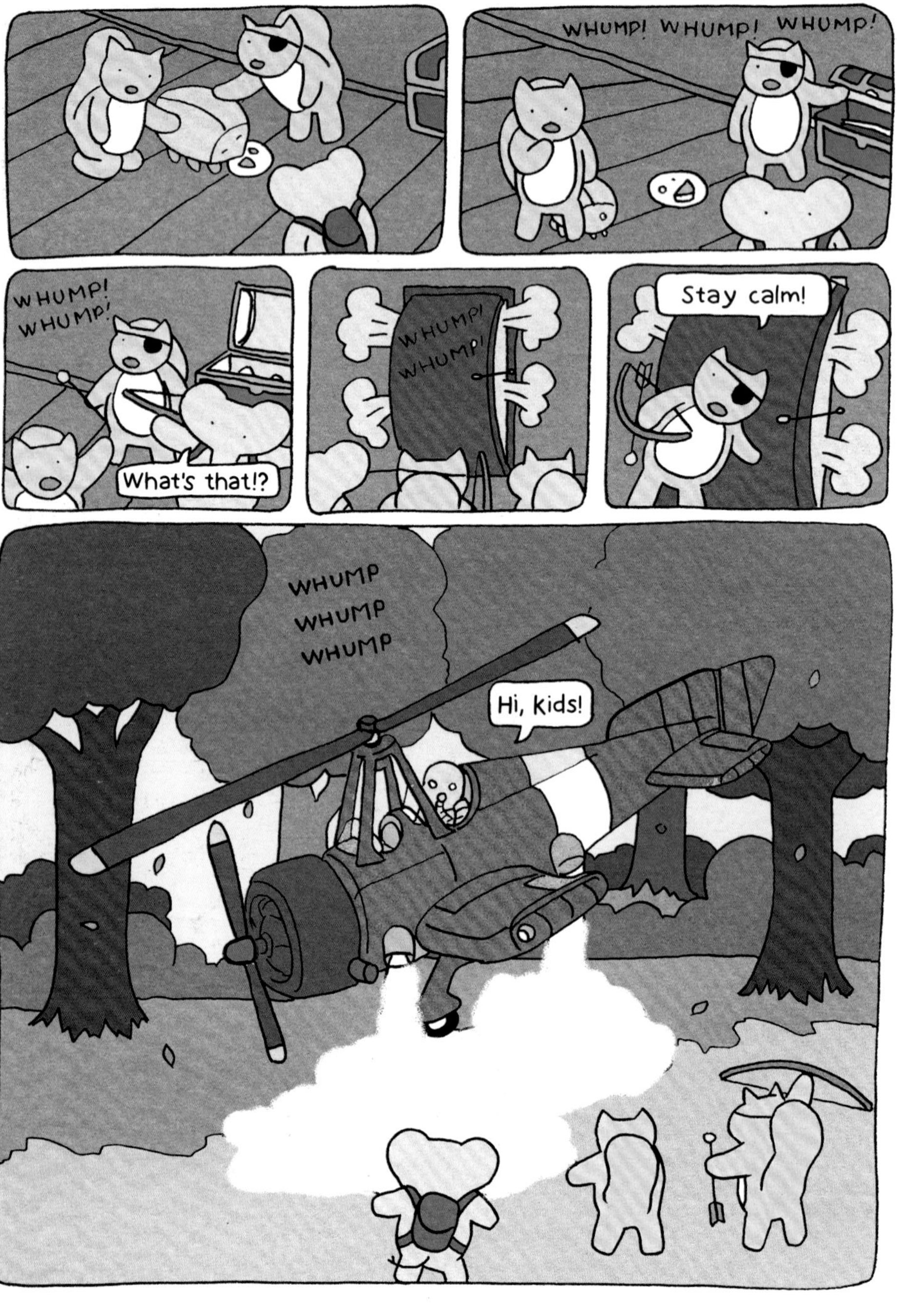
WHUMP! WHUMP! WHUMP!
WHUMP! WHUMP!
What's that!?
WHUMP! WHUMP!
Stay calm!
WHUMP
WHUMP
WHUMP
Hi, kids!

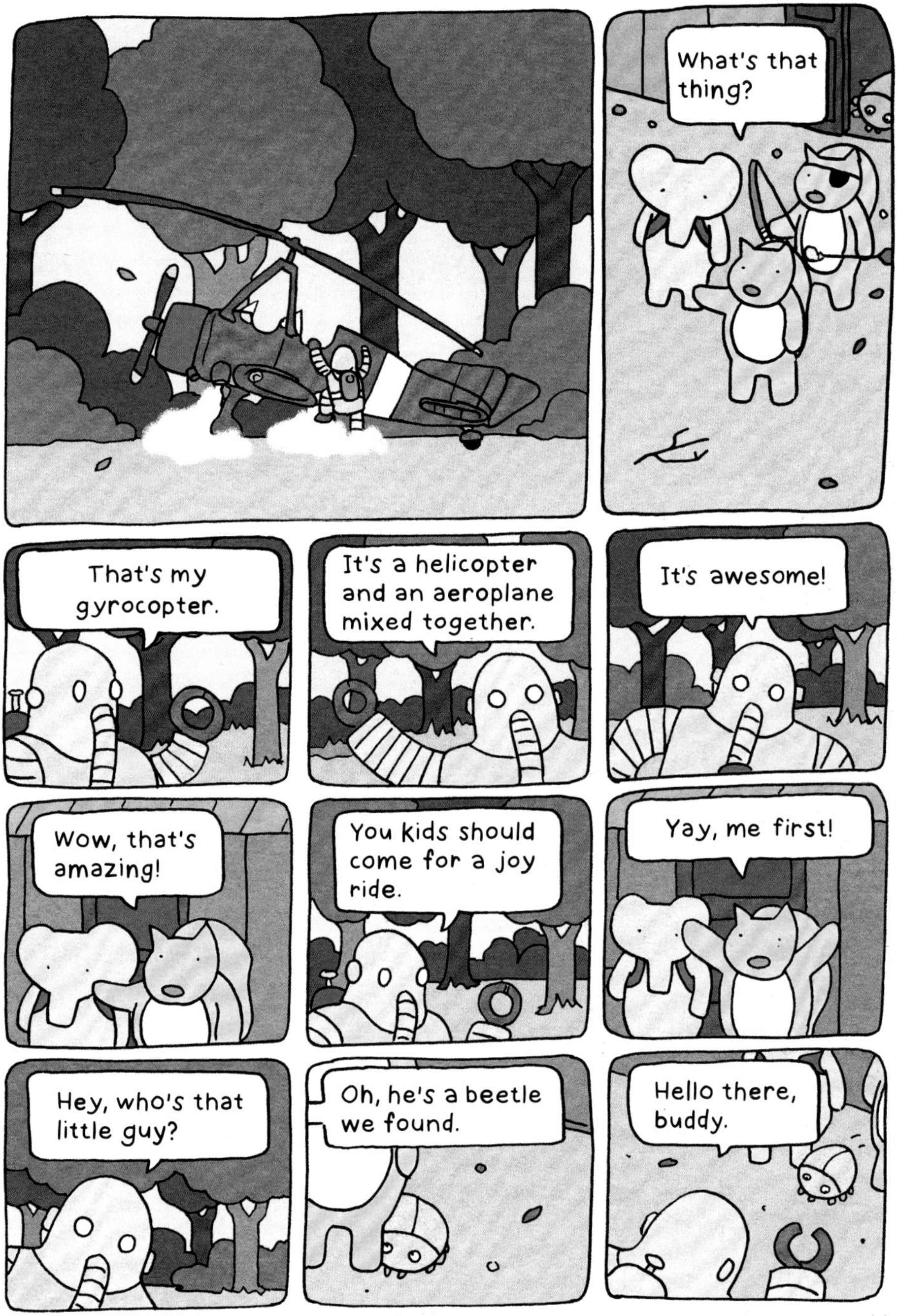
What's that thing?
That's my gyrocopter.
It's a helicopter and an aeroplane mixed together.
It's awesome!
Wow, that's amazing!
You kids should come for a joy ride.
Yay, me first!
Hey, who's that little guy?
Oh, he's a beetle we found.
Hello there, buddy.

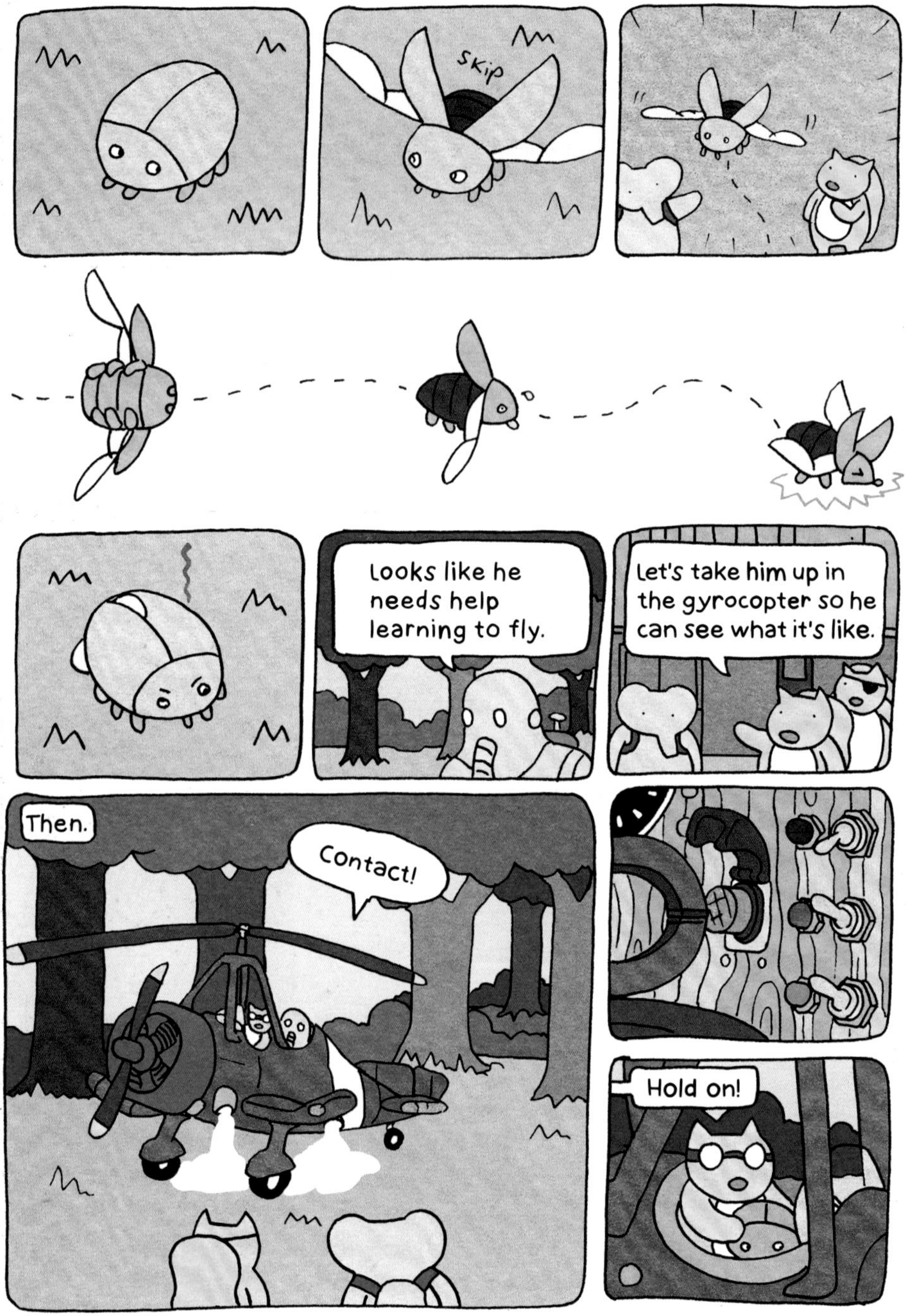
SKIP
Looks like he needs help learning to fly.
Let's take him up in the gyrocopter so he can see what it's like.
Then.
Contact!
Hold on!

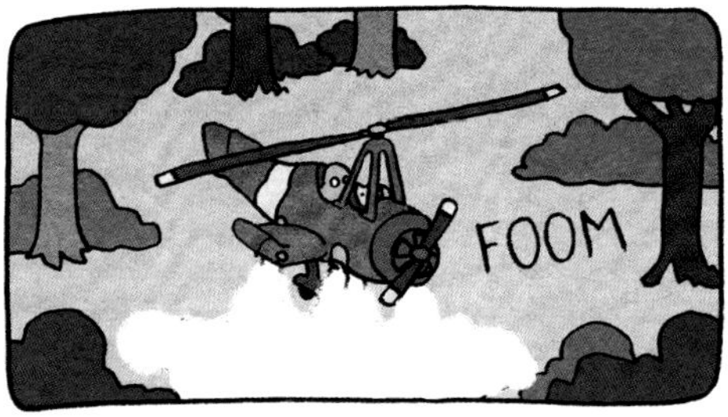
FOOM

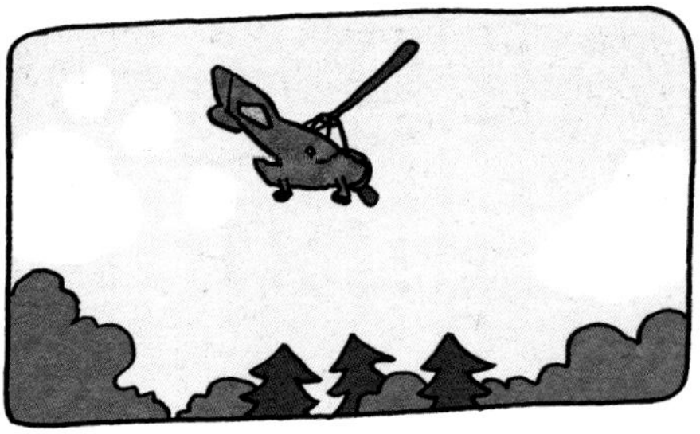

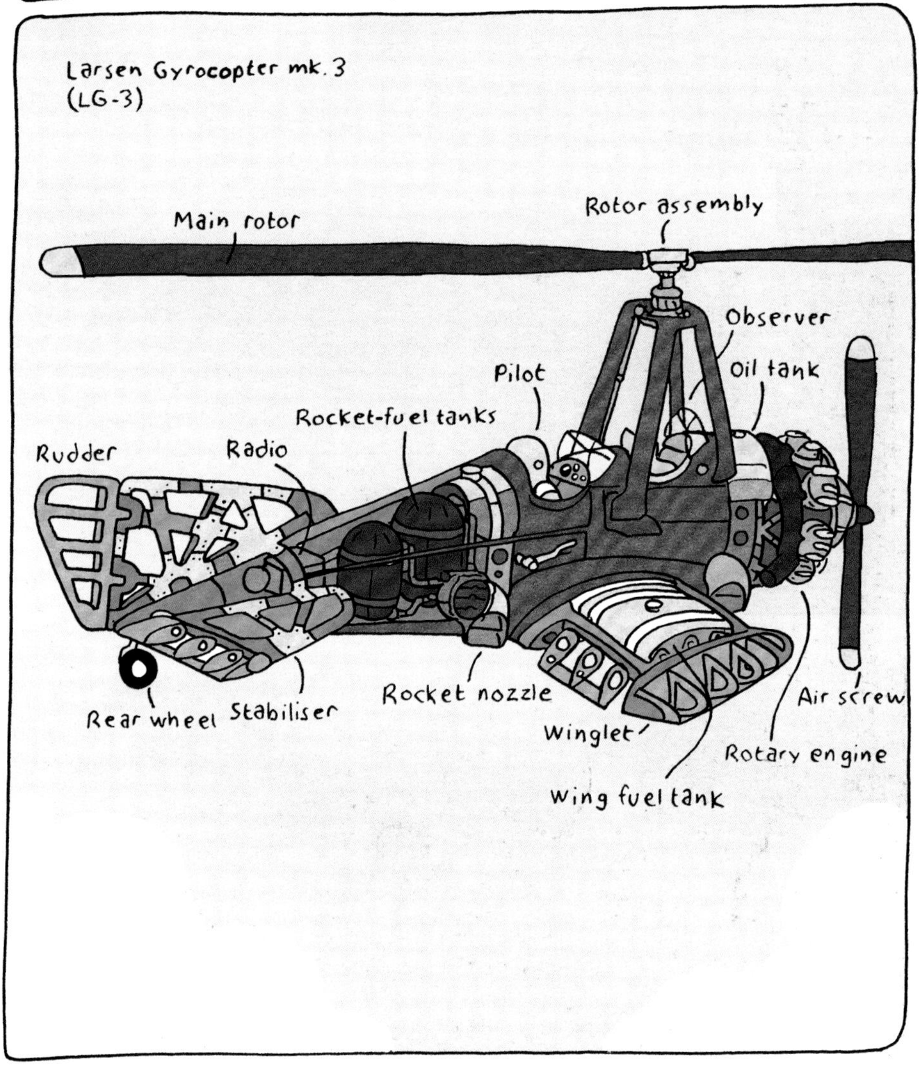
Larsen Gyrocopter mk. 3
(LG-3)
Main rotor
Rotor assembly
Observer
Pilot
Oil tank
Rocket-fuel tanks
Rudder
Radio
Rear wheel
Stabiliser
Rocket nozzle
Winglet
Wing fuel tank
Rotary engine
Air screw

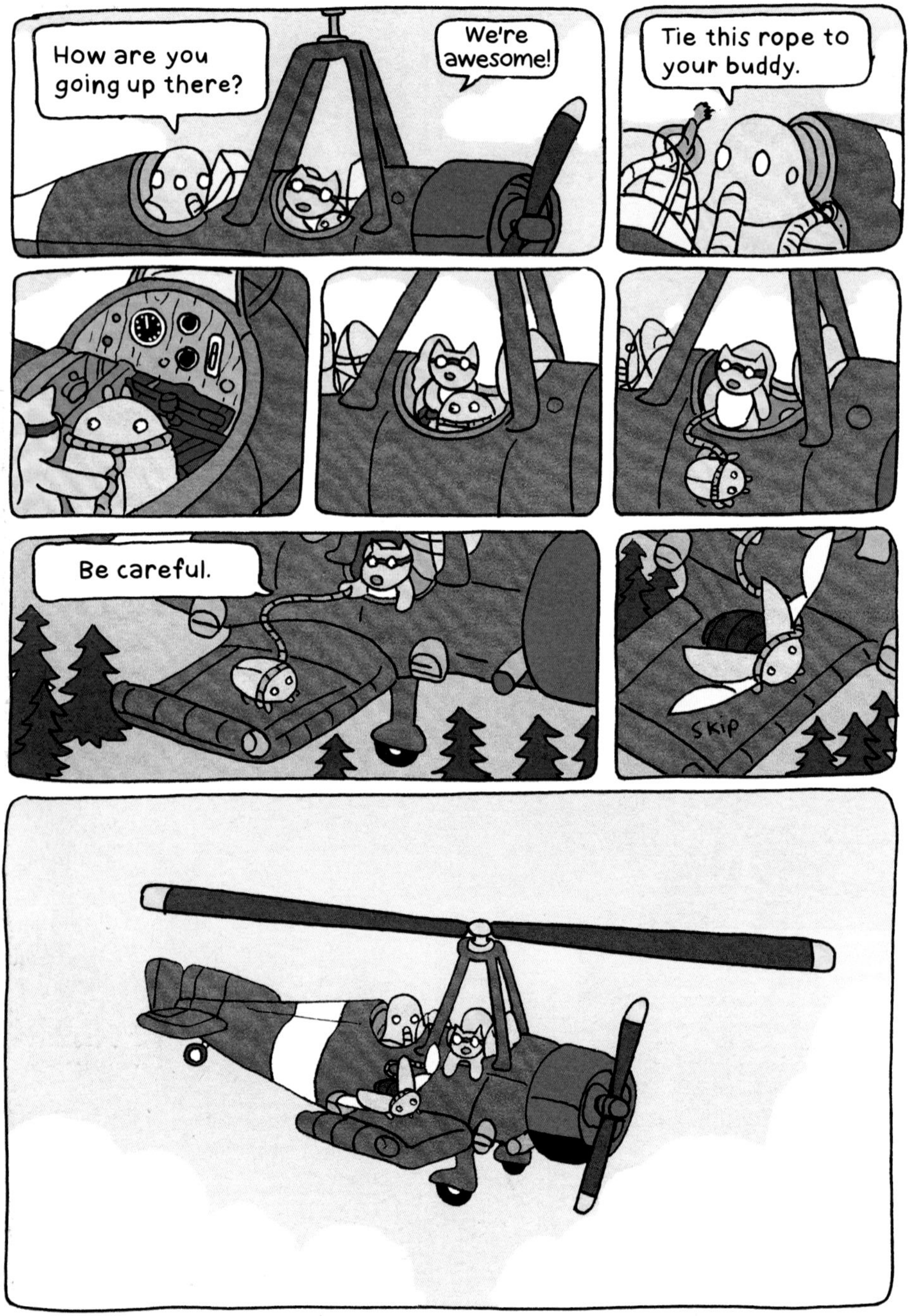
How are you going up there?
We're awesome!
Tie this rope to your buddy.
Be careful.
SKIP

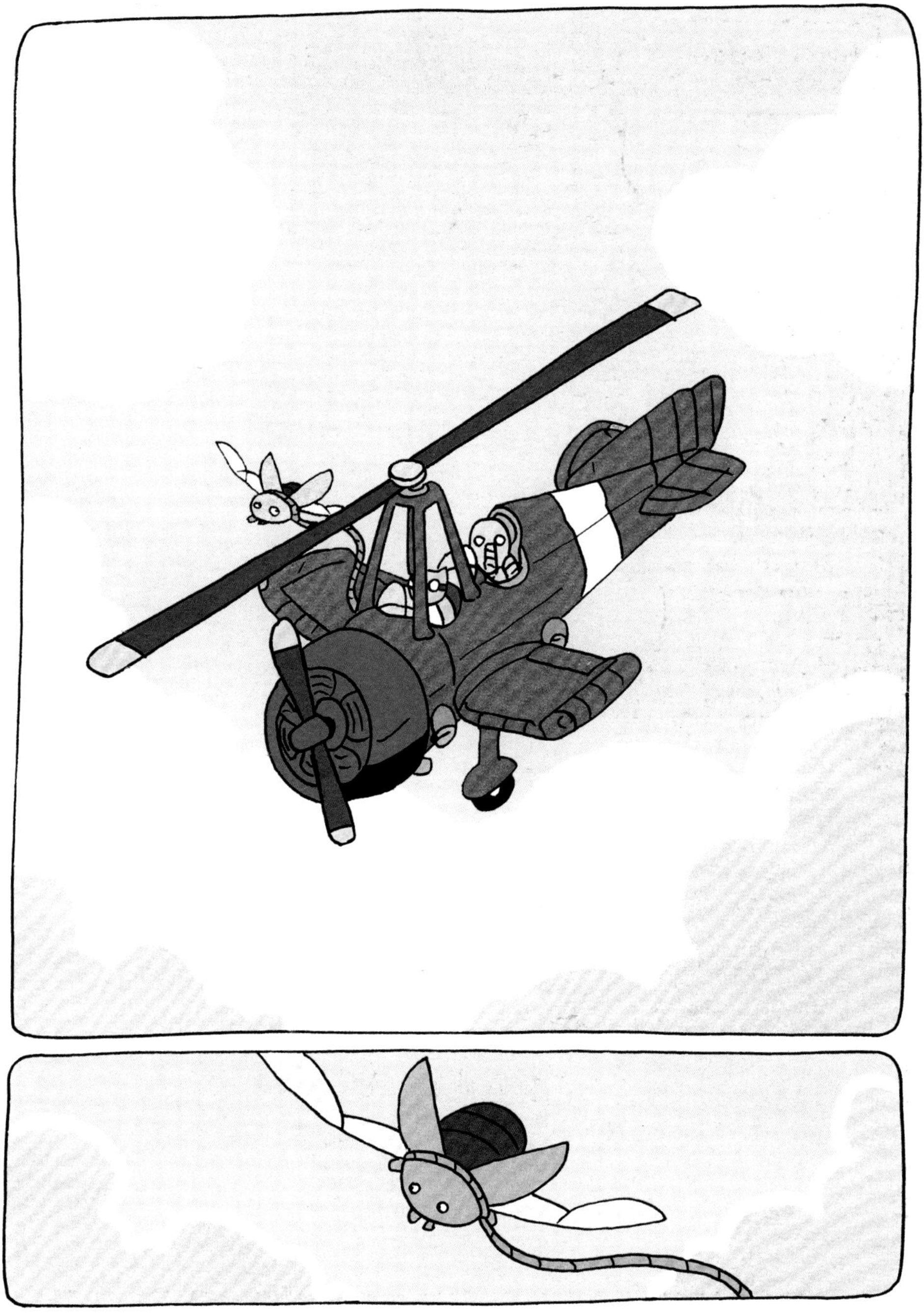

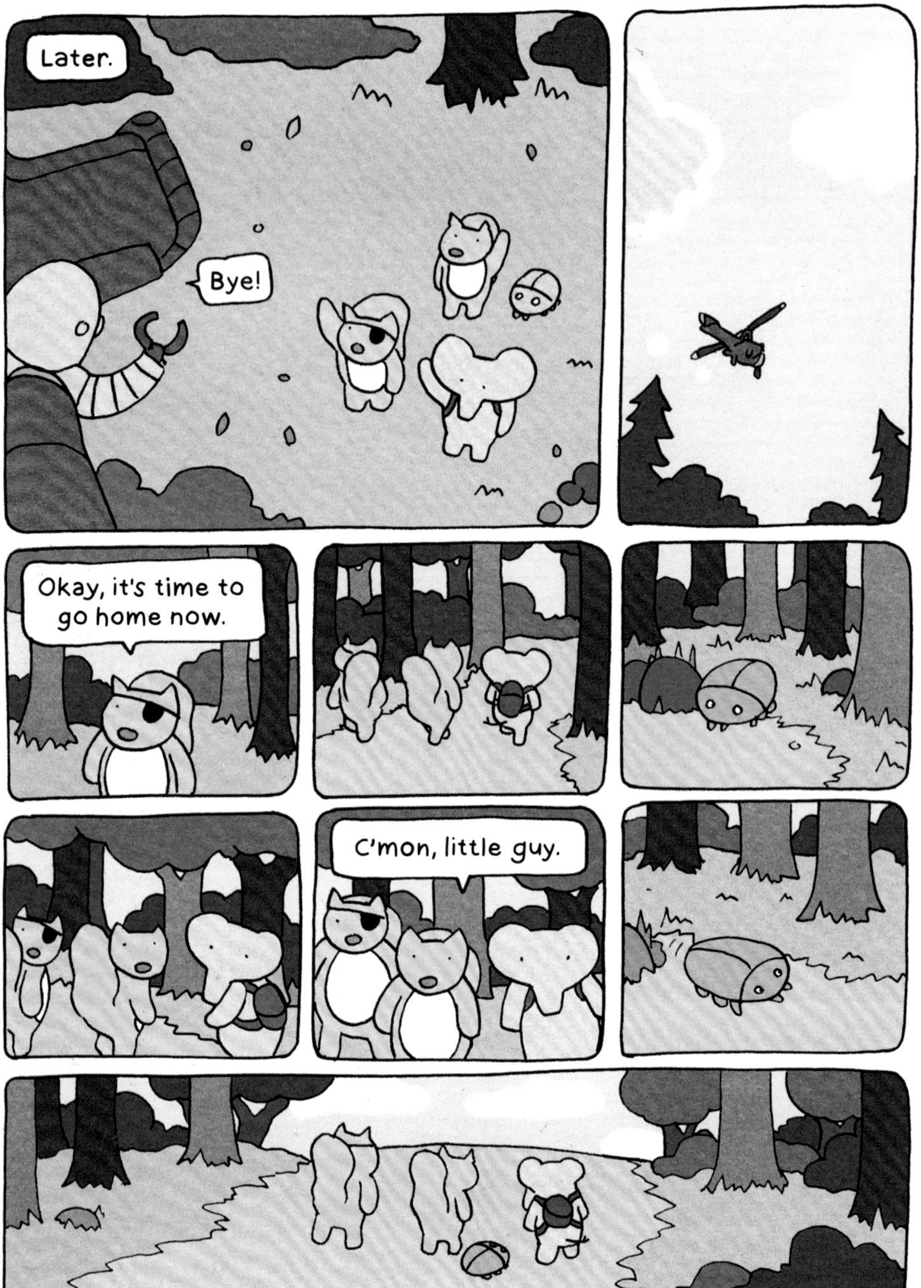
Later.
Bye!
Okay, it's time to go home now.
C'mon, little guy.

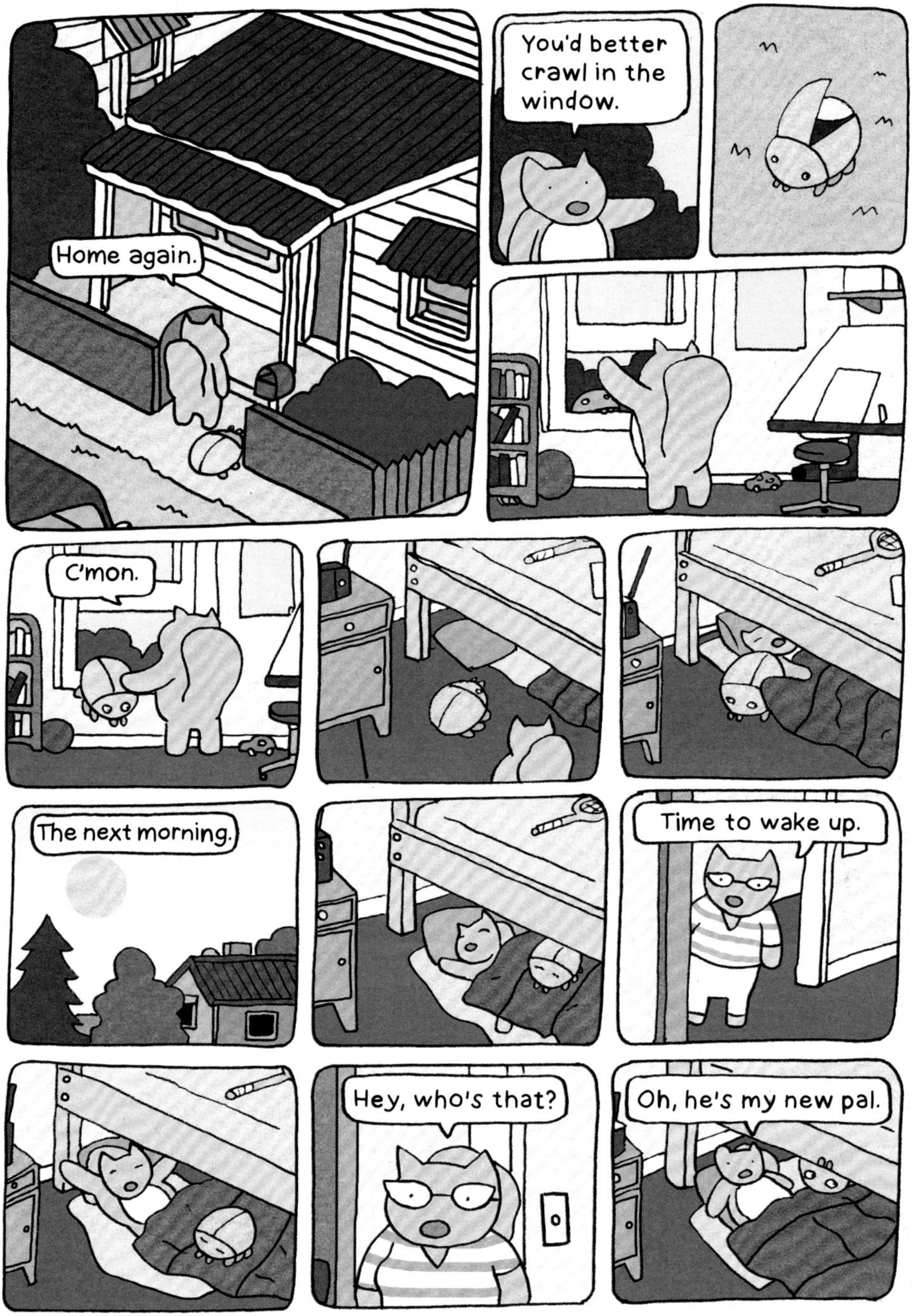
Home again.
You'd better crawl in the window.
C'mon.
The next morning.
Time to wake up.
Hey, who's that?
Oh, he's my new pal.

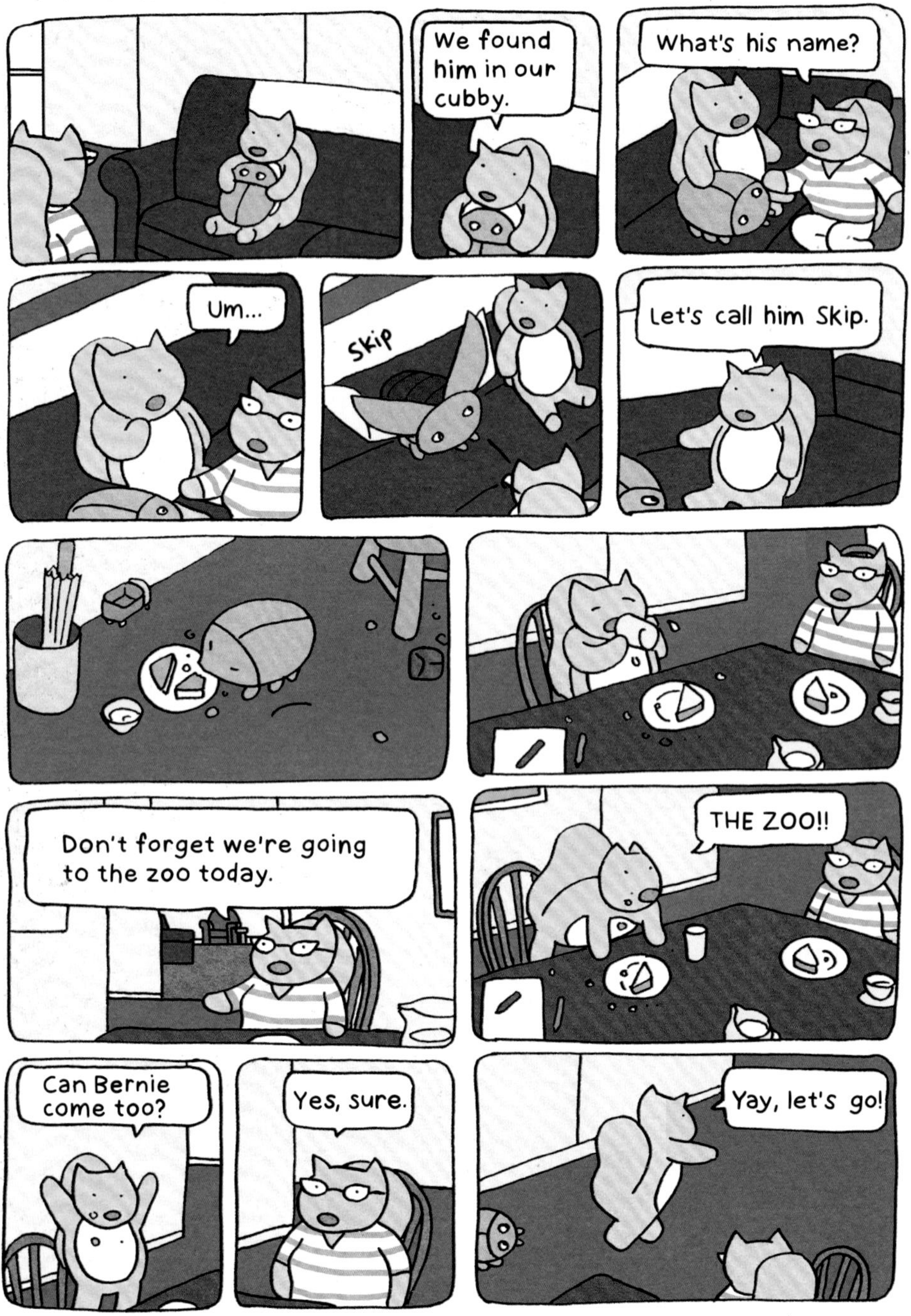
We found him in our cubby.
What's his name?
Um...
SKIP
Let's call him Skip.
Don't forget we're going to the zoo today.
THE ZOO!!
Can Bernie come too?
Yes, sure.
Yay, let's go!

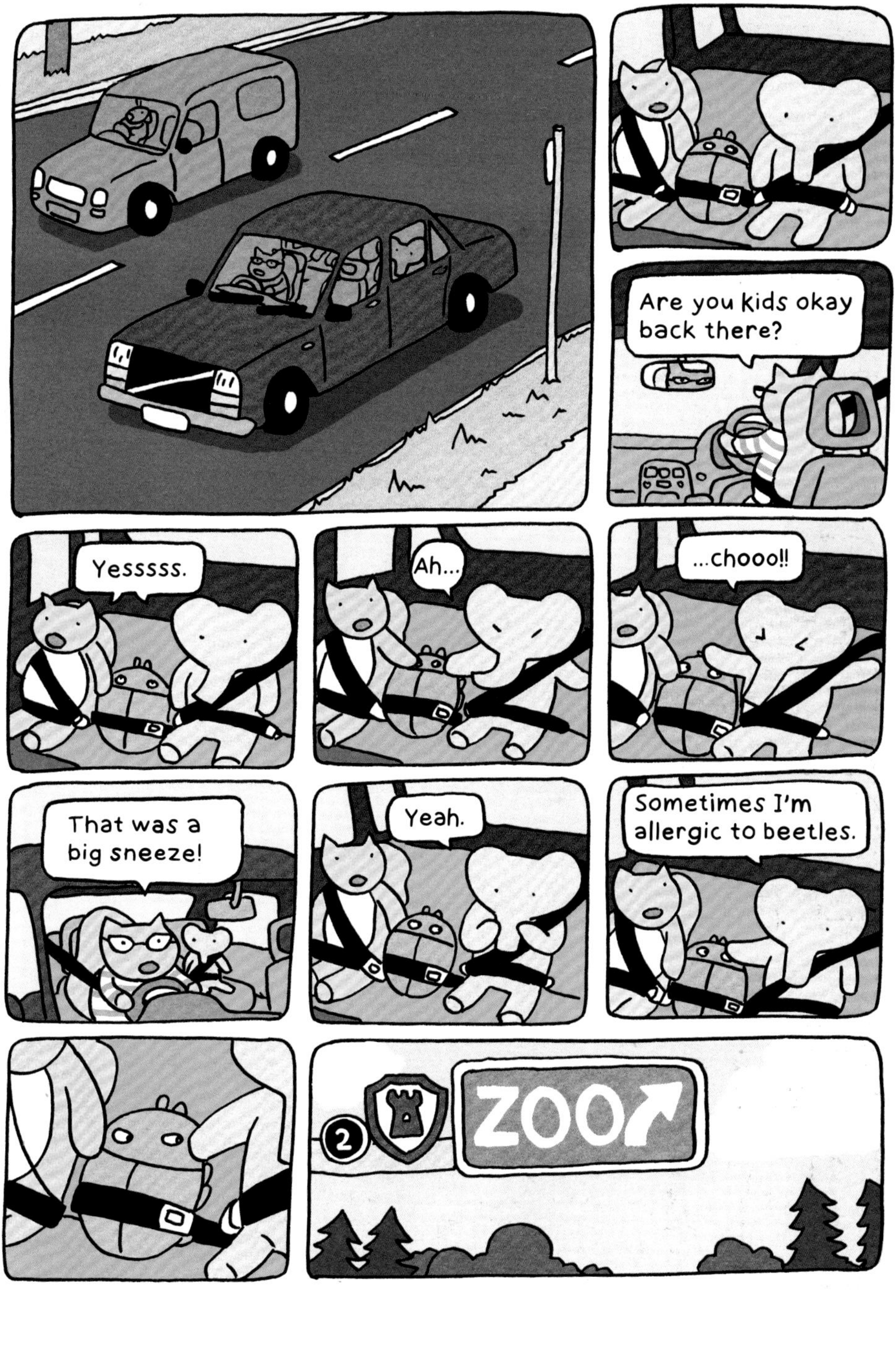
Are you kids okay back there?
Yesssss.
Ah...
...chooo!!
That was a big sneeze!
Yeah.
Sometimes I'm allergic to beetles.
2
ZOO

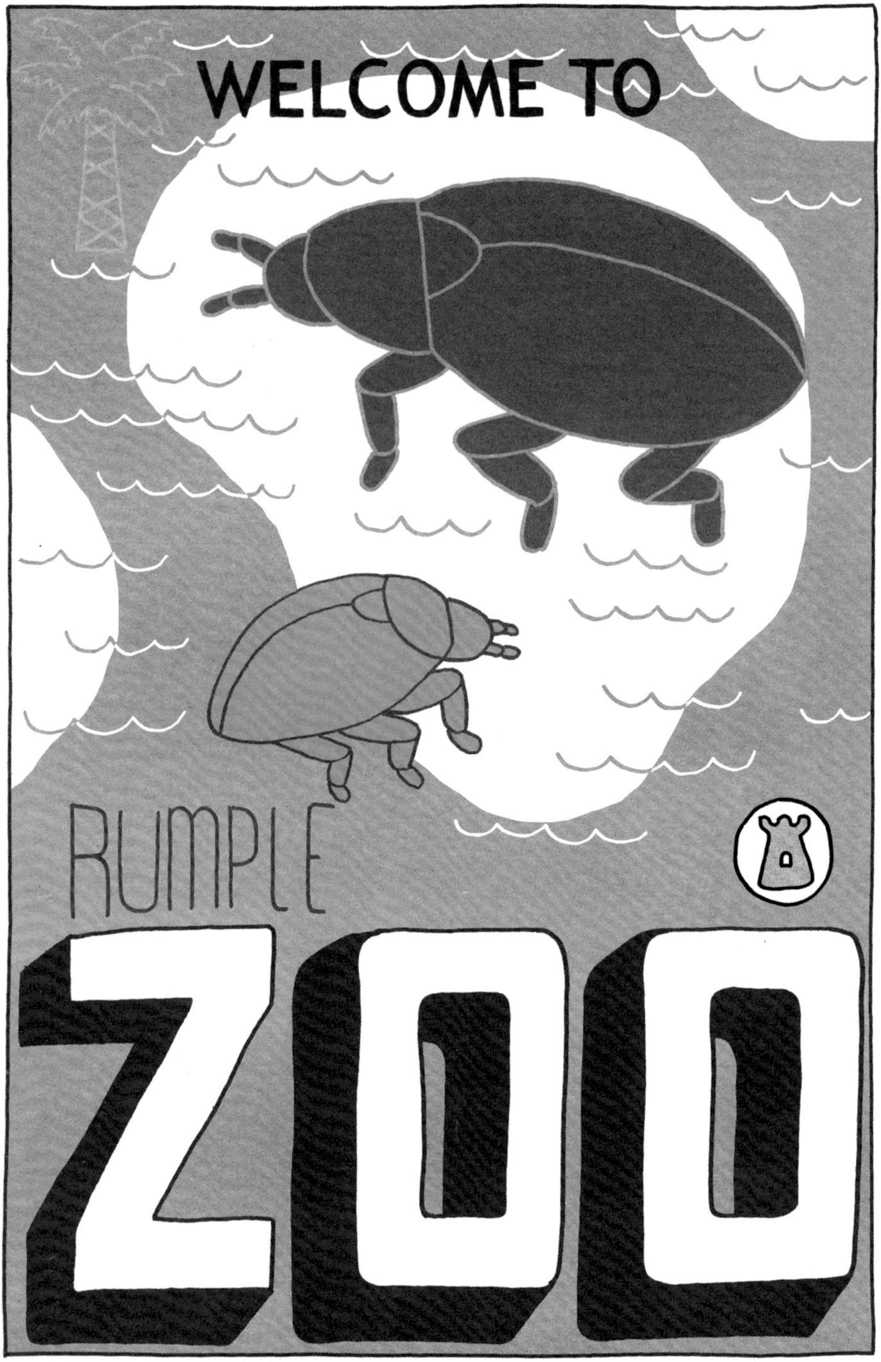
WELCOME TO
RUMPLE
ZOO

Chapter 6

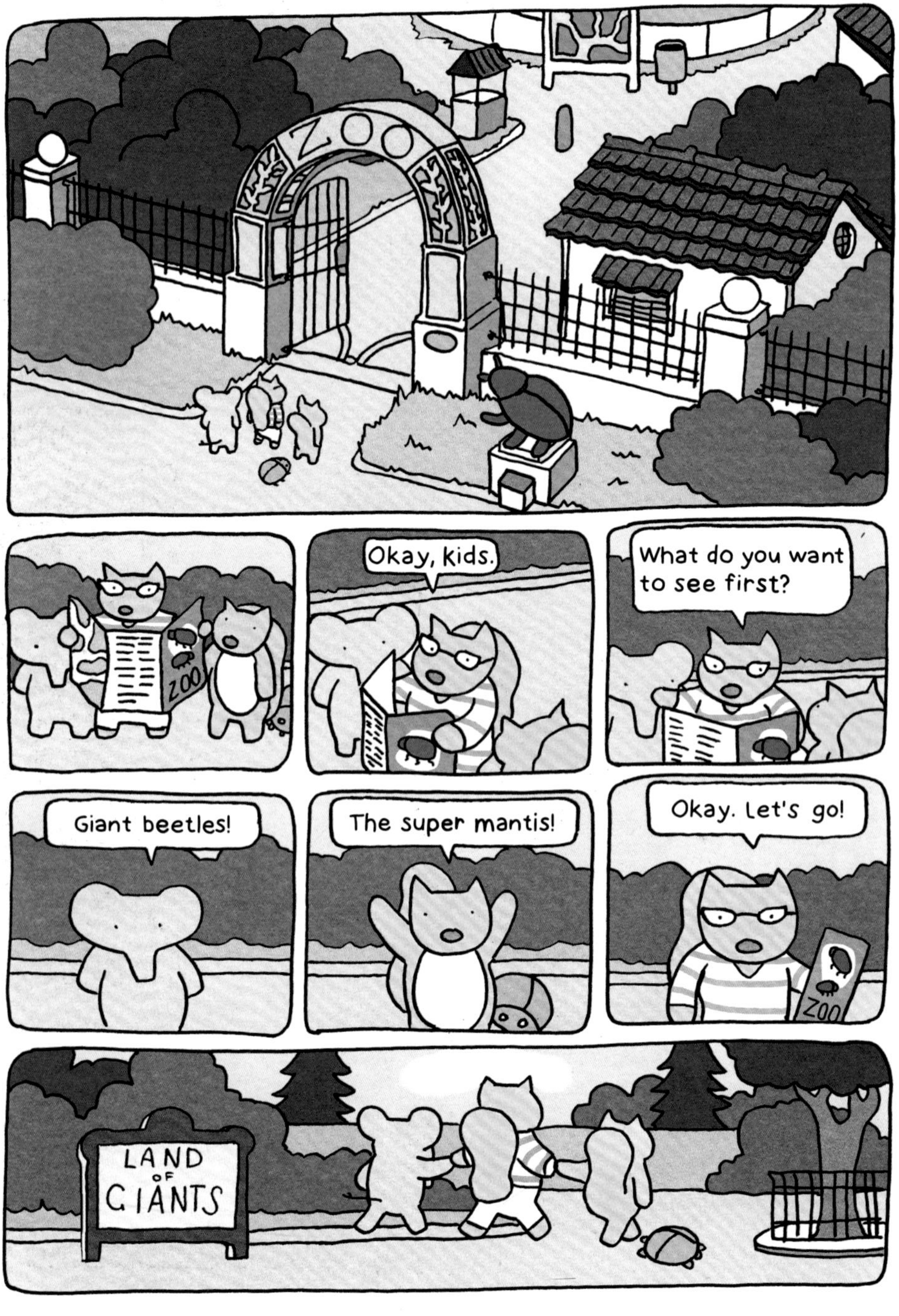
ZOO
ZOO
Okay, kids.
What do you want to see first?
Giant beetles!
The super mantis!
Okay. Let's go!
ZOO
LAND of GIANTS

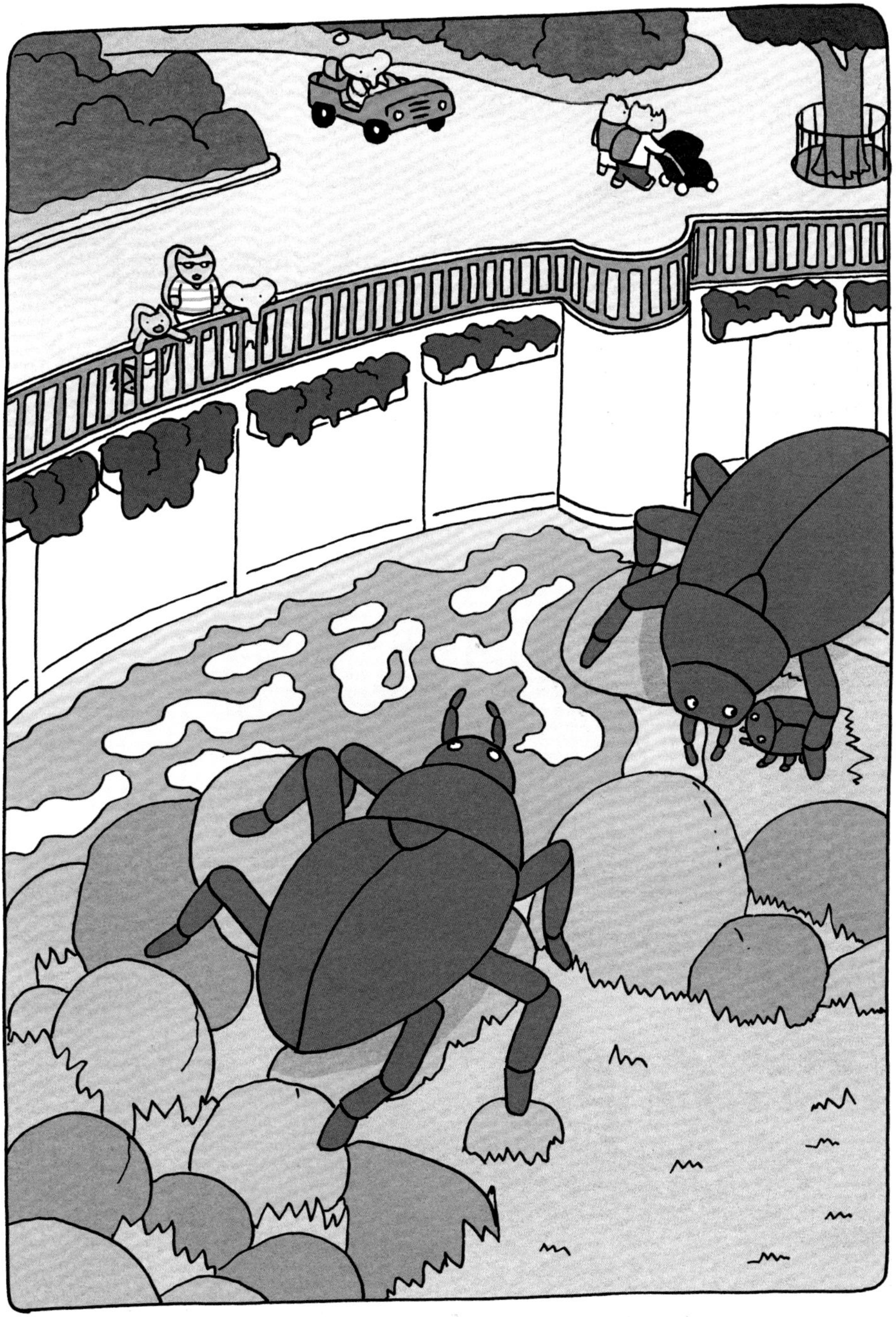

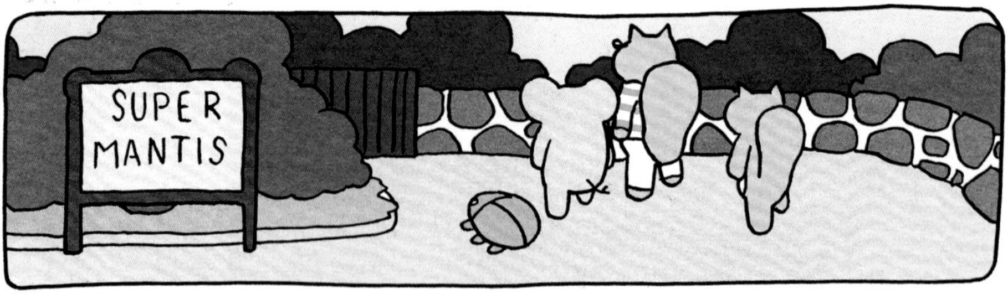
SUPER
MANTIS

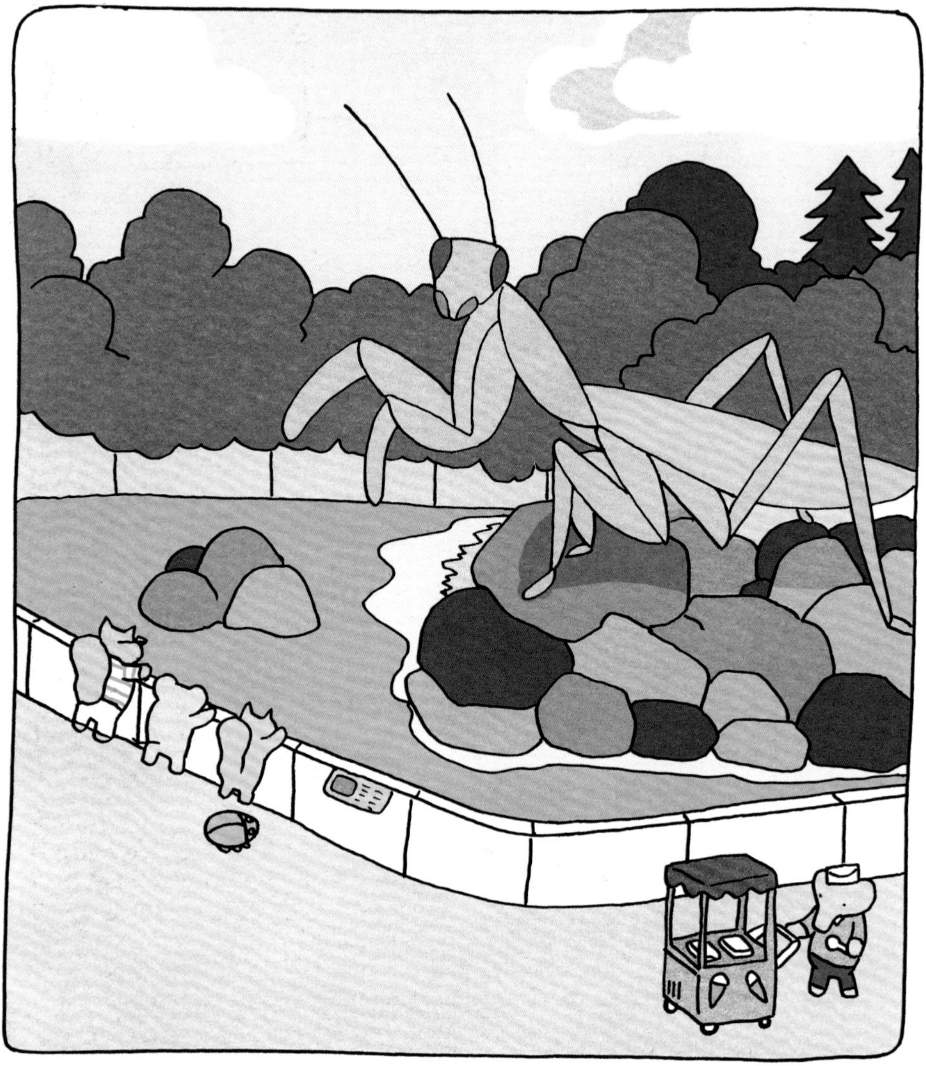

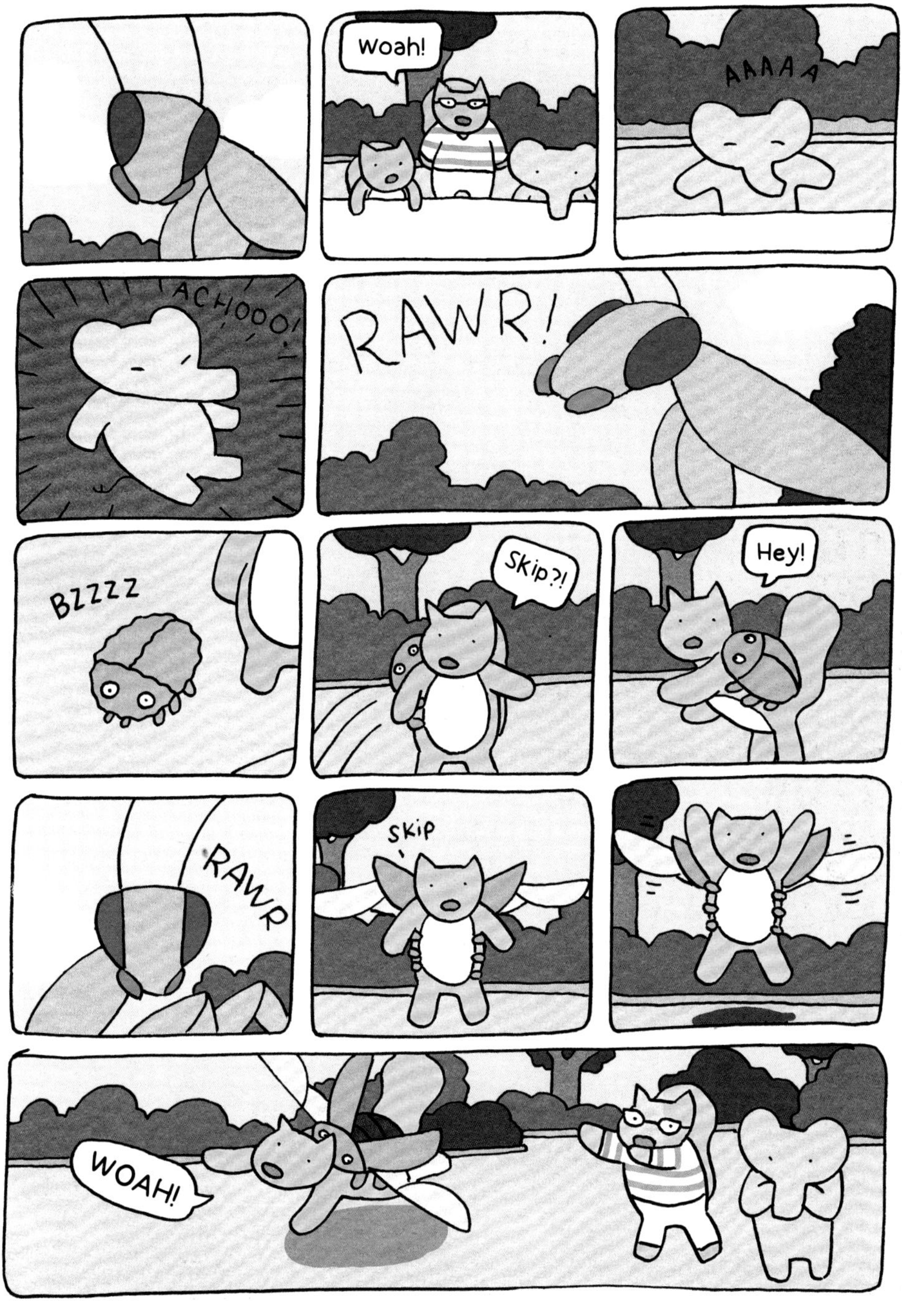
Woah!
AAAAA
ACHOOO!
RAWR!
BZZZZ
Skip?!
Hey!
RAWR
SKIP
WOAH!

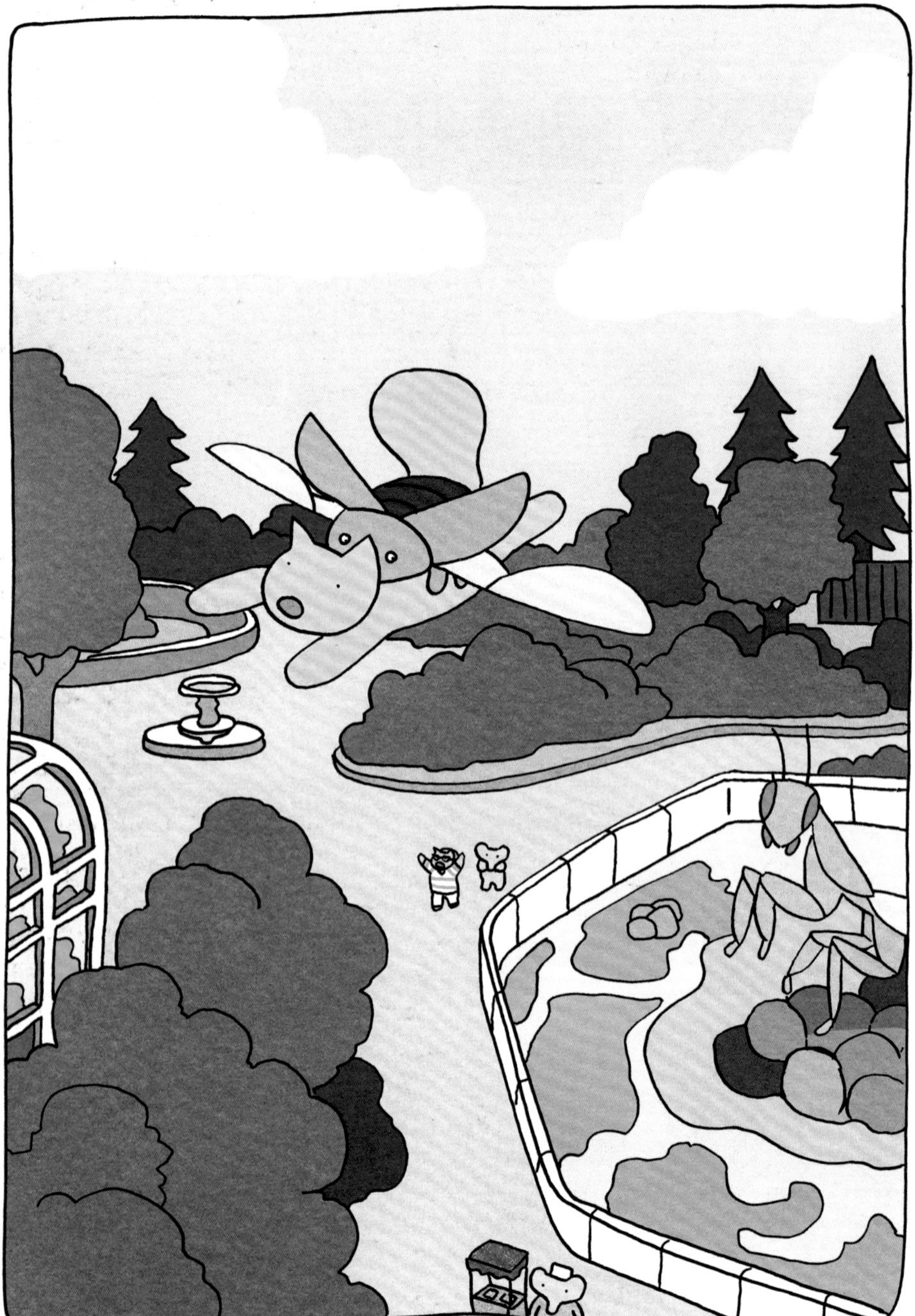

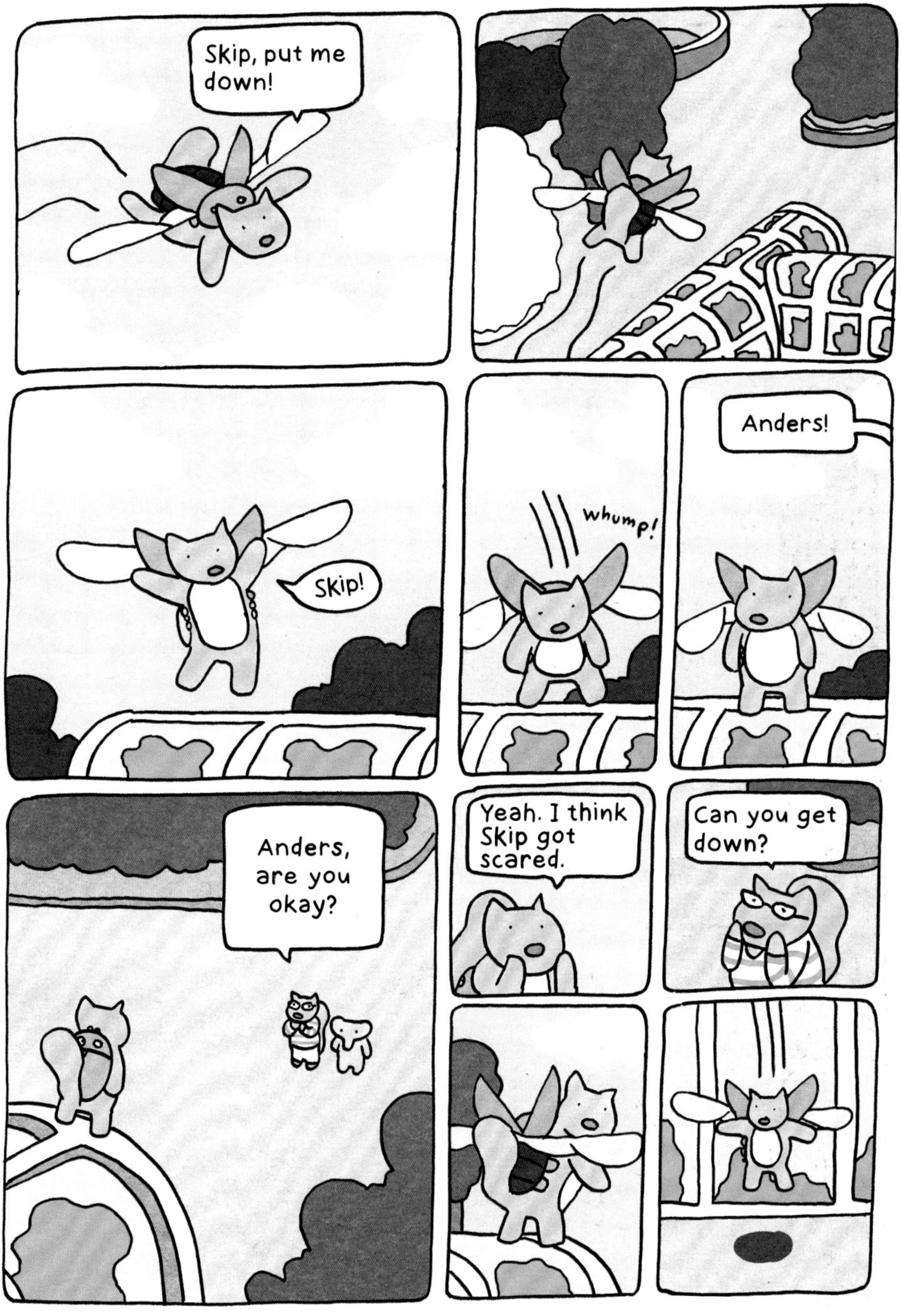
Skip, put me down!
Skip!
whump!
Anders!
Anders, are you okay?
Yeah. I think Skip got scared.
Can you get down?

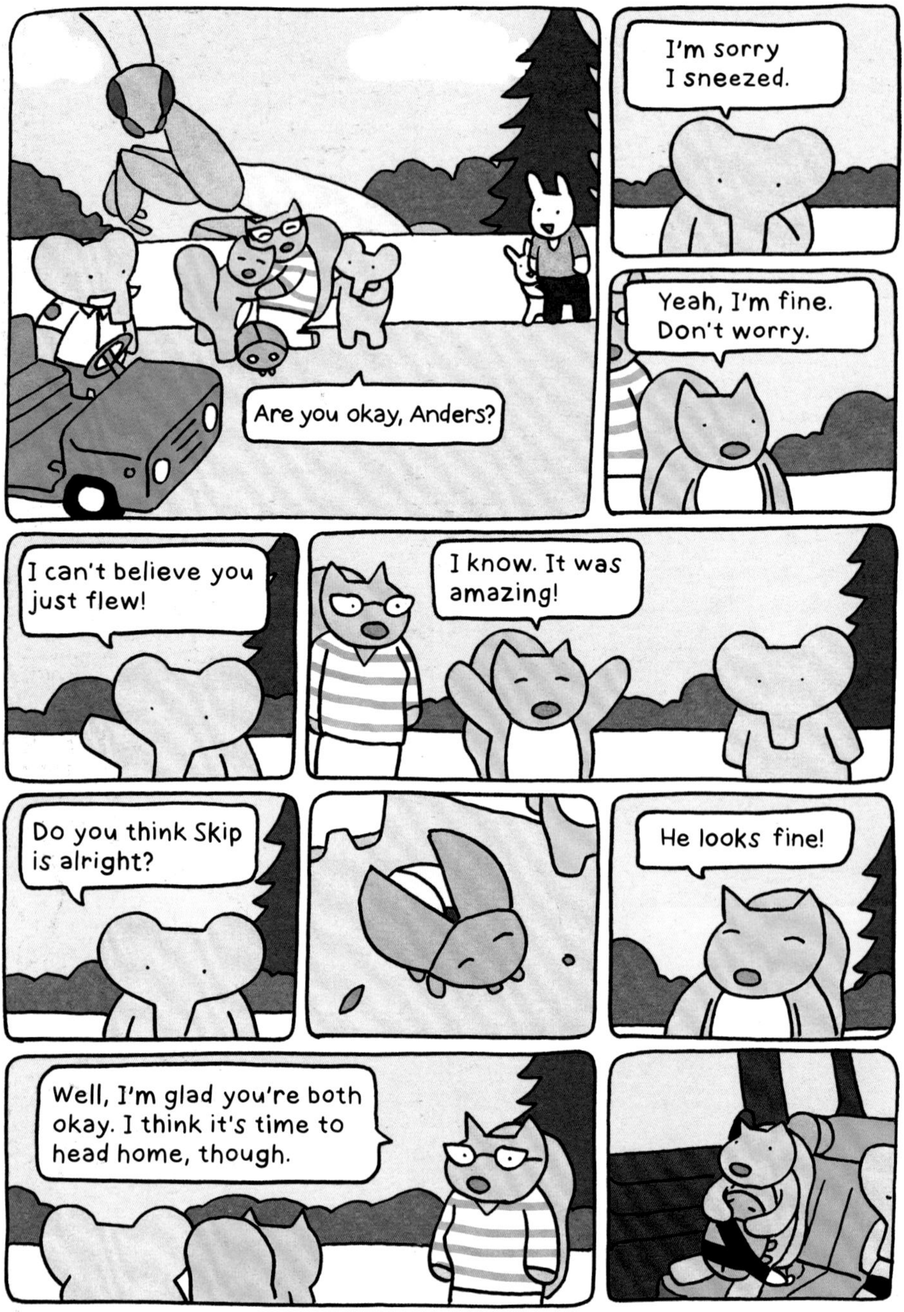
Are you okay, Anders?
I'm sorry I sneezed.
Yeah, I'm fine. Don't worry.
I can't believe you just flew!
I know. It was amazing!
Do you think Skip is alright?
He looks fine!
Well, I'm glad you're both okay. I think it's time to head home, though.

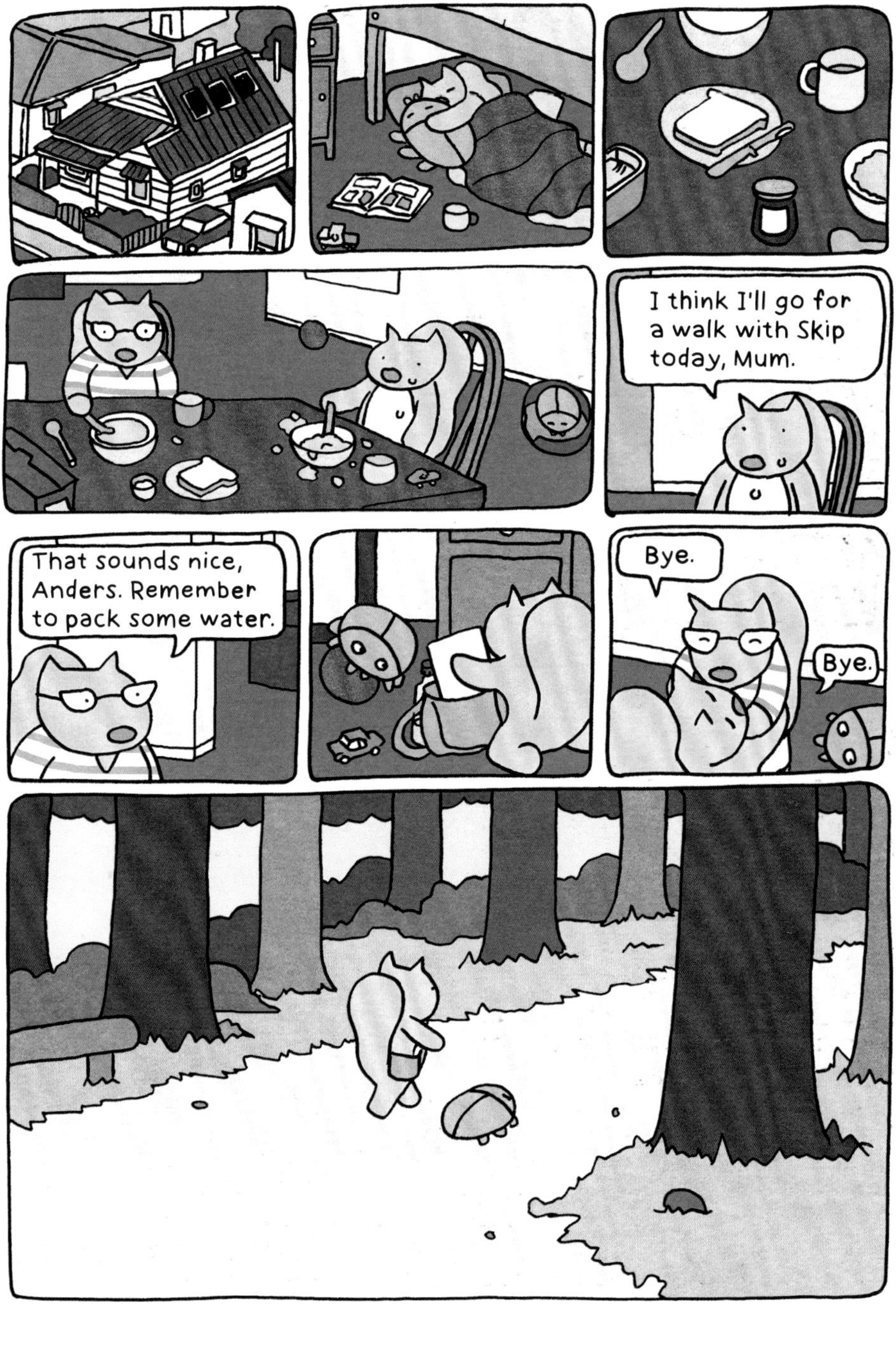
I think I'll go for a walk with Skip today, Mum.
That sounds nice, Anders. Remember to pack some water.
Bye.
Bye.

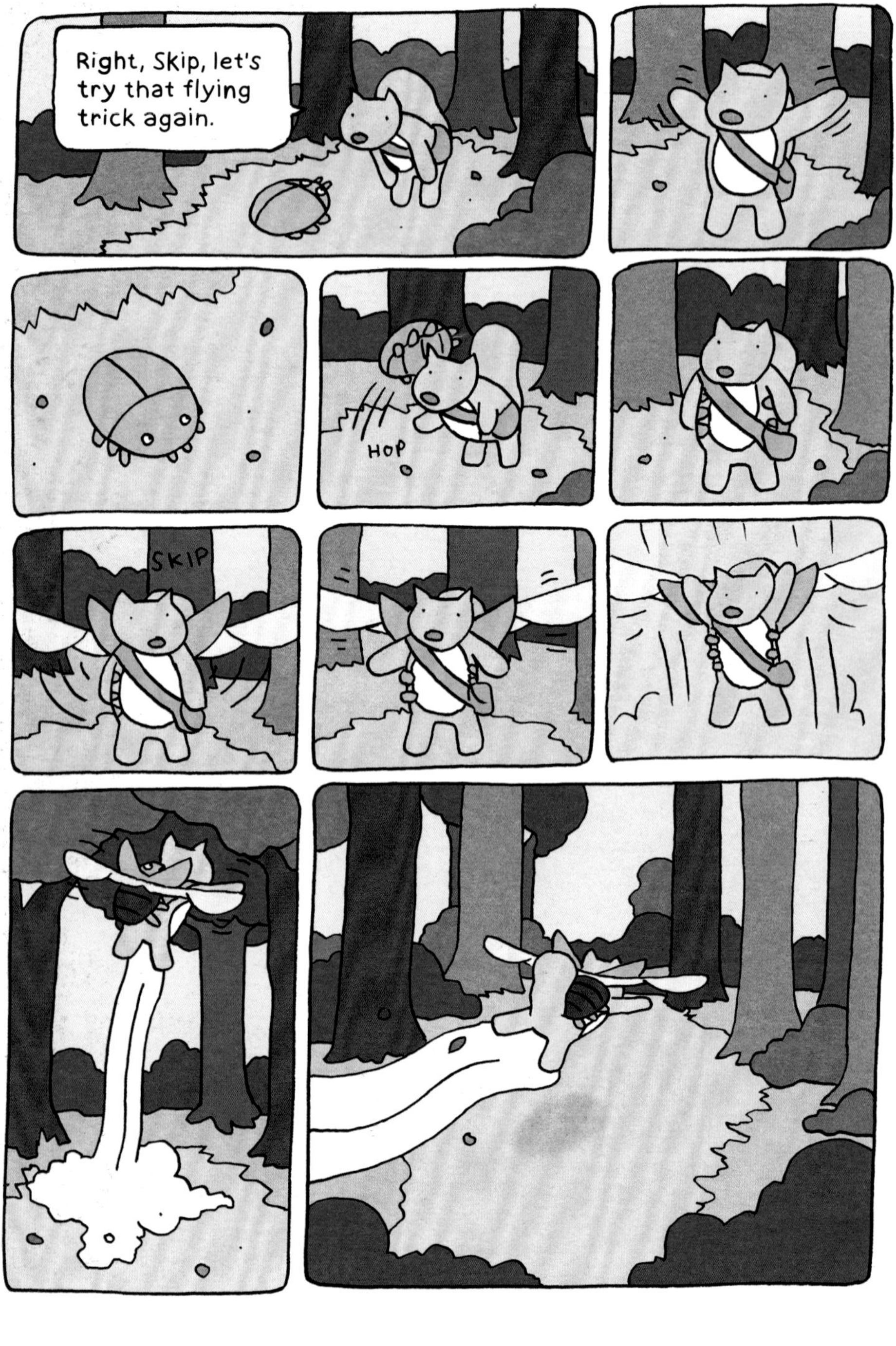
Right, Skip, let's try that flying trick again.
HOP
SKIP

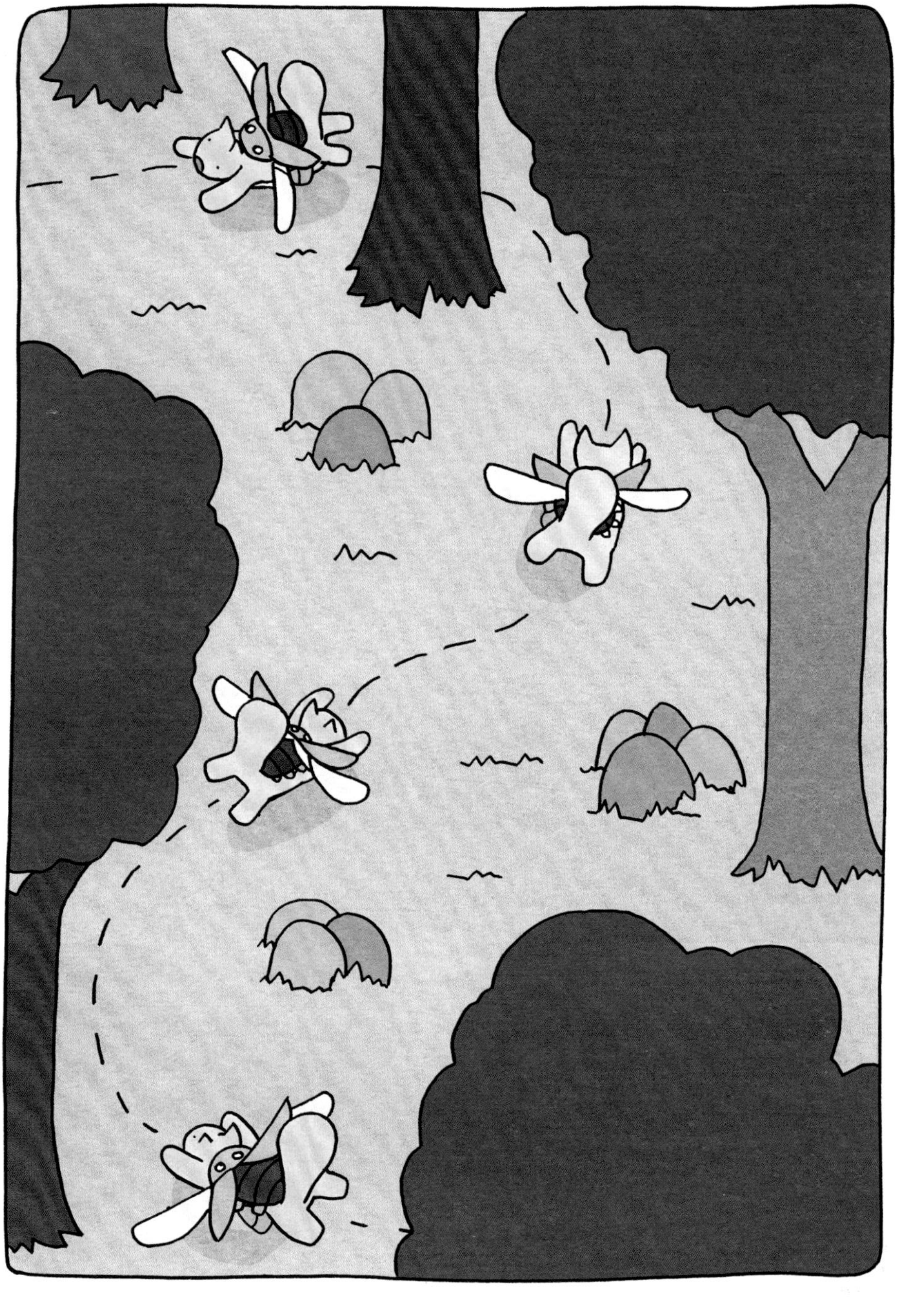

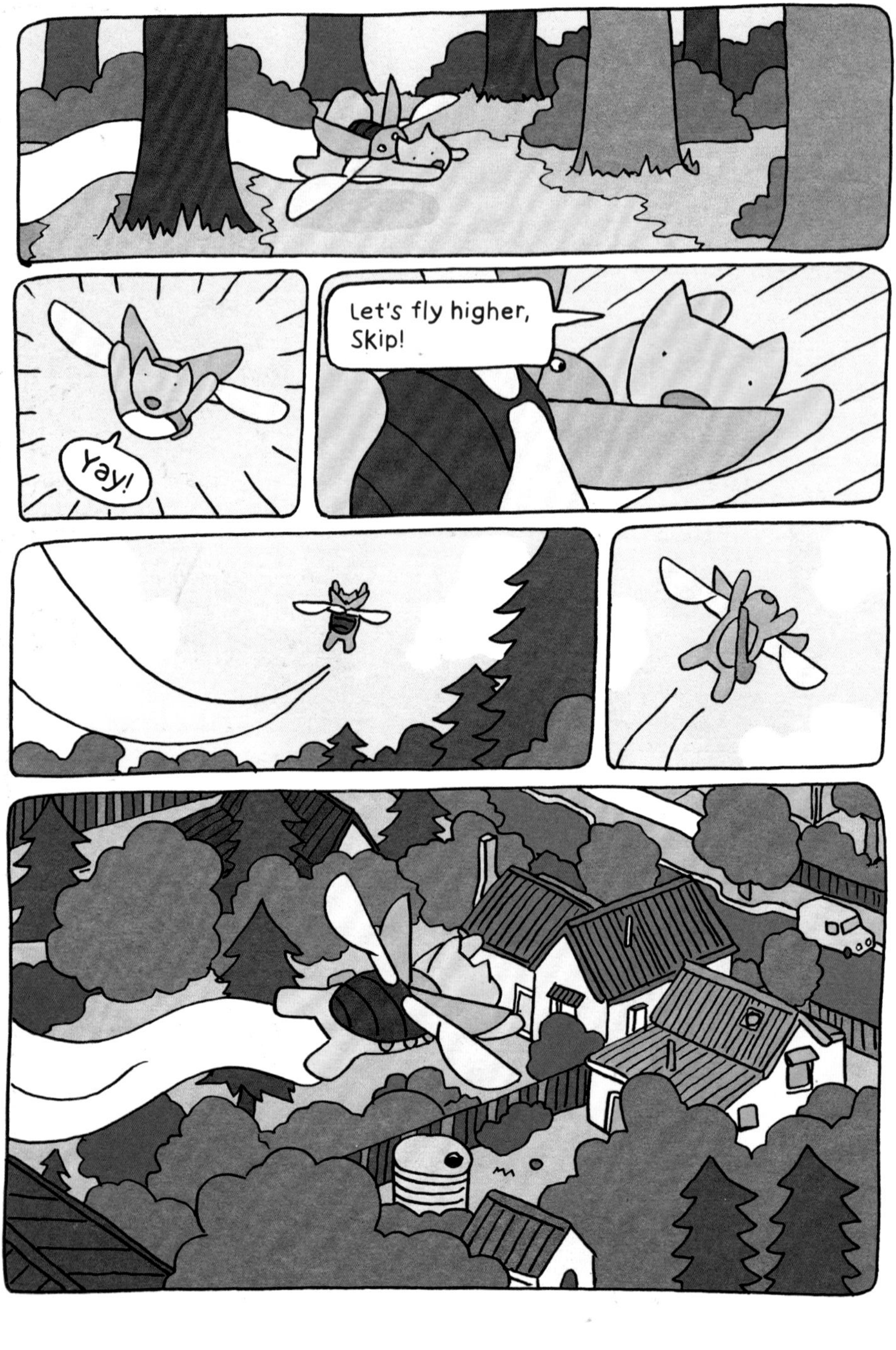
Yay!
Let's fly higher, Skip!

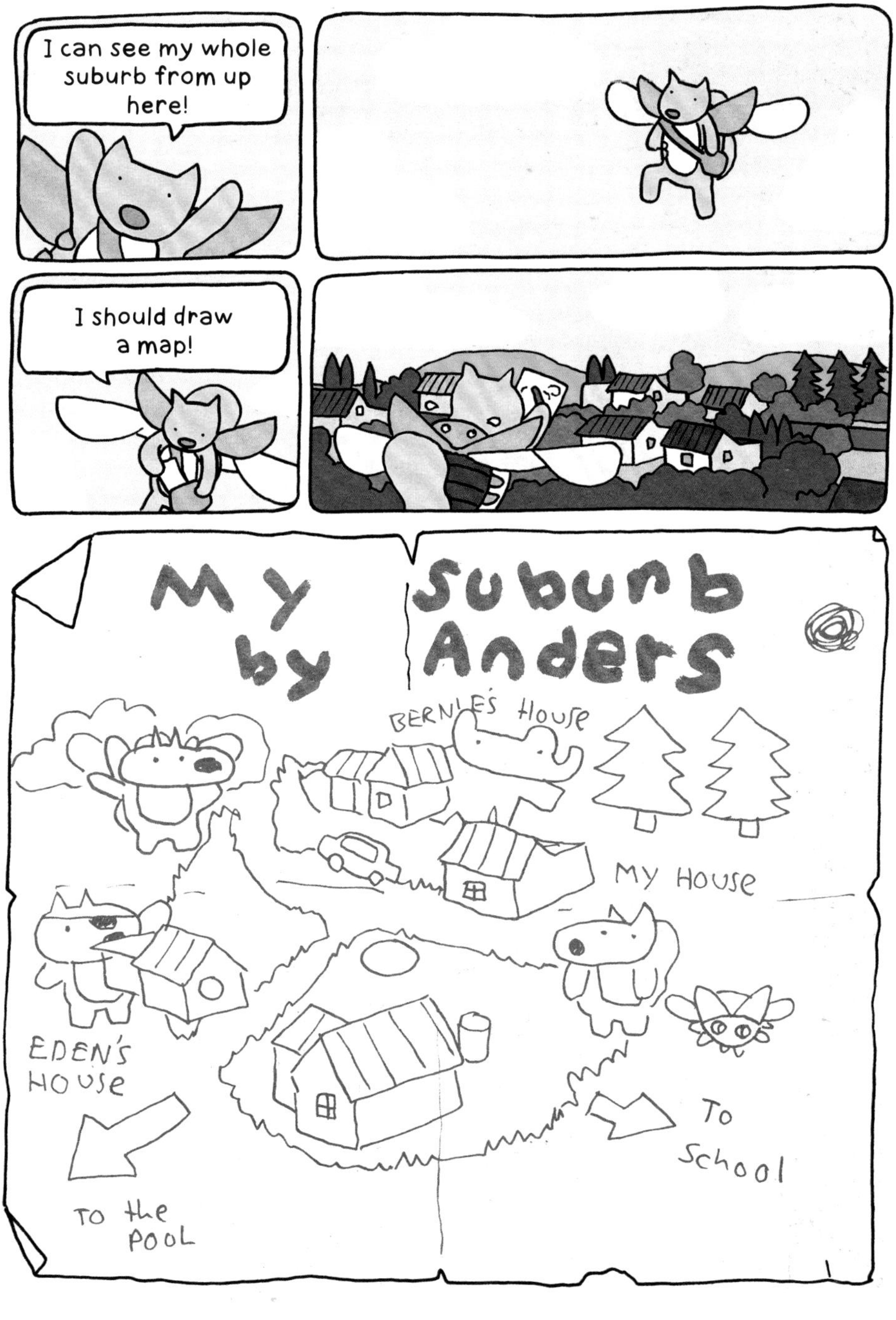
I can see my whole suburb from up here!
I should draw a map!
My Suburb by Anders
BERNIE'S HOUSE
MY HOUSE
EDEN'S HOUSE
TO the POOL
TO School

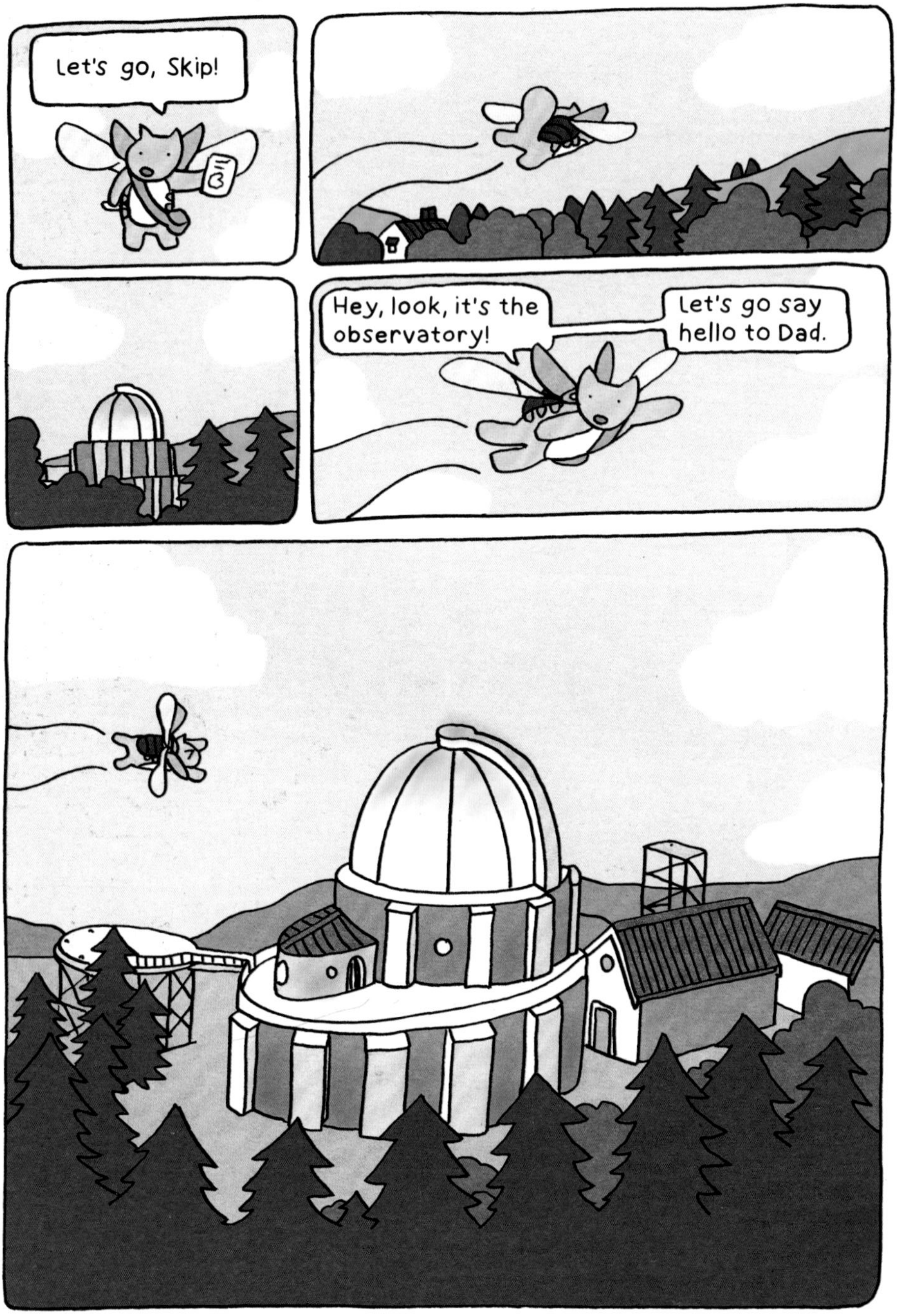
Let's go, Skip!
Hey, look, it's the observatory!
Let's go say hello to Dad.

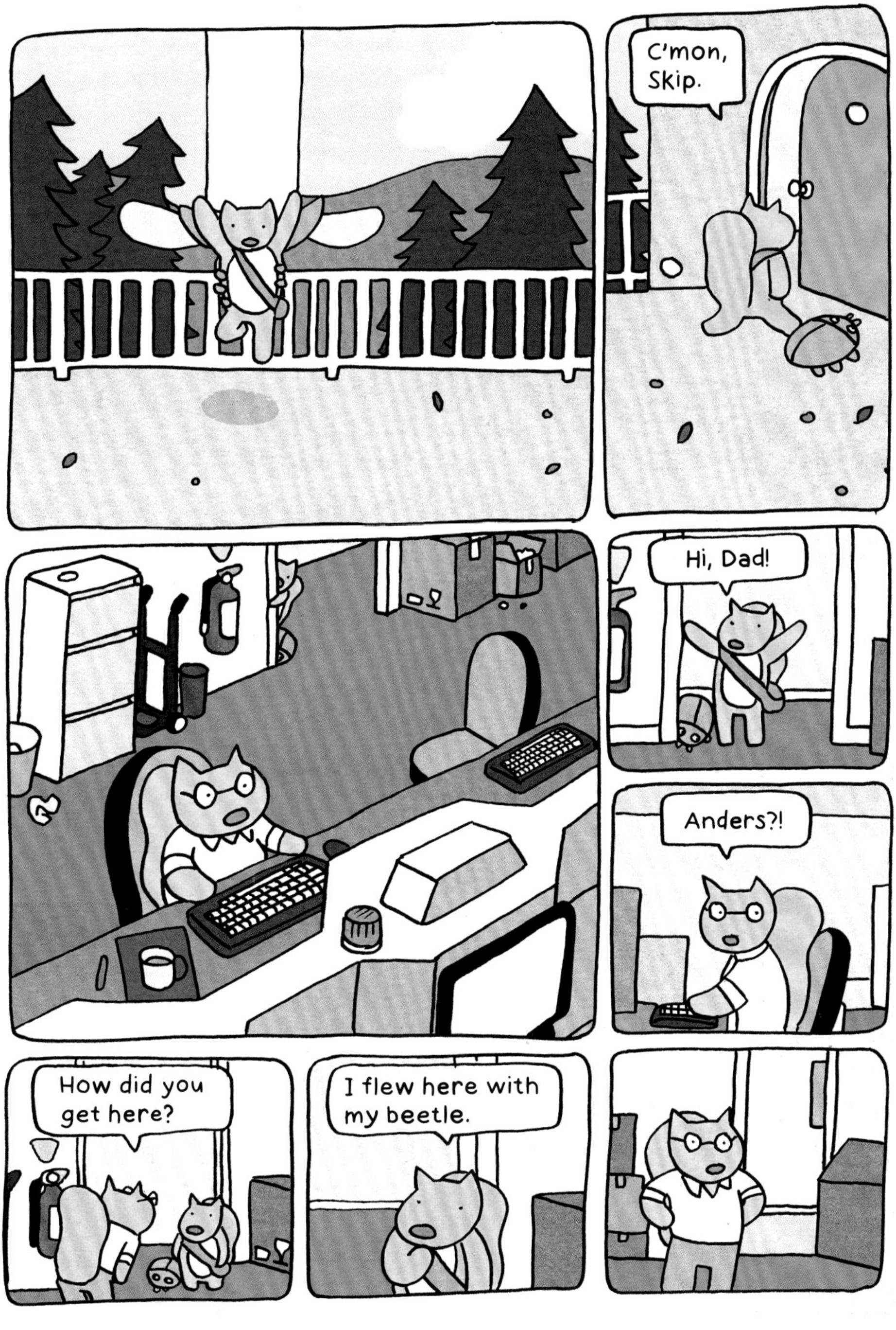
C'mon, Skip.
Hi, Dad!
Anders?!
How did you get here?
I flew here with my beetle.

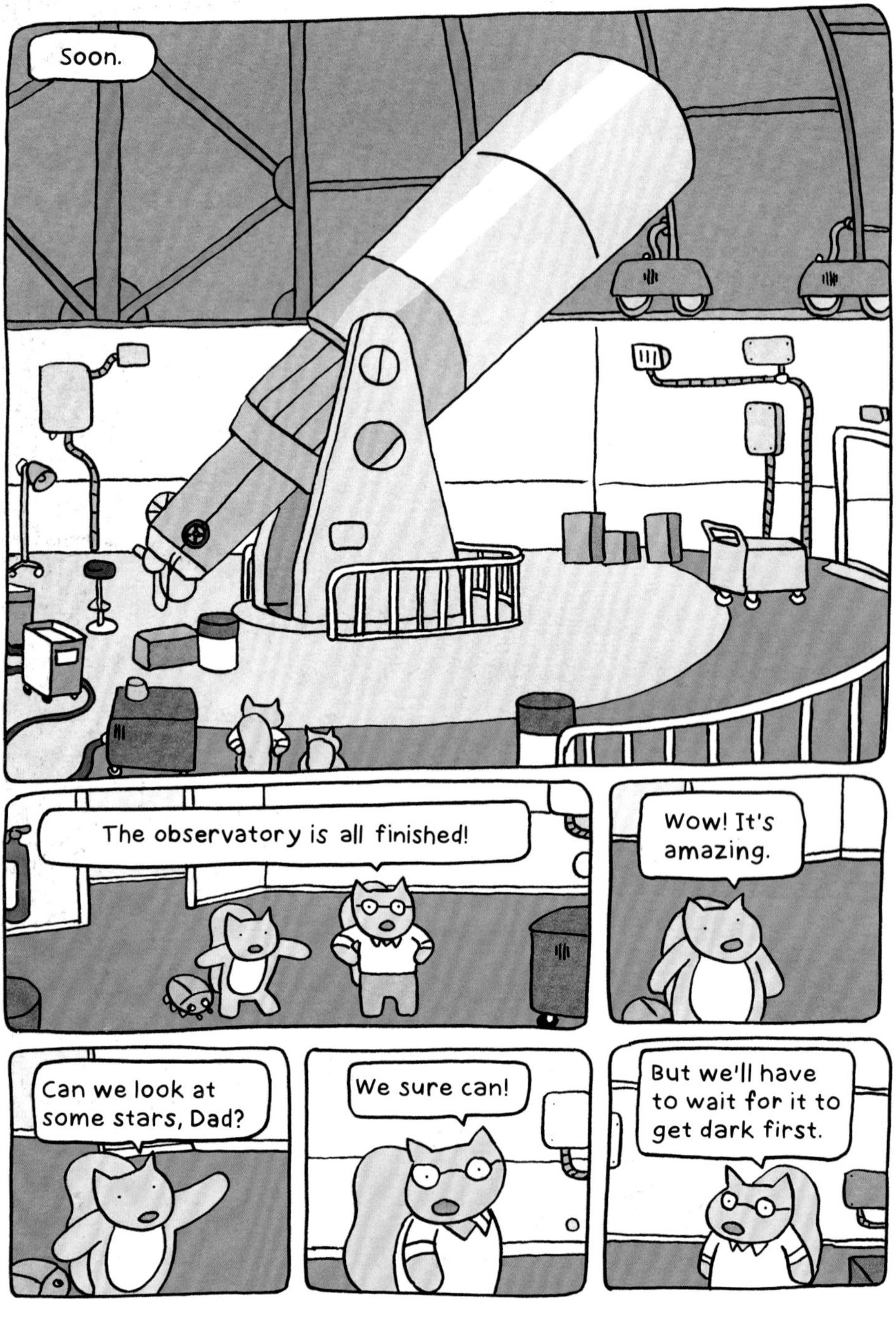
Soon.
The observatory is all finished!
Wow! It's amazing.
Can we look at some stars, Dad?
We sure can!
But we'll have to wait for it to get dark first.

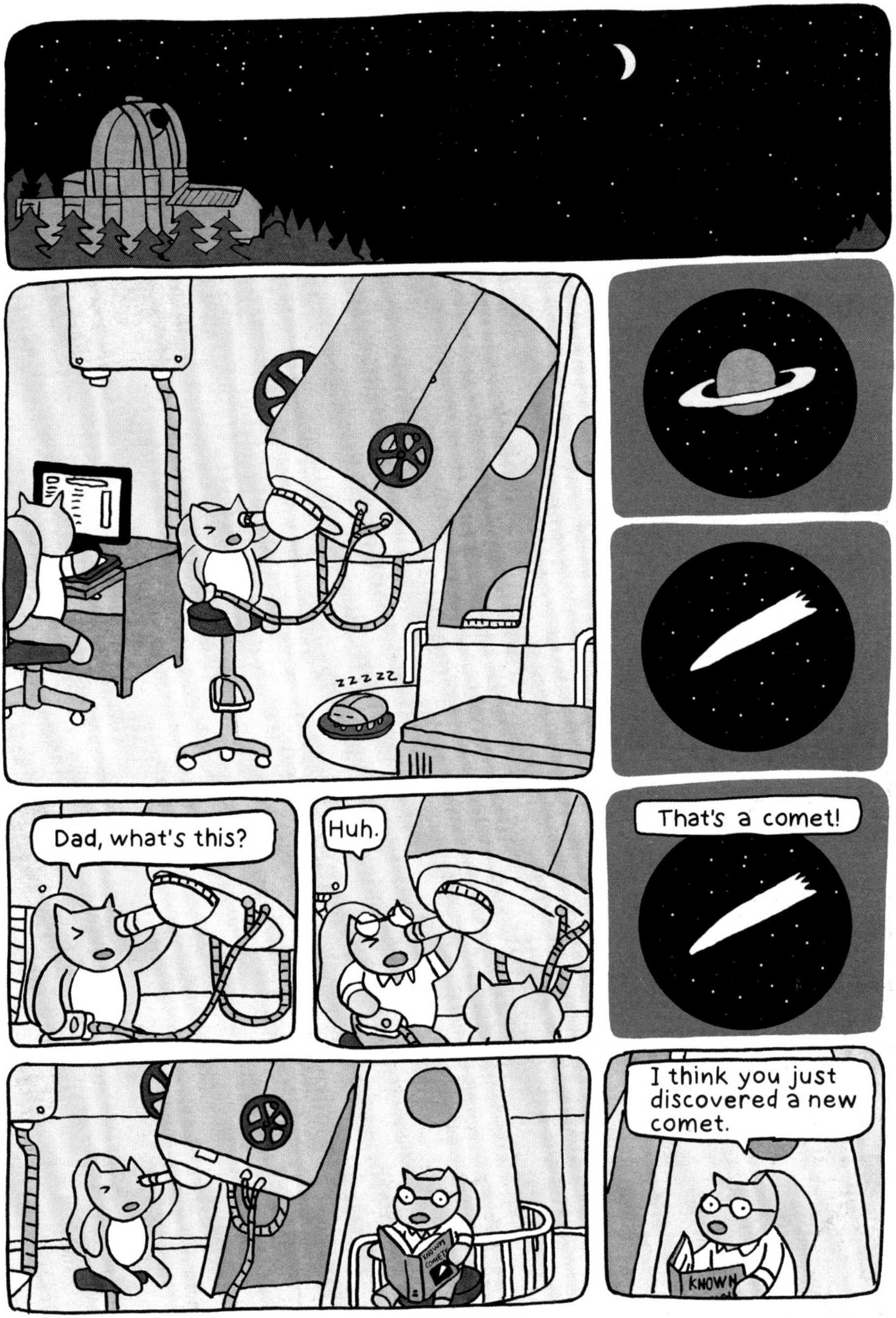
zzzzz
Dad, what's this?
Huh.
That's a comet!
KNOWN COMETS
I think you just discovered a new comet.
KNOWN

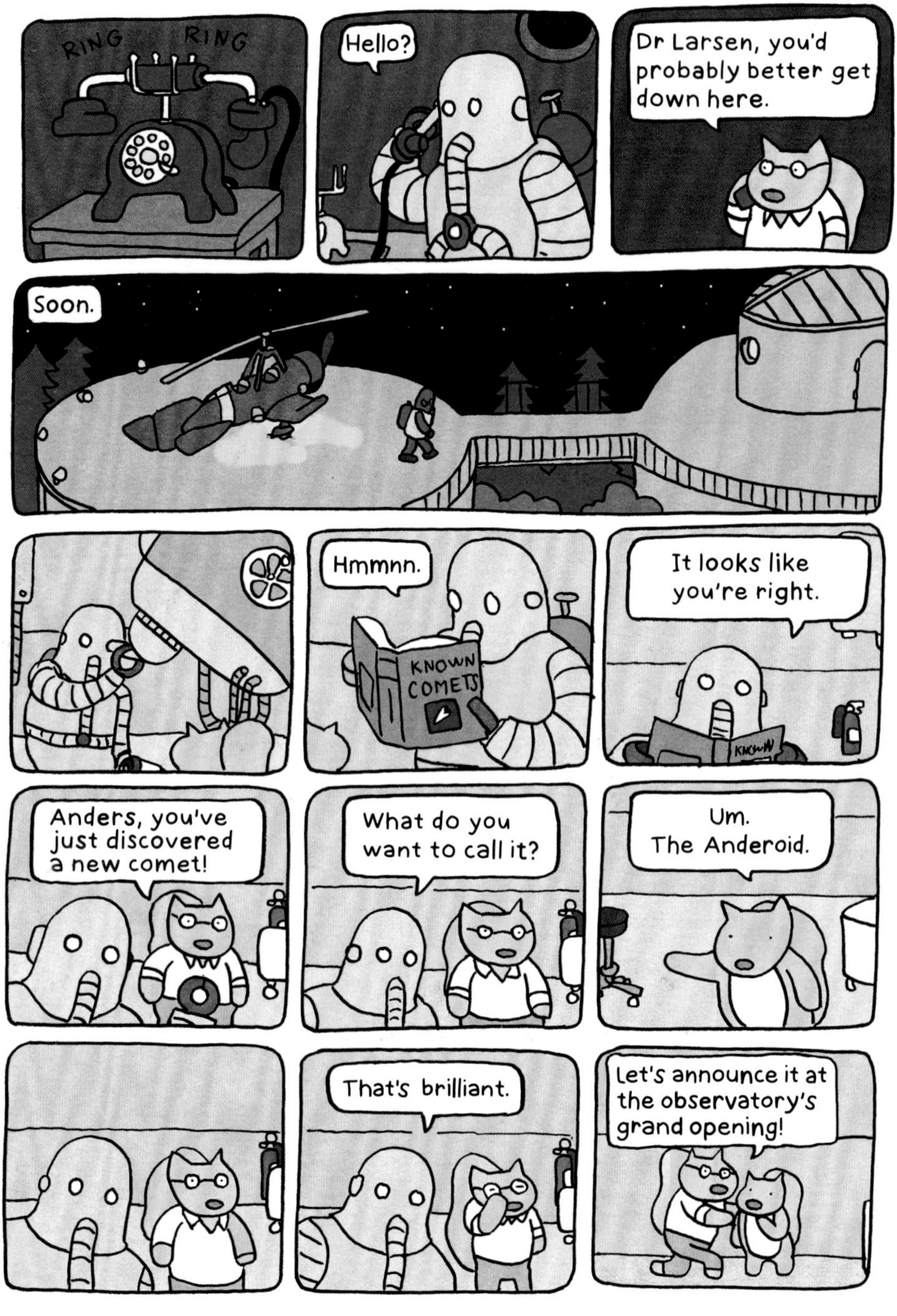
RING RING
Hello?
Dr Larsen, you'd probably better get down here.
Soon.
Hmmnn.
KNOWN COMETS
It looks like you're right.
Anders, you've just discovered a new comet!
What do you want to call it?
Um.
The Anderoid.
That's brilliant.
Let's announce it at the observatory's grand opening!

Chapter 7

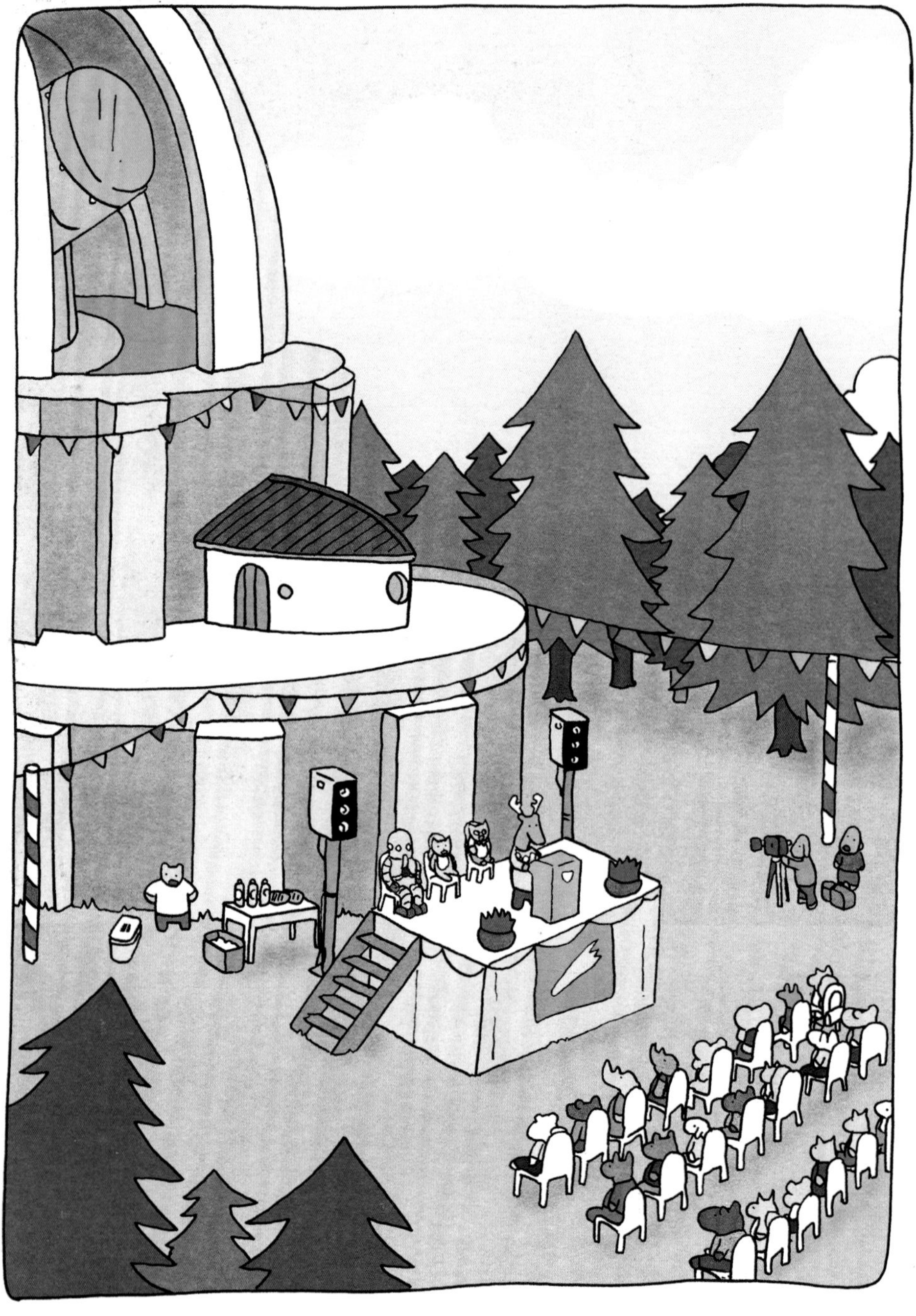

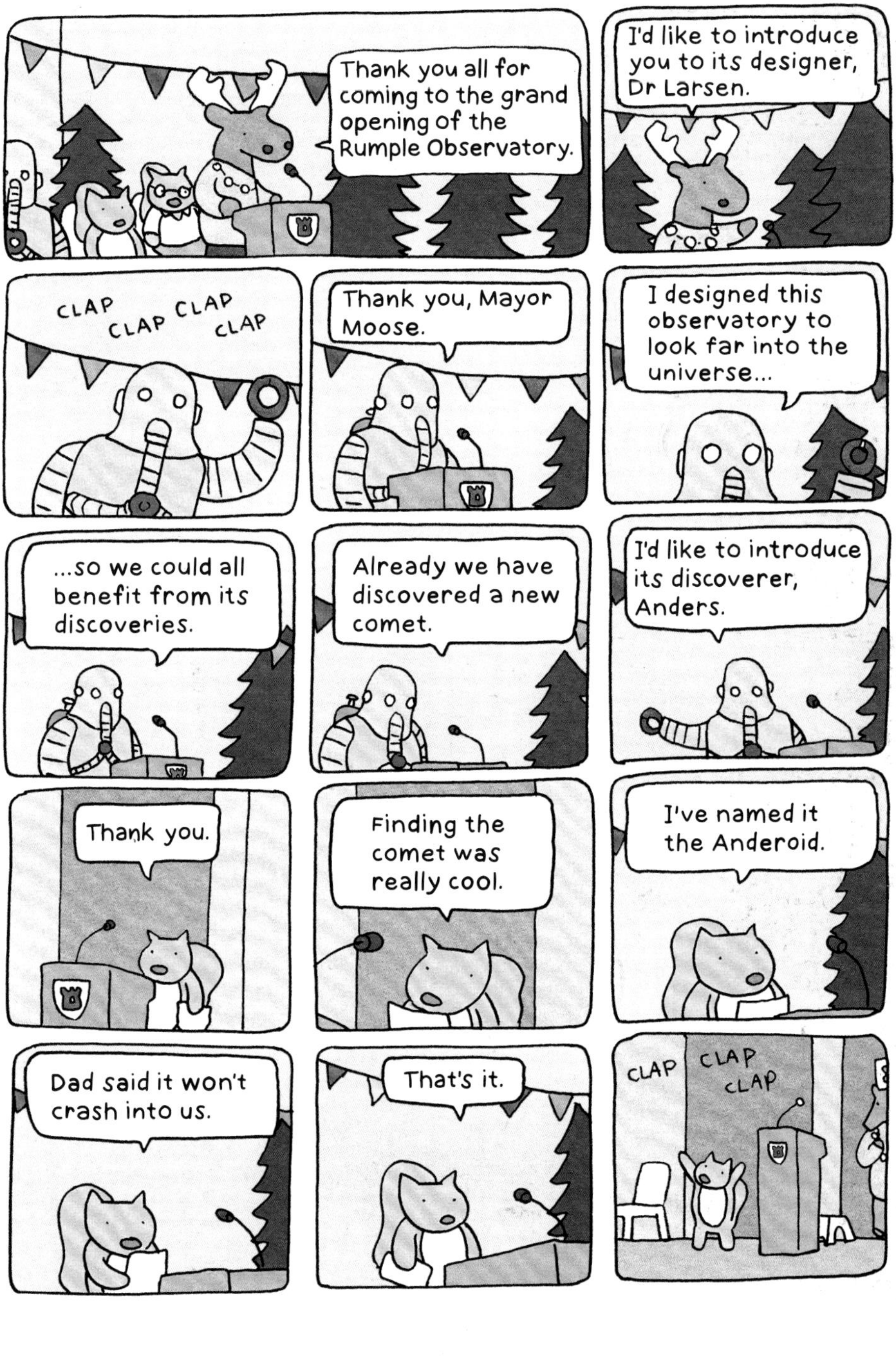
Thank you all for coming to the grand opening of the Rumple Observatory.
I'd like to introduce you to its designer, Dr Larsen.
CLAP CLAP CLAP CLAP
Thank you, Mayor Moose.
I designed this observatory to look far into the universe...
...so we could all benefit from its discoveries.
Already we have discovered a new comet.
I'd like to introduce its discoverer, Anders.
Thank you.
Finding the comet was really cool.
I've named it the Anderoid.
Dad said it won't crash into us.
That's it.
CLAP CLAP CLAP

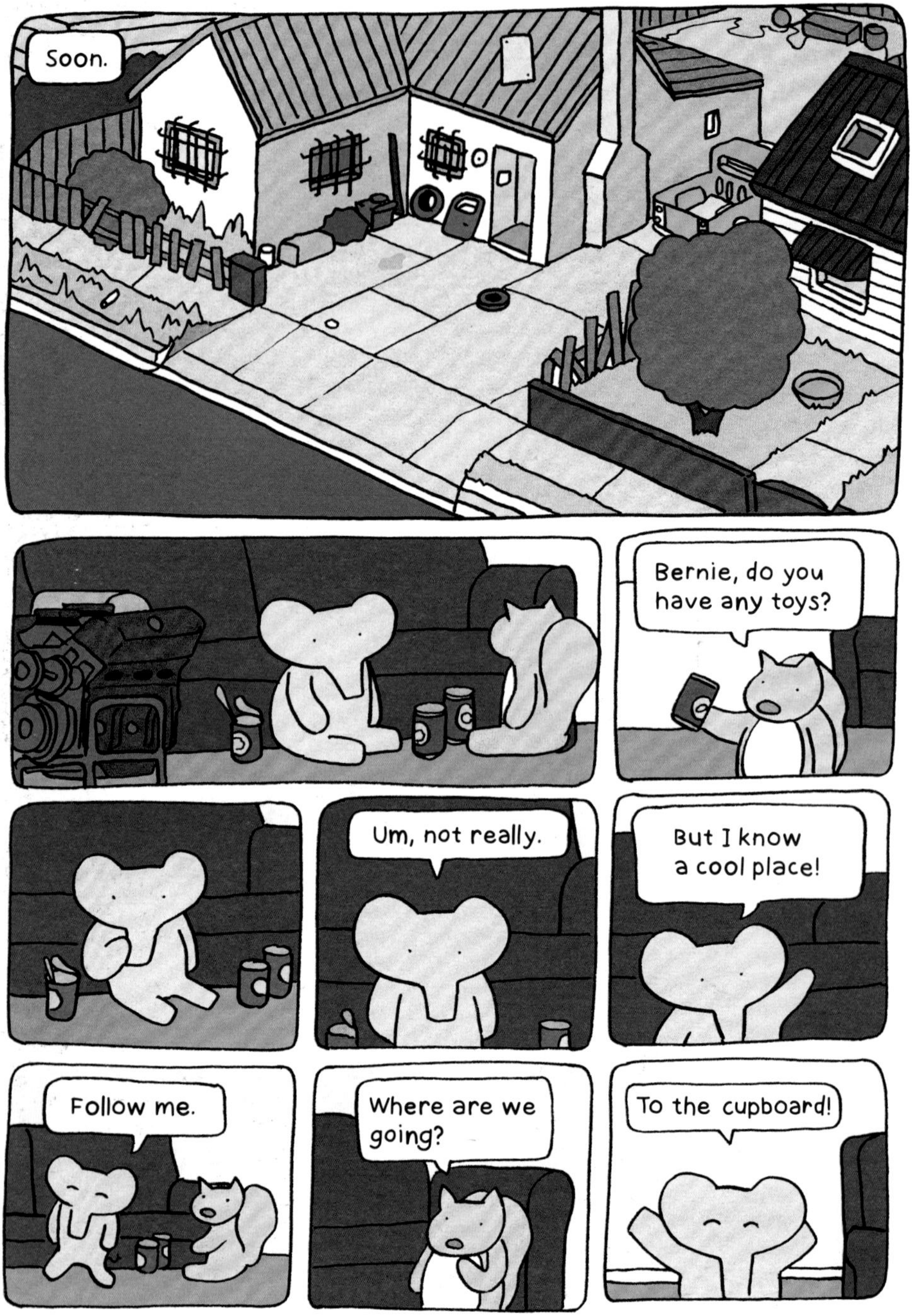
Soon.
Bernie, do you have any toys?
Um, not really.
But I know a cool place!
Follow me.
Where are we going?
To the cupboard!

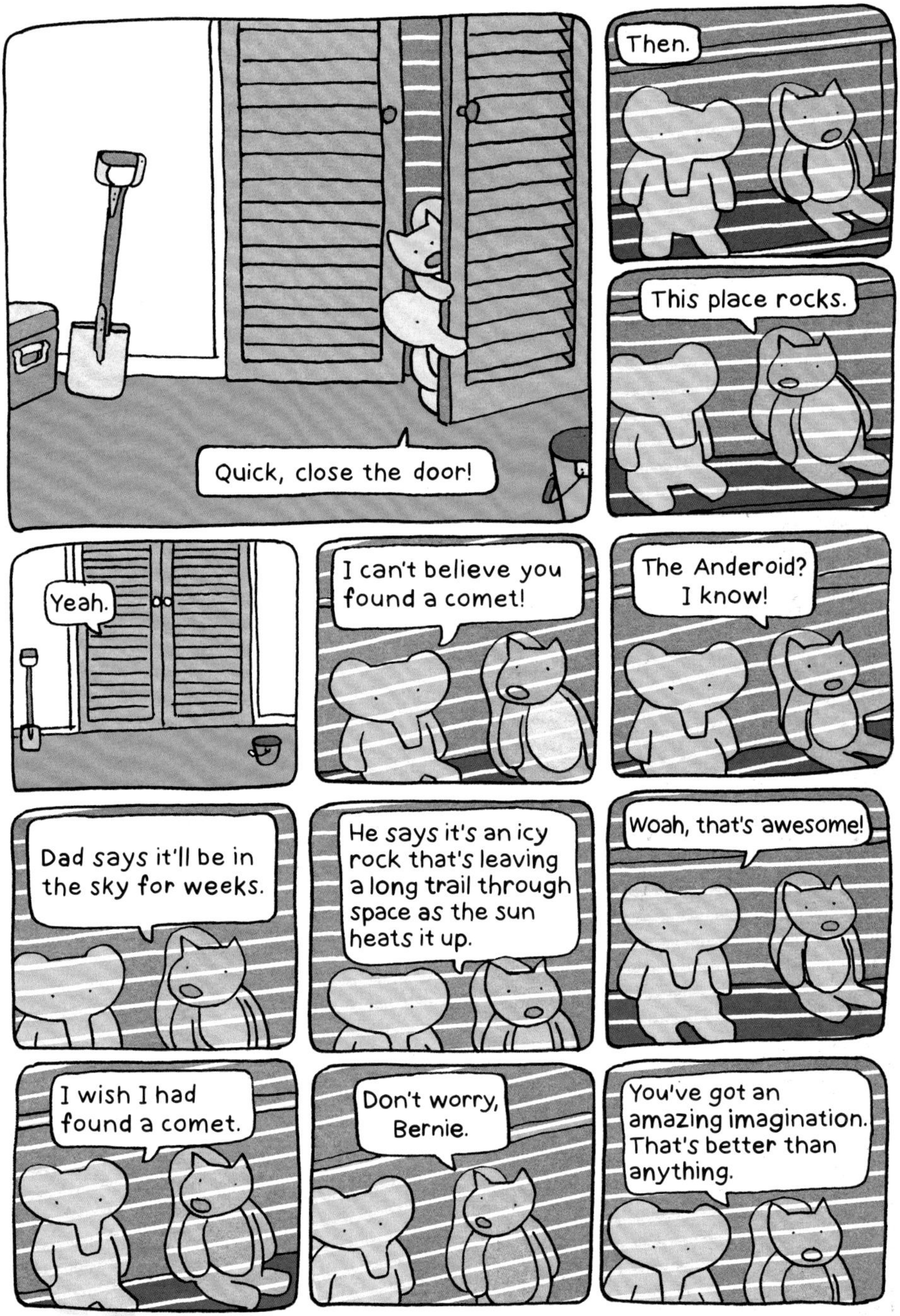
Quick, close the door!
Then.
This place rocks.
Yeah.
I can't believe you found a comet!
The Anderoid? I know!
Dad *says* it'll be in the sky for weeks.
He *says* it's an icy rock that's leaving a long trail through space as the sun heats it up.
Woah, that's awesome!
I wish I had found a comet.
Don't worry, Bernie.
You've got an amazing imagination. That's better than anything.

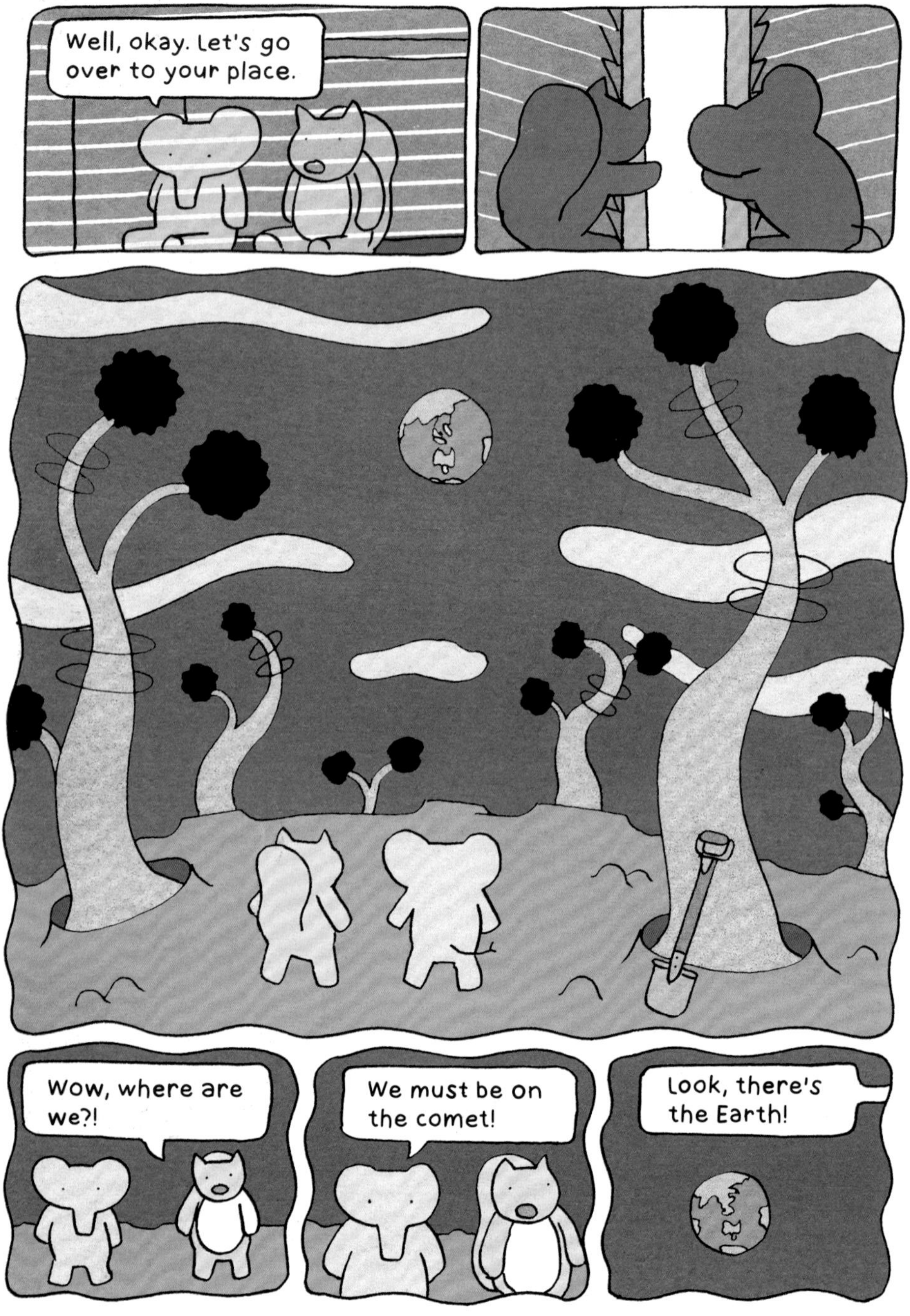
Well, okay. Let's go over to your place.
Wow, where are we?!
We must be on the comet!
Look, there's the Earth!

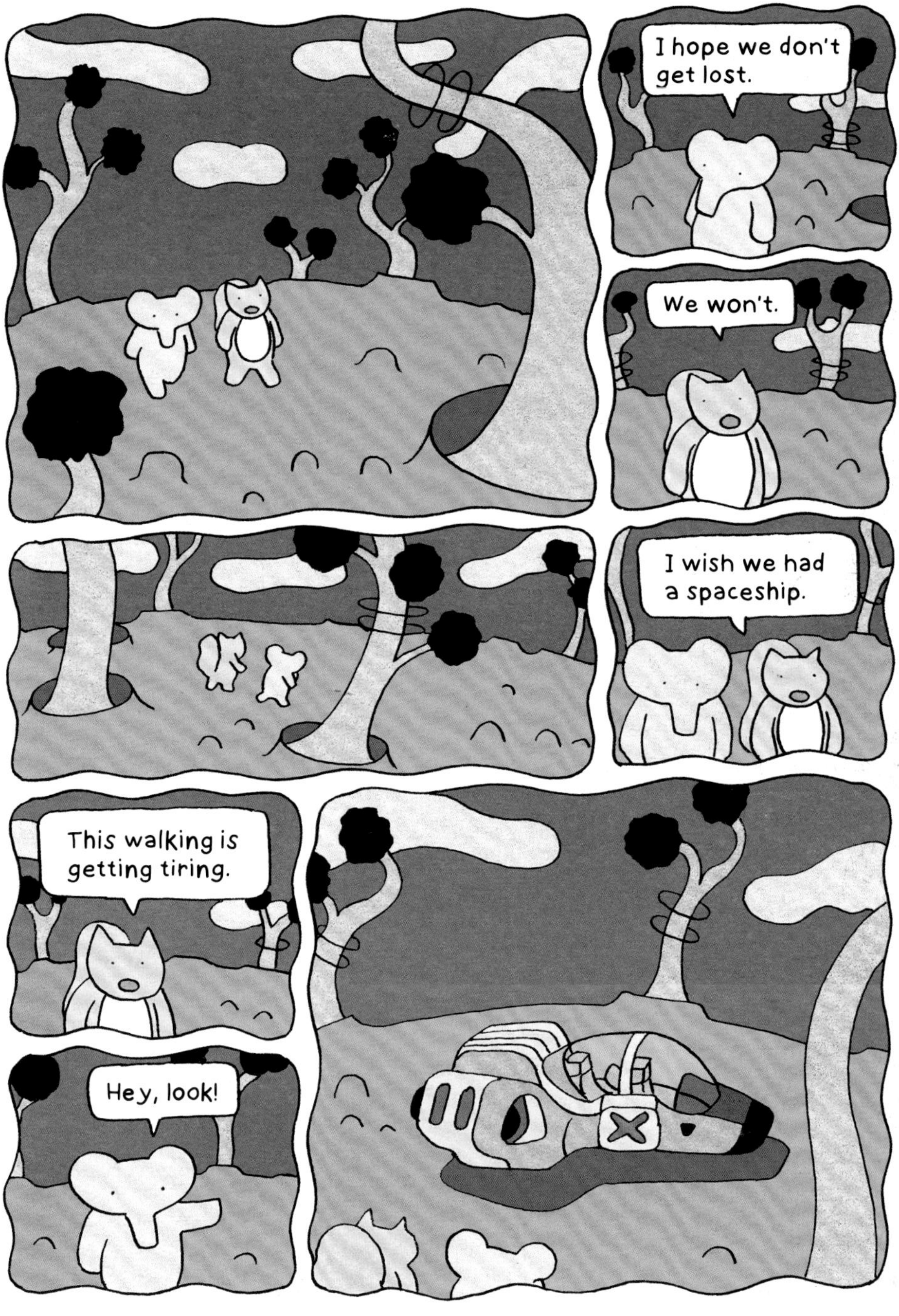
I hope we don't get lost.
We won't.
I wish we had a spaceship.
This walking is getting tiring.
Hey, look!

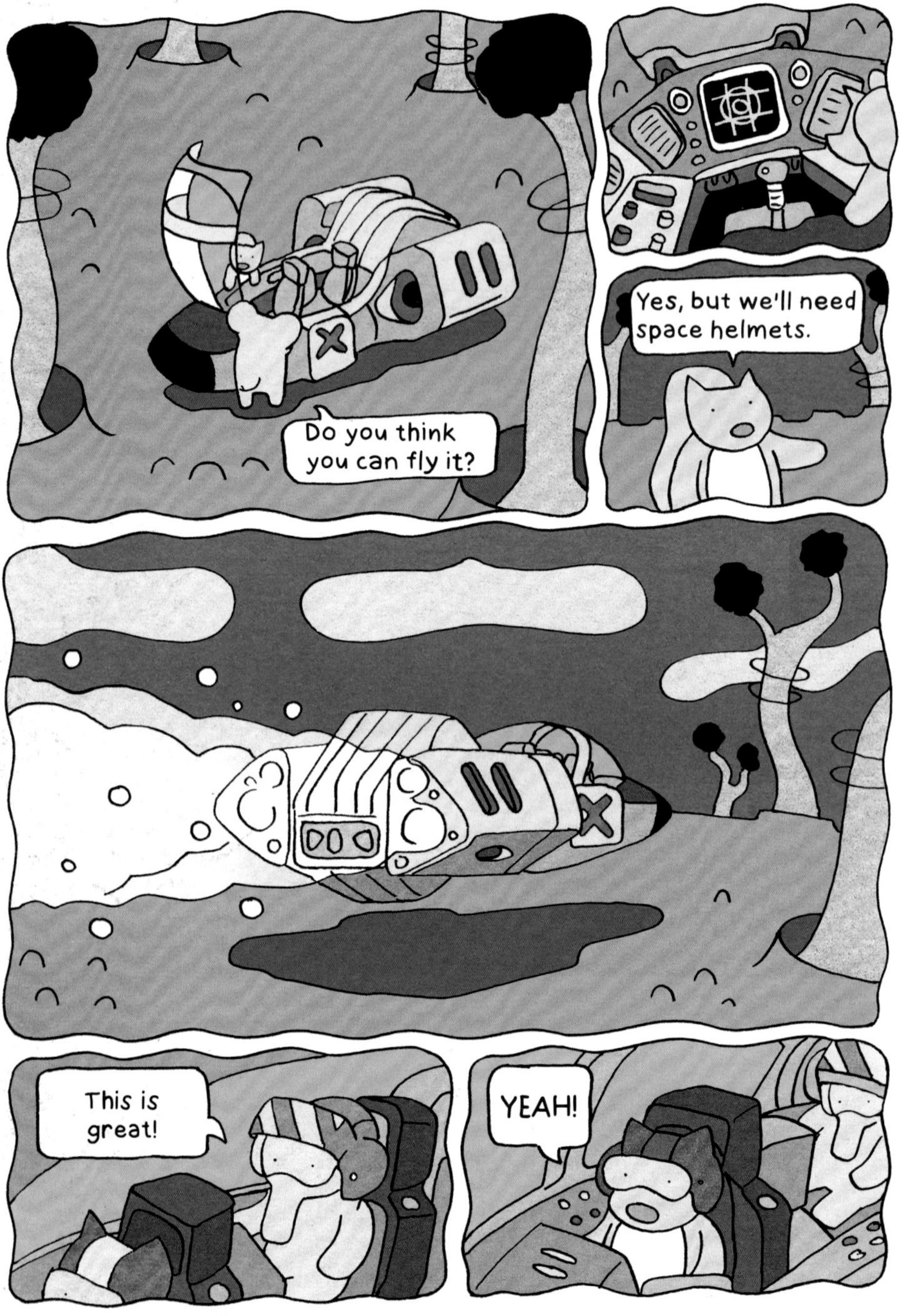
Do you think you can fly it?
Yes, but we'll need space helmets.
This is great!
YEAH!

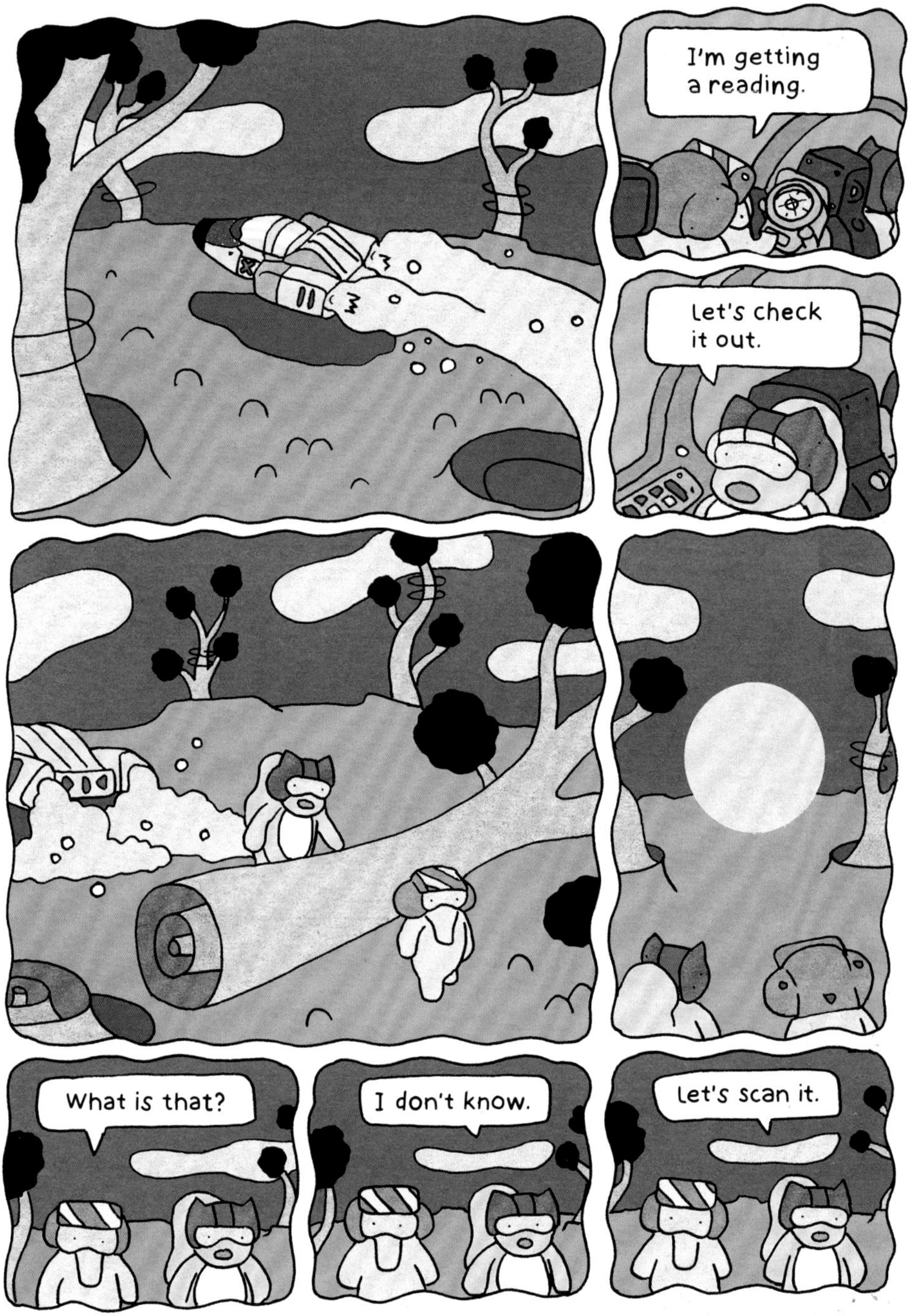
I'm getting a reading.
Let's check it out.
What is that?
I don't know.
Let's scan it.

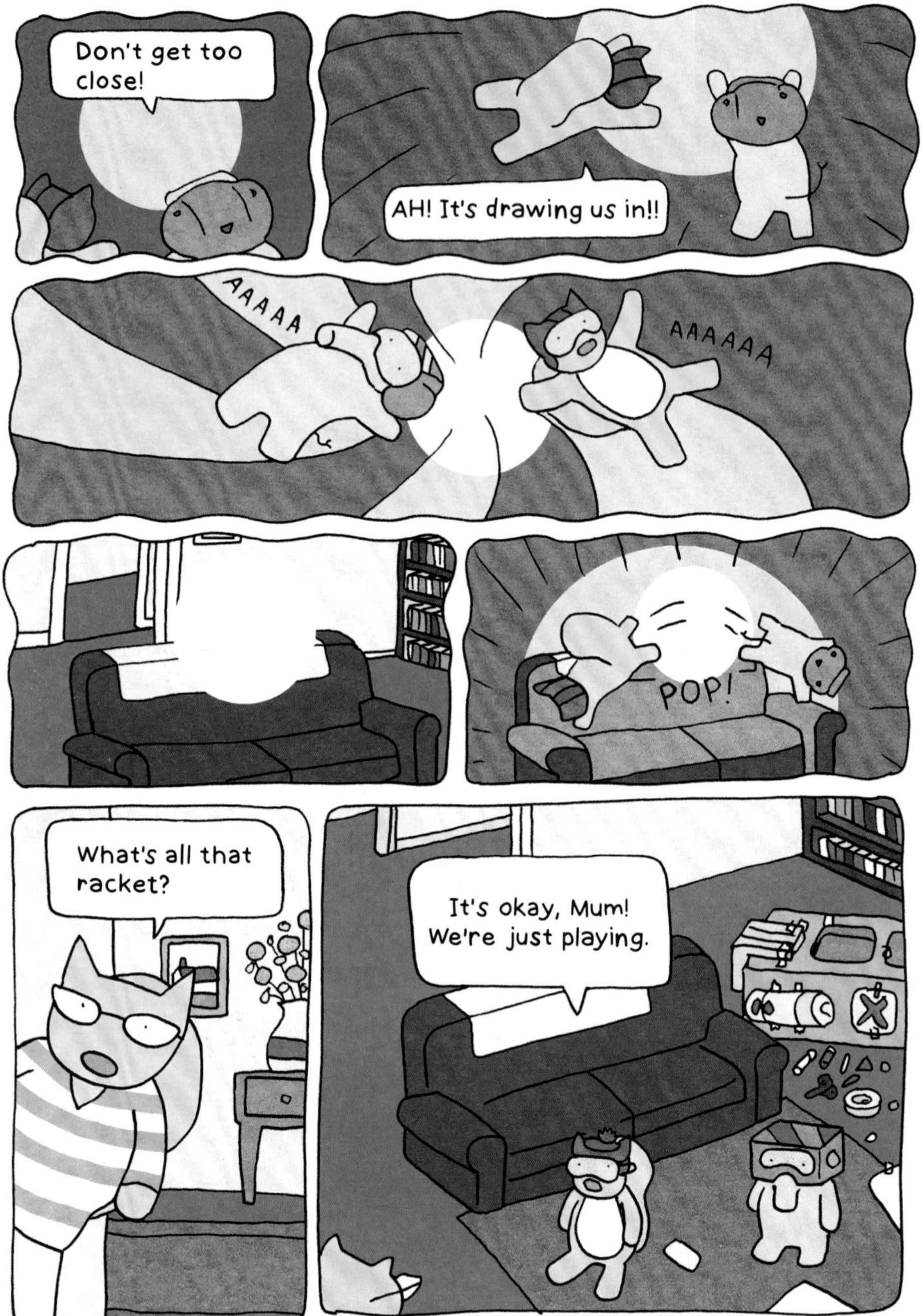
Don't get too close!
AH! It's drawing us in!!
AAAAA
AAAAAA
POP!
What's all that racket?
It's okay, Mum! We're just playing.

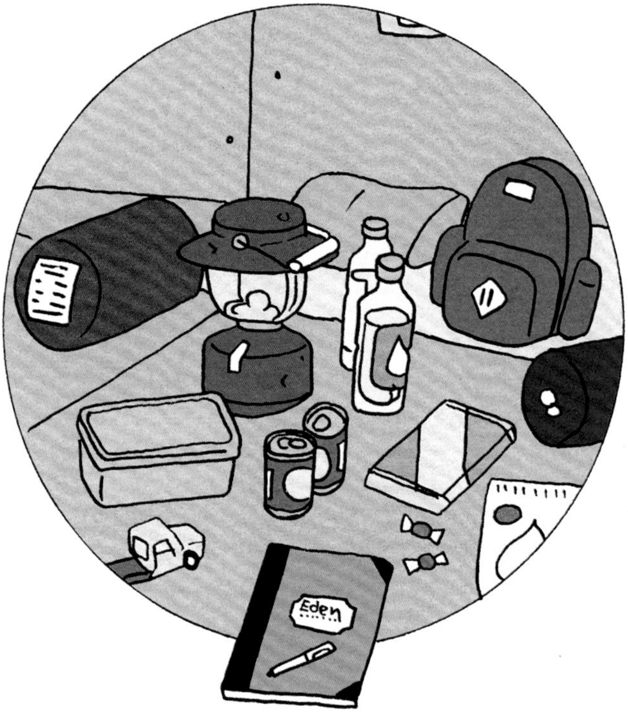
Eden

Chapter 8

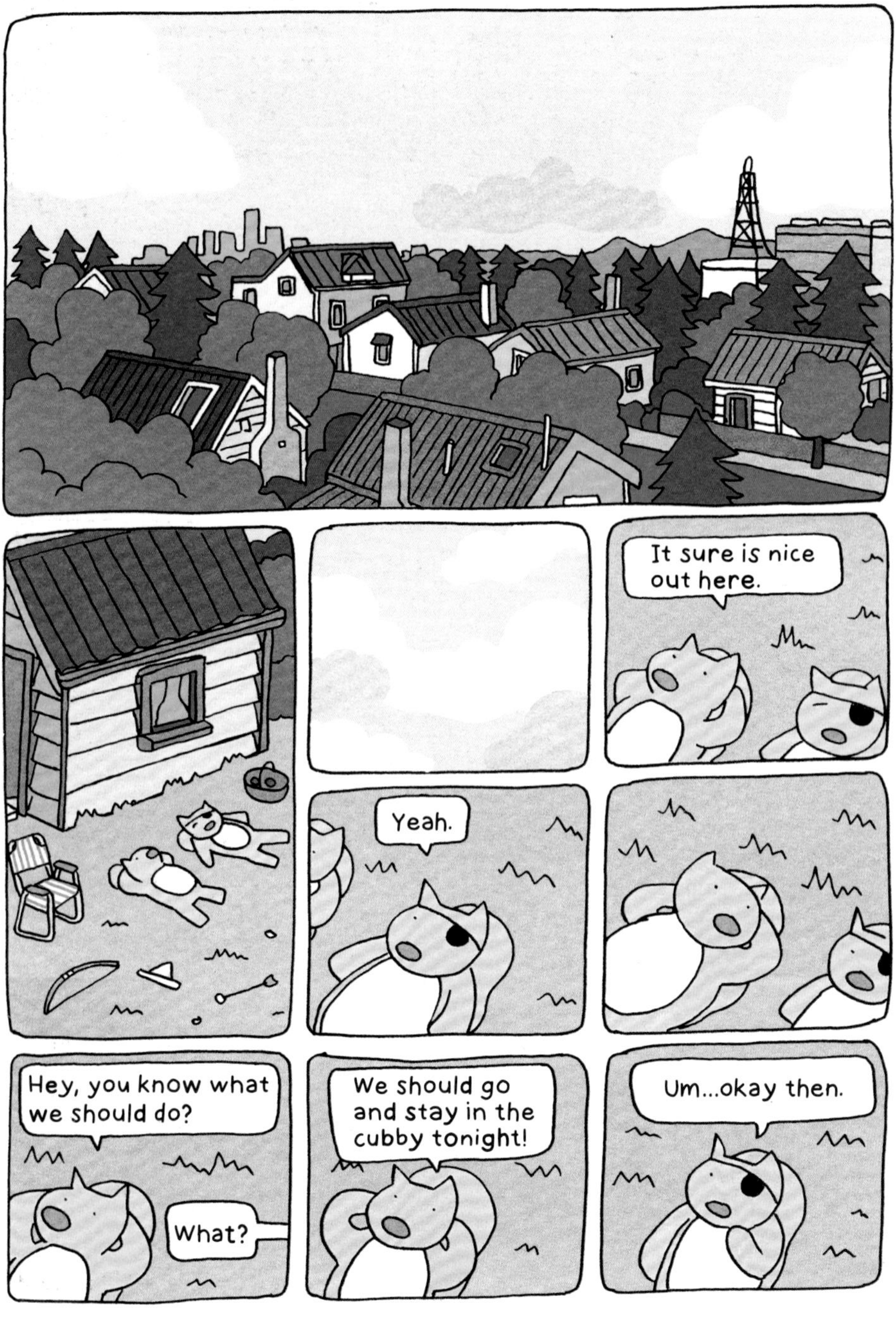
It sure is nice out here.
Yeah.
Hey, you know what we should do?
What?
We should go and stay in the cubby tonight!
Um...okay then.

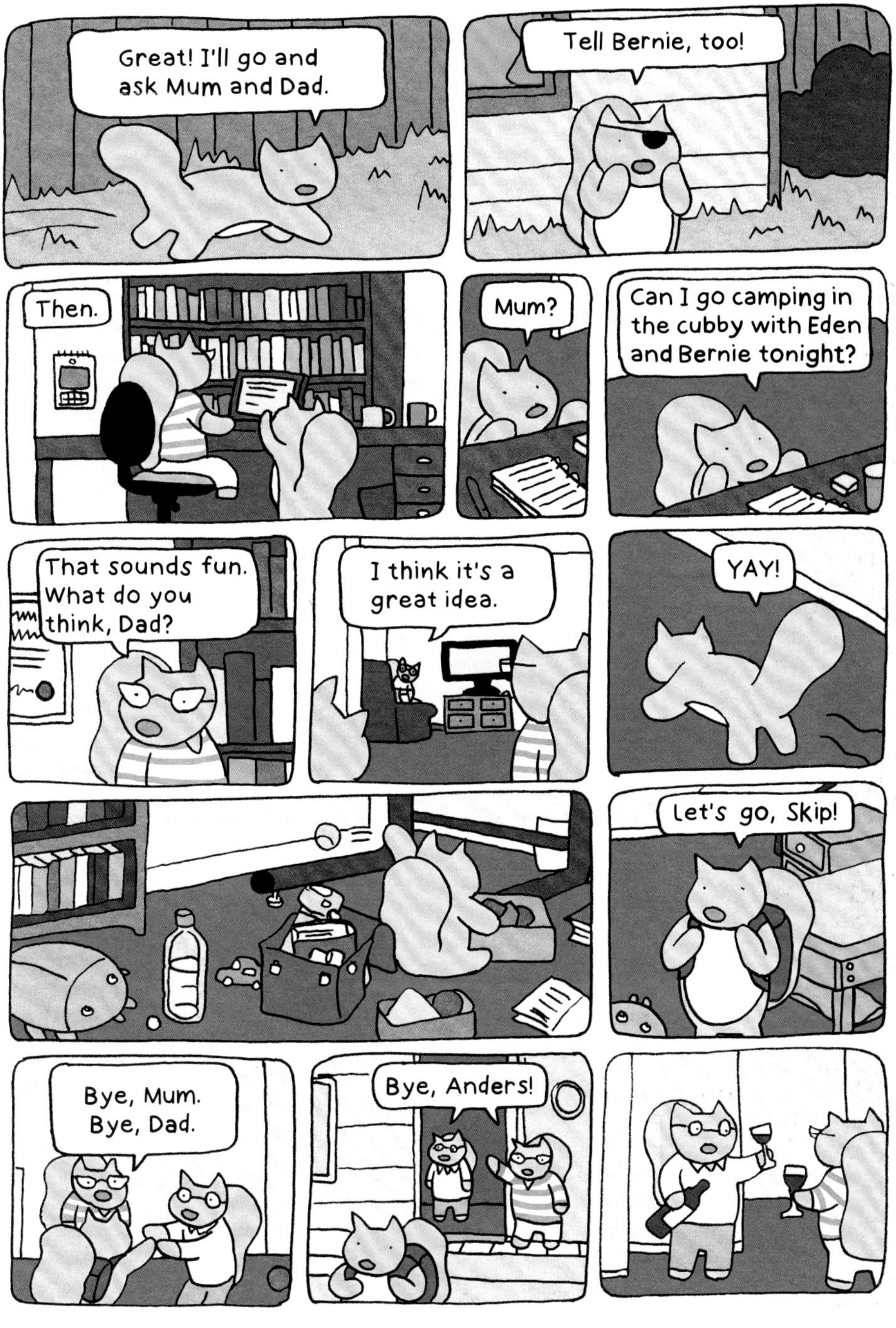
Great! I'll go and ask Mum and Dad.
Tell Bernie, too!
Then.
Mum?
Can I go camping in the cubby with Eden and Bernie tonight?
That sounds fun. What do you think, Dad?
I think it's a great idea.
YAY!
Let's go, Skip!
Bye, Mum. Bye, Dad.
Bye, Anders!

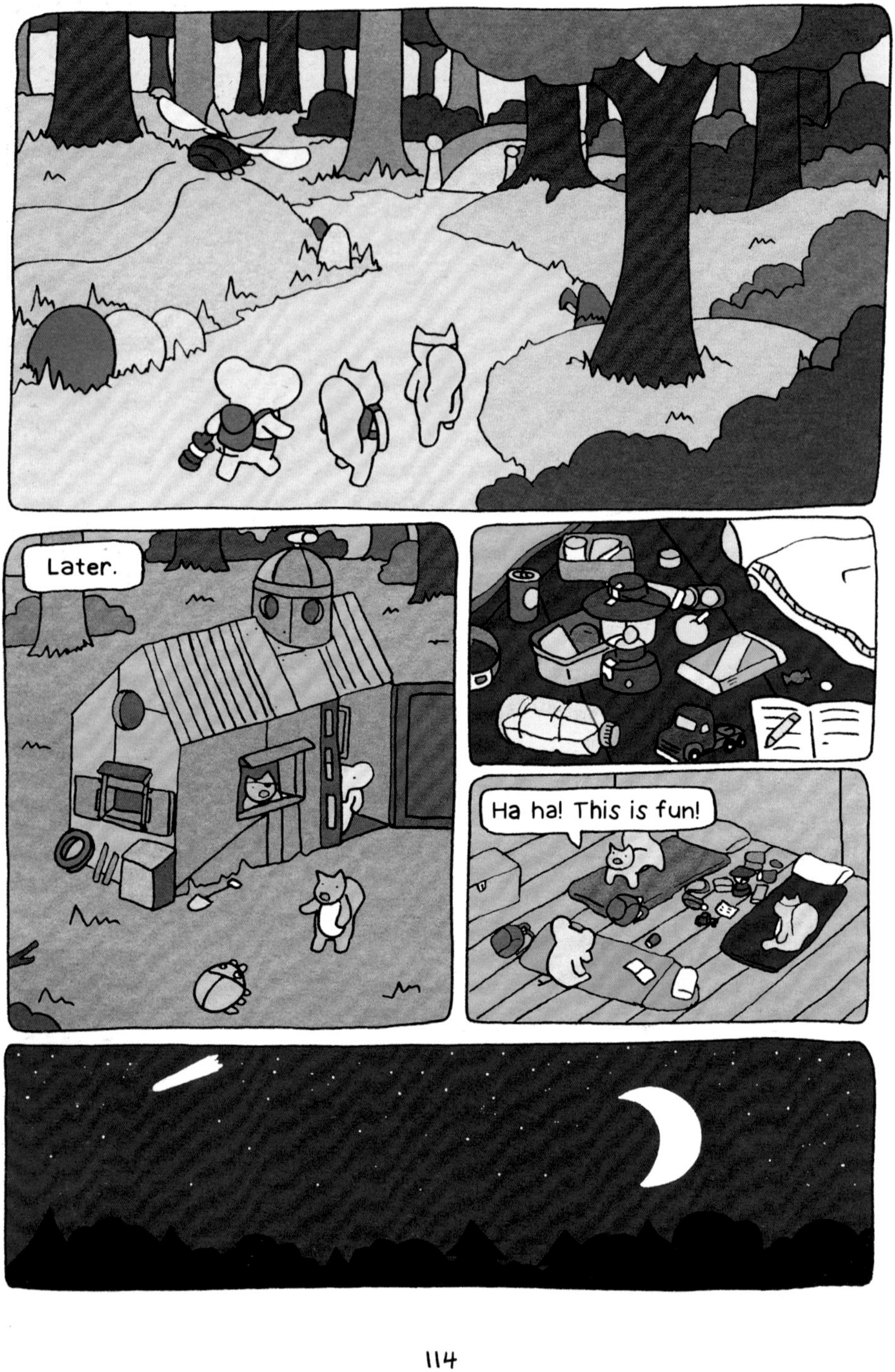
Later.
Ha ha! This is fun!

This cubby is the best thing ever!

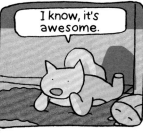
I know, it's awesome.

I'd live here if I could.

Me too.

I'd miss all my stuff.

So would I.

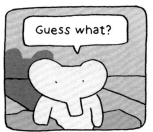
Guess what?

What?

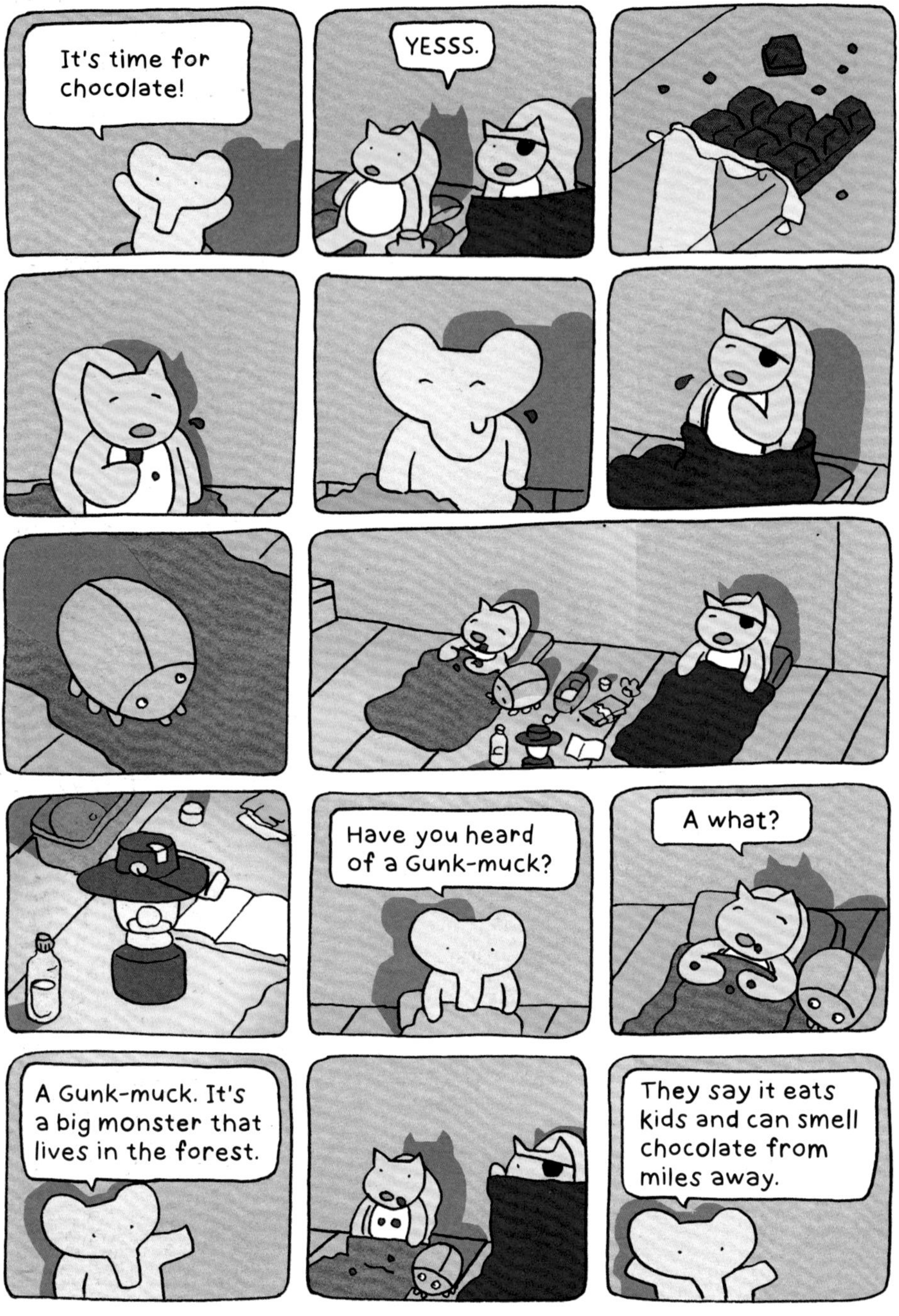
It's time for chocolate!
YESSS.
Have you heard of a Gunk-muck?
A what?
A Gunk-muck. It's a big monster that lives in the forest.
They say it eats kids and can smell chocolate from miles away.

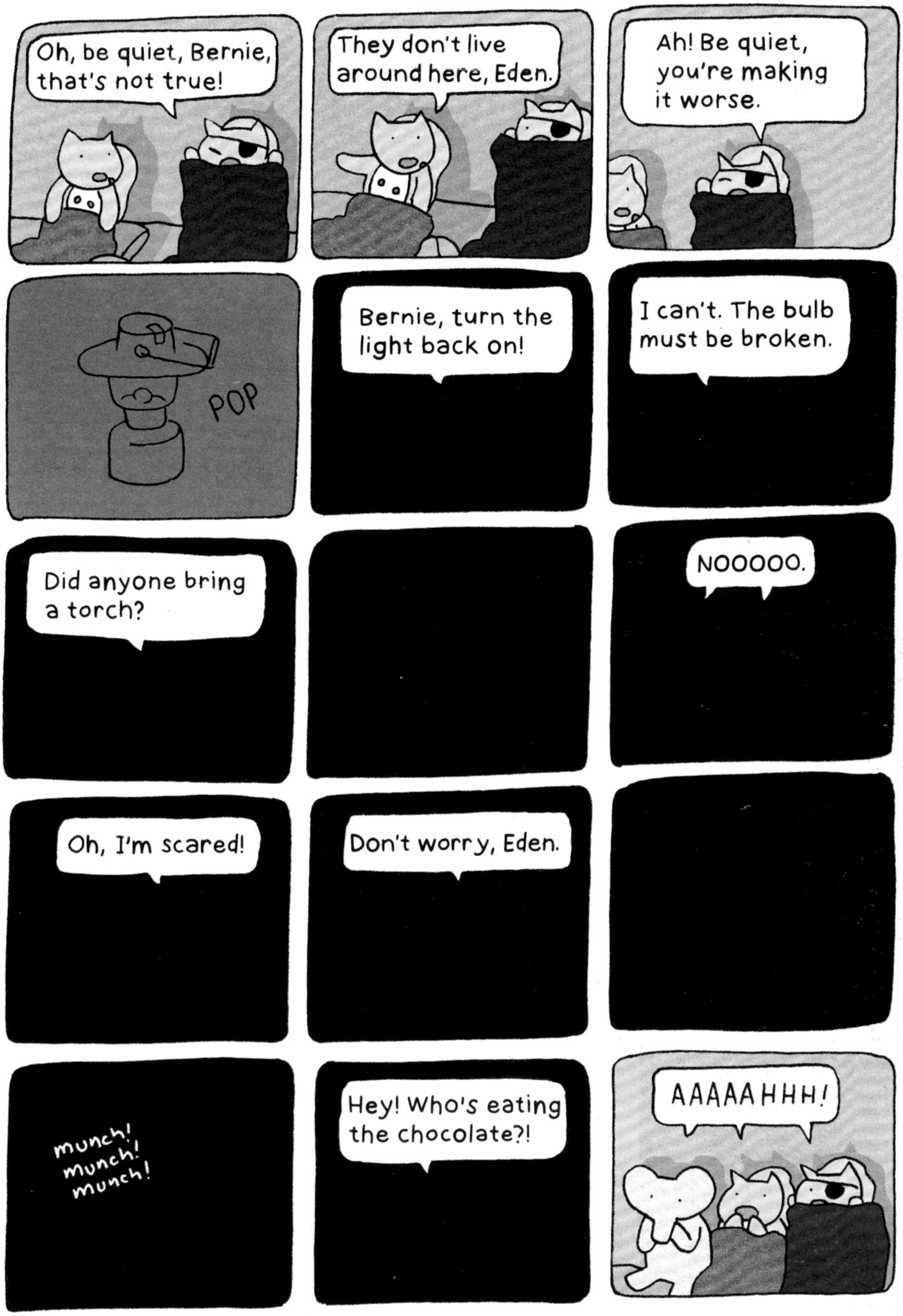

Oh, be quiet, Bernie, that's not true!
They don't live around here, Eden.
Ah! Be quiet, you're making it worse.
POP
Bernie, turn the light back on!
I can't. The bulb must be broken.
Did anyone bring a torch?
NOOOOO.
Oh, I'm scared!
Don't worry, Eden.
munch! munch! munch!
Hey! Who's eating the chocolate?!
AAAAAHHH!

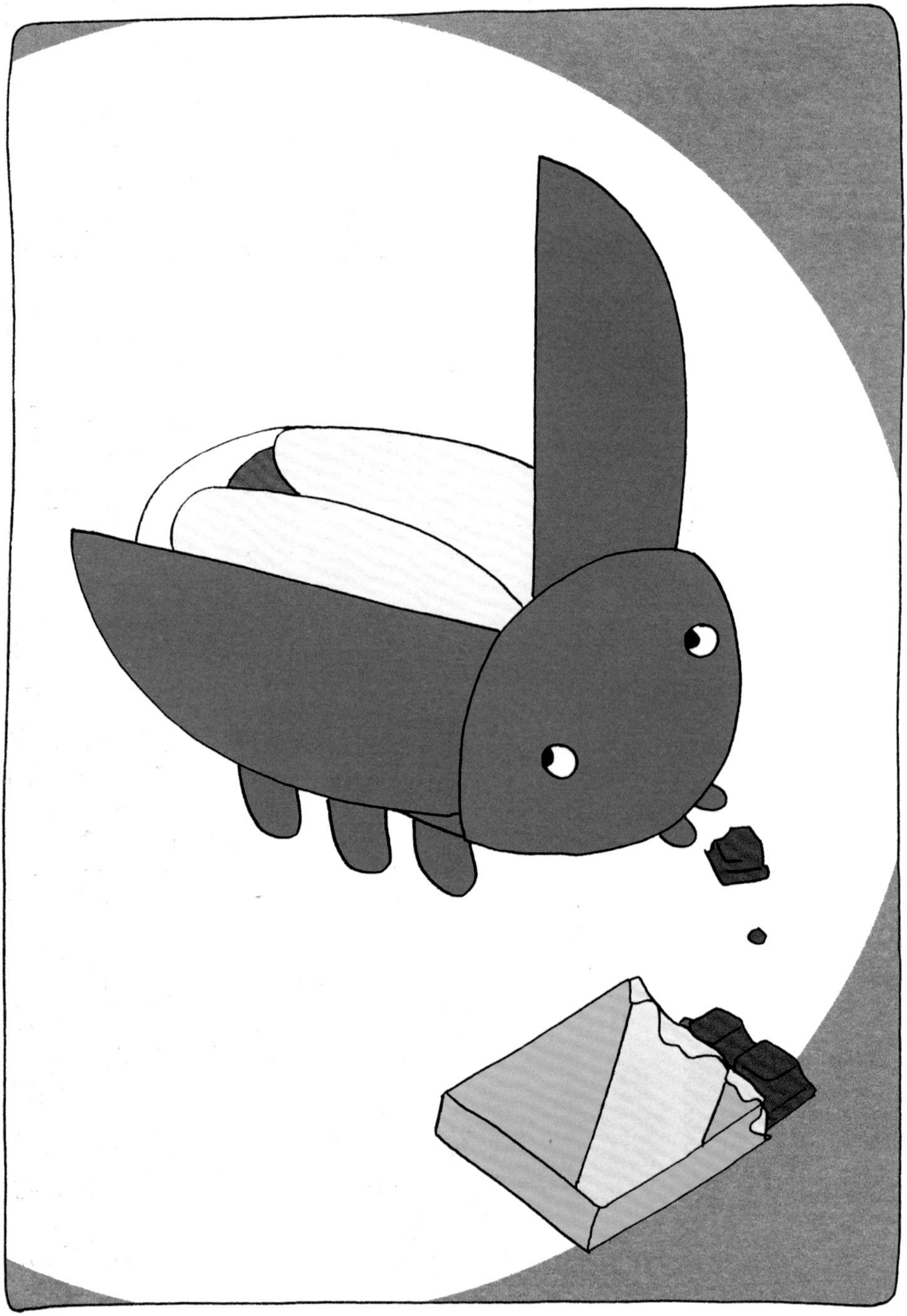

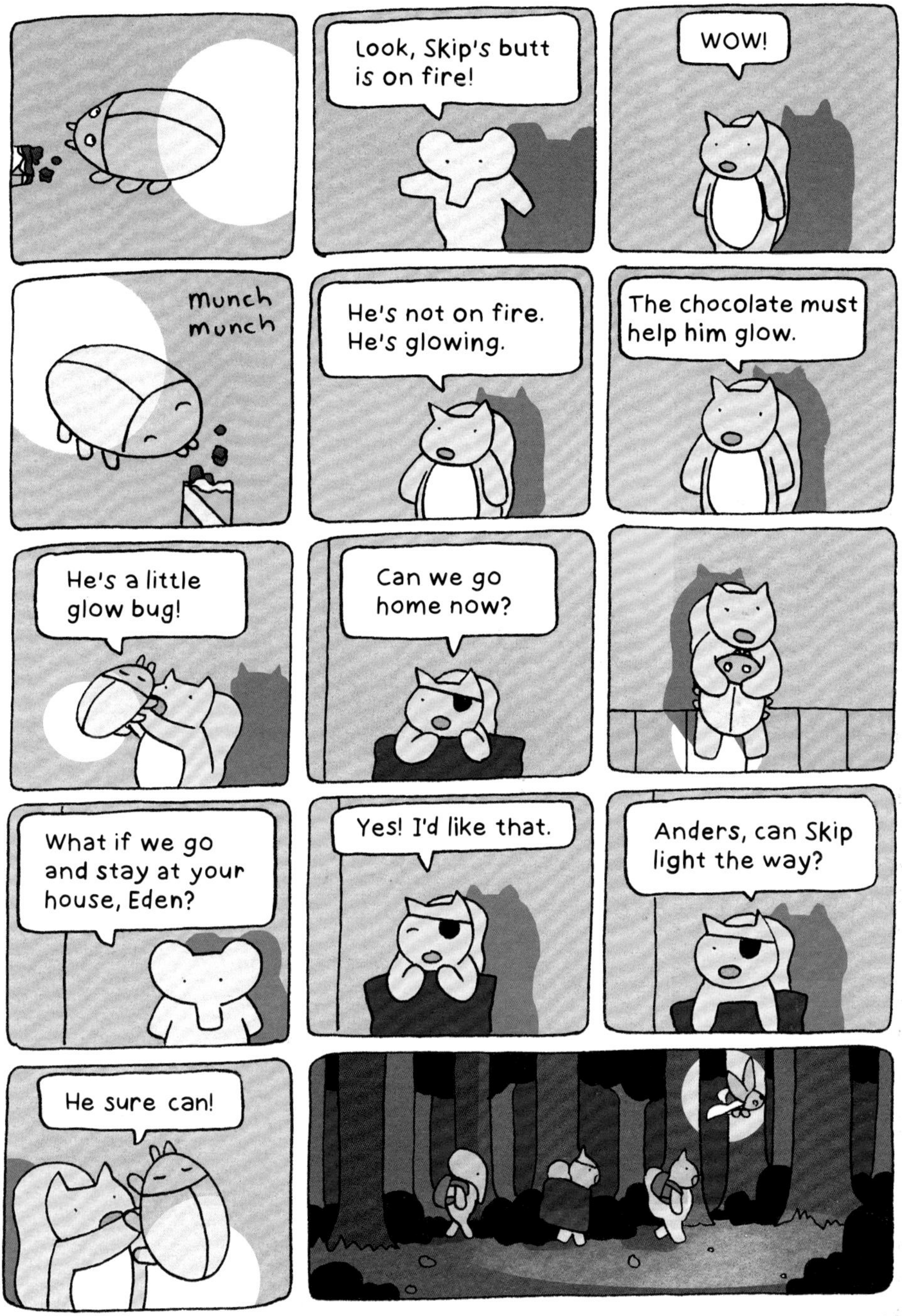
Look, Skip's butt is on fire!
WOW!
munch munch
He's not on fire. He's glowing.
The chocolate must help him glow.
He's a little glow bug!
Can we go home now?
What if we go and stay at your house, Eden?
Yes! I'd like that.
Anders, can Skip light the way?
He sure can!

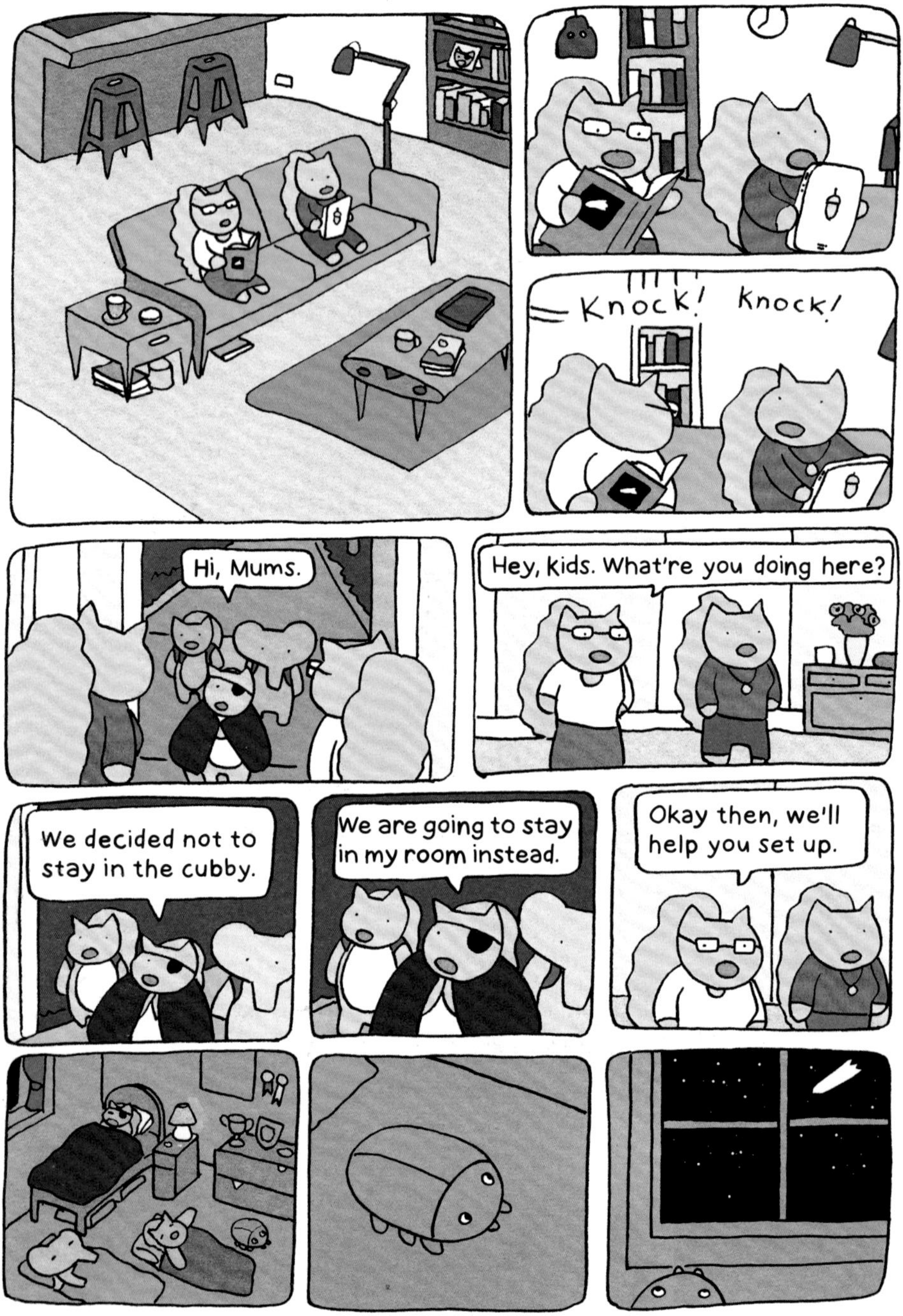
Knock! Knock!
Hi, Mums.
Hey, kids. What're you doing here?
We decided not to stay in the cubby.
We are going to stay in my room instead.
Okay then, we'll help you set up.

Chapter 9

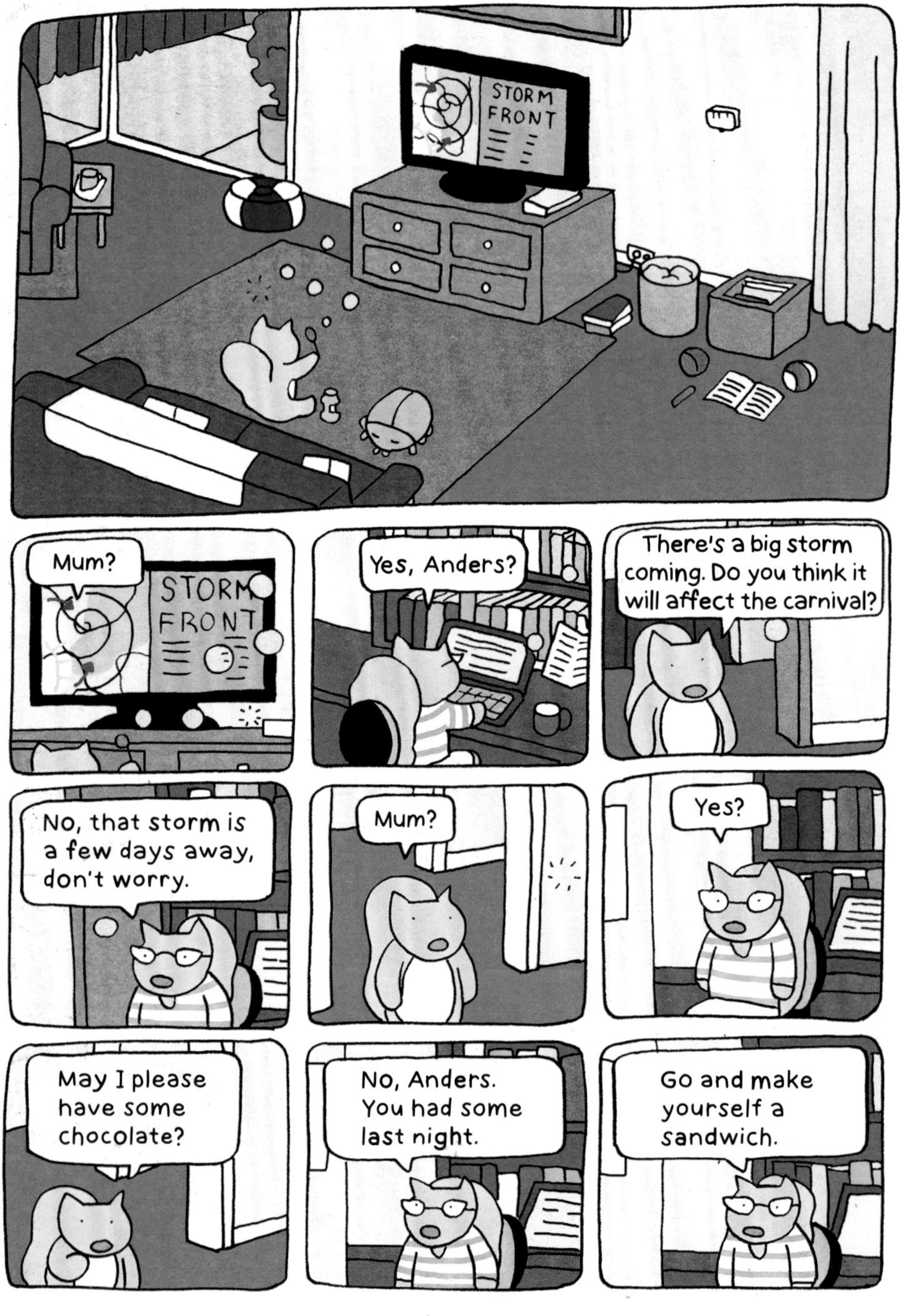
STORM FRONT
Mum?
STORM FRONT
Yes, Anders?
There's a big storm coming. Do you think it will affect the carnival?
No, that storm is a few days away, don't worry.
Mum?
Yes?
May I please have some chocolate?
No, Anders. You had some last night.
Go and make yourself a sandwich.

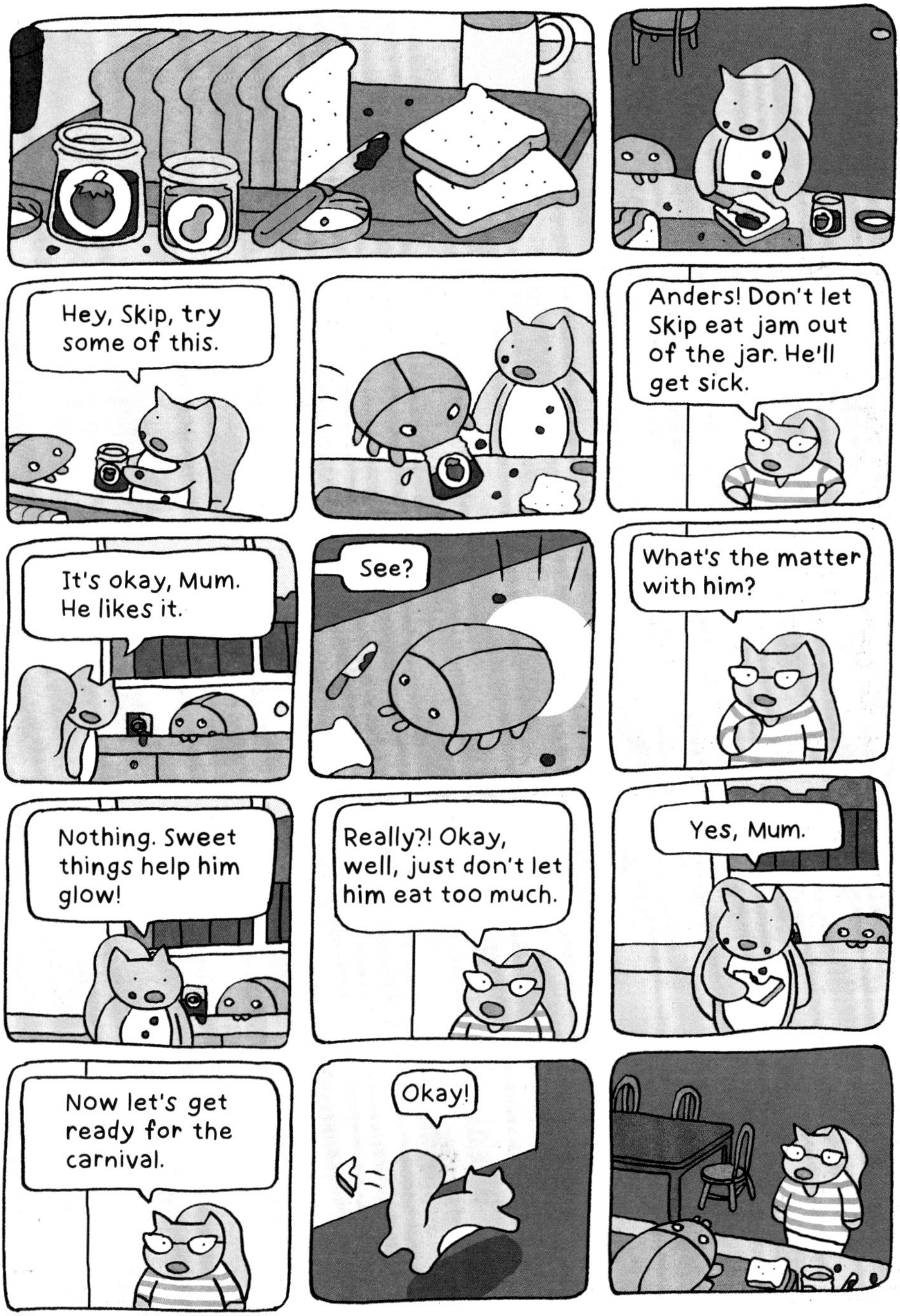
Hey, Skip, try some of this.
Anders! Don't let Skip eat jam out of the jar. He'll get sick.
It's okay, Mum. He likes it.
See?
What's the matter with him?
Nothing. Sweet things help him glow!
Really?! Okay, well, just don't let him eat too much.
Yes, Mum.
Now let's get ready for the carnival.
Okay!

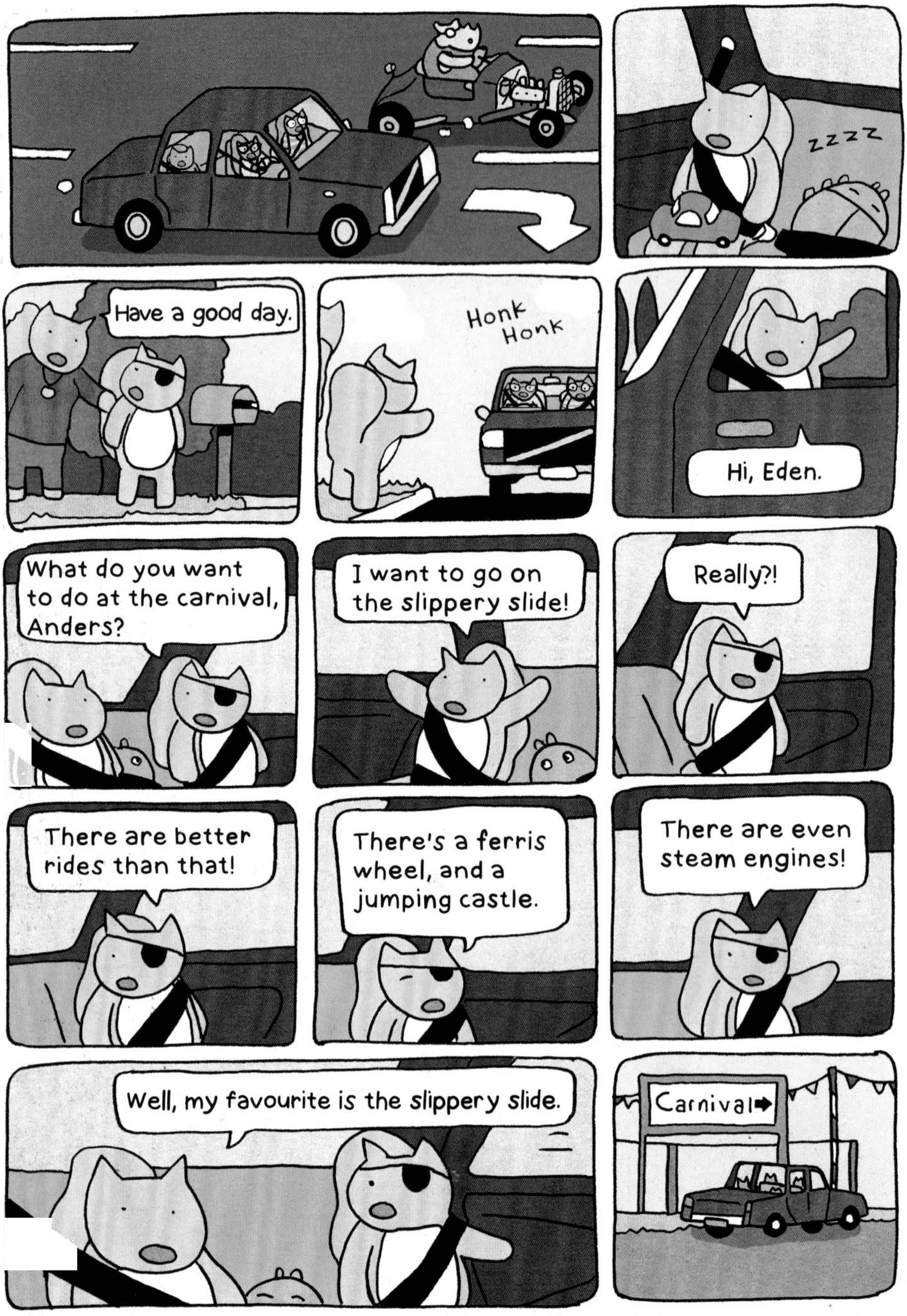
ZZZZ
Have a good day.
Honk
Honk
Hi, Eden.
What do you want to do at the carnival, Anders?
I want to go on the slippery slide!
Really?!
There are better rides than that!
There's a ferris wheel, and a jumping castle.
There are even steam engines!
Well, my favourite is the slippery slide.
Carnival

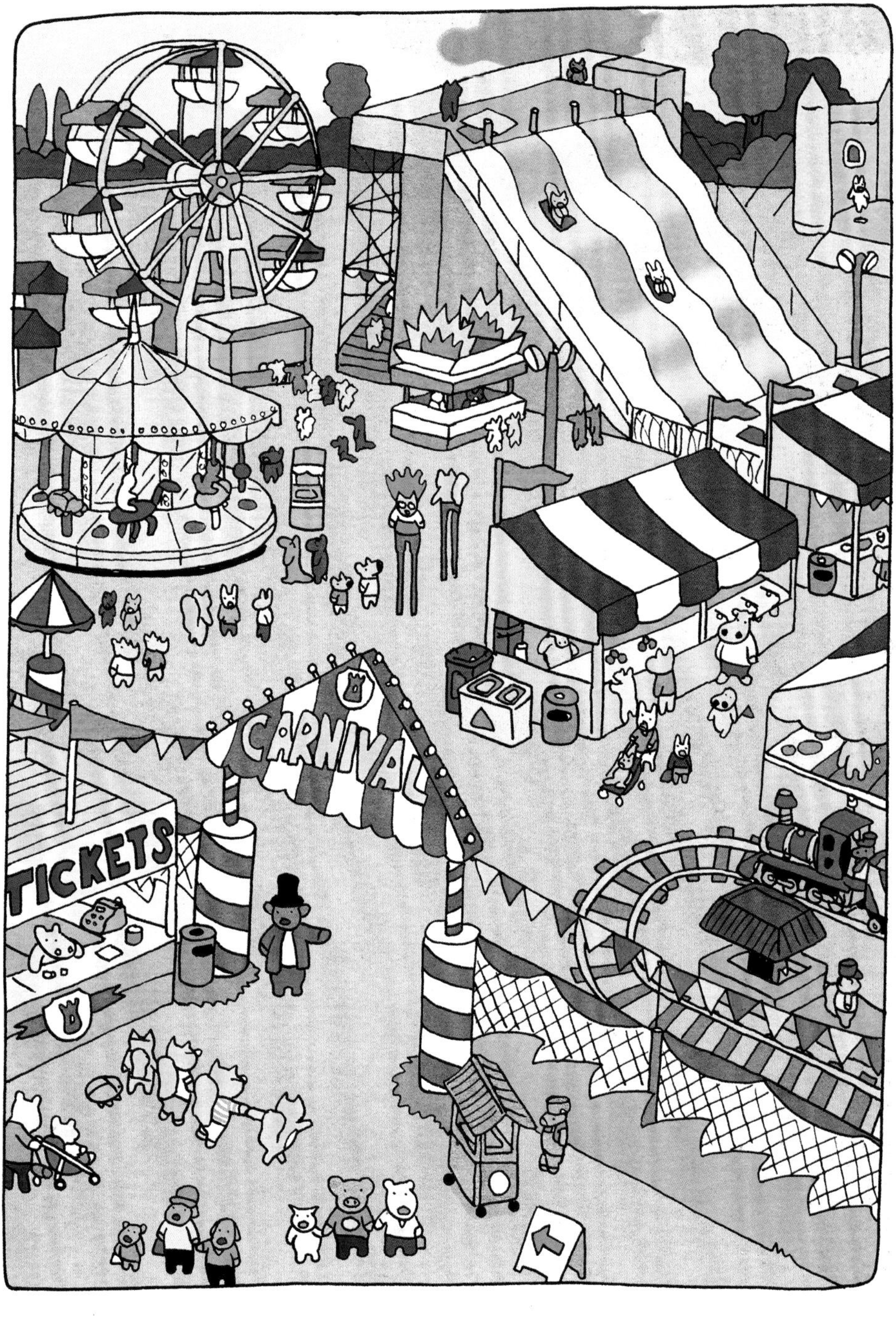
CARNIVAL
TICKETS

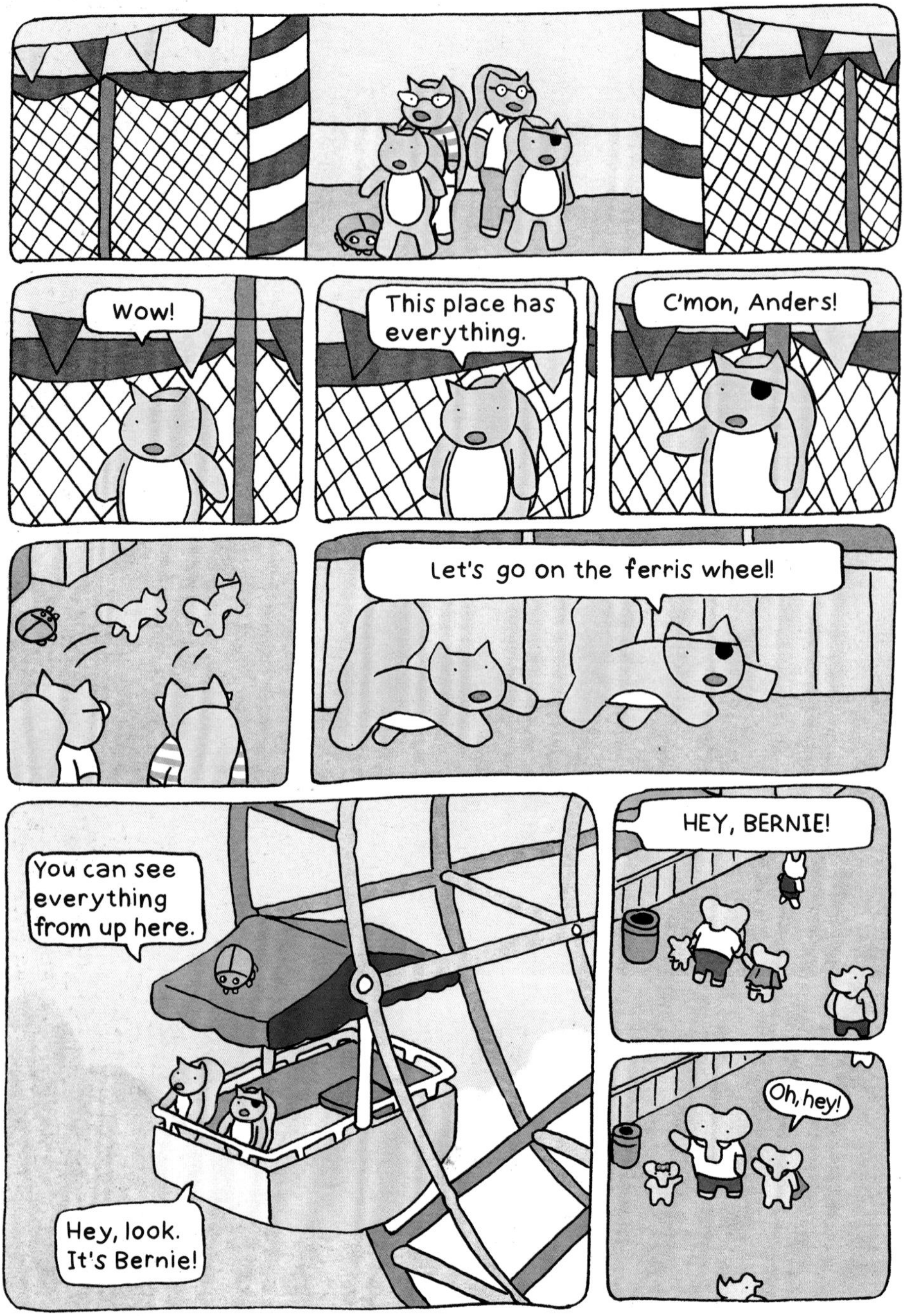

Wow!
This place has everything.
C'mon, Anders!
Let's go on the ferris wheel!
You can see everything from up here.
Hey, look. It's Bernie!
HEY, BERNIE!
Oh, hey!

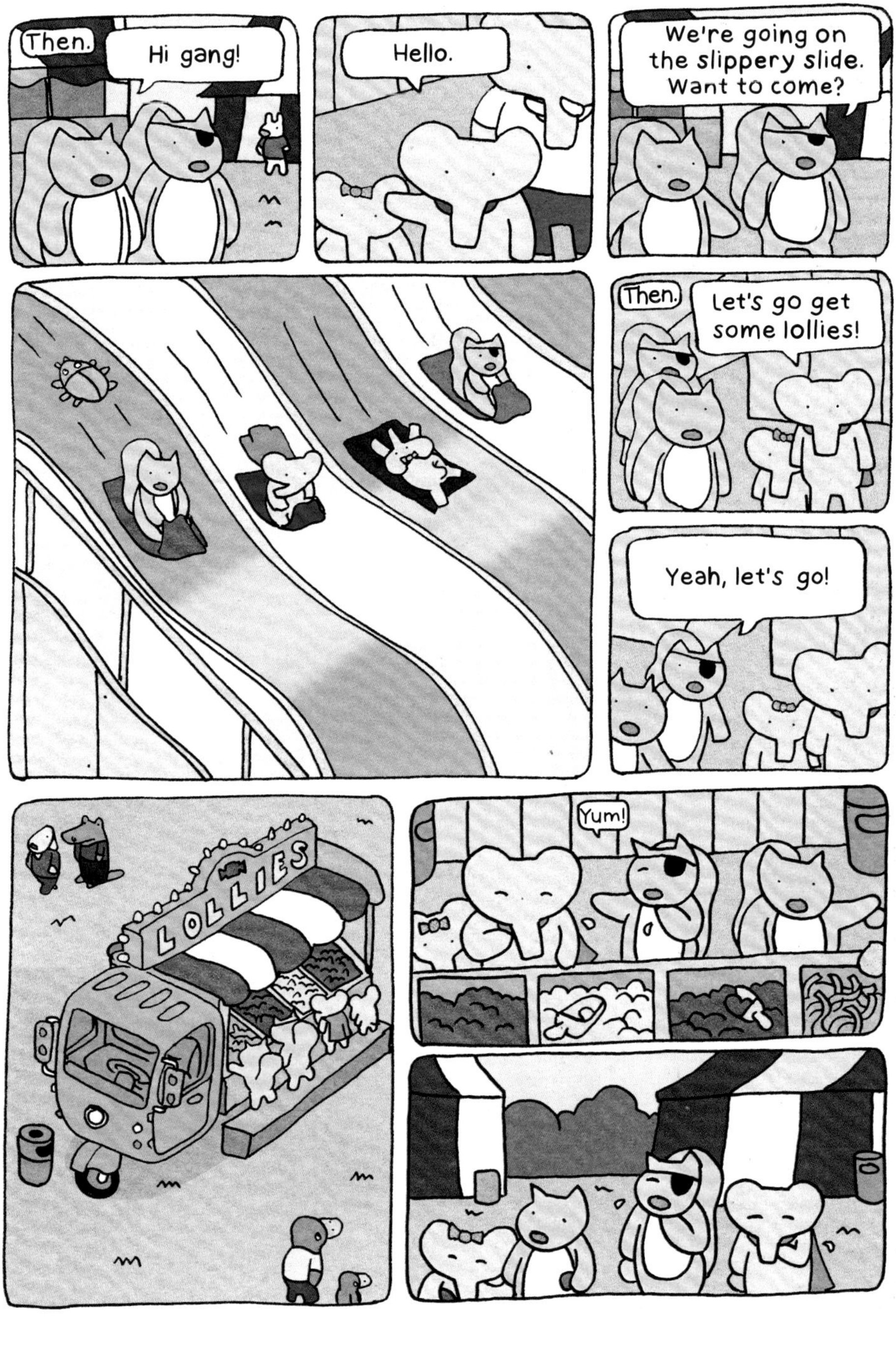
Then.
Hi gang!
Hello.
We're going on the slippery slide. Want to come?
Then.
Let's go get some lollies!
Yeah, let's go!
LOLLIES
Yum!

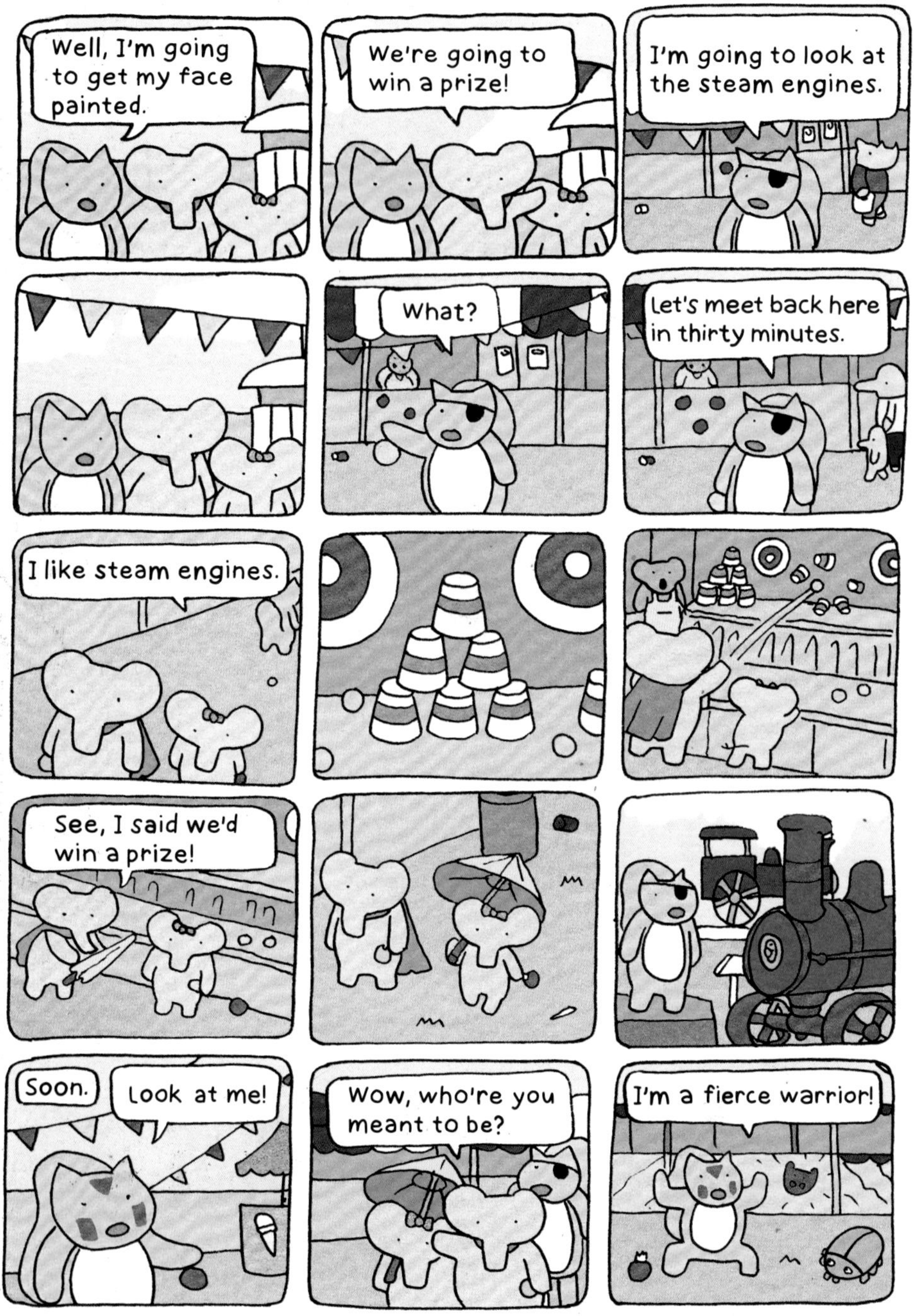
Well, I'm going to get my face painted.
We're going to win a prize!
I'm going to look at the steam engines.
What?
Let's meet back here in thirty minutes.
I like steam engines.
See, I said we'd win a prize!
Soon.
Look at me!
Wow, who're you meant to be?
I'm a fierce warrior!

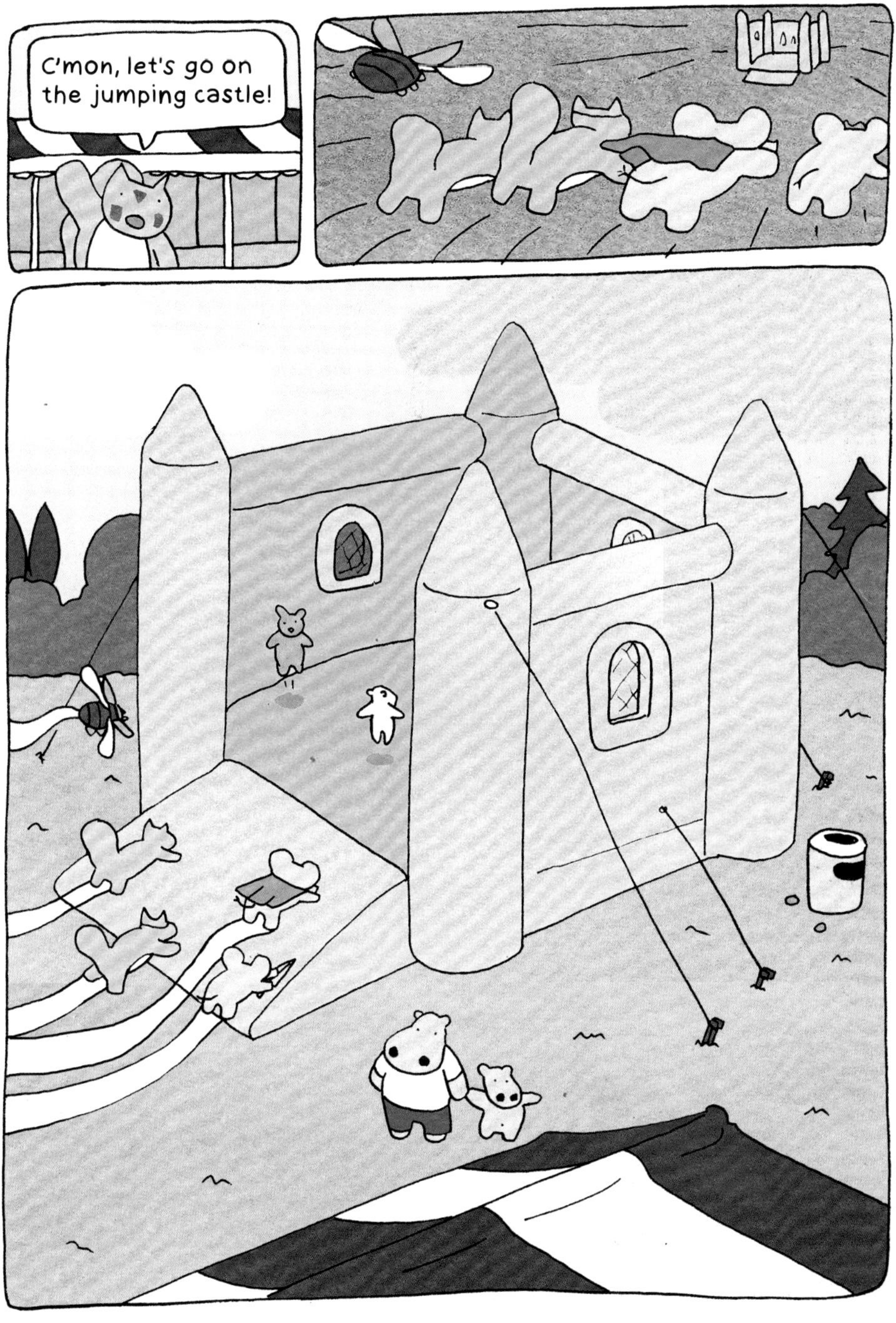
C'mon, let's go on the jumping castle!

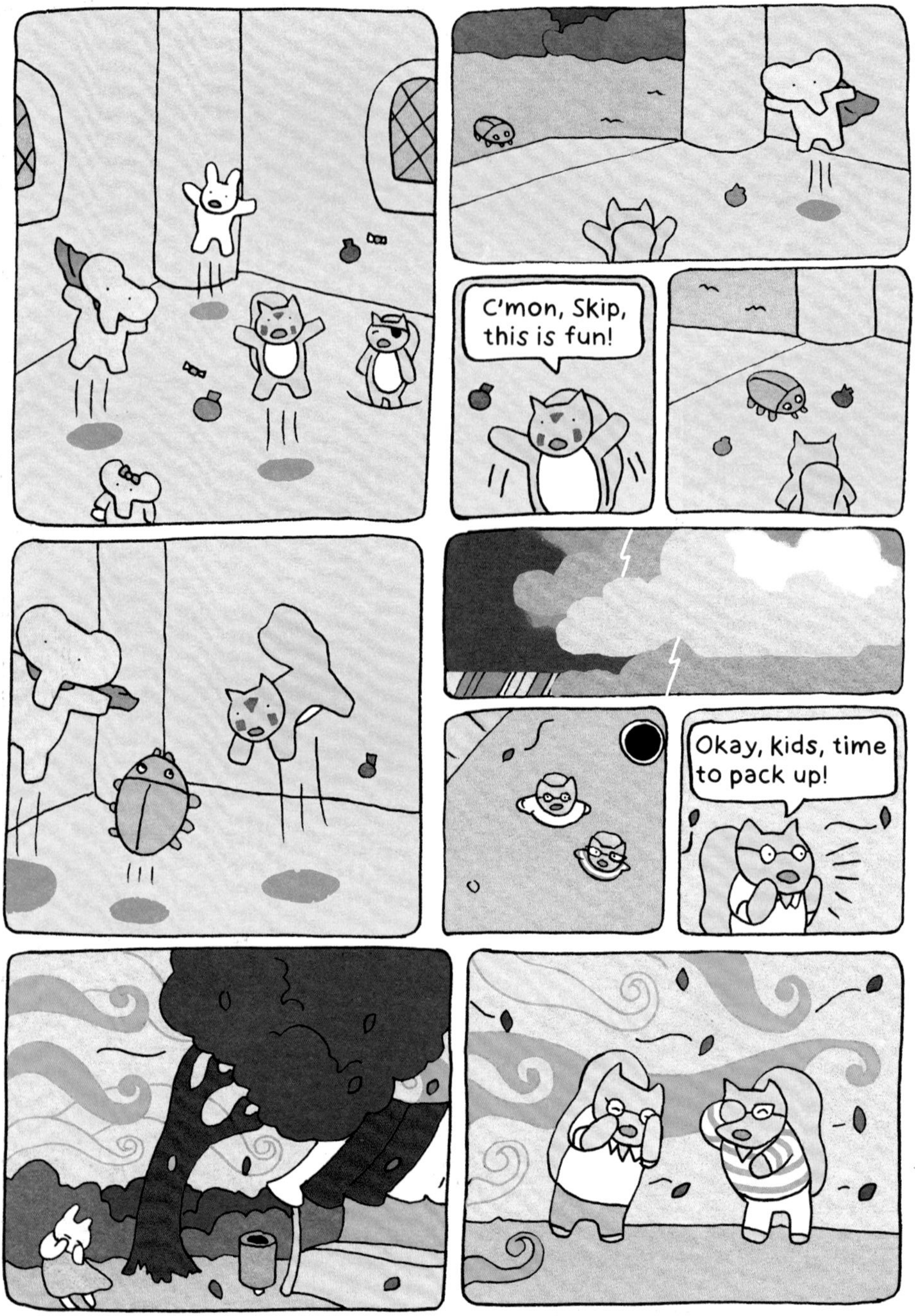
C'mon, Skip, this is fun!
Okay, kids, time to pack up!

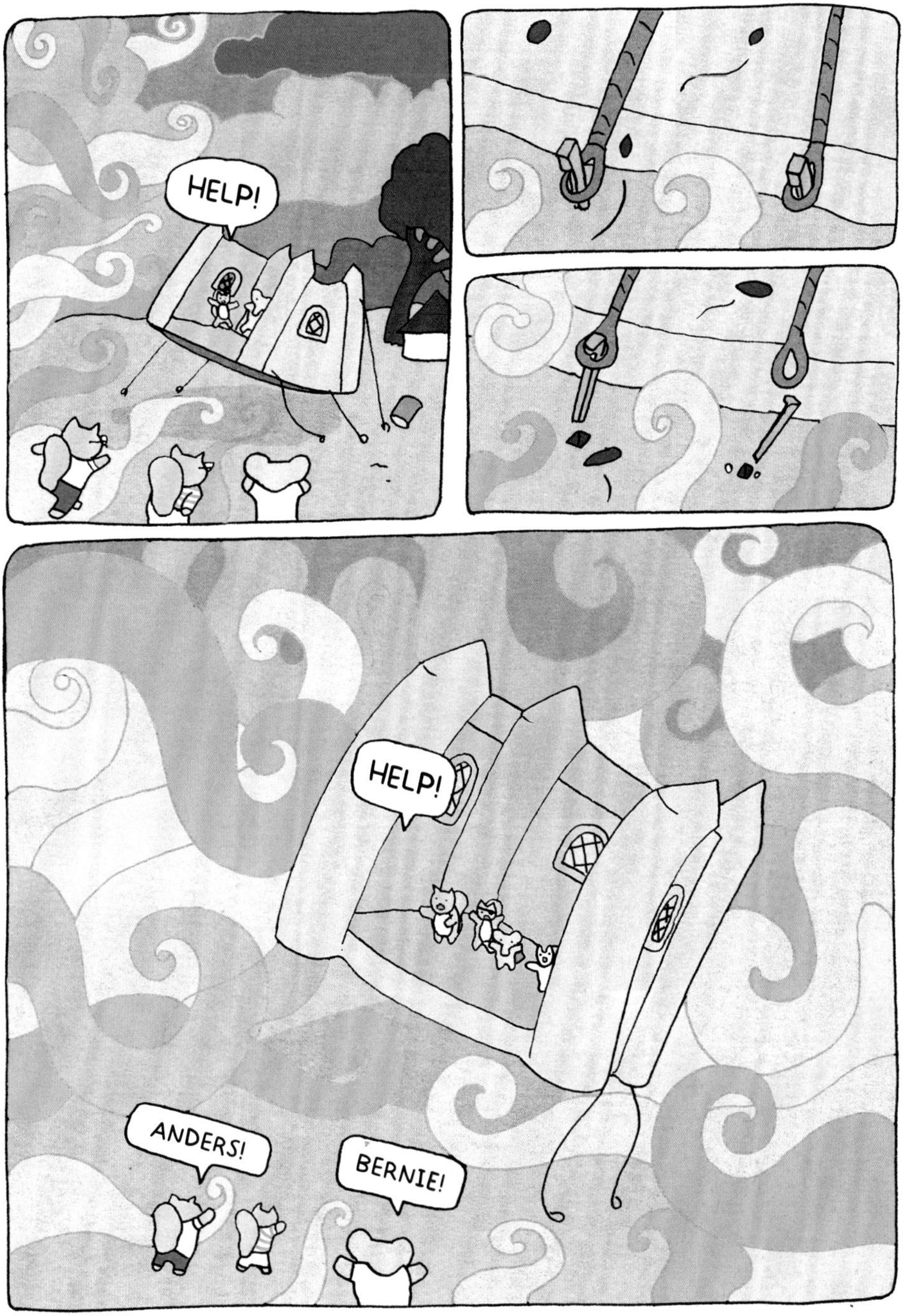
HELP!
HELP!
ANDERS!
BERNIE!

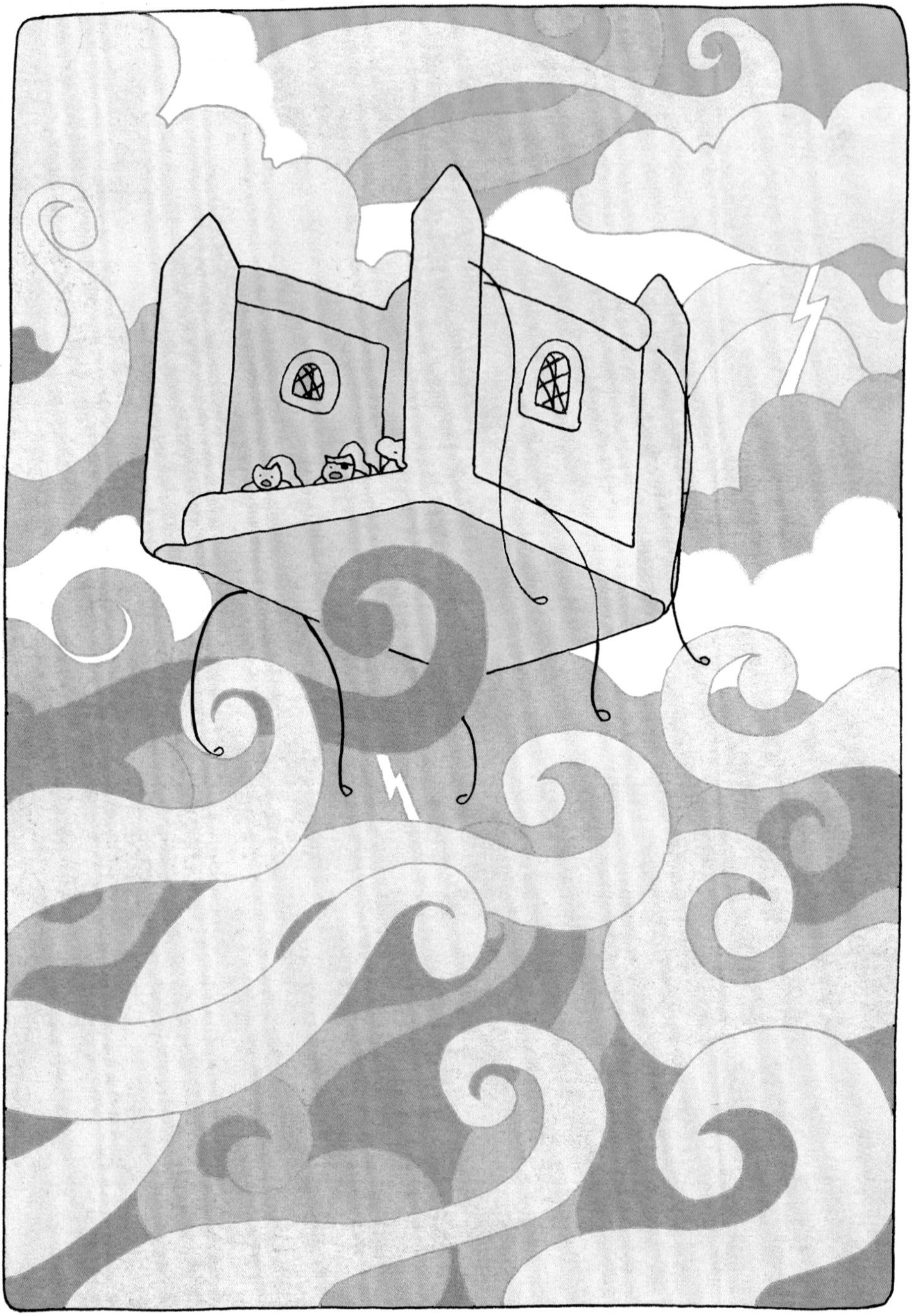

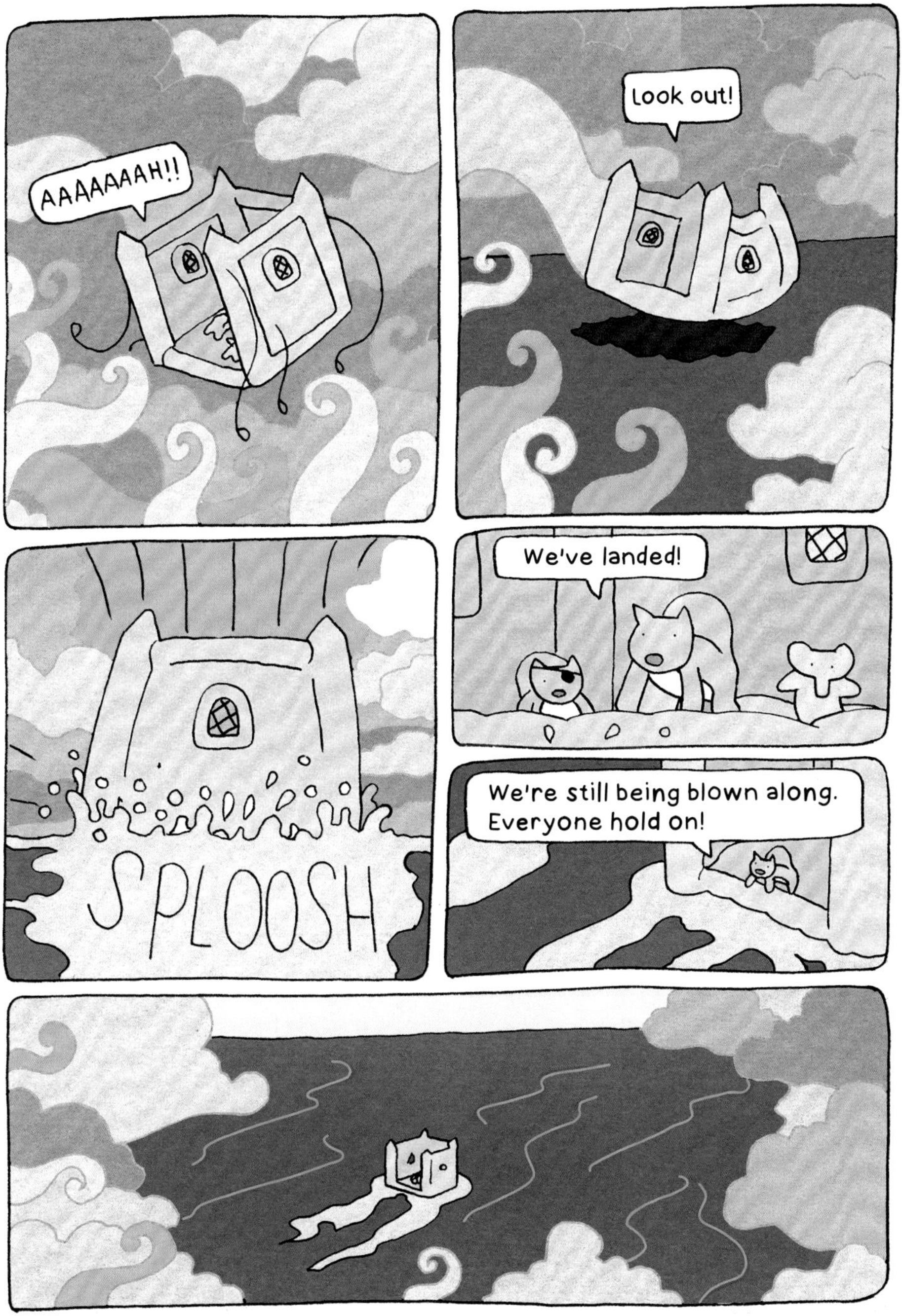
AAAAAAAH!!
Look out!
SPLOOSH
We've landed!
We're still being blown along. Everyone hold on!

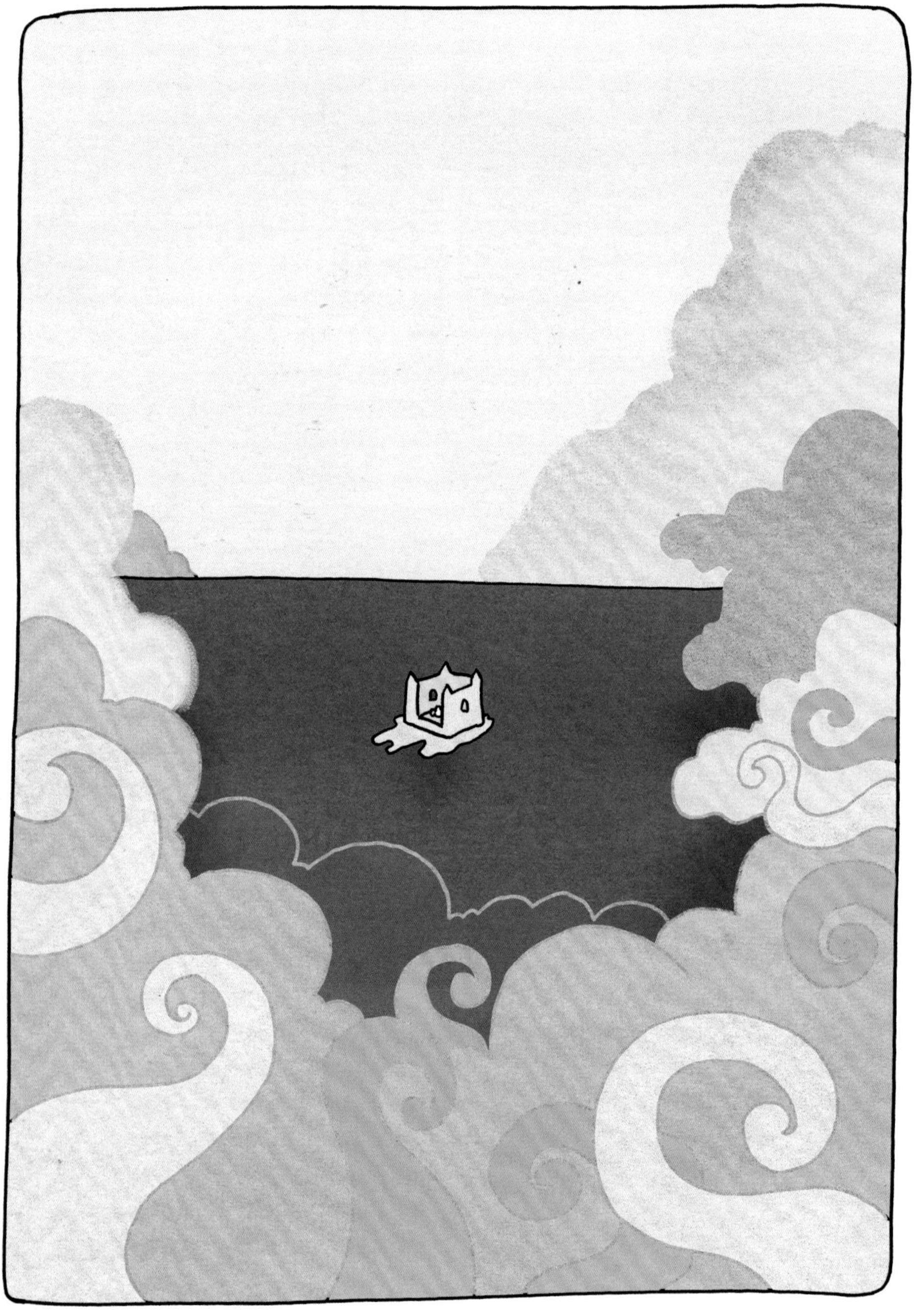

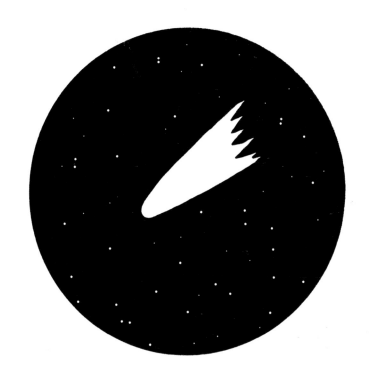

Chapter 10

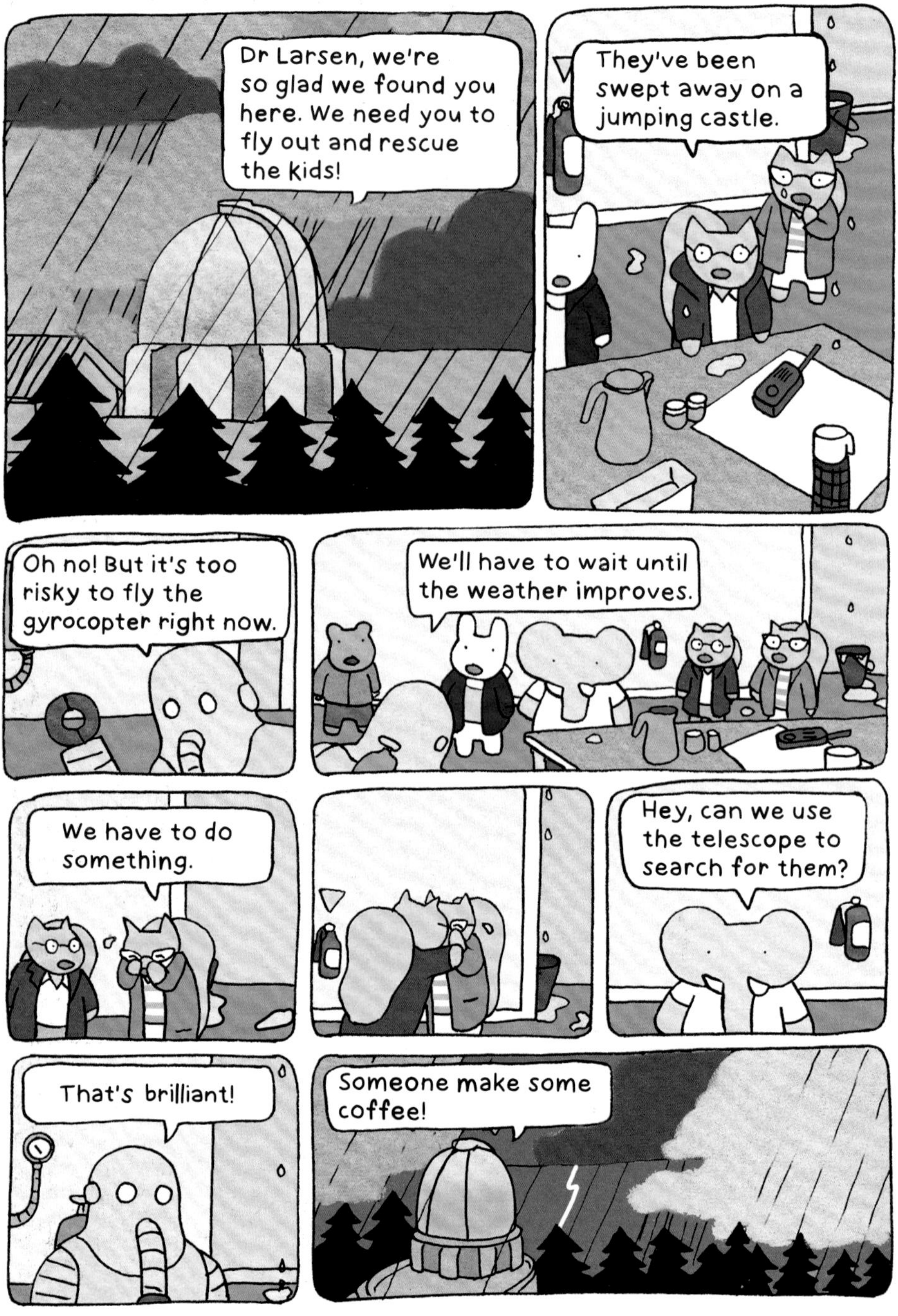
Dr Larsen, we're so glad we found you here. We need you to fly out and rescue the kids!
They've been swept away on a jumping castle.
Oh no! But it's too risky to fly the gyrocopter right now.
We'll have to wait until the weather improves.
We have to do something.
Hey, can we use the telescope to search for them?
That's brilliant!
Someone make some coffee!

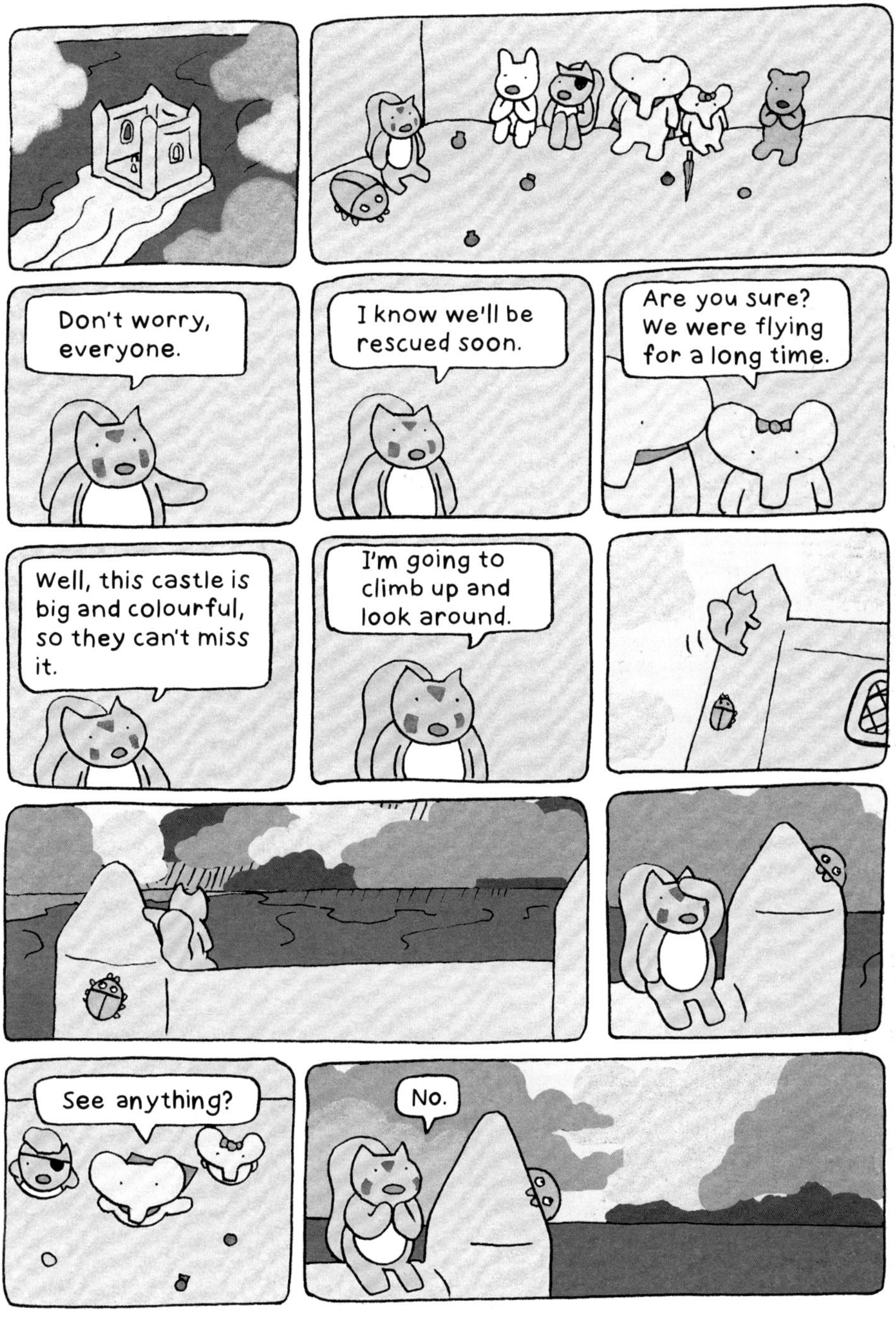

Don't worry, everyone.
I know we'll be rescued soon.
Are you sure? We were flying for a long time.
Well, this castle is big and colourful, so they can't miss it.
I'm going to climb up and look around.
See anything?
No.

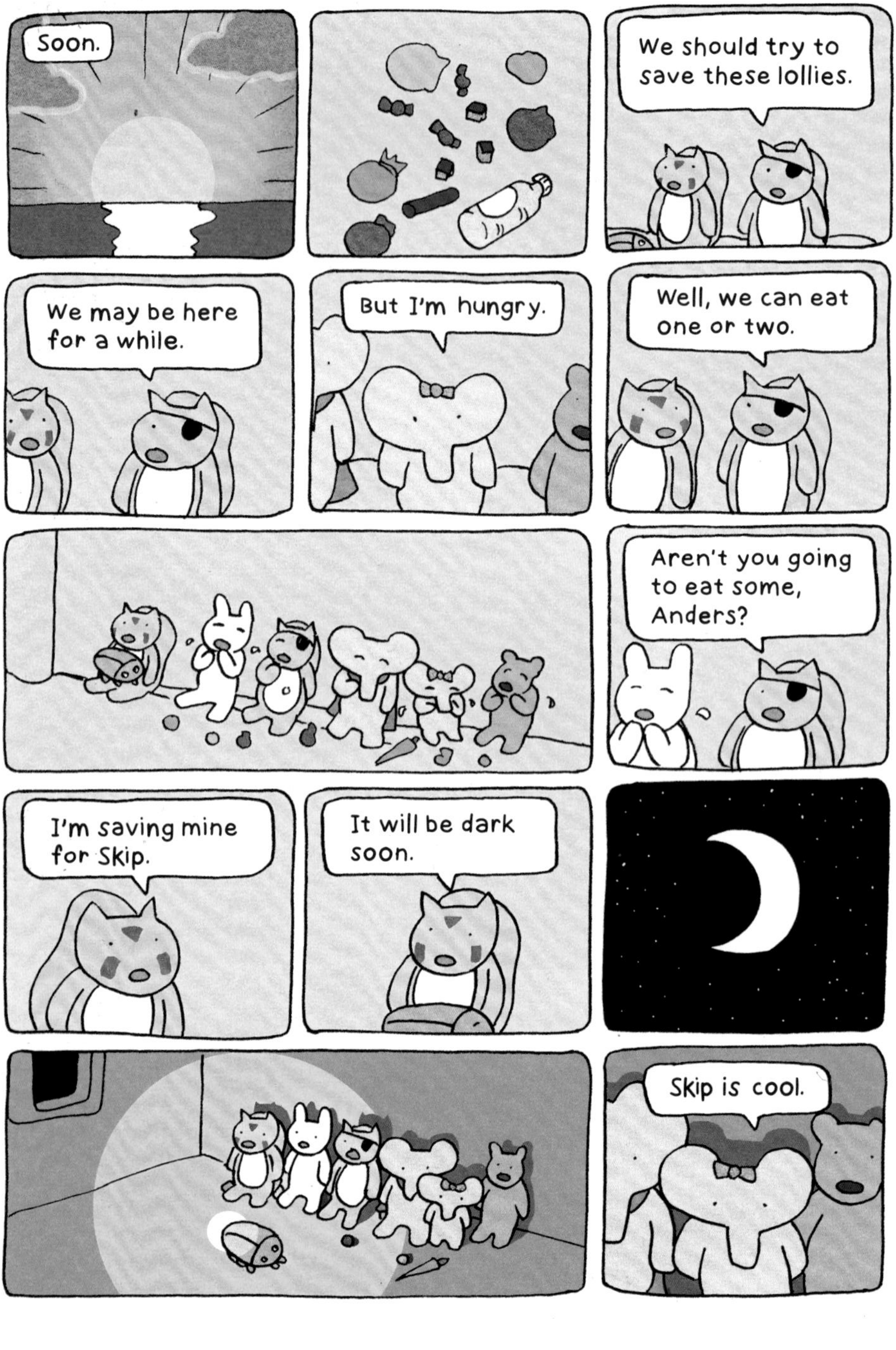
Soon.
We should try to save these lollies.
We may be here for a while.
But I'm hungry.
Well, we can eat one or two.
Aren't you going to eat some, Anders?
I'm saving mine for Skip.
It will be dark soon.
Skip is cool.

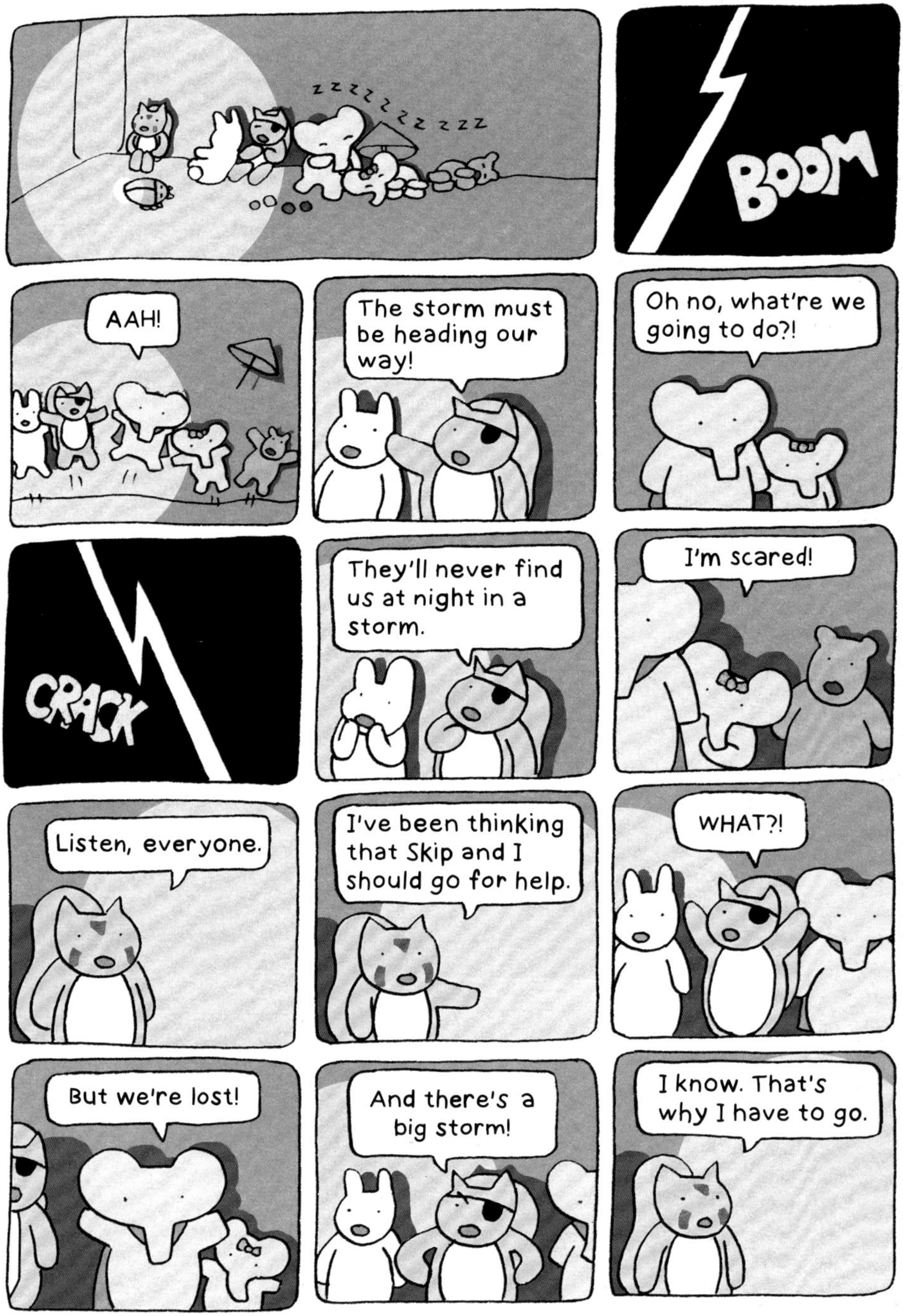

ZZZZZZZZZZZ
BOOM
AAH!
The storm must be heading our way!
Oh no, what're we going to do?!
CRACK
They'll never find us at night in a storm.
I'm scared!
Listen, everyone.
I've been thinking that Skip and I should go for help.
WHAT?!
But we're lost!
And there's a big storm!
I know. That's why I have to go.

But it'll be dark without Skip.

I know.

And there's something else I have to ask.

I think Skip and I should take the rest of the lollies with us.

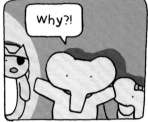
Why?!

To give Skip energy to fly and make light.

But we'll get hungry and it will be dark.

Anders is right. It's our best chance for rescue.

Let's vote on it. I vote to give the lollies to Anders so he can fly home.

All those in favour raise your hand.

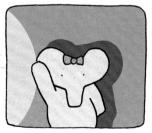

Okay. Anders, it's up to you and Skip.

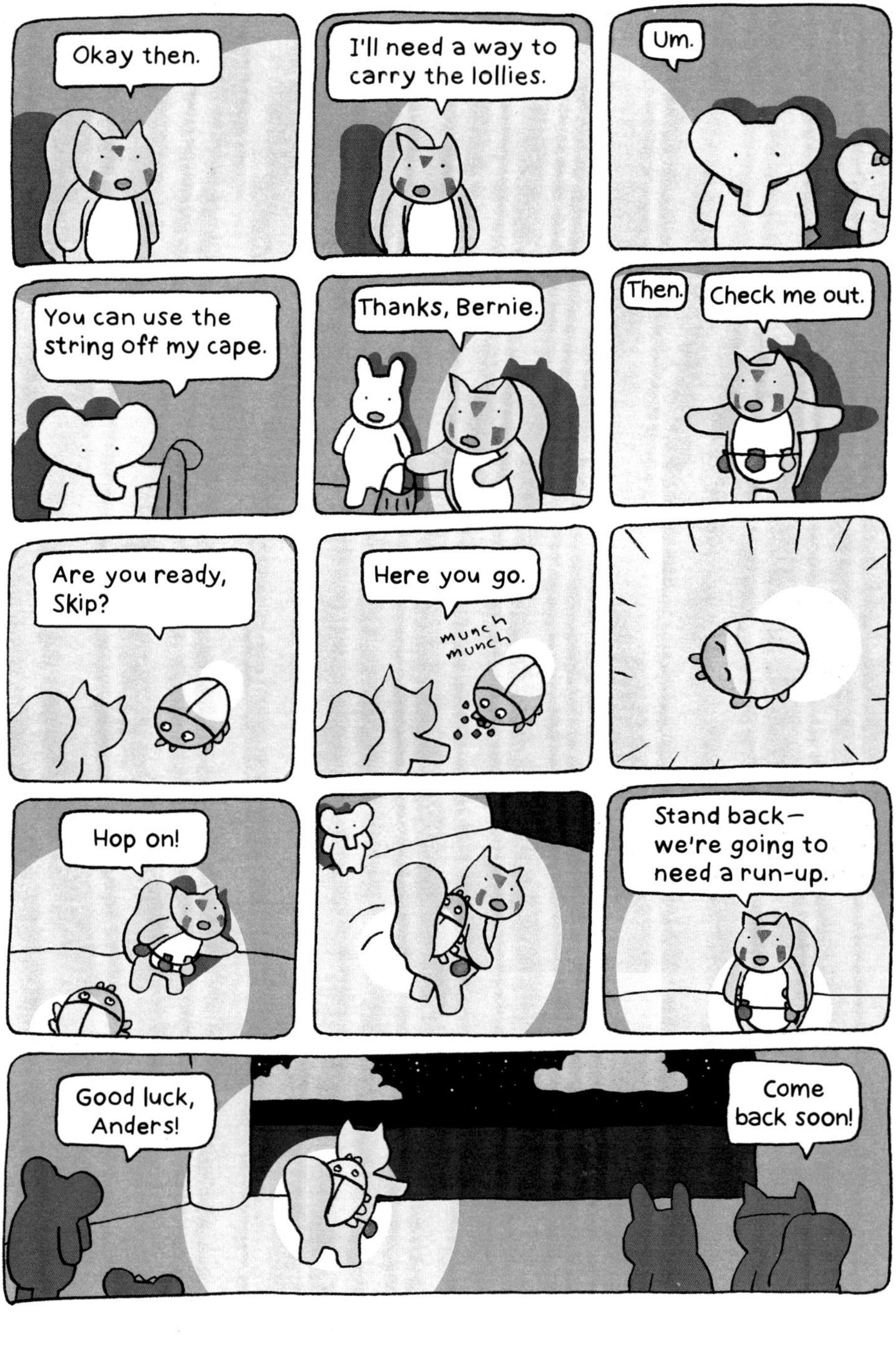
Okay then.
I'll need a way to carry the lollies.
Um.
You can use the string off my cape.
Thanks, Bernie.
Then.
Check me out.
Are you ready, Skip?
Here you go.
munch munch
Hop on!
Stand back— we're going to need a run-up.
Good luck, Anders!
Come back soon!

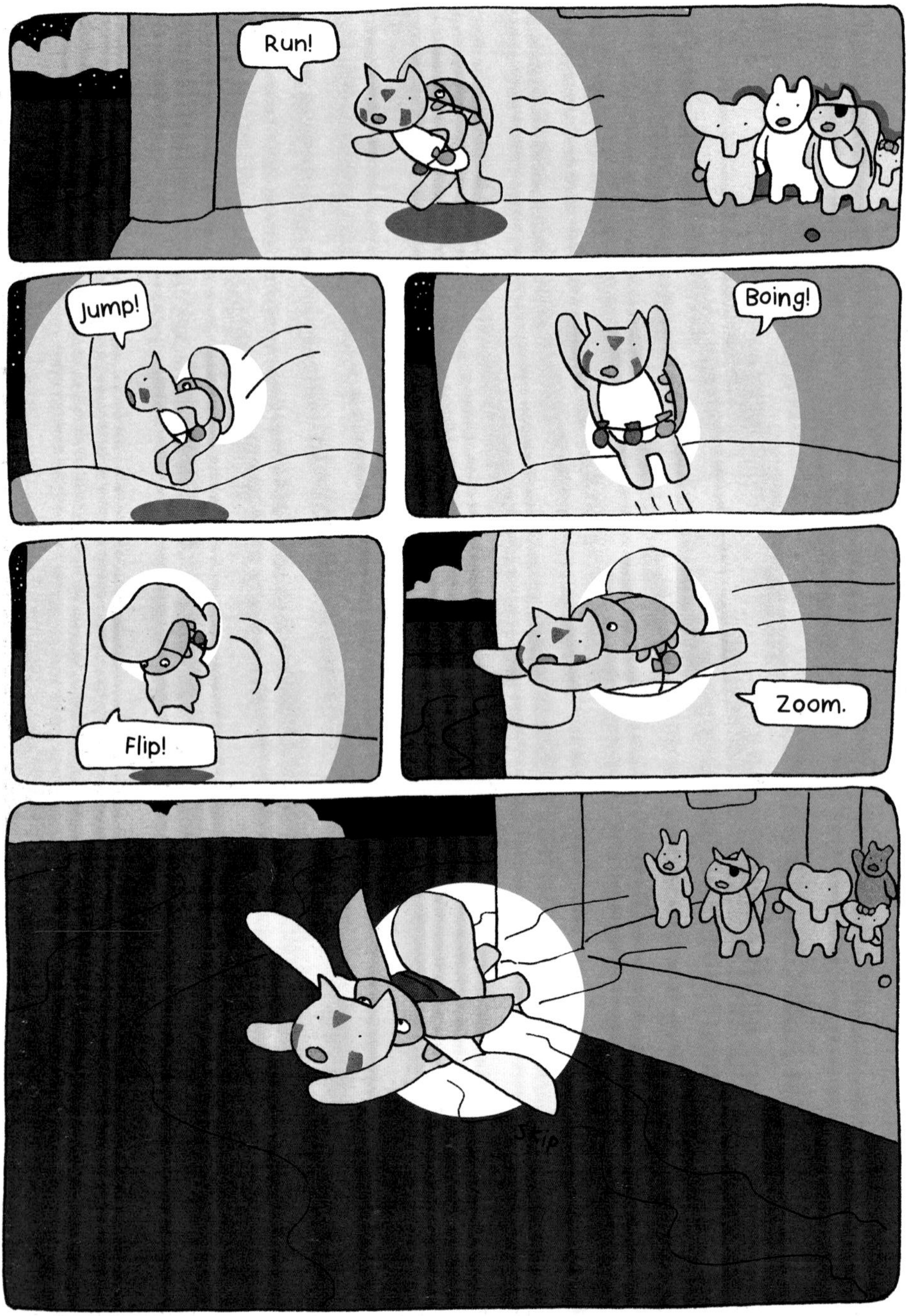
Run!
Jump!
Boing!
Flip!
Zoom.

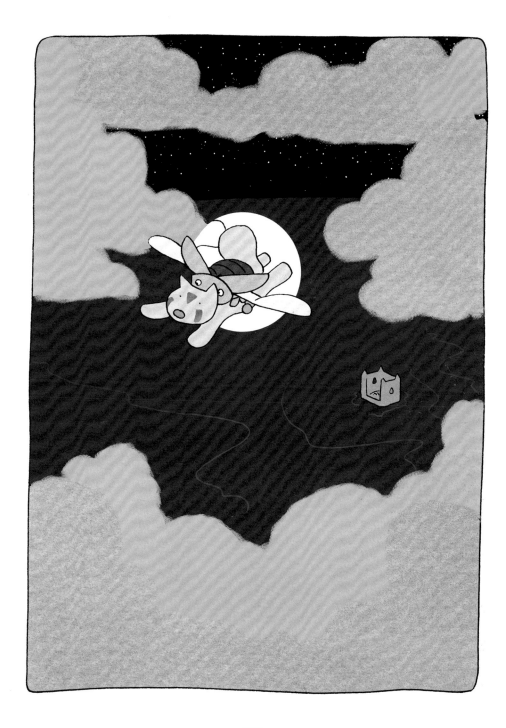

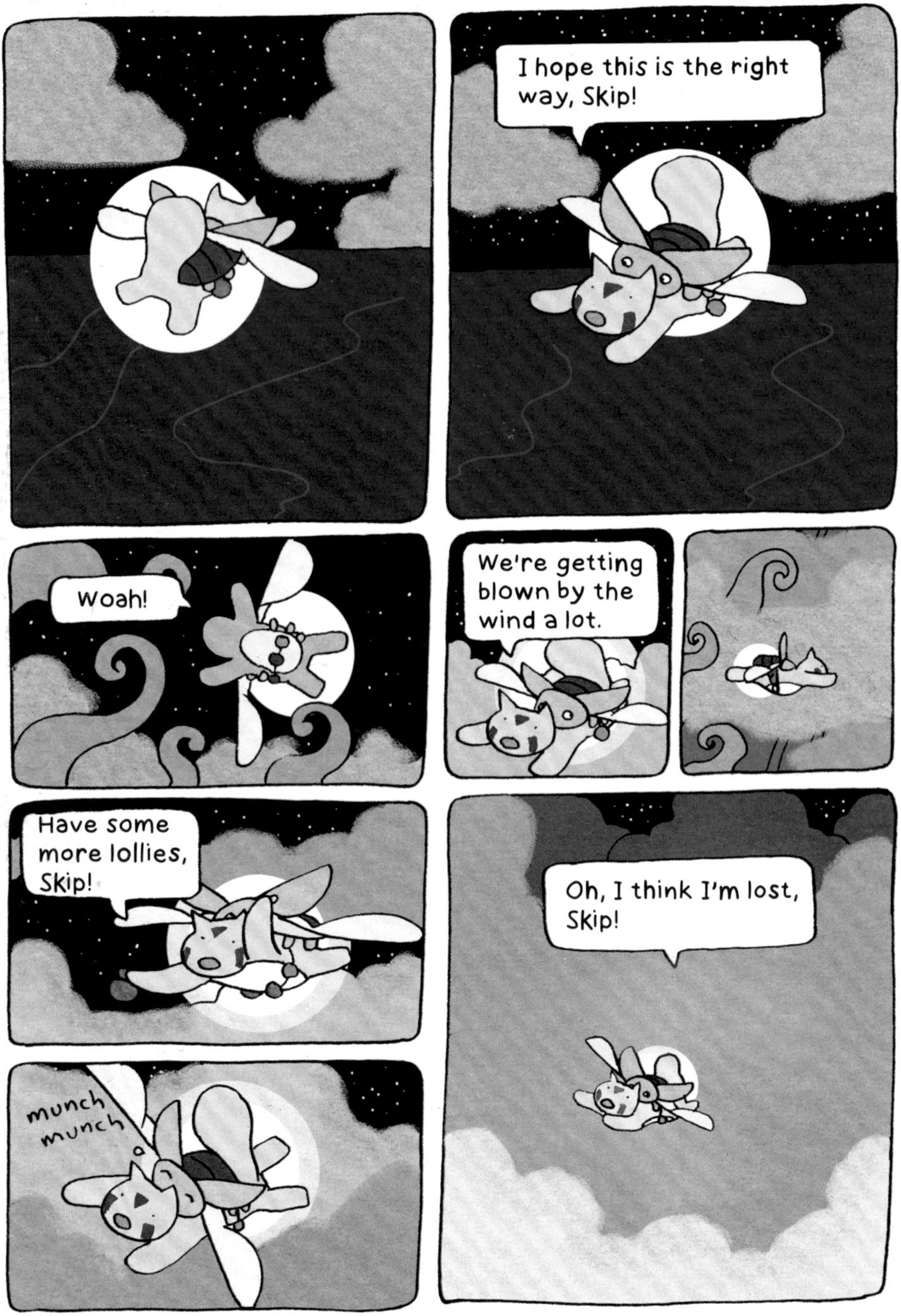
I hope this is the right way, Skip!
Woah!
We're getting blown by the wind a lot.
Have some more lollies, Skip!
Oh, I think I'm lost, Skip!
munch munch

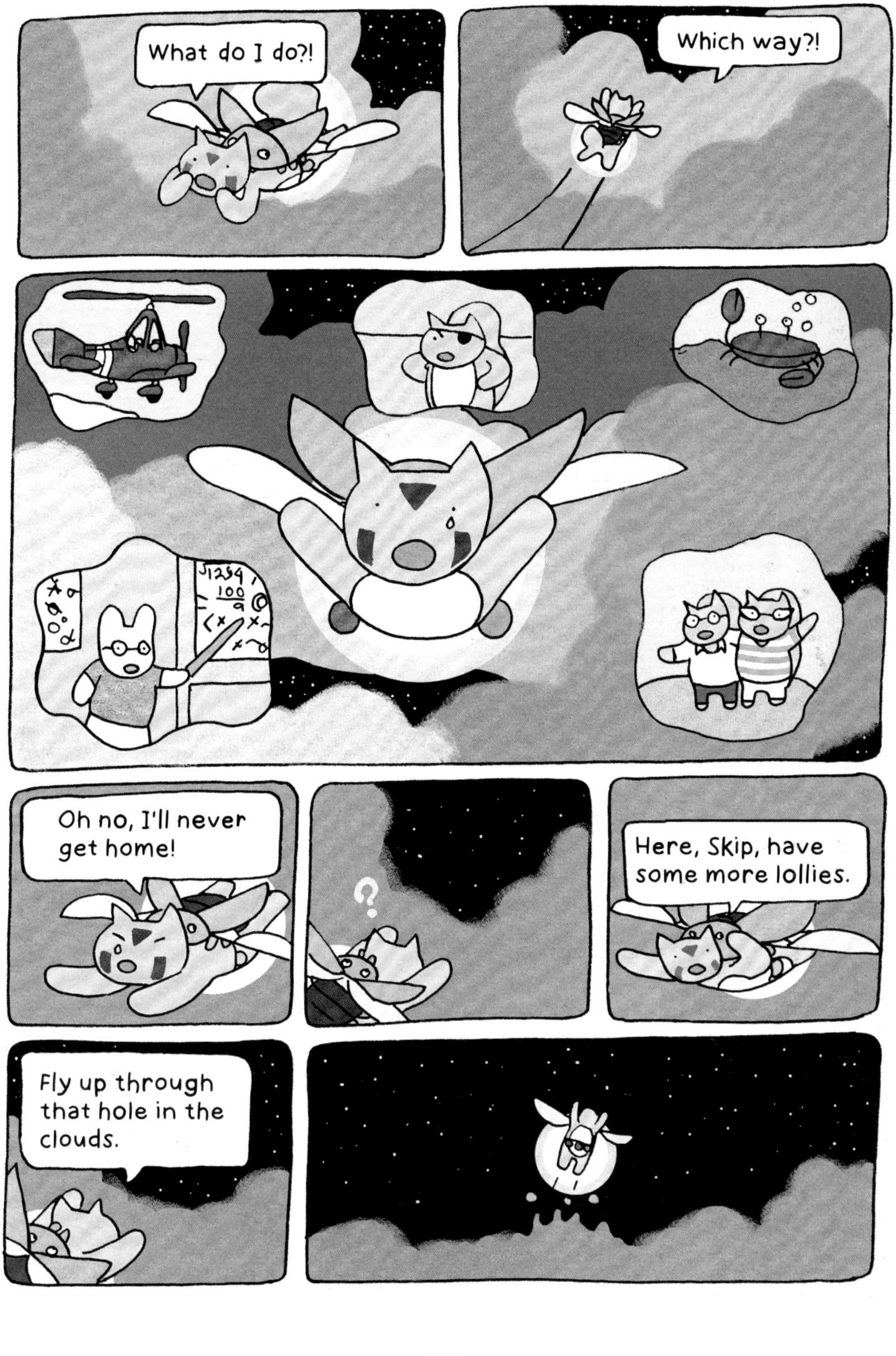
What do I do?!
Which way?!
Oh no, I'll never get home!
?
Here, Skip, have some more lollies.
Fly up through that hole in the clouds.

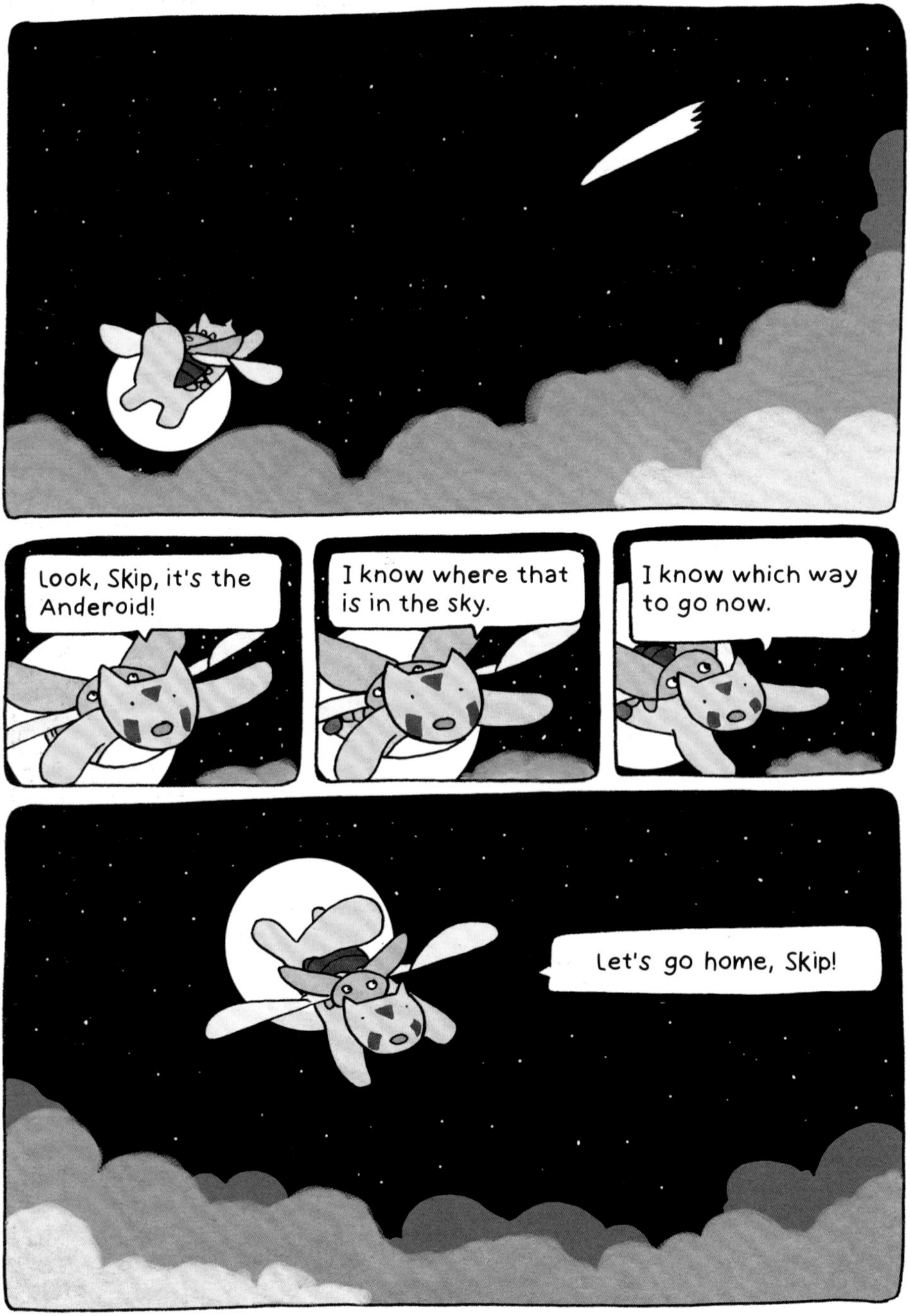
Look, Skip, it's the Anderoid!
I know where that is in the sky.
I know which way to go now.
Let's go home, Skip!

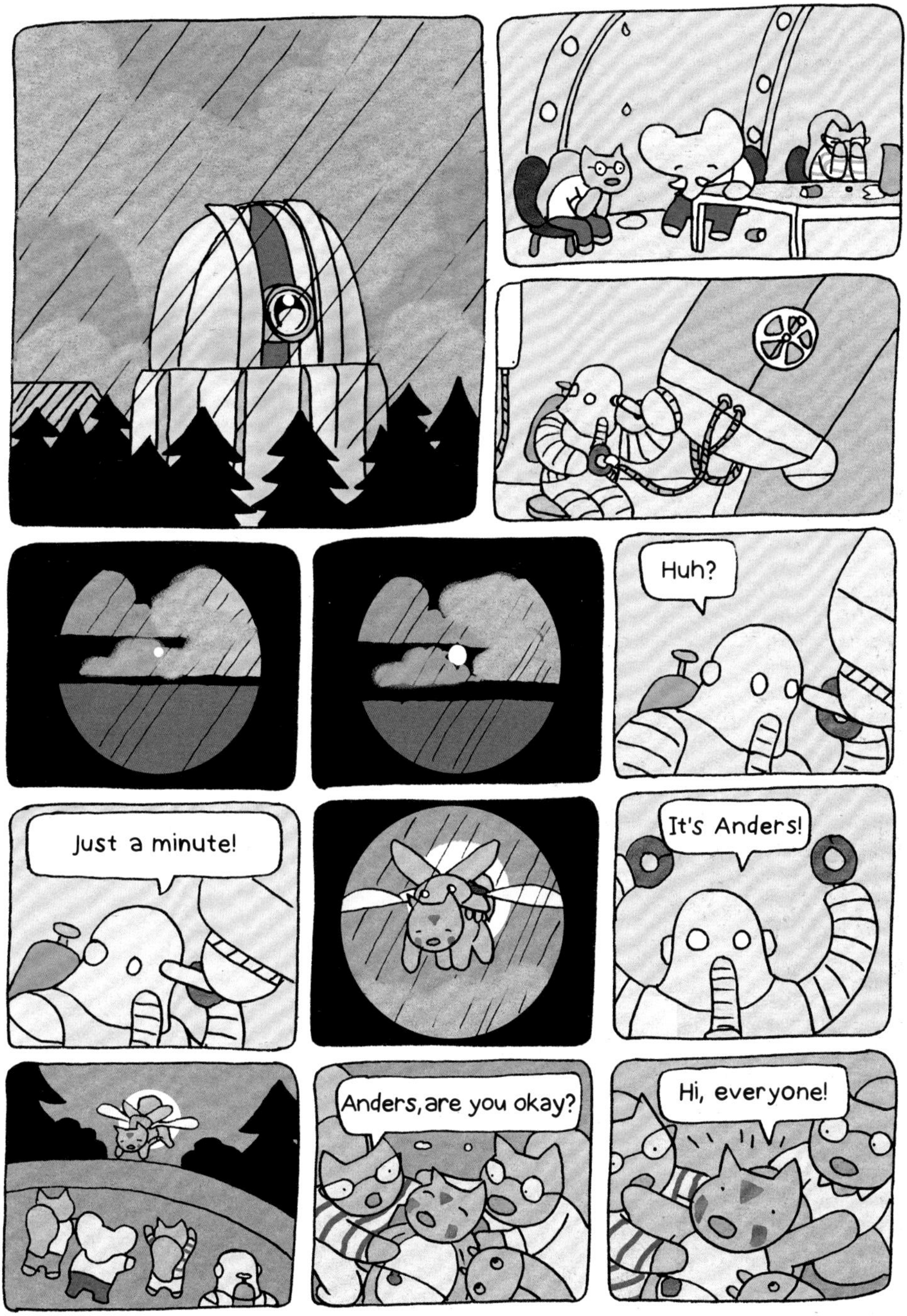
Huh?
Just a minute!
It's Anders!
Anders, are you okay?
Hi, everyone!

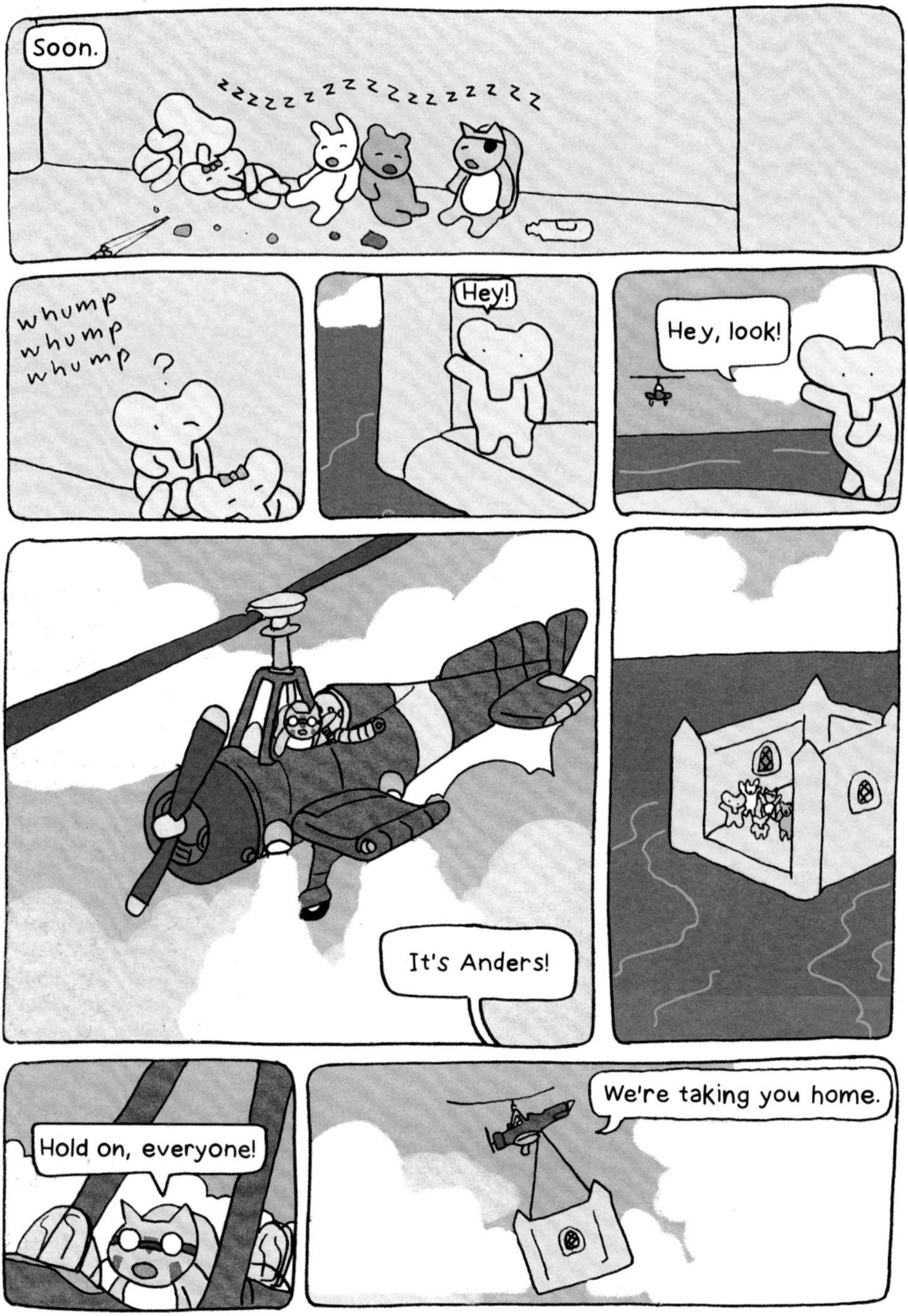
Soon.
zzzzzzzzzzzzzzzzz
whump
whump
whump
?
Hey!
Hey, look!
It's Anders!
Hold on, everyone!
We're taking you home.

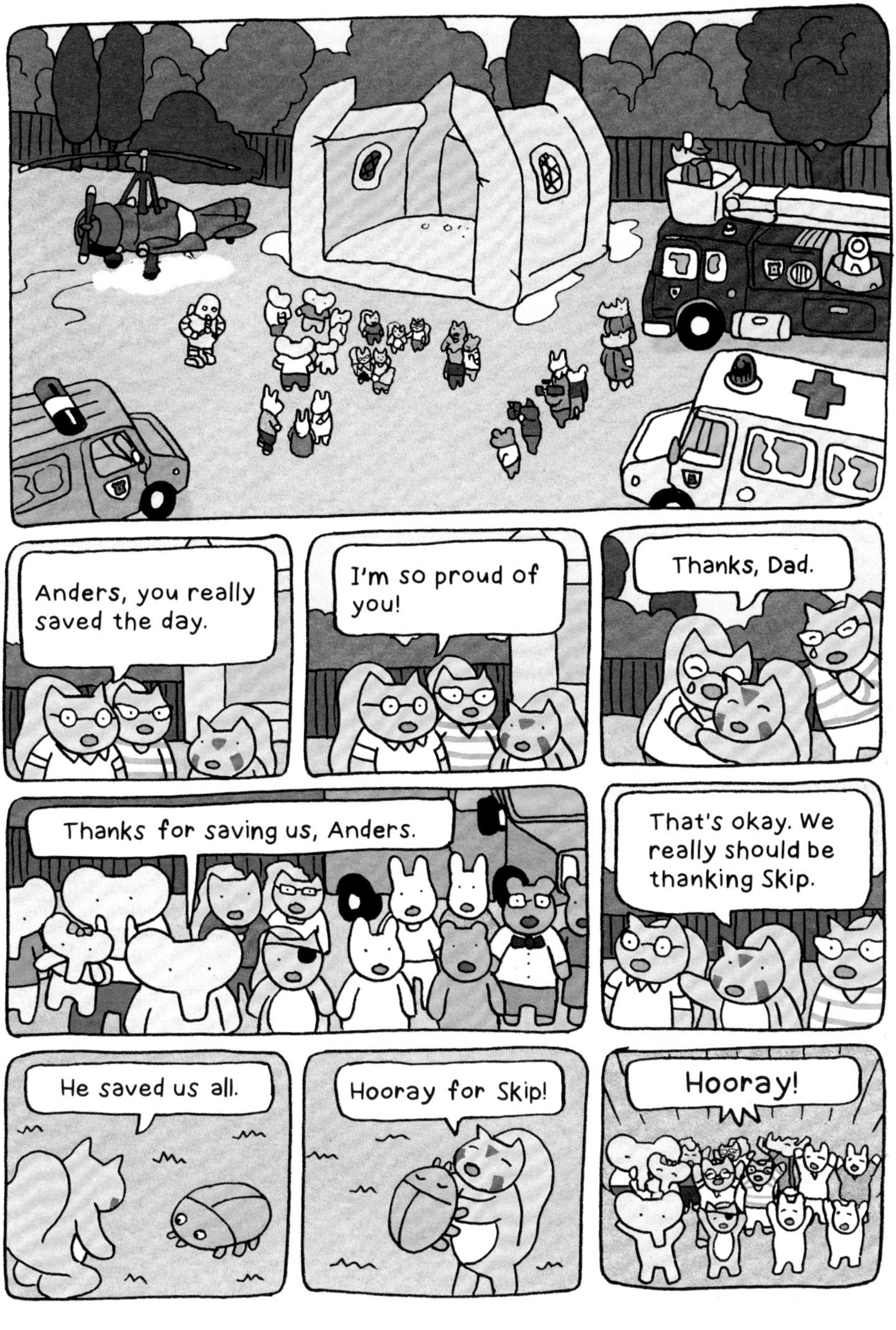
Anders, you really saved the day.
I'm so proud of you!
Thanks, Dad.
Thanks for saving us, Anders.
That's okay. We really should be thanking Skip.
He saved us all.
Hooray for Skip!
Hooray!

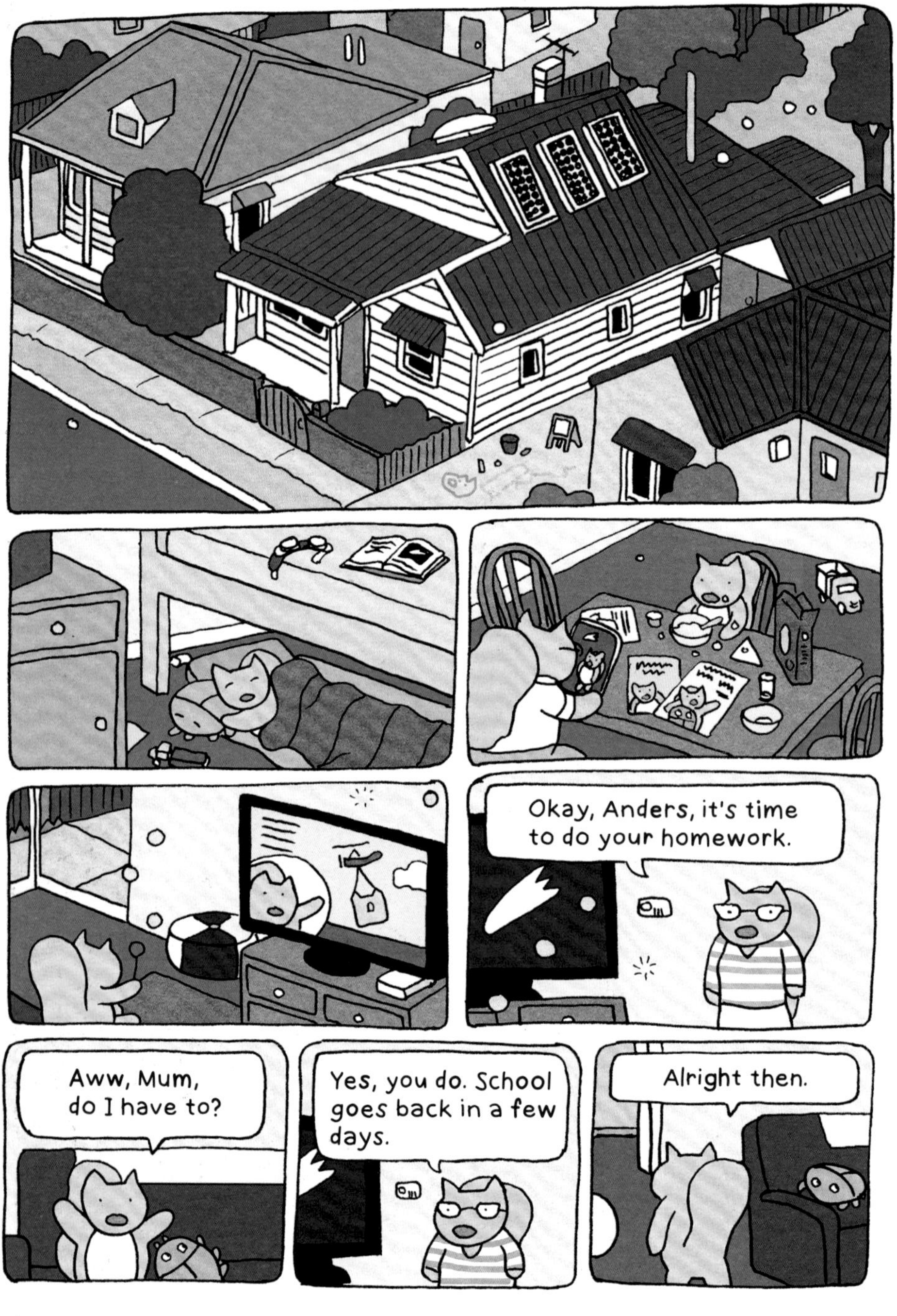
Okay, Anders, it's time to do your homework.
Aww, Mum, do I have to?
Yes, you do. School goes back in a few days.
Alright then.

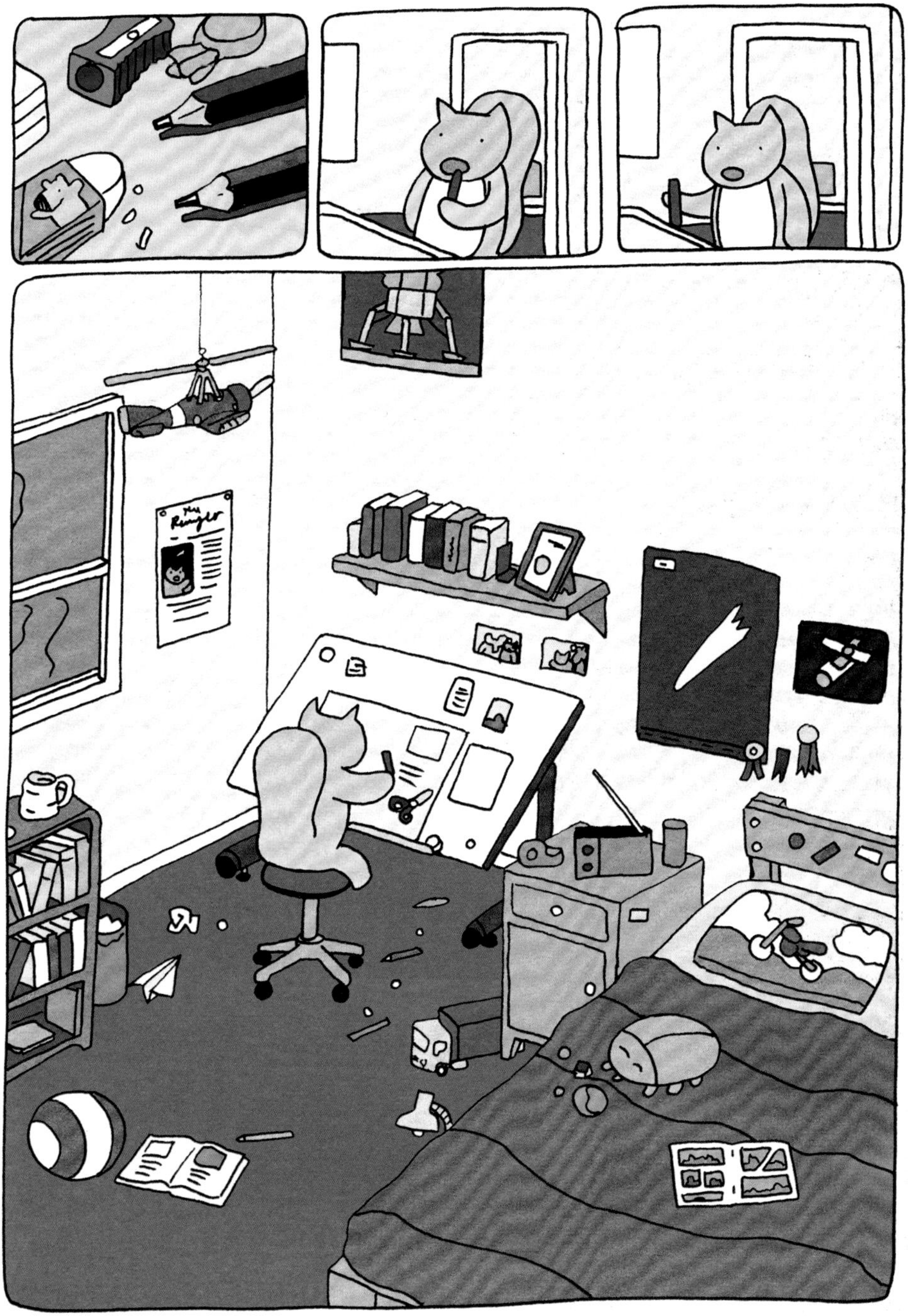

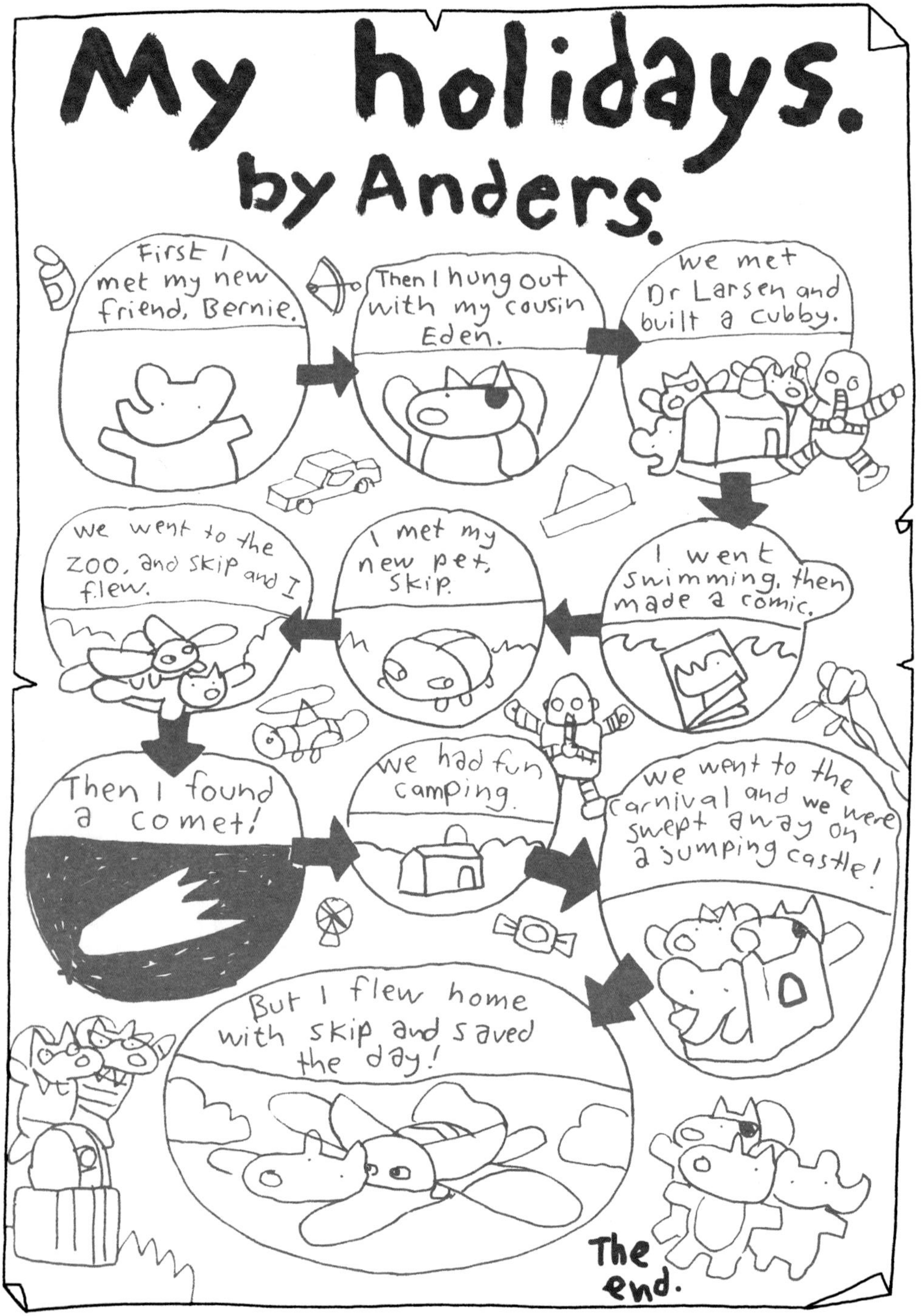
My holidays.
by Anders.
First I met my new friend, Bernie.
Then I hung out with my cousin Eden.
We met Dr Larsen and built a cubby.
I went swimming, then made a comic.
I met my new pet, Skip.
We went to the zoo, and Skip and I flew.
Then I found a comet!
We had fun camping.
We went to the carnival and we were swept away on a jumping castle!
But I flew home with Skip and saved the day!
The end.

What is a COMET?

A comet is a large icy ball of dirt and ice that zooms through space.

As it flies closer to the sun, it heats up.

This causes the comet to leave a trail of gas and dust behind it for thousands of kilometres.

100m

60 Kms

Comets range in size and can sometimes be seen from Earth.

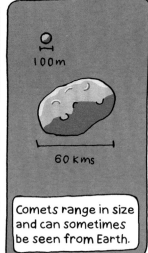

As the comet flies through the solar system, the tail will turn away from the sun and grow longer.

Earth

Sun

There are over 5000 known comets, with more and more being discovered frequently.

ANDERS
and the
VOLCANO

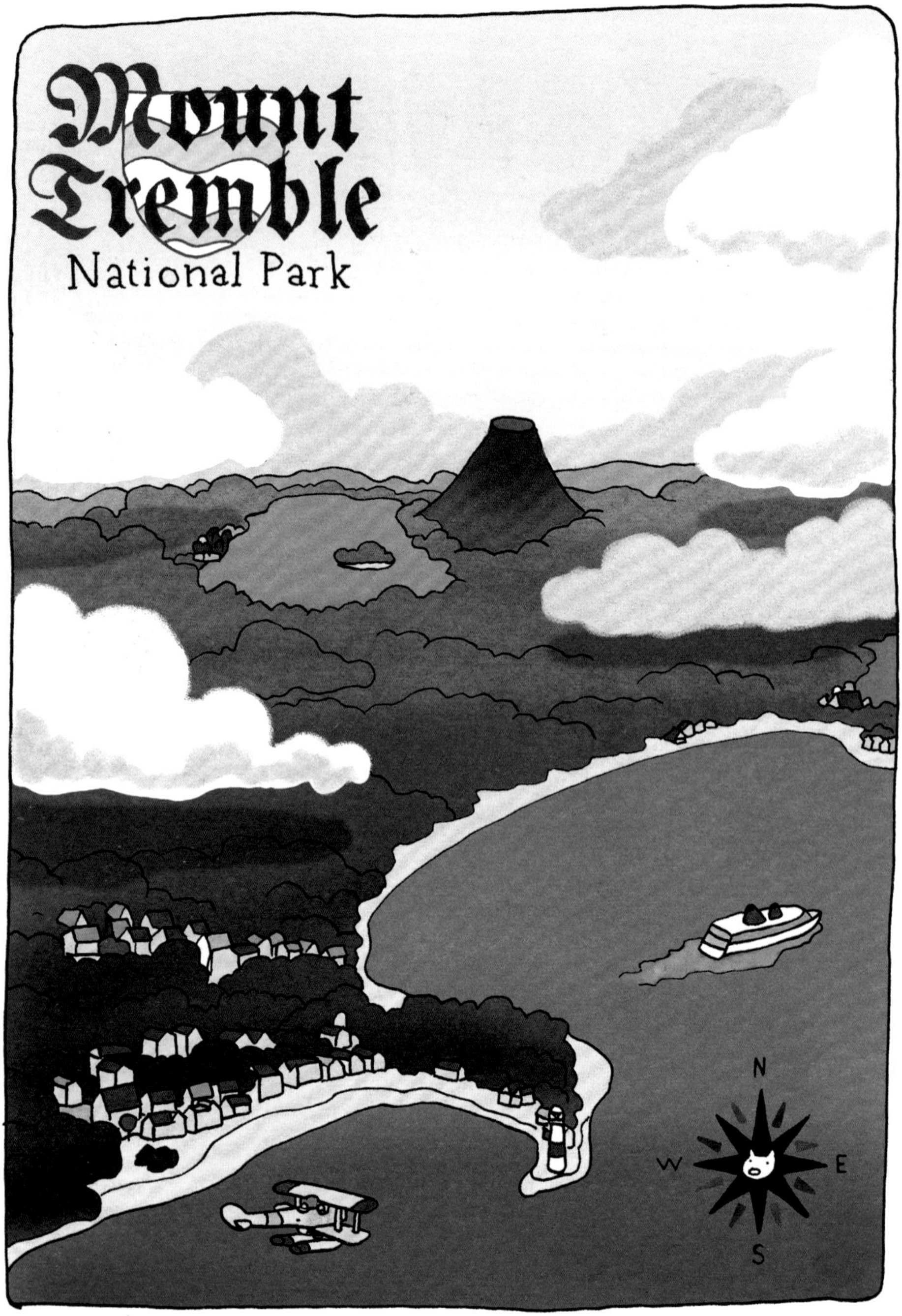
Mount Tremble
National Park
N
W
E
S

Chapter 1

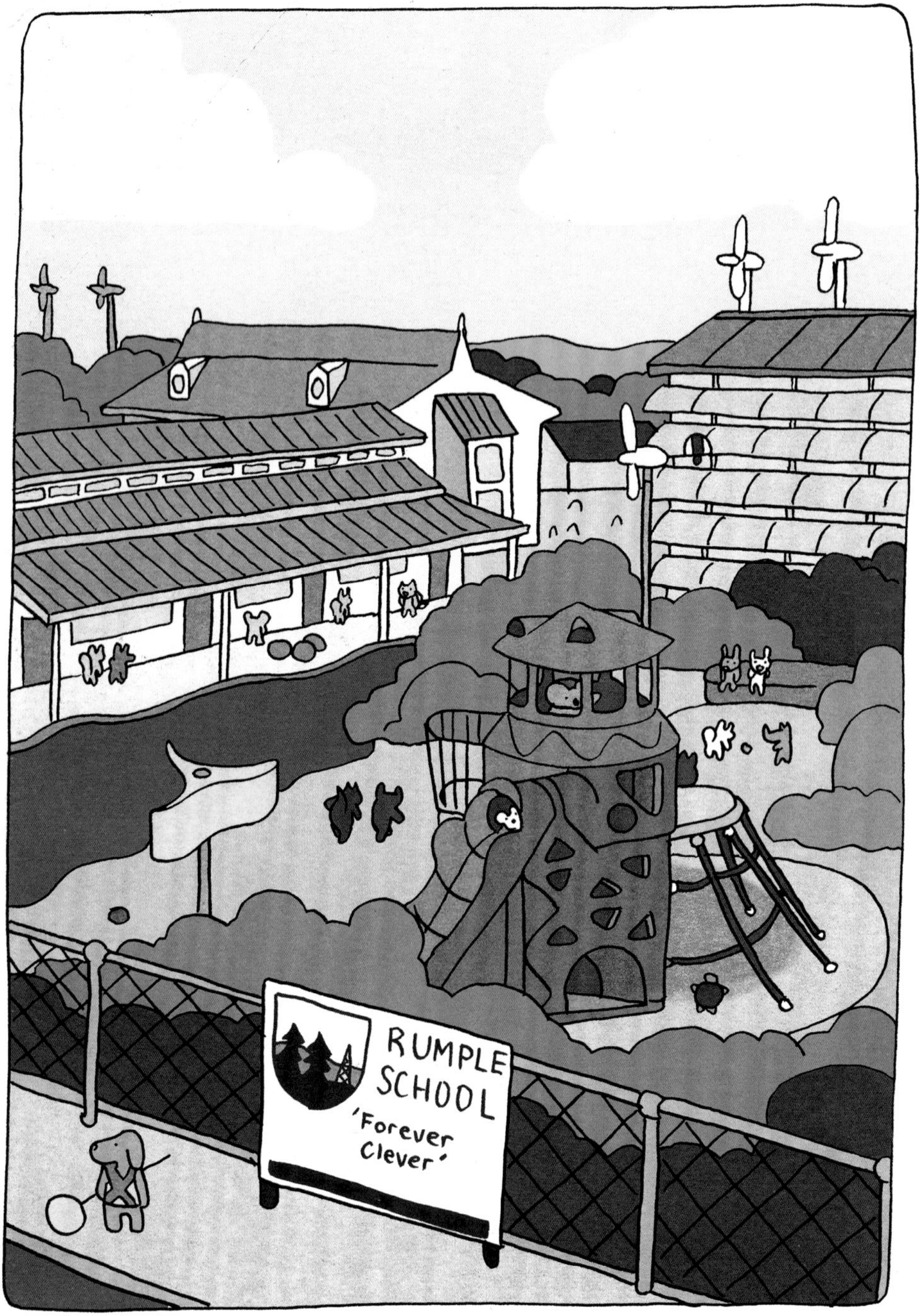
RUMPLE
SCHOOL
'Forever
Clever'

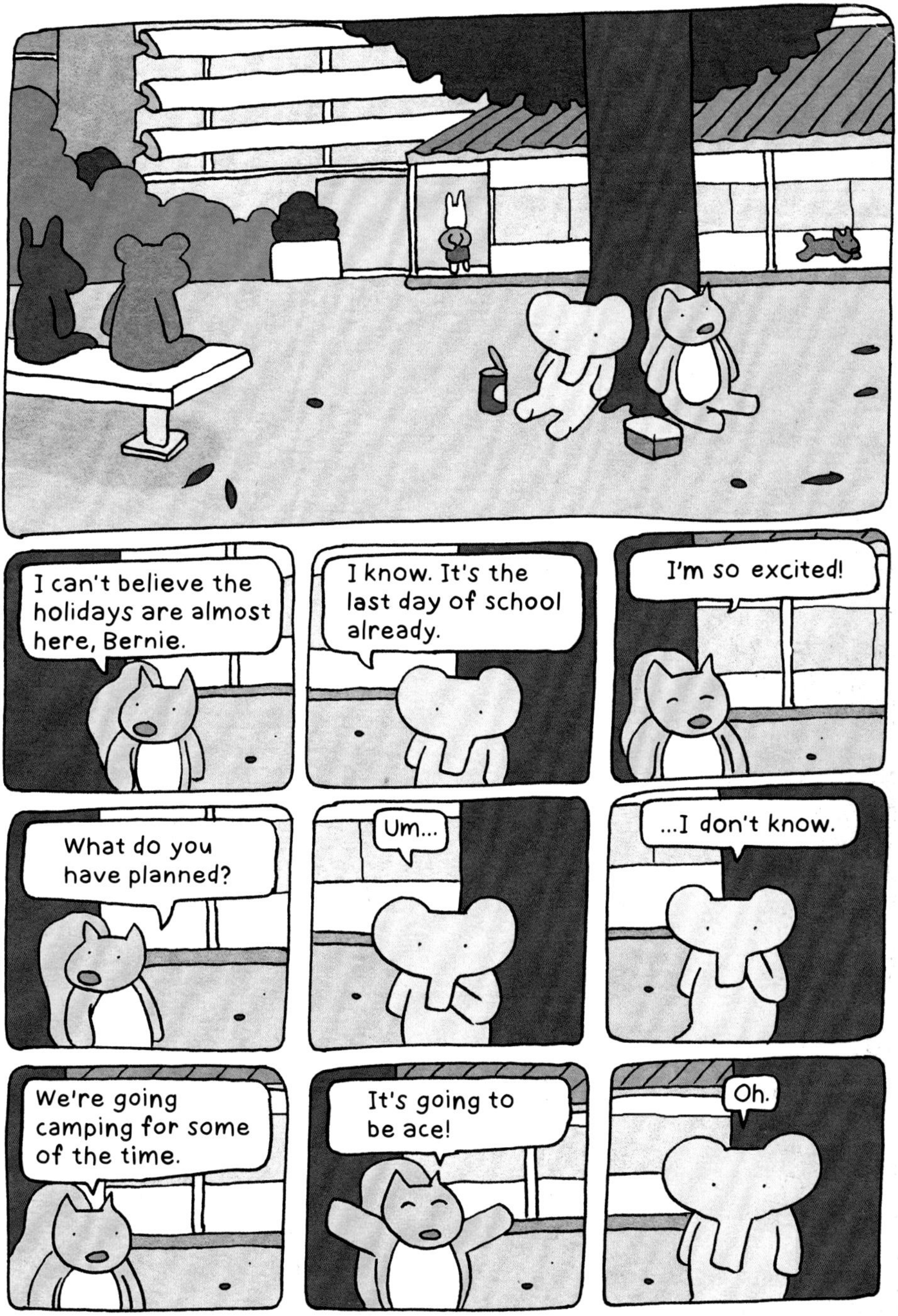
I can't believe the holidays are almost here, Bernie.
I know. It's the last day of school already.
I'm so excited!
What do you have planned?
Um...
...I don't know.
We're going camping for some of the time.
It's going to be ace!
Oh.

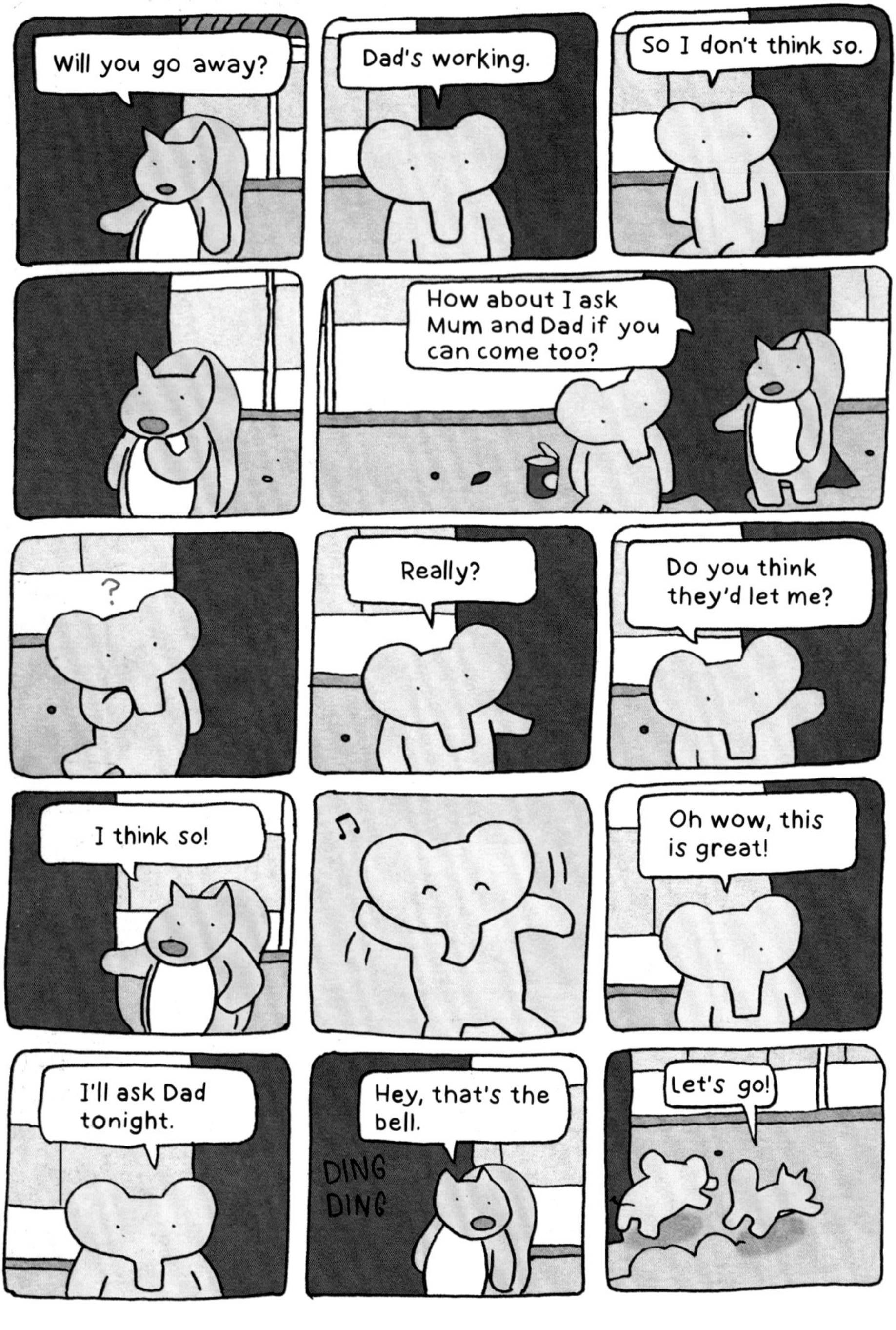

Will you go away?
Dad's working.
So I don't think so.
How about I ask Mum and Dad if you can come too?
?
Really?
Do you think they'd let me?
I think so!
Oh wow, this is great!
I'll ask Dad tonight.
Hey, that's the bell.
DING DING
Let's go!

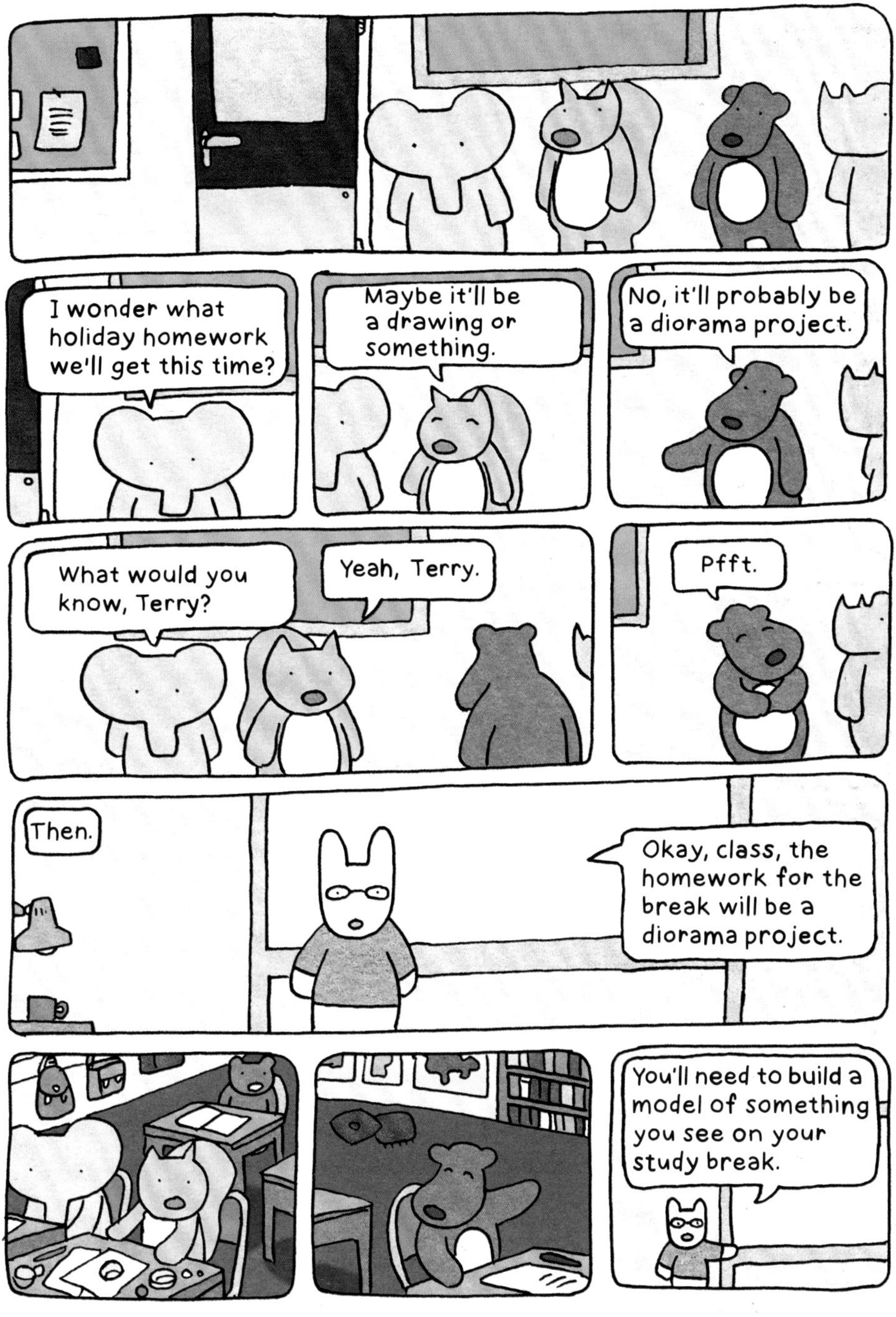
I wonder what holiday homework we'll get this time?
Maybe it'll be a drawing or something.
No, it'll probably be a diorama project.
What would you know, Terry?
Yeah, Terry.
Pfft.
Then.
Okay, class, the homework for the break will be a diorama project.
You'll need to build a model of something you see on your study break.

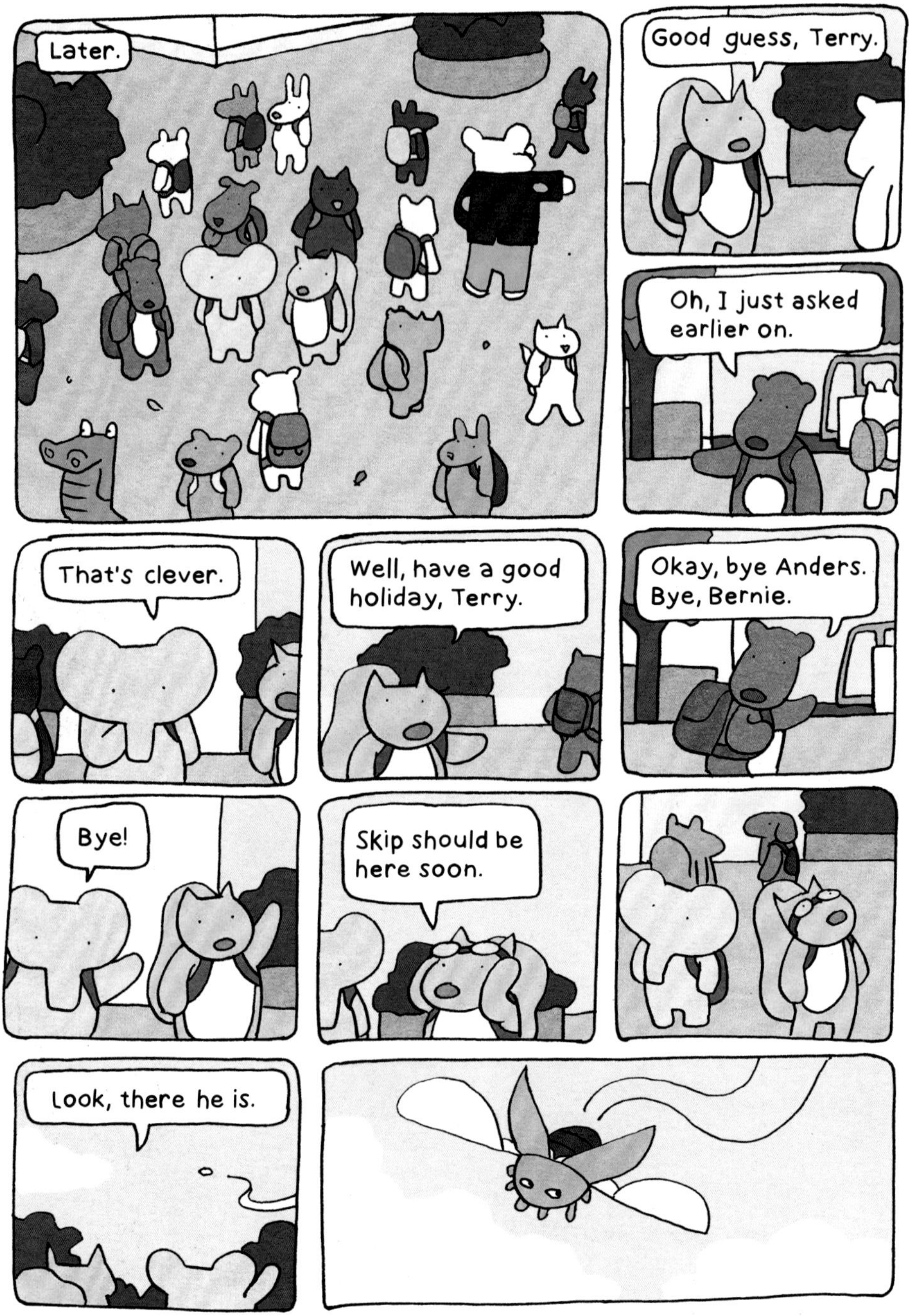
Later.
Good guess, Terry.
Oh, I just asked earlier on.
That's clever.
Well, have a good holiday, Terry.
Okay, bye Anders. Bye, Bernie.
Bye!
Skip should be here soon.
Look, there he is.

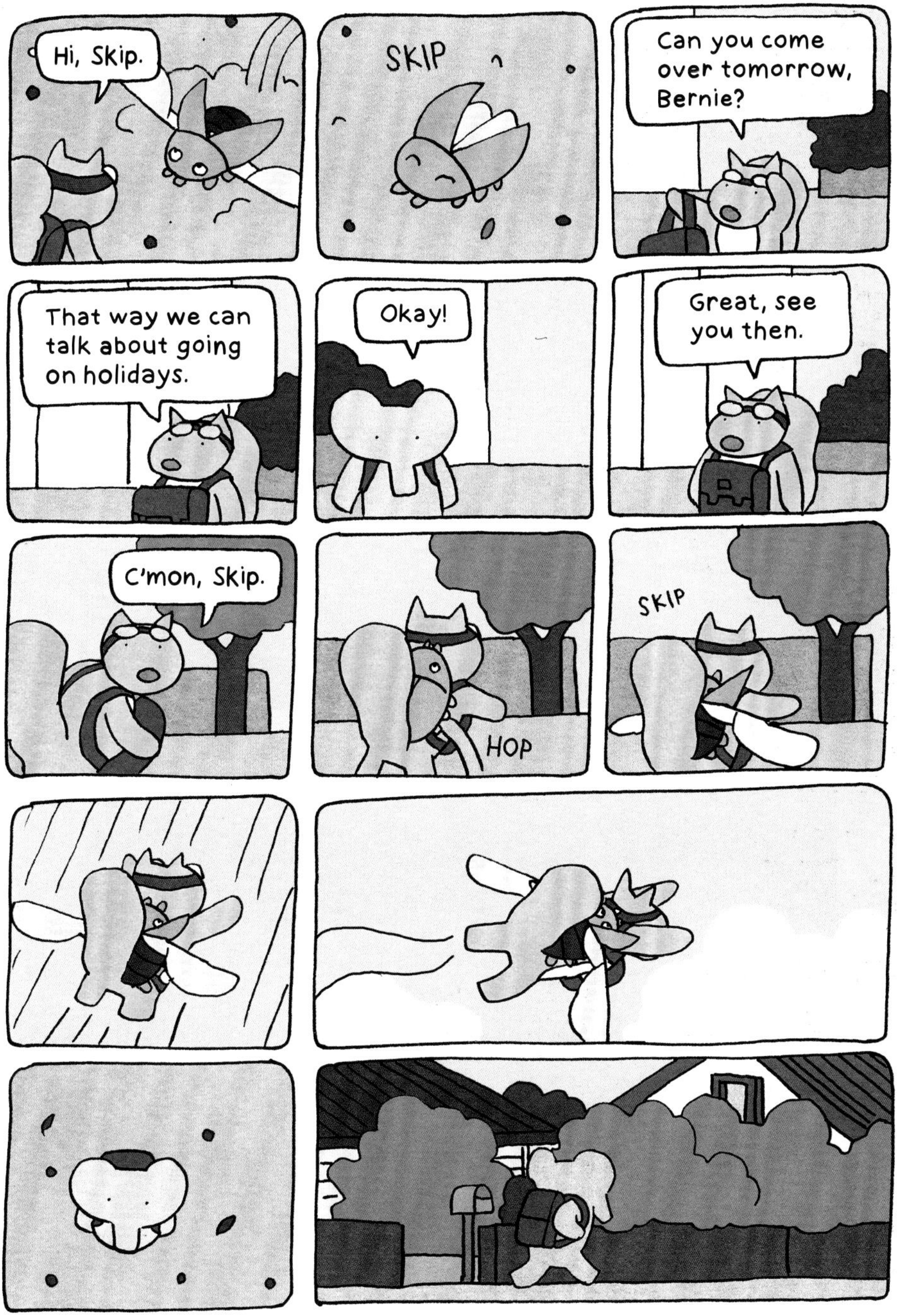
Hi, Skip.
SKIP
Can you come over tomorrow, Bernie?
That way we can talk about going on holidays.
Okay!
Great, see you then.
C'mon, Skip.
HOP
SKIP

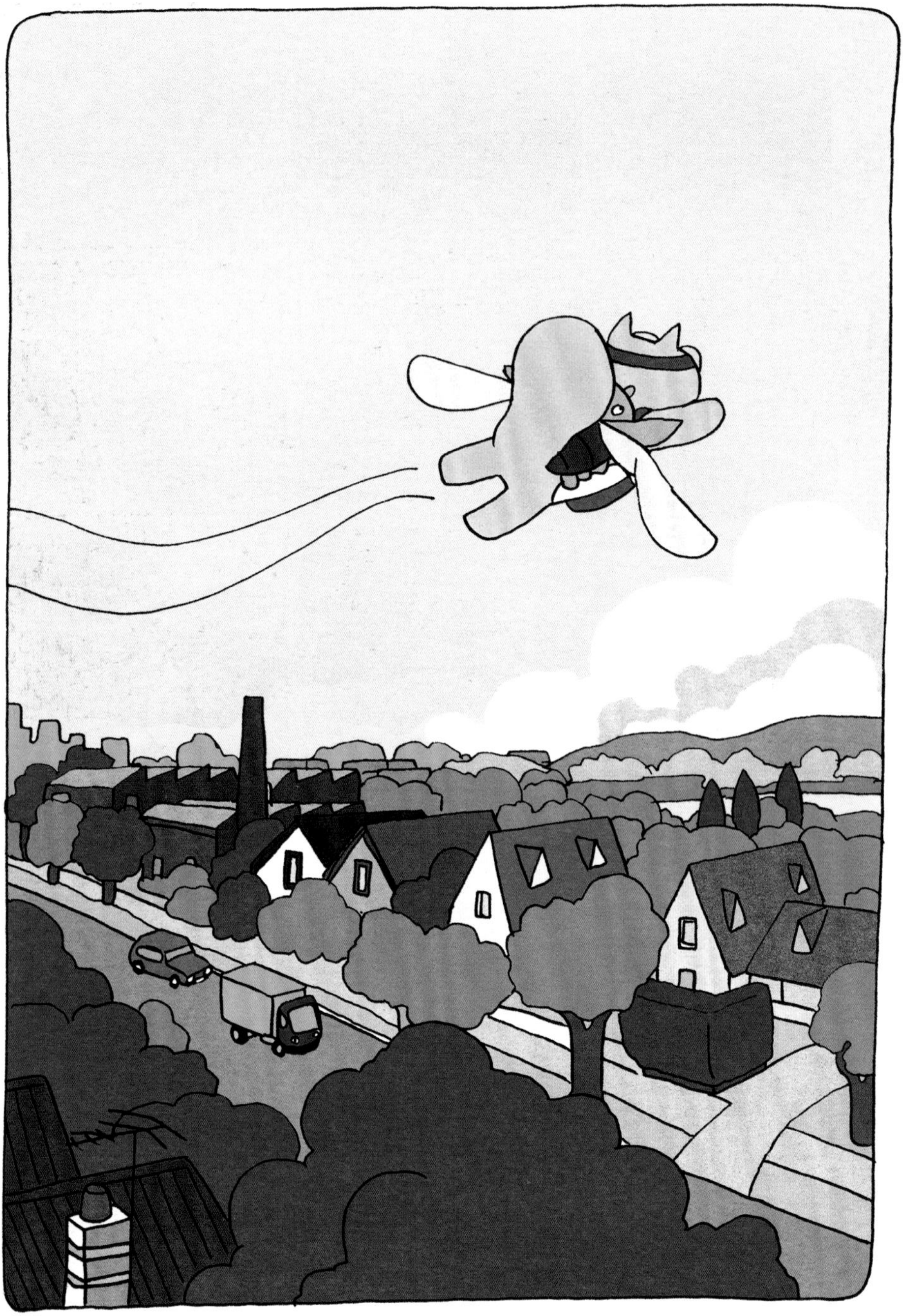

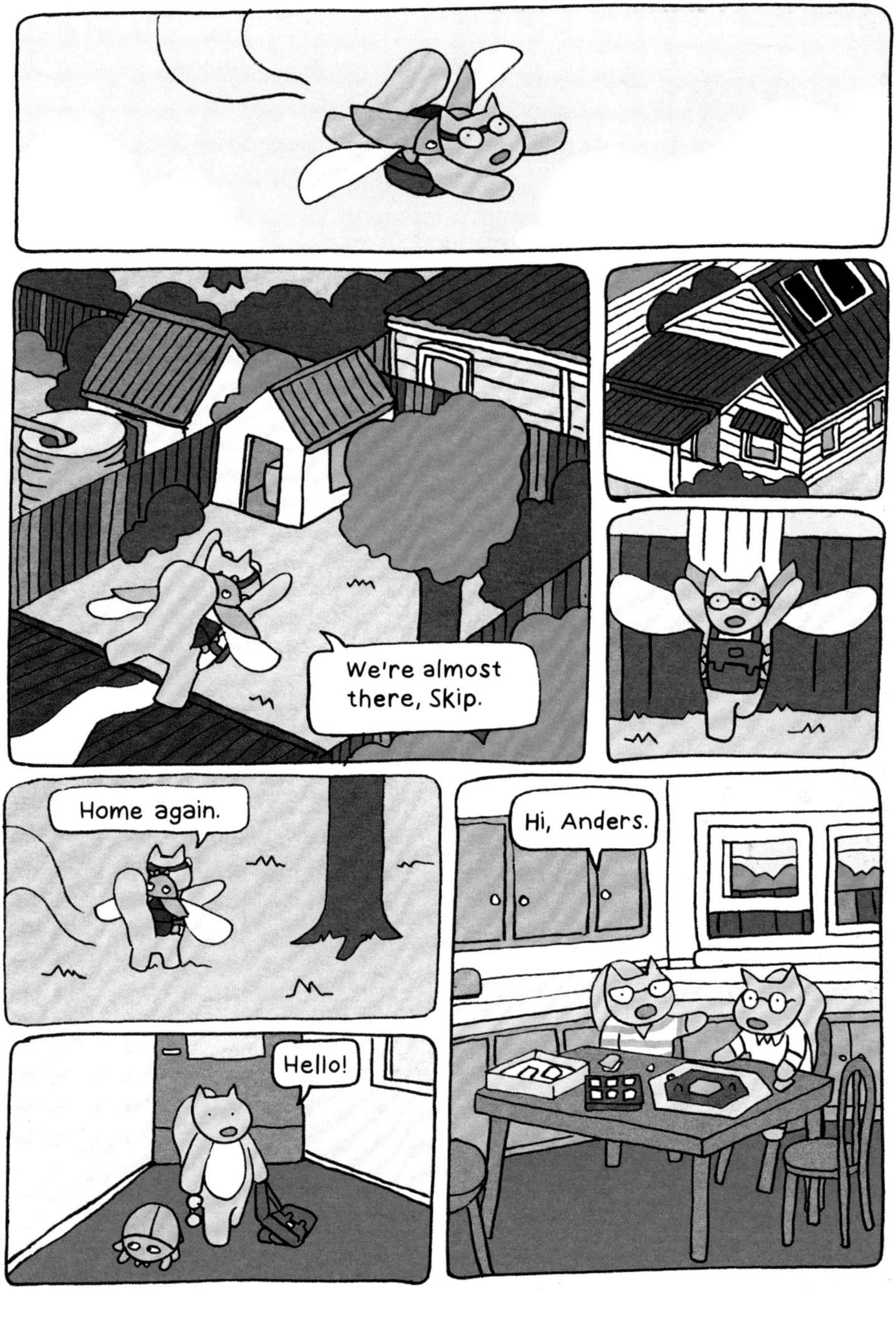
We're almost there, Skip.
Home again.
Hi, Anders.
Hello!

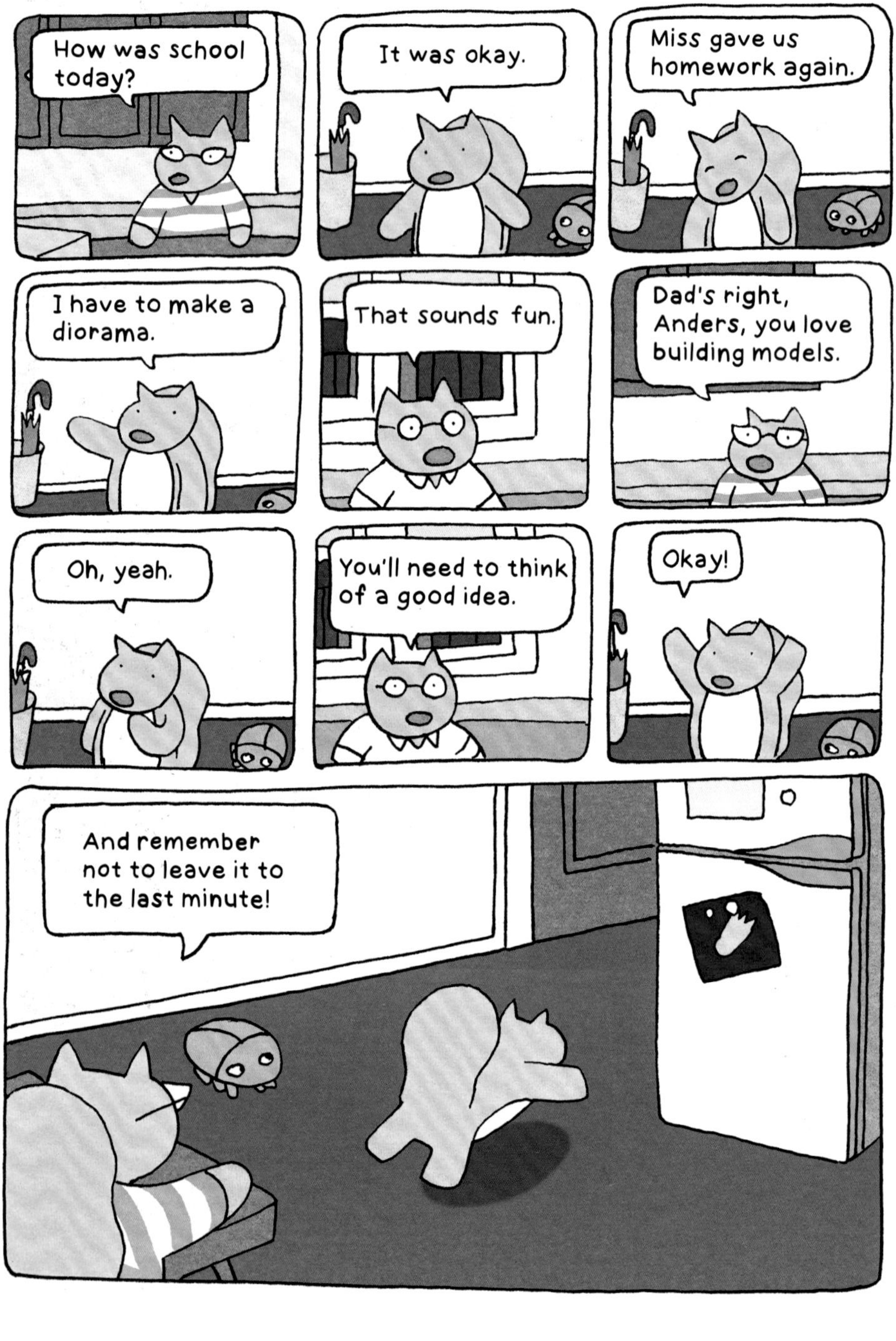
How was school today?
It was okay.
Miss gave us homework again.
I have to make a diorama.
That sounds fun.
Dad's right, Anders, you love building models.
Oh, yeah.
You'll need to think of a good idea.
Okay!
And remember not to leave it to the last minute!

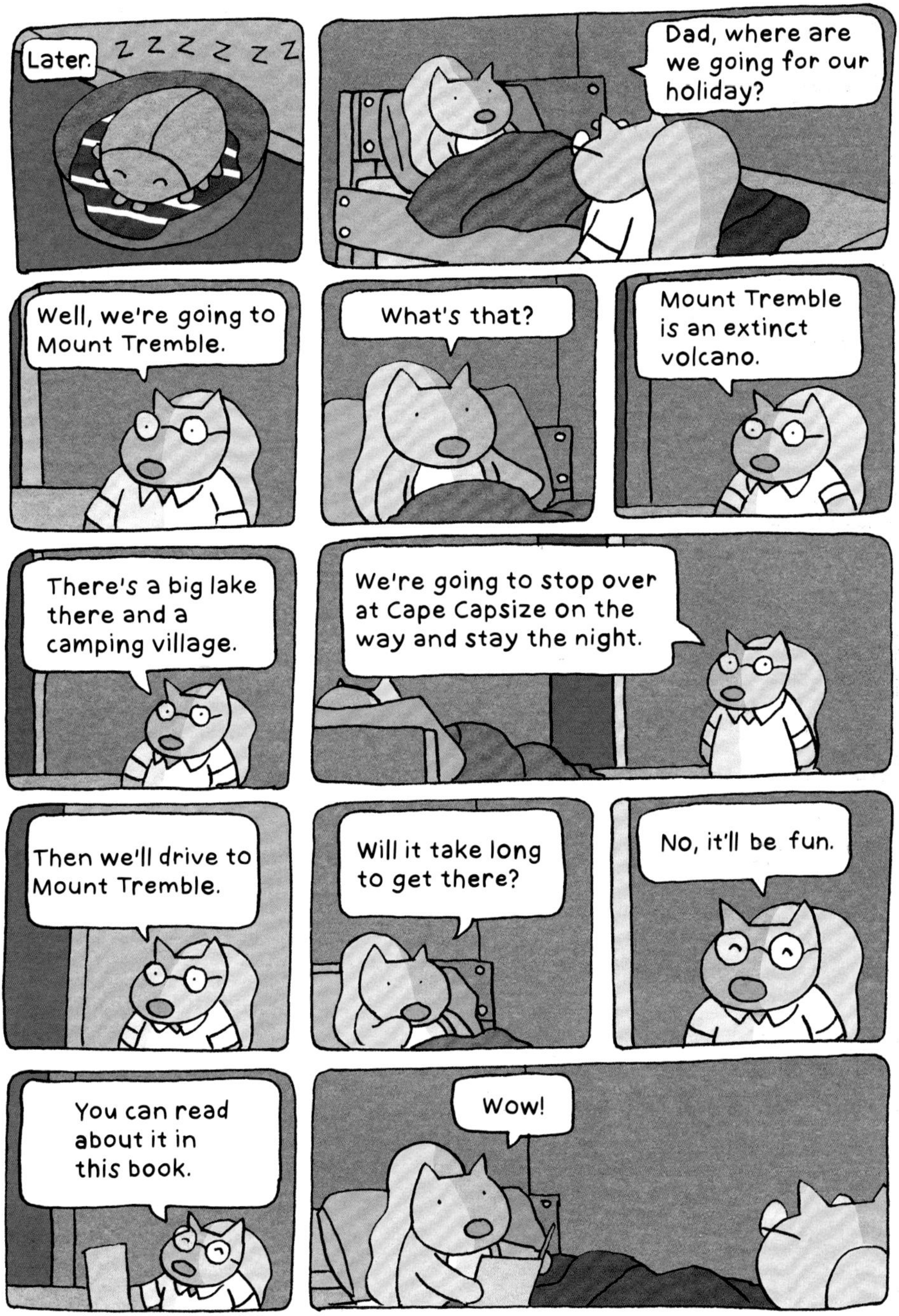
Later.
Z Z Z Z Z Z
Dad, where are we going for our holiday?
Well, we're going to Mount Tremble.
What's that?
Mount Tremble is an extinct volcano.
There's a big lake there and a camping village.
We're going to stop over at Cape Capsize on the way and stay the night.
Then we'll drive to Mount Tremble.
Will it take long to get there?
No, it'll be fun.
You can read about it in this book.
Wow!

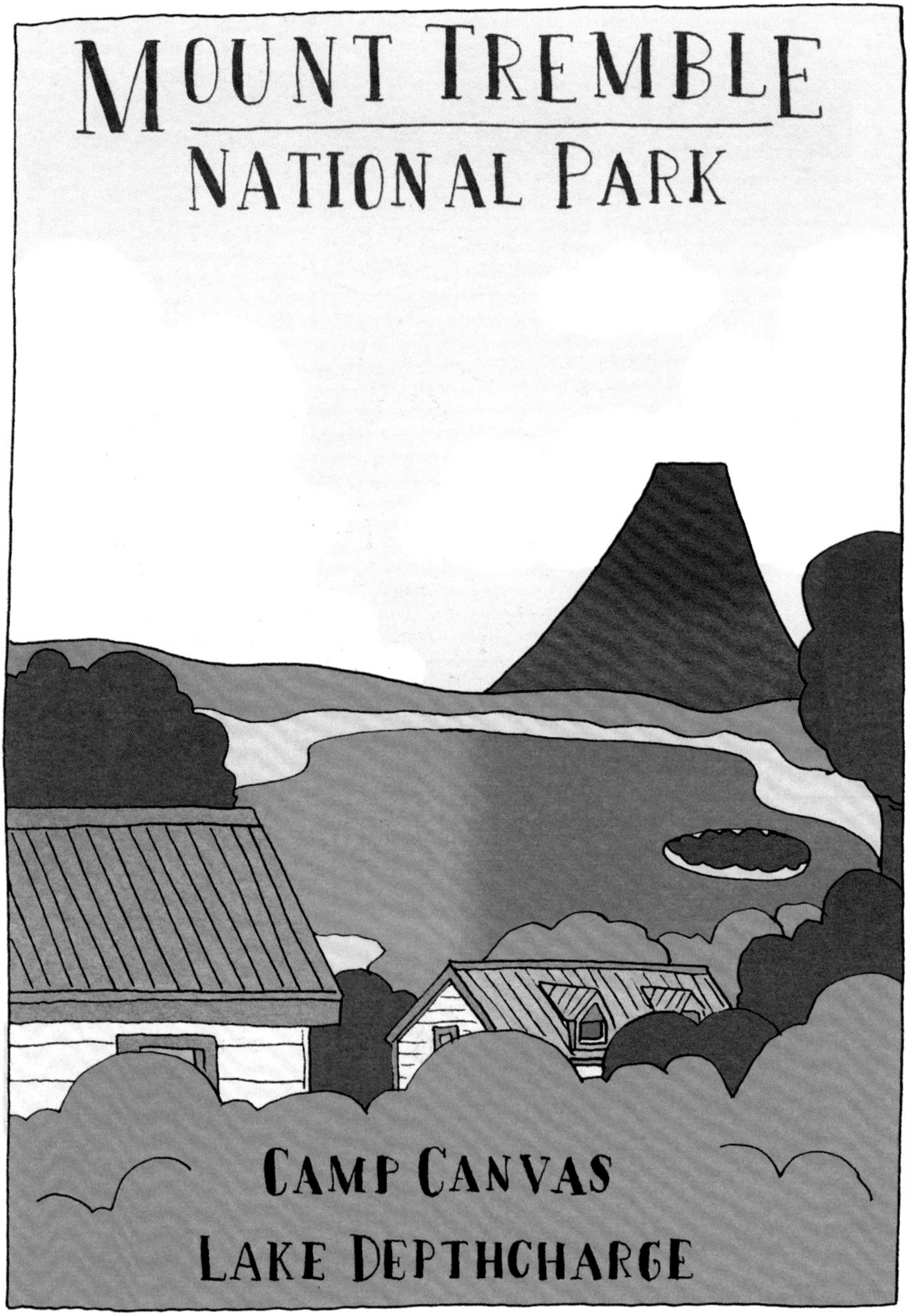
MOUNT TREMBLE
NATIONAL PARK
CAMP CANVAS
LAKE DEPTHCHARGE

Chapter 2

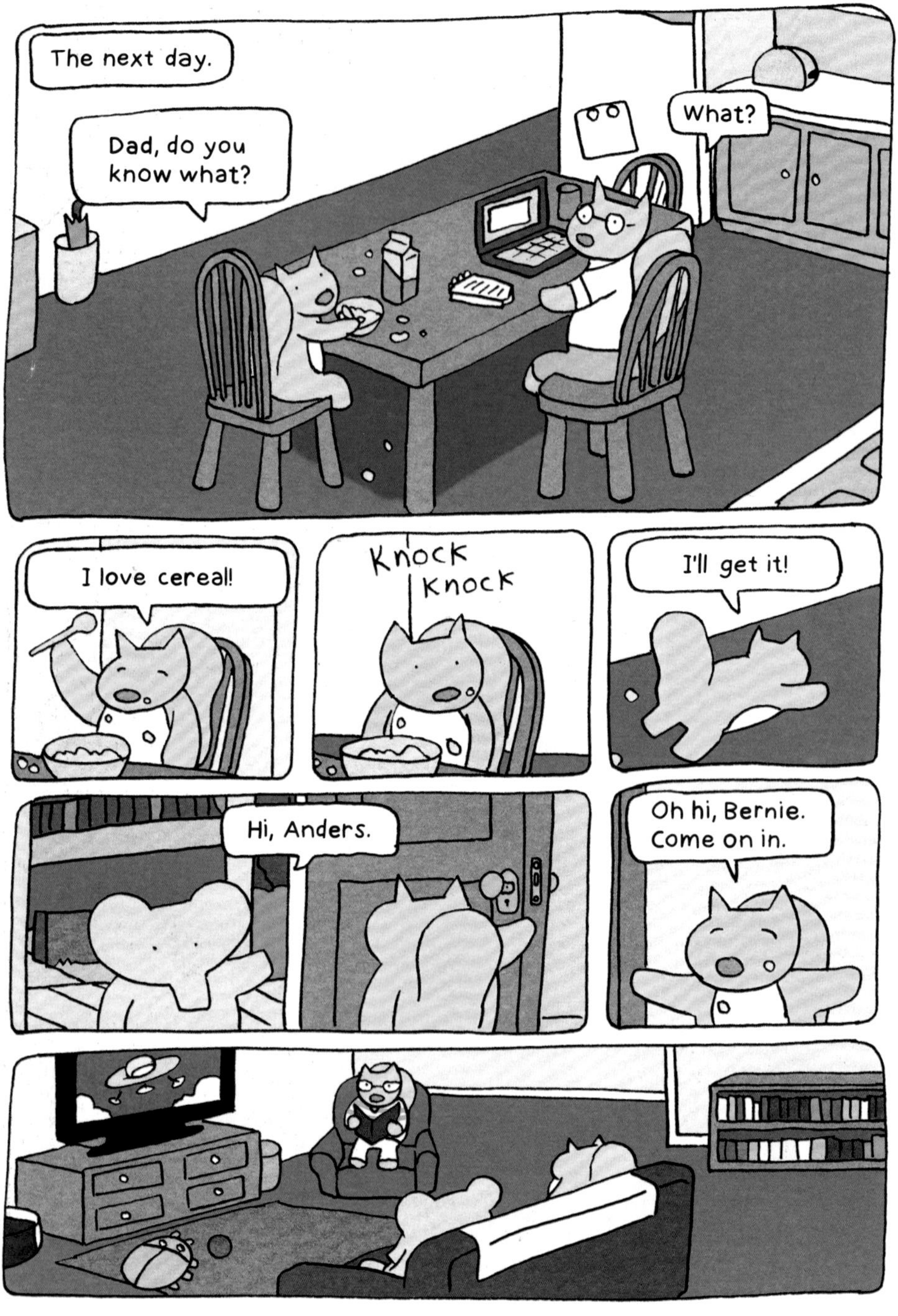

The next day.
Dad, do you know what?
What?
I love cereal!
Knock Knock
I'll get it!
Hi, Anders.
Oh hi, Bernie. Come on in.

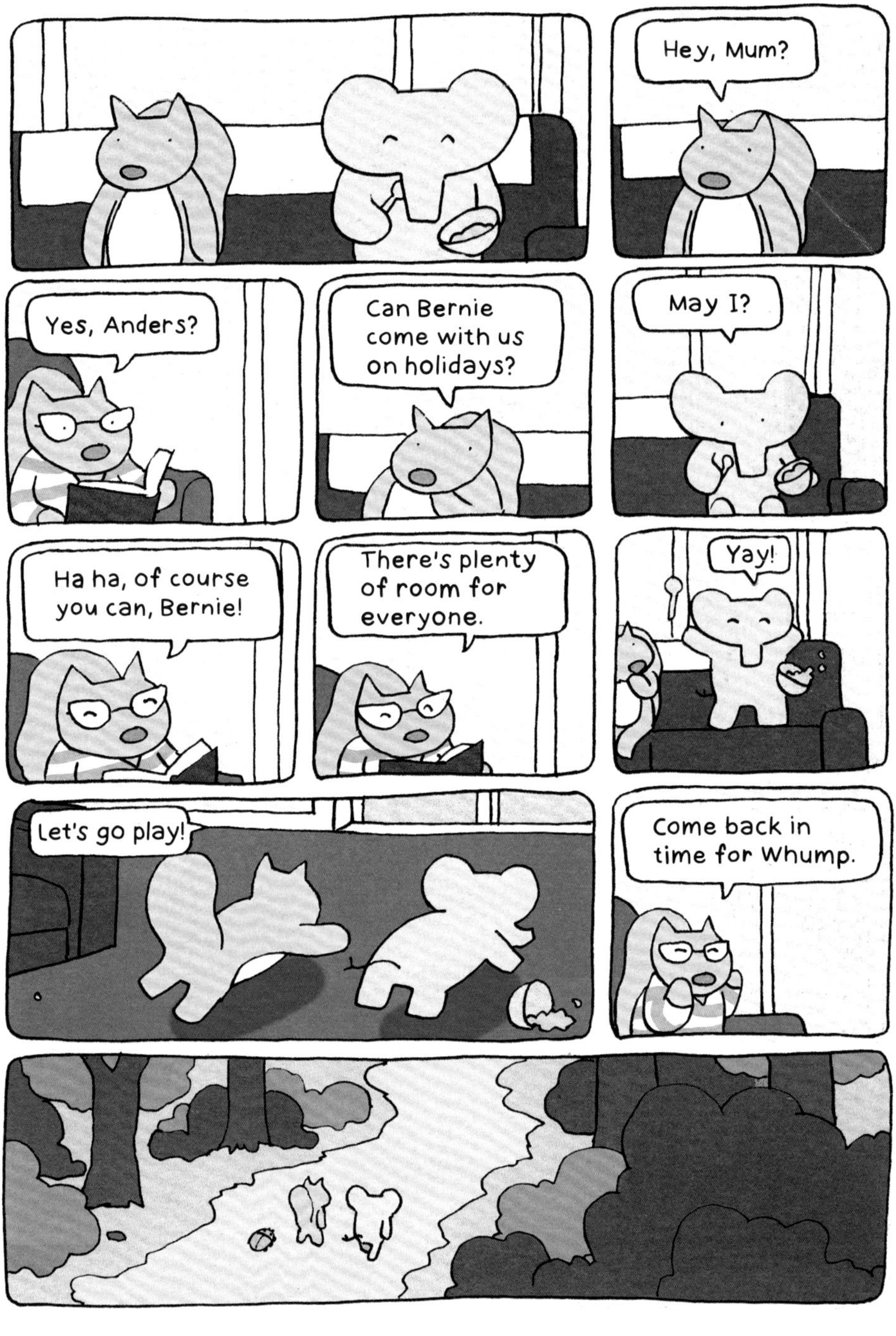
Hey, Mum?
Yes, Anders?
Can Bernie come with us on holidays?
May I?
Ha ha, of course you can, Bernie!
There's plenty of room for everyone.
Yay!
Let's go play!
Come back in time for Whump.

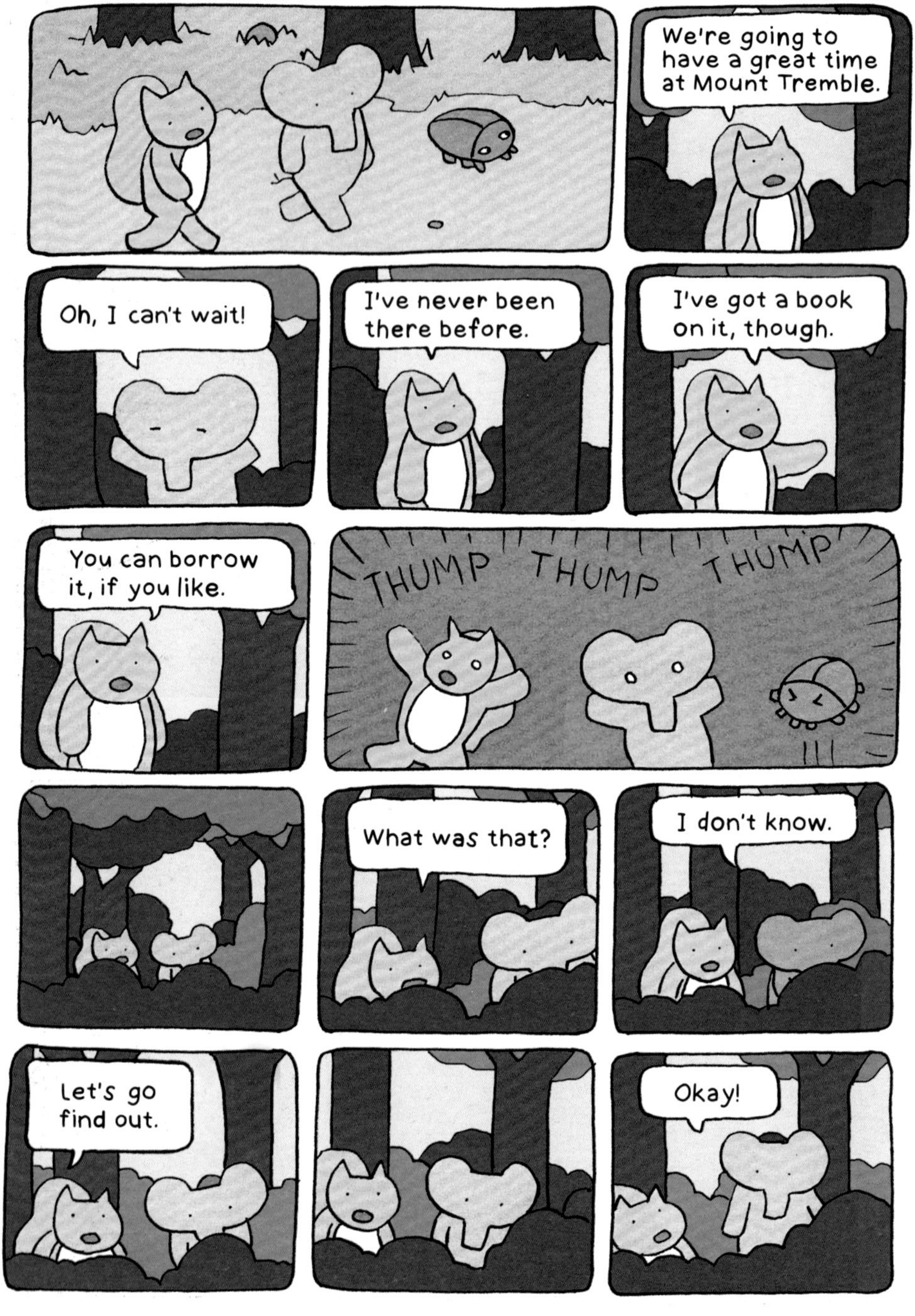
We're going to have a great time at Mount Tremble.
Oh, I can't wait!
I've never been there before.
I've got a book on it, though.
You can borrow it, if you like.
THUMP THUMP THUMP
What was that?
I don't know.
Let's go find out.
Okay!

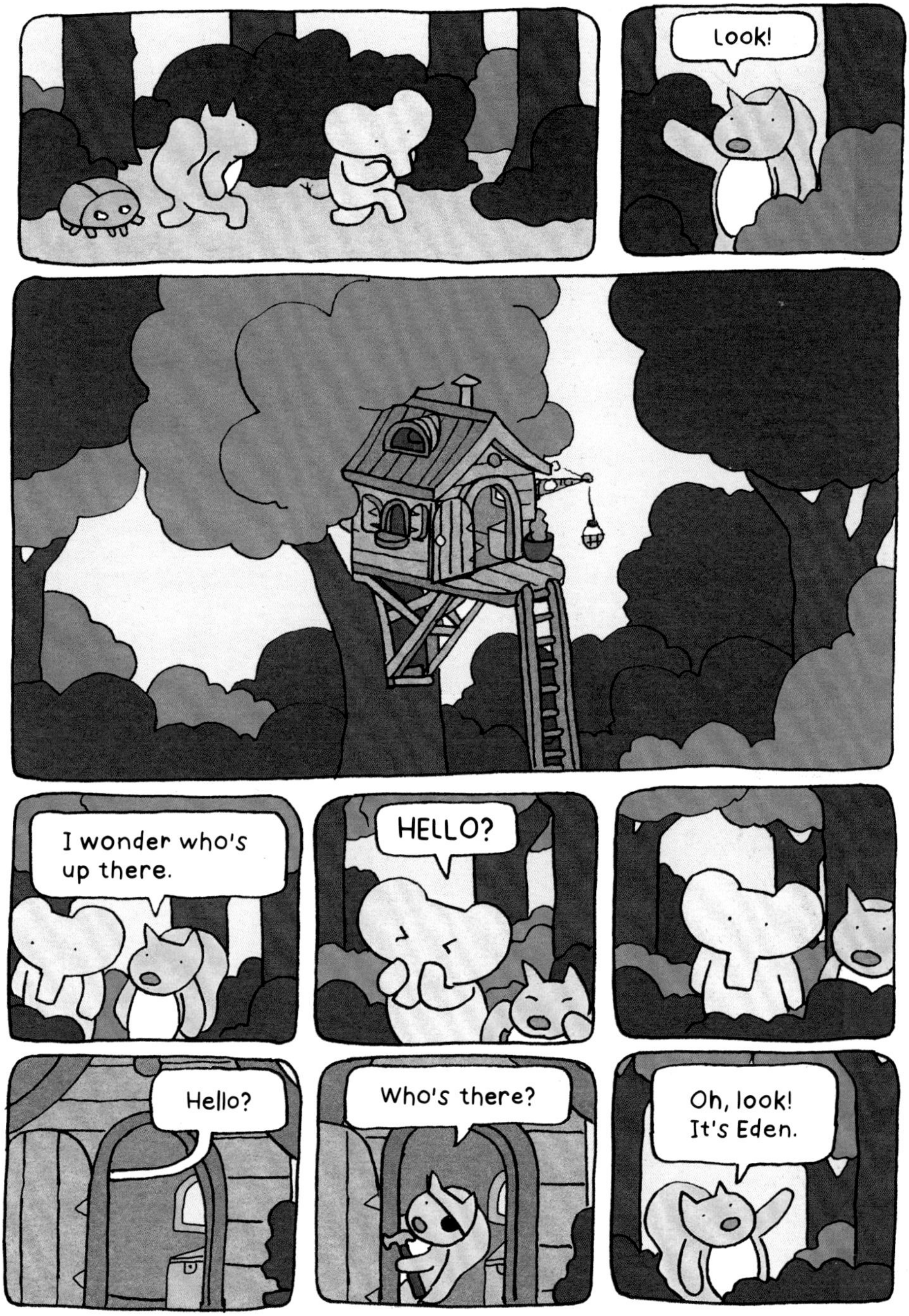
Look!
I wonder who's up there.
HELLO?
Hello?
Who's there?
Oh, look! It's Eden.

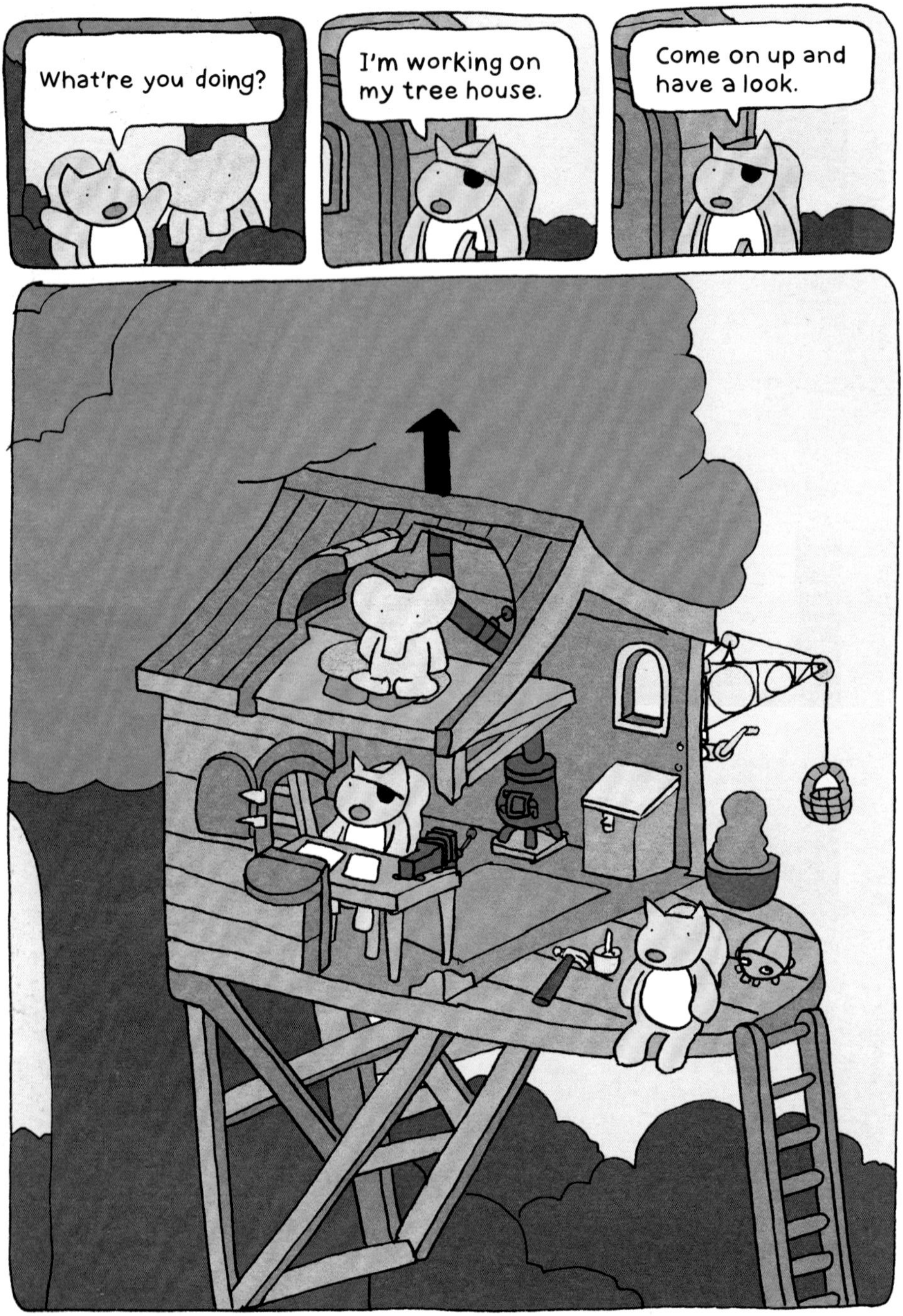
What're you doing?
I'm working on my tree house.
Come on up and have a look.

This place is amazing, Eden.

Did you build it all by yourself?

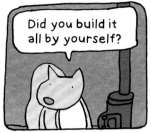

I sure did!

Mum helped me with the plans...

...and some of the other stuff.

But I did all the hammering!

There's lots of room for storage.

We already have a cubby, though.

Why did you build this tree house?

Oh, I just wanted my own room.

Hey, look, it's nearly time for Whump!

It is too.

Let's go, Skip.

See you there.

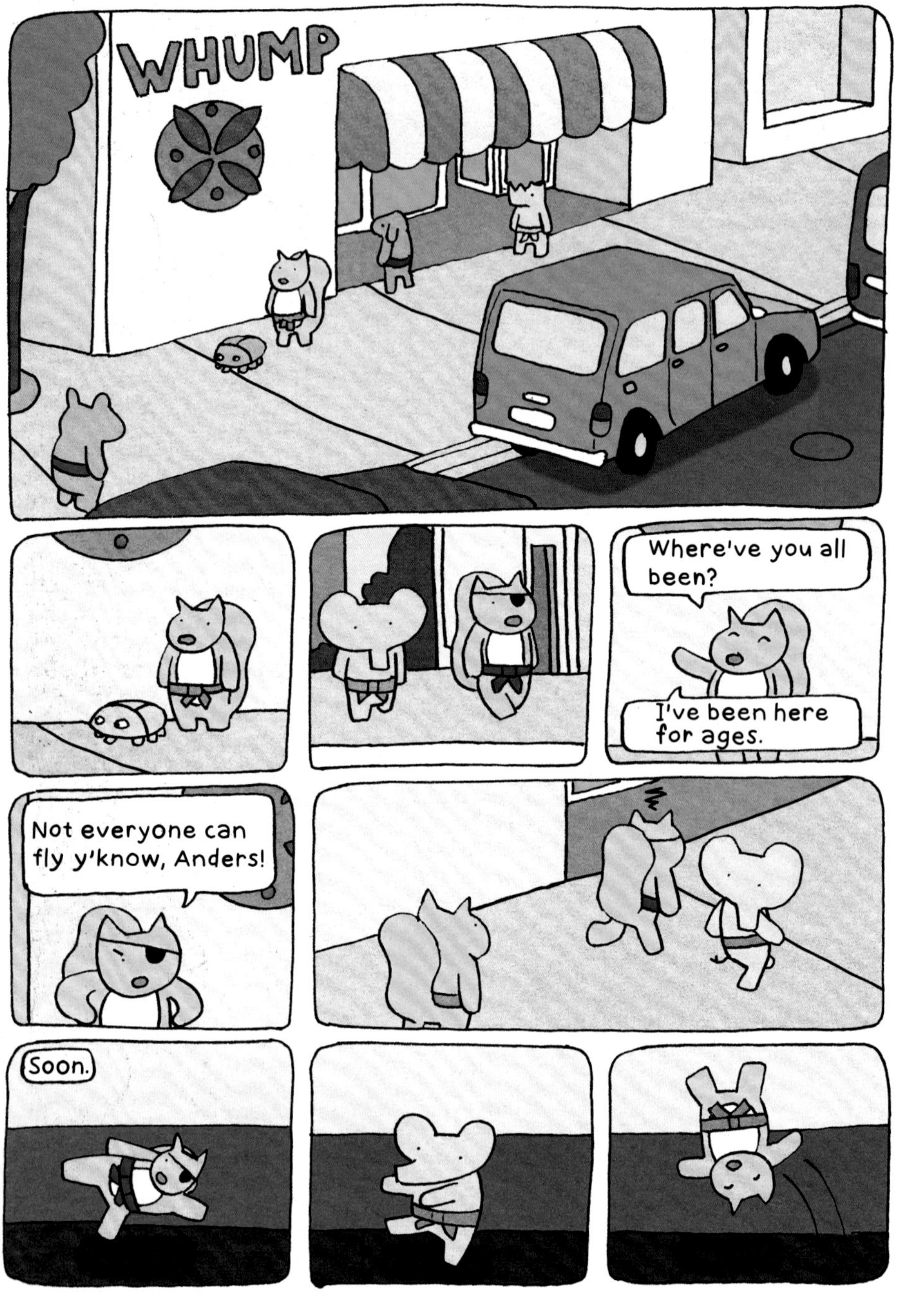
WHUMP
Where've you all been?
I've been here for ages.
Not everyone can fly y'know, Anders!
Soon.

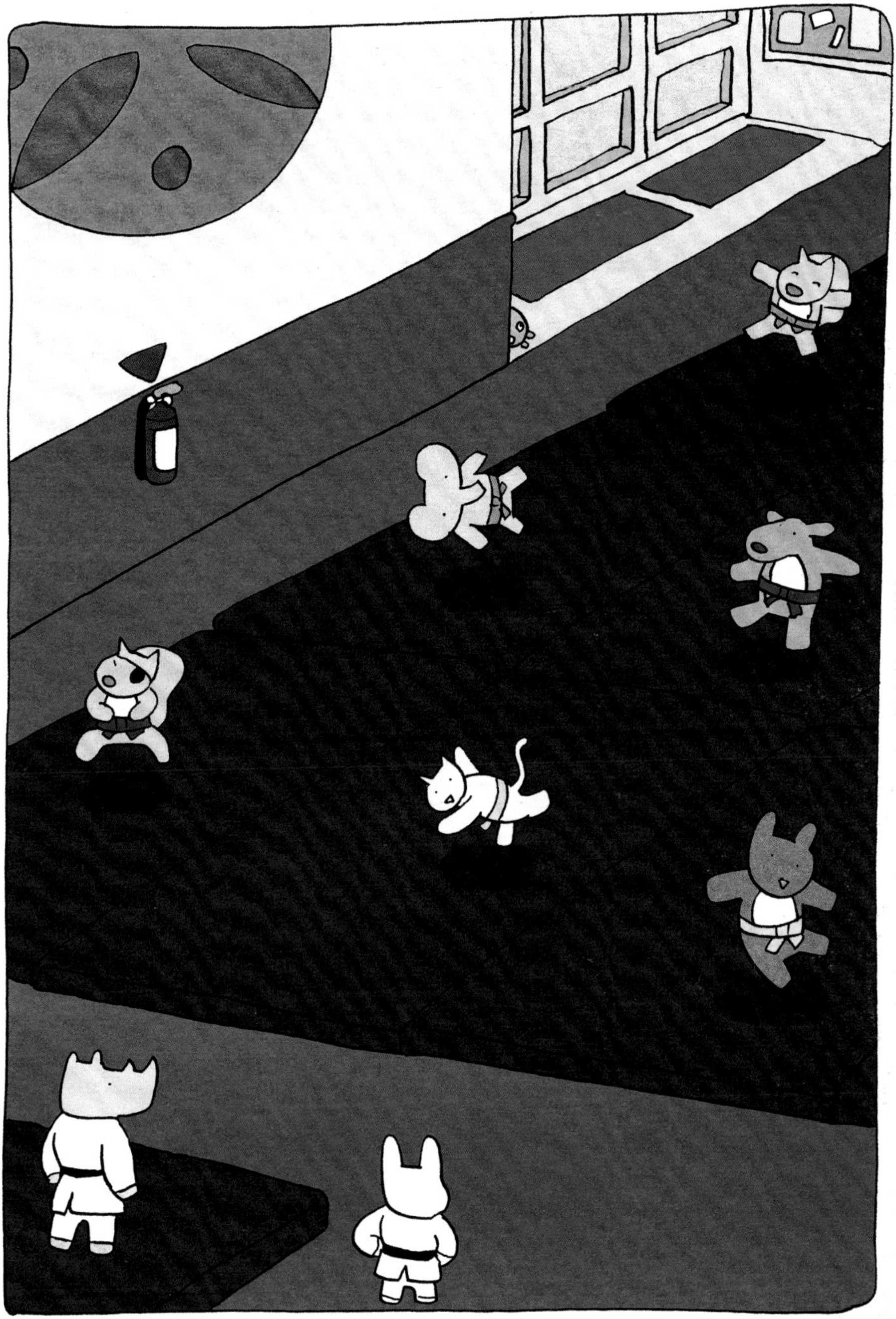

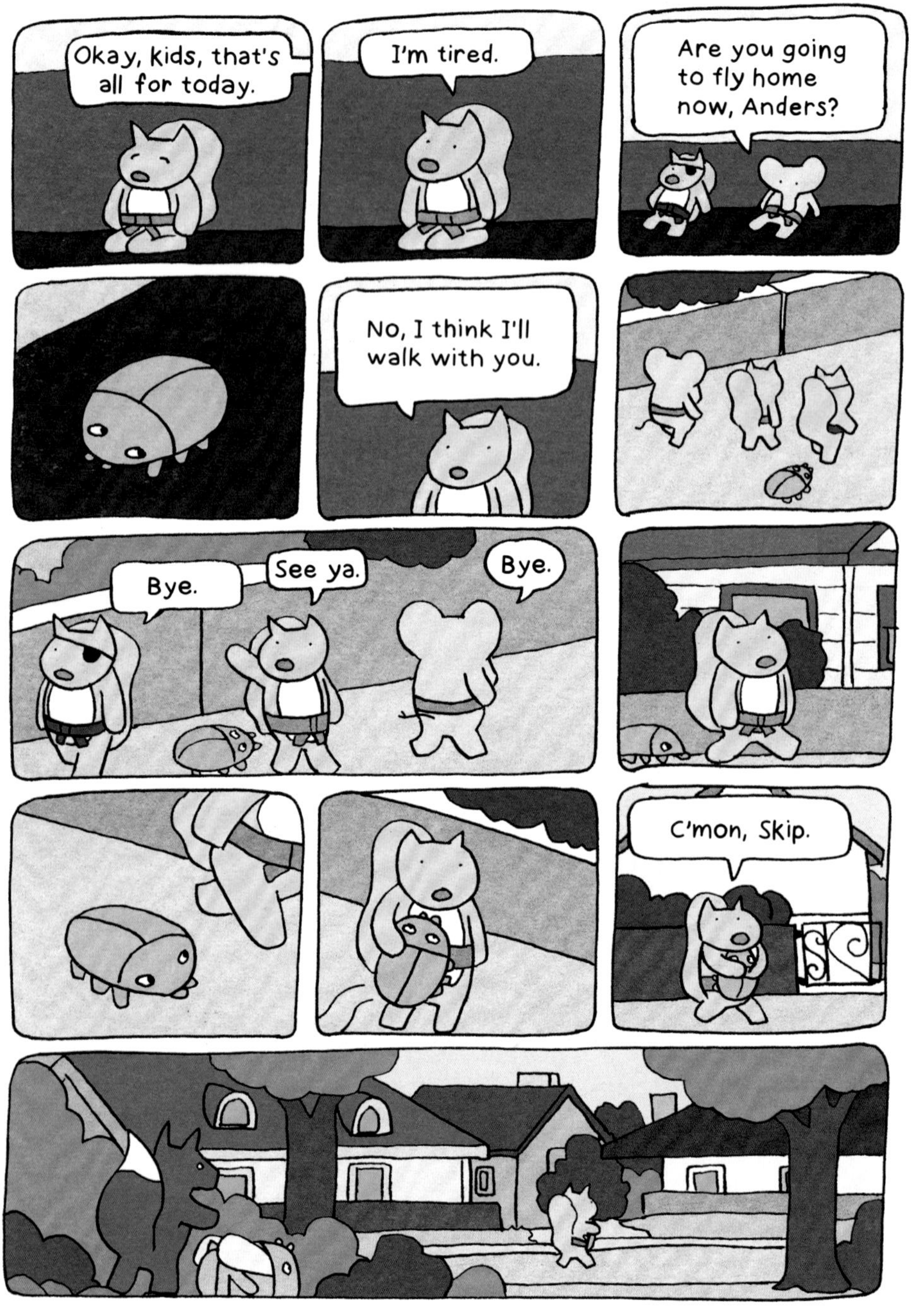
Okay, kids, that's all for today.
I'm tired.
Are you going to fly home now, Anders?
No, I think I'll walk with you.
Bye.
See ya.
Bye.
C'mon, Skip.

Chapter 3

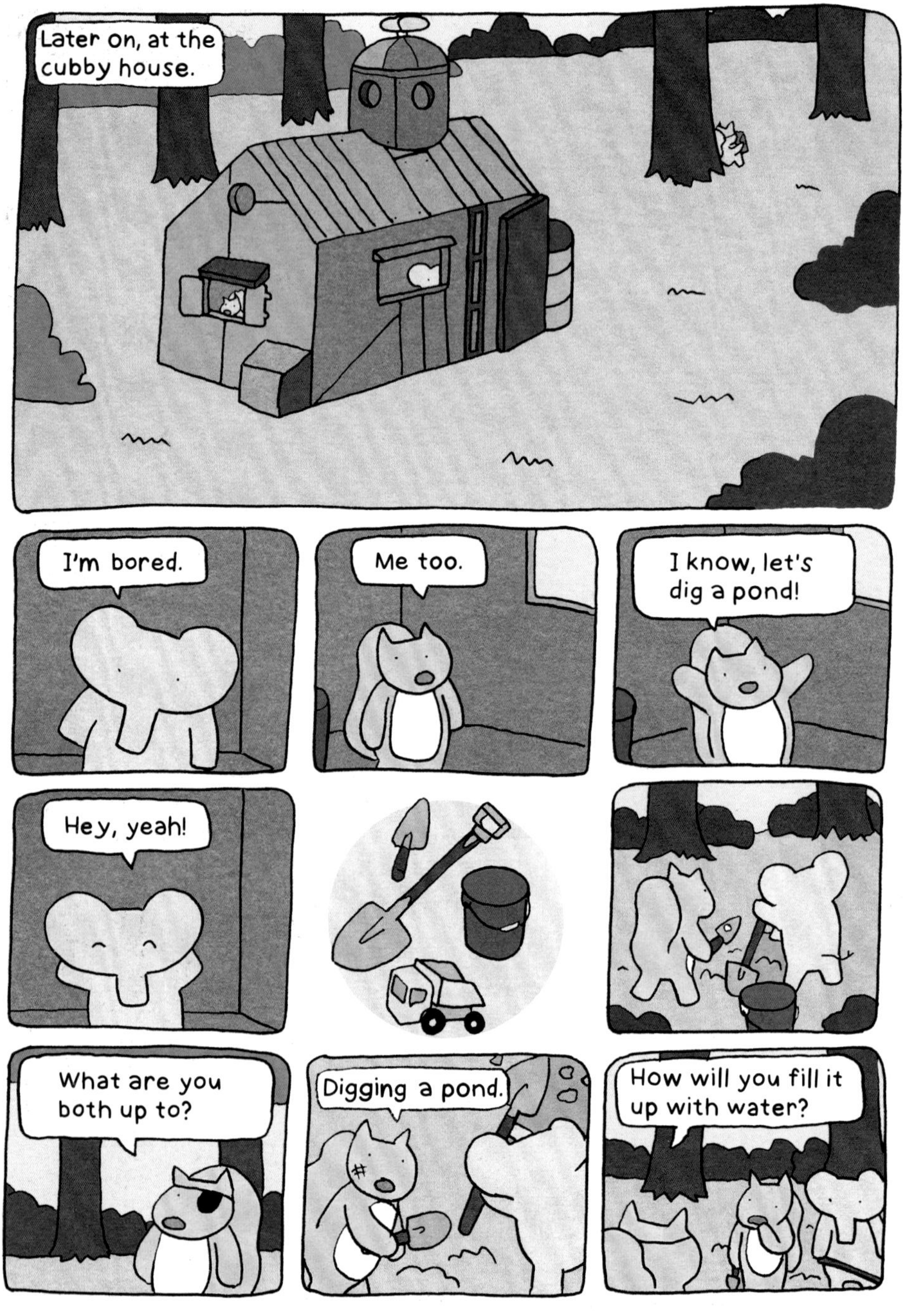
Later on, at the cubby house.
I'm bored.
Me too.
I know, let's dig a pond!
Hey, yeah!
What are you both up to?
Digging a pond.
How will you fill it up with water?

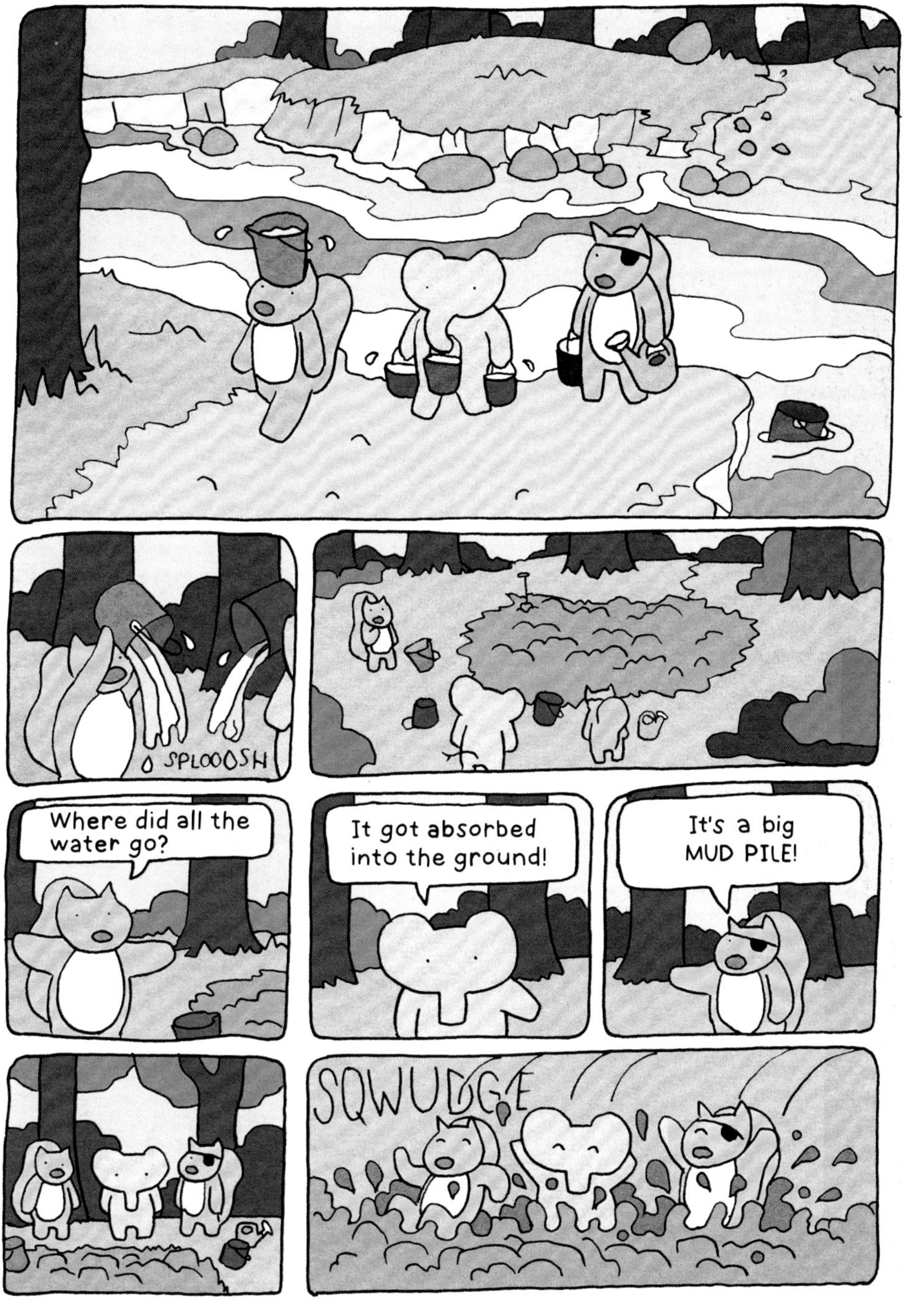
SPLOOOSH
Where did all the water go?
It got absorbed into the ground!
It's a big MUD PILE!
SQWUDGE

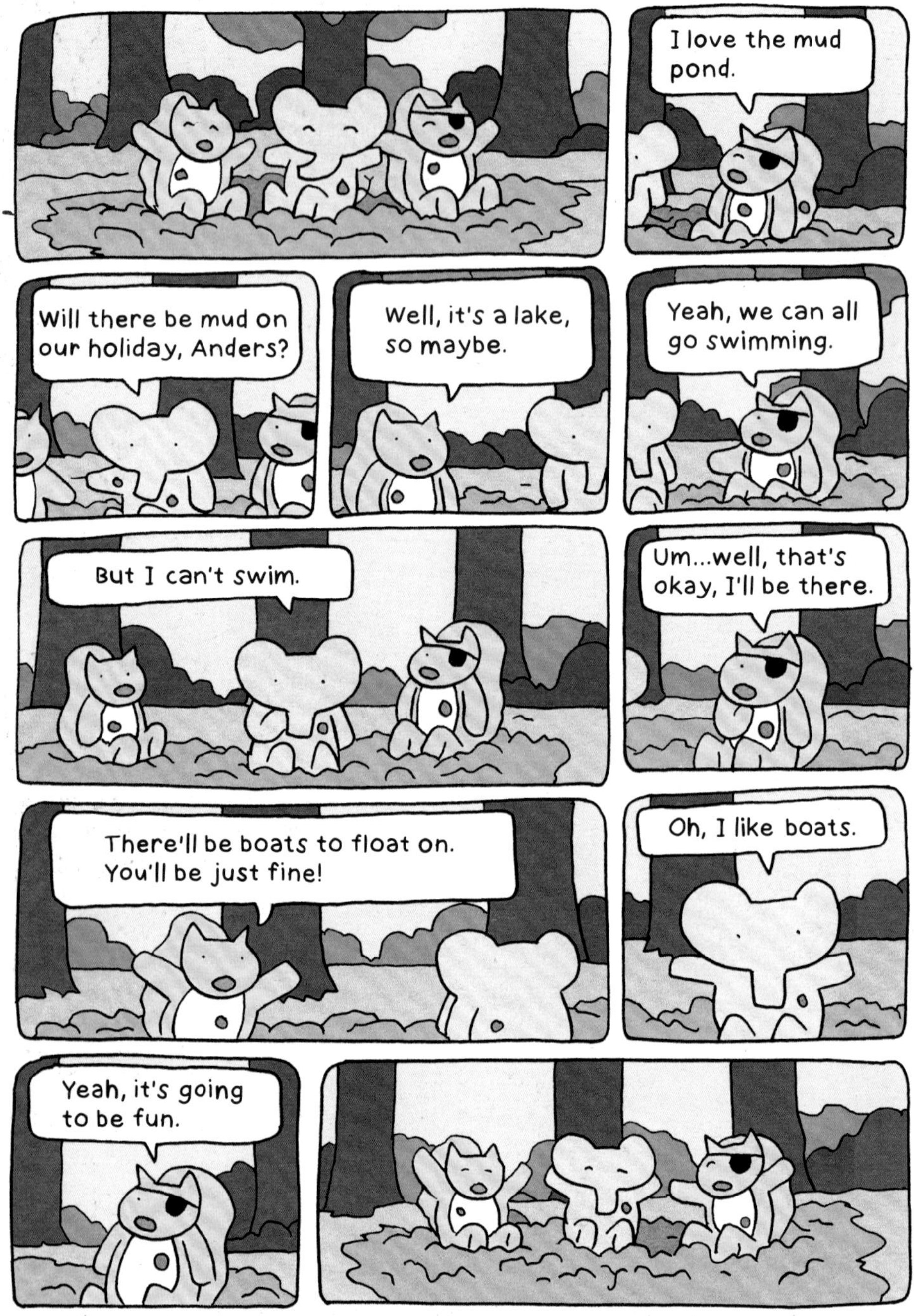
I love the mud pond.
Will there be mud on our holiday, Anders?
Well, it's a lake, so maybe.
Yeah, we can all go swimming.
But I can't swim.
Um...well, that's okay, I'll be there.
There'll be boats to float on. You'll be just fine!
Oh, I like boats.
Yeah, it's going to be fun.

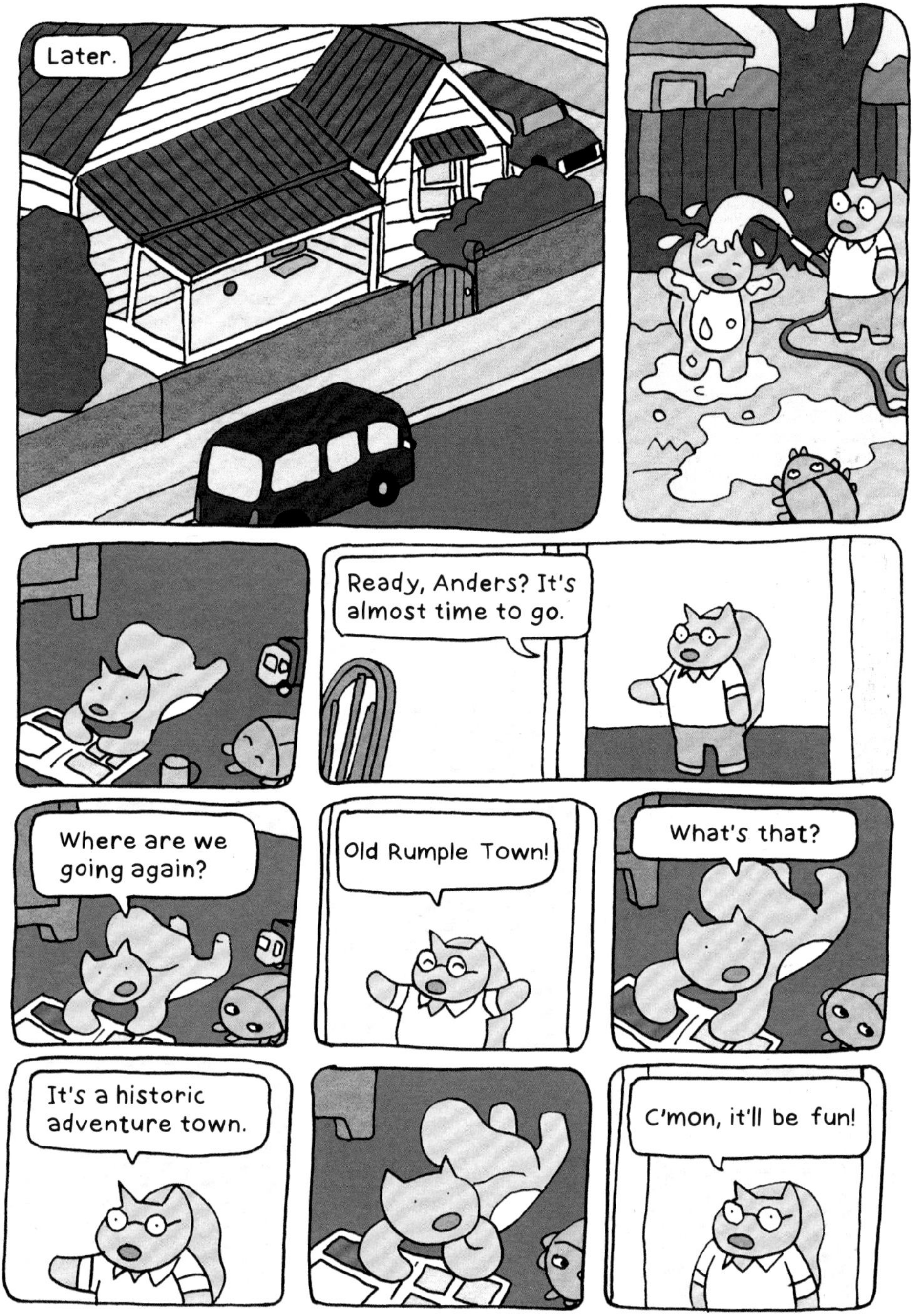
Later.
Ready, Anders? It's almost time to go.
Where are we going again?
Old Rumple Town!
What's that?
It's a historic adventure town.
C'mon, it'll be fun!

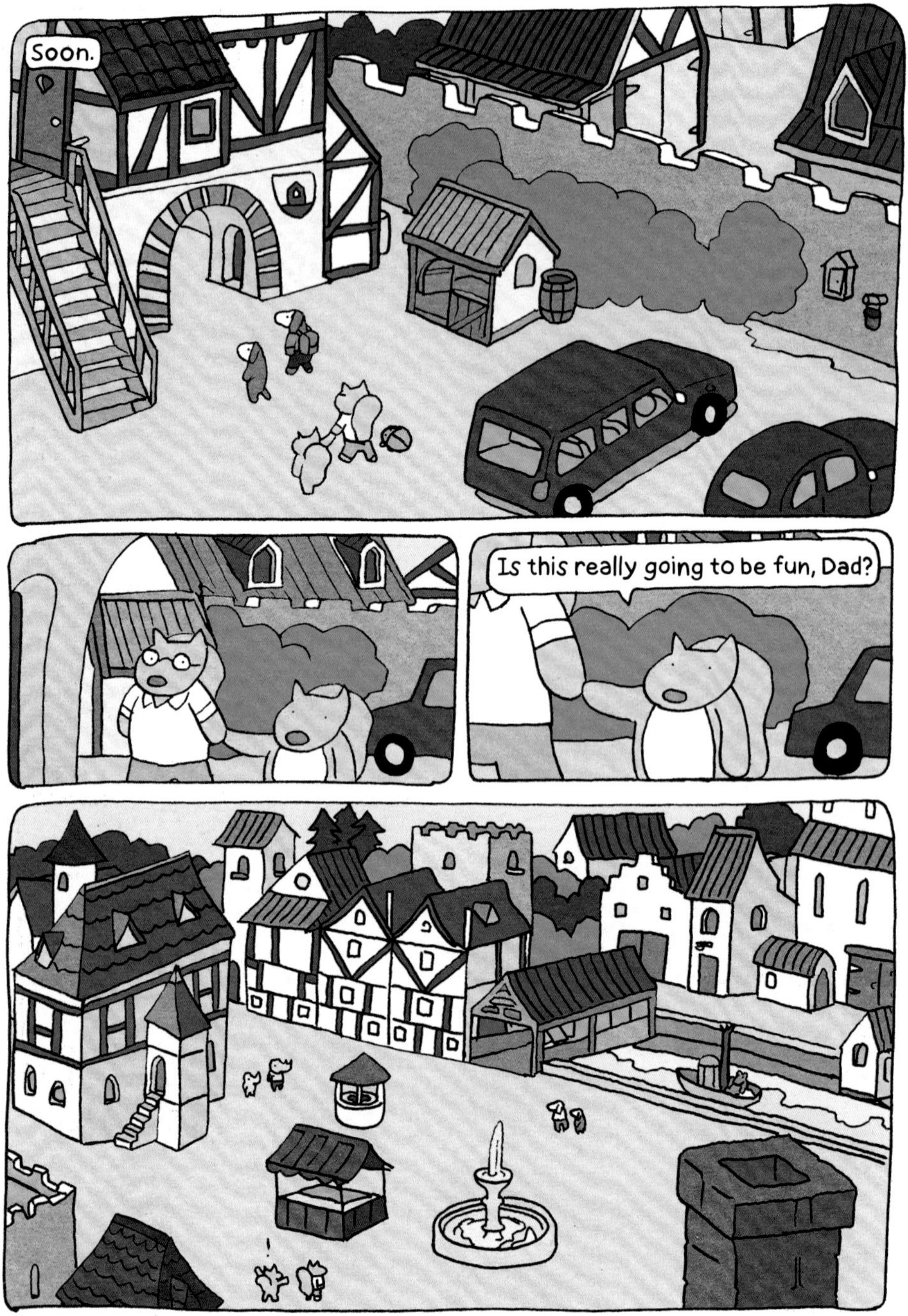
Soon.
Is this really going to be fun, Dad?

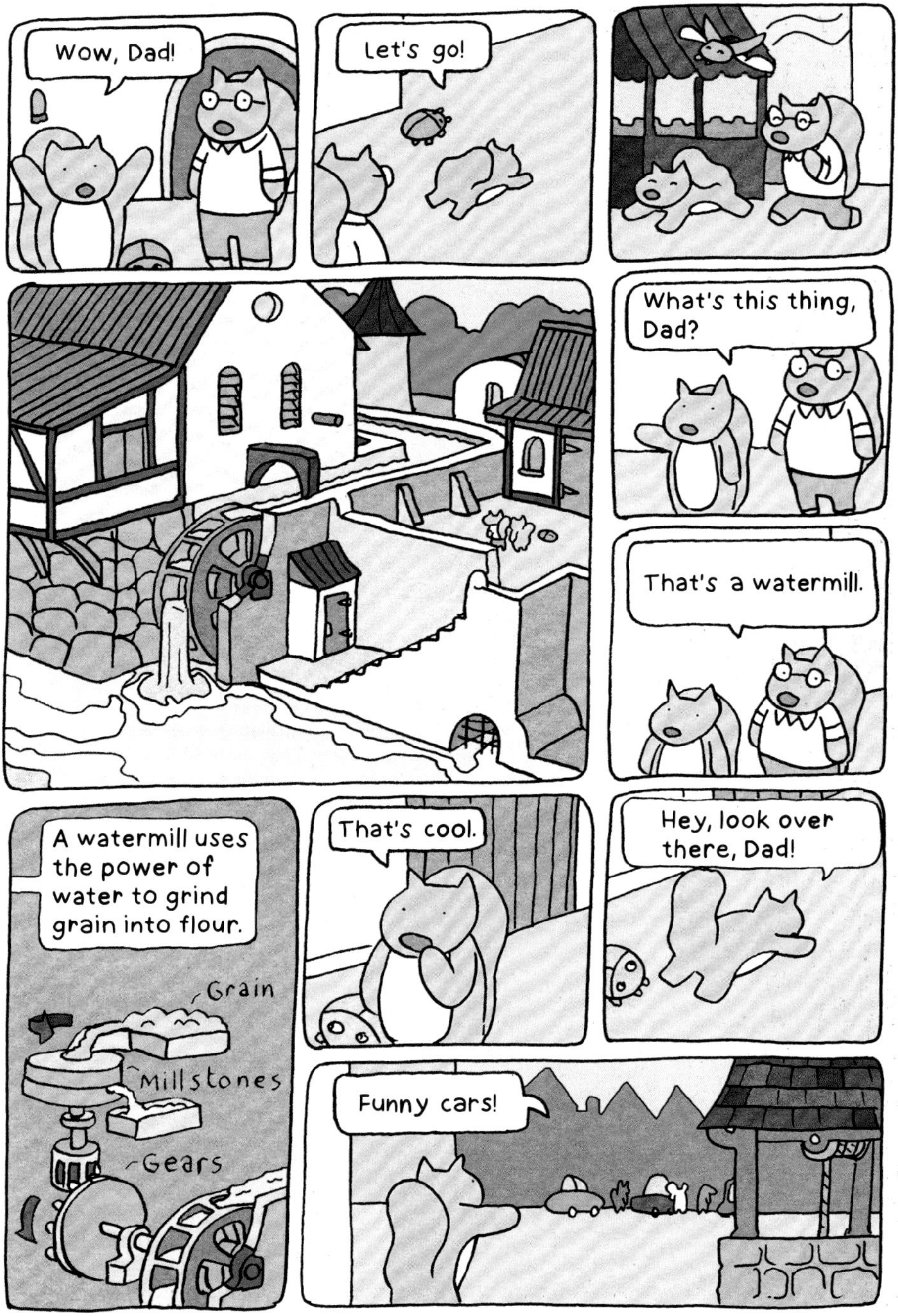
Wow, Dad!
Let's go!
What's this thing, Dad?
That's a watermill.
A watermill uses the power of water to grind grain into flour.
Grain
Millstones
Gears
That's cool.
Hey, look over there, Dad!
Funny cars!

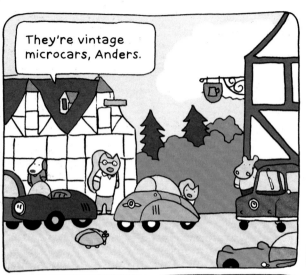

They're vintage microcars, Anders.

Ha! Tiny cars!

Hi, Anders.

Hi!

Hey, look Anders, that kid has a little friend like Skip.

Woah!

I'm going to say hi.

Hello, I'm Anders.

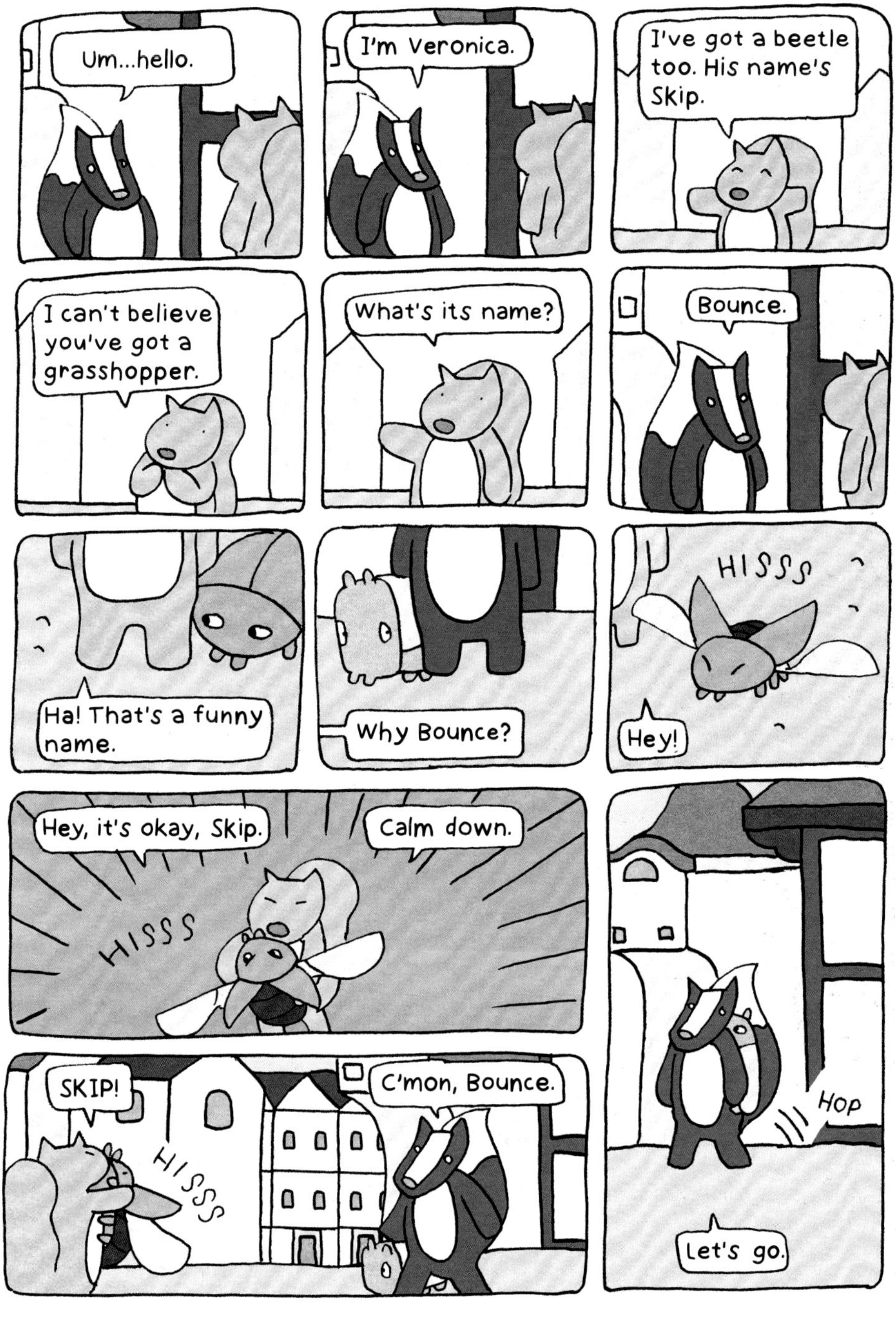
Um...hello.
I'm Veronica.
I've got a beetle too. His name's Skip.
I can't believe you've got a grasshopper.
What's its name?
Bounce.
Ha! That's a funny name.
Why Bounce?
HISSS
Hey!
Hey, it's okay, Skip.
Calm down.
HISSS
SKIP!
HISSS
C'mon, Bounce.
HOP
Let's go.

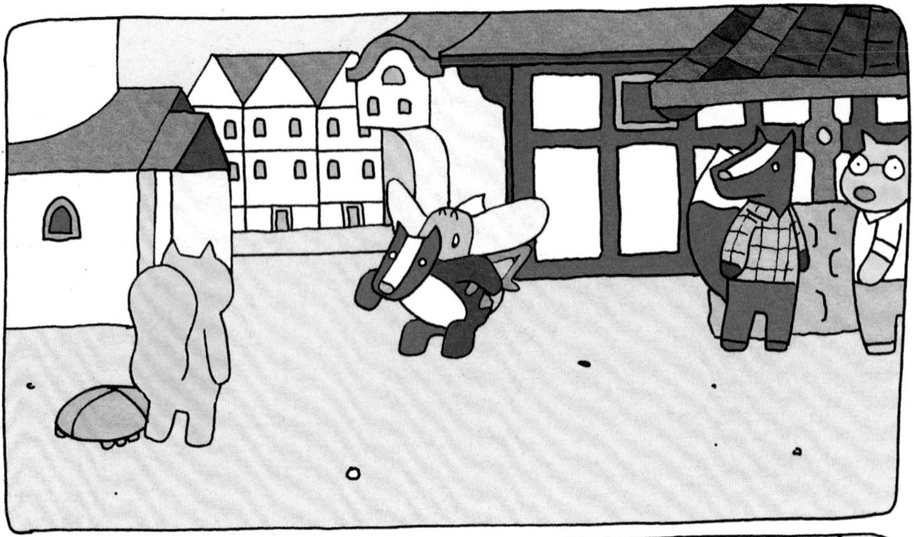

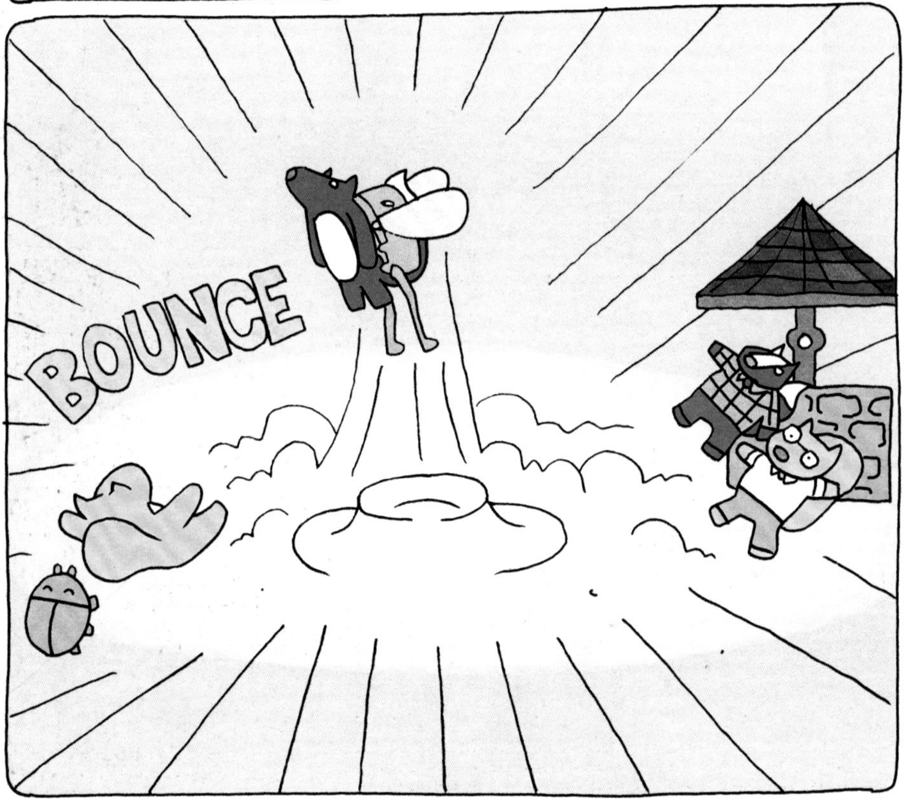
BOUNCE

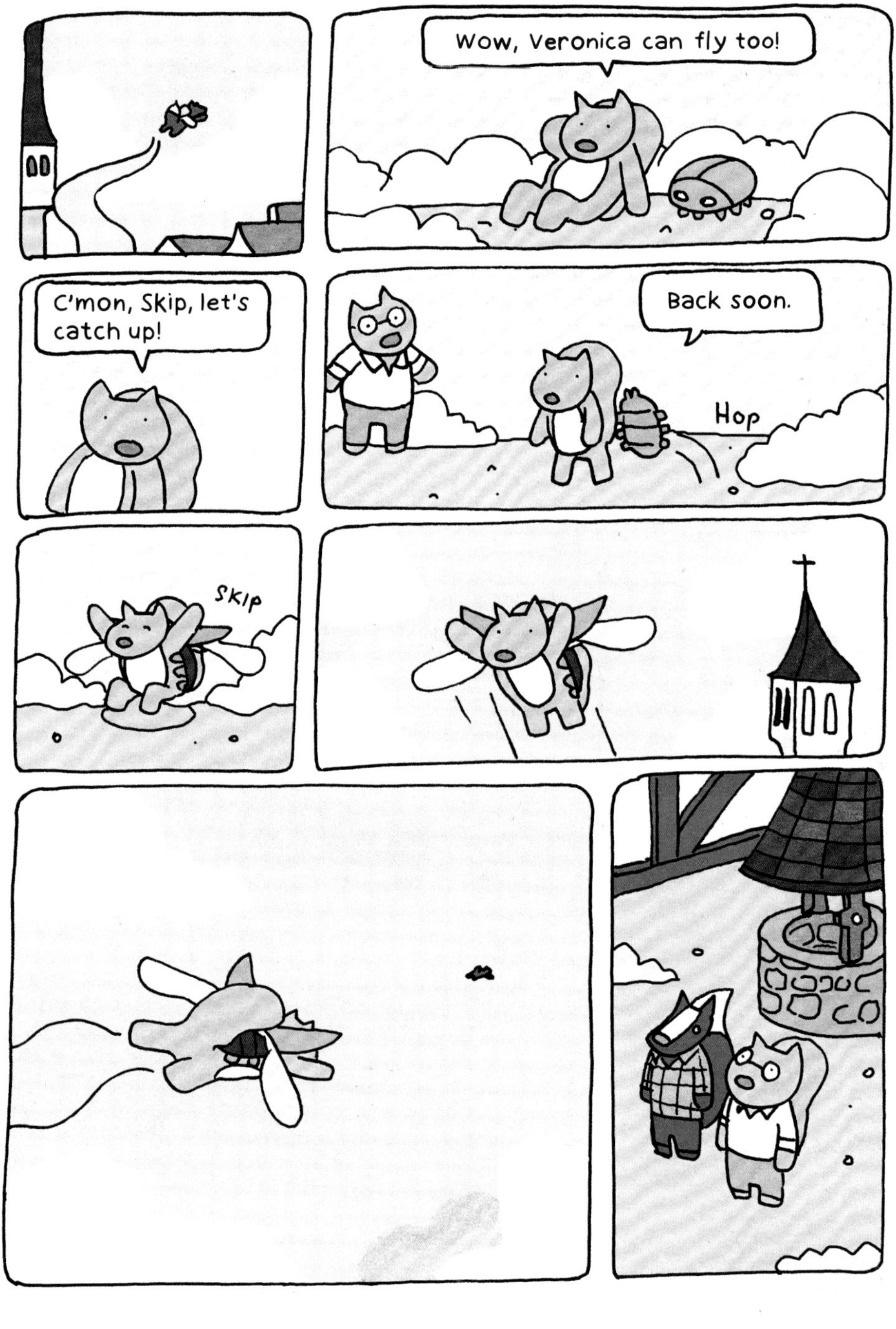
Wow, Veronica can fly too!
C'mon, Skip, let's catch up!
Back soon.
Hop
SKIP

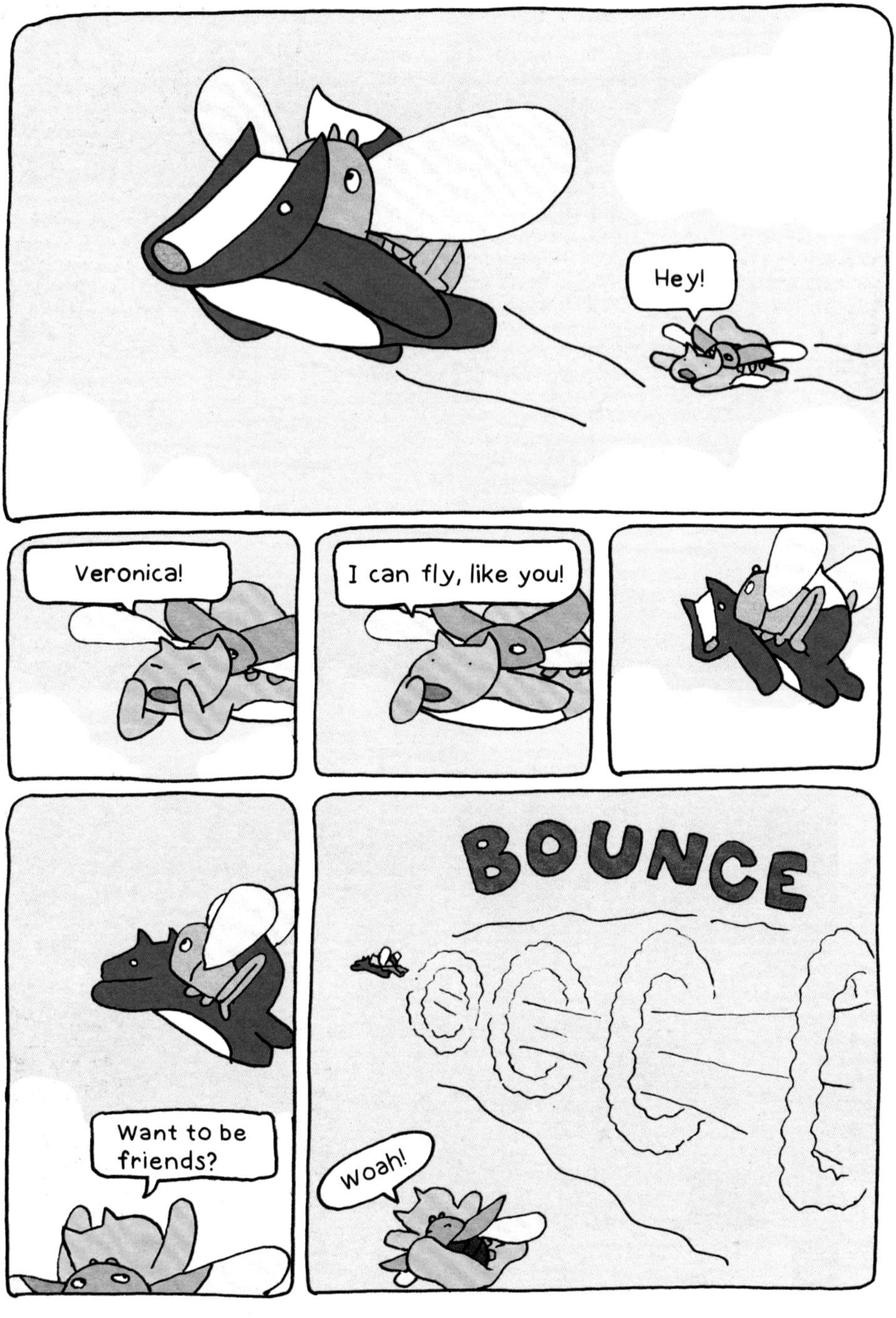
Hey!
Veronica!
I can fly, like you!
Want to be friends?
BOUNCE
Woah!

Bounce must make some kind of shock wave.

Let's go, Skip.

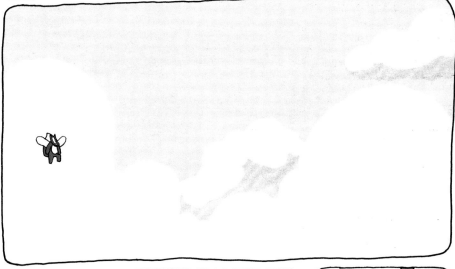

Are you okay, Anders?

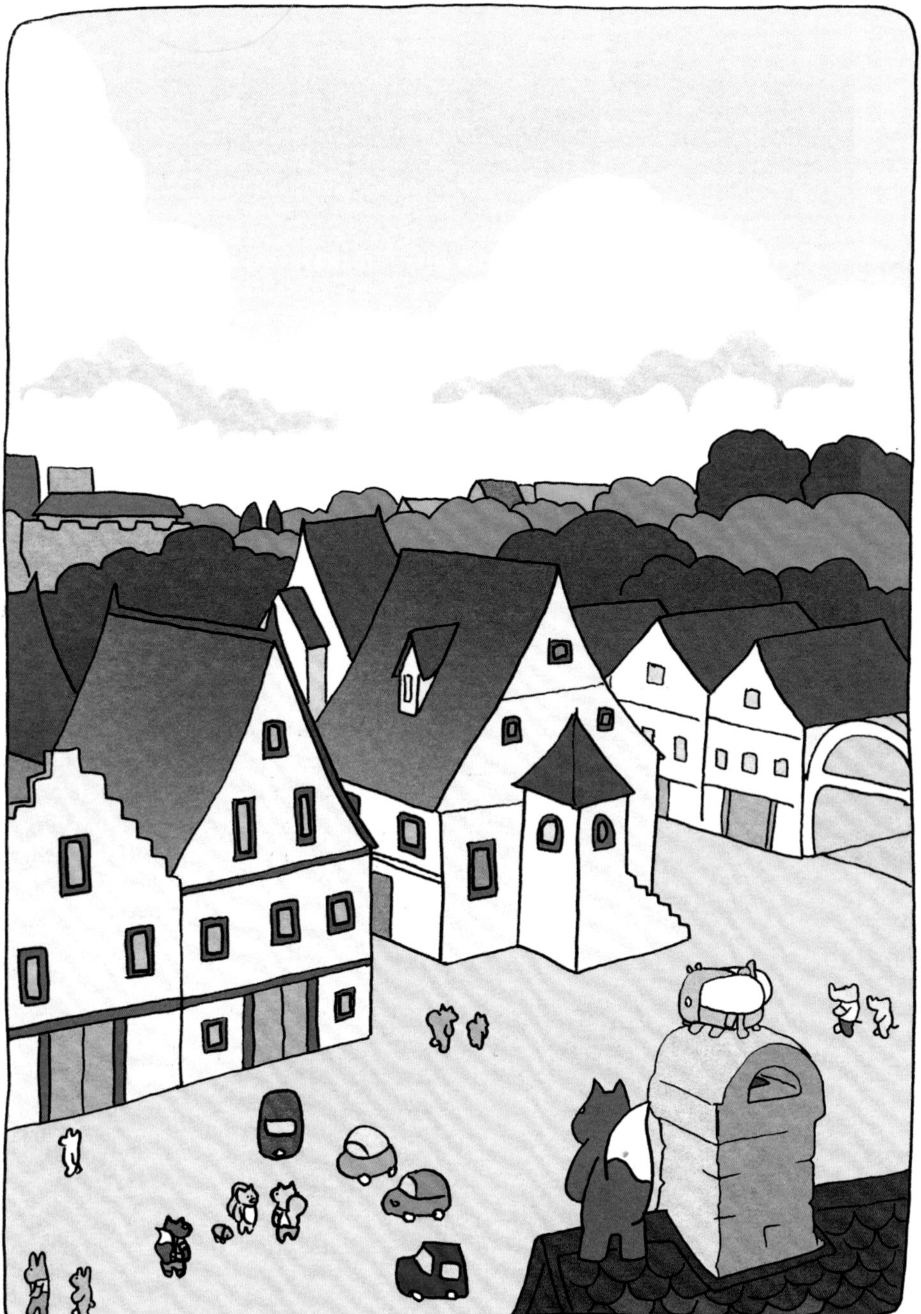

Chapter 4

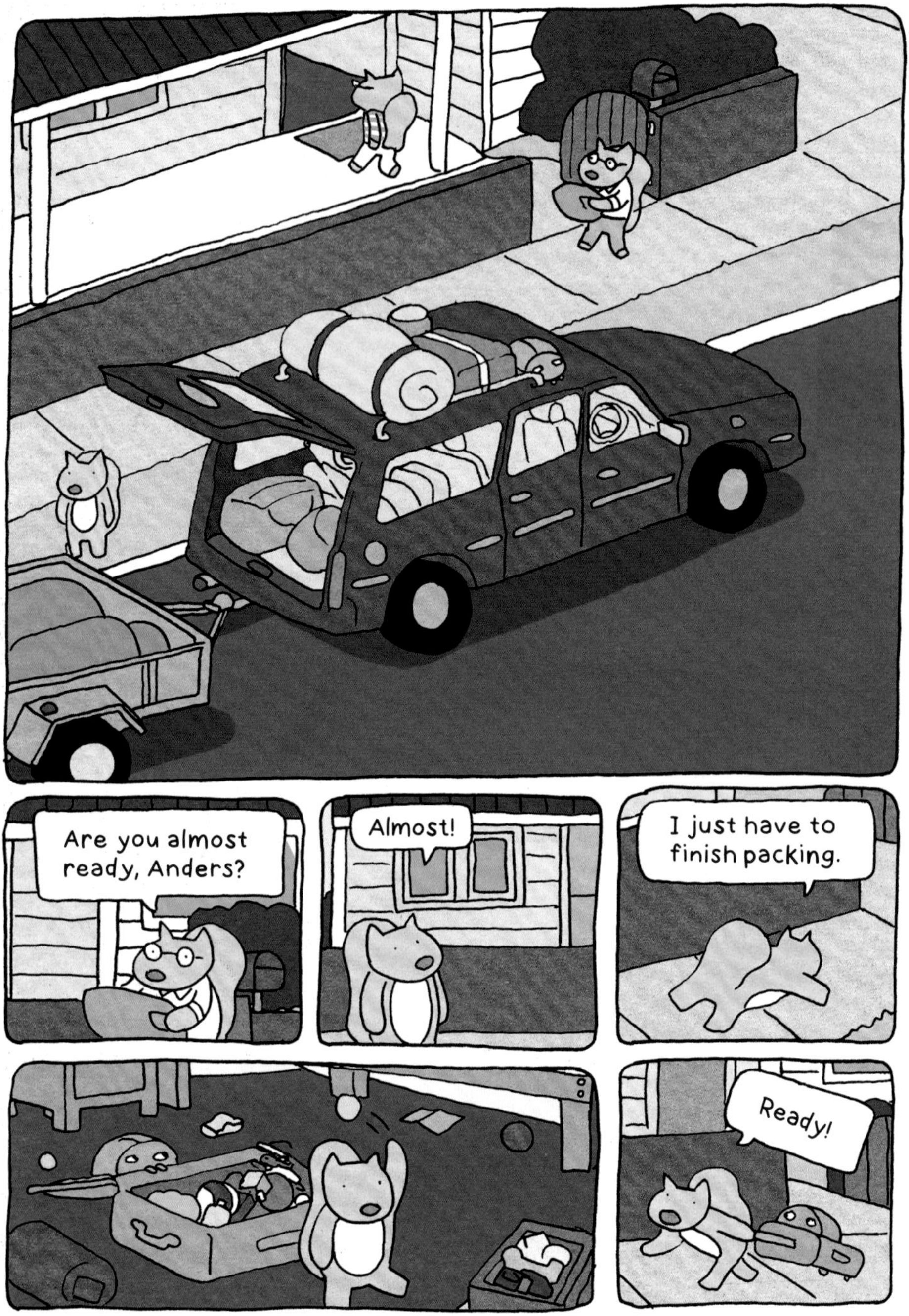
Are you almost ready, Anders?
Almost!
I just have to finish packing.
Ready!

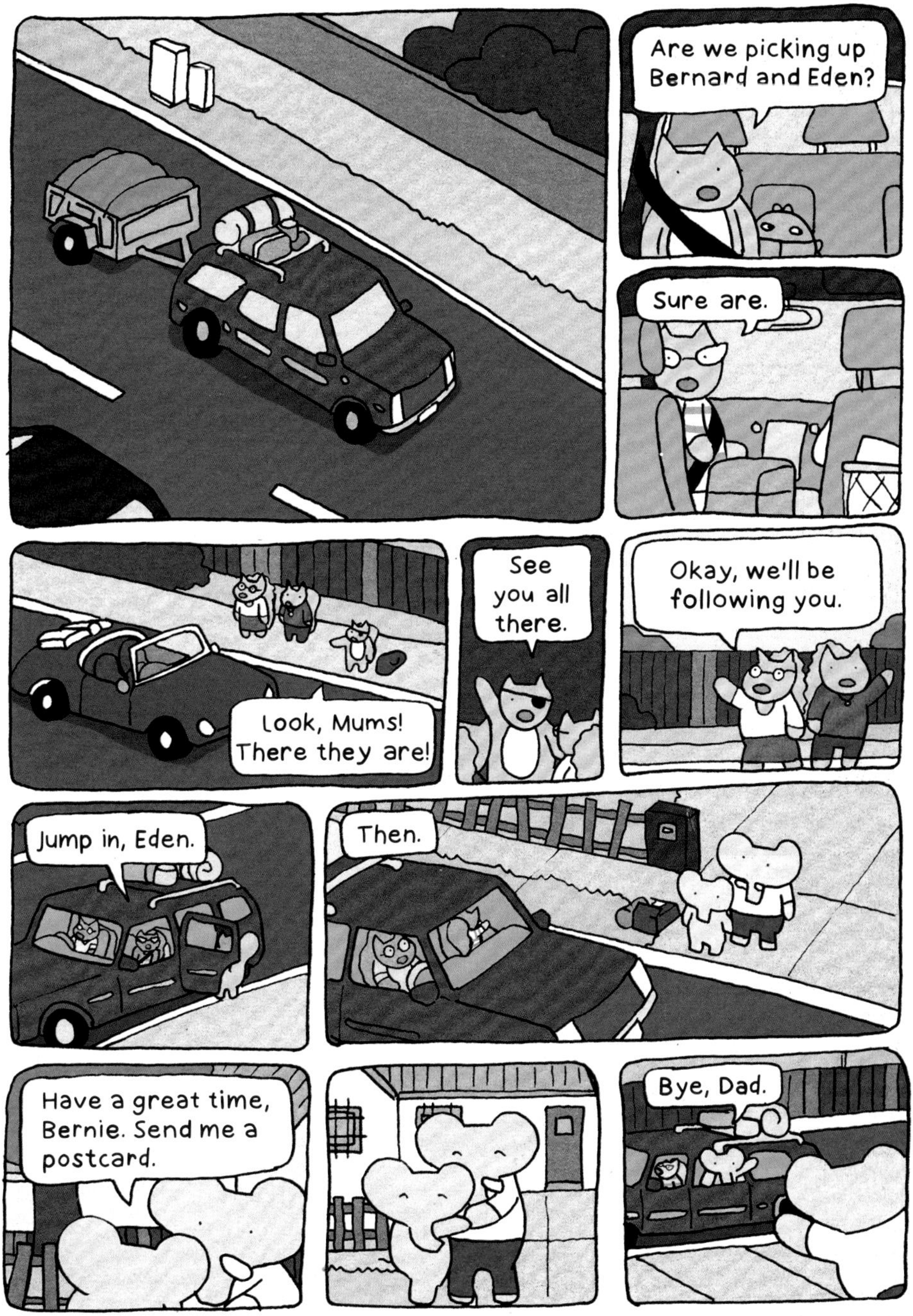
Are we picking up Bernard and Eden?
Sure are.
Look, Mums! There they are!
See you all there.
Okay, we'll be following you.
Jump in, Eden.
Then.
Have a great time, Bernie. Send me a postcard.
Bye, Dad.

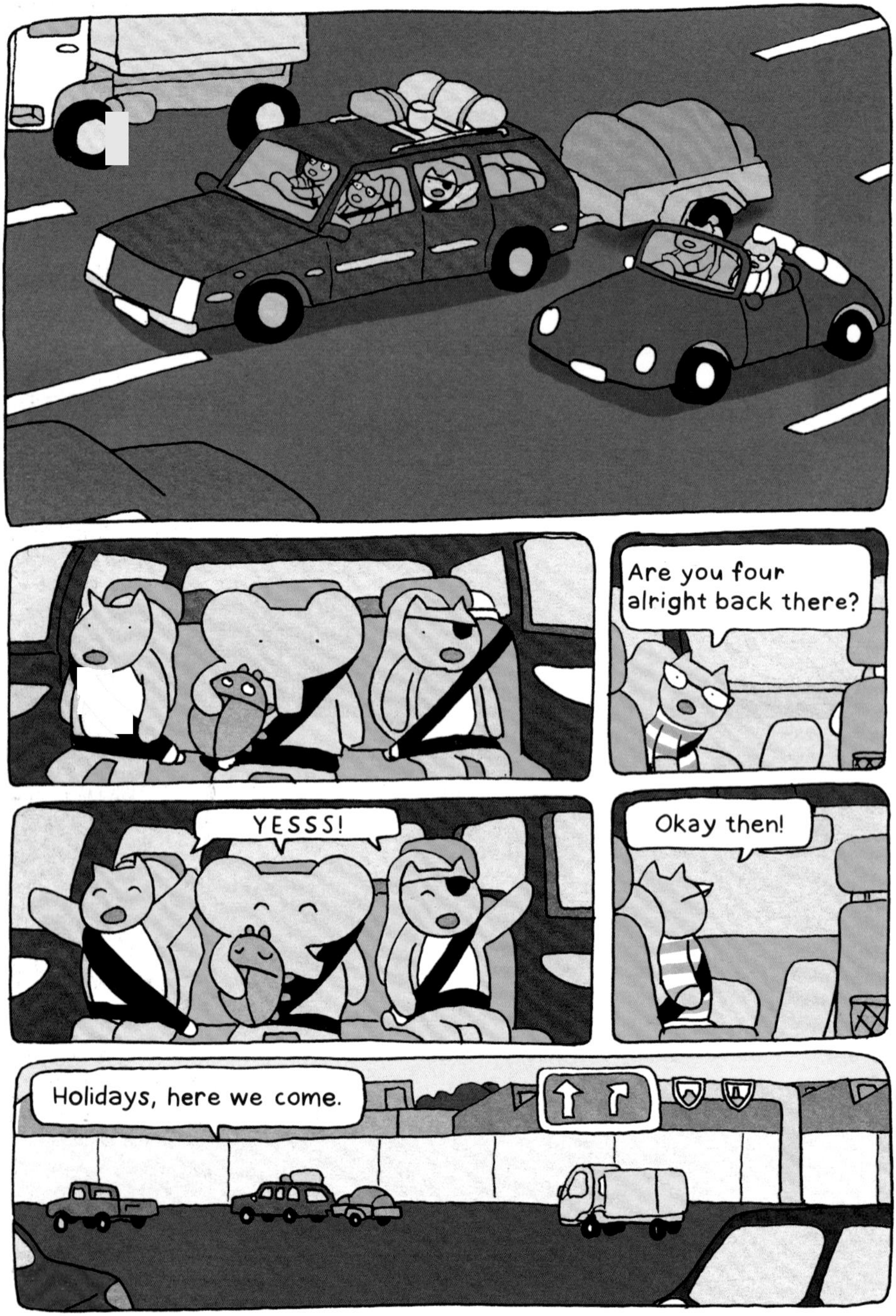
Are you four alright back there?
YESSS!
Okay then!
Holidays, here we come.

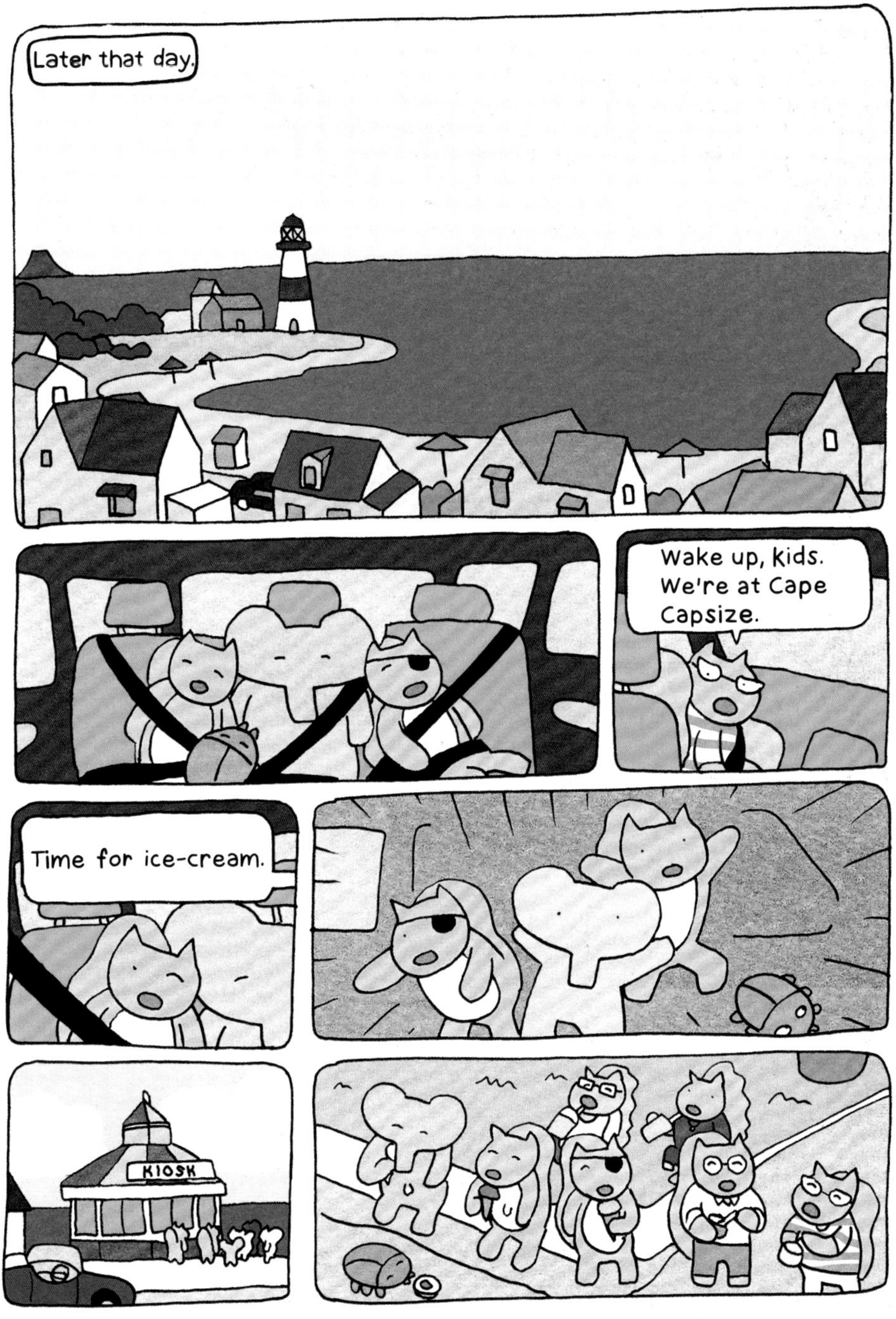
Later that day.
Wake up, kids.
We're at Cape
Capsize.
Time for ice-cream.
KIOSK

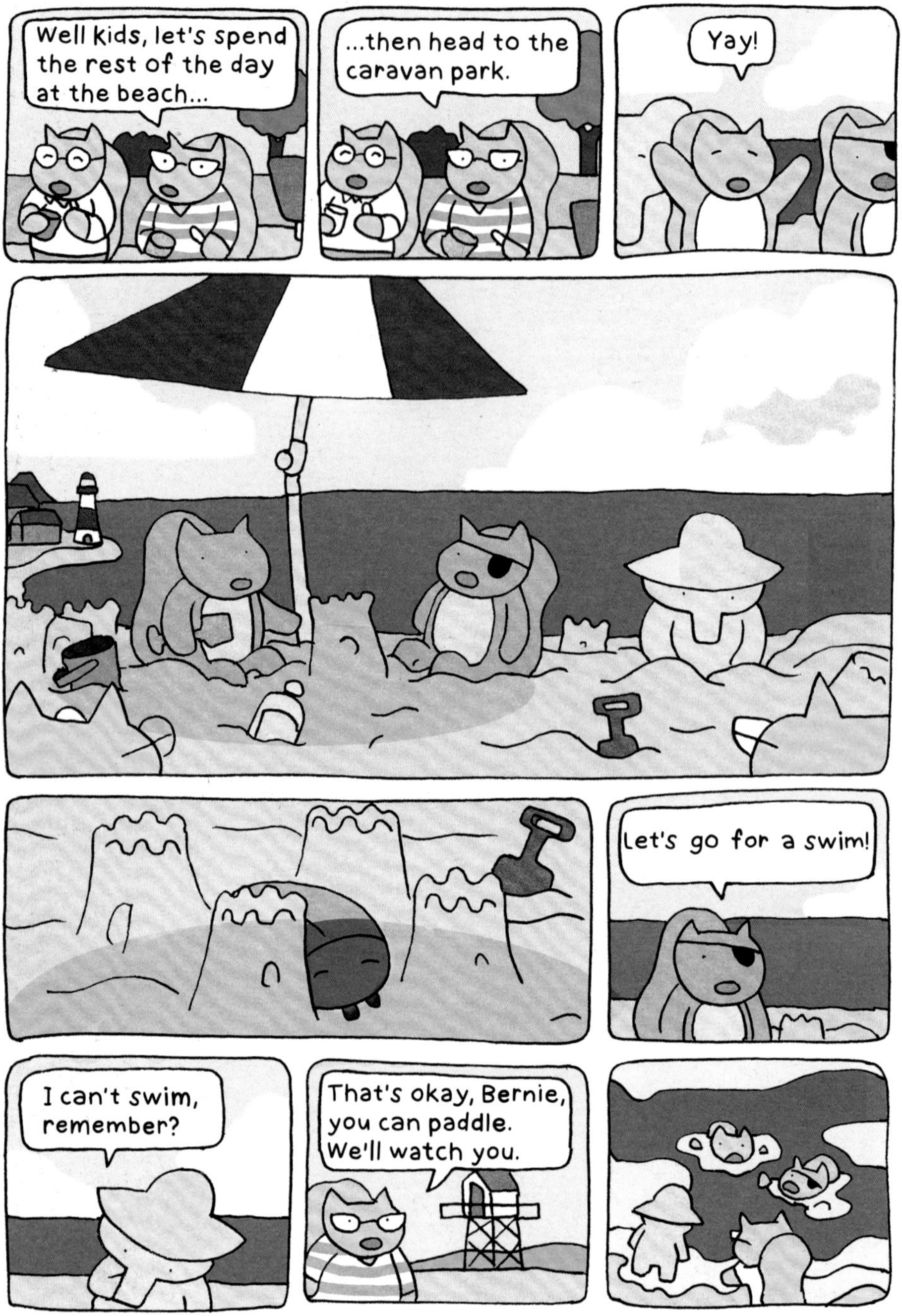
Well kids, let's spend the rest of the day at the beach...
...then head to the caravan park.
Yay!
Let's go for a swim!
I can't swim, remember?
That's okay, Bernie, you can paddle. We'll watch you.

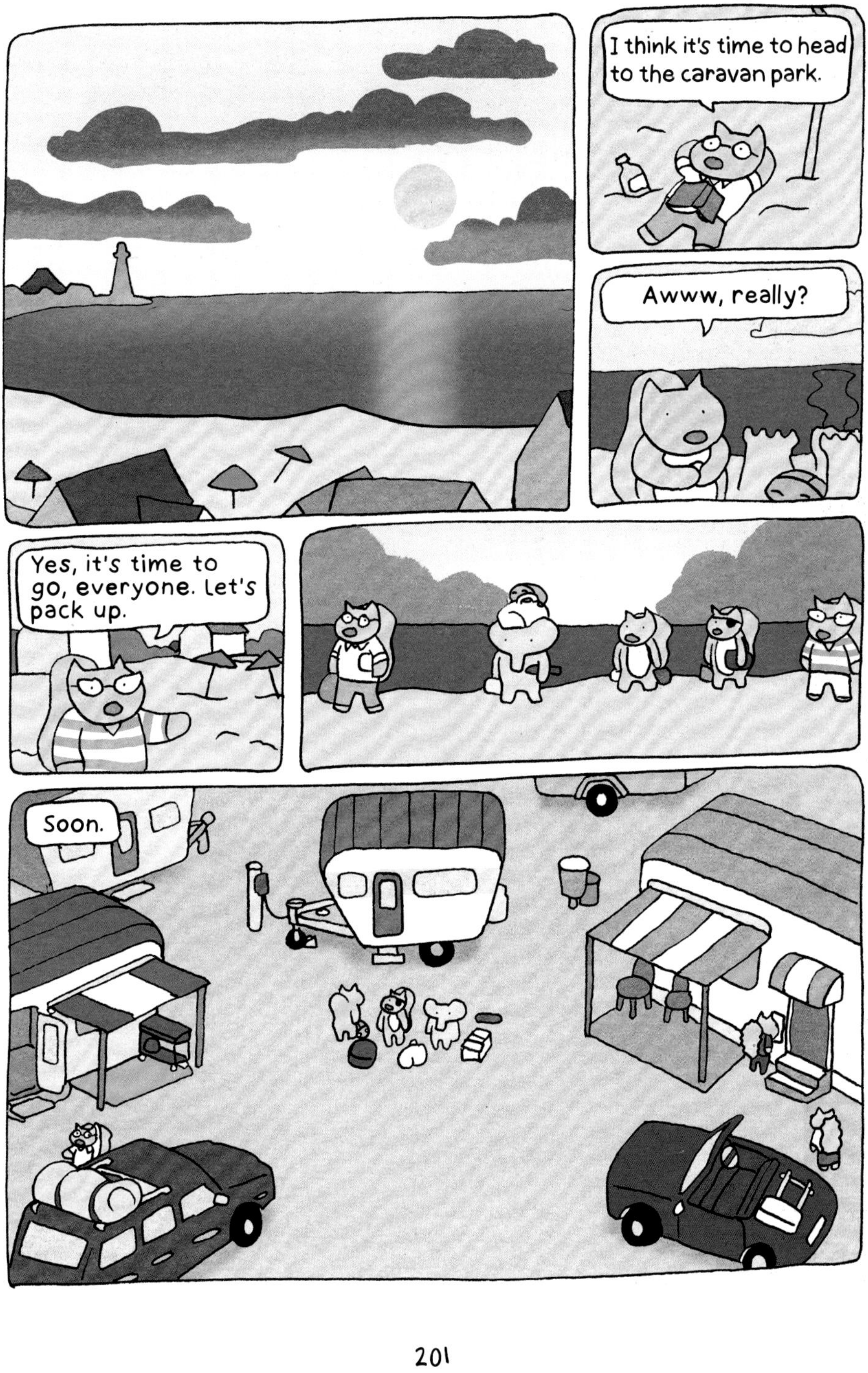
I think it's time to head to the caravan park.
Awww, really?
Yes, it's time to go, everyone. Let's pack up.
Soon.

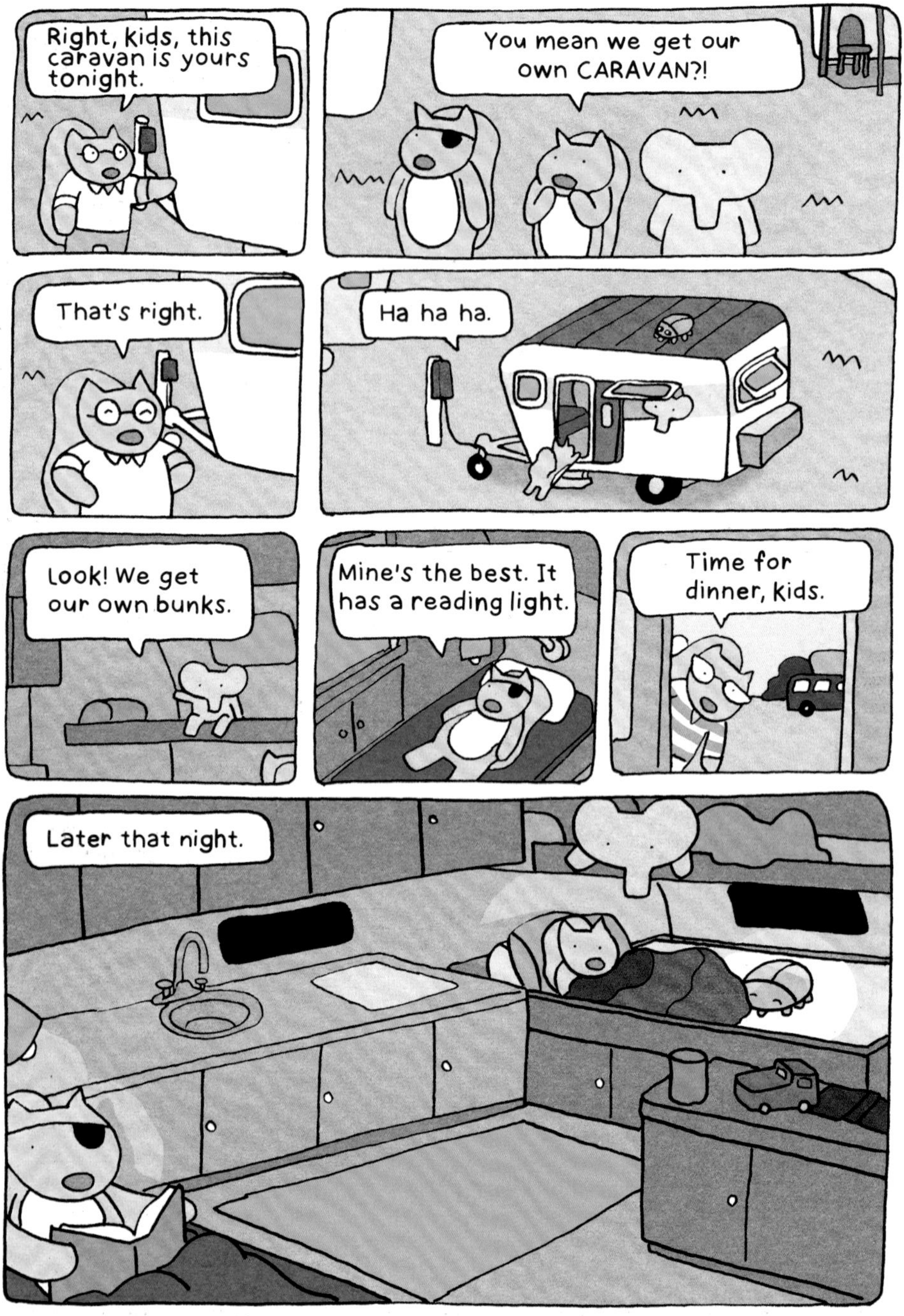
Right, kids, this caravan is yours tonight.
You mean we get our own CARAVAN?!
That's right.
Ha ha ha.
Look! We get our own bunks.
Mine's the best. It has a reading light.
Time for dinner, kids.
Later that night.

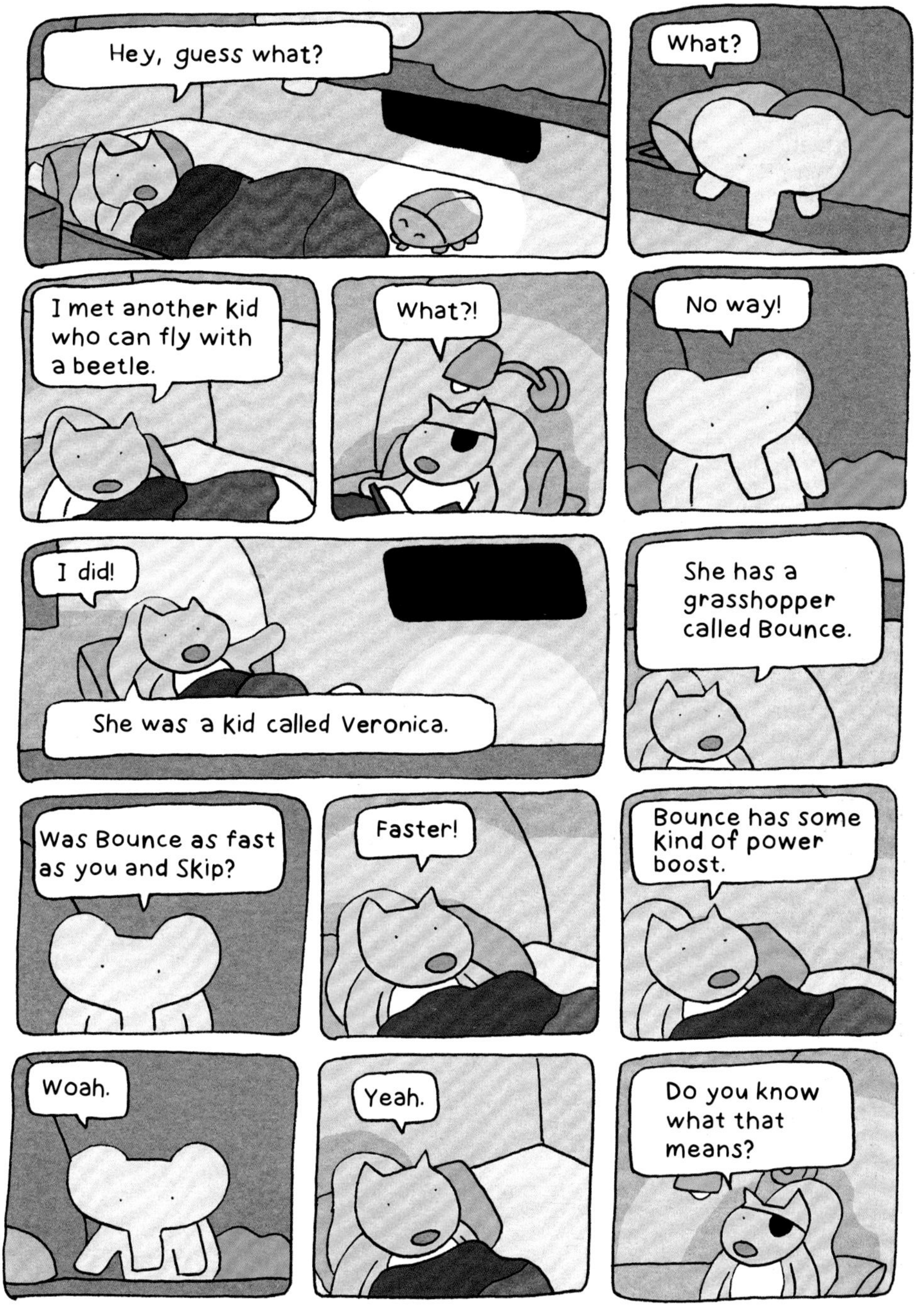
Hey, guess what?
What?
I met another kid who can fly with a beetle.
What?!
No way!
I did!
She was a kid called Veronica.
She has a grasshopper called Bounce.
Was Bounce as fast as you and Skip?
Faster!
Bounce has some kind of power boost.
Woah.
Yeah.
Do you know what that means?

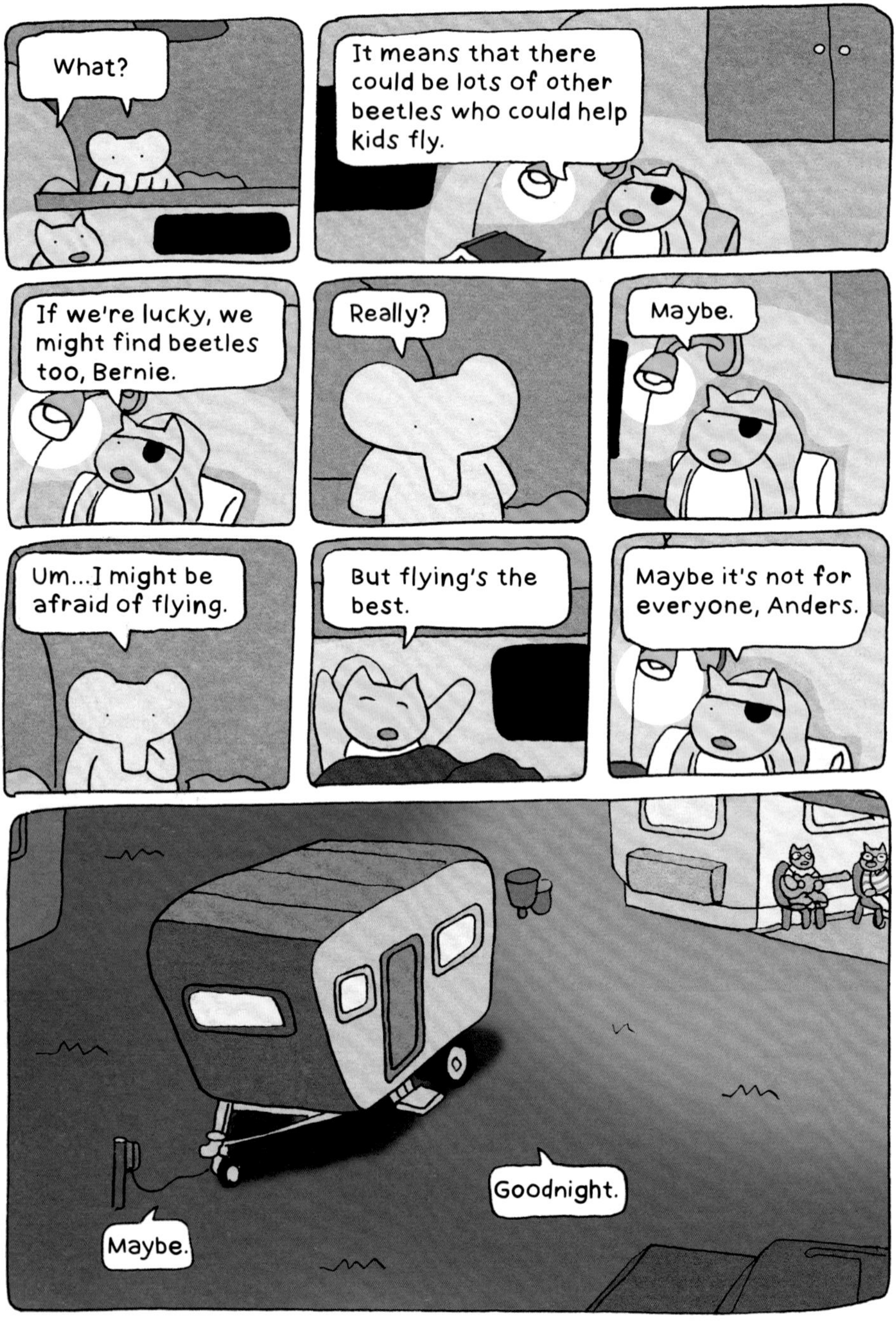
What?
It means that there could be lots of other beetles who could help kids fly.
If we're lucky, we might find beetles too, Bernie.
Really?
Maybe.
Um...I might be afraid of flying.
But flying's the best.
Maybe it's not for everyone, Anders.
Maybe.
Goodnight.

Chapter 5

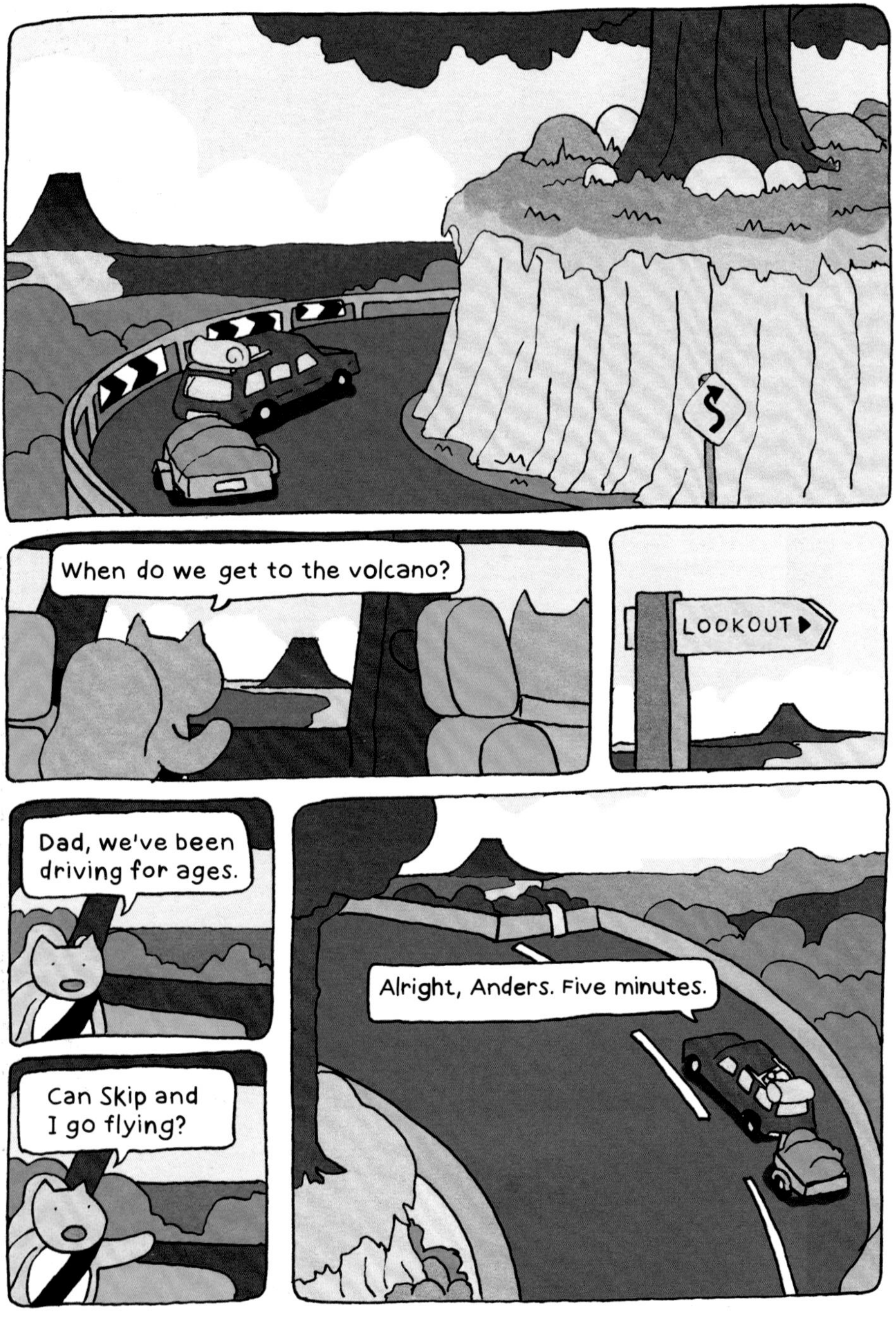
When do we get to the volcano?
LOOKOUT
Dad, we've been driving for ages.
Can Skip and I go flying?
Alright, Anders. Five minutes.

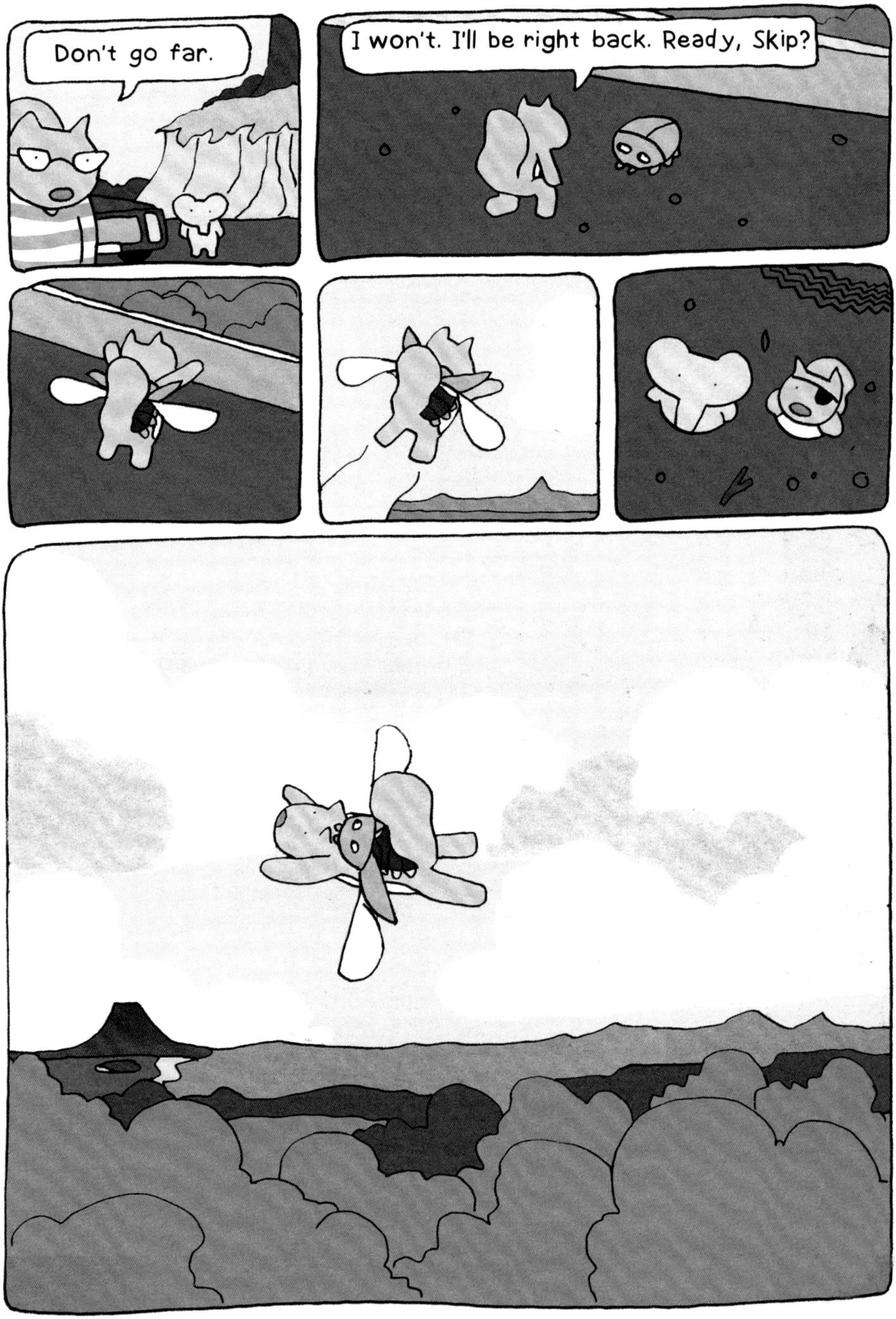
Don't go far.
I won't. I'll be right back. Ready, Skip?

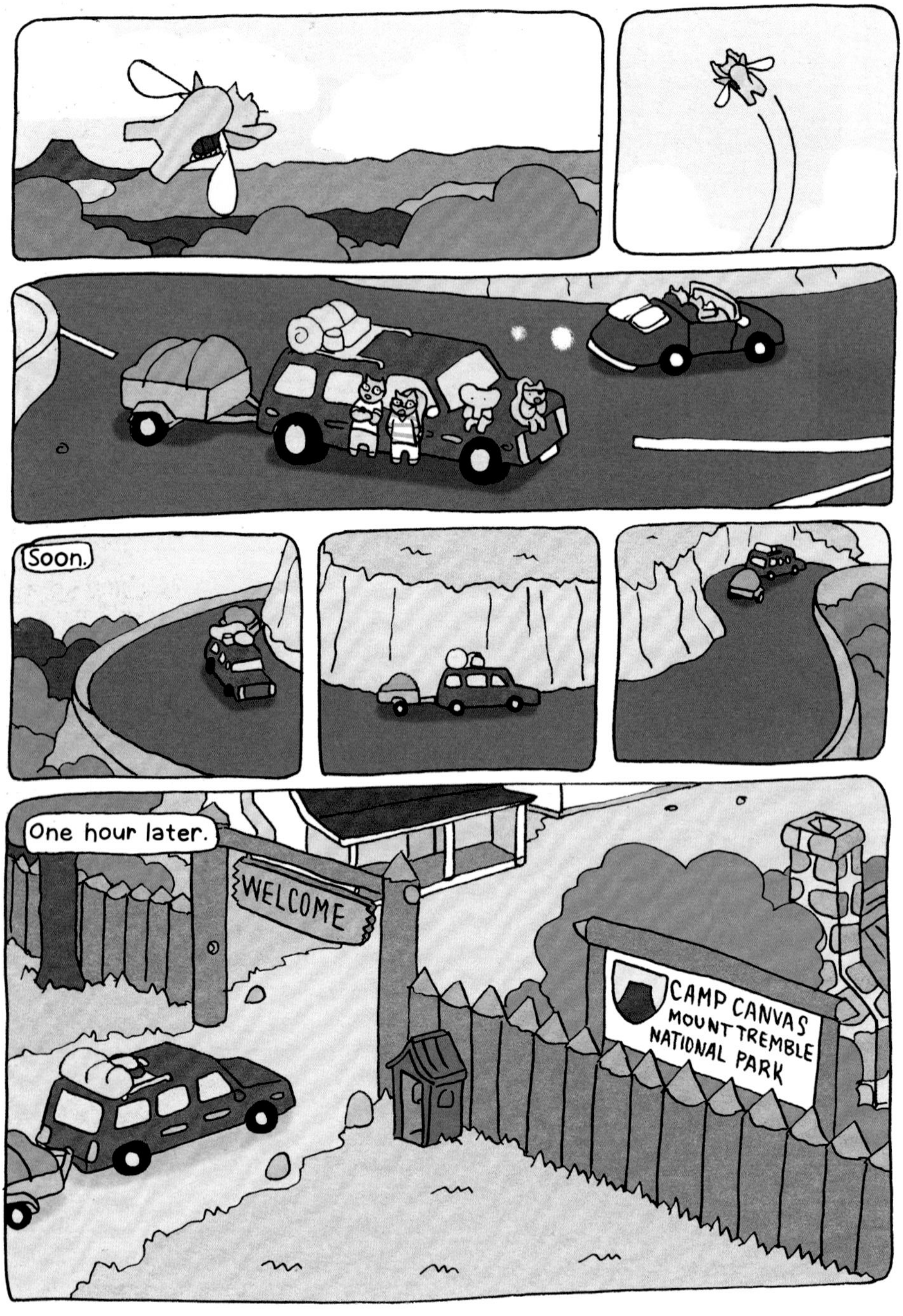
Soon.
One hour later.
WELCOME
CAMP CANVAS
MOUNT TREMBLE
NATIONAL PARK

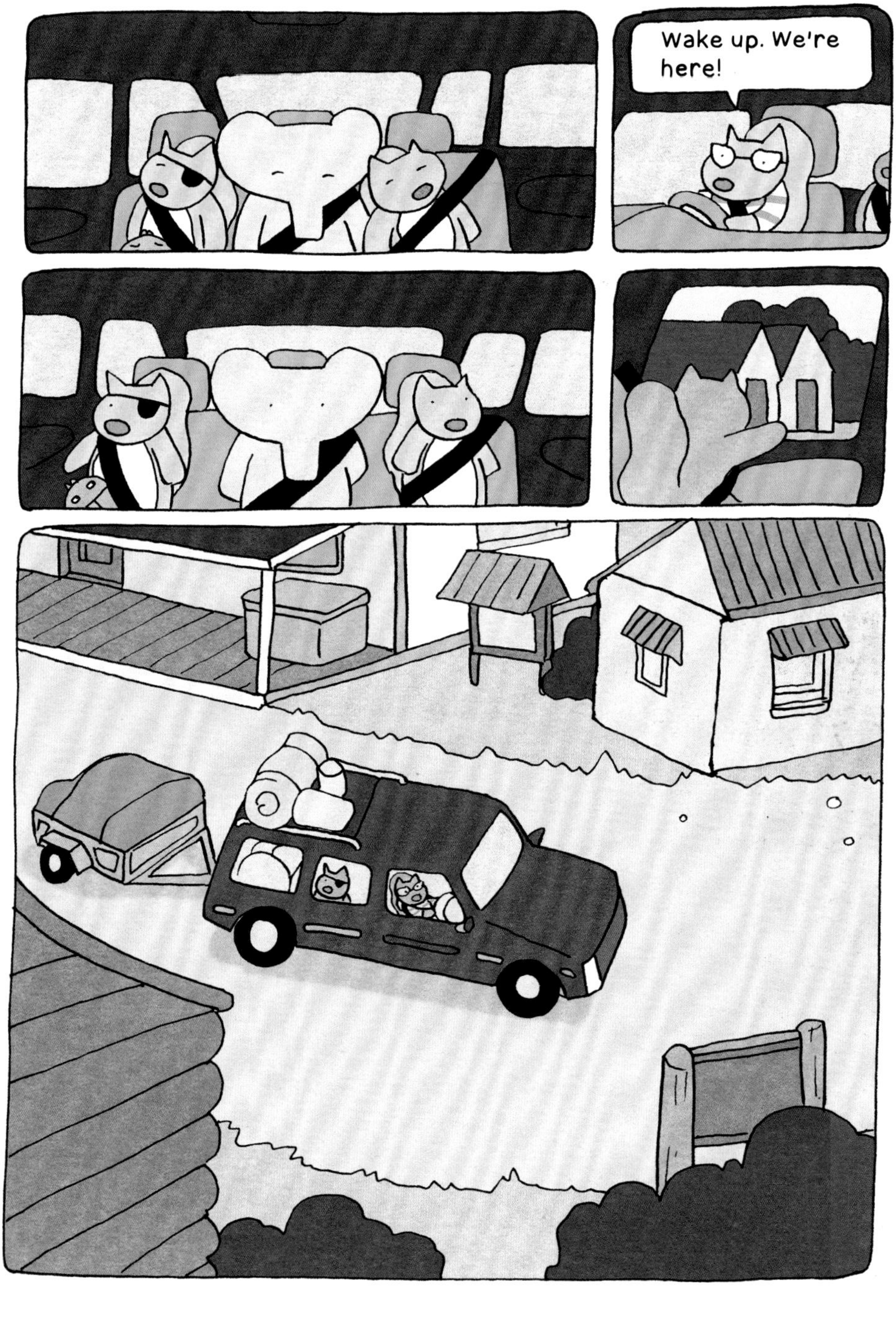
Wake up. We're here!

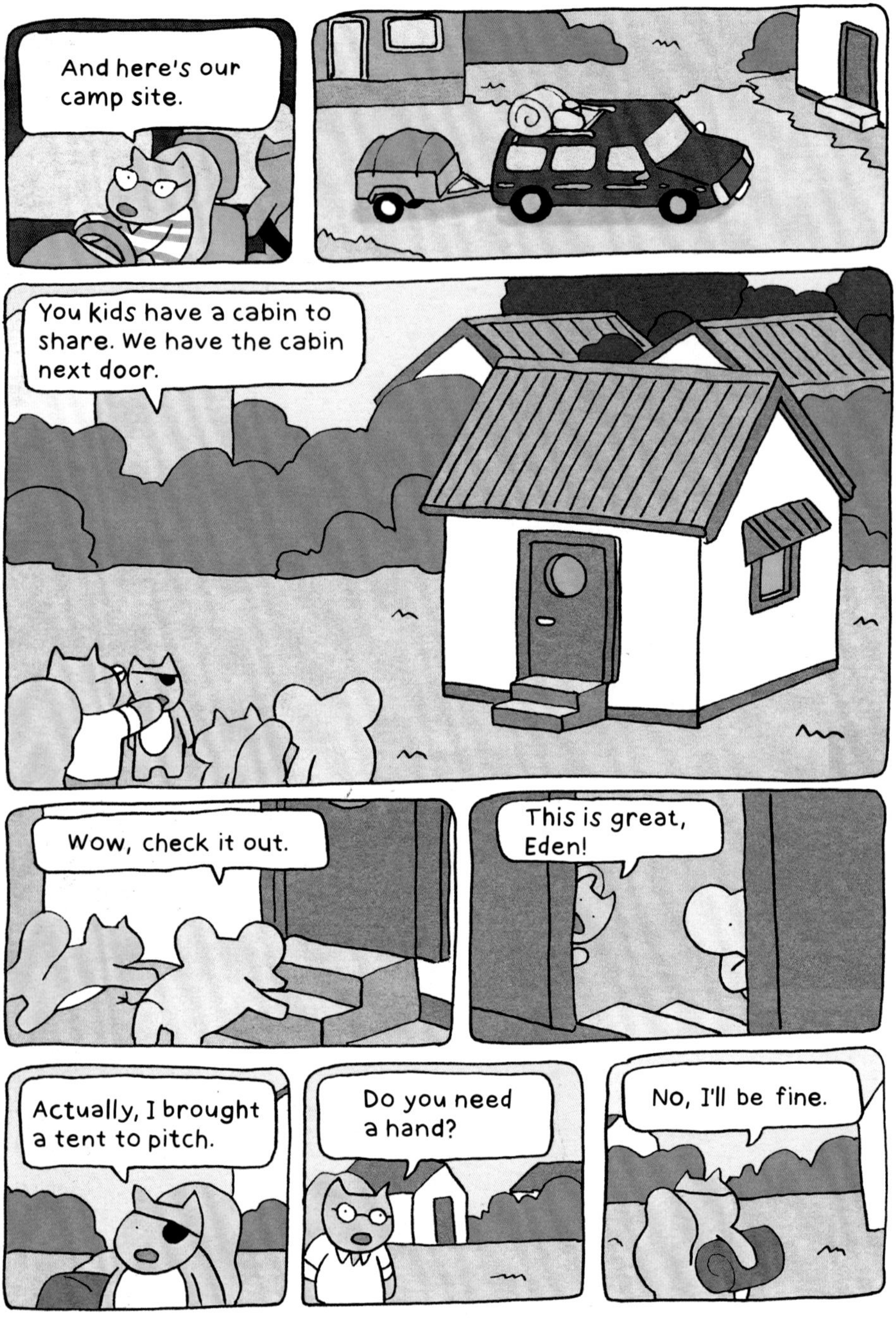
And here's our camp site.
You kids have a cabin to share. We have the cabin next door.
Wow, check it out.
This is great, Eden!
Actually, I brought a tent to pitch.
Do you need a hand?
No, I'll be fine.

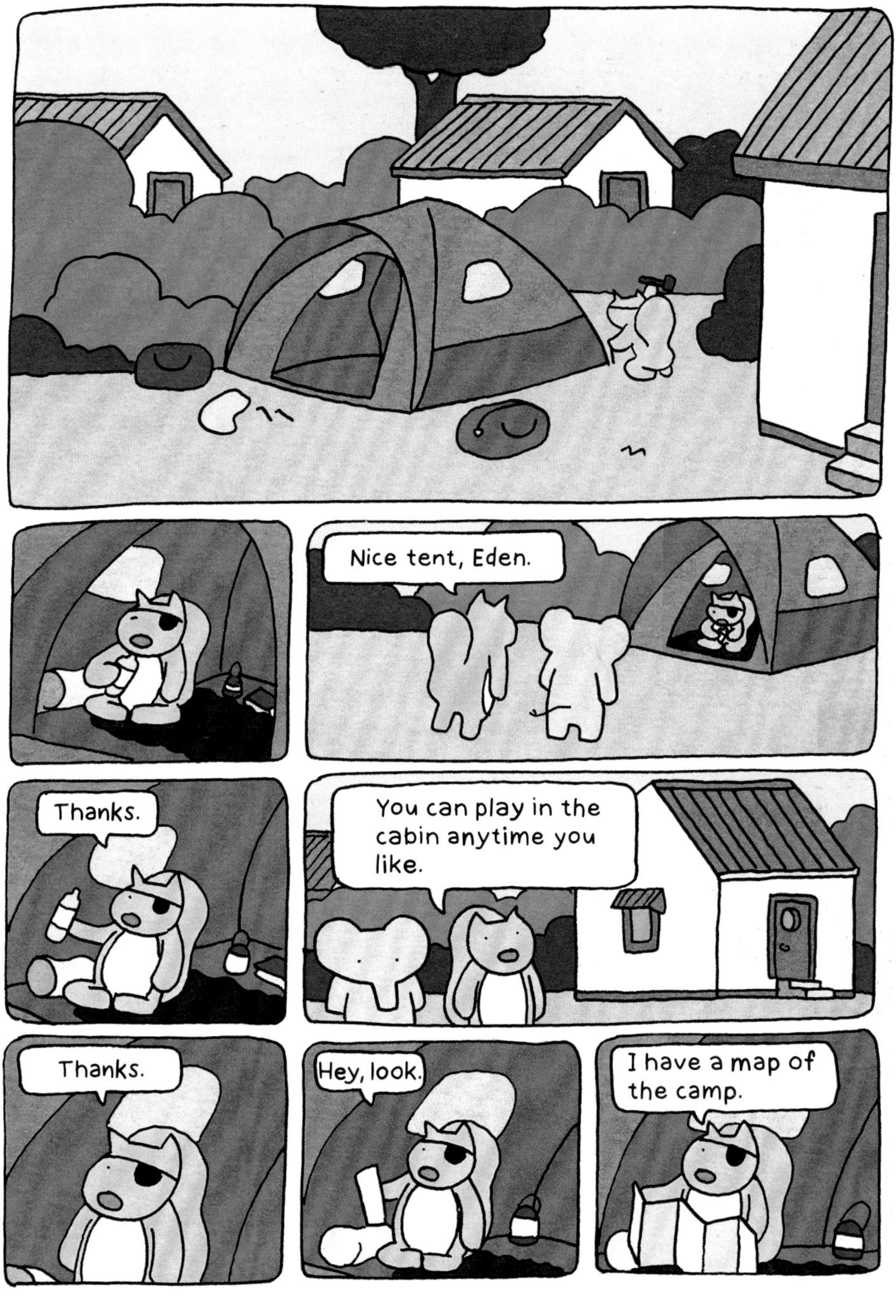
Nice tent, Eden.
Thanks.
You can play in the cabin anytime you like.
Thanks.
Hey, look.
I have a map of the camp.

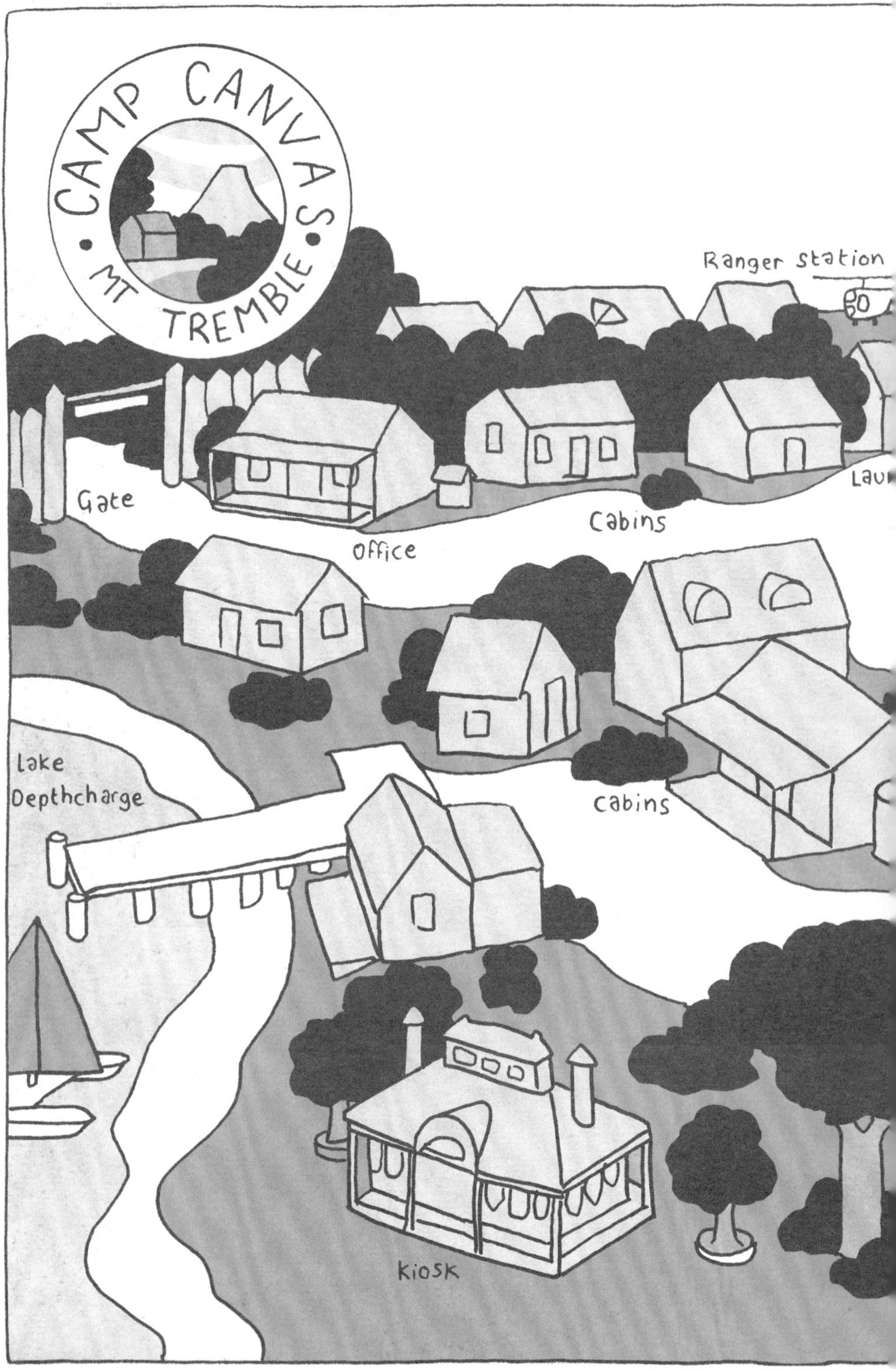
CAMP CANVAS
MT TREMBLE
Ranger station
Gate
Office
Cabins
Cabins
Lake Depthcharge
Kiosk

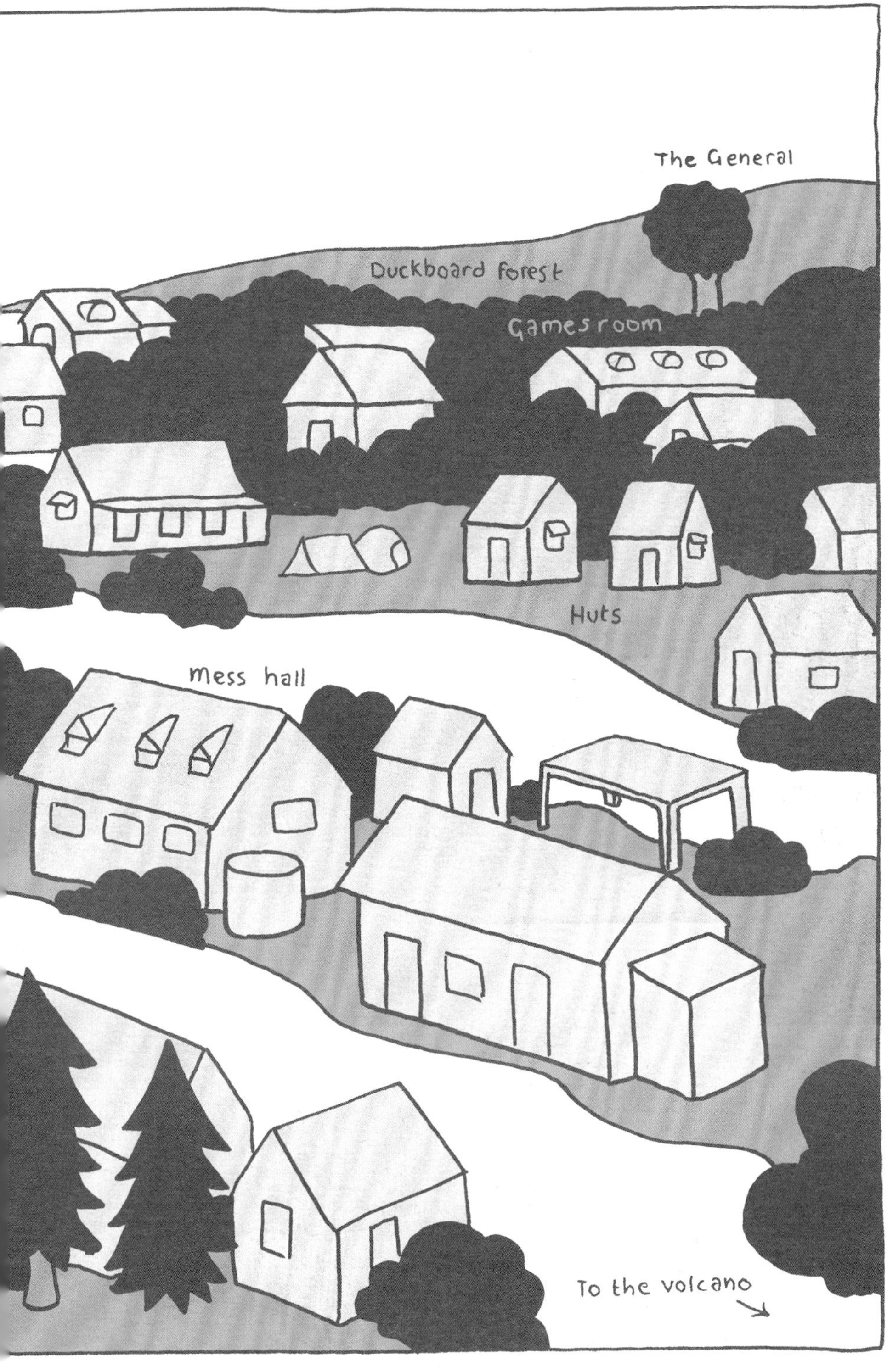
The General
Duckboard forest
Gamesroom
Huts
mess hall
To the volcano

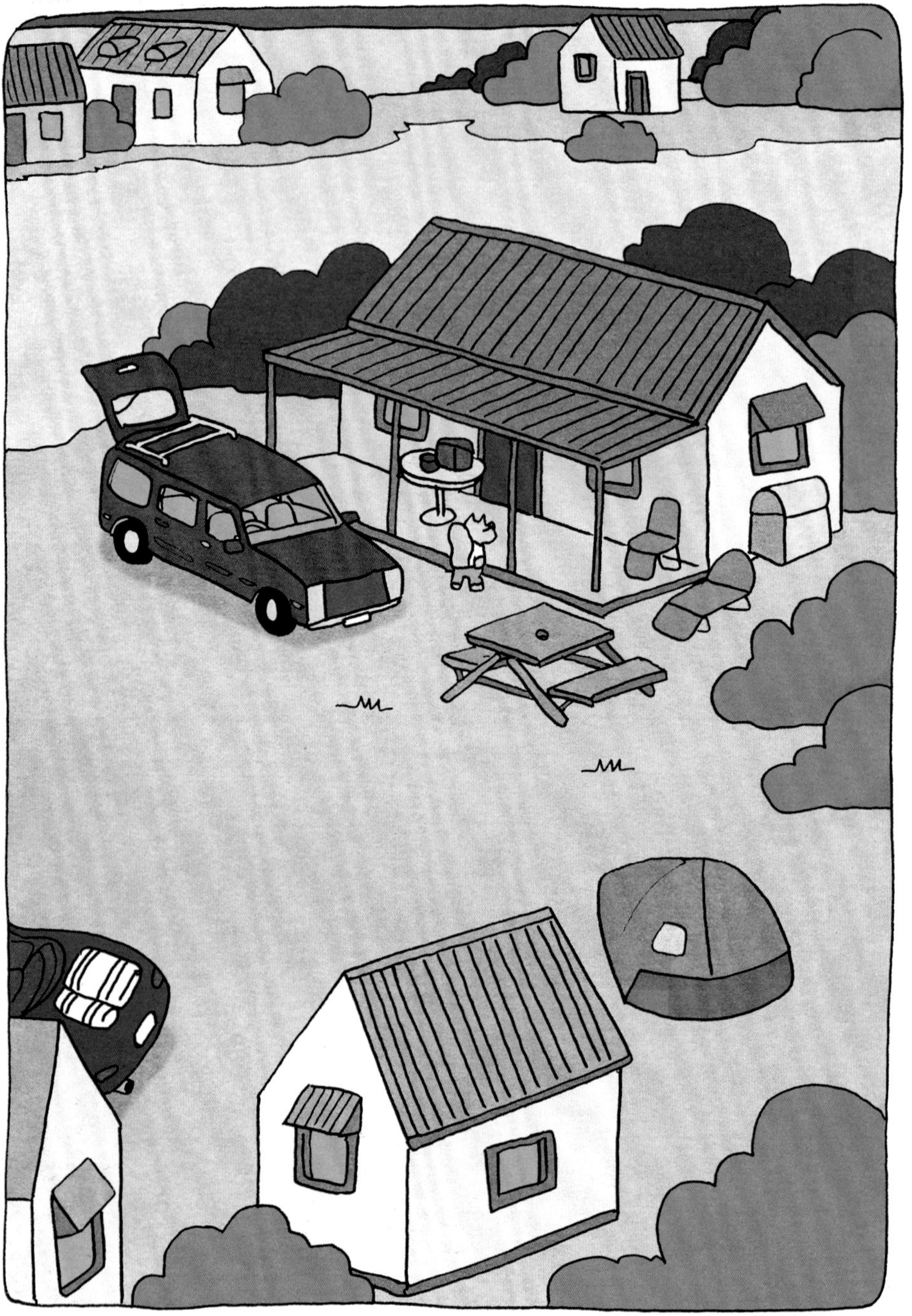

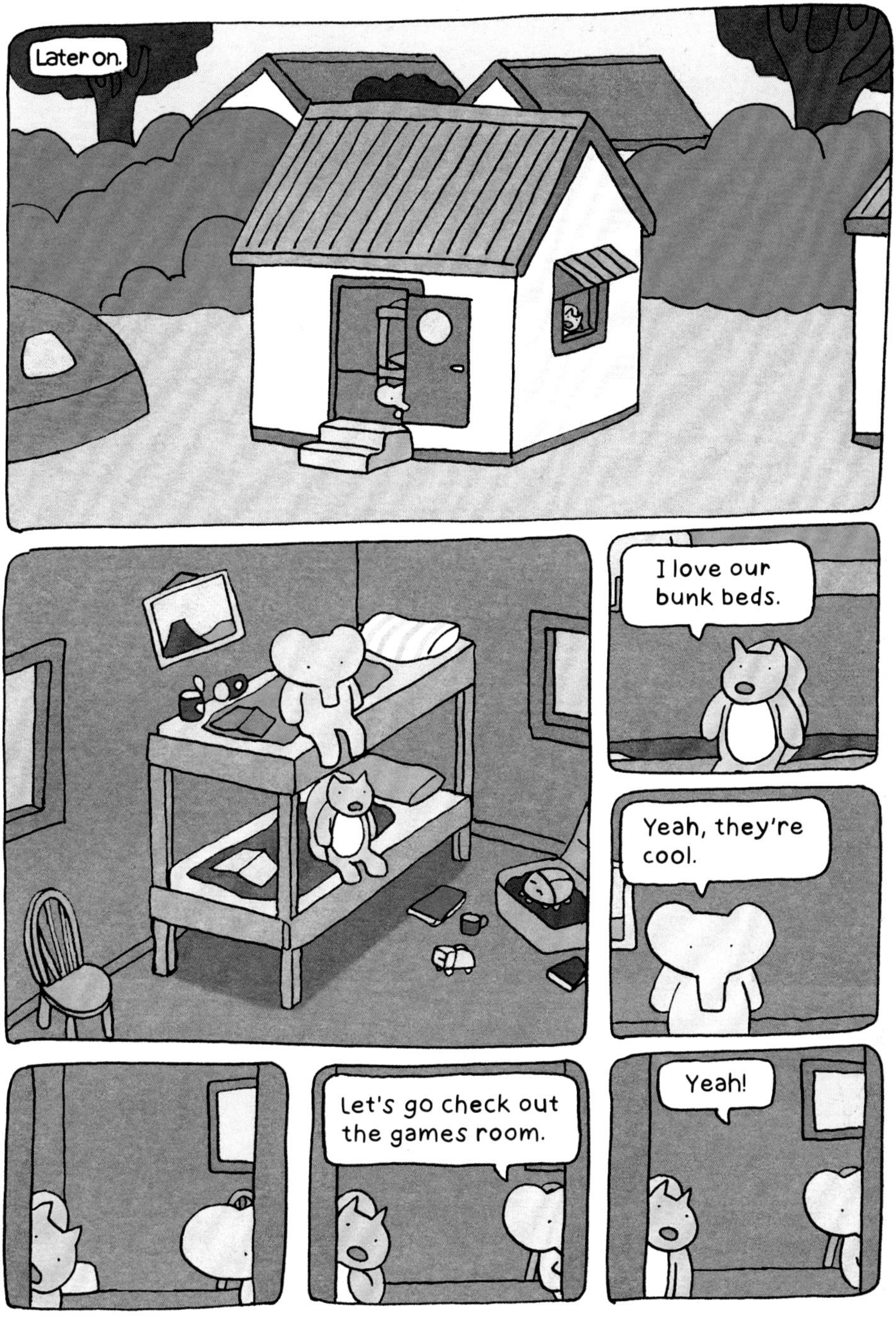
Later on.
I love our bunk beds.
Yeah, they're cool.
Let's go check out the games room.
Yeah!

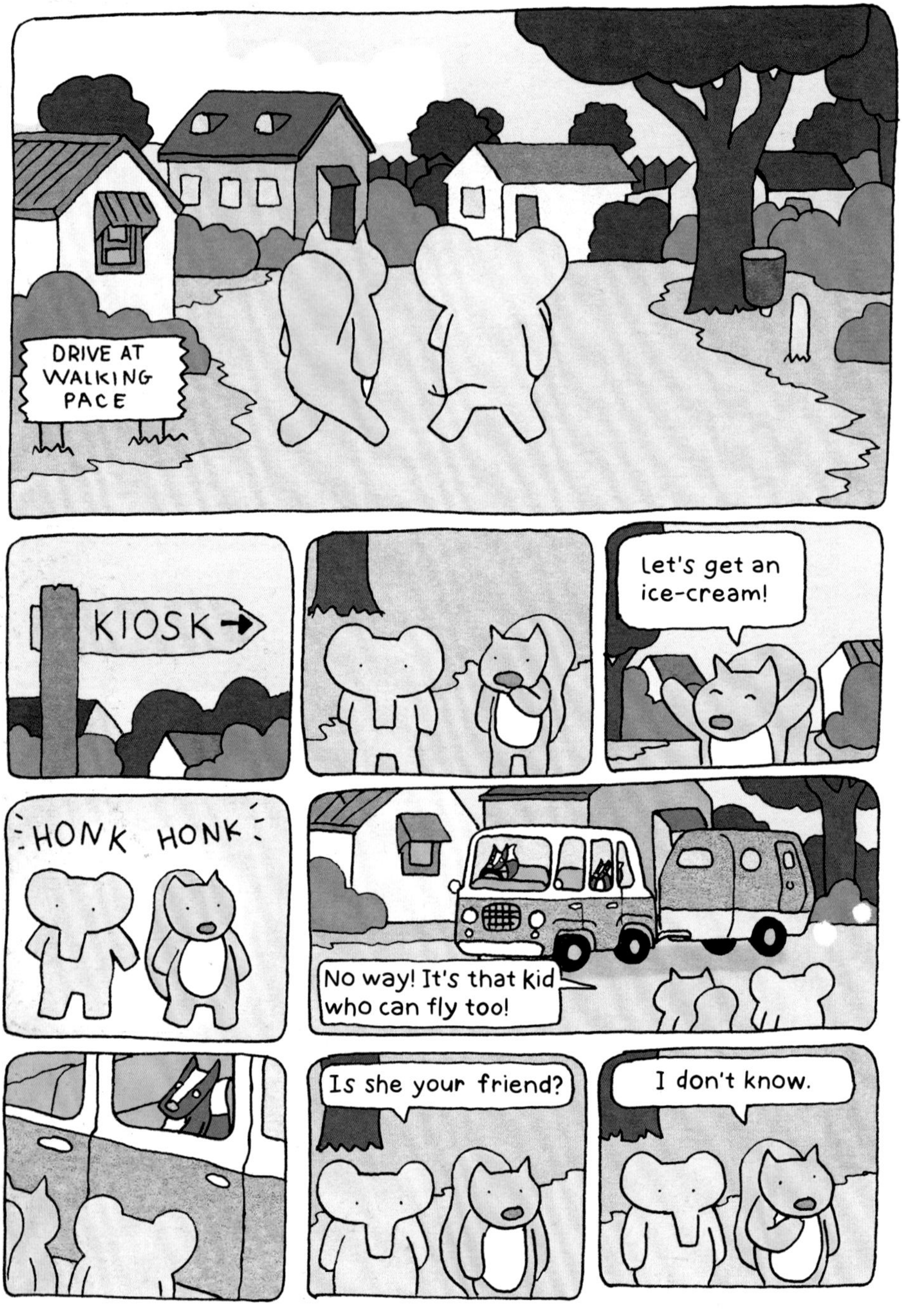
DRIVE AT WALKING PACE
KIOSK
Let's get an ice-cream!
HONK HONK
No way! It's that kid who can fly too!
Is she your friend?
I don't know.

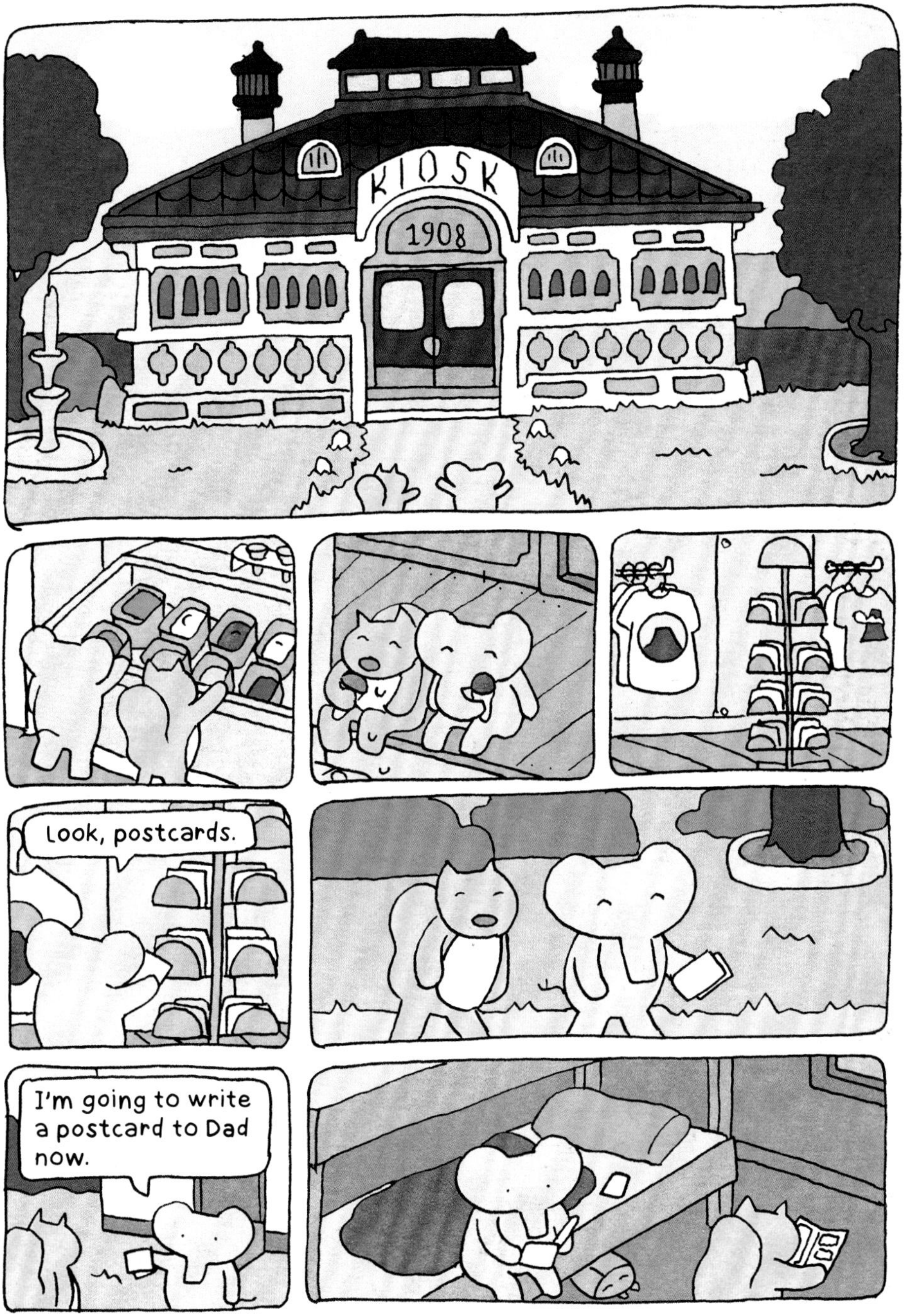
KIOSK
1908
Look, postcards.
I'm going to write a postcard to Dad now.

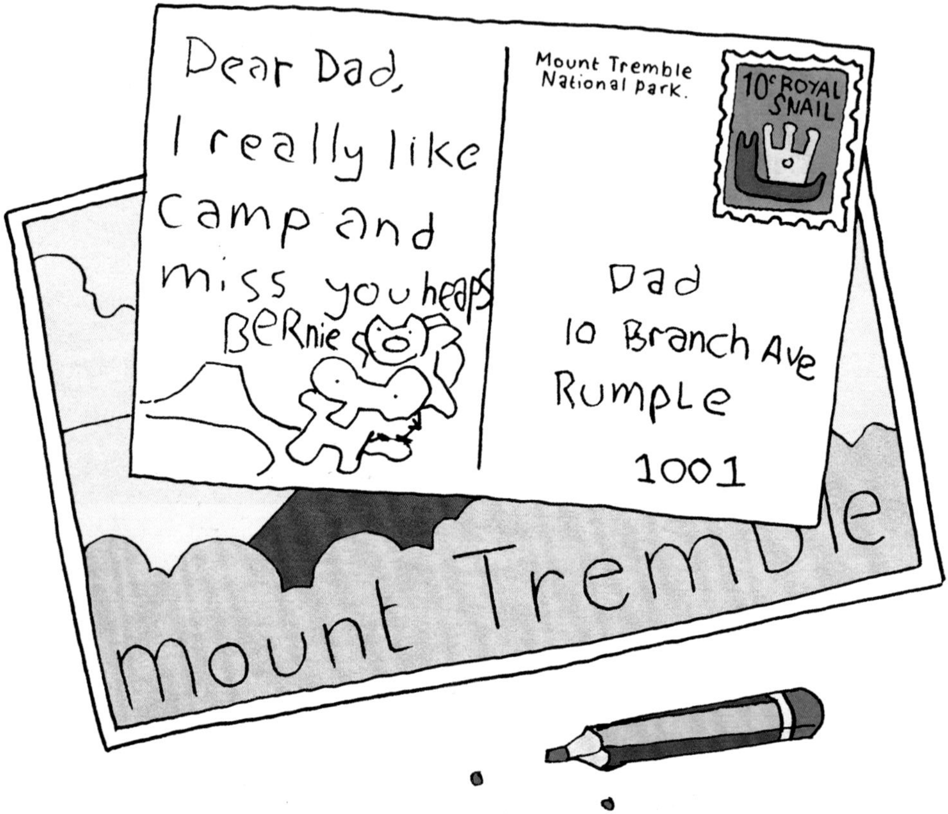
Dear Dad,
I really like camp and miss you heaps
BERnie
Mount Tremble
National park.
10c ROYAL SNAIL
Dad
10 Branch Ave
Rumple
1001
mount Tremble

Chapter 6

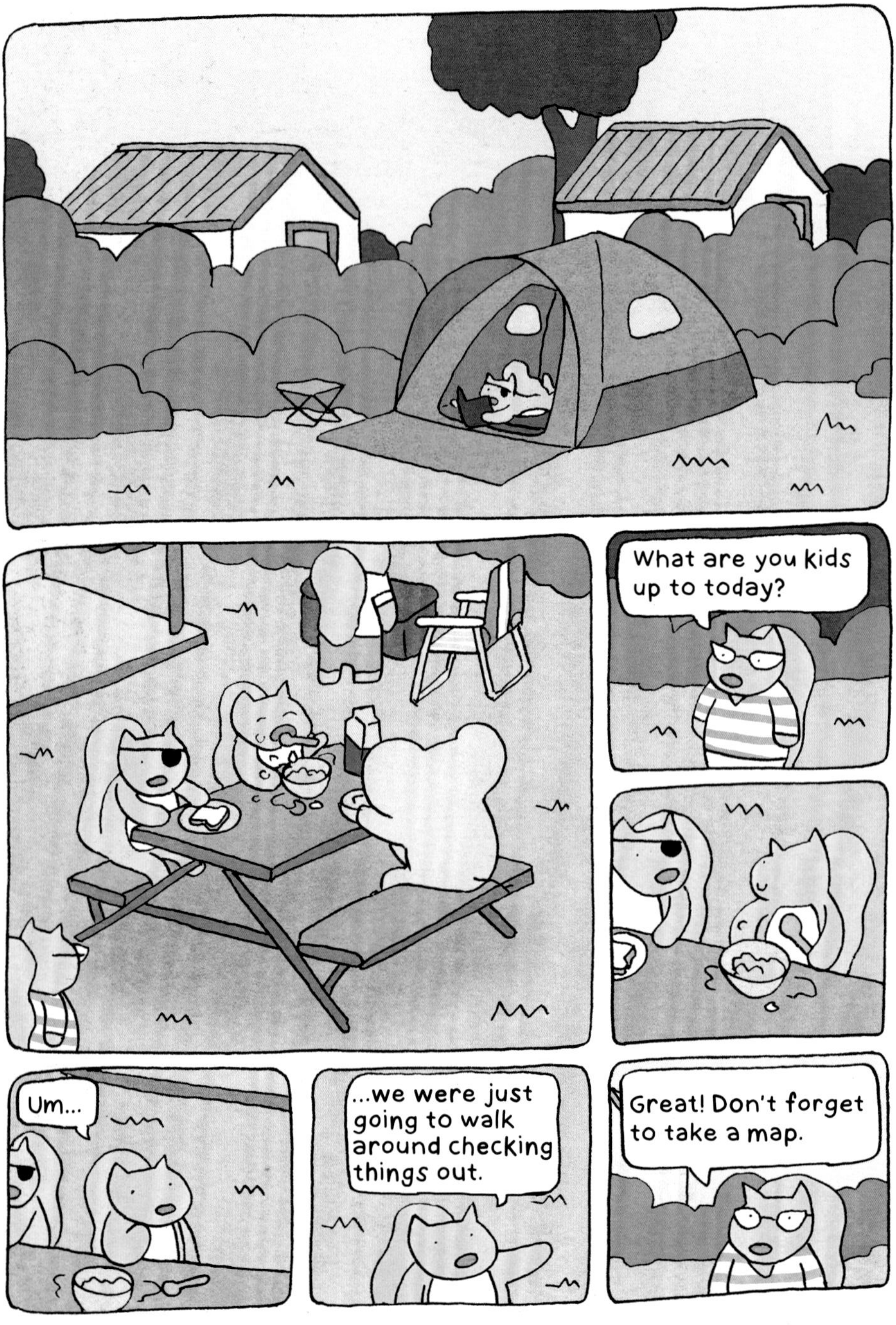
What are you kids up to today?
Um...
...we were just going to walk around checking things out.
Great! Don't forget to take a map.

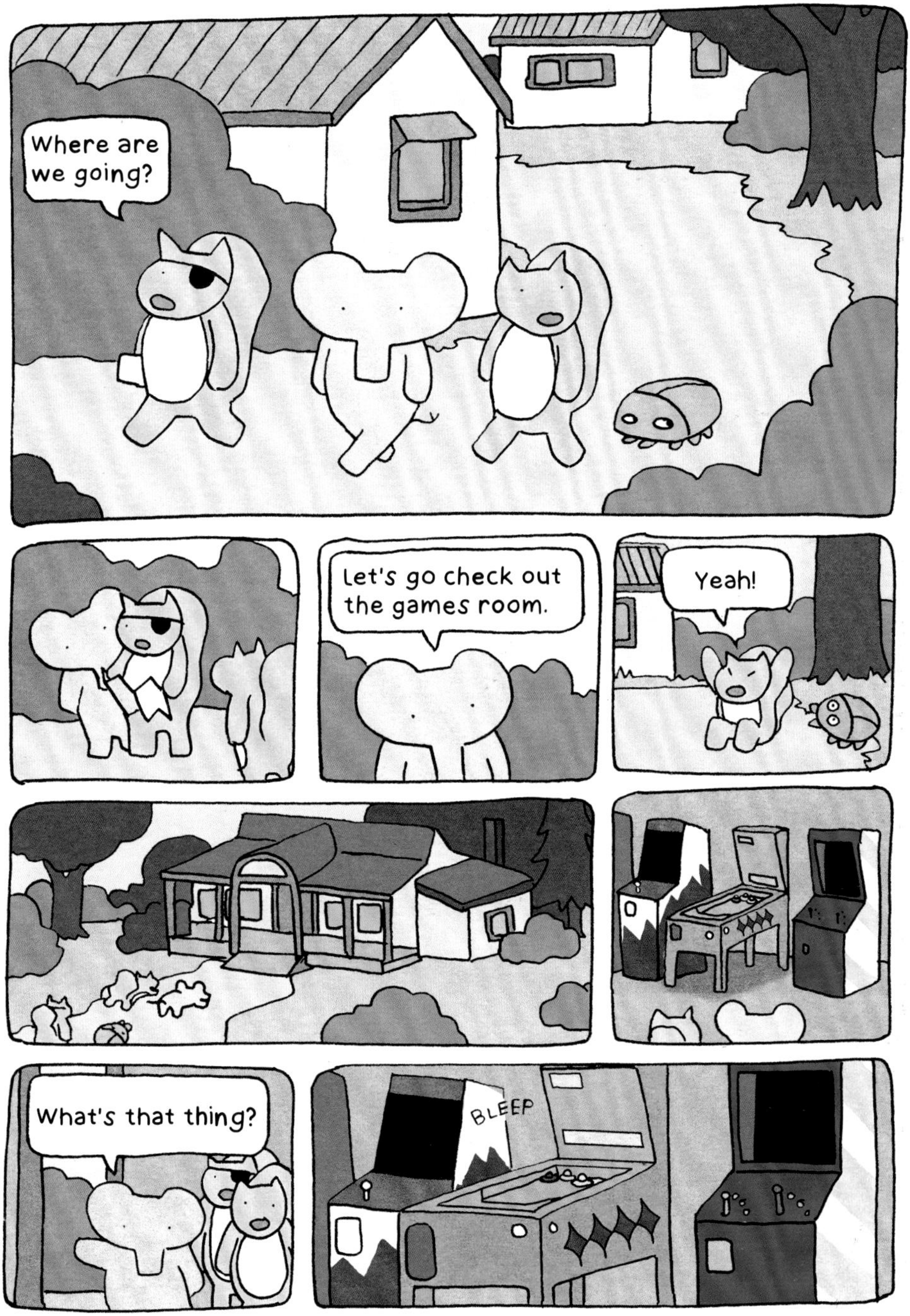
Where are we going?
Let's go check out the games room.
Yeah!
What's that thing?
BLEEP

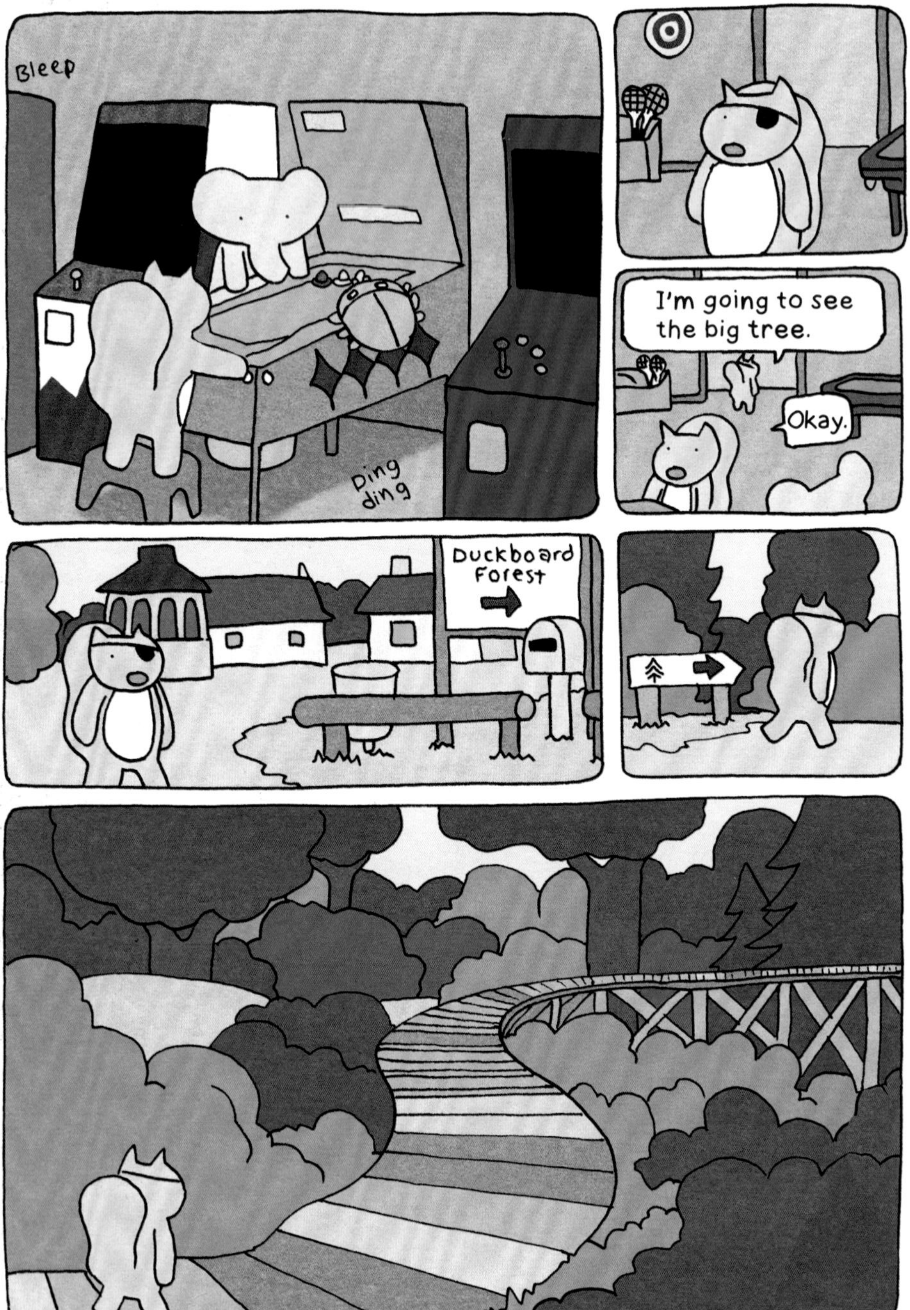
Bleep
Ding ding
I'm going to see the big tree.
Okay.
Duckboard Forest

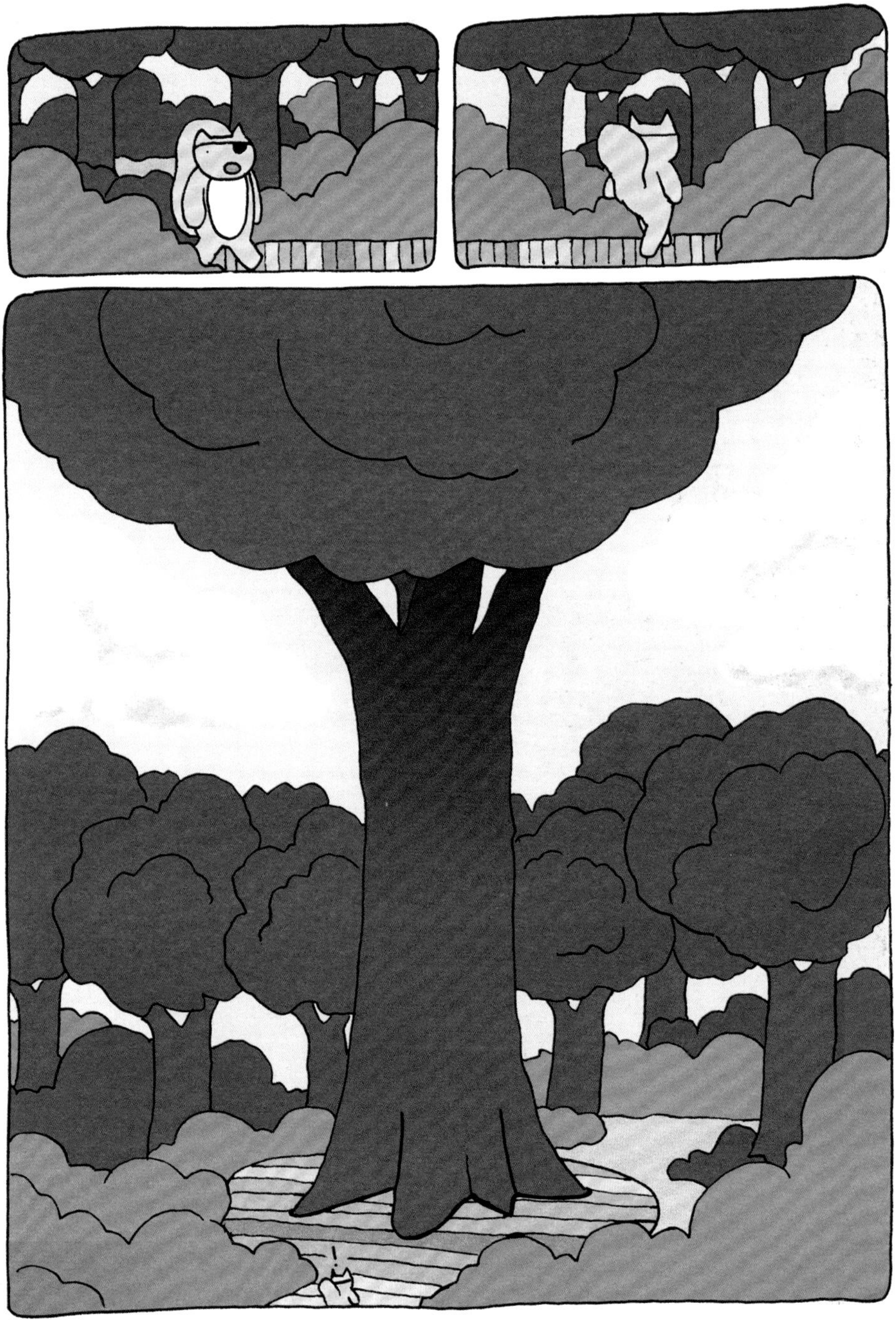

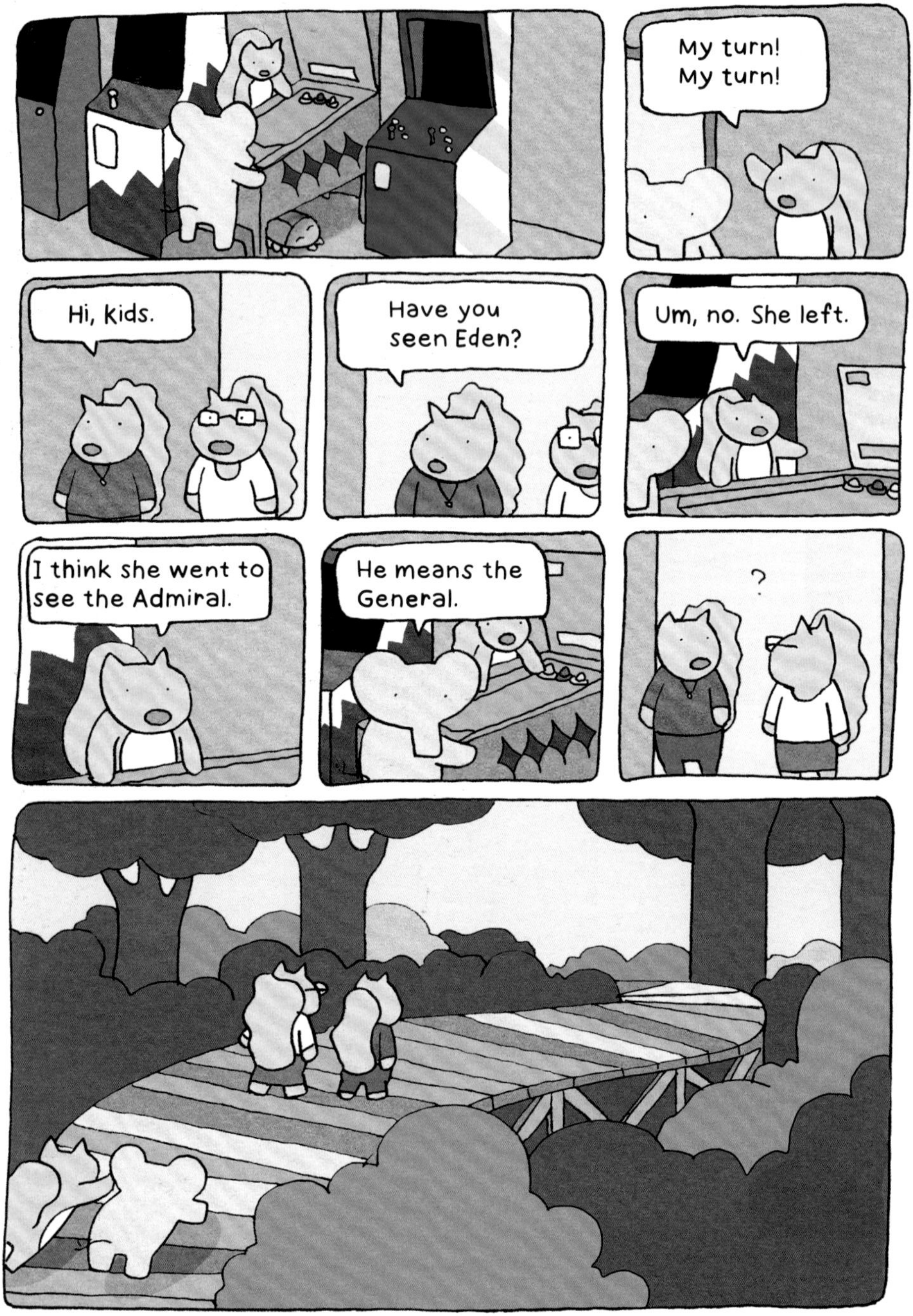
My turn! My turn!
Hi, kids.
Have you seen Eden?
Um, no. She left.
I think she went to see the Admiral.
He means the General.
?

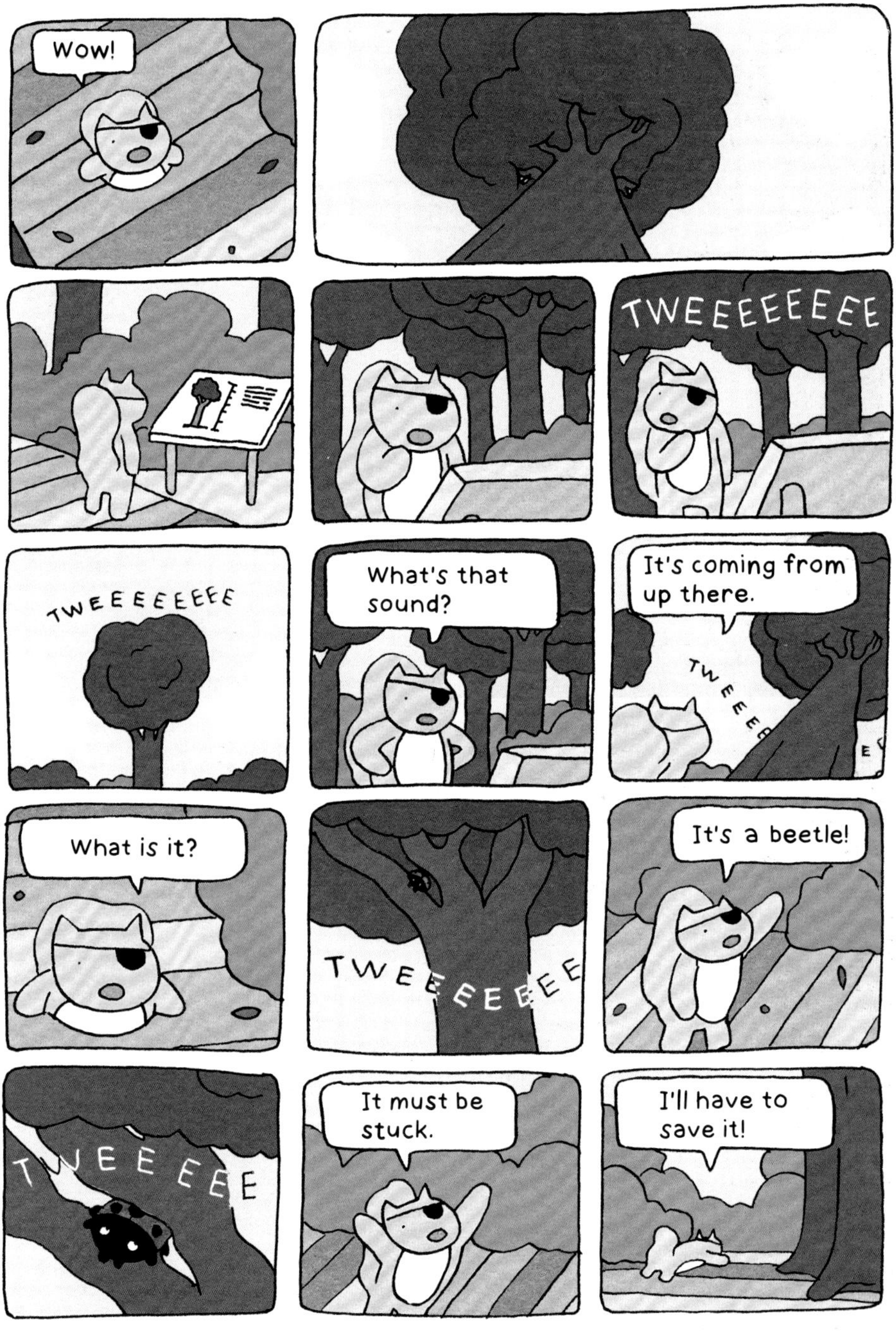
Wow!
TWEEEEEEEE
TWEEEEEEEE
What's that sound?
It's coming from up there.
What is it?
TWEEEEEEEE
It's a beetle!
TWEEEEEE
It must be stuck.
I'll have to save it!

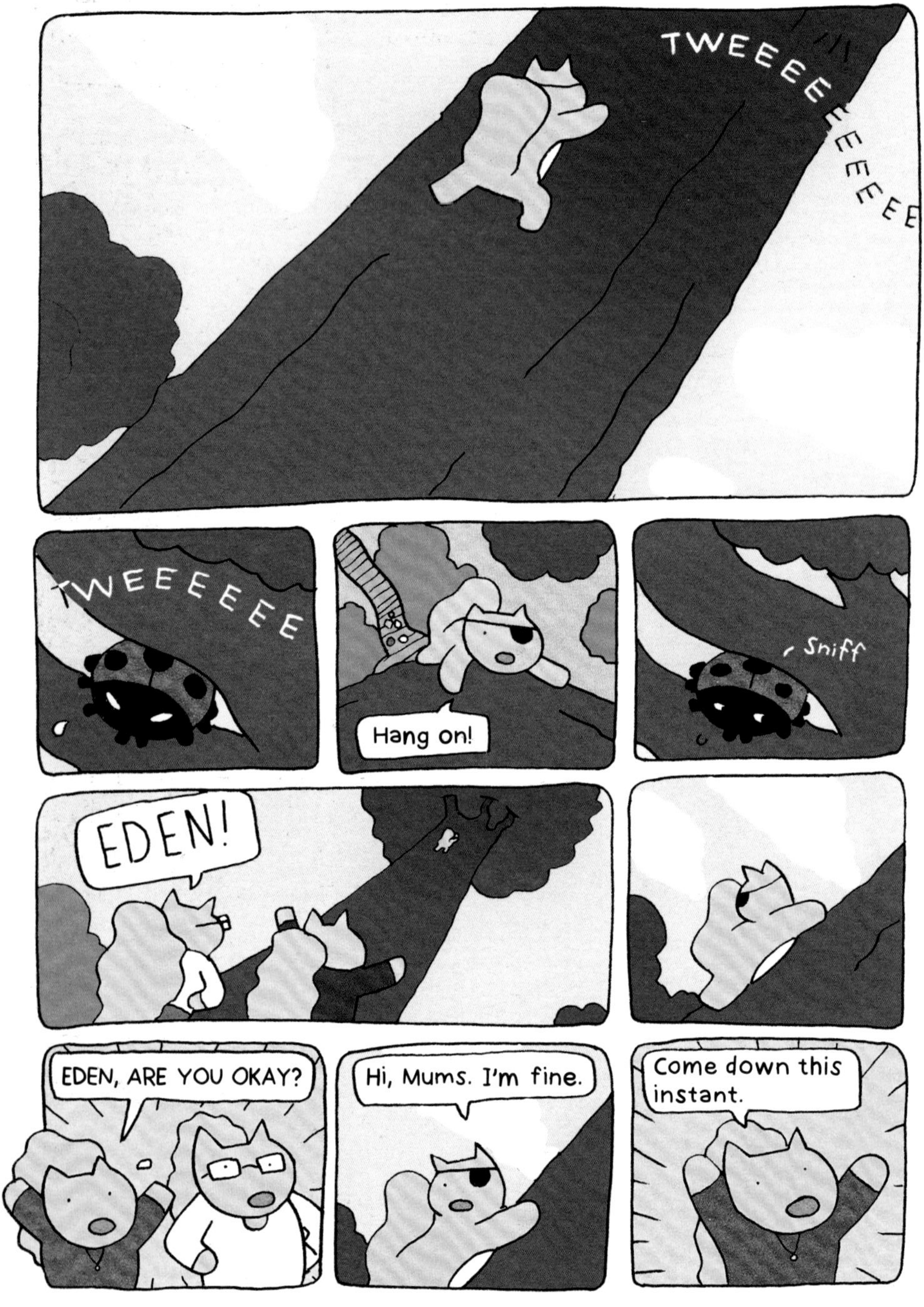
TWEEEEEEEEEE
TWEEEEEEEE
Hang on!
Sniff
EDEN!
EDEN, ARE YOU OKAY?
Hi, Mums. I'm fine.
Come down this instant.

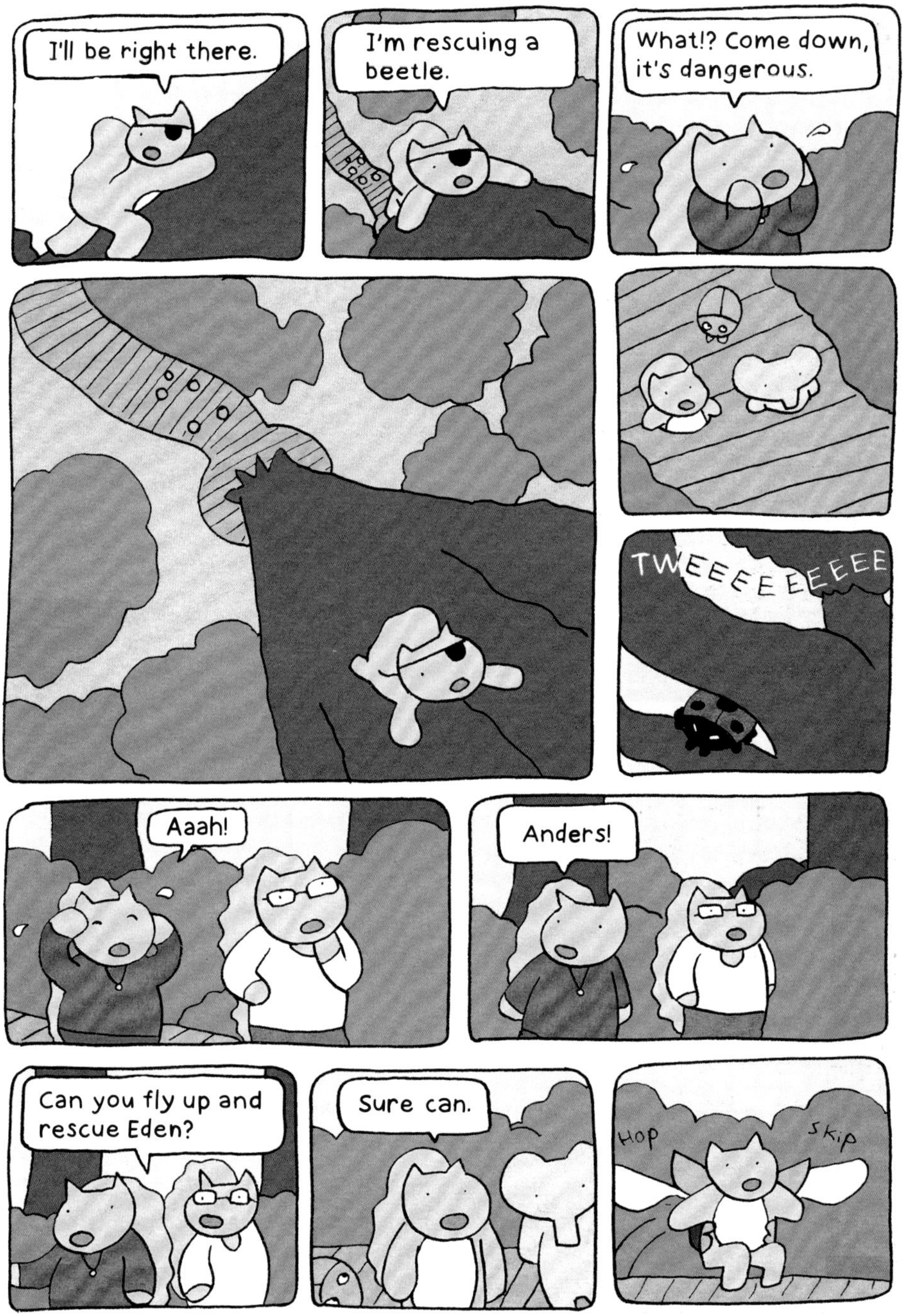
I'll be right there.
I'm rescuing a beetle.
What!? Come down, it's dangerous.
TWEEEEEEEEEE
Aaah!
Anders!
Can you fly up and rescue Eden?
Sure can.
Hop
Skip

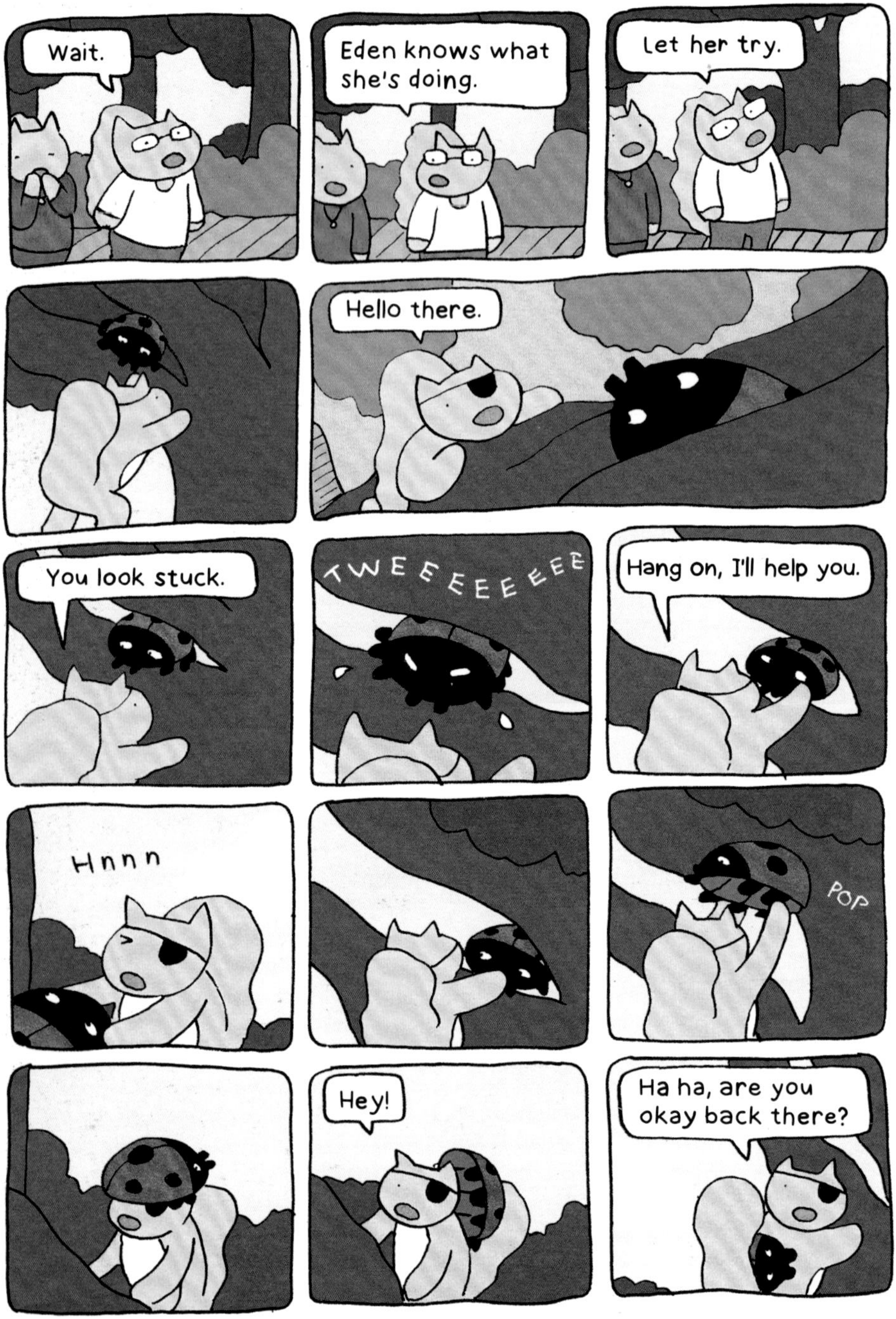
Wait.
Eden knows what she's doing.
Let her try.
Hello there.
You look stuck.
TWEEEEEEEEE
Hang on, I'll help you.
Hnnn
POP
Hey!
Ha ha, are you okay back there?

We're coming down now!

Be careful!

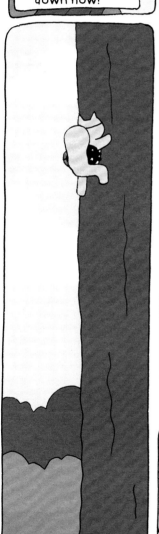

Almost there.

Eden!

Are you hurt?

No, I'm fine.

This little beetle was stuck in the tree.

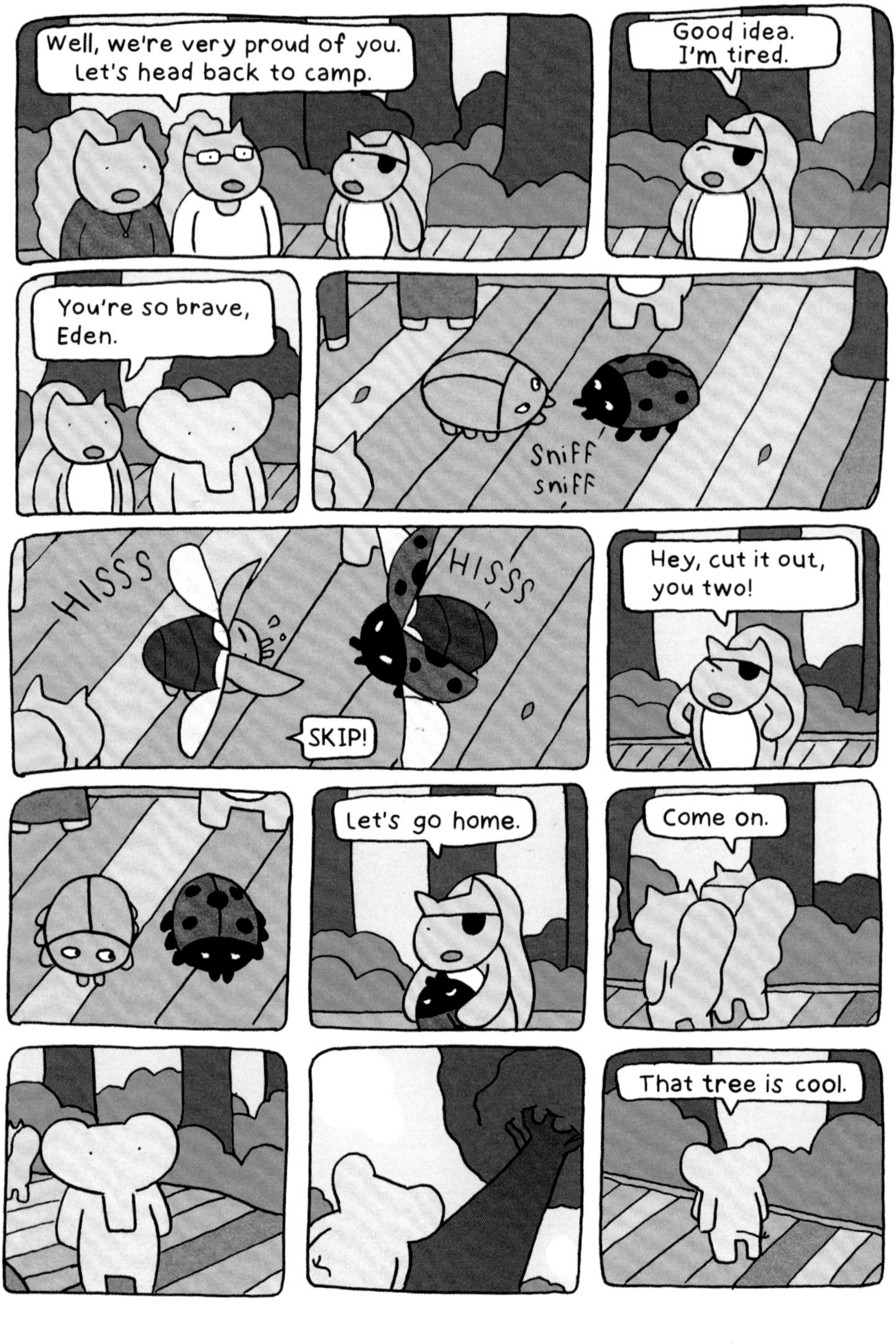
Well, we're very proud of you. Let's head back to camp.
Good idea. I'm tired.
You're so brave, Eden.
Sniff sniff
HISSS
HISSS
SKIP!
Hey, cut it out, you two!
Let's go home.
Come on.
That tree is cool.

Chapter 7

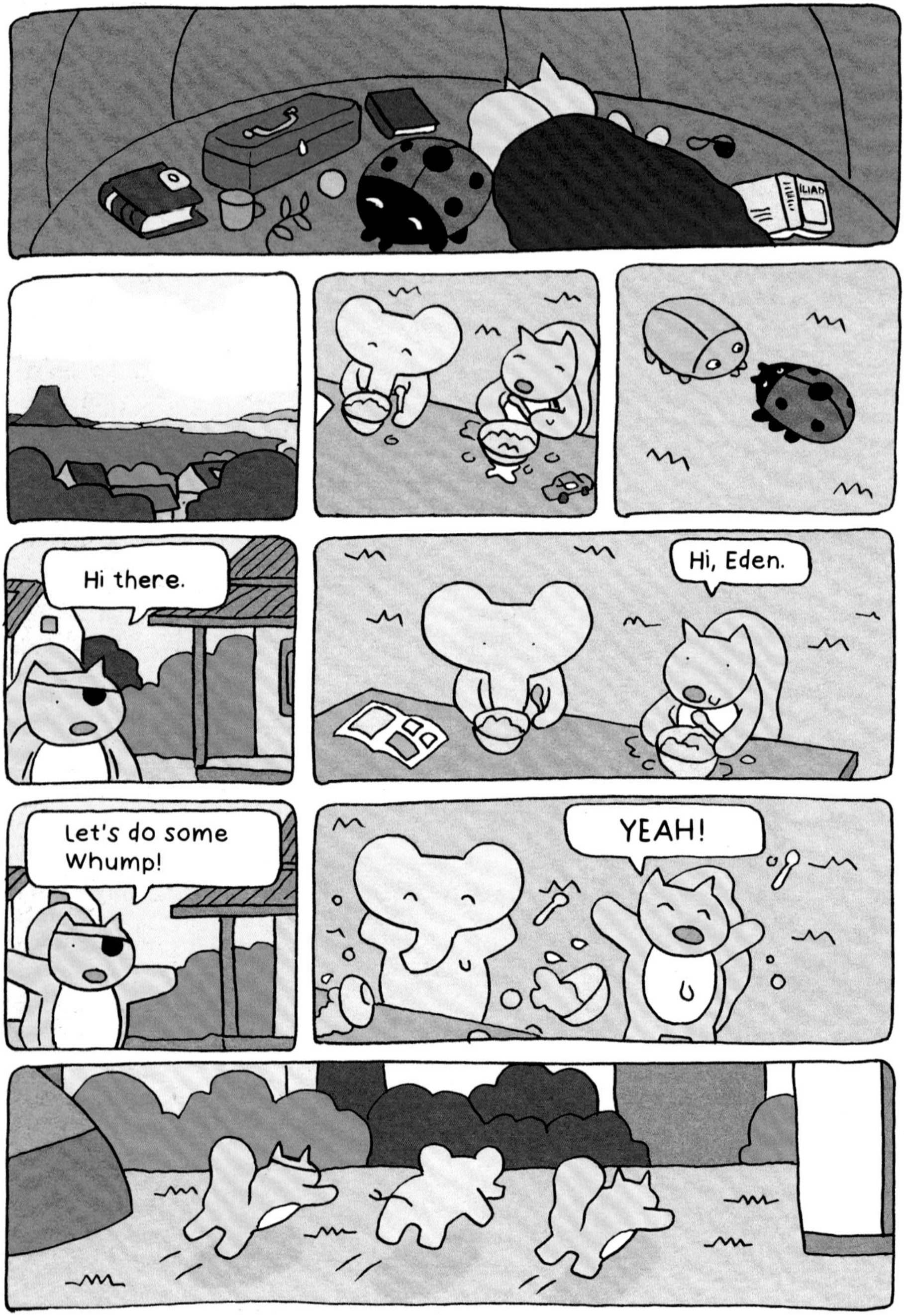
ILIAD
Hi there.
Hi, Eden.
Let's do some Whump!
YEAH!

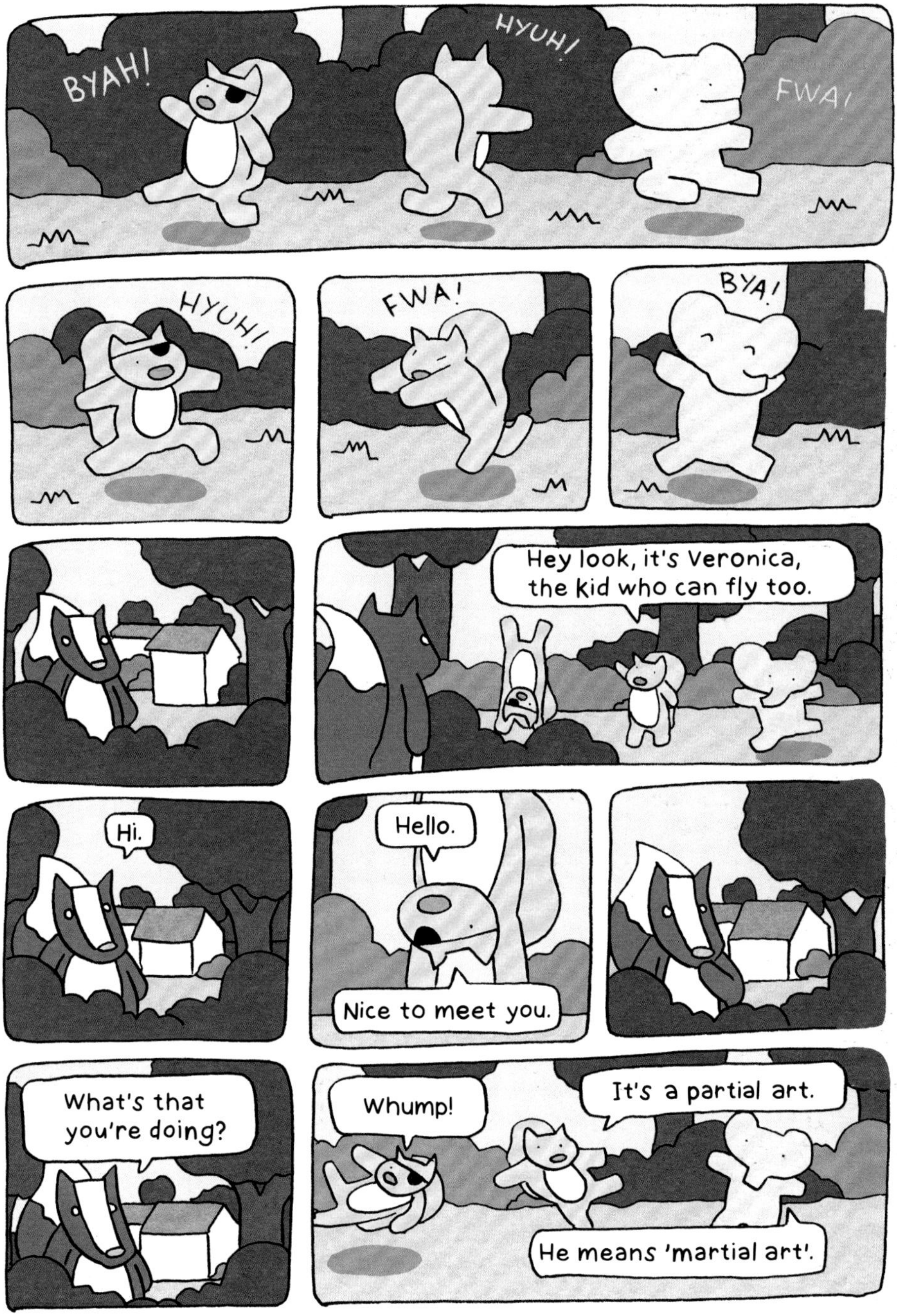
BYAH!
HYUH!
FWA!
HYUH!
FWA!
BYA!
Hey look, it's Veronica, the kid who can fly too.
Hi.
Hello.
Nice to meet you.
What's that you're doing?
Whump!
It's a partial art.
He means 'martial art'.

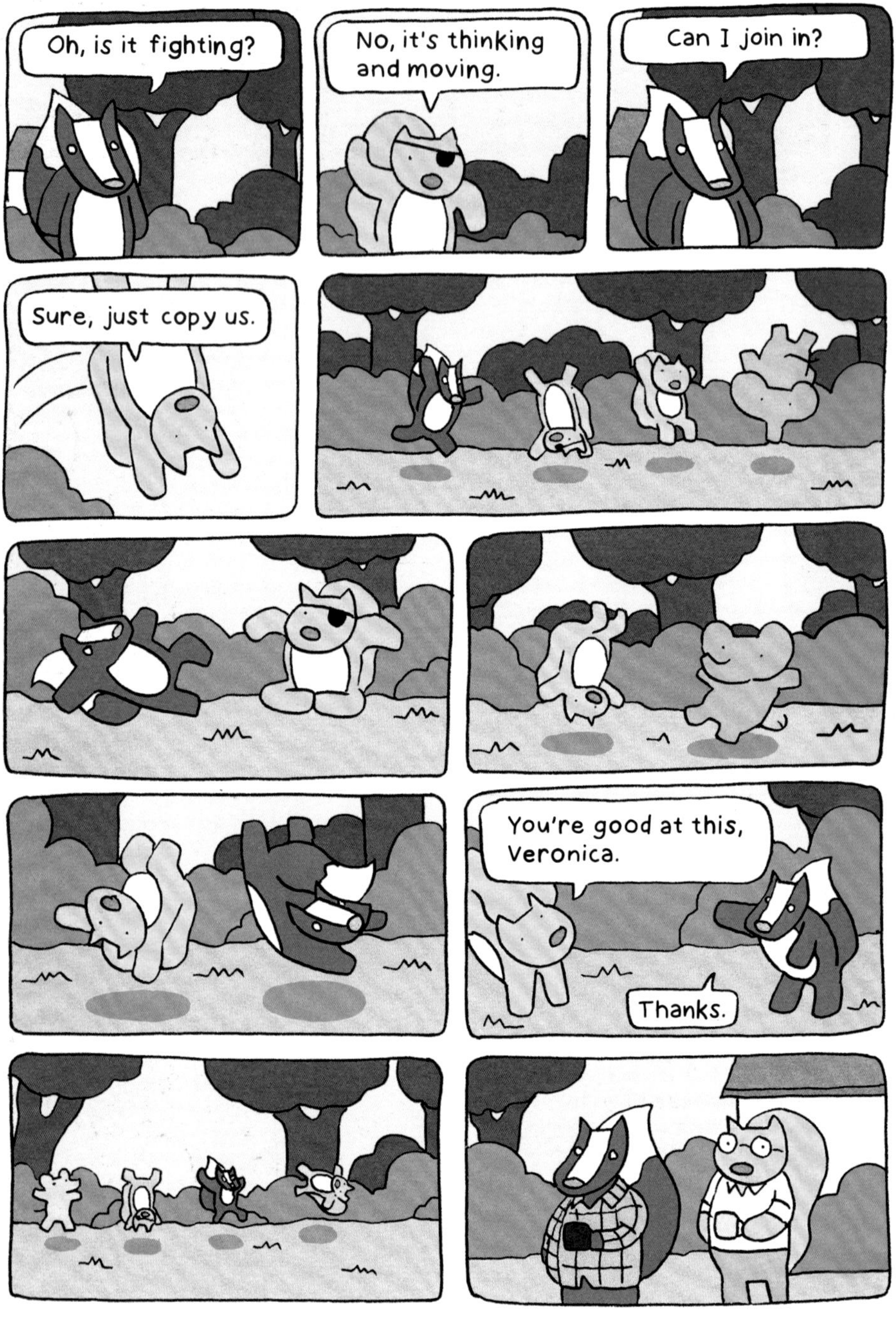
Oh, is it fighting?
No, it's thinking and moving.
Can I join in?
Sure, just copy us.
You're good at this, Veronica.
Thanks.

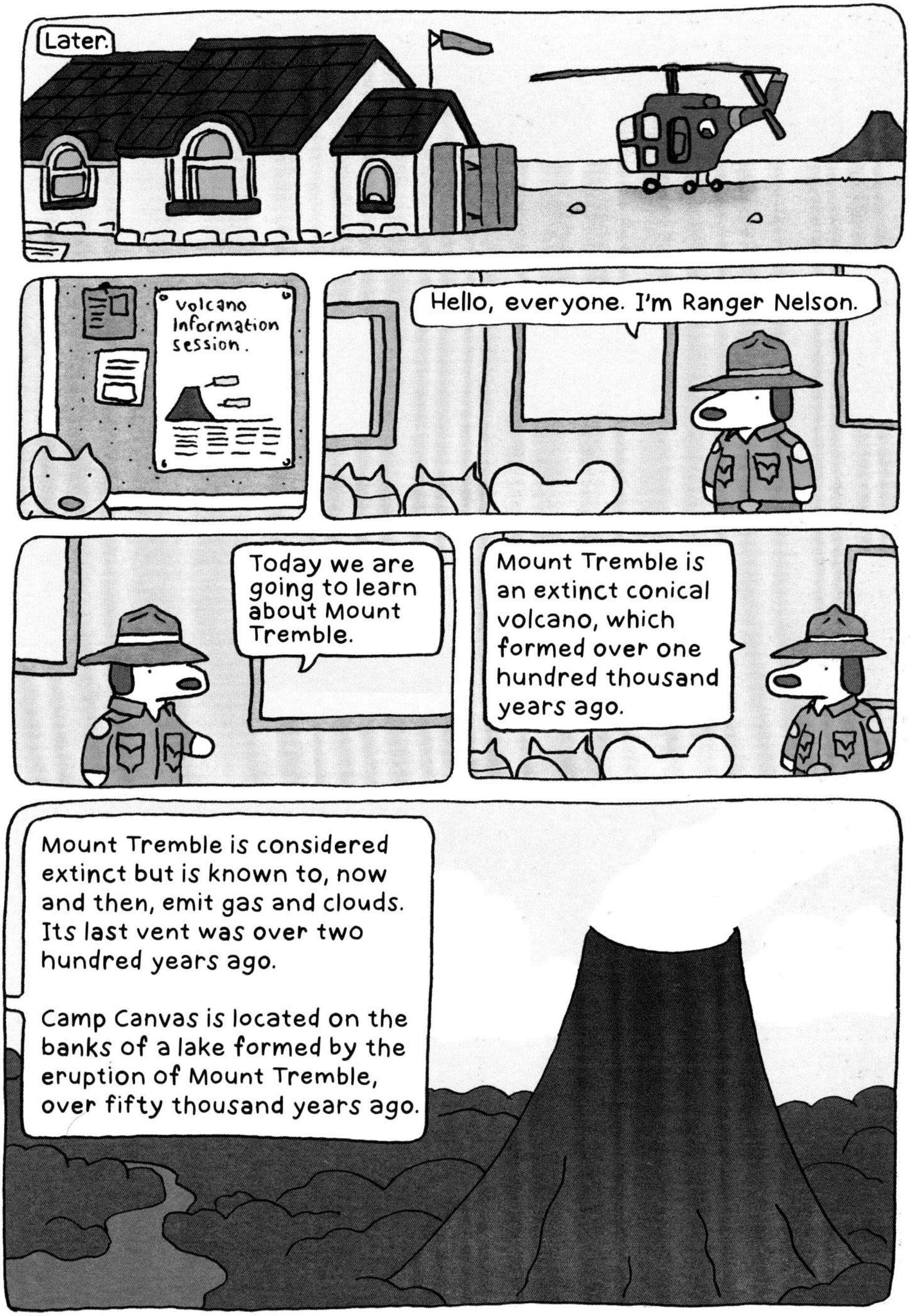
Later.
Volcano Information session.
Hello, everyone. I'm Ranger Nelson.
Today we are going to learn about Mount Tremble.
Mount Tremble is an extinct conical volcano, which formed over one hundred thousand years ago.
Mount Tremble is considered extinct but is known to, now and then, emit gas and clouds. Its last vent was over two hundred years ago.
Camp Canvas is located on the banks of a lake formed by the eruption of Mount Tremble, over fifty thousand years ago.

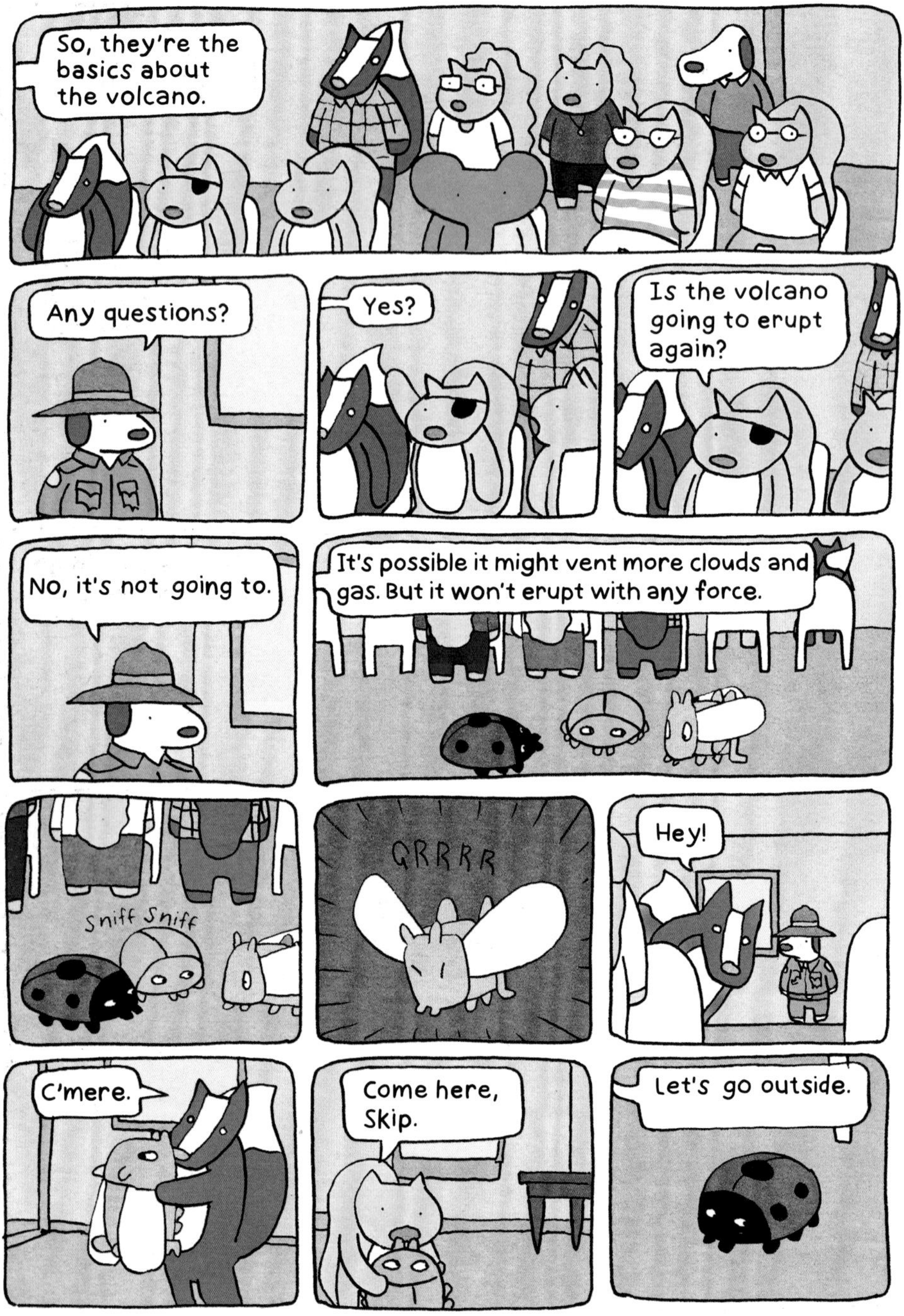
So, they're the basics about the volcano.
Any questions?
Yes?
Is the volcano going to erupt again?
No, it's not going to.
It's possible it might vent more clouds and gas. But it won't erupt with any force.
Sniff Sniff
GRRRR
Hey!
C'mere.
Come here, Skip.
Let's go outside.

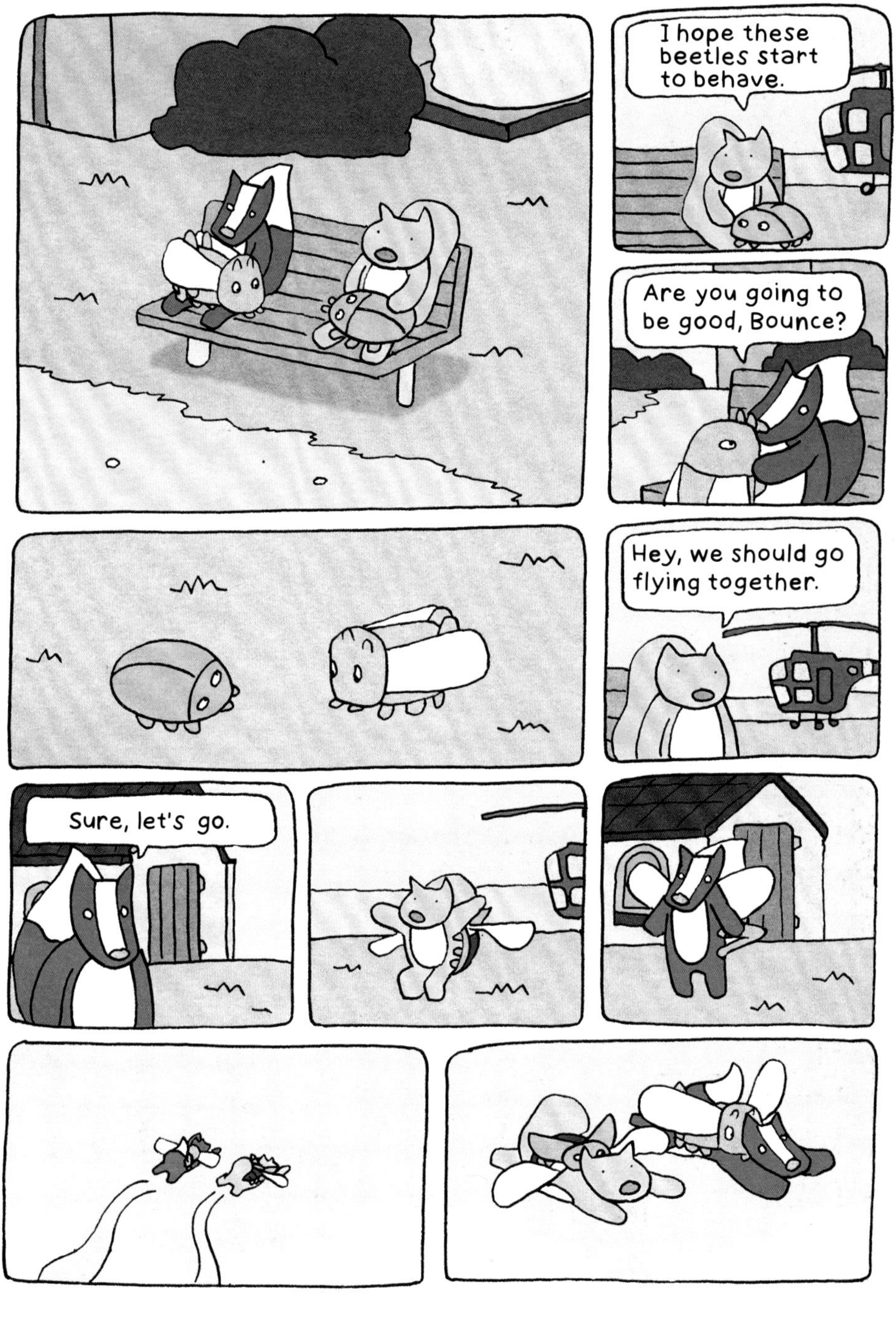
I hope these beetles start to behave.
Are you going to be good, Bounce?
Hey, we should go flying together.
Sure, let's go.

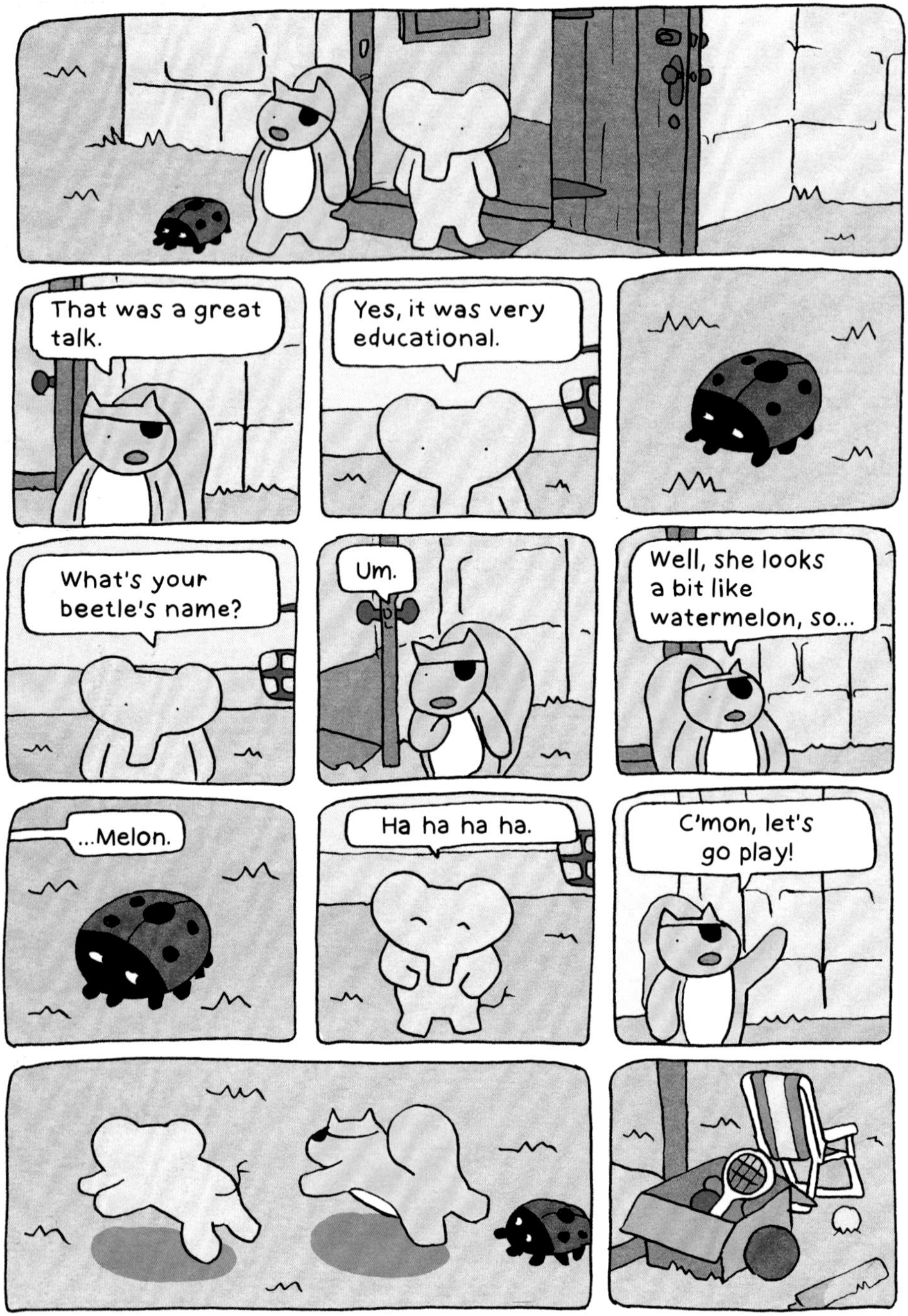
That was a great talk.
Yes, it was very educational.
What's your beetle's name?
Um.
Well, she looks a bit like watermelon, so...
...Melon.
Ha ha ha ha.
C'mon, let's go play!

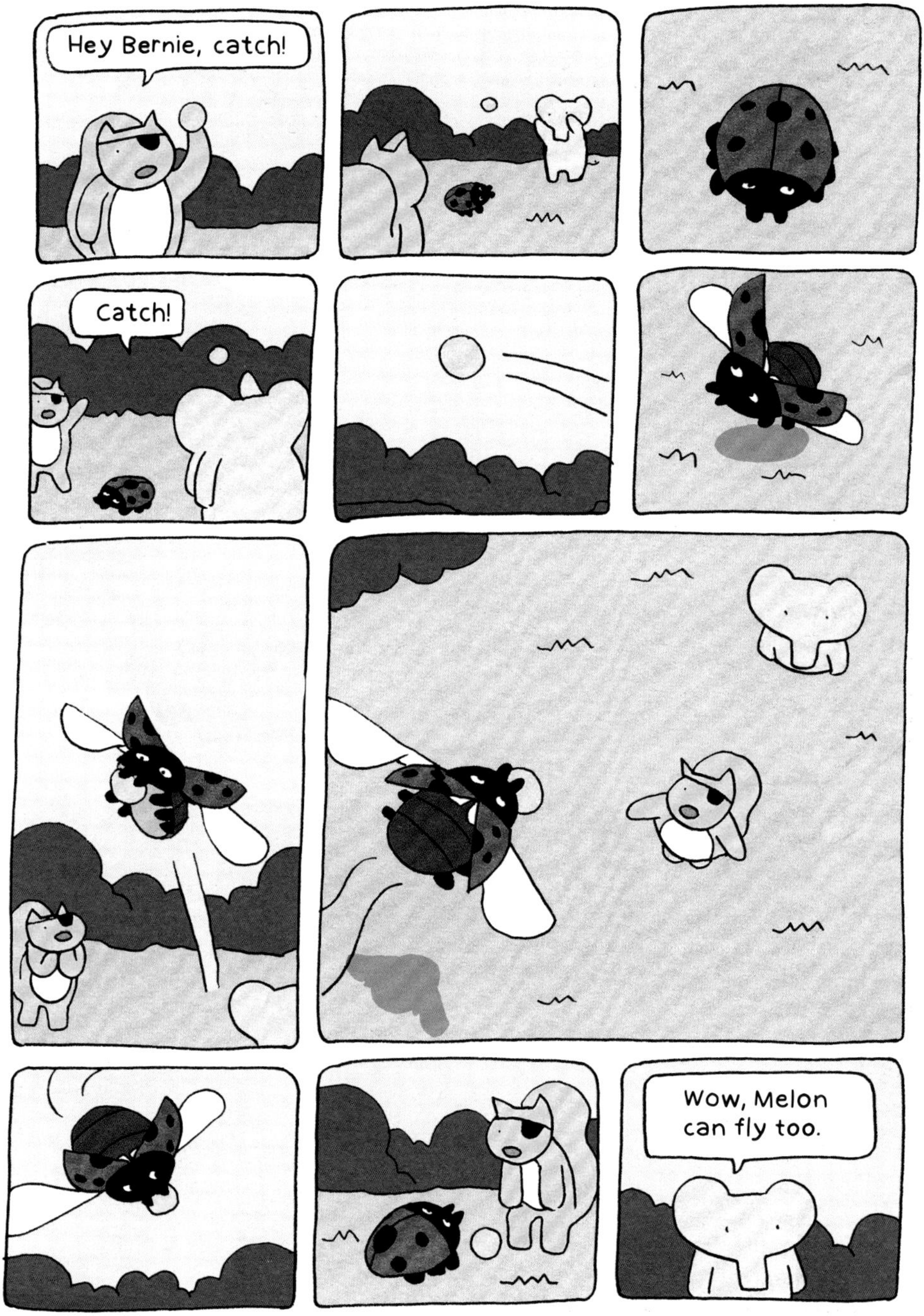
Hey Bernie, catch!
Catch!
Wow, Melon can fly too.

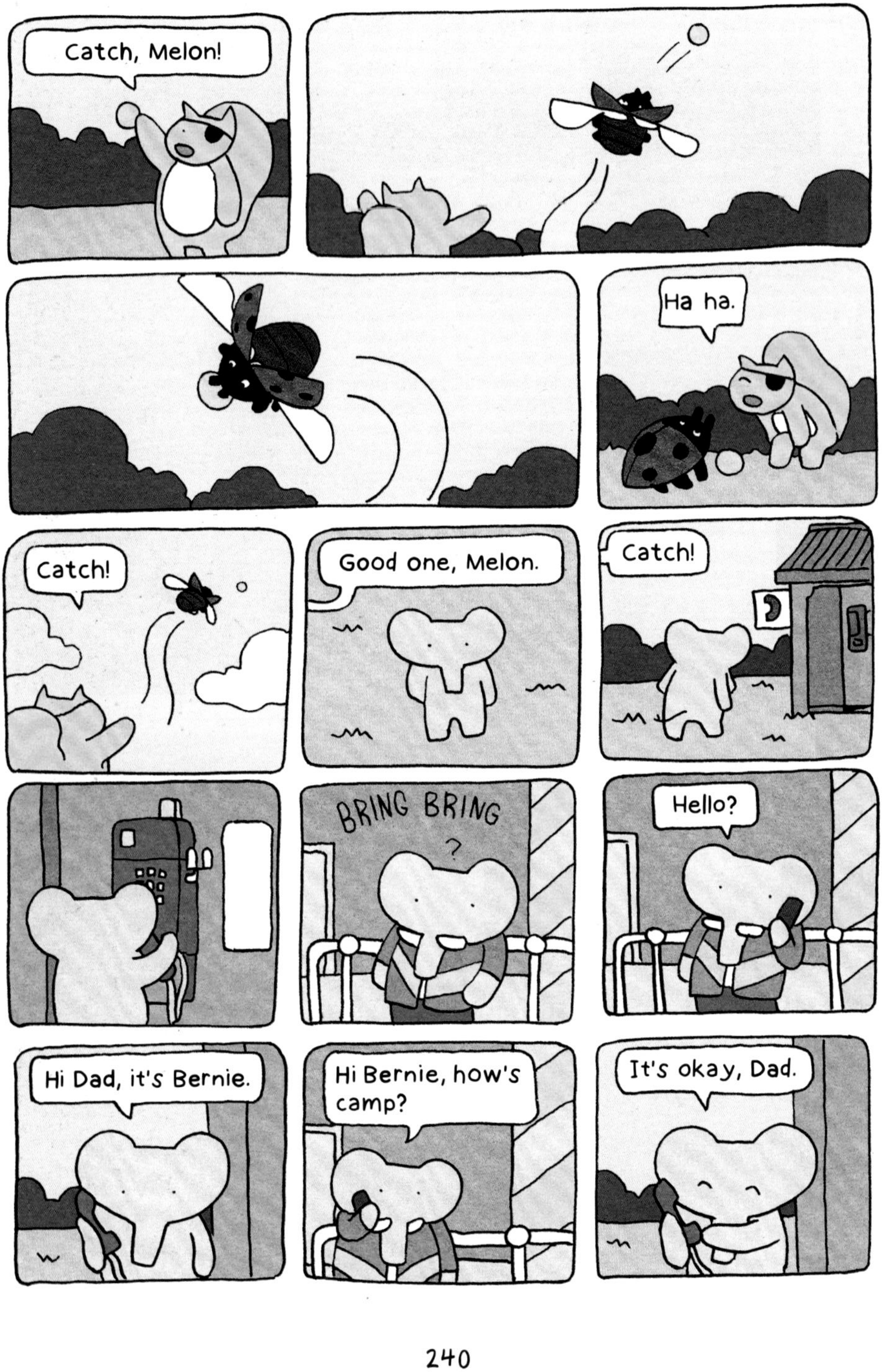
Catch, Melon!
Ha ha.
Catch!
Good one, Melon.
Catch!
BRING BRING
?
Hello?
Hi Dad, it's Bernie.
Hi Bernie, how's camp?
It's okay, Dad.

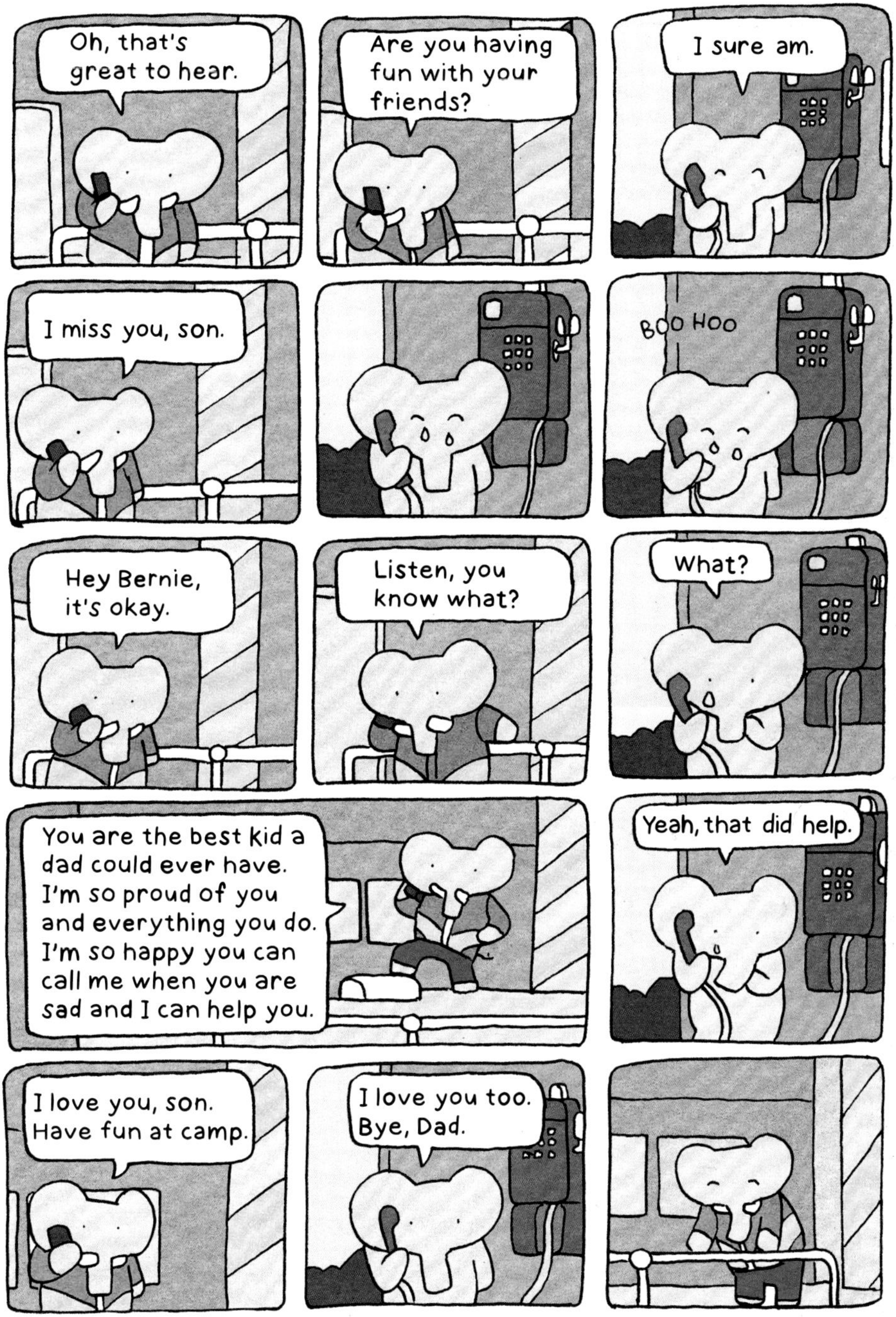
Oh, that's great to hear.
Are you having fun with your friends?
I sure am.
I miss you, son.
BOO HOO
Hey Bernie, it's okay.
Listen, you know what?
What?
You are the best kid a dad could ever have. I'm so proud of you and everything you do. I'm so happy you can call me when you are sad and I can help you.
Yeah, that did help.
I love you, son. Have fun at camp.
I love you too. Bye, Dad.

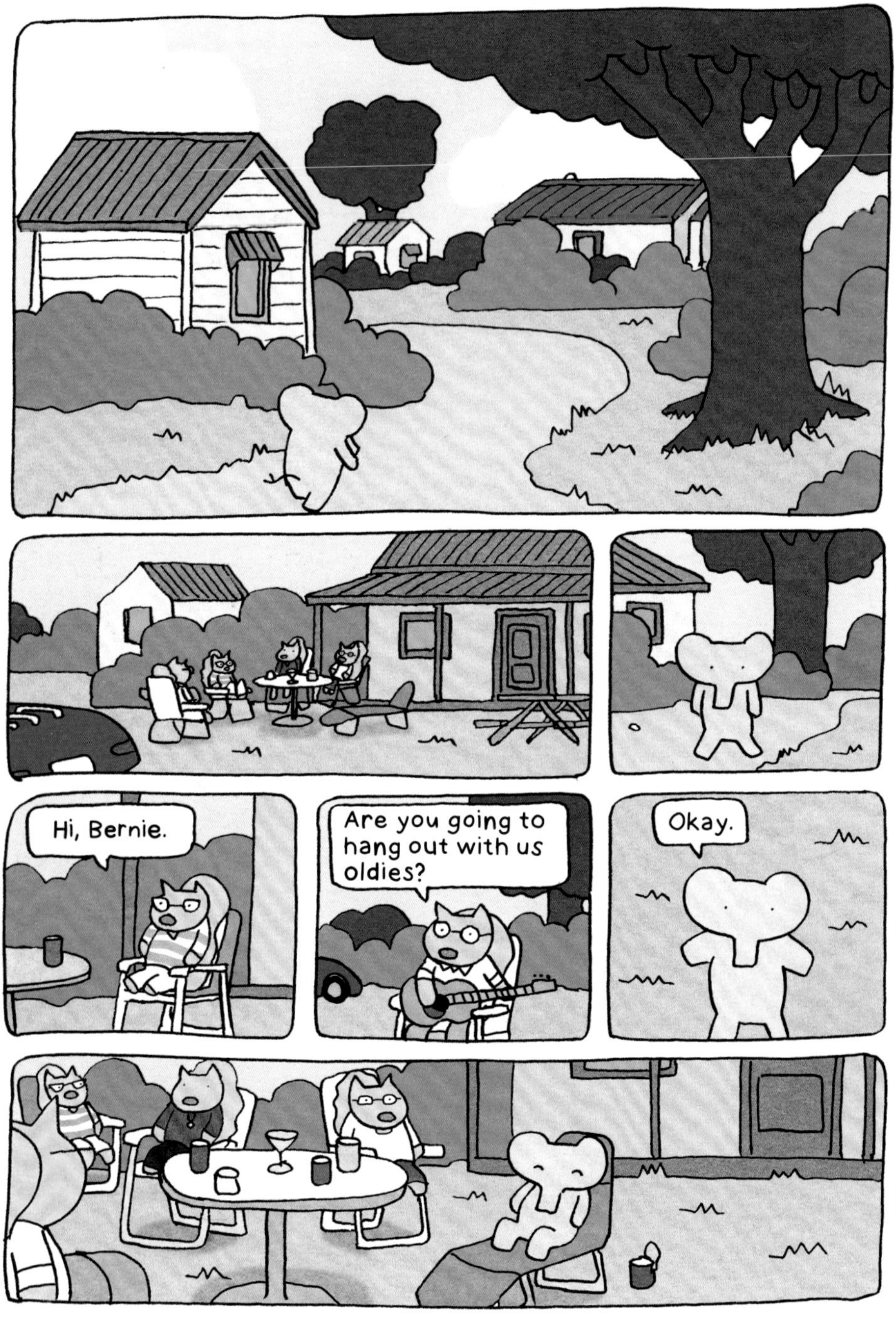
Hi, Bernie.
Are you going to hang out with us oldies?
Okay.

Chapter 8

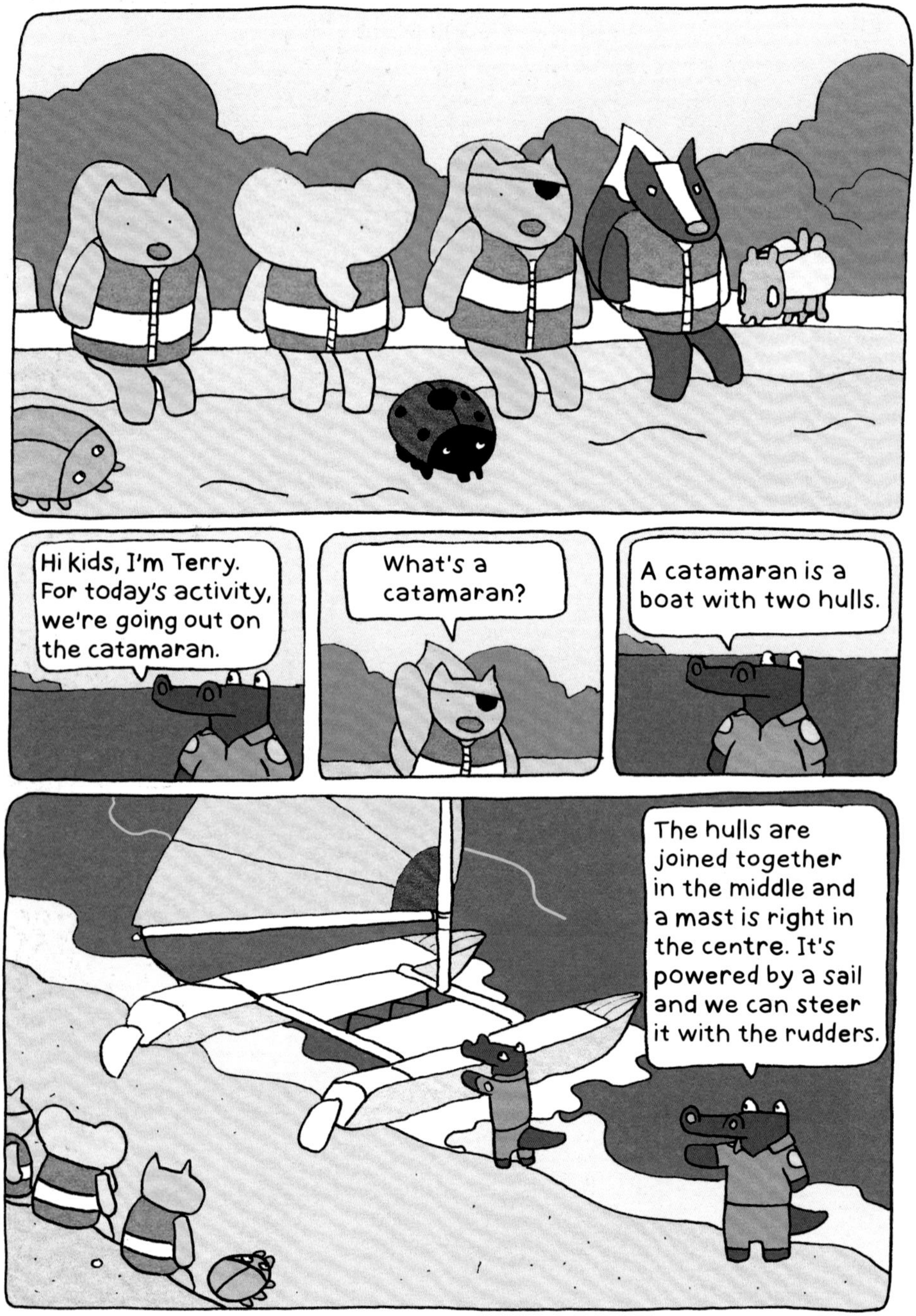
Hi kids, I'm Terry. For today's activity, we're going out on the catamaran.
What's a catamaran?
A catamaran is a boat with two hulls.
The hulls are joined together in the middle and a mast is right in the centre. It's powered by a sail and we can steer it with the rudders.

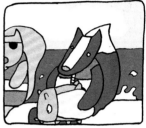

What's your beetle's name again?

Bounce.

Why Bounce?

Because she can bounce really high. Sometimes when Bounce has a burst of speed it makes a big shock wave.

Bounce is awesome.

Hold on! It's getting choppy!

Ha ha ha ha.

SPLASH
AAAAAH!

HISSS!

No, Bounce!

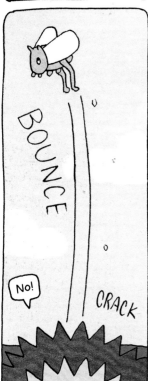
BOUNCE
No!
CRACK

Bounce, come back!

Oh no, look!

Bounce broke the boat.

Whoops!

Don't worry, kids. I'm just calling for help now.

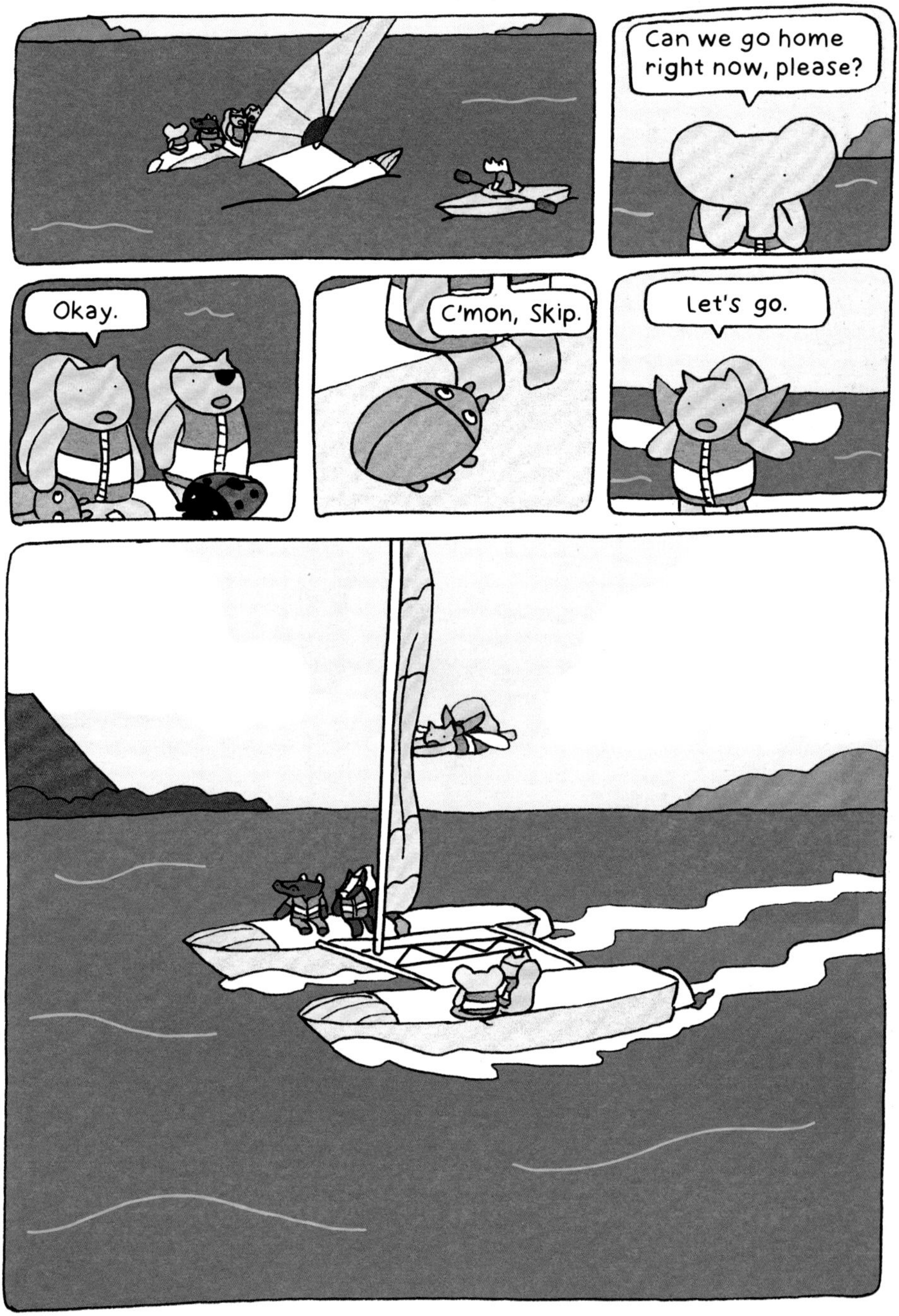
Can we go home right now, please?
Okay.
C'mon, Skip.
Let's go.

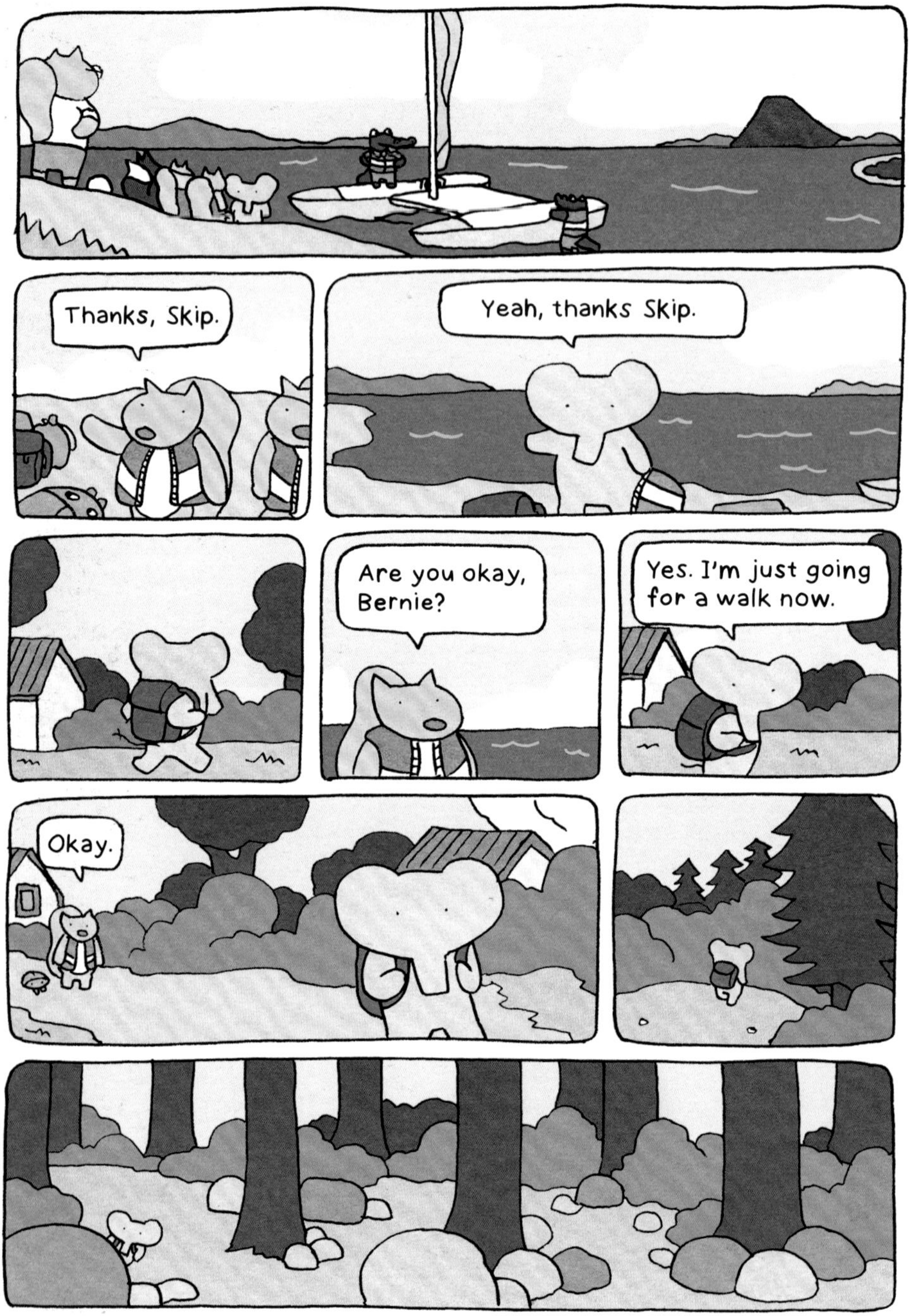
Thanks, Skip.
Yeah, thanks Skip.
Are you okay, Bernie?
Yes. I'm just going for a walk now.
Okay.

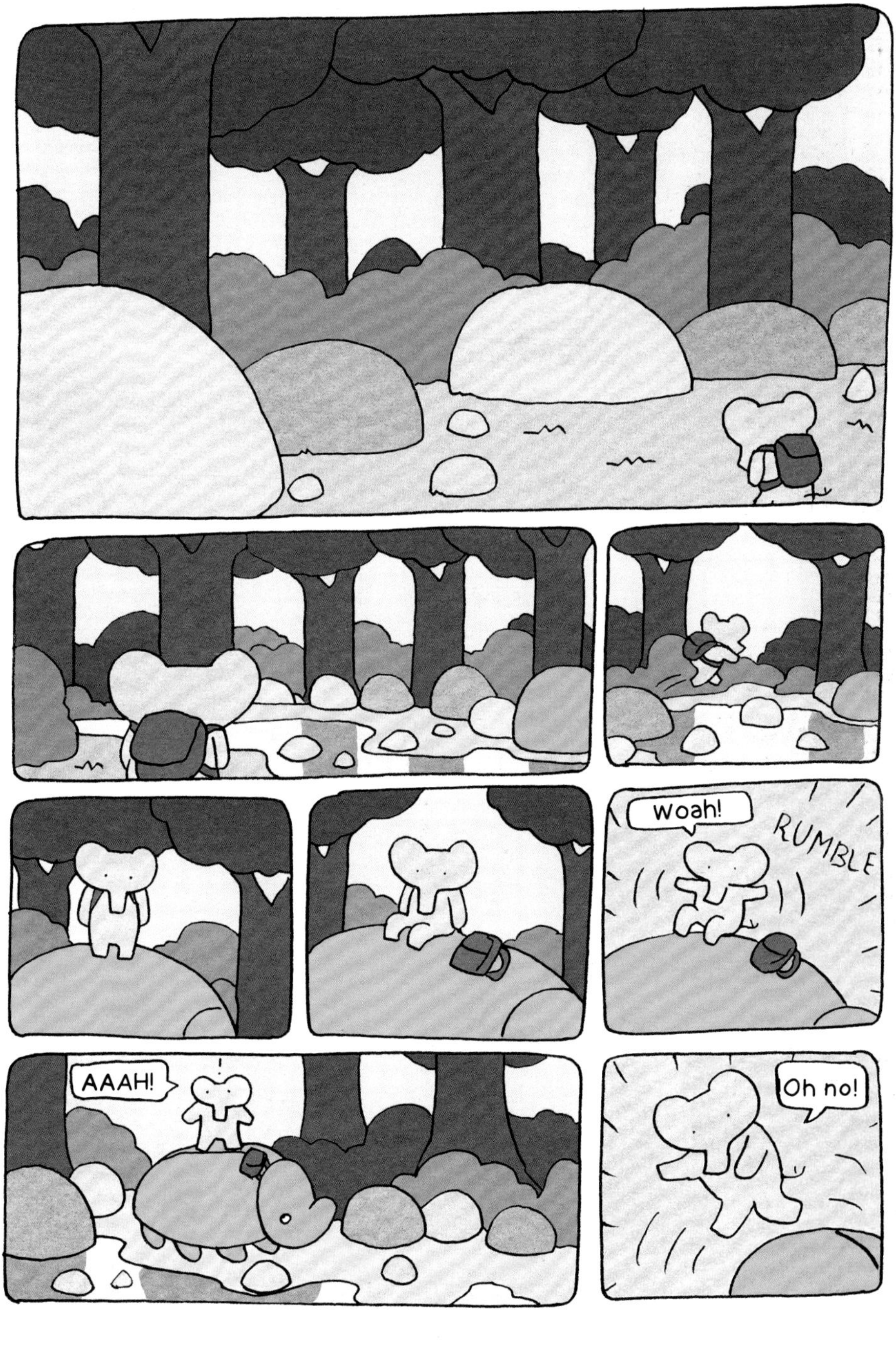
Woah!
RUMBLE
AAAH!
Oh no!

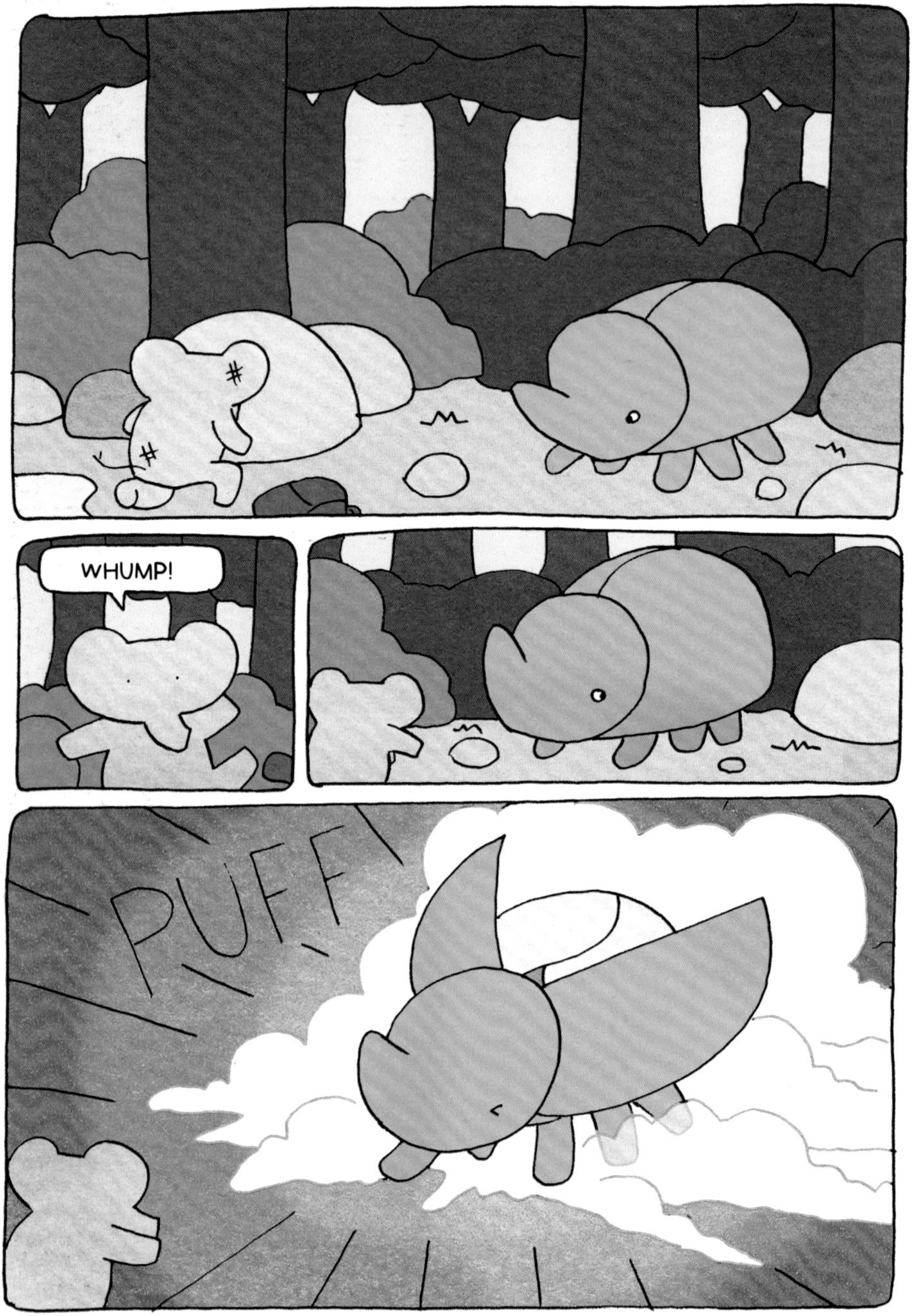
WHUMP!
PUFF!

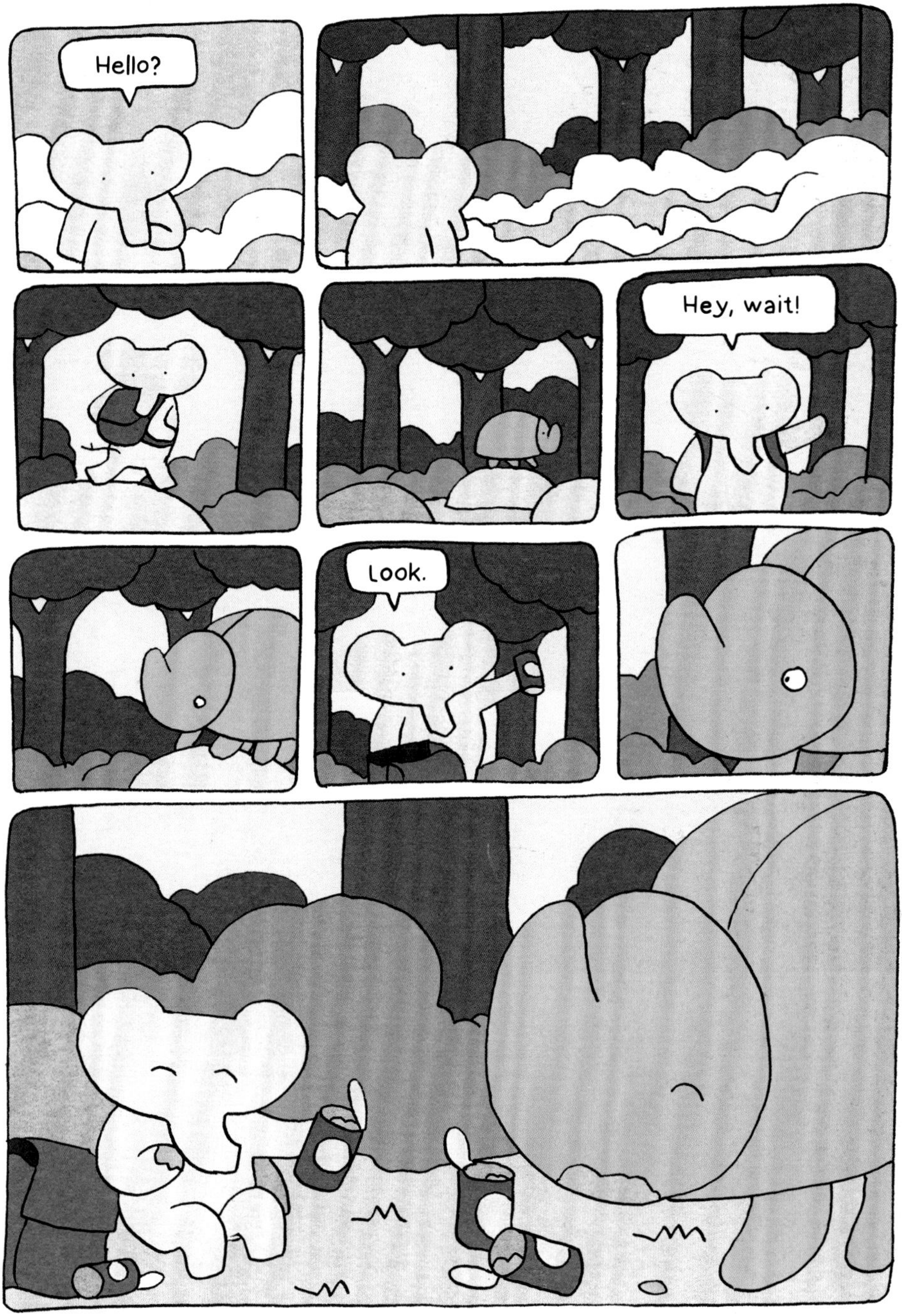
Hello?
Hey, wait!
Look.

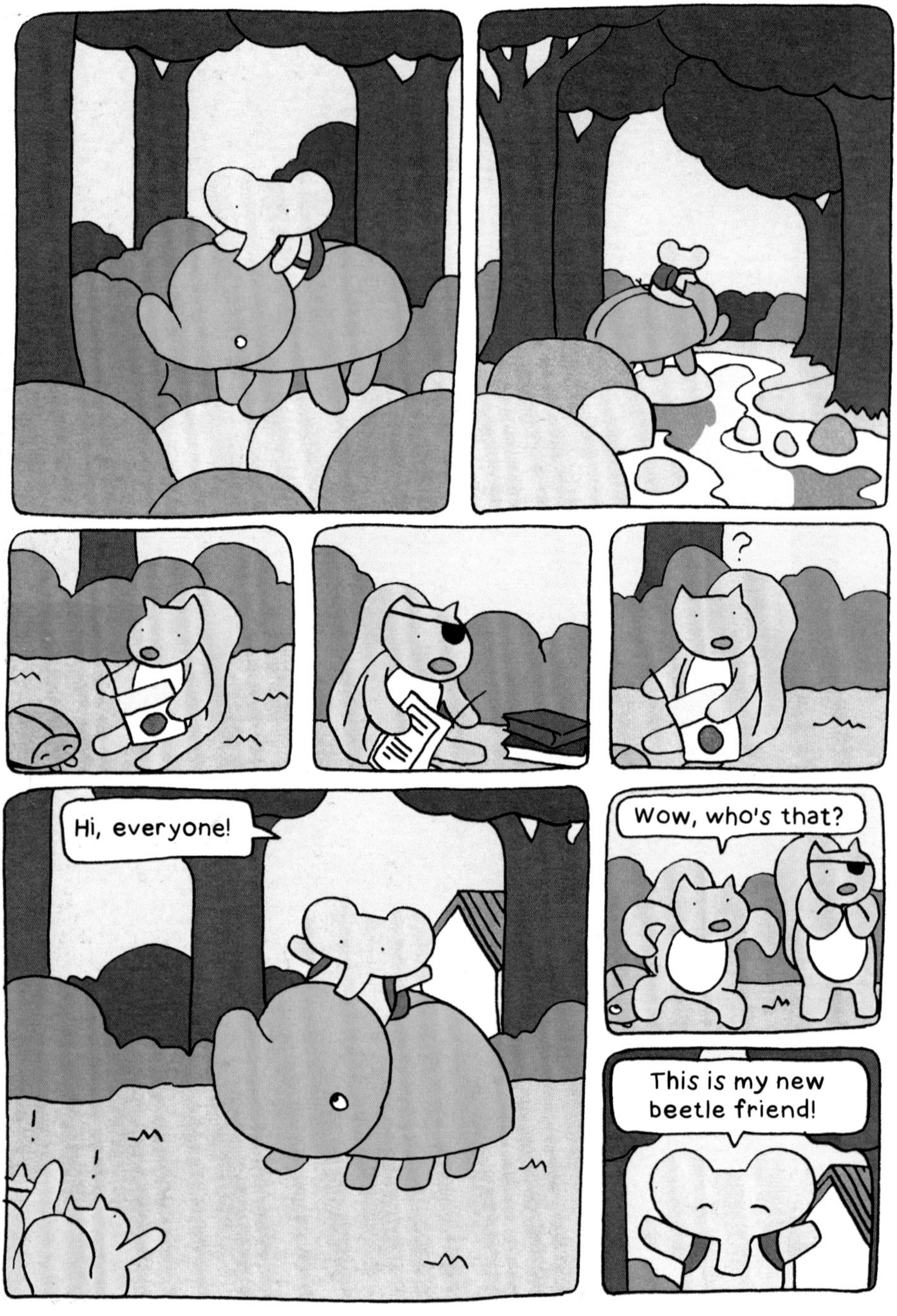
?
Hi, everyone!
!
!
Wow, who's that?
This is my new beetle friend!

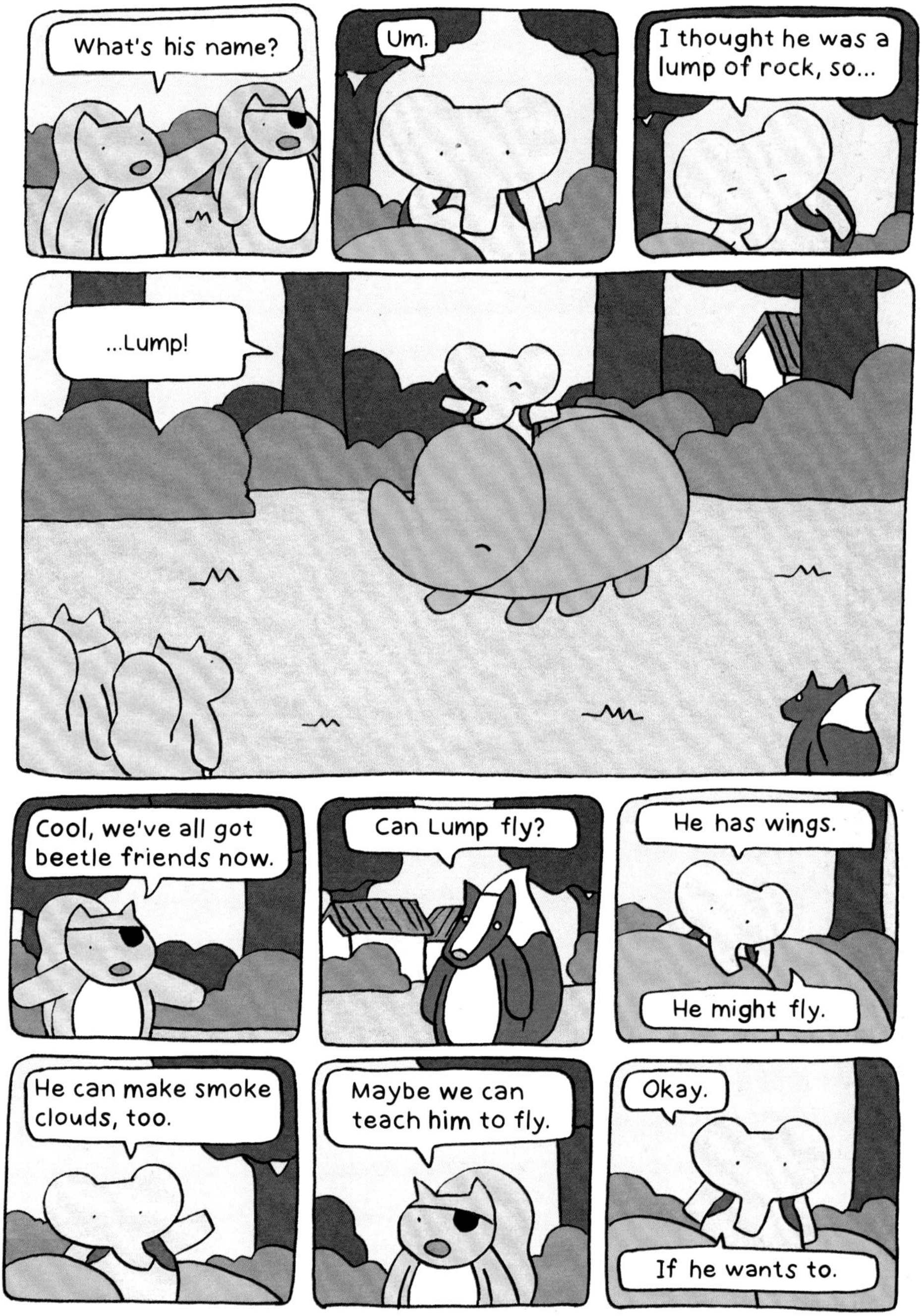
What's his name?
Um.
I thought he was a lump of rock, so...
...Lump!
Cool, we've all got beetle friends now.
Can Lump fly?
He has wings.
He might fly.
He can make smoke clouds, too.
Maybe we can teach him to fly.
Okay.
If he wants to.

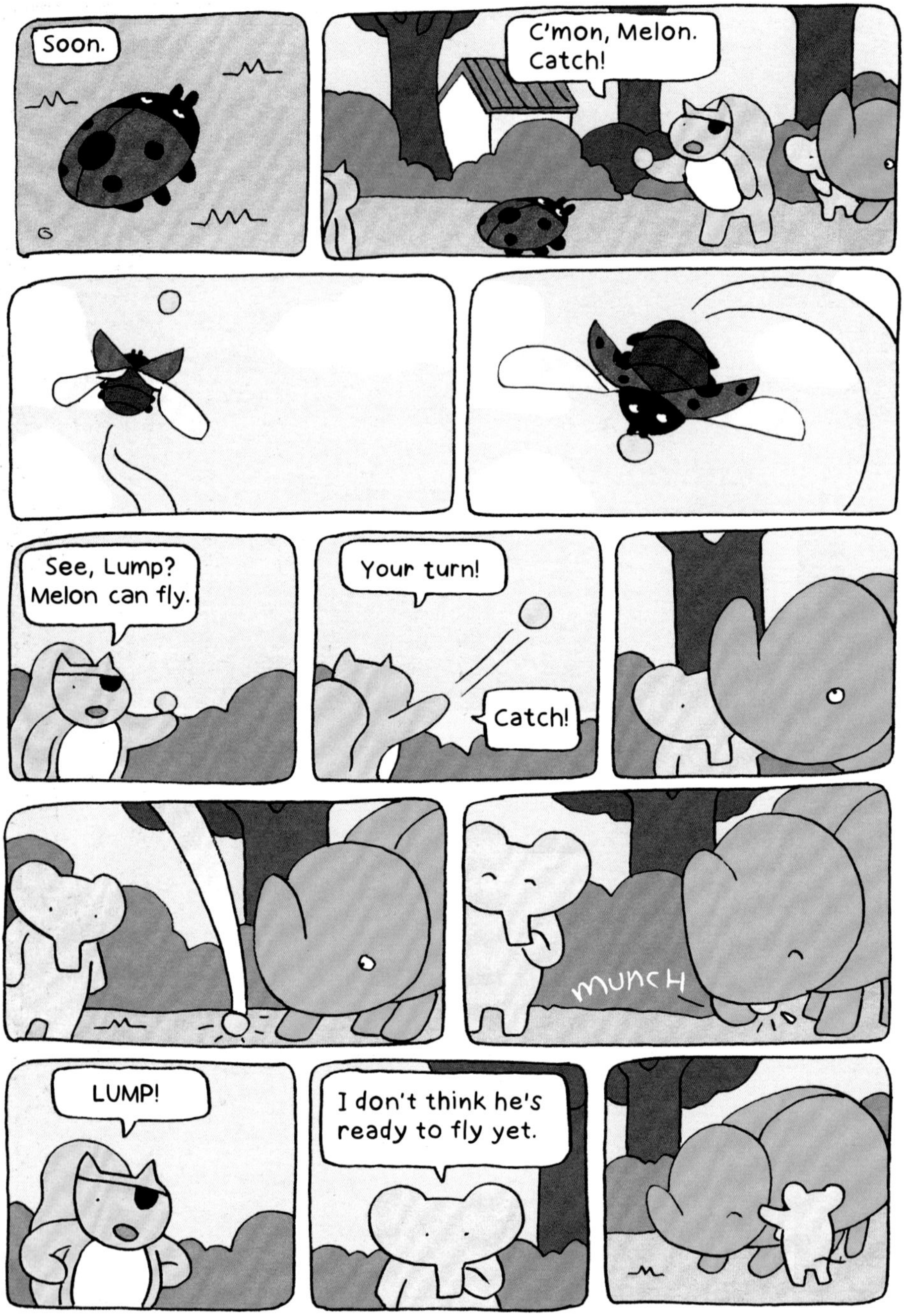
Soon.
C'mon, Melon. Catch!
See, Lump? Melon can fly.
Your turn!
Catch!
MUNCH
LUMP!
I don't think he's ready to fly yet.

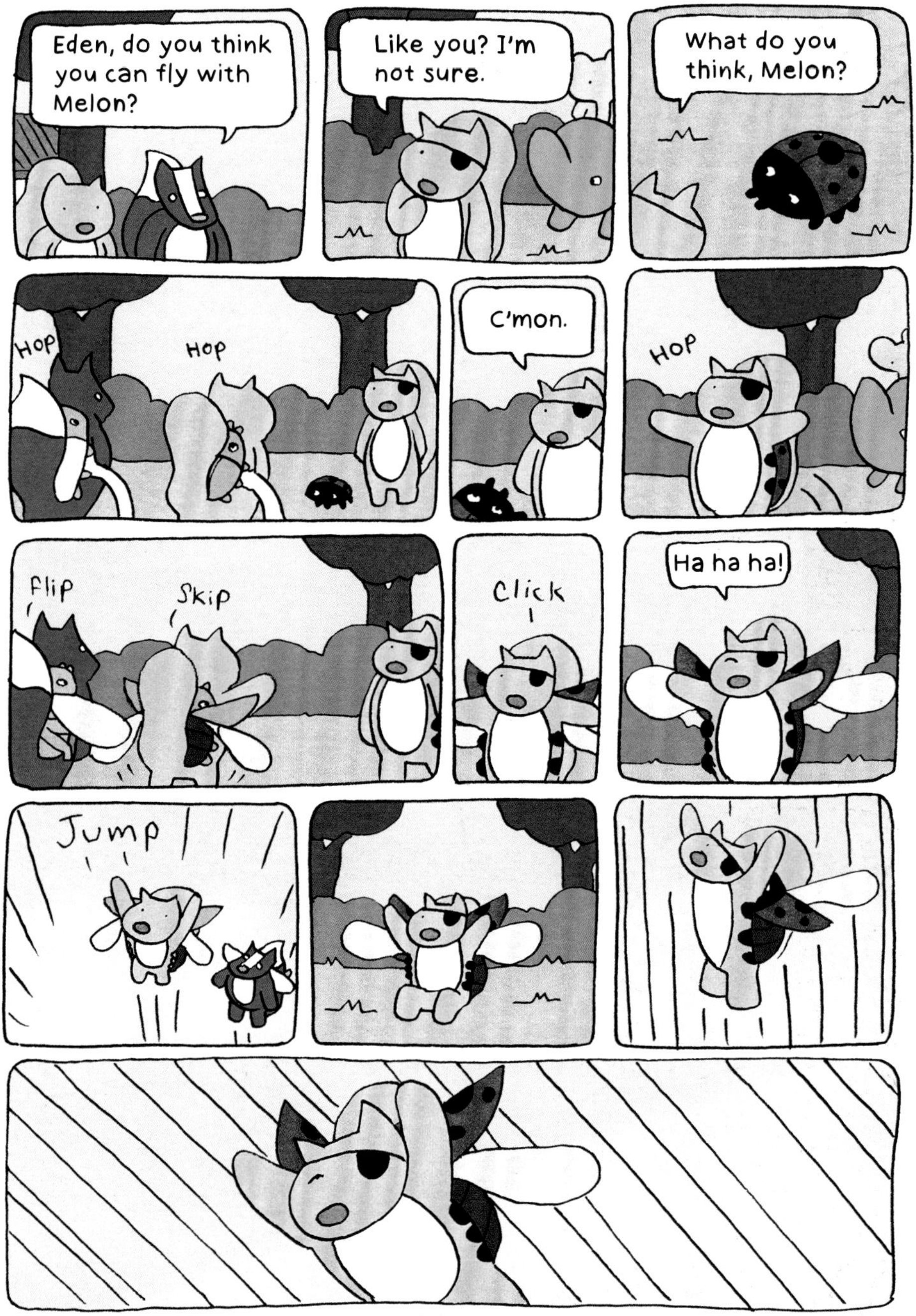
Eden, do you think you can fly with Melon?
Like you? I'm not sure.
What do you think, Melon?
HOP
HOP
C'mon.
HOP
flip
Skip
Click
Ha ha ha!
Jump

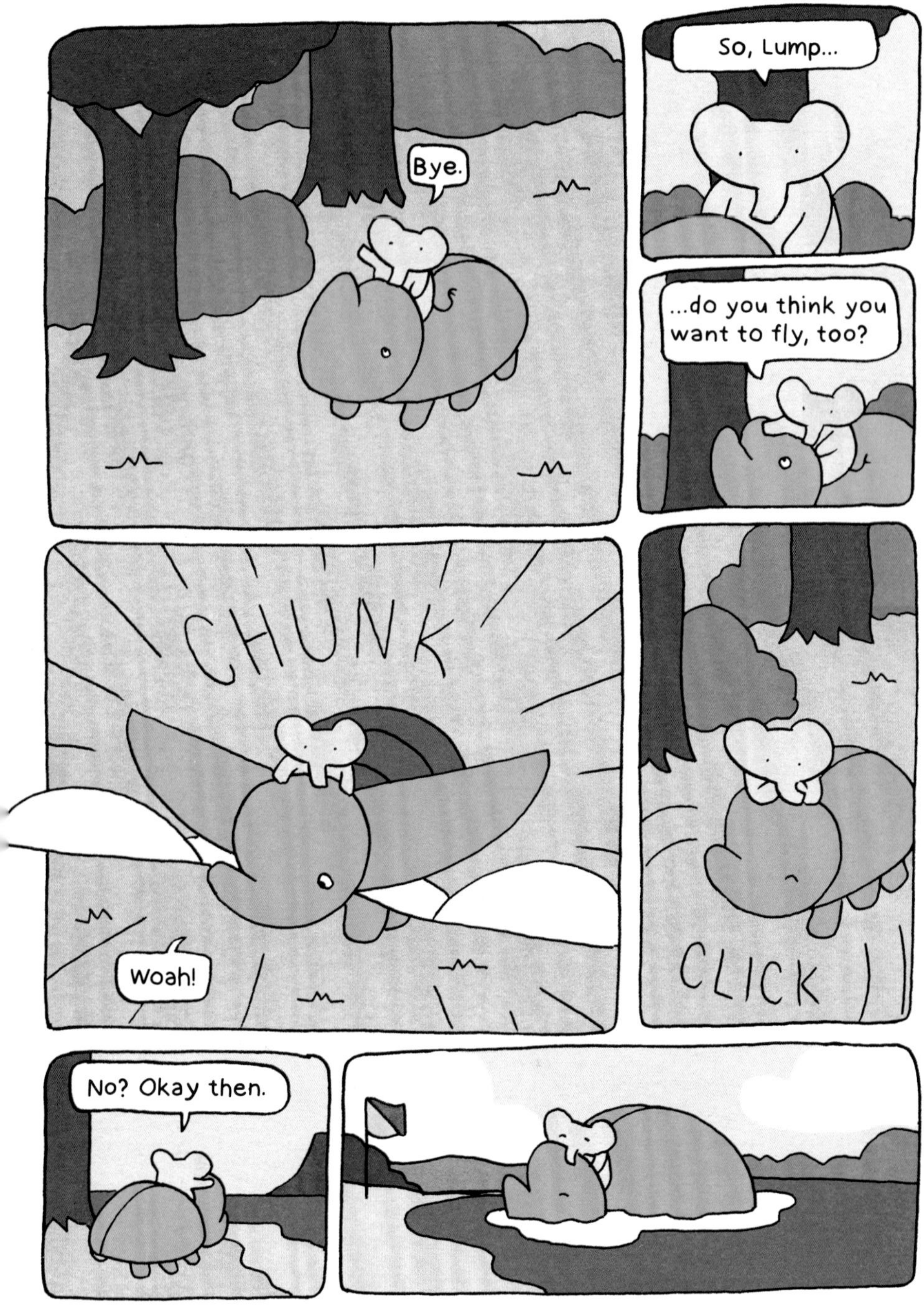
Bye.
So, Lump...
...do you think you want to fly, too?
CHUNK
Woah!
CLICK
No? Okay then.

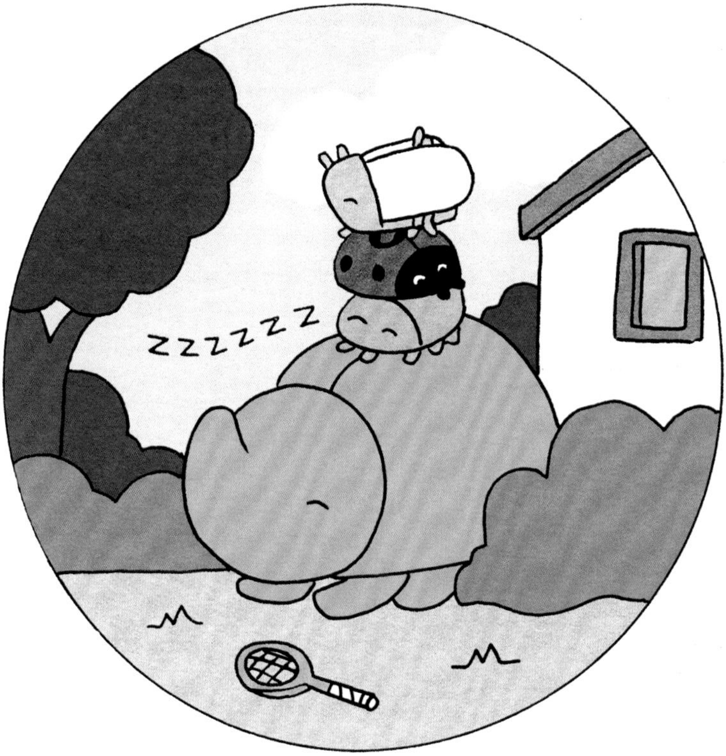
ZZZZZZ

Chapter 9

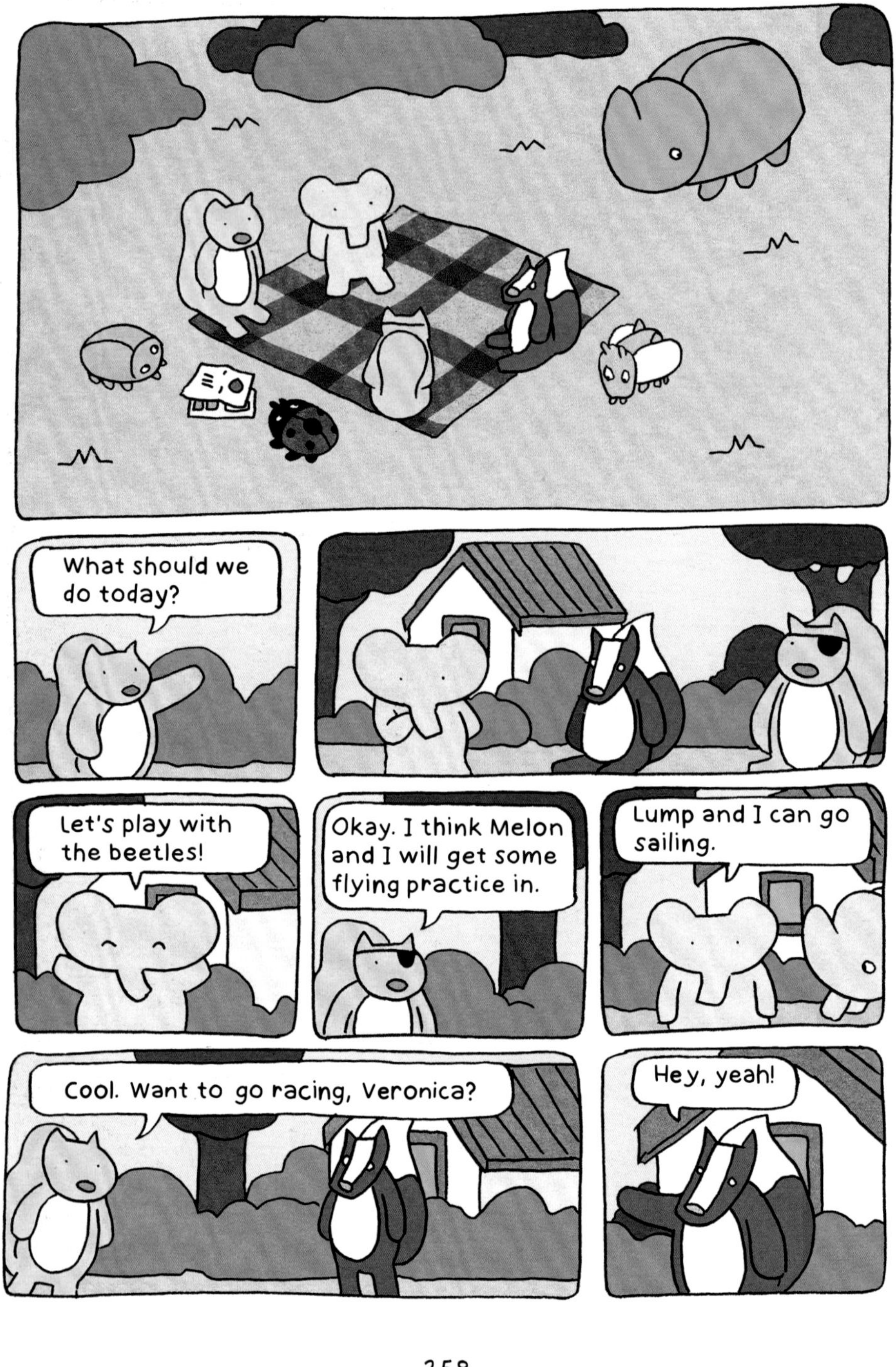
What should we do today?
Let's play with the beetles!
Okay. I think Melon and I will get some flying practice in.
Lump and I can go sailing.
Cool. Want to go racing, Veronica?
Hey, yeah!

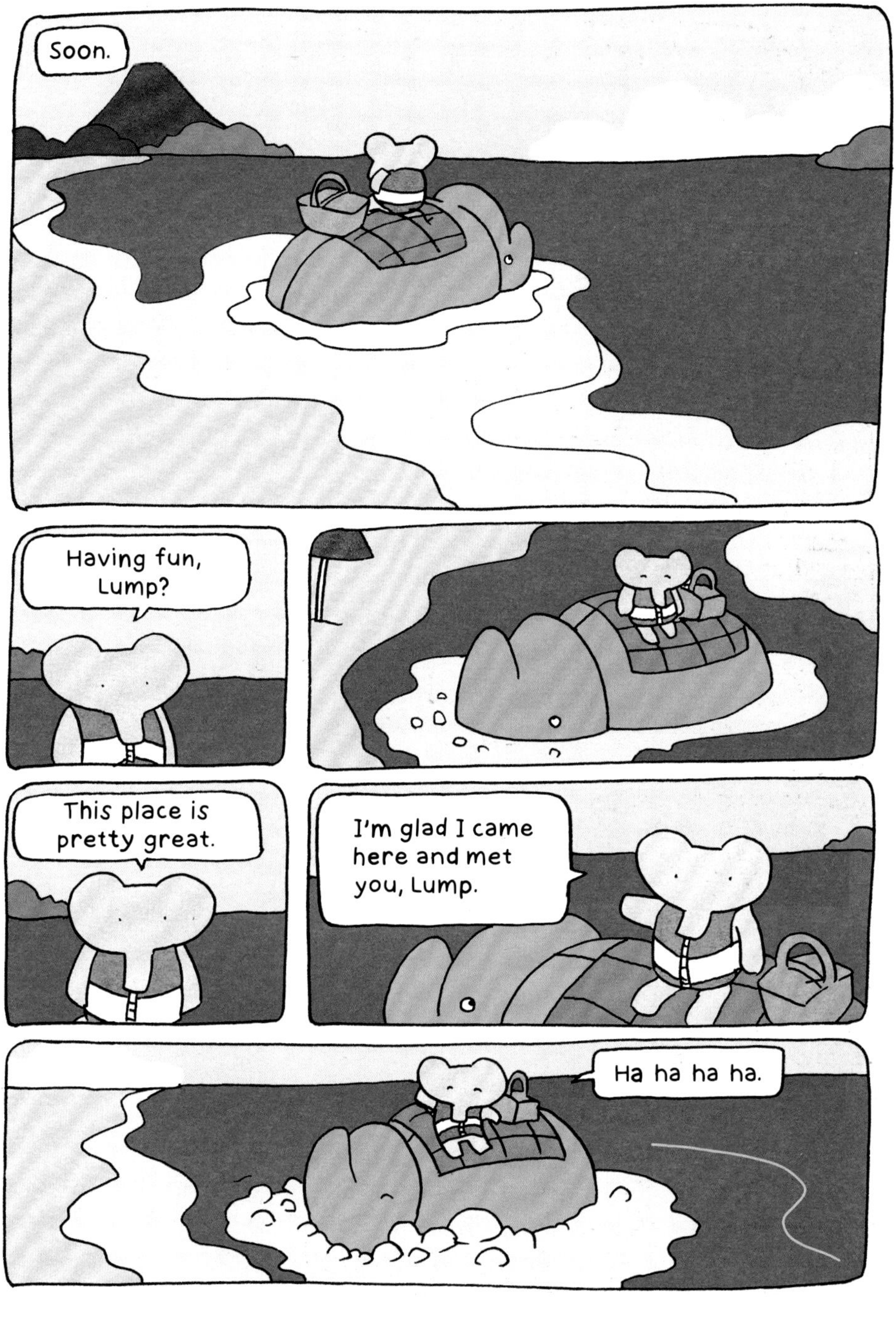
Soon.
Having fun, Lump?
This place is pretty great.
I'm glad I came here and met you, Lump.
Ha ha ha ha.

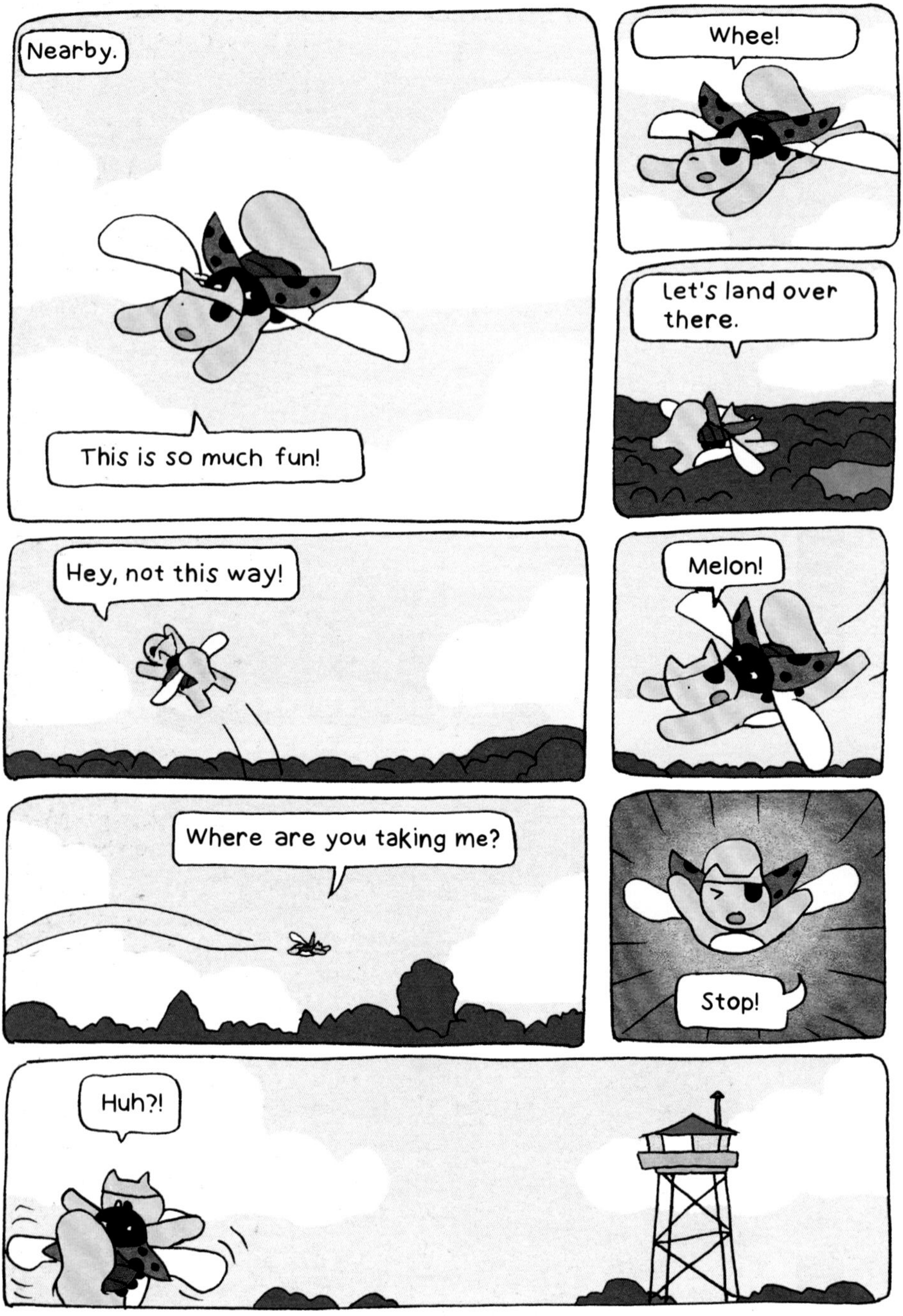
Nearby.
This is so much fun!
Whee!
Let's land over there.
Hey, not this way!
Melon!
Where are you taking me?
Stop!
Huh?!

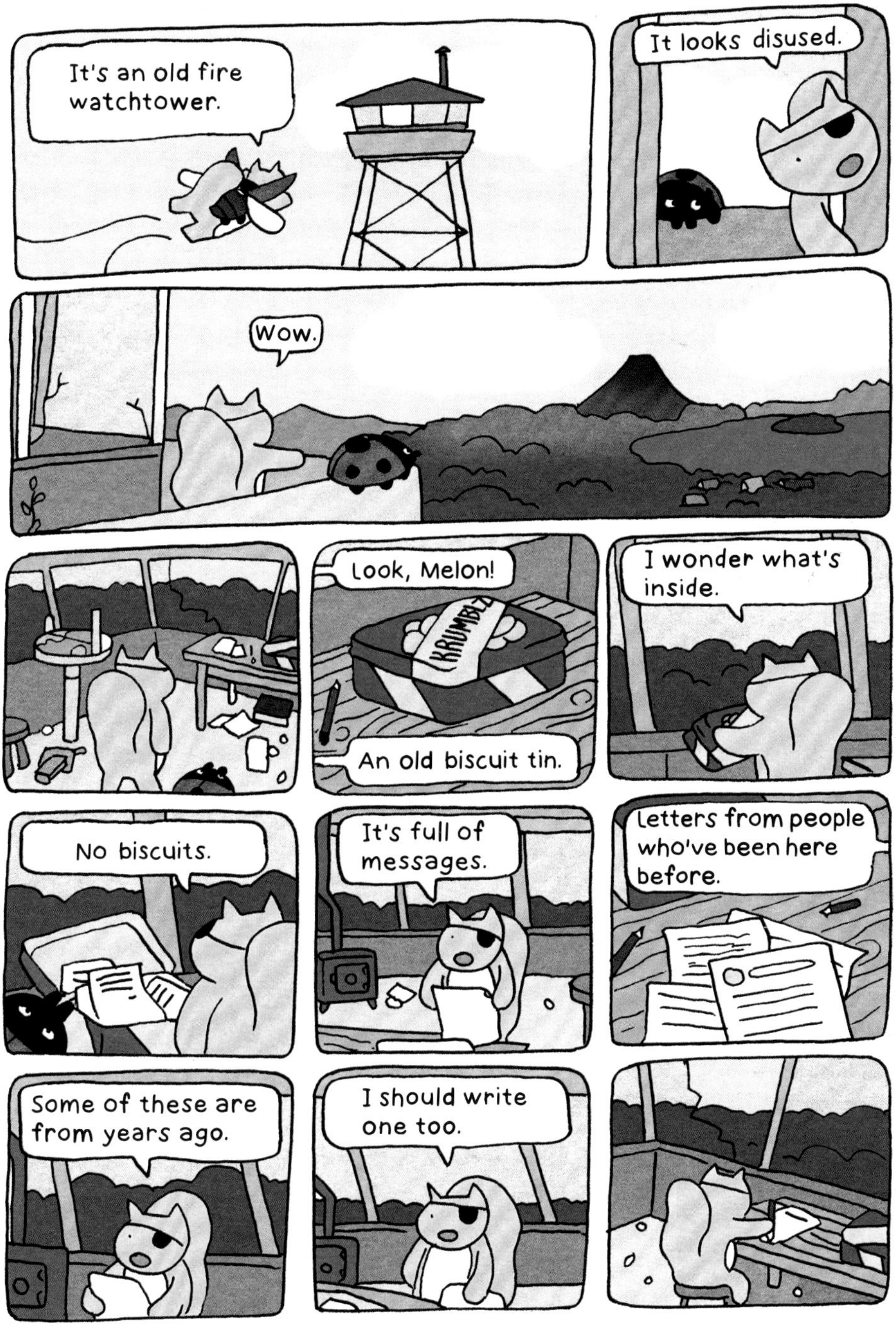
It's an old fire watchtower.
It looks disused.
Wow.
Look, Melon!
KRUMBLZ
An old biscuit tin.
I wonder what's inside.
No biscuits.
It's full of messages.
Letters from people who've been here before.
Some of these are from years ago.
I should write one too.

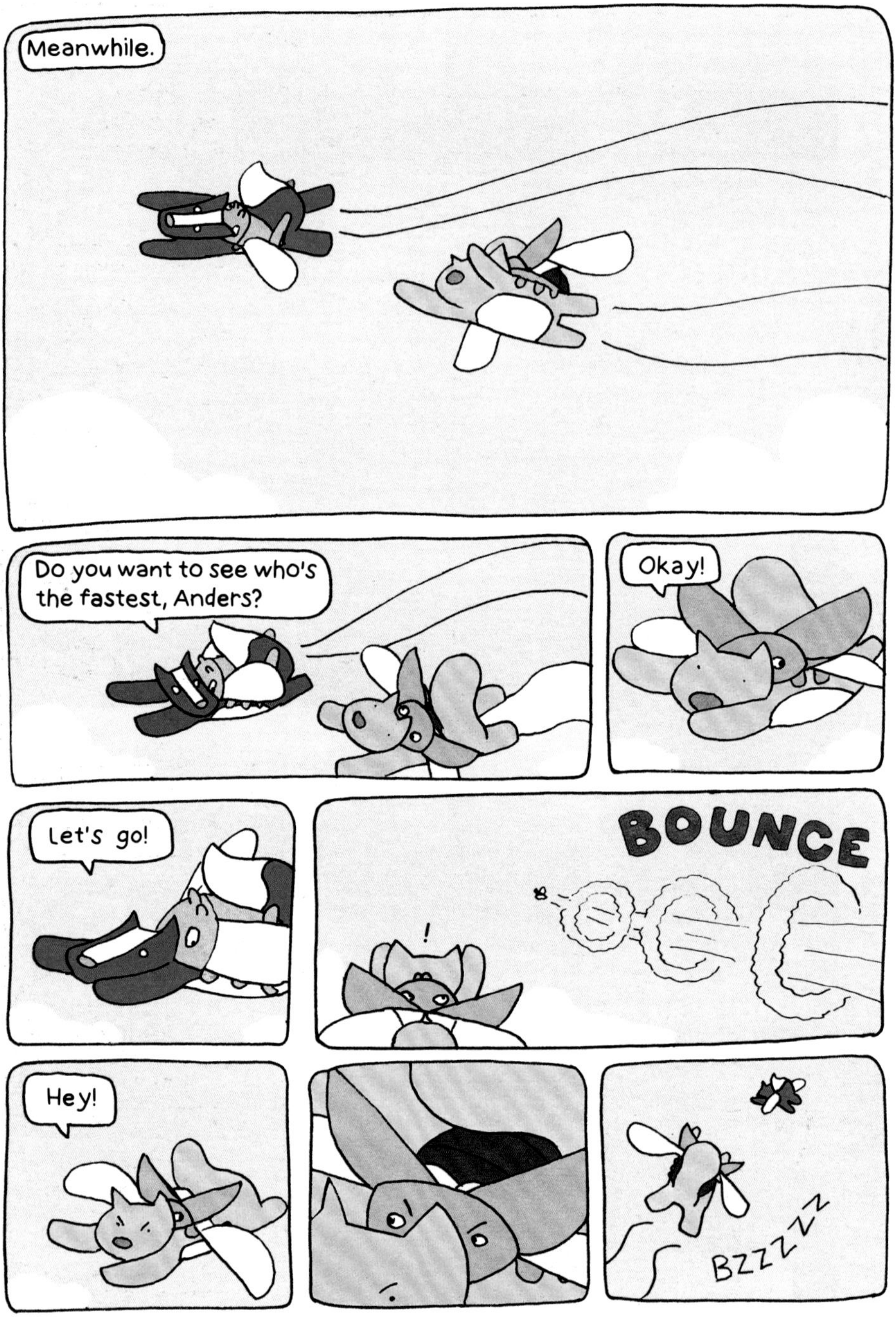
Meanwhile.
Do you want to see who's the fastest, Anders?
Okay!
Let's go!
BOUNCE
!
Hey!
BZZZZZ

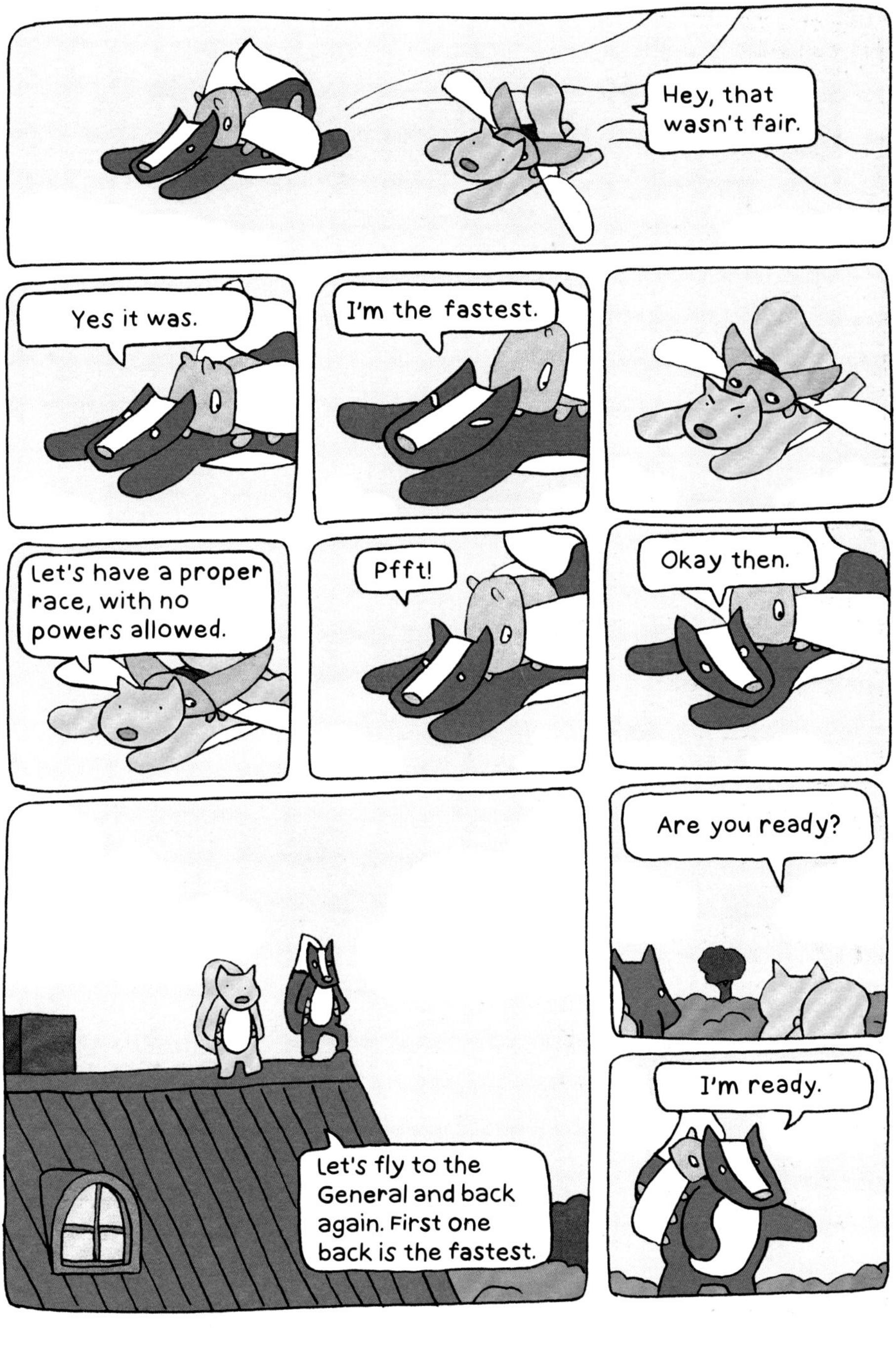
Hey, that wasn't fair.
Yes it was.
I'm the fastest.
Let's have a proper race, with no powers allowed.
Pfft!
Okay then.
Let's fly to the General and back again. First one back is the fastest.
Are you ready?
I'm ready.

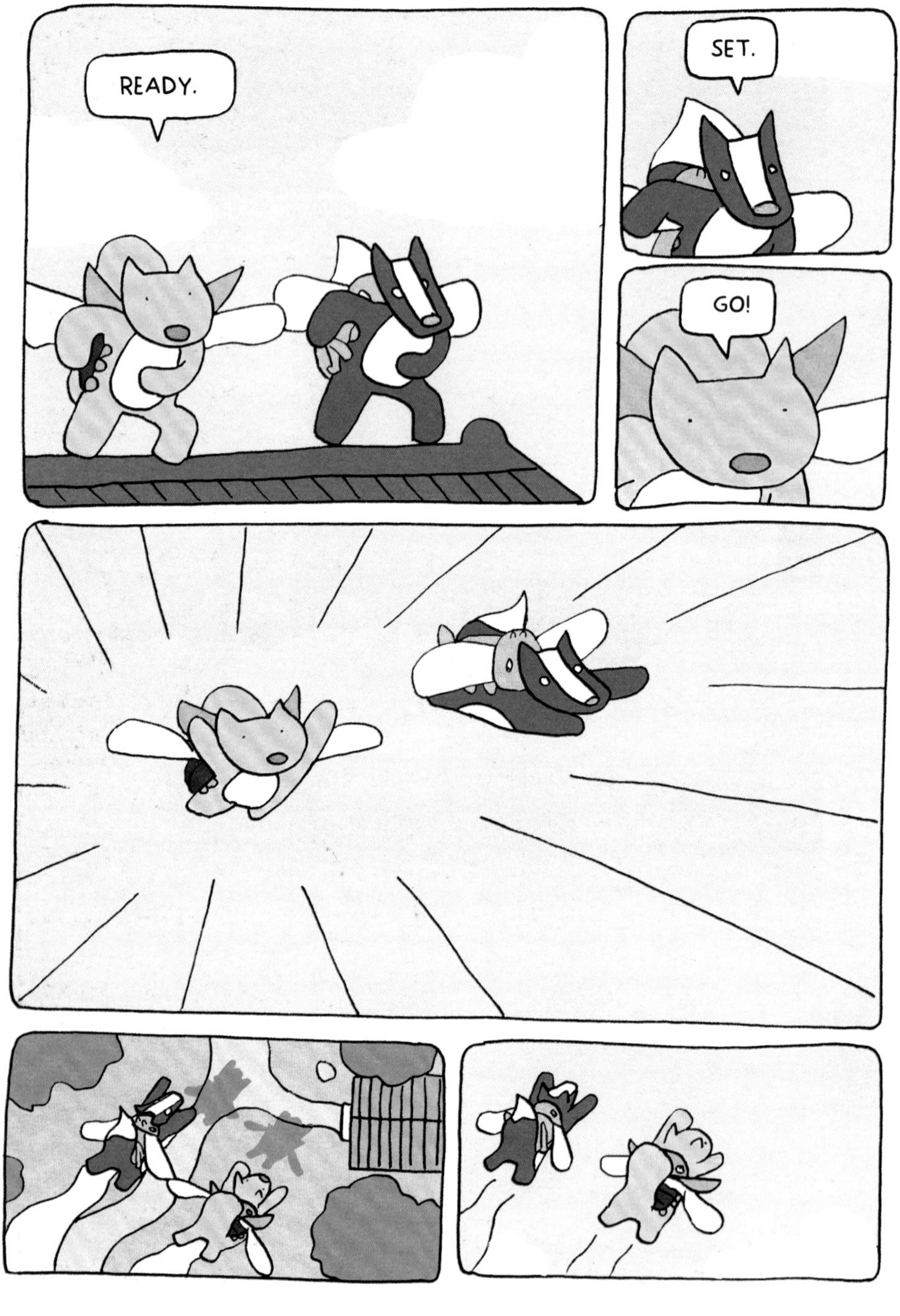
READY.
SET.
GO!

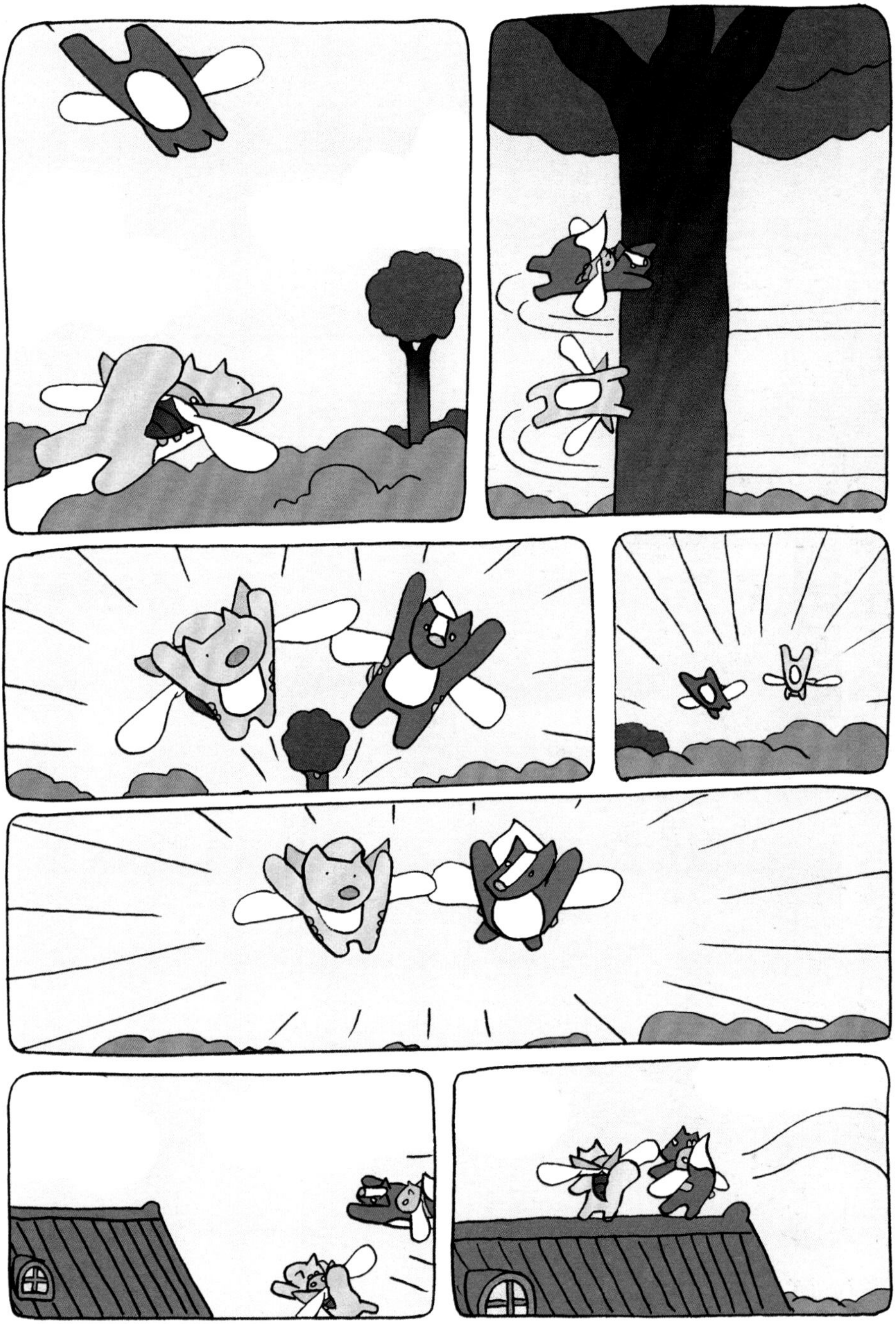

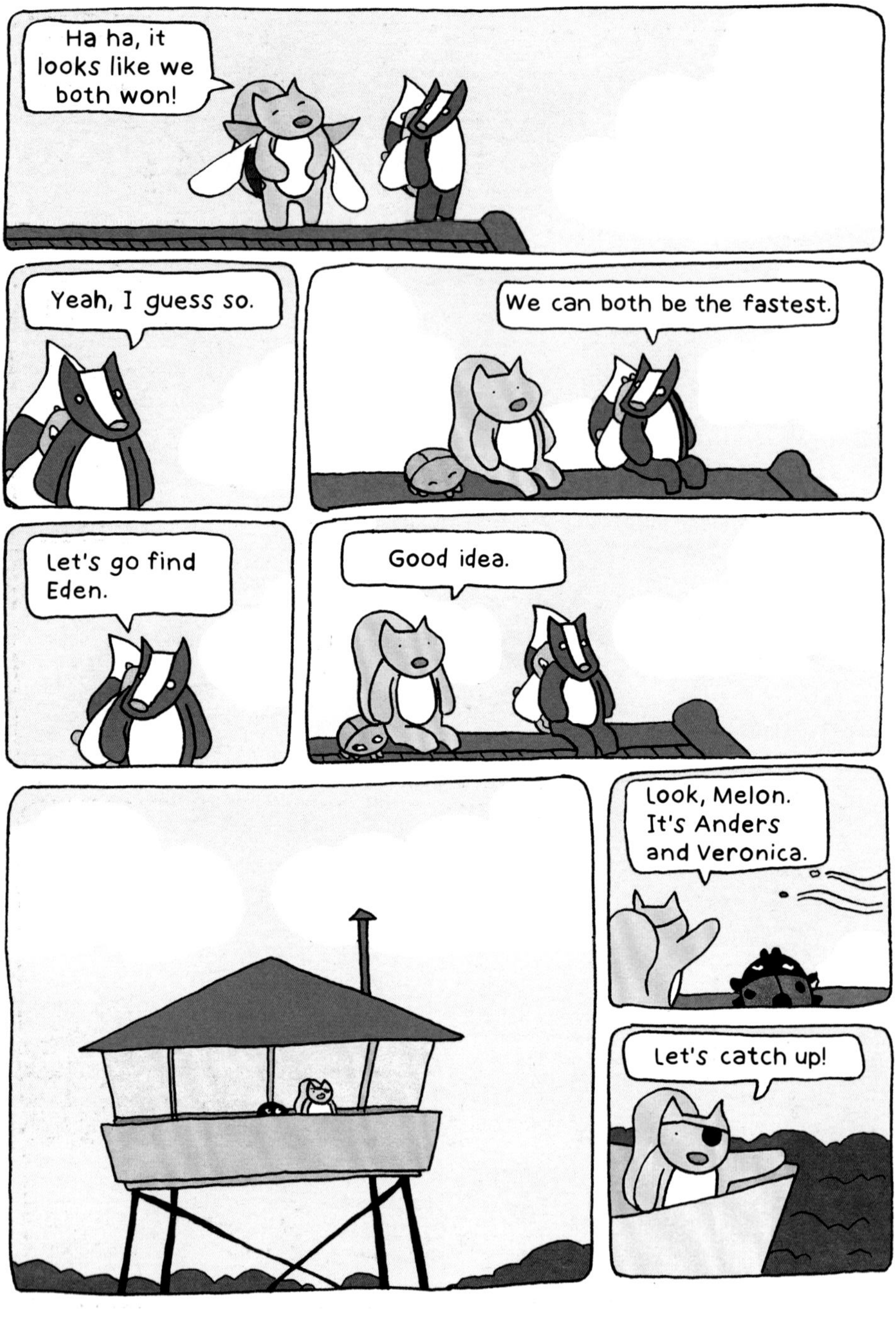
Ha ha, it looks like we both won!
Yeah, I guess so.
We can both be the fastest.
Let's go find Eden.
Good idea.
Look, Melon. It's Anders and Veronica.
Let's catch up!

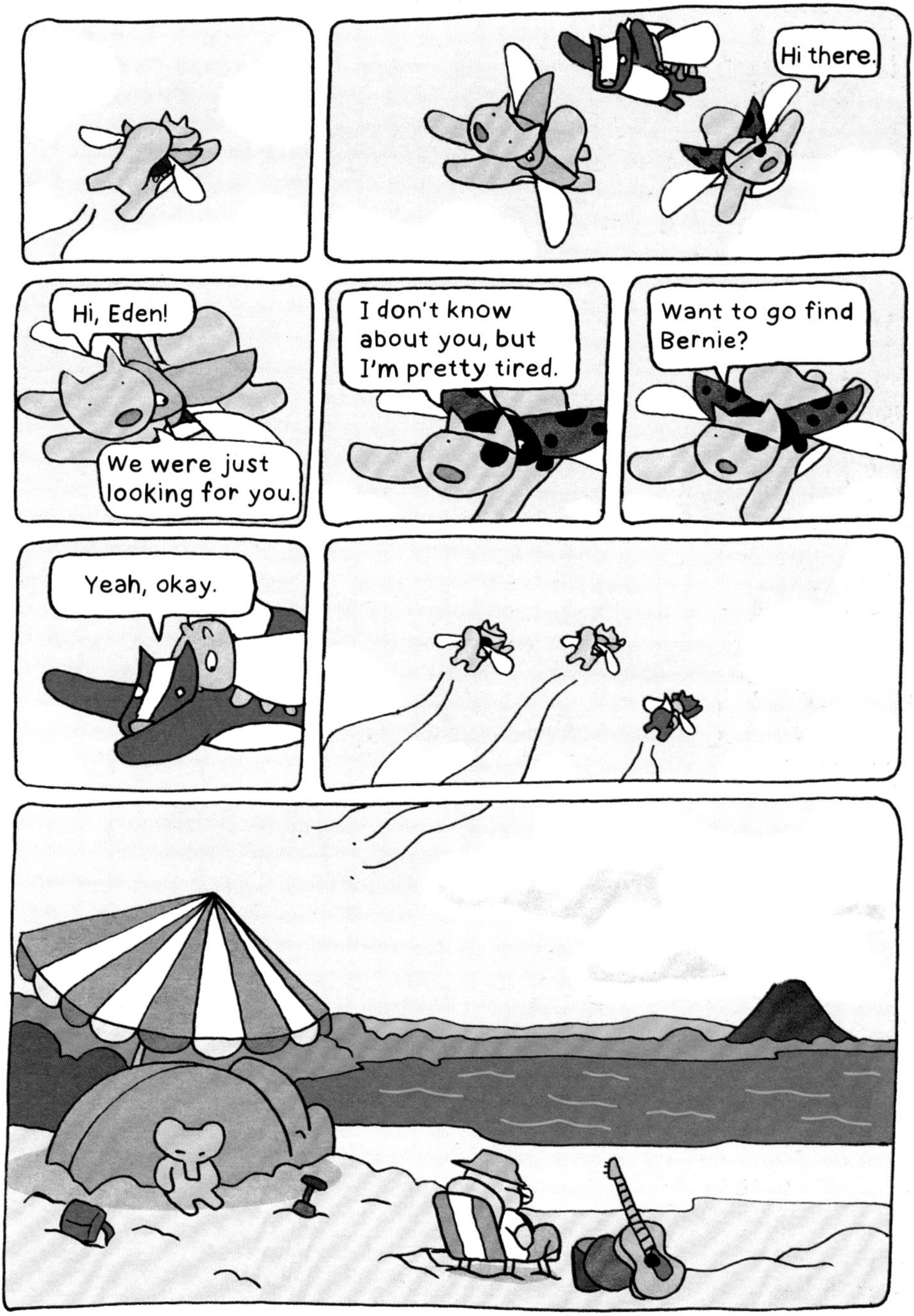
Hi there.
Hi, Eden!
We were just looking for you.
I don't know about you, but I'm pretty tired.
Want to go find Bernie?
Yeah, okay.

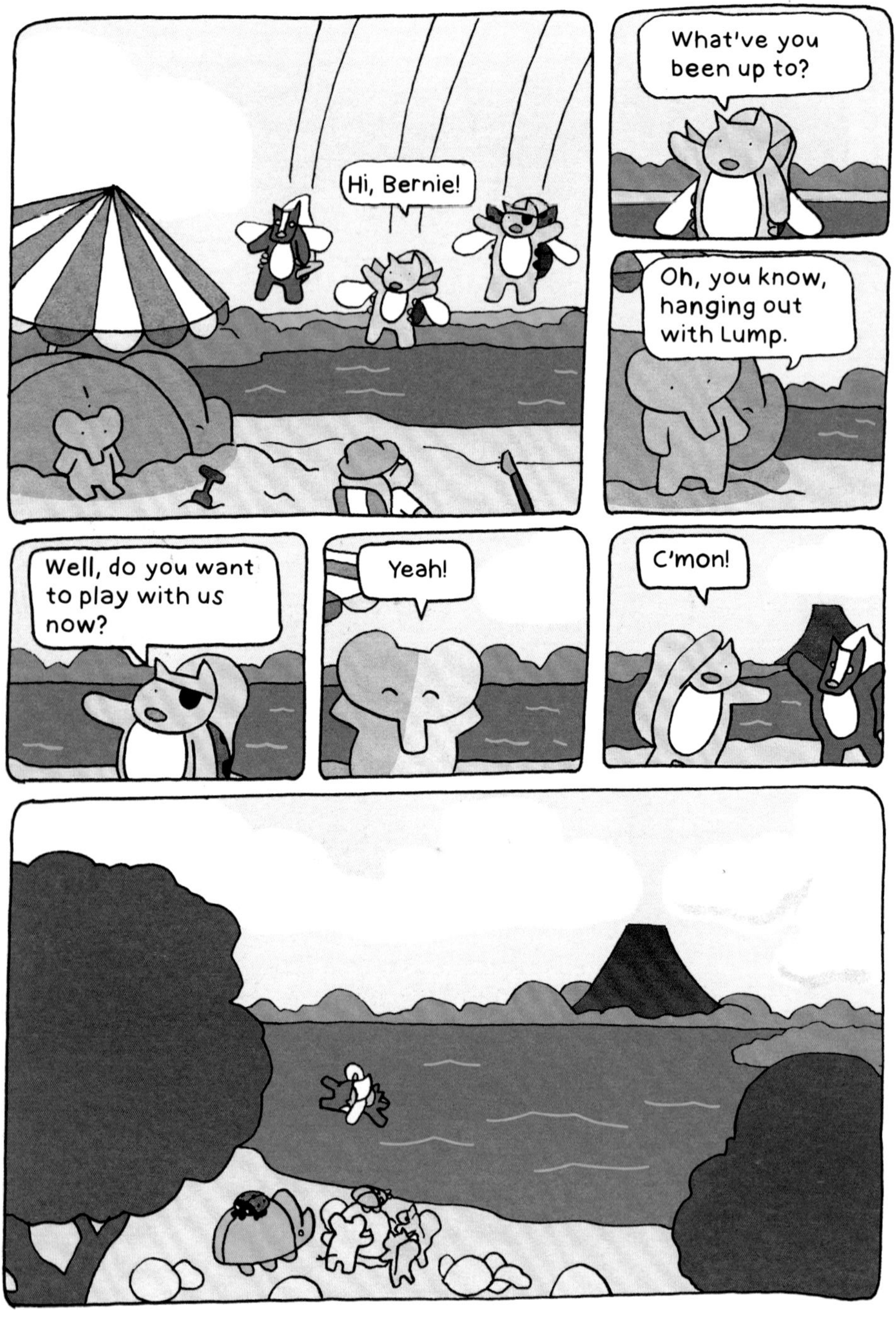
Hi, Bernie!
What've you been up to?
Oh, you know, hanging out with Lump.
Well, do you want to play with us now?
Yeah!
C'mon!

Chapter 10

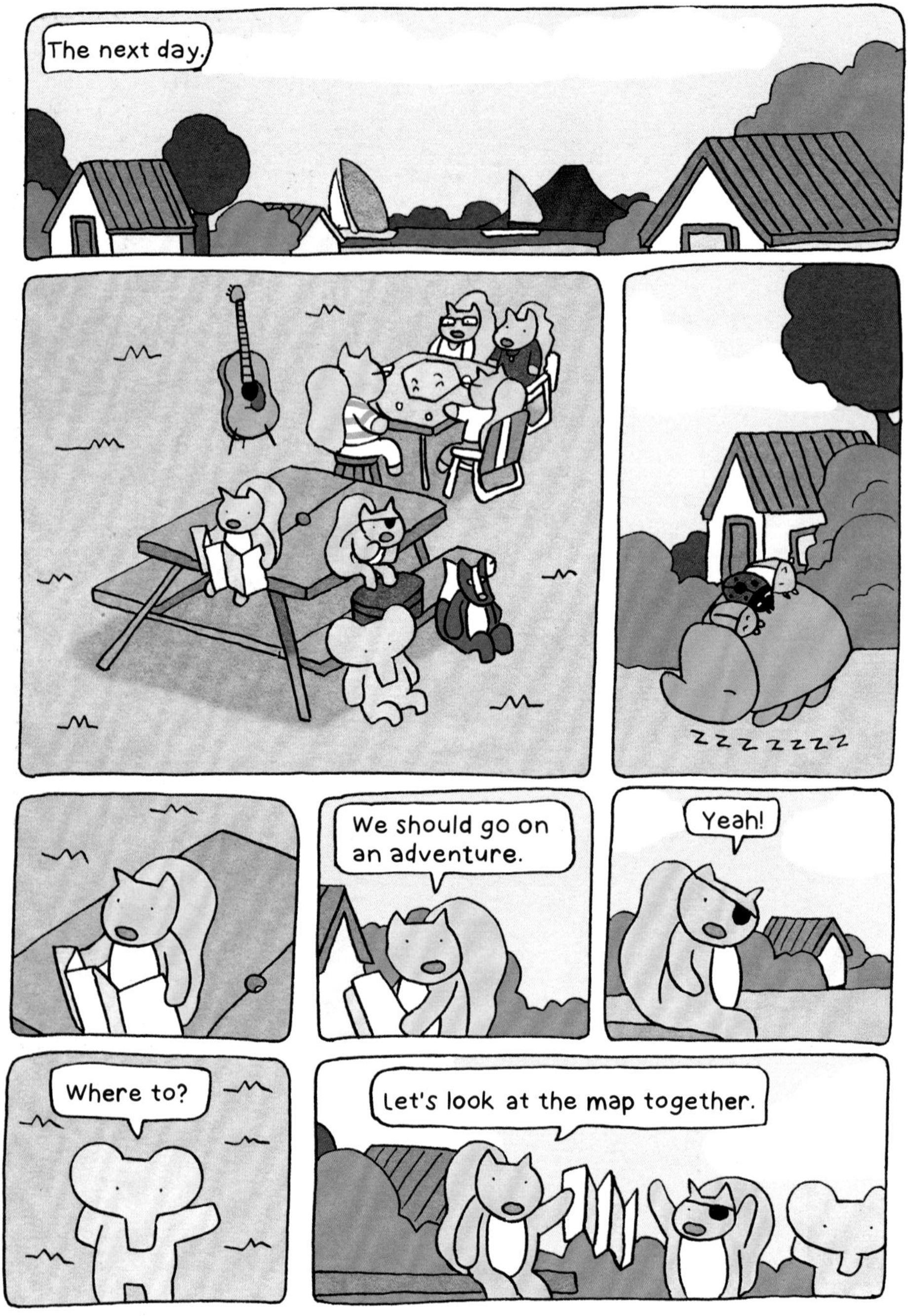
The next day.
ZZZZZZZ
We should go on an adventure.
Yeah!
Where to?
Let's look at the map together.

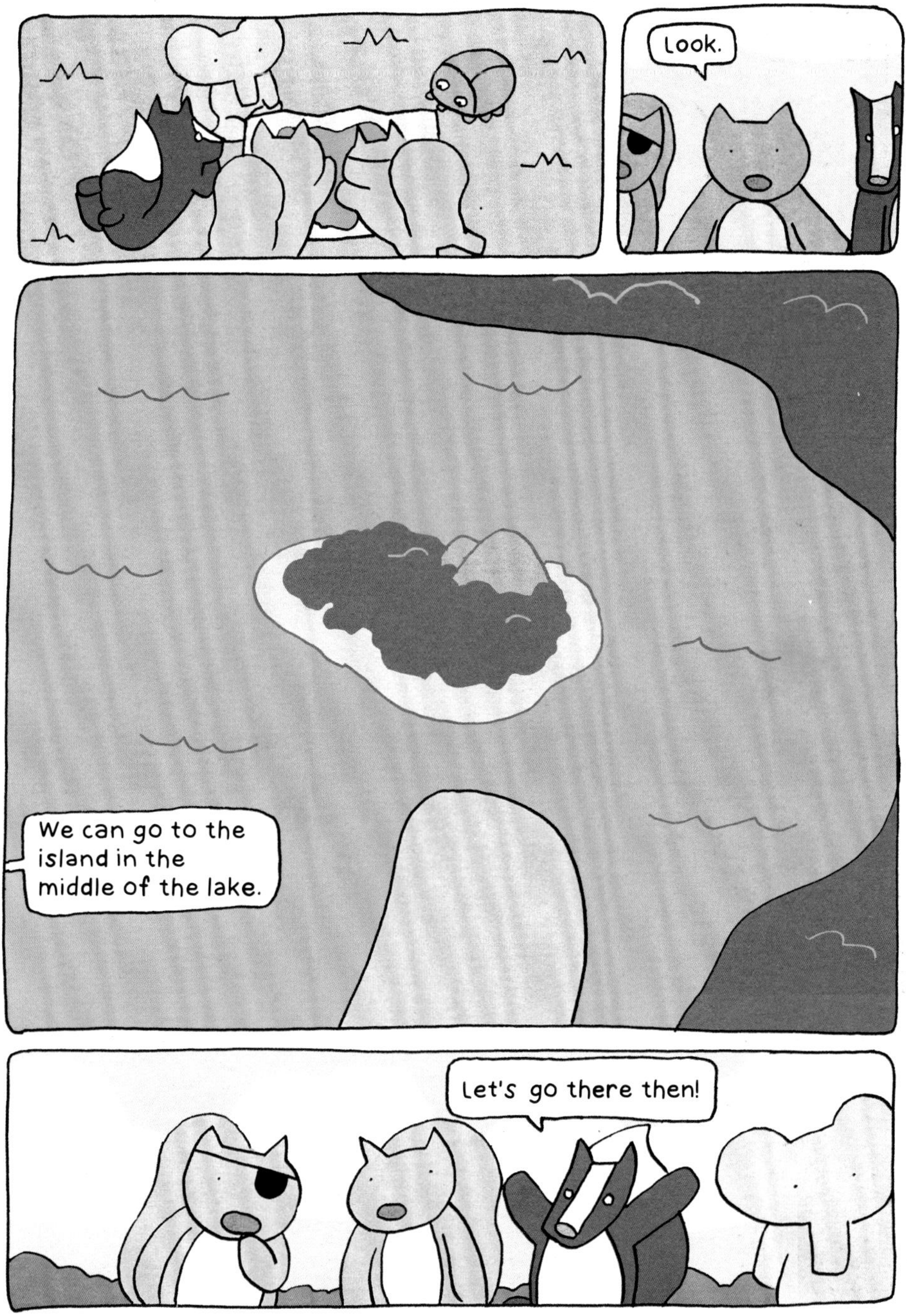
Look.
We can go to the island in the middle of the lake.
Let's go there then!

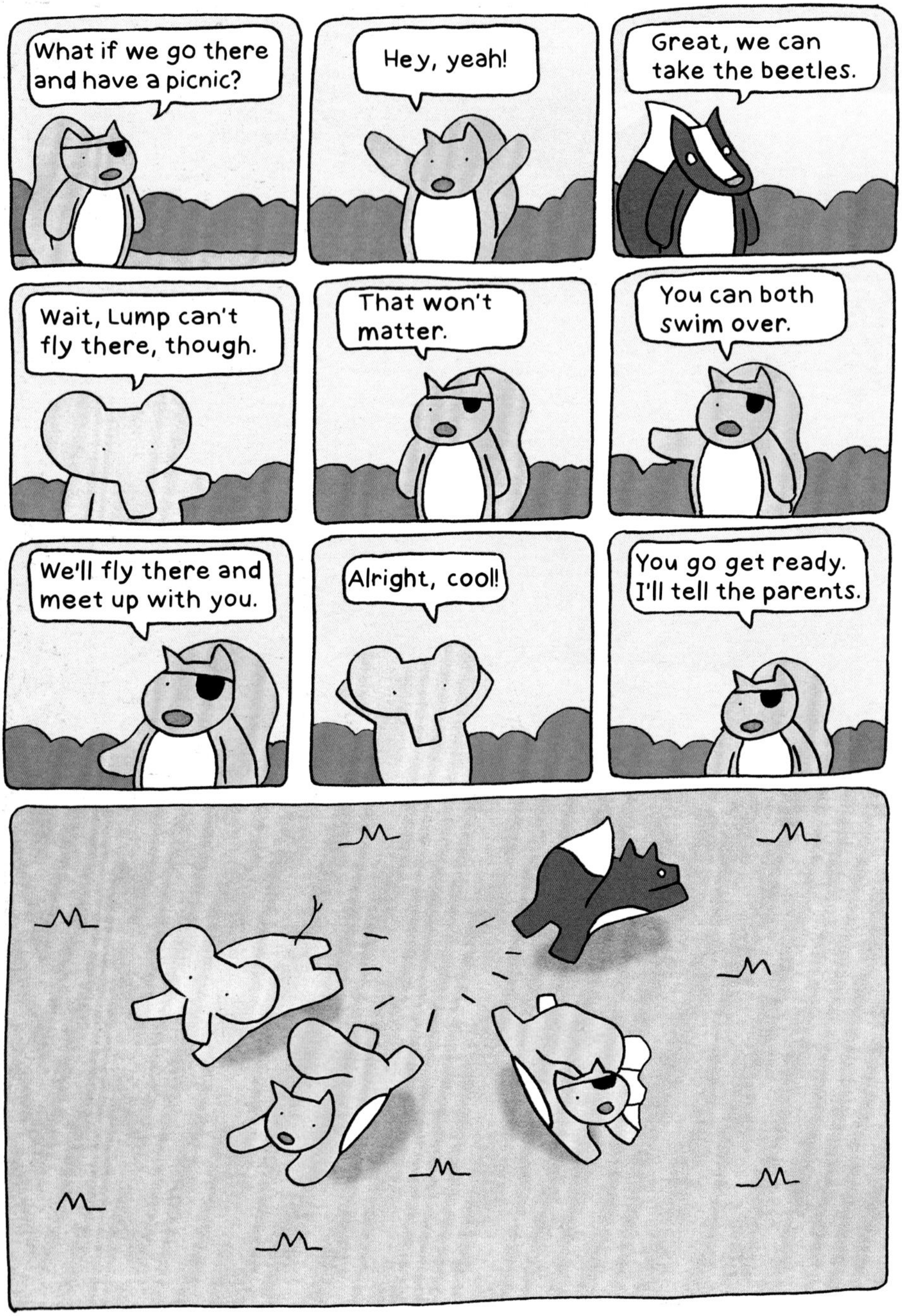
What if we go there and have a picnic?
Hey, yeah!
Great, we can take the beetles.
Wait, Lump can't fly there, though.
That won't matter.
You can both swim over.
We'll fly there and meet up with you.
Alright, cool!
You go get ready. I'll tell the parents.

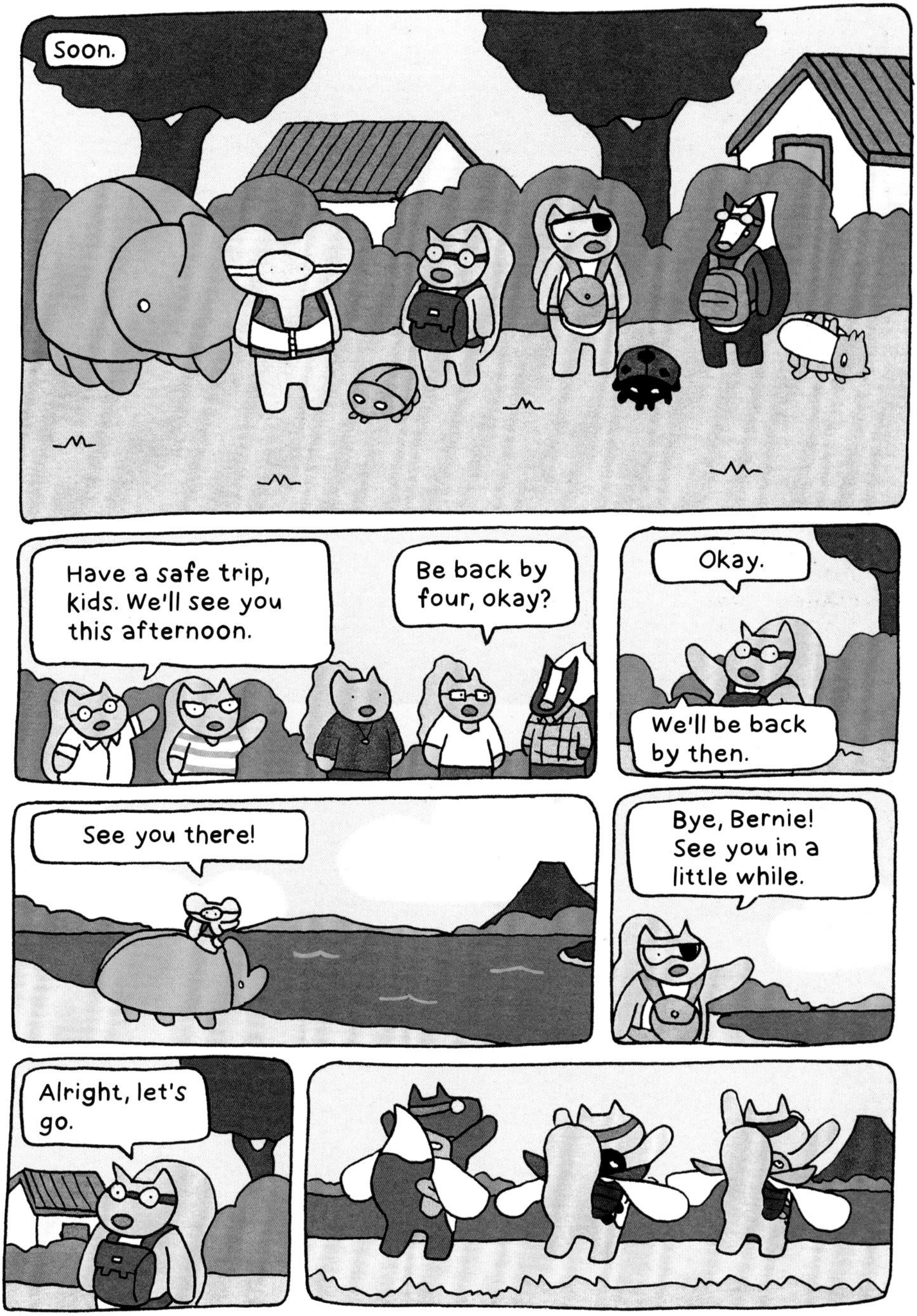
Soon.
Have a safe trip, kids. We'll see you this afternoon.
Be back by four, okay?
Okay.
We'll be back by then.
See you there!
Bye, Bernie! See you in a little while.
Alright, let's go.

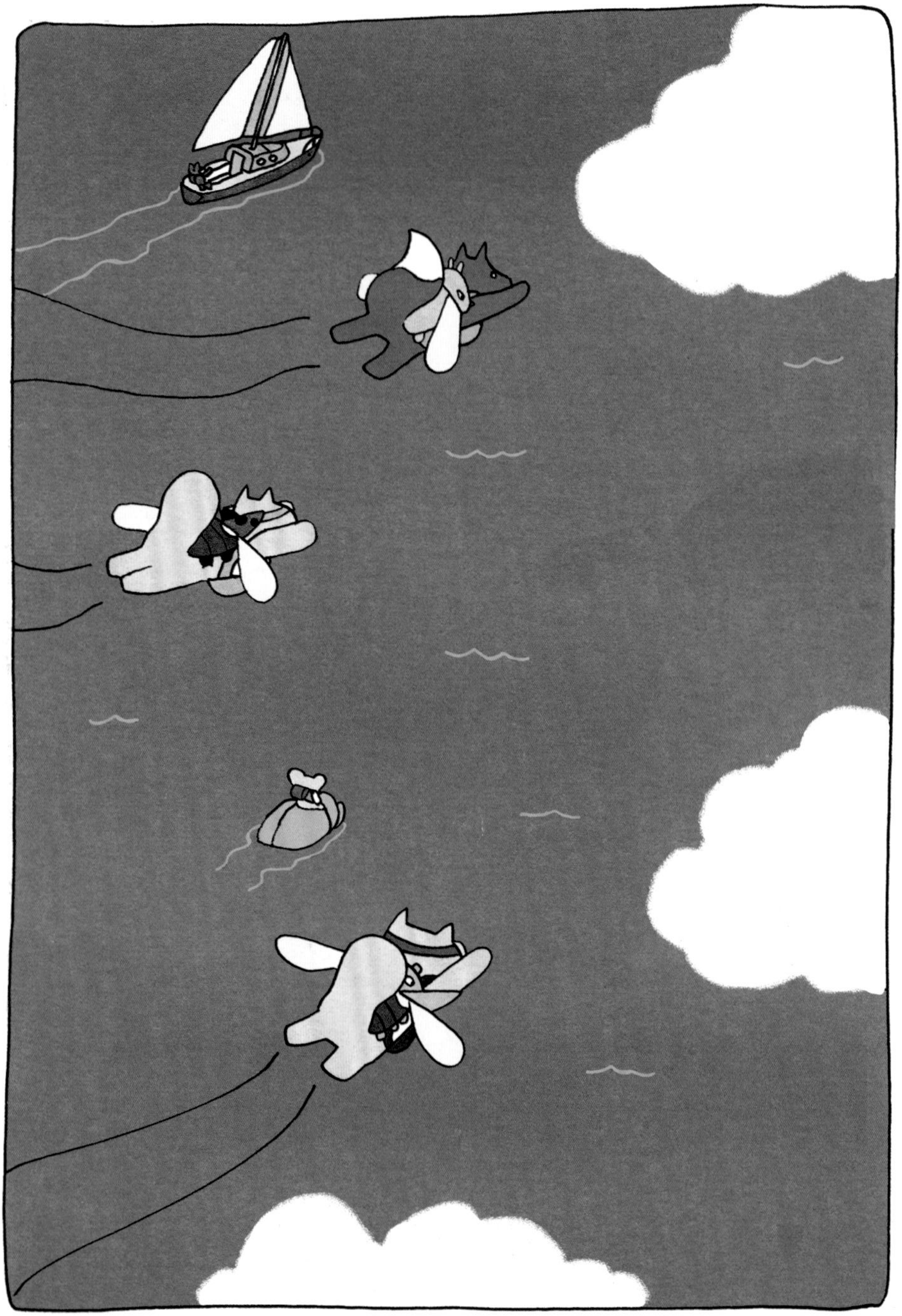

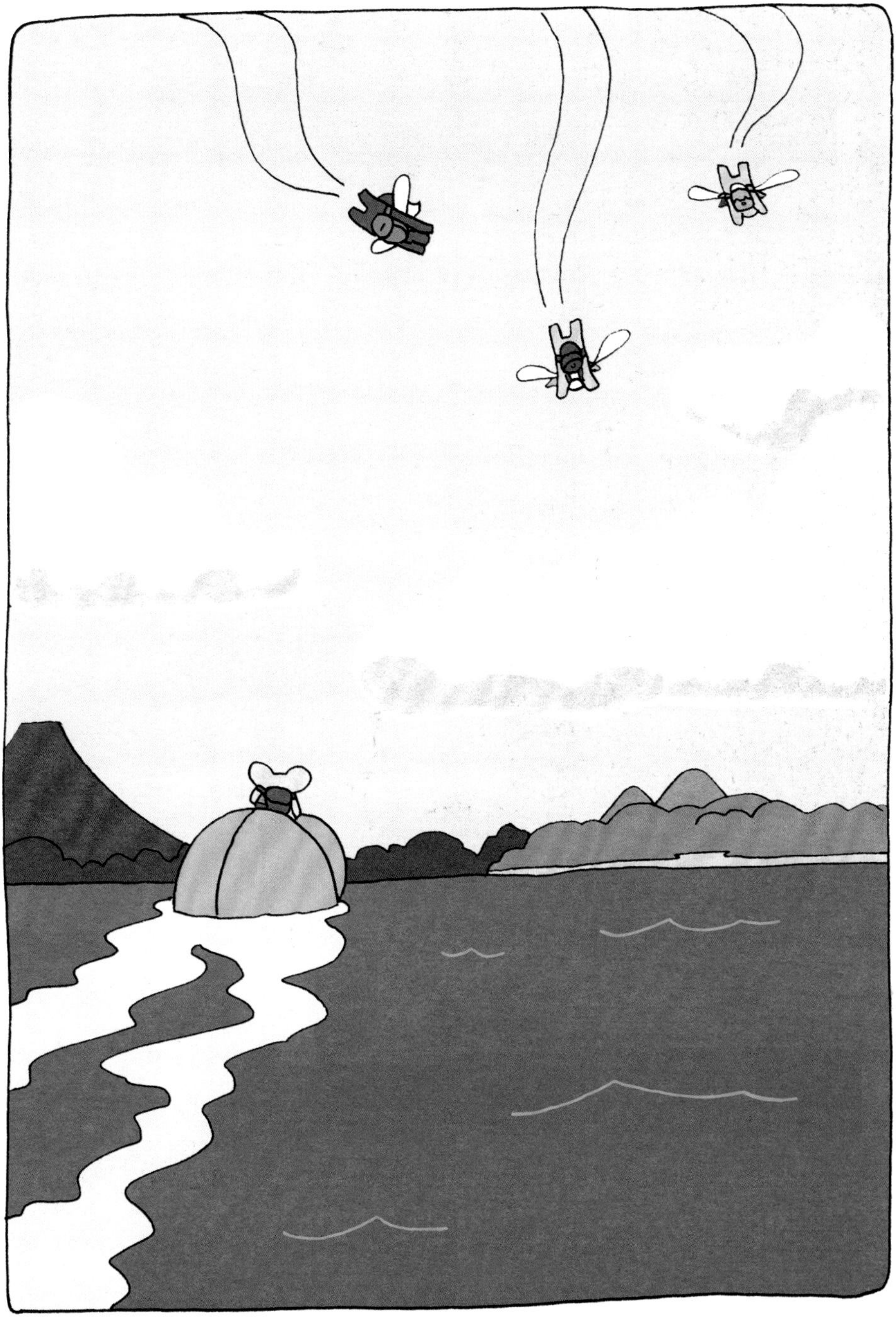

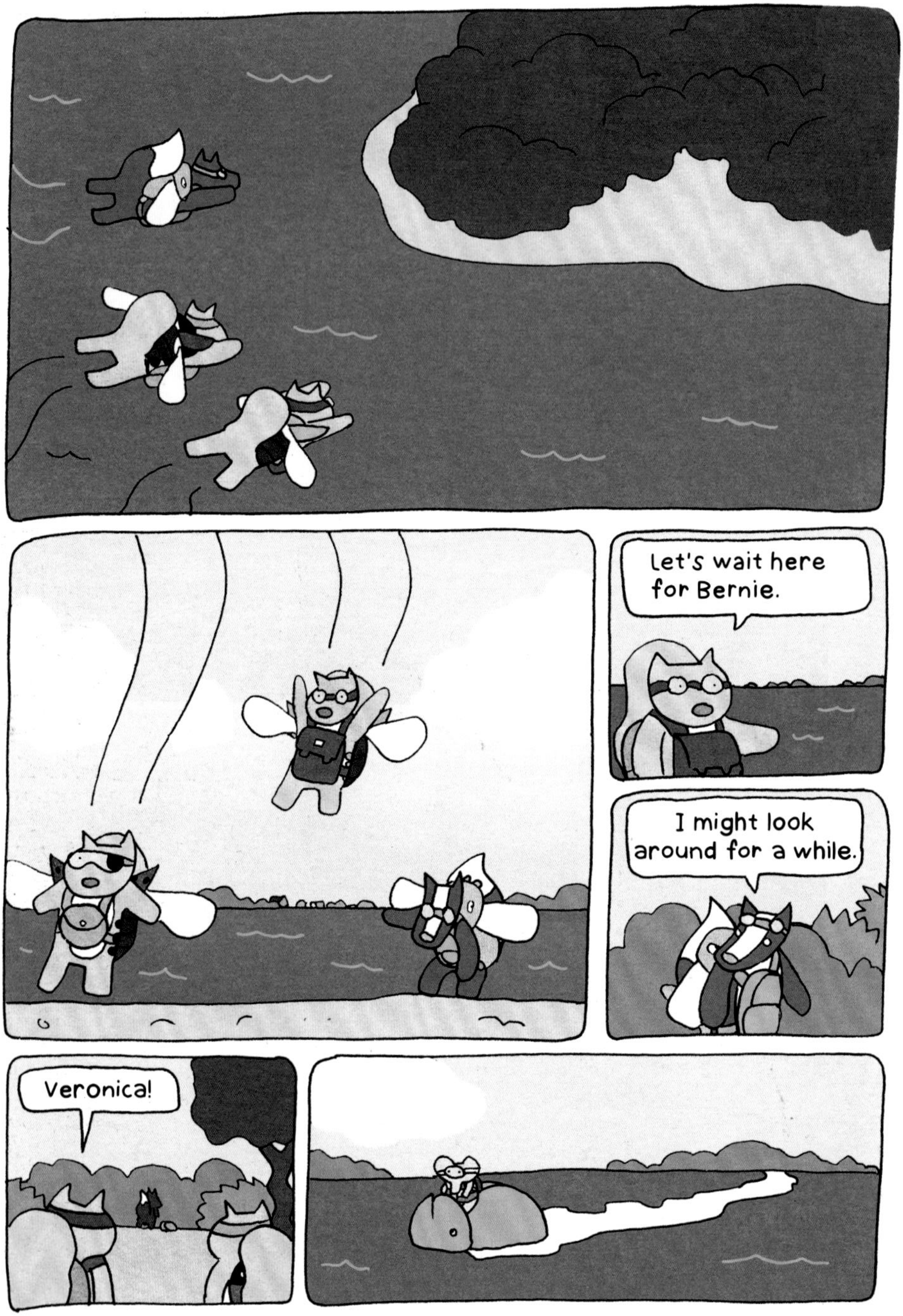
Let's wait here for Bernie.
I might look around for a while.
Veronica!

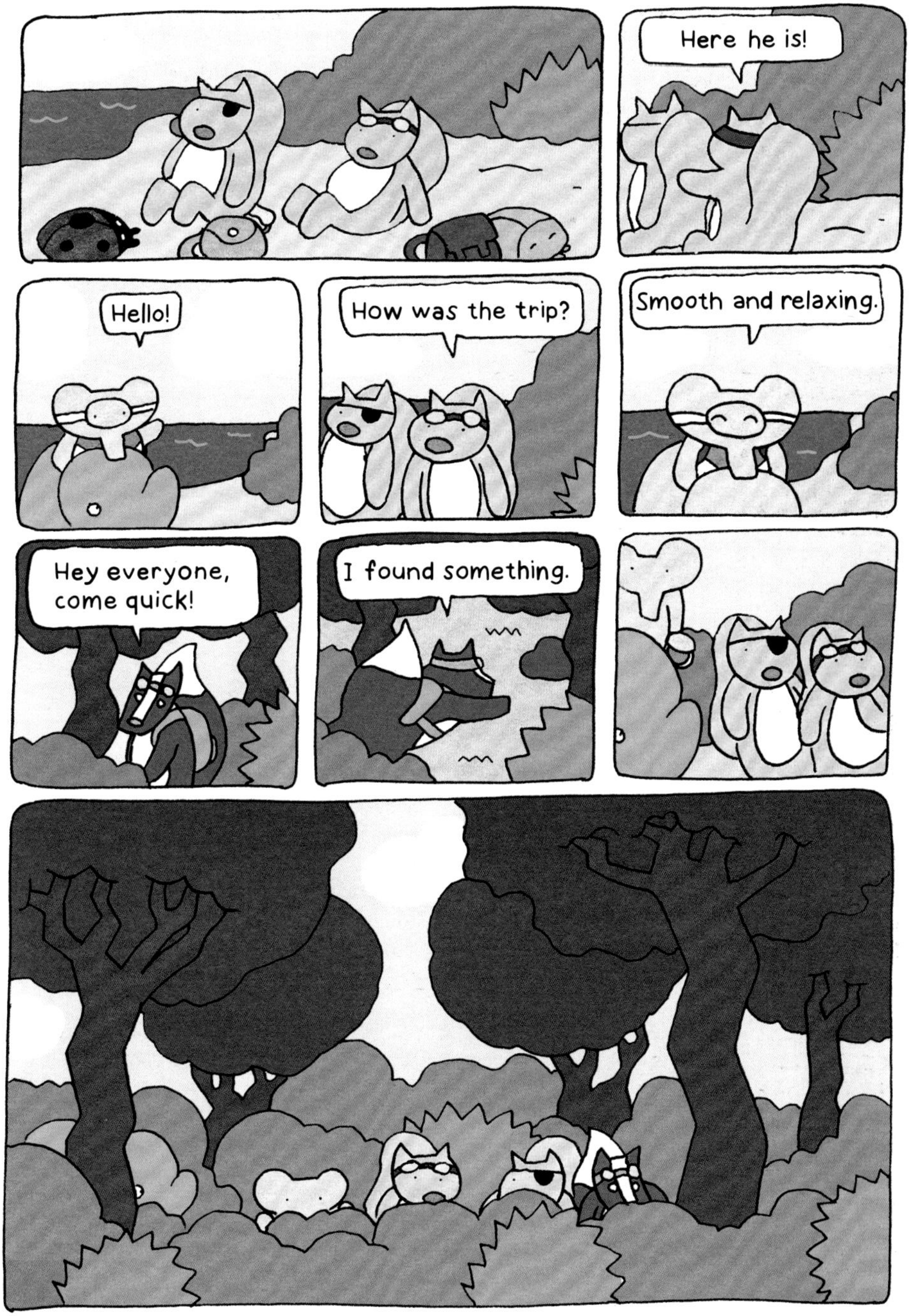
Here he is!
Hello!
How was the trip?
Smooth and relaxing.
Hey everyone, come quick!
I found something.

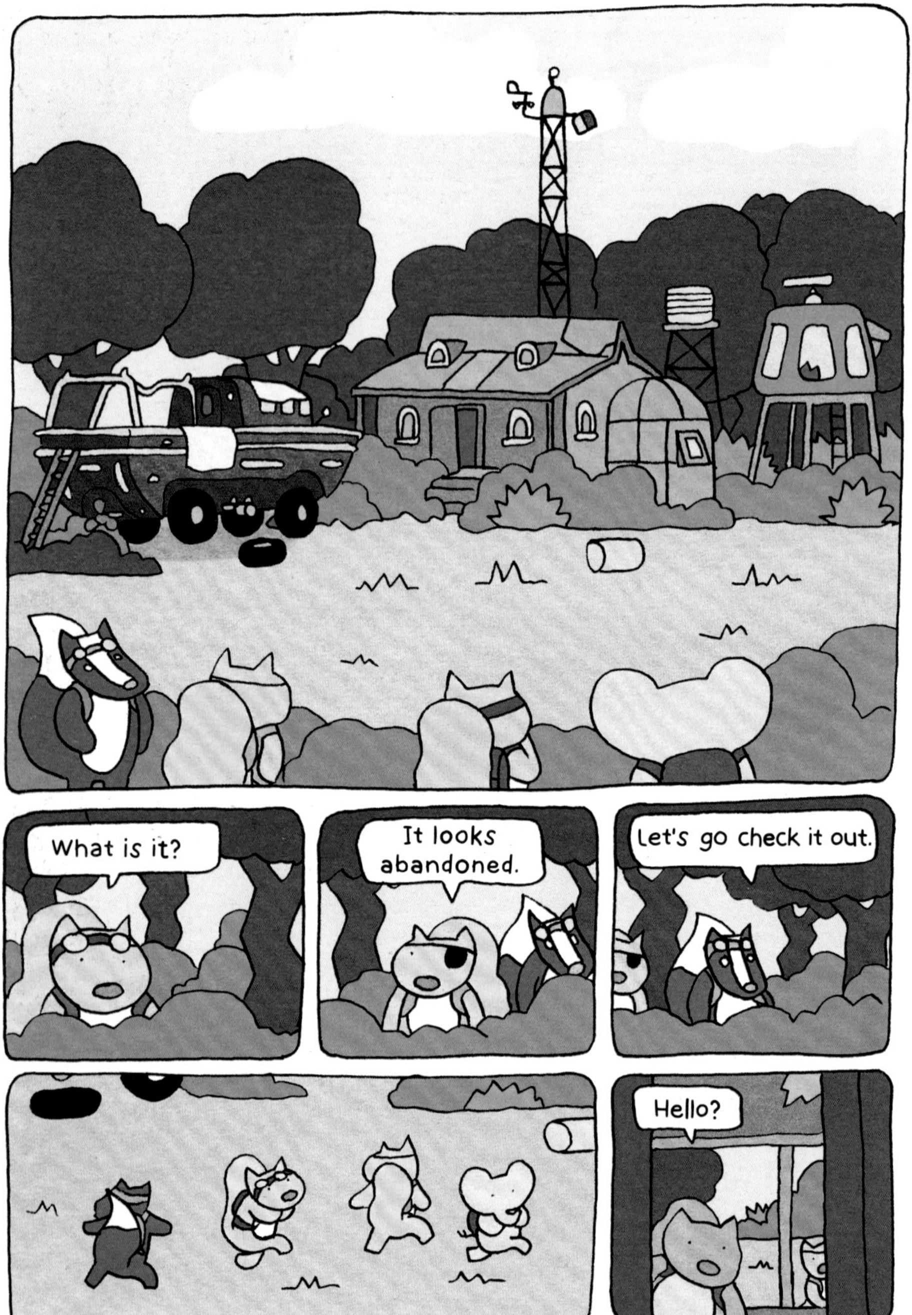
What is it?
It looks abandoned.
Let's go check it out.
Hello?

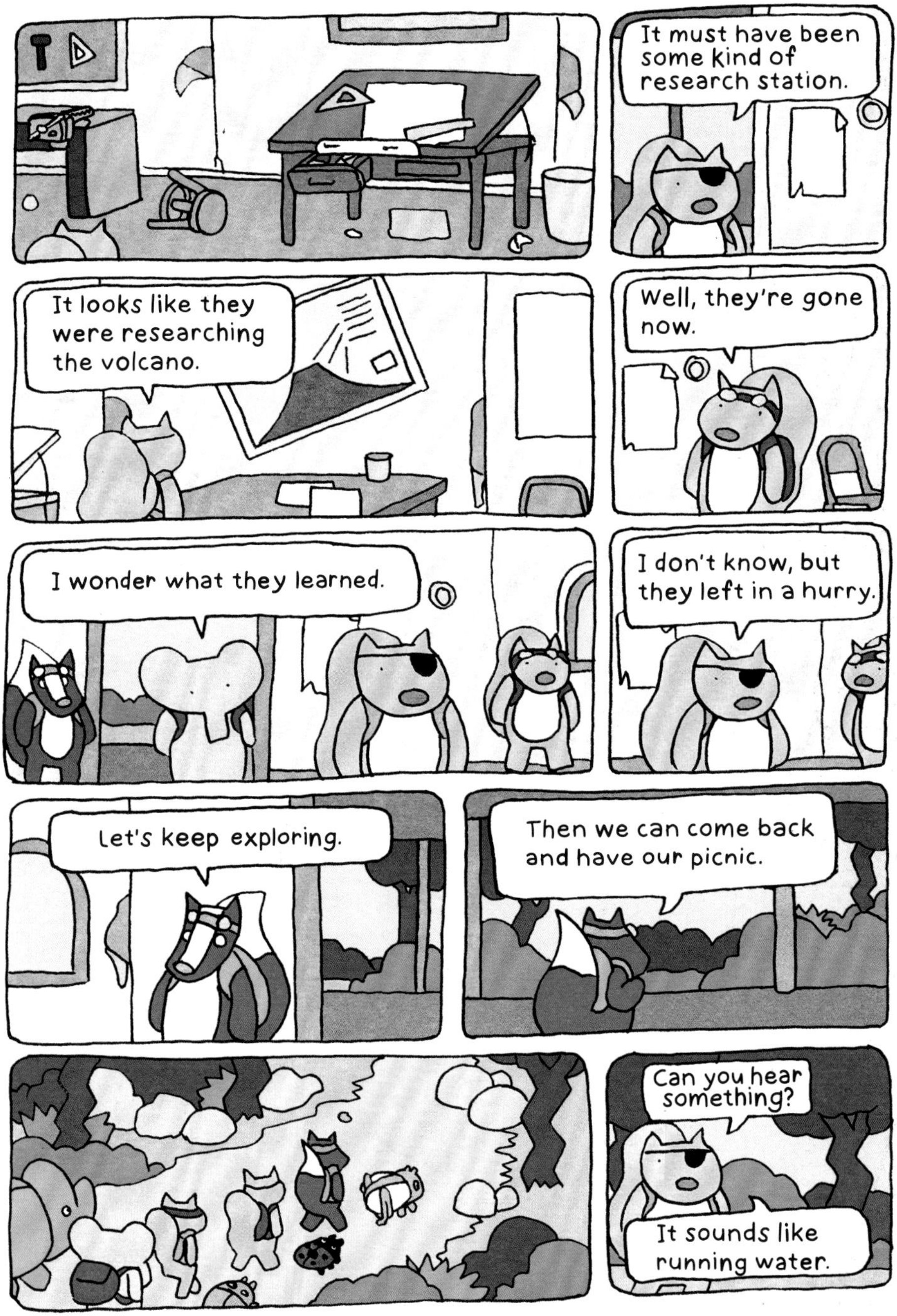
It must have been some kind of research station.
It looks like they were researching the volcano.
Well, they're gone now.
I wonder what they learned.
I don't know, but they left in a hurry.
Let's keep exploring.
Then we can come back and have our picnic.
Can you hear something?
It sounds like running water.

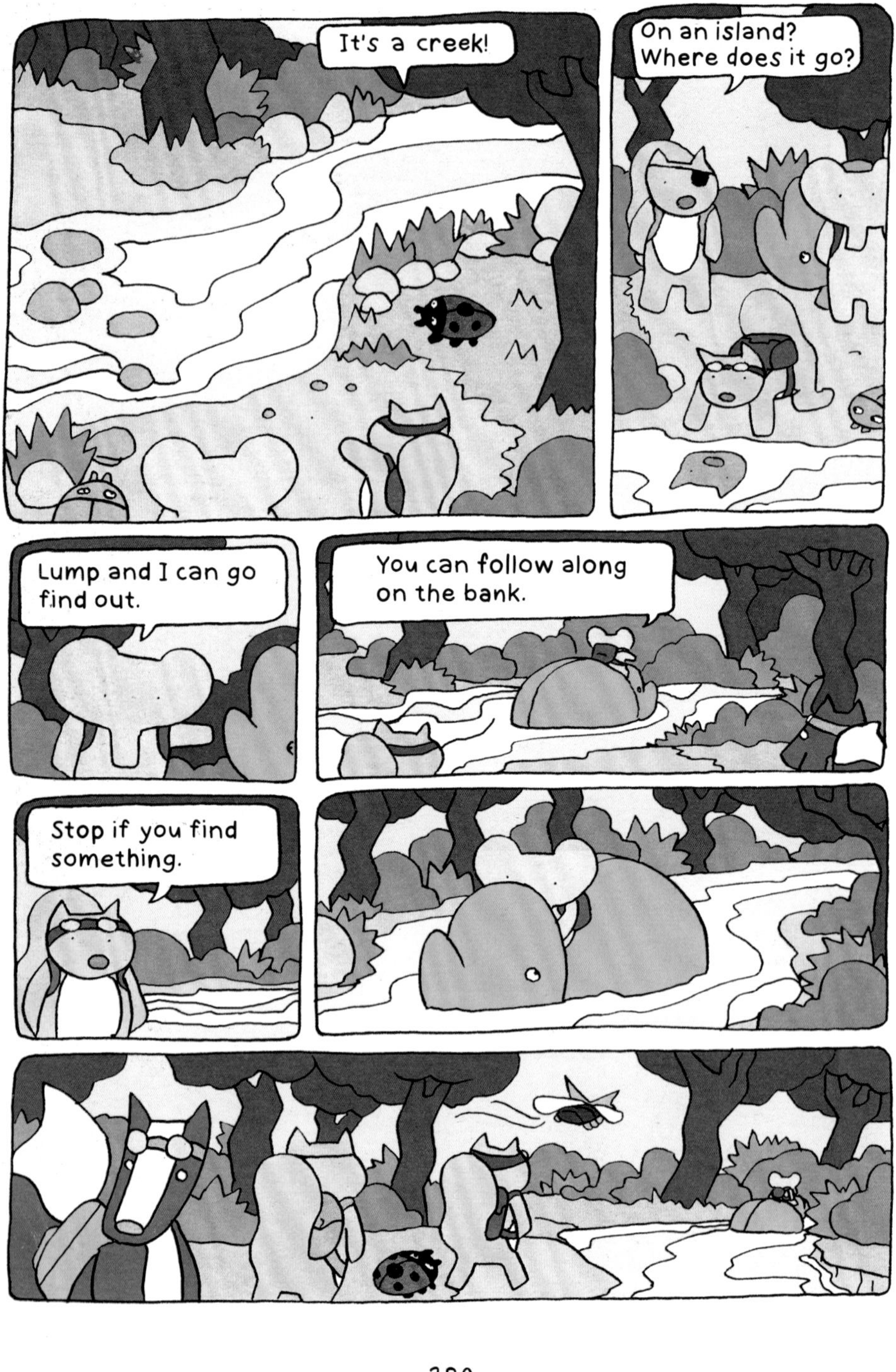
It's a creek!
On an island? Where does it go?
Lump and I can go find out.
You can follow along on the bank.
Stop if you find something.

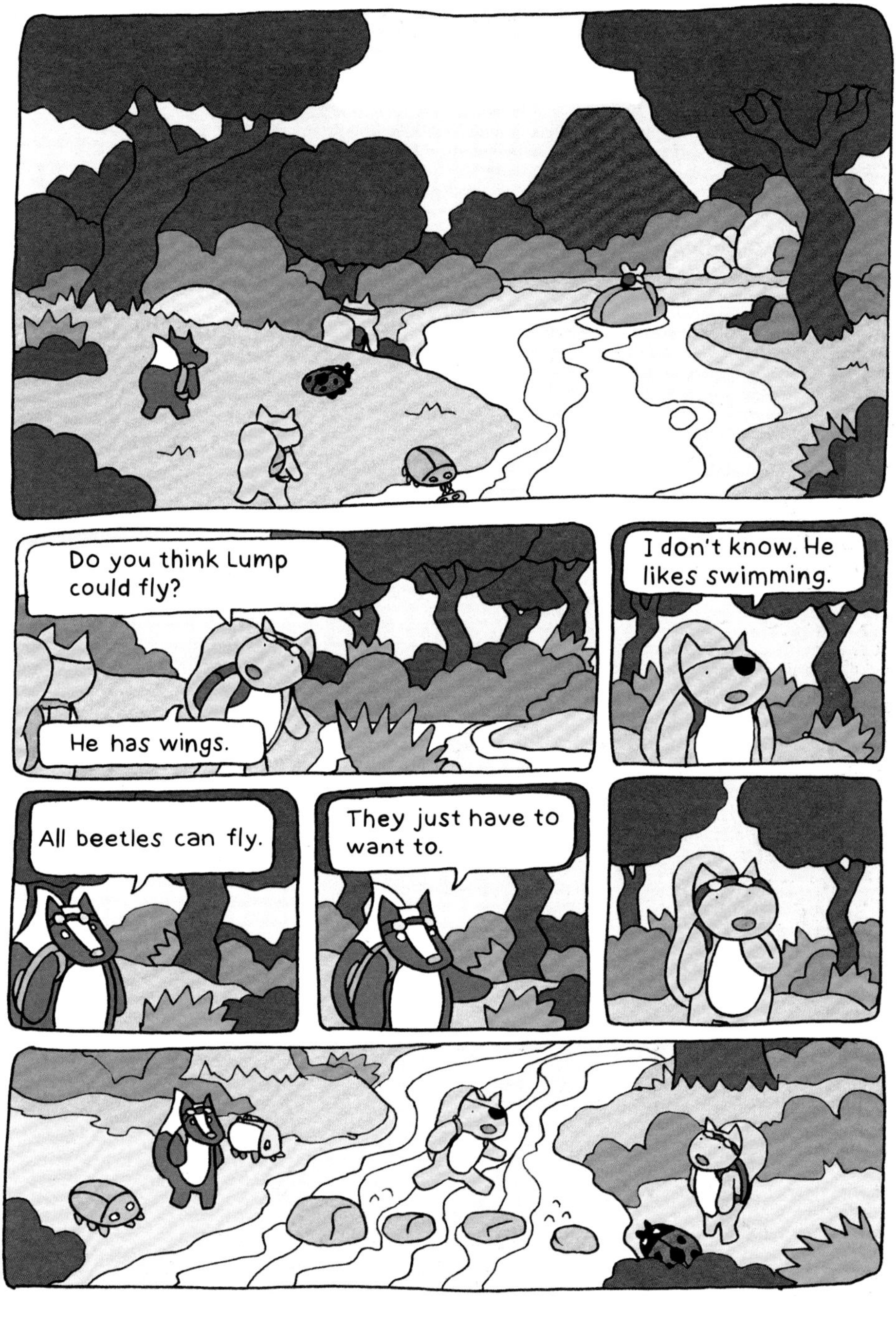
Do you think Lump could fly?
He has wings.
I don't know. He likes swimming.
All beetles can fly.
They just have to want to.

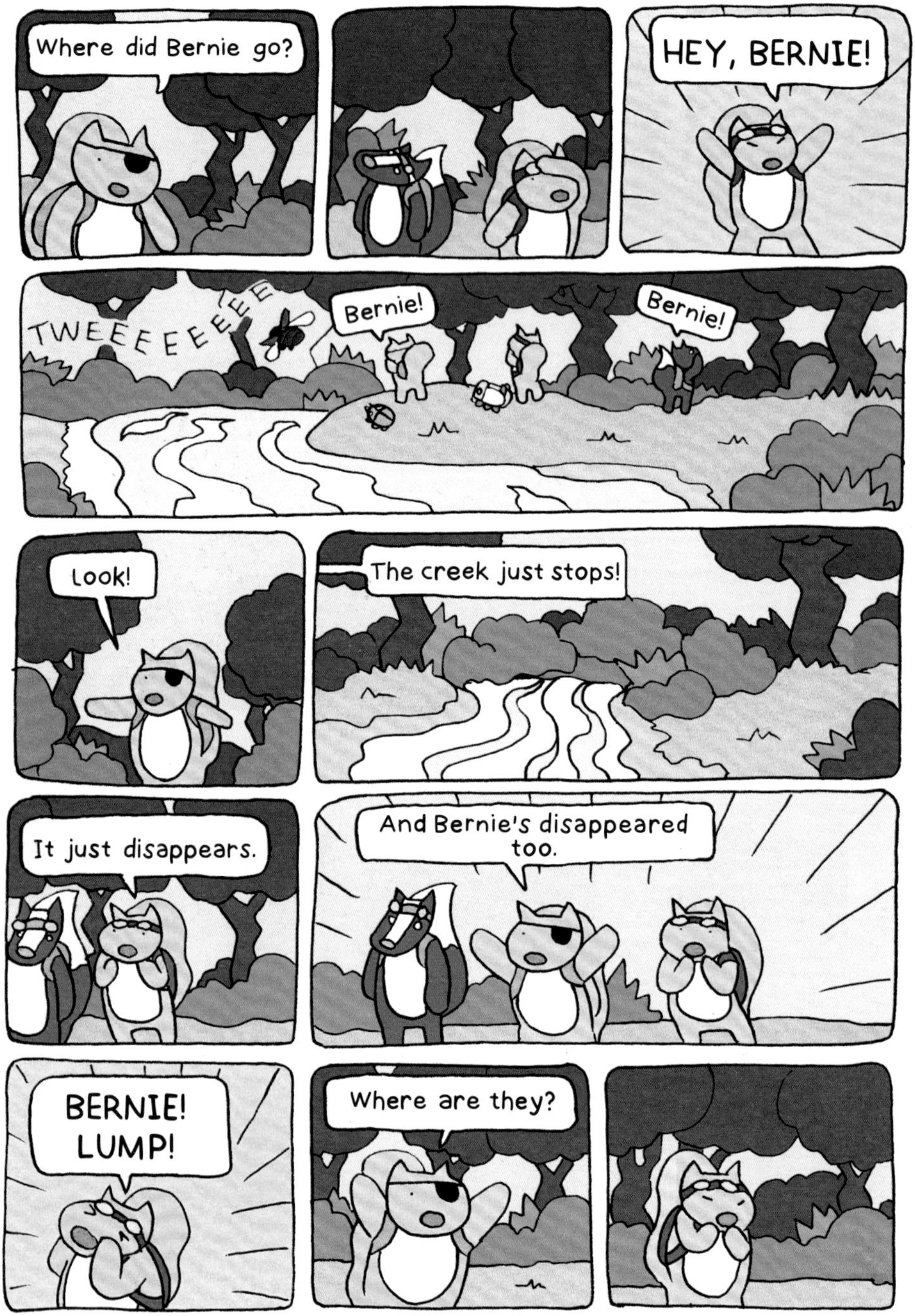
Where did Bernie go?
HEY, BERNIE!
TWEEEEEEEEEE
Bernie!
Bernie!
Look!
The creek just stops!
It just disappears.
And Bernie's disappeared too.
BERNIE! LUMP!
Where are they?

Chapter 11

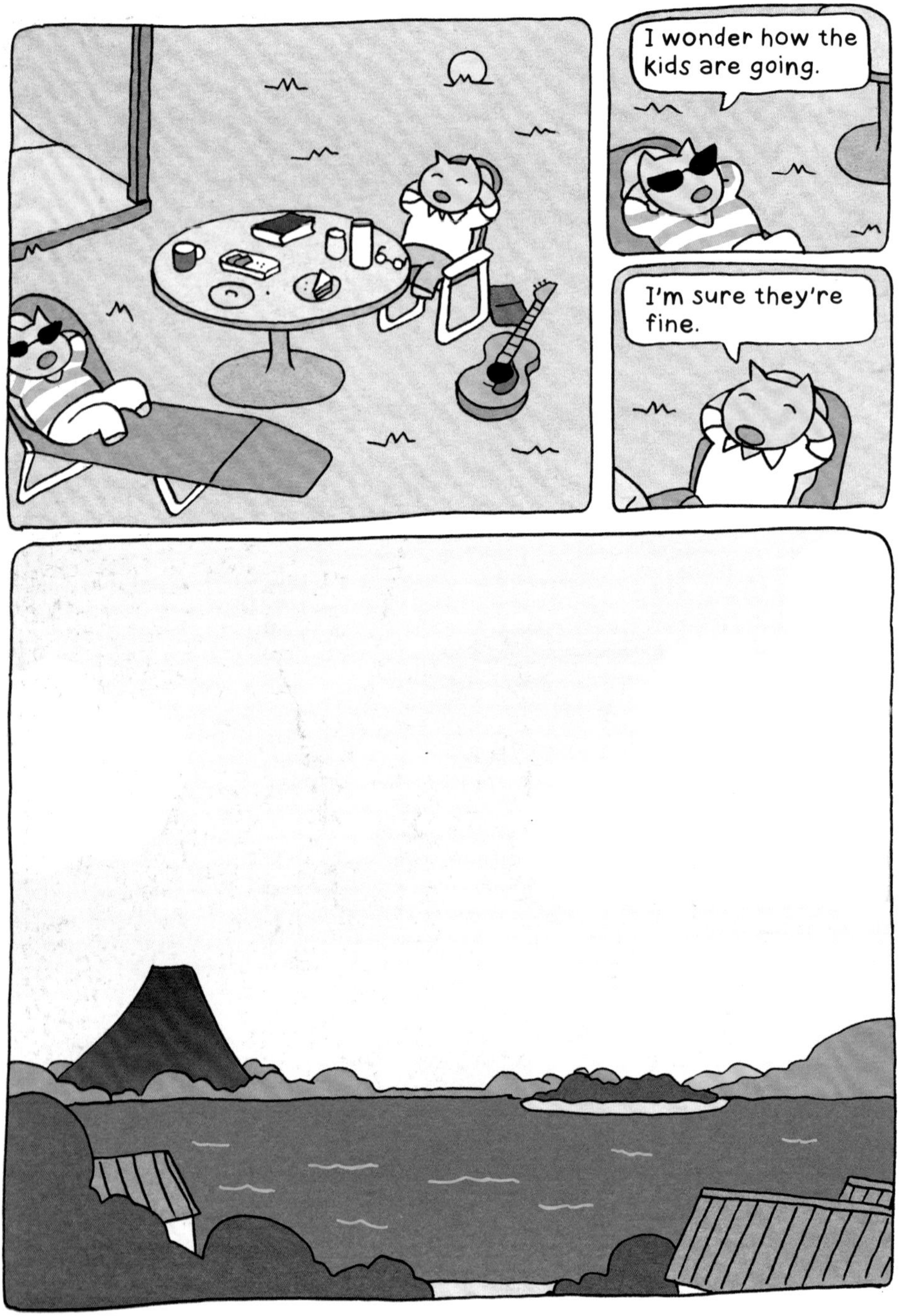
I wonder how the kids are going.
I'm sure they're fine.

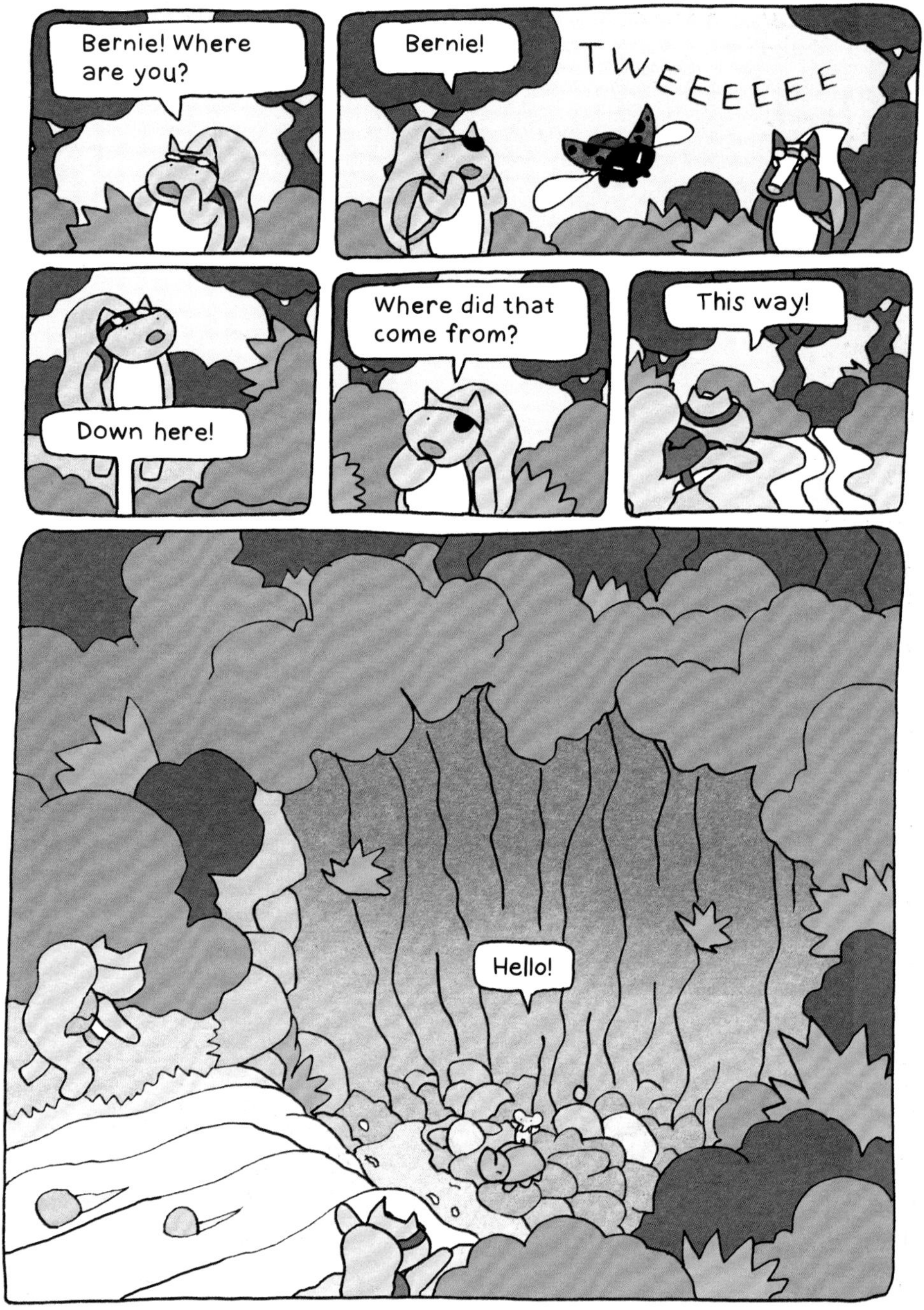
Bernie! Where are you?
Bernie!
TWEEEEEEE
Down here!
Where did that come from?
This way!
Hello!

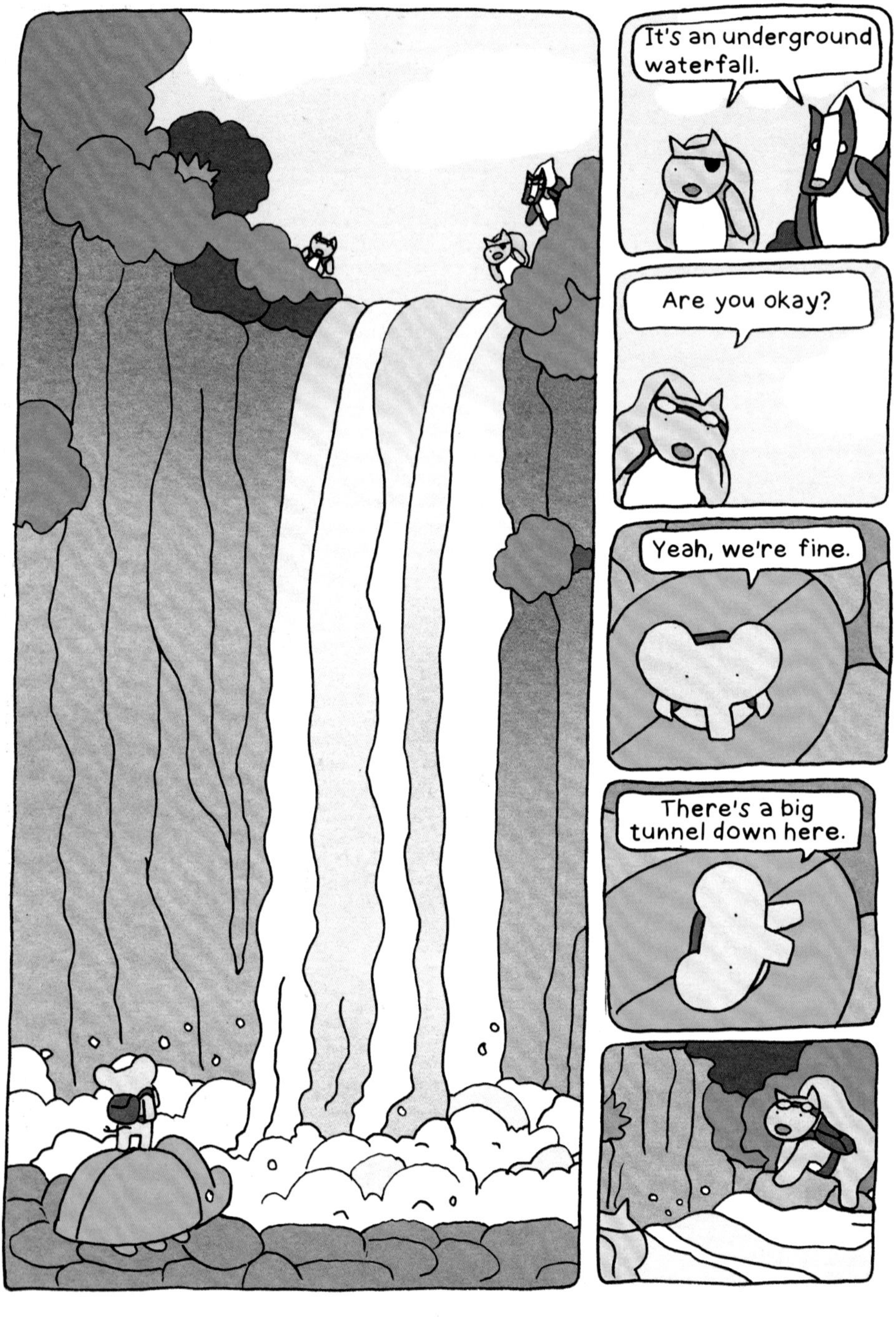
It's an underground waterfall.
Are you okay?
Yeah, we're fine.
There's a big tunnel down here.

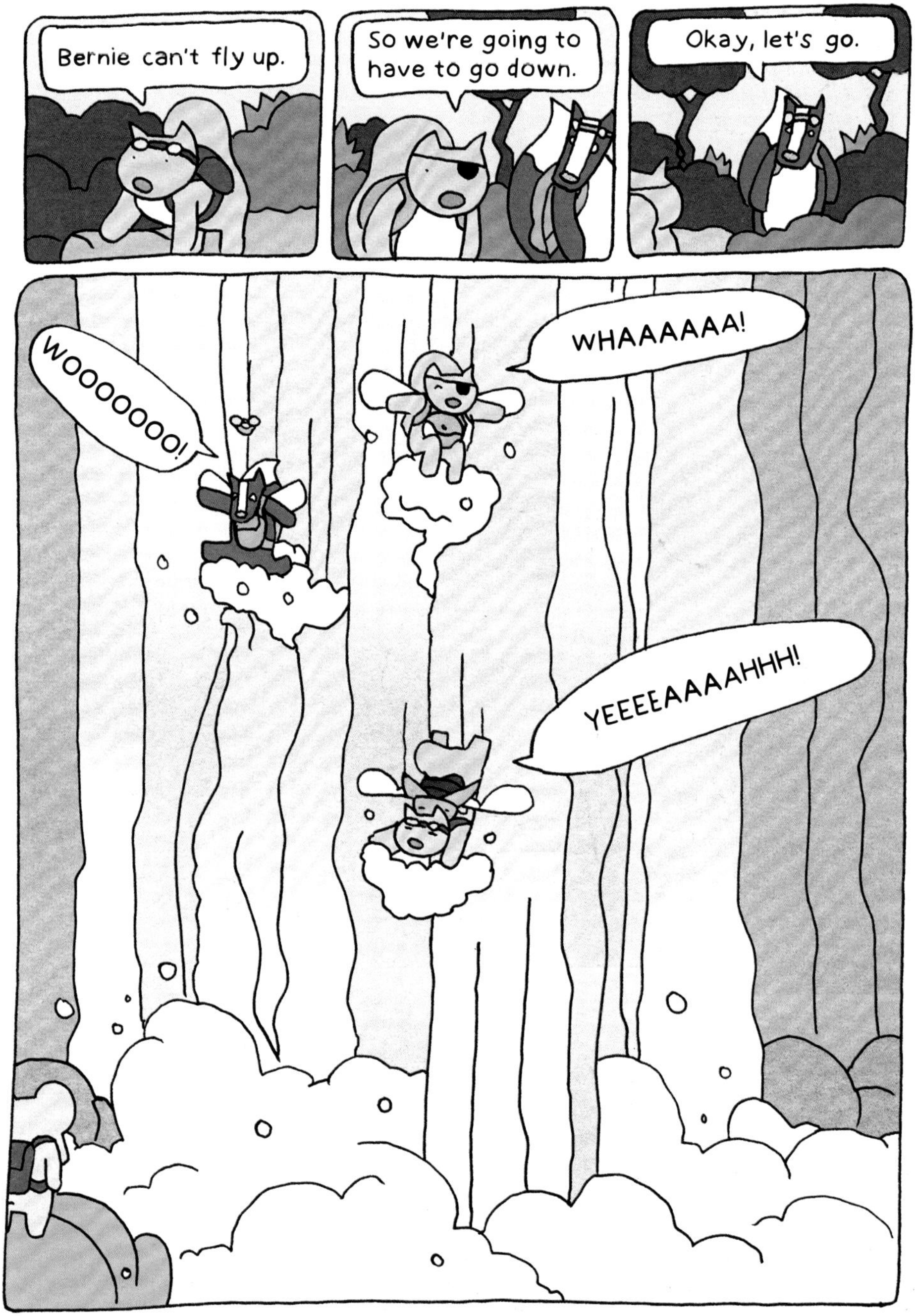
Bernie can't fly up.
So we're going to have to go down.
Okay, let's go.
WOOOOOOO!
WHAAAAAA!
YEEEEAAAAHHH!

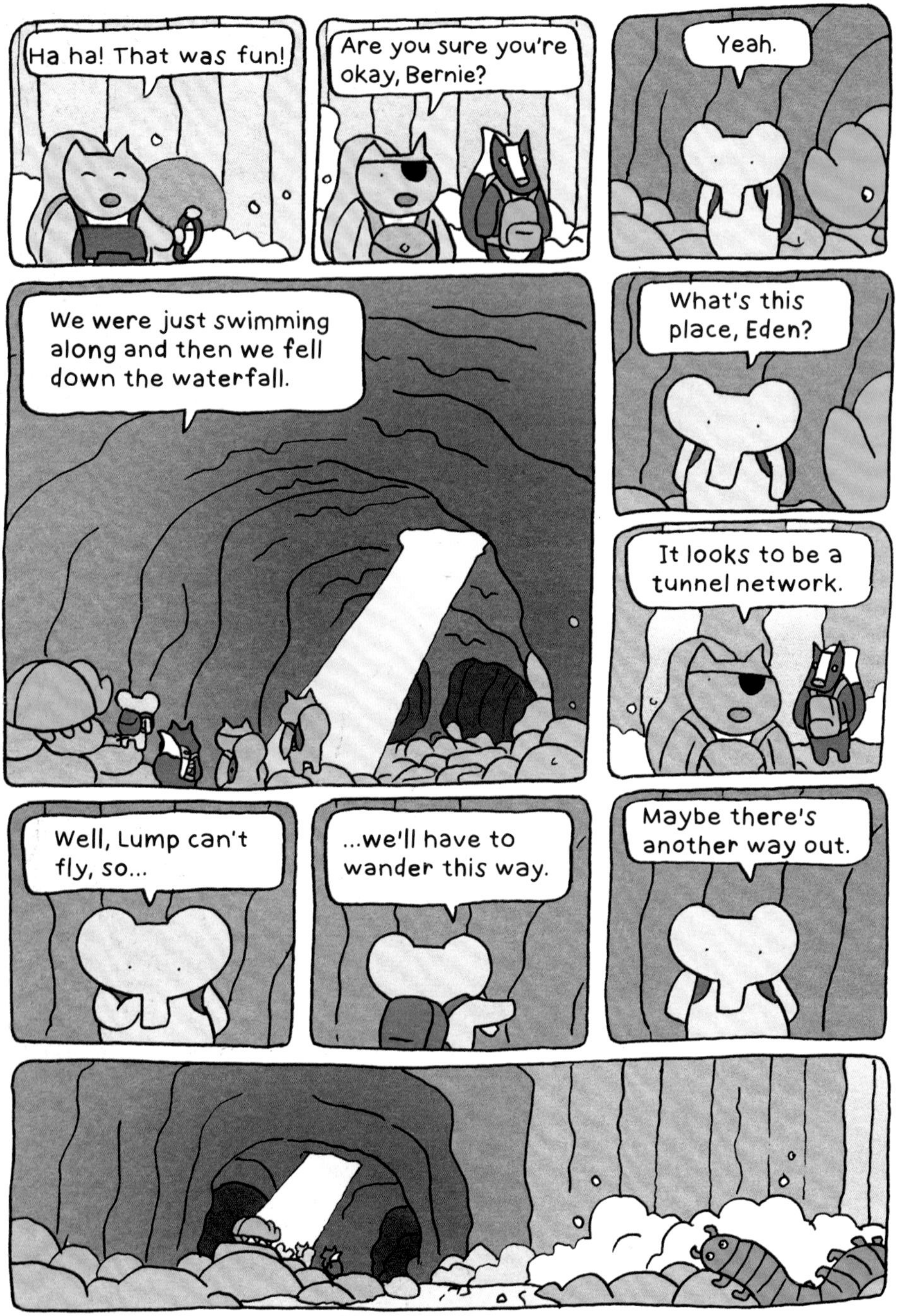
Ha ha! That was fun!
Are you sure you're okay, Bernie?
Yeah.
We were just swimming along and then we fell down the waterfall.
What's this place, Eden?
It looks to be a tunnel network.
Well, Lump can't fly, so...
...we'll have to wander this way.
Maybe there's another way out.

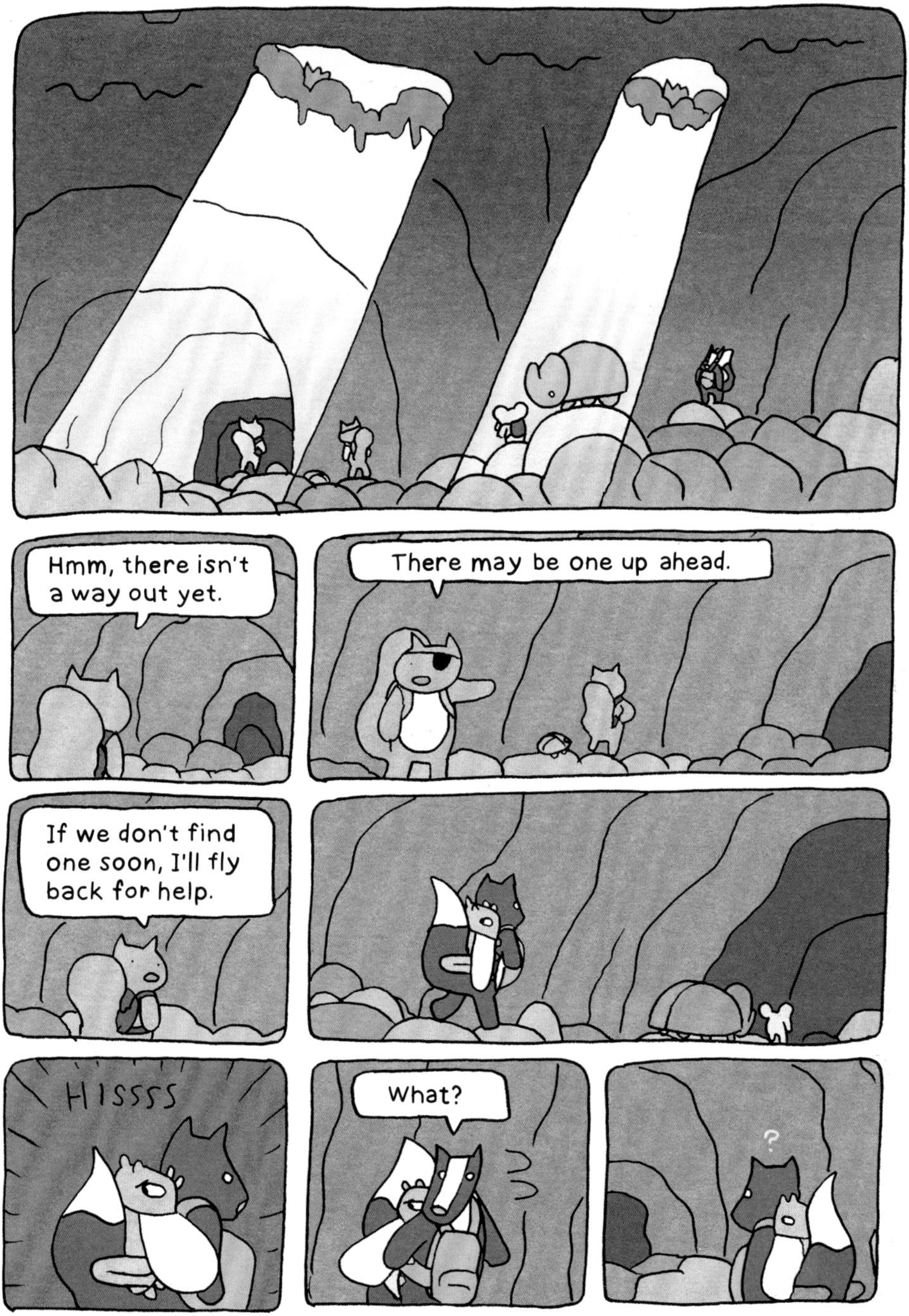
Hmm, there isn't a way out yet.
There may be one up ahead.
If we don't find one soon, I'll fly back for help.
HISSSS
What?
?

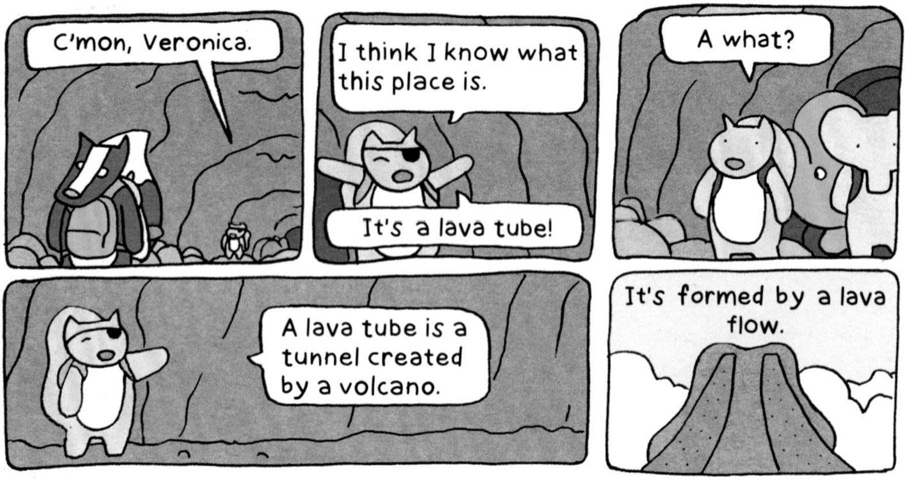
C'mon, Veronica.
I think I know what this place is.
It's a lava tube!
A what?
A lava tube is a tunnel created by a volcano.
It's formed by a lava flow.

When a flow of lava forms a channel, the walls can build up and harden.

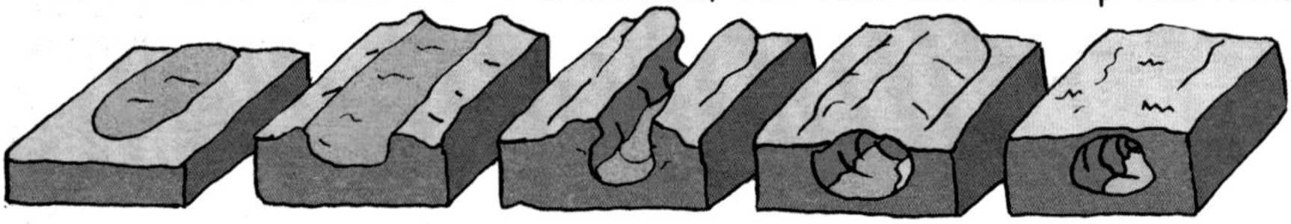

This wall can get bigger and form a tunnel over the channel.

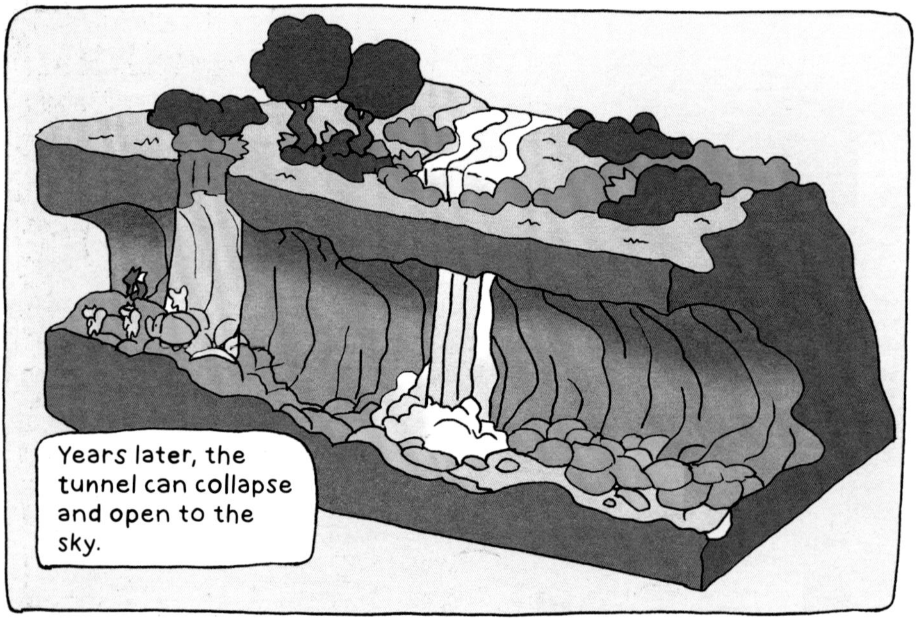
Years later, the tunnel can collapse and open to the sky.

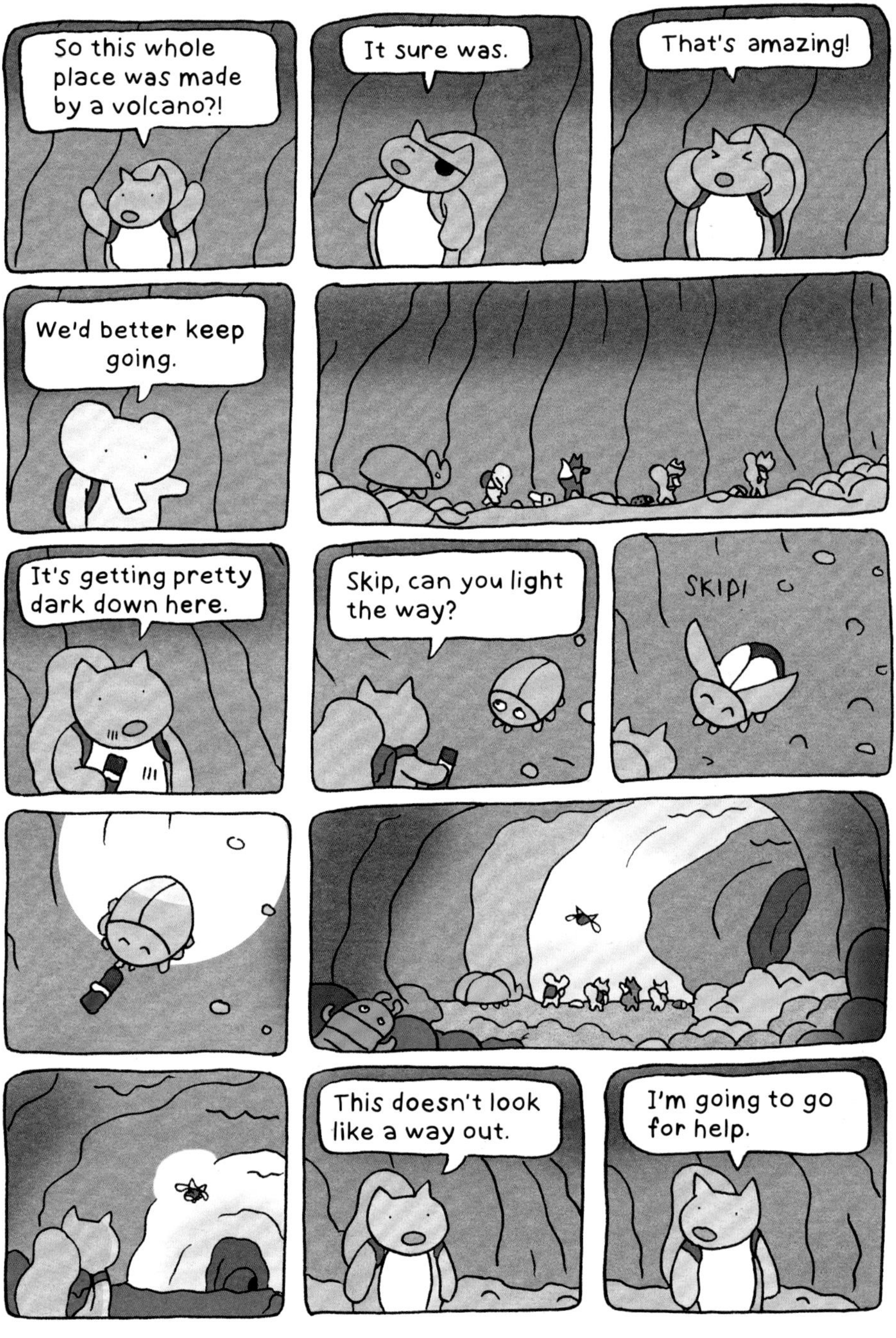
So this whole place was made by a volcano?!
It sure was.
That's amazing!
We'd better keep going.
It's getting pretty dark down here.
Skip, can you light the way?
SKIP!
This doesn't look like a way out.
I'm going to go for help.

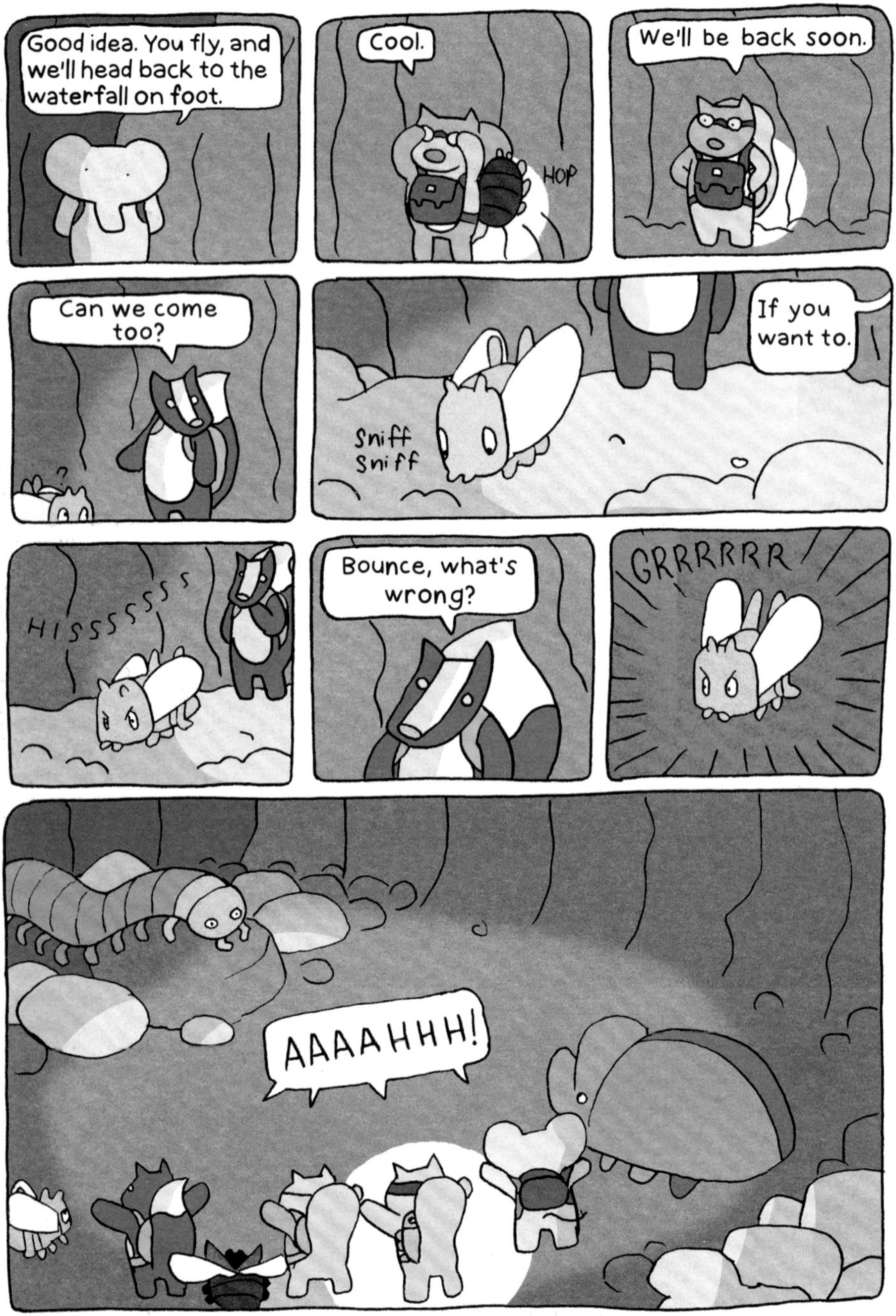
Good idea. You fly, and we'll head back to the waterfall on foot.
Cool.
HOP
We'll be back soon.
Can we come too?
?
If you want to.
Sniff Sniff
HISSSSSSS
Bounce, what's wrong?
GRRRRRR
AAAAHHH!

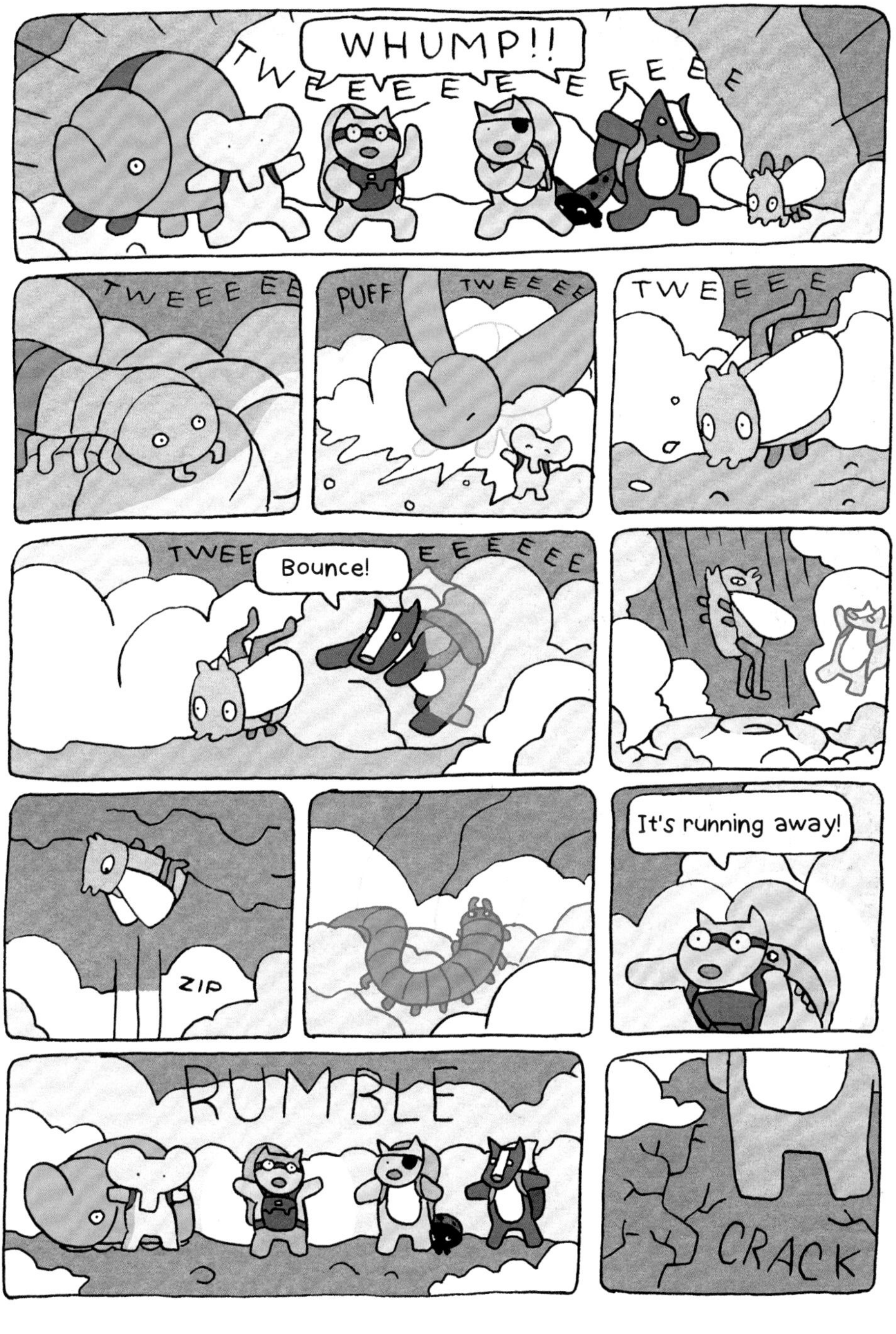
WHUMP!!
TWEEEEEEEEEE
TWEEEEE
PUFF
TWEEEE
TWEEEE
TWEE
Bounce!
EEEEEE
ZIP
It's running away!
RUMBLE
CRACK

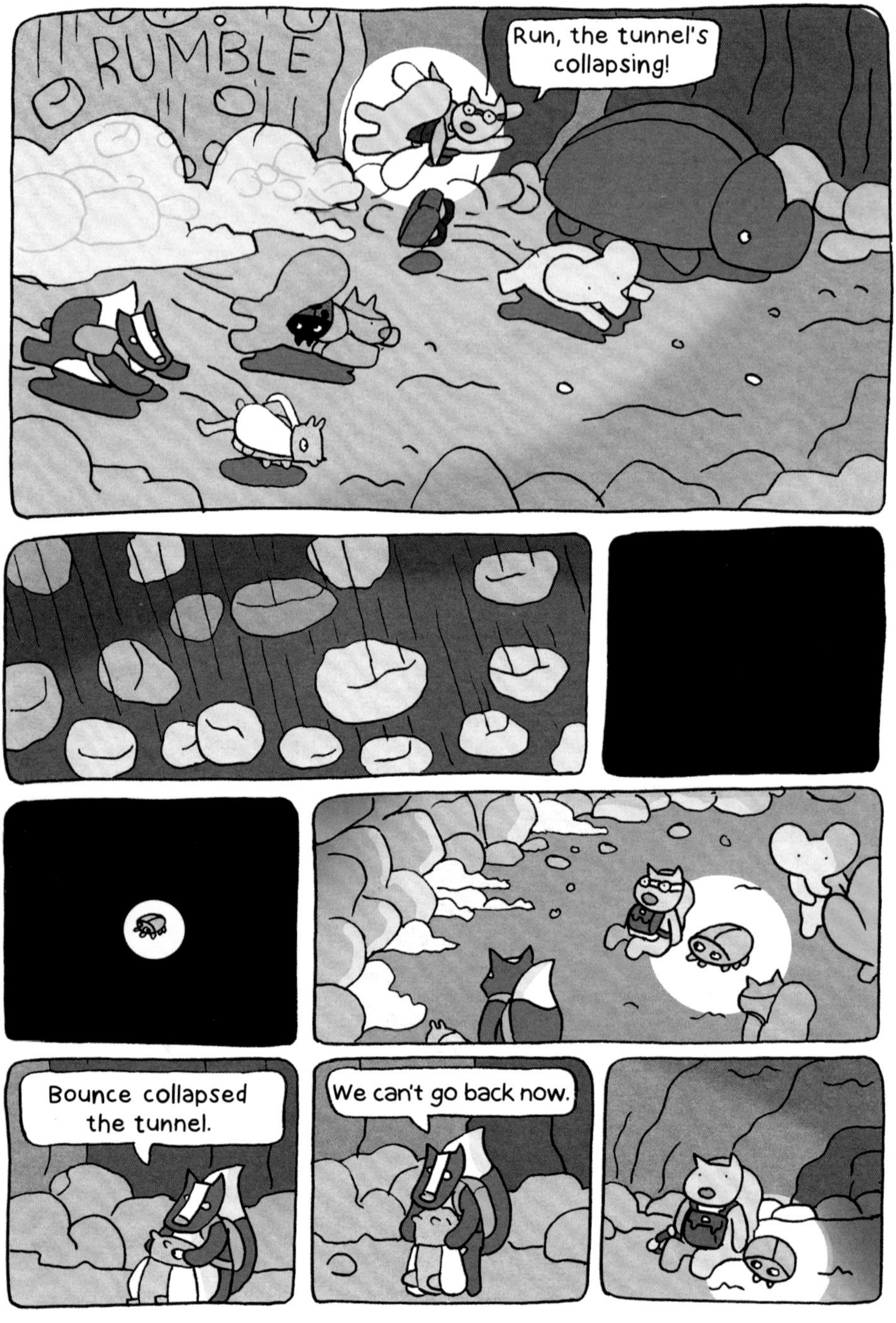
RUMBLE
Run, the tunnel's collapsing!
Bounce collapsed the tunnel.
We can't go back now.

Chapter 12

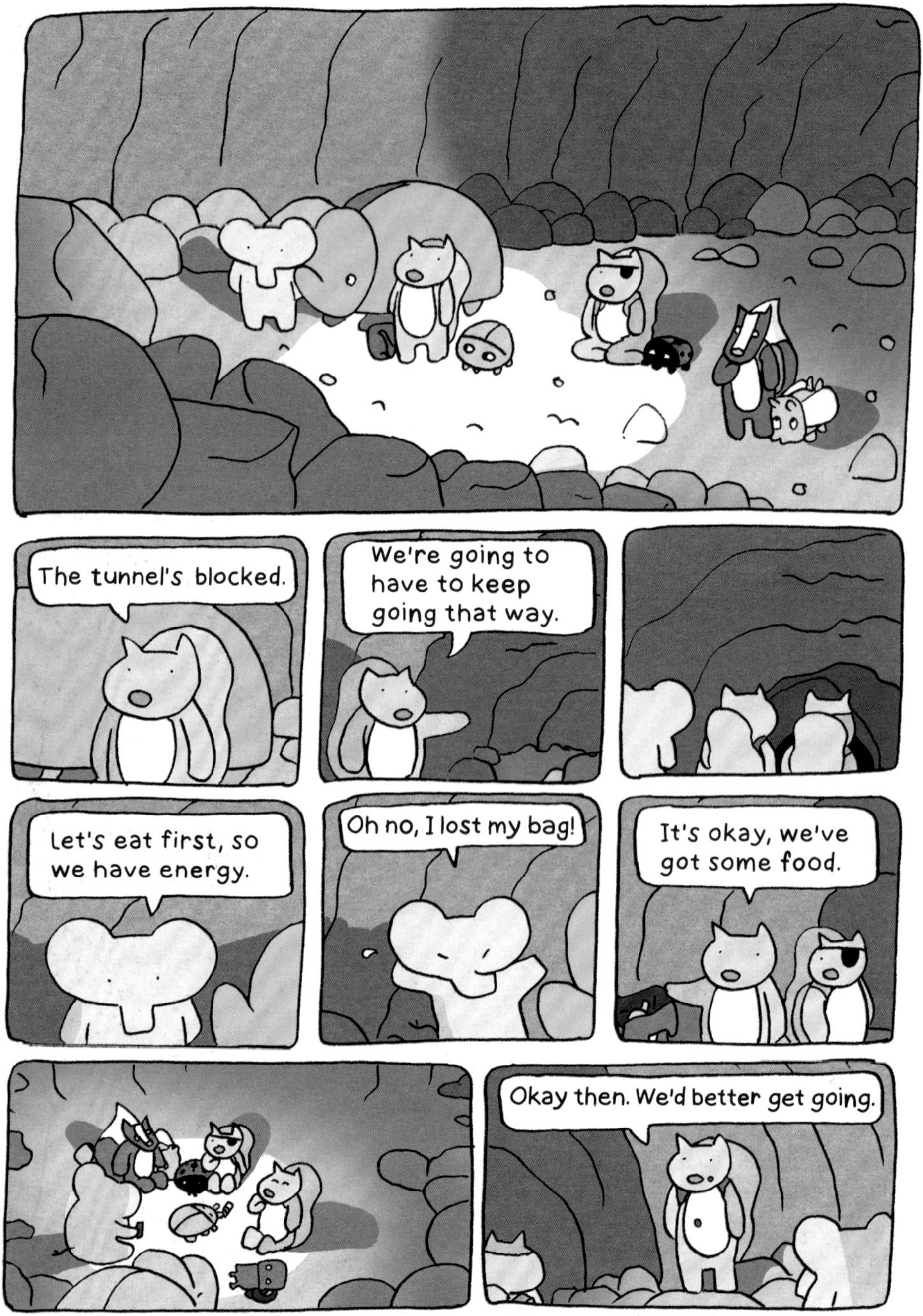
The tunnel's blocked.
We're going to have to keep going that way.
Let's eat first, so we have energy.
Oh no, I lost my bag!
It's okay, we've got some food.
Okay then. We'd better get going.

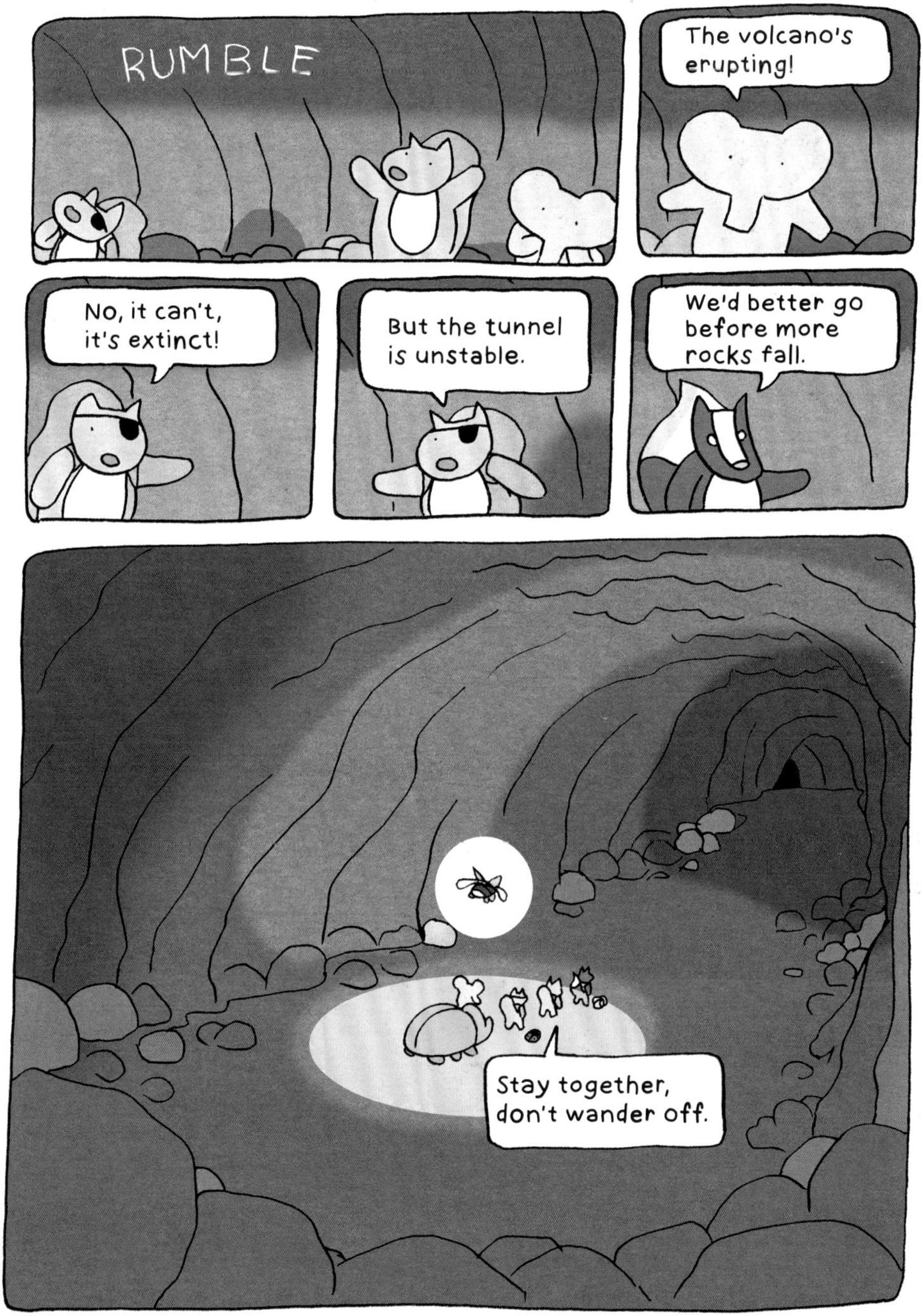
RUMBLE
The volcano's erupting!
No, it can't, it's extinct!
But the tunnel is unstable.
We'd better go before more rocks fall.
Stay together, don't wander off.

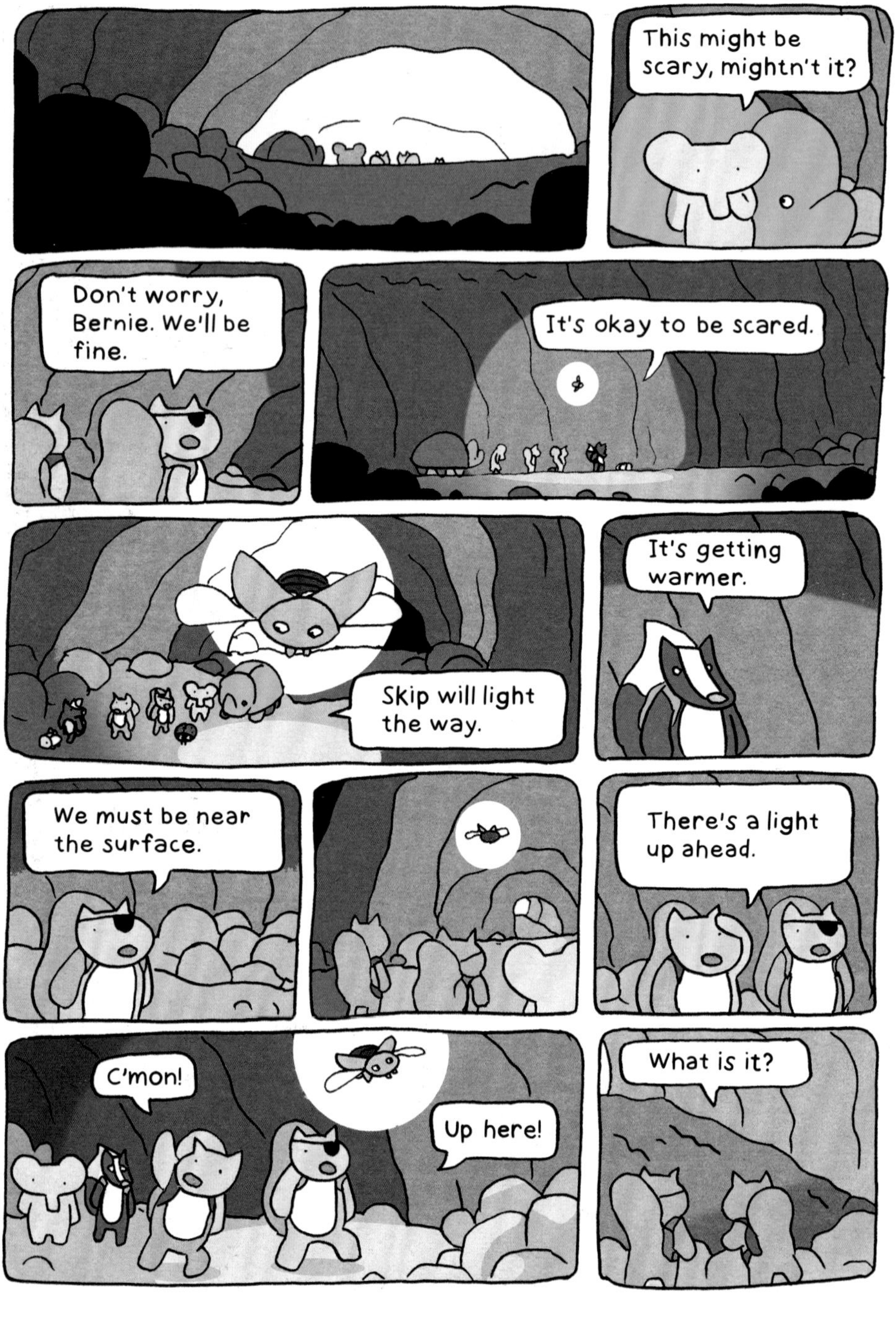
This might be scary, mightn't it?
Don't worry, Bernie. We'll be fine.
It's okay to be scared.
Skip will light the way.
It's getting warmer.
We must be near the surface.
There's a light up ahead.
C'mon!
Up here!
What is it?

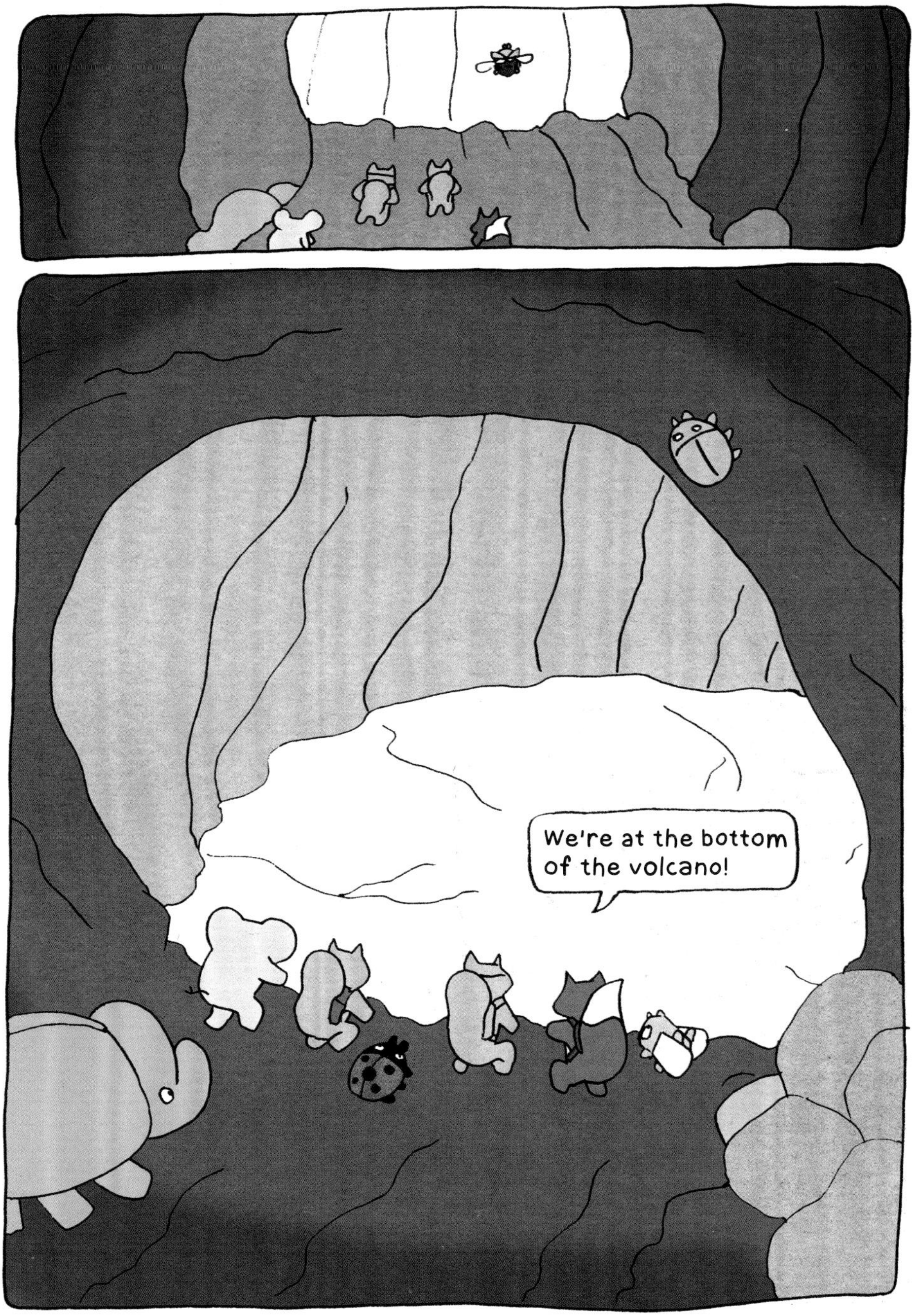
We're at the bottom of the volcano!

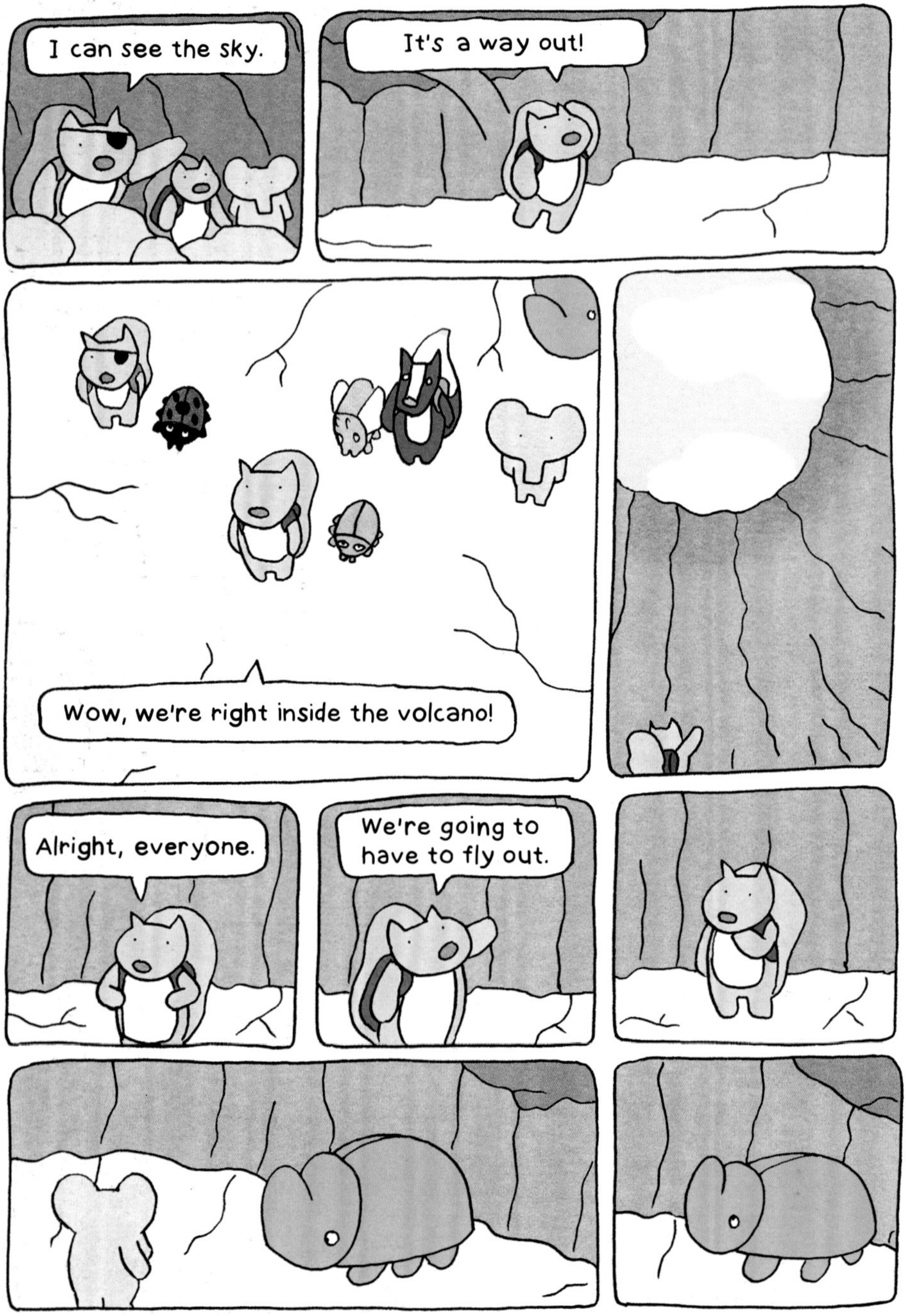
I can see the sky.
It's a way out!
Wow, we're right inside the volcano!
Alright, everyone.
We're going to have to fly out.

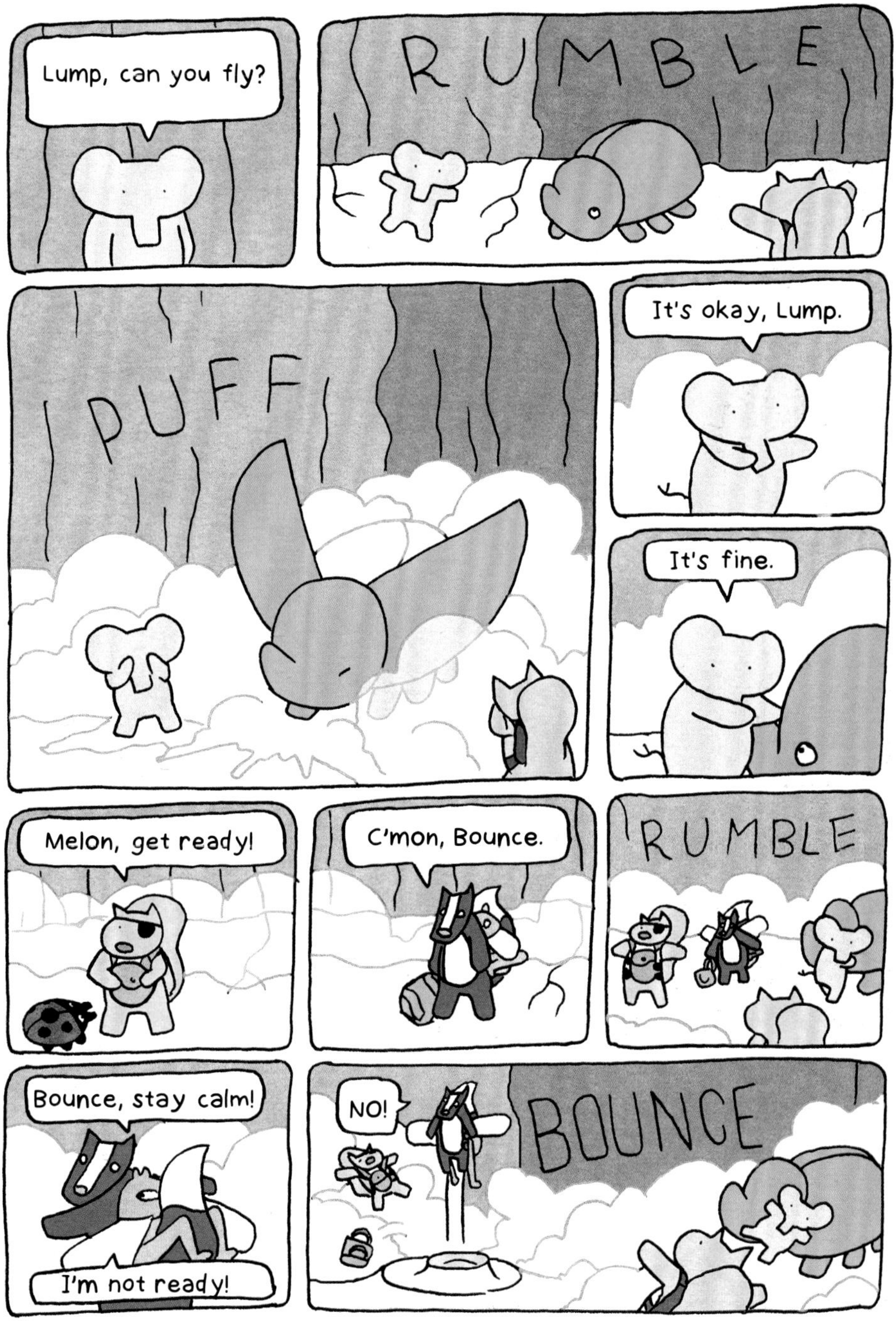

Lump, can you fly?
RUMBLE
PUFF
It's okay, Lump.
It's fine.
Melon, get ready!
C'mon, Bounce.
RUMBLE
Bounce, stay calm!
I'm not ready!
NO!
BOUNCE

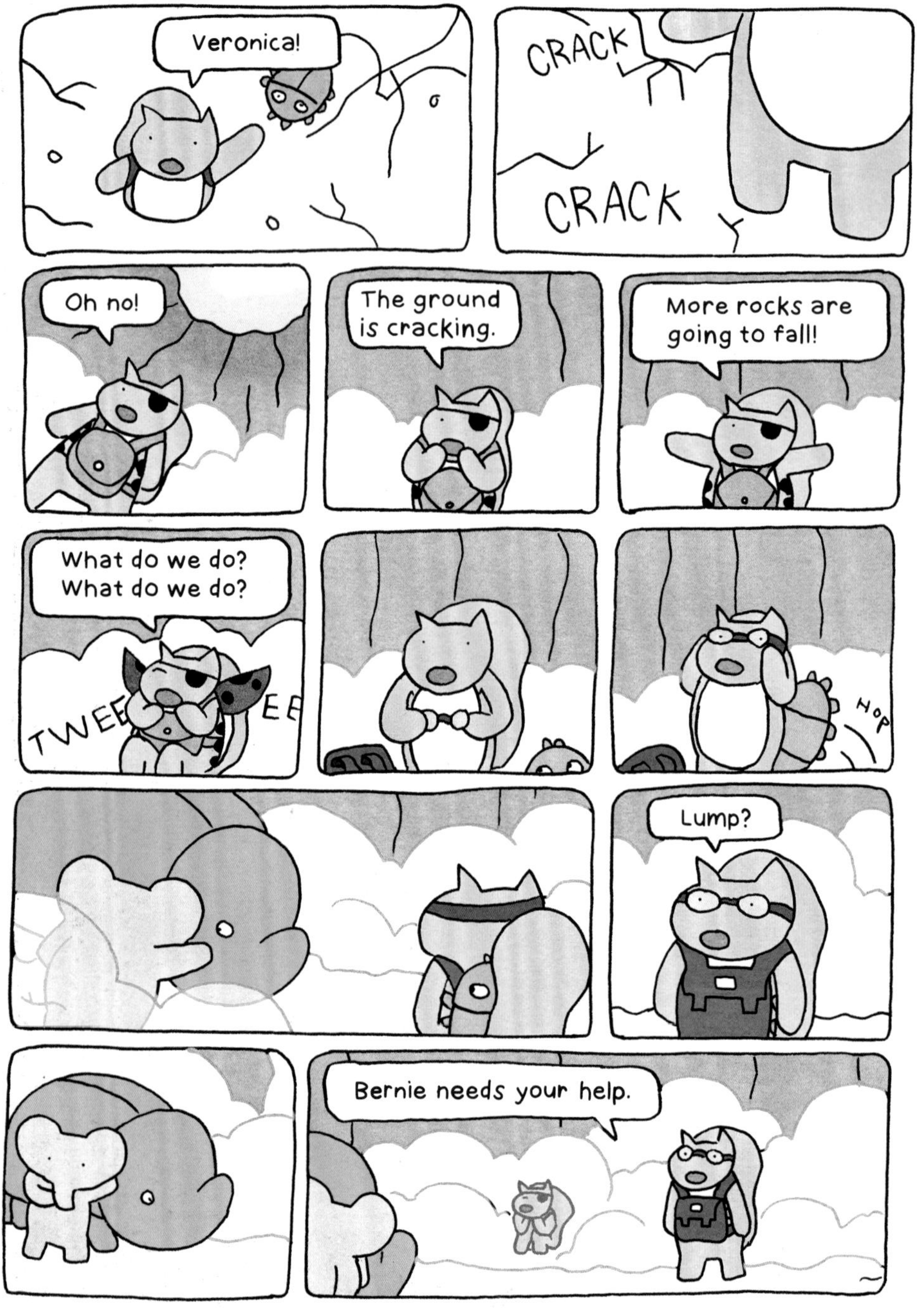
Veronica!
CRACK
CRACK
Oh no!
The ground is cracking.
More rocks are going to fall!
What do we do? What do we do?
TWEE
EE
HOP
Lump?
Bernie needs your help.

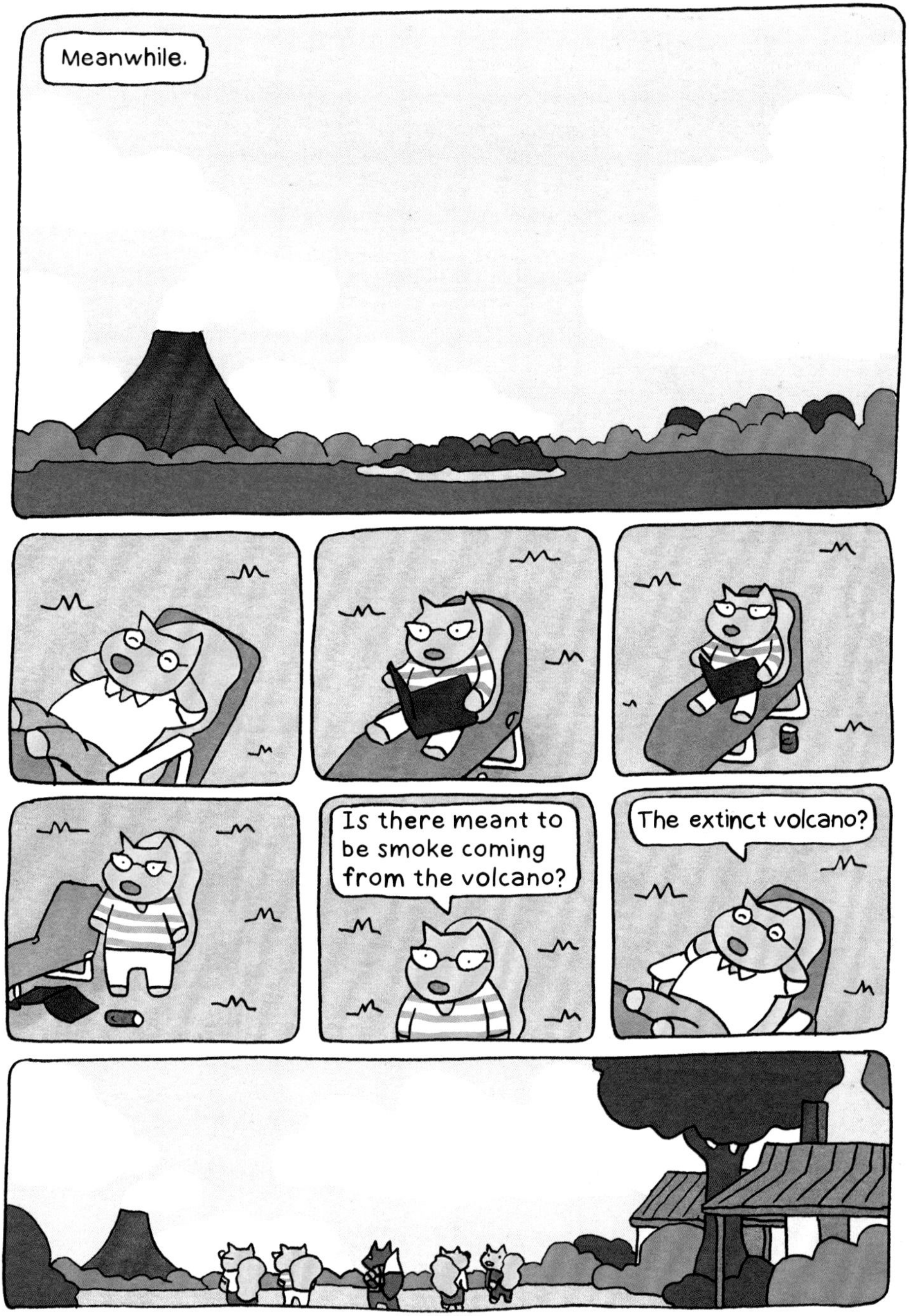
Meanwhile.
Is there meant to be smoke coming from the volcano?
The extinct volcano?

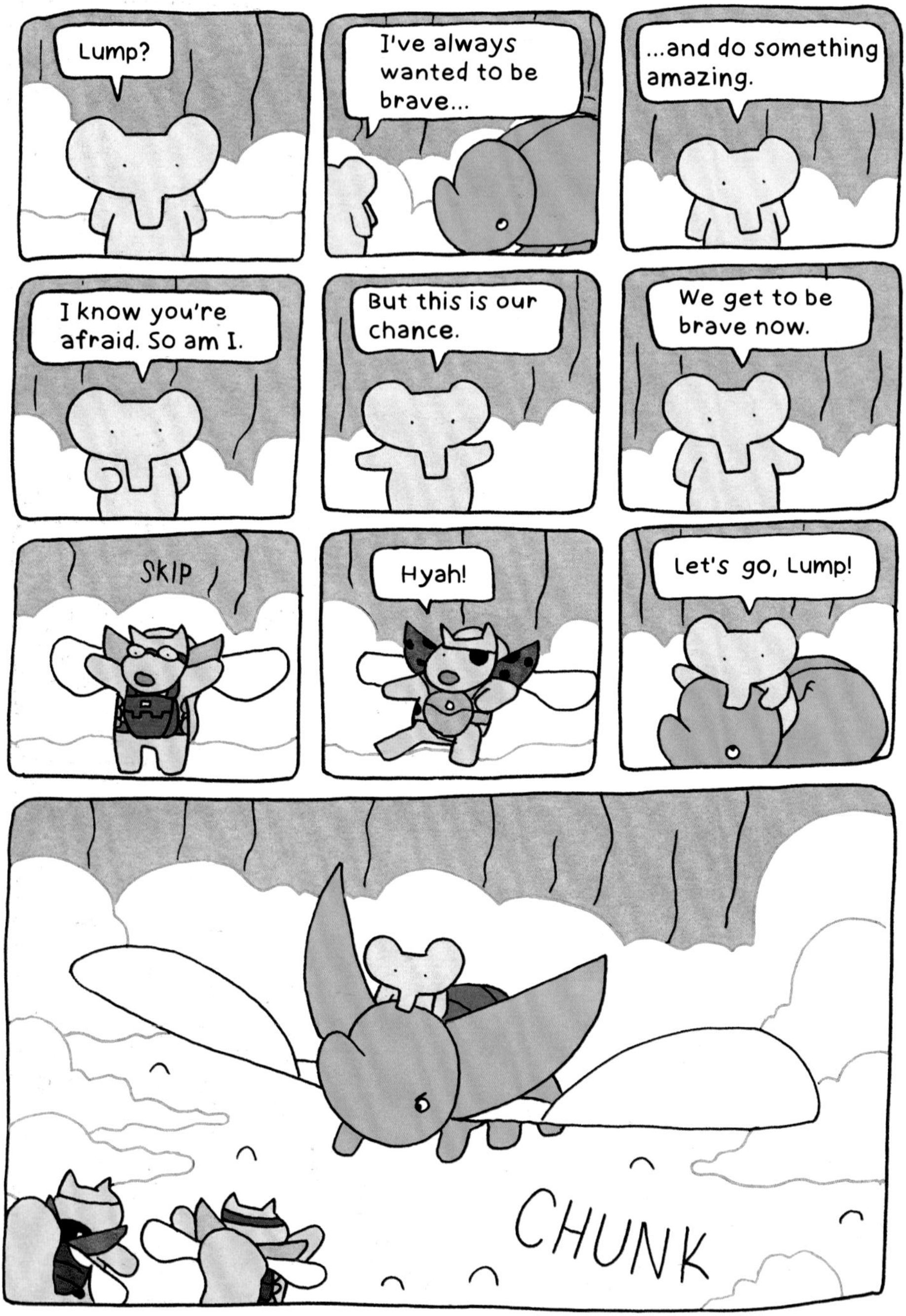
Lump?
I've always wanted to be brave...
...and do something amazing.
I know you're afraid. So am I.
But this is our chance.
We get to be brave now.
SKIP
Hyah!
Let's go, Lump!
CHUNK

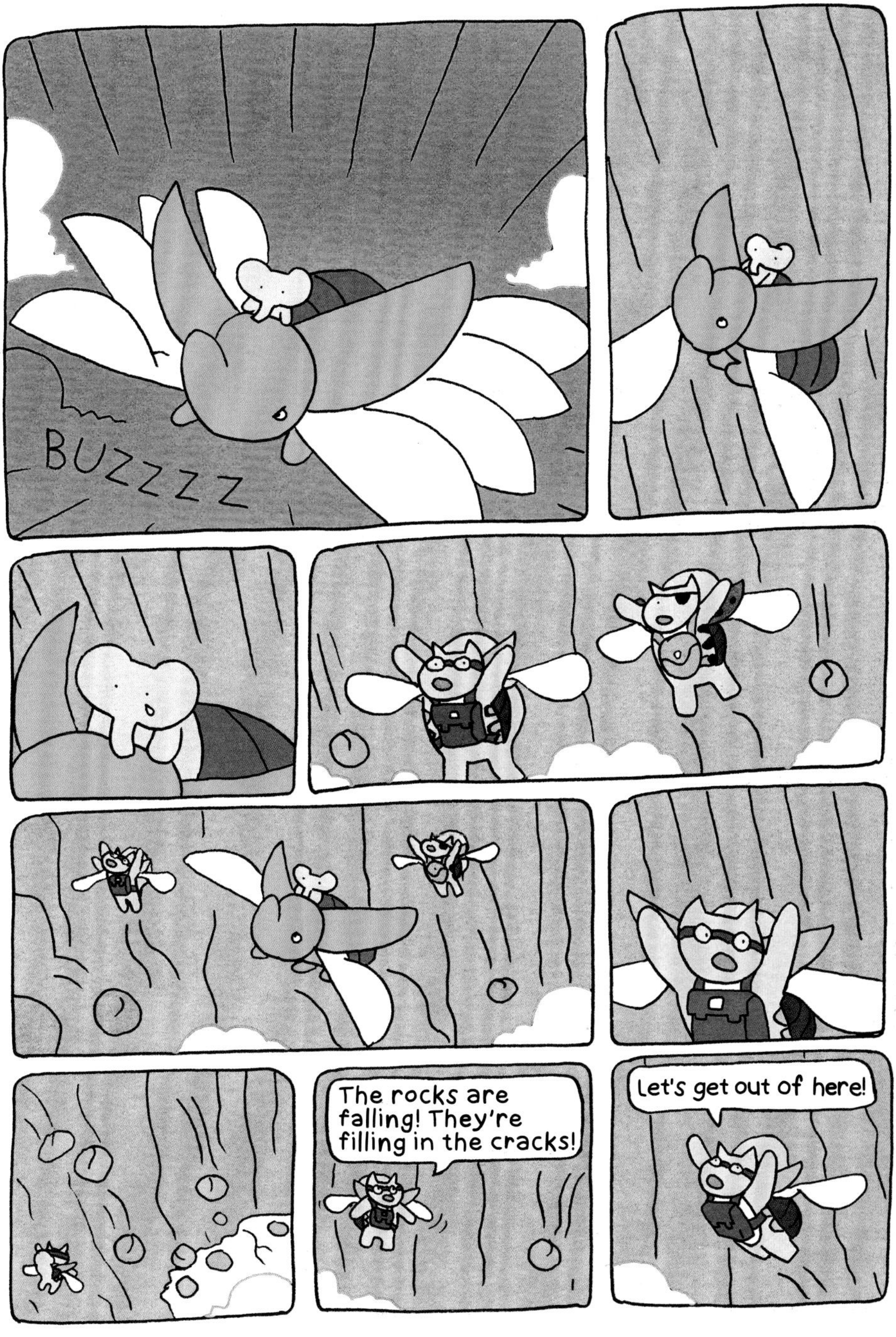
BUZZZZZ
The rocks are falling! They're filling in the cracks!
Let's get out of here!

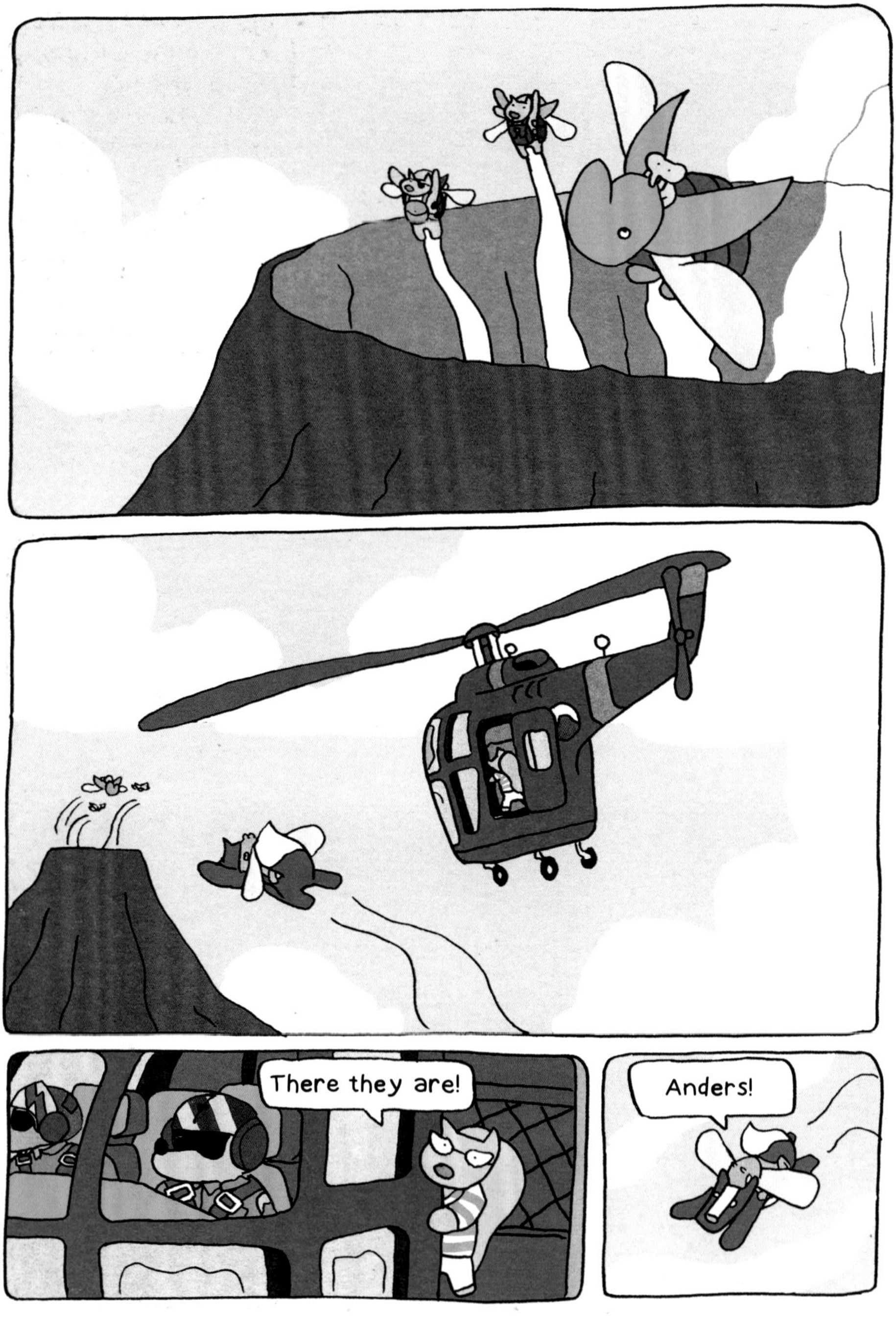
There they are!
Anders!

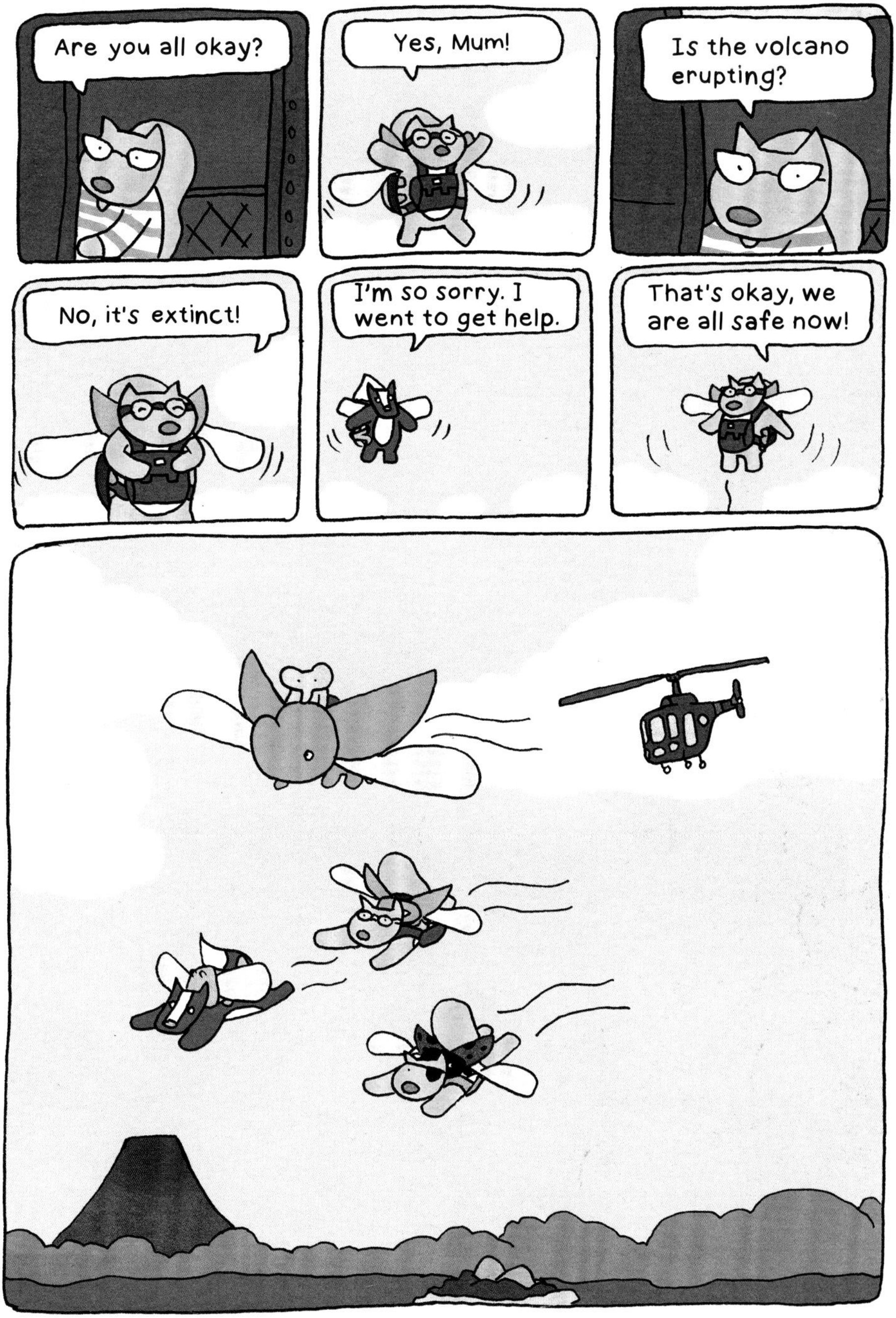
Are you all okay?
Yes, Mum!
Is the volcano erupting?
No, it's extinct!
I'm so sorry. I went to get help.
That's okay, we are all safe now!

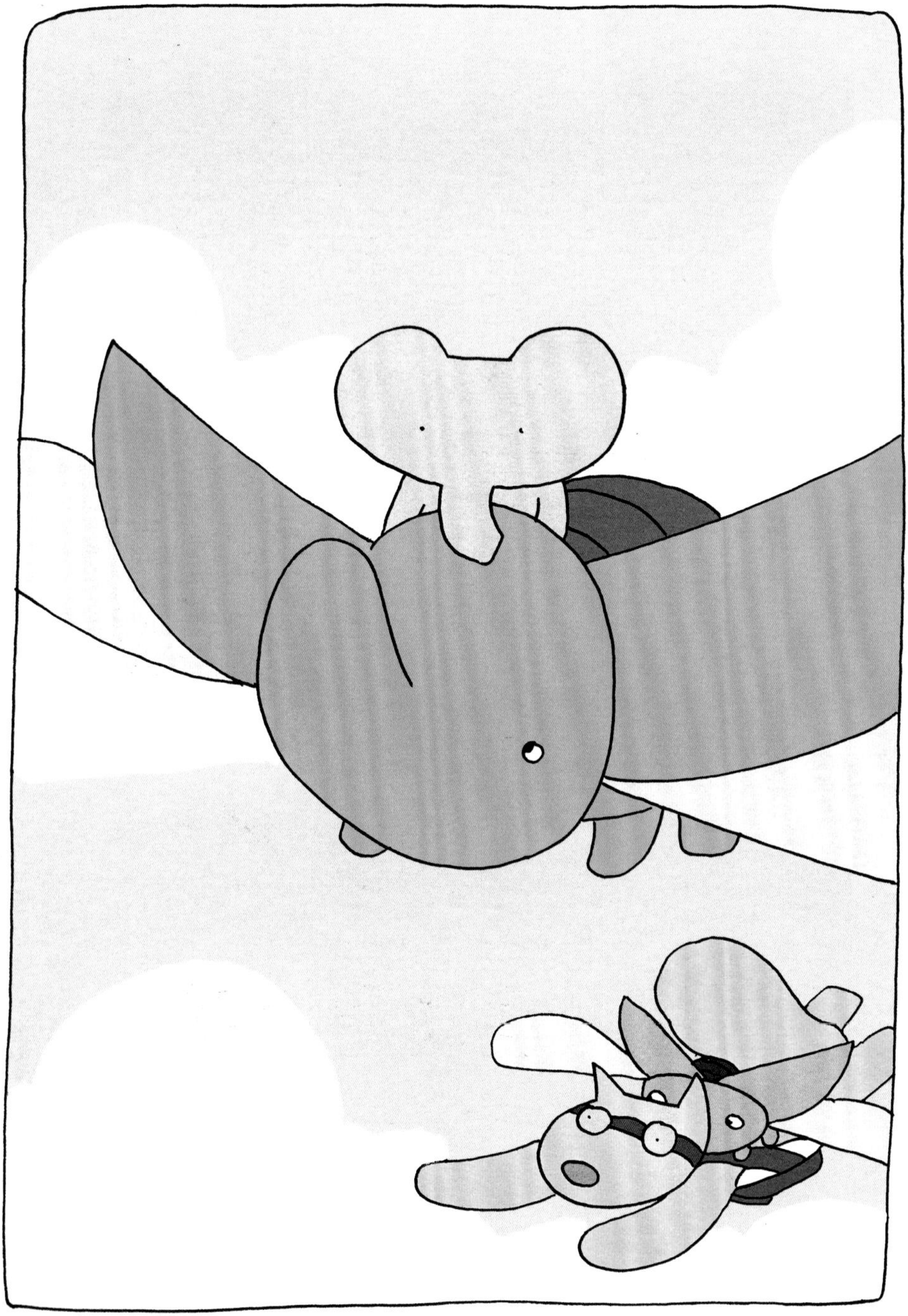

Chapter 13

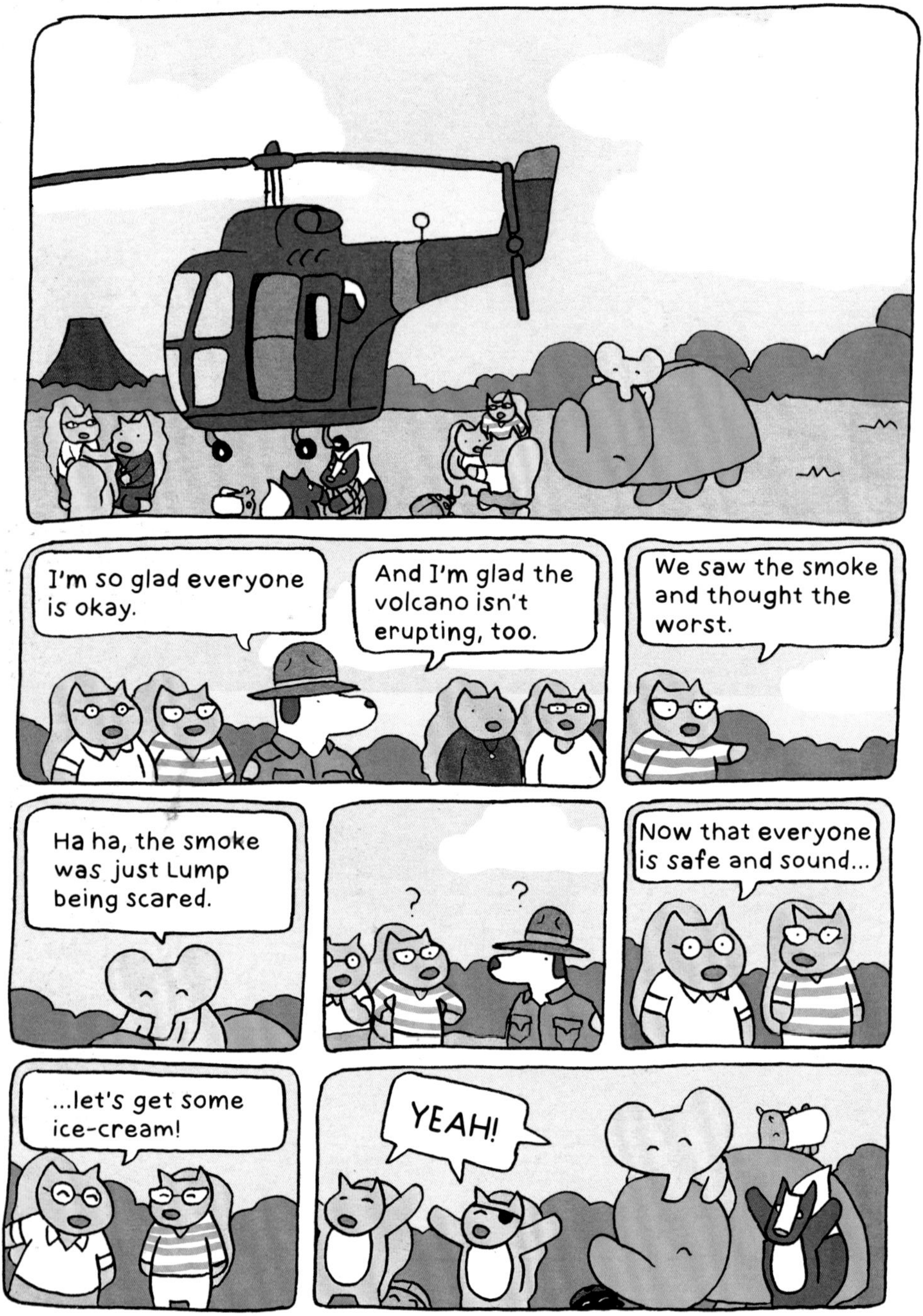

I'm so glad everyone is okay.
And I'm glad the volcano isn't erupting, too.
We saw the smoke and thought the worst.
Ha ha, the smoke was just Lump being scared.
?
?
Now that everyone is safe and sound...
...let's get some ice-cream!
YEAH!

The next day.

This is the best holiday ever.

Thanks for inviting me, Anders.

That's okay, Bernie.

Hey kids, it's time to start packing up. We have to drive home soon.

Awwwww, Mum.

Come on, Anders. It's time to go.

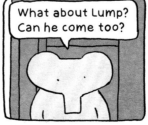

What about Lump? Can he come too?

Yes. I was going to tell you about that.

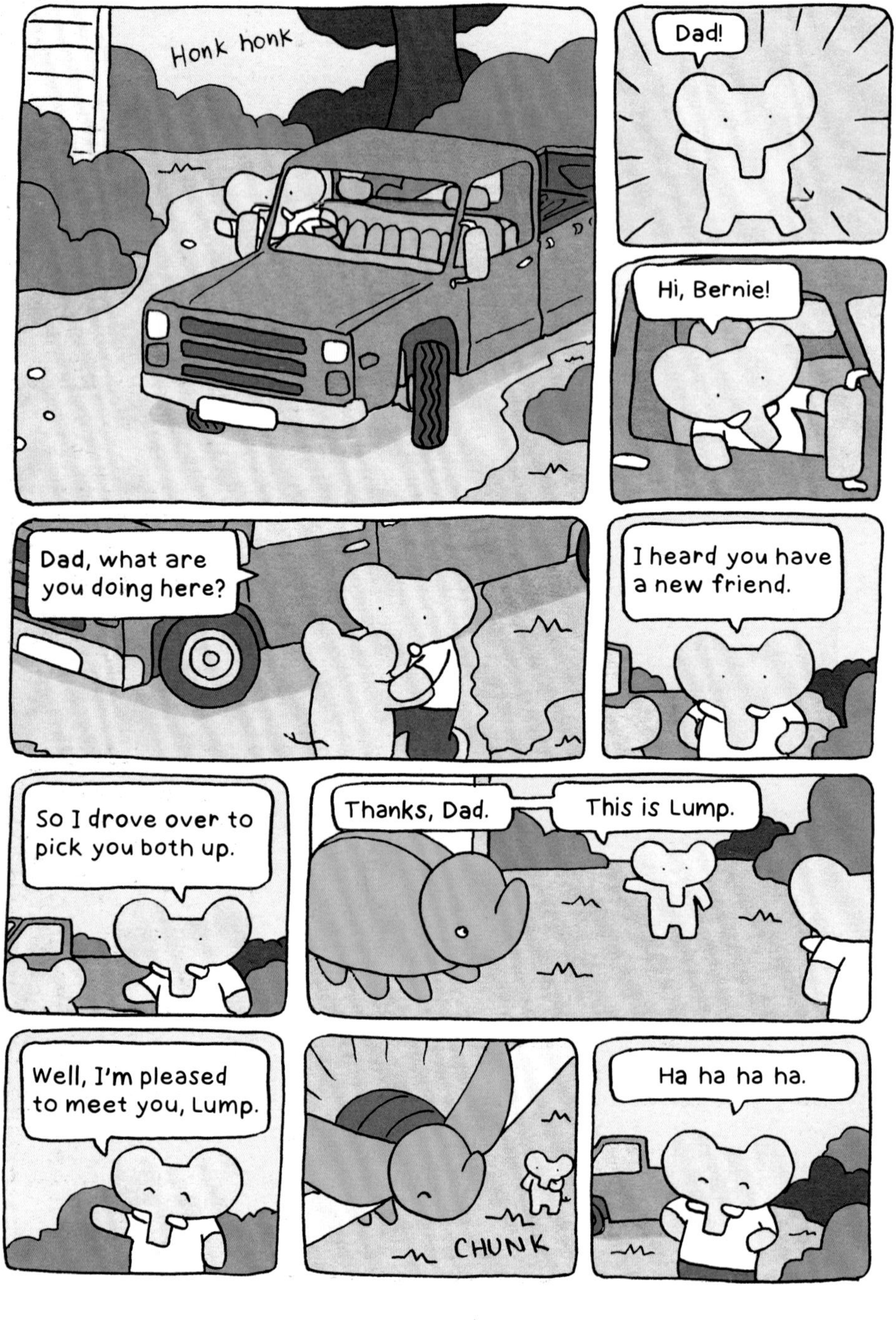
Honk honk
Dad!
Hi, Bernie!
Dad, what are you doing here?
I heard you have a new friend.
So I drove over to pick you both up.
Thanks, Dad.
This is Lump.
Well, I'm pleased to meet you, Lump.
CHUNK
Ha ha ha ha.

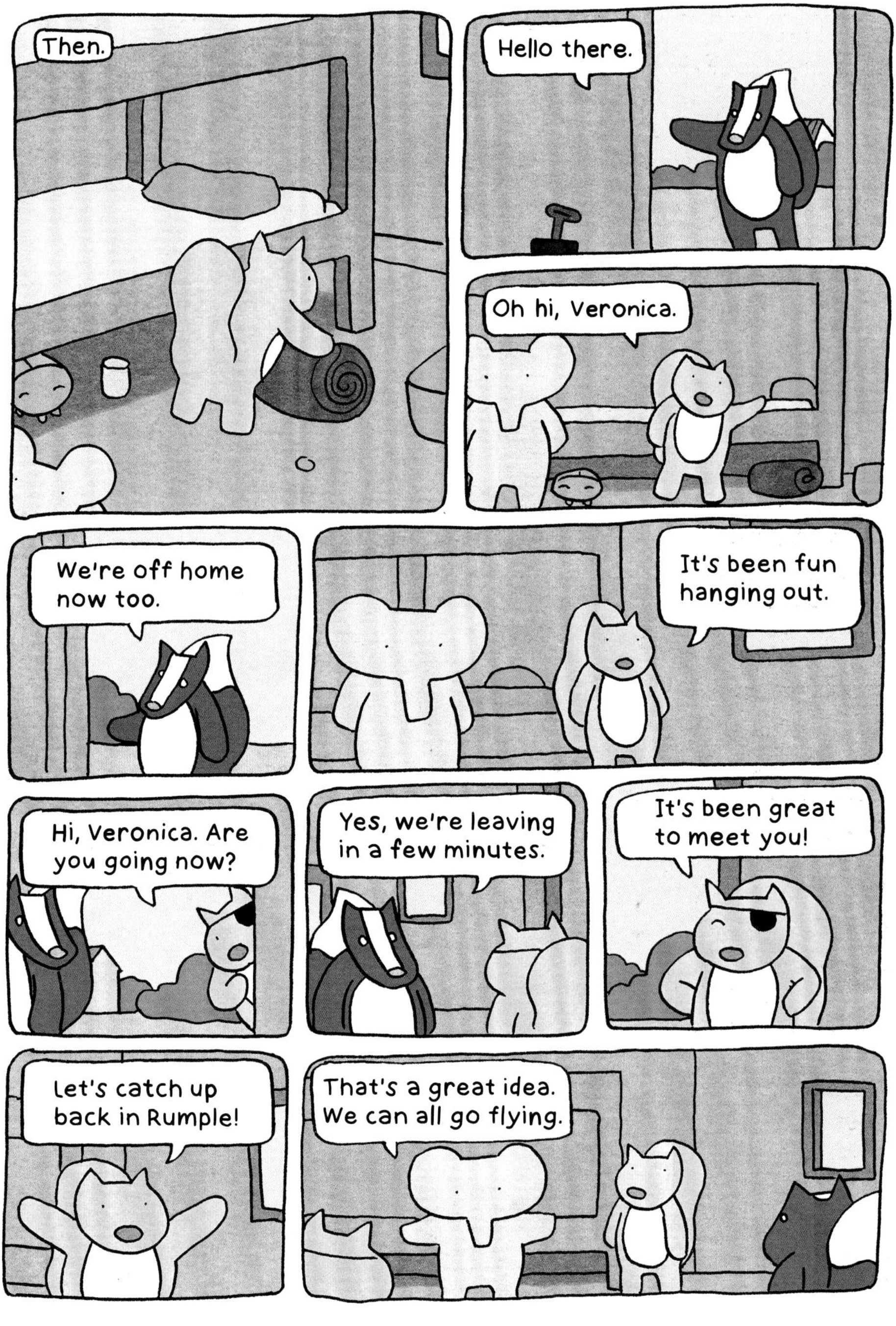

Then.
Hello there.
Oh hi, Veronica.
We're off home now too.
It's been fun hanging out.
Hi, Veronica. Are you going now?
Yes, we're leaving in a few minutes.
It's been great to meet you!
Let's catch up back in Rumple!
That's a great idea. We can all go flying.

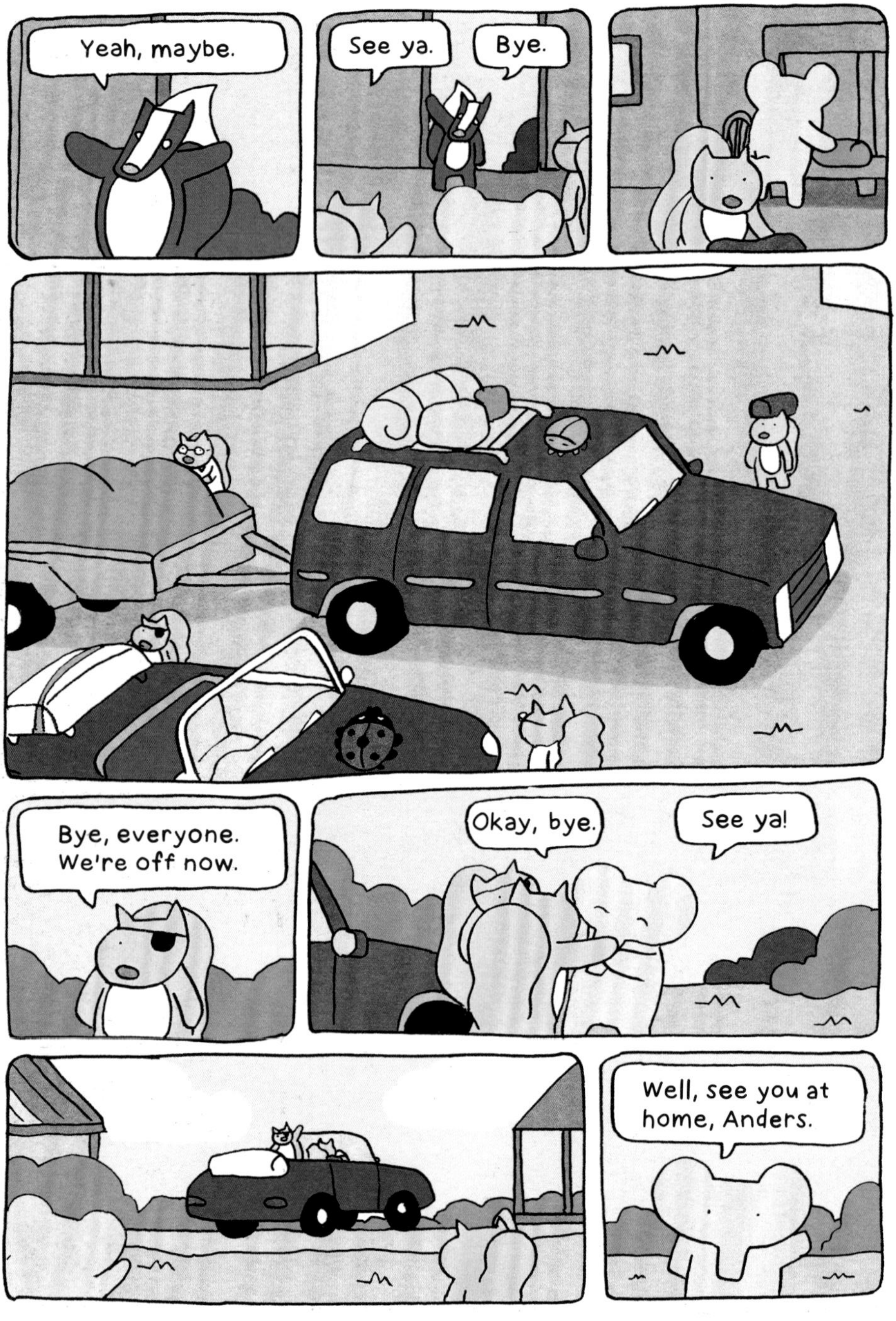
Yeah, maybe.
See ya.
Bye.
Bye, everyone. We're off now.
Okay, bye.
See ya!
Well, see you at home, Anders.

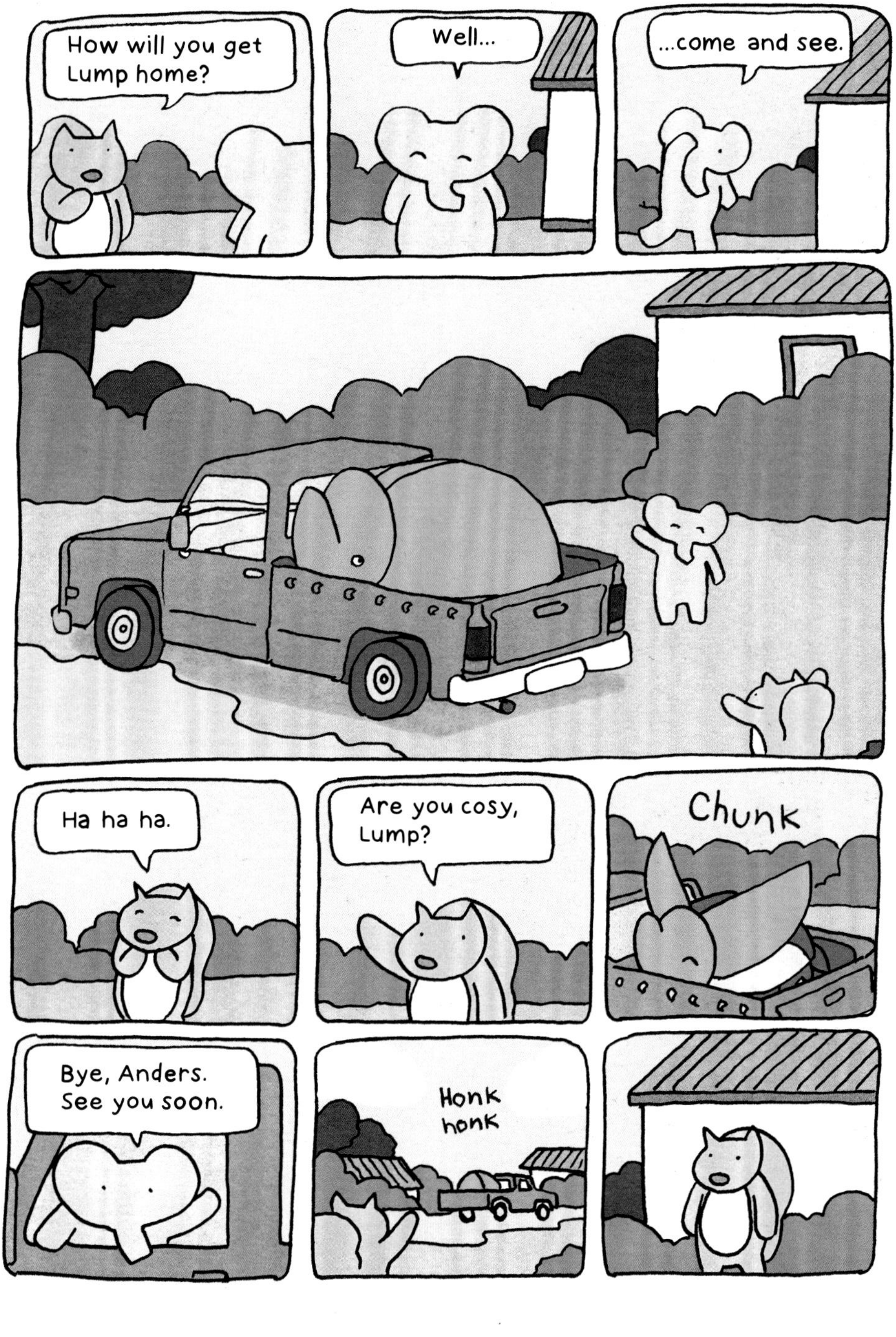
How will you get Lump home?
Well...
...come and see.
Ha ha ha.
Are you cosy, Lump?
Chunk
Bye, Anders. See you soon.
Honk honk

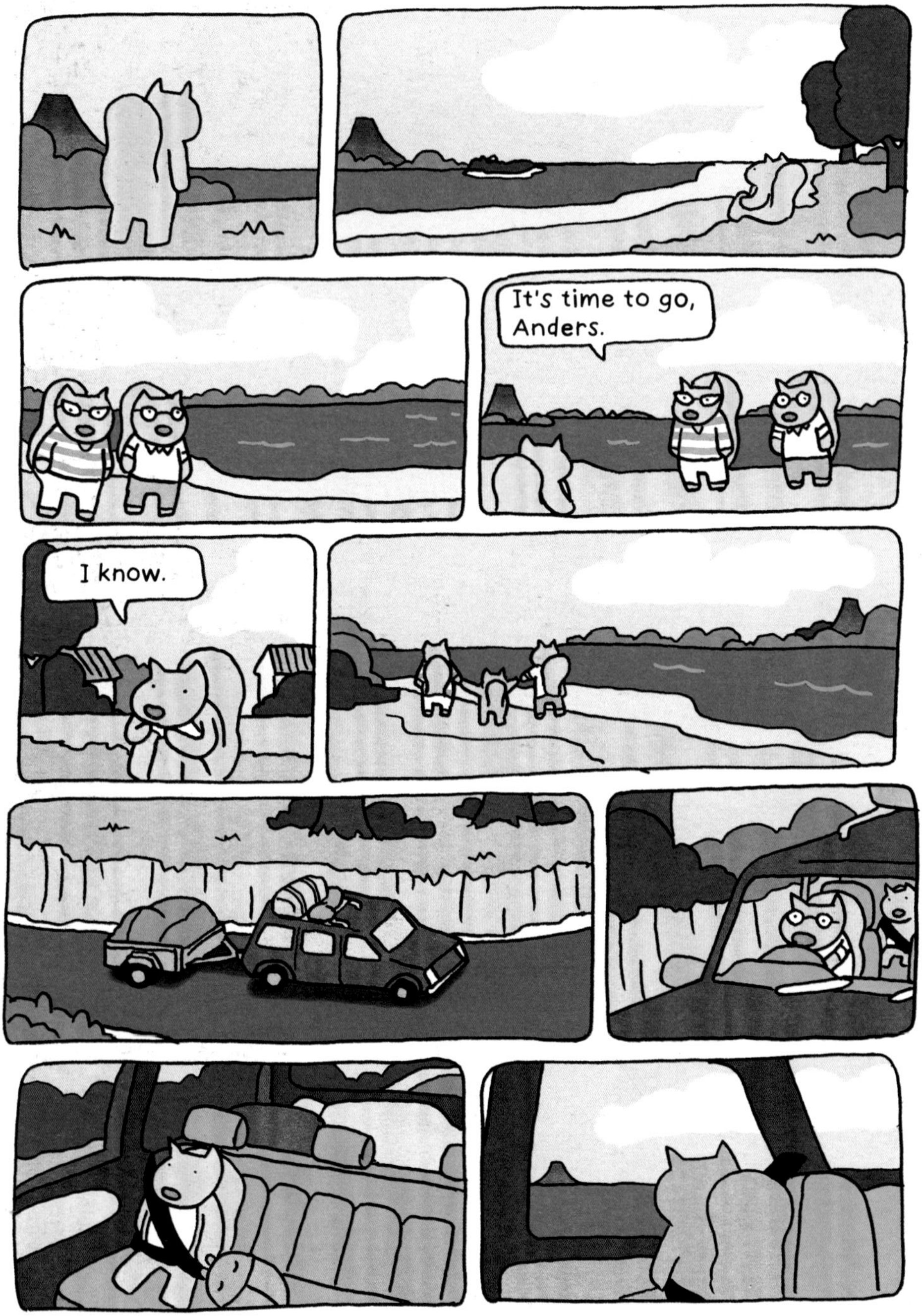
It's time to go, Anders.
I know.

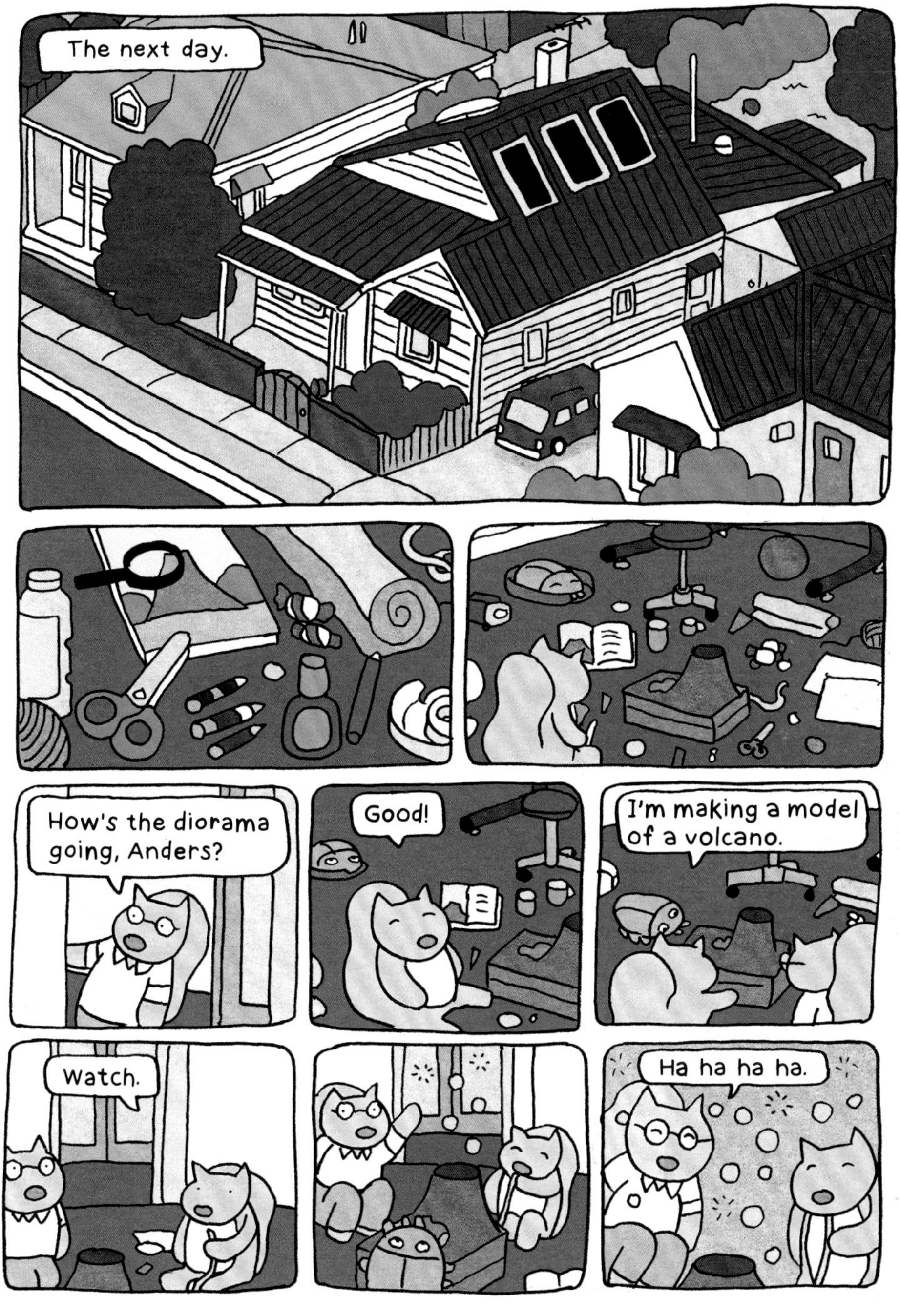
The next day.
How's the diorama going, Anders?
Good!
I'm making a model of a volcano.
Watch.
Ha ha ha ha.

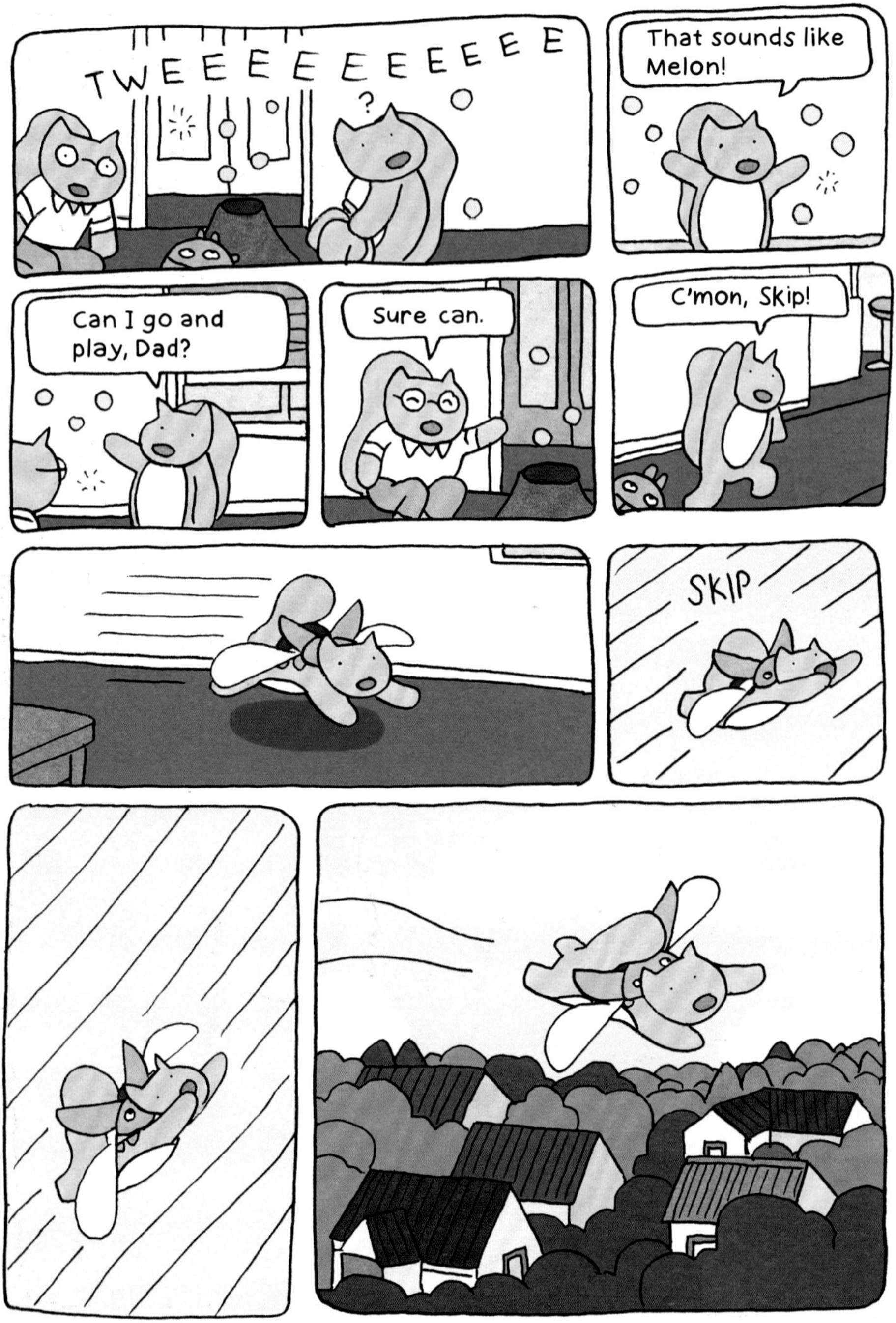
TWEEEEEEEEEEE
That sounds like Melon!
Can I go and play, Dad?
Sure can.
C'mon, Skip!
SKIP

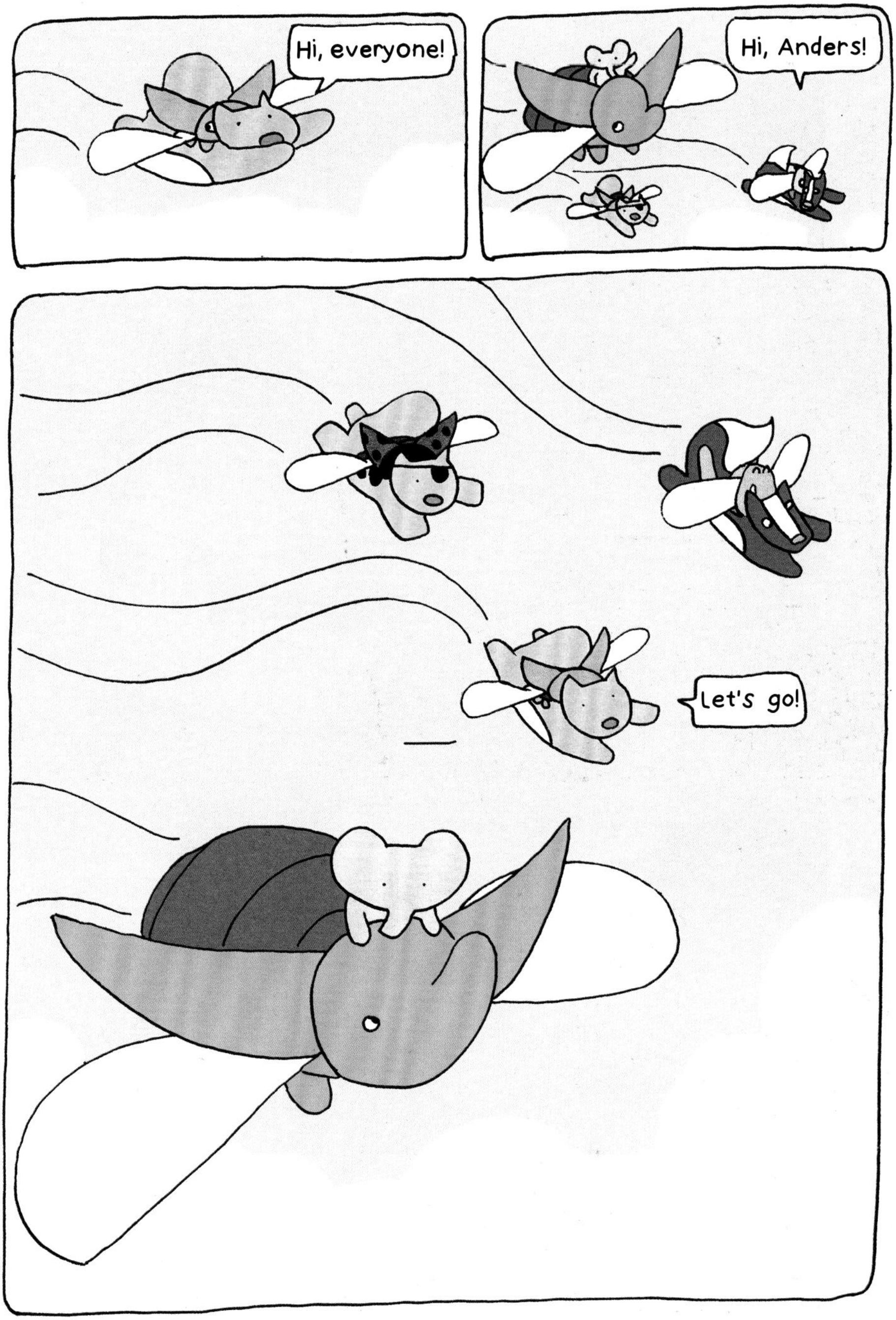
Hi, everyone!
Hi, Anders!
Let's go!

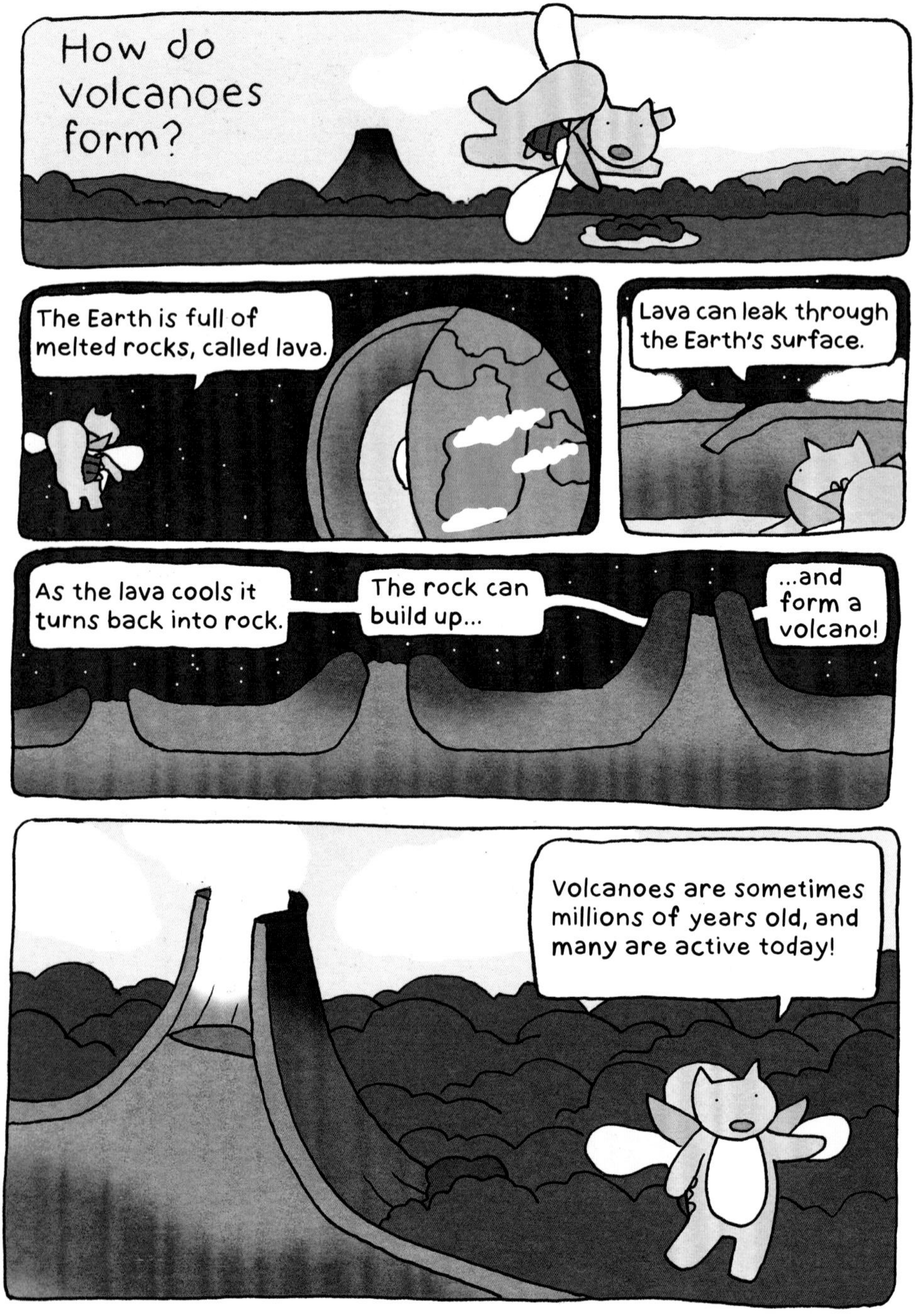
How do volcanoes form?
The Earth is full of melted rocks, called lava.
Lava can leak through the Earth's surface.
As the lava cools it turns back into rock.
The rock can build up...
...and form a volcano!
Volcanoes are sometimes millions of years old, and many are active today!

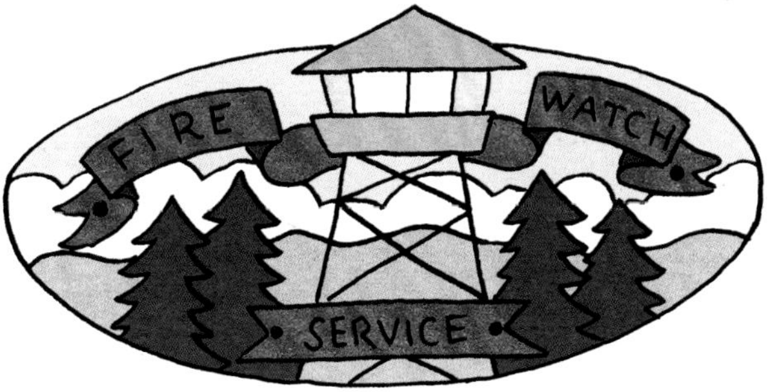
FIRE
WATCH
SERVICE

Dear Visitor,

I found this place by accident, after my beetle, Melon, led me here.

I think that it's quite wonderful that this place exists and people choose to leave messages for other visitors who chance upon it.

You can see the whole Mt Tremble area from here, and I am reminded of the beauty of nature and the mystery of the volcano.

I hope you find a beetle too, so you can see this magical place from the skies.

Eden

ANDERS
and the
CASTLE

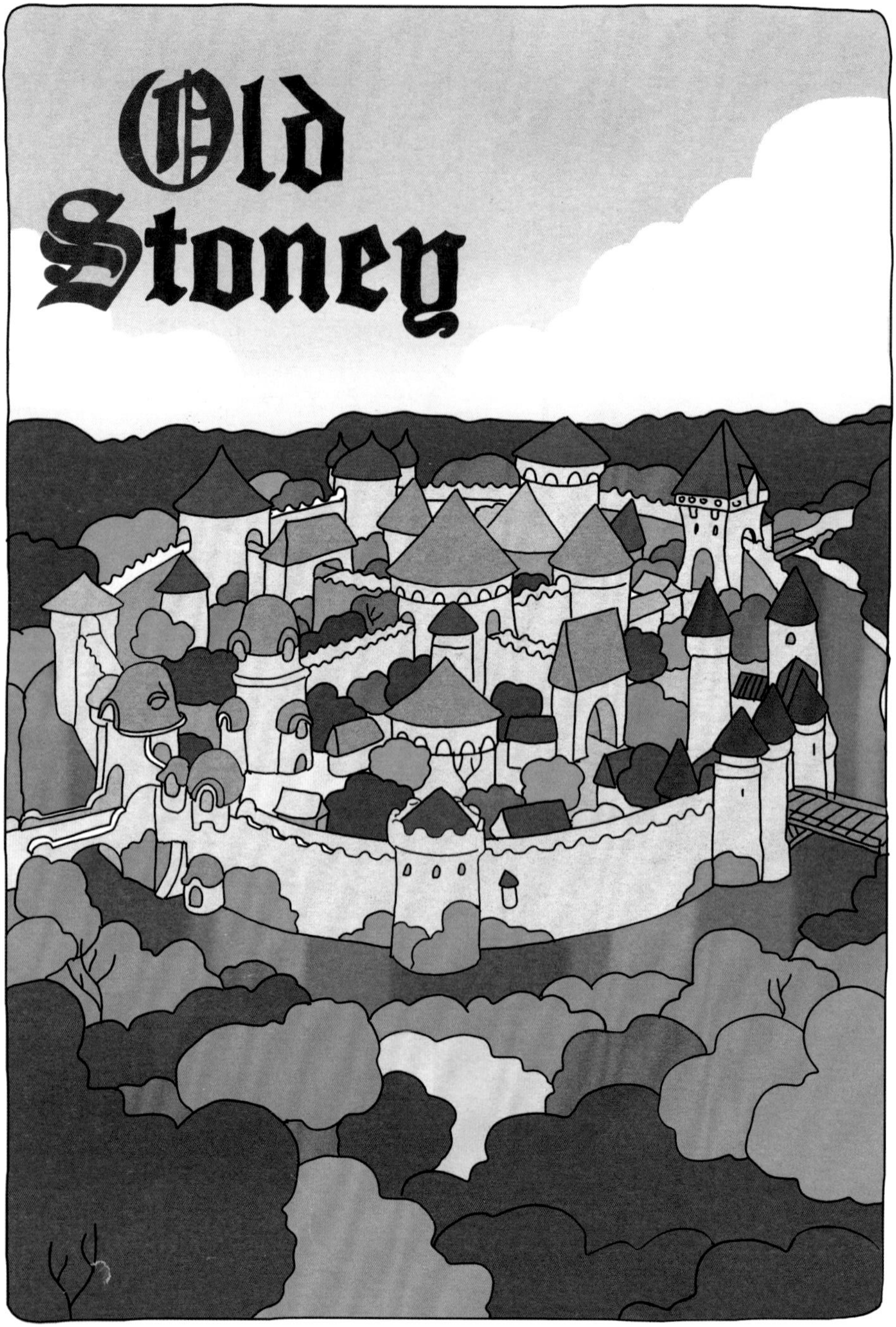
Old
Stoney

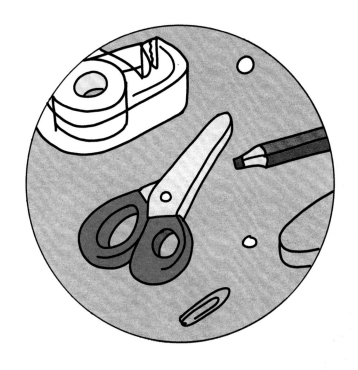

Chapter 1

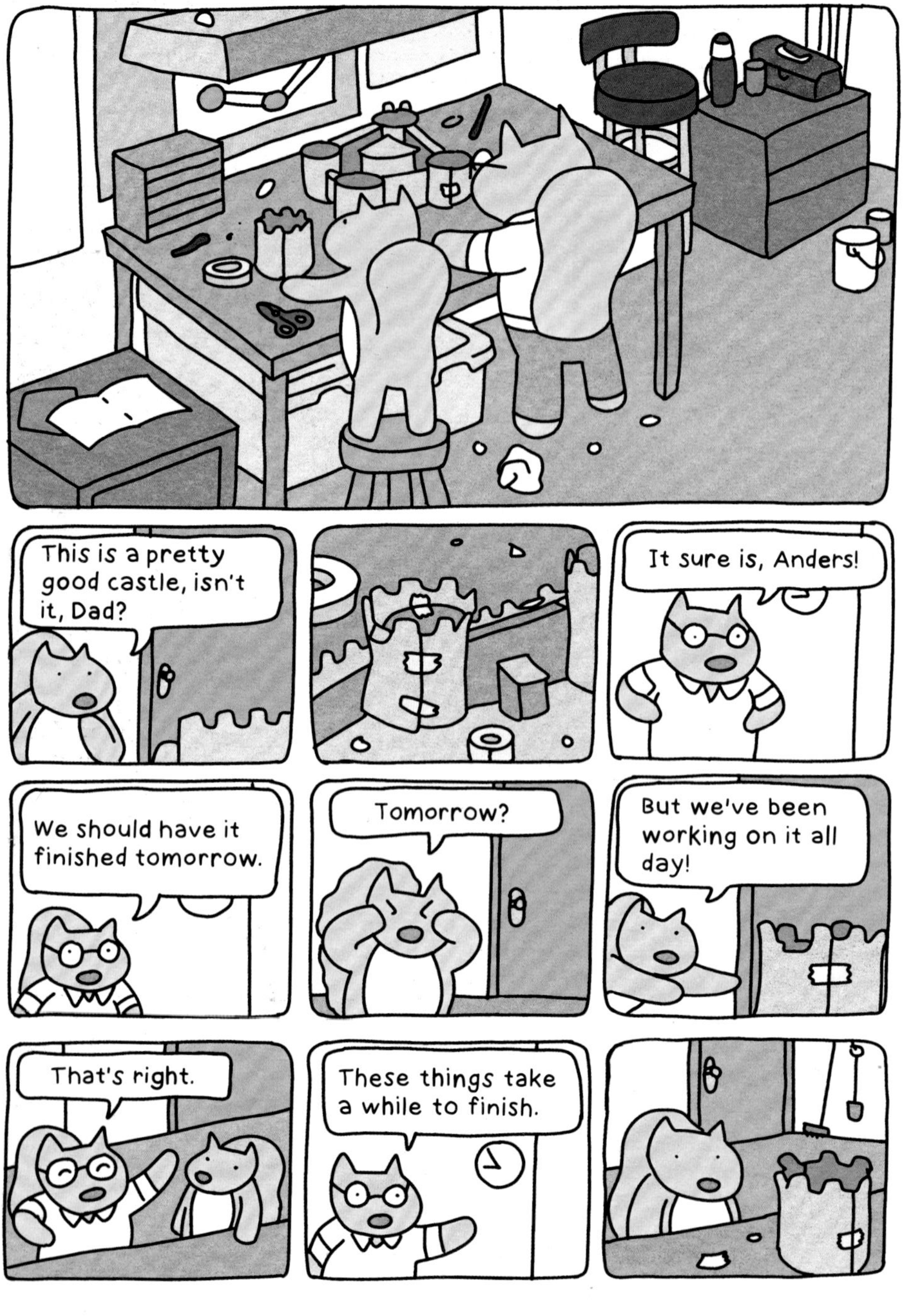

This is a pretty good castle, isn't it, Dad?
It sure is, Anders!
We should have it finished tomorrow.
Tomorrow?
But we've been working on it all day!
That's right.
These things take a while to finish.

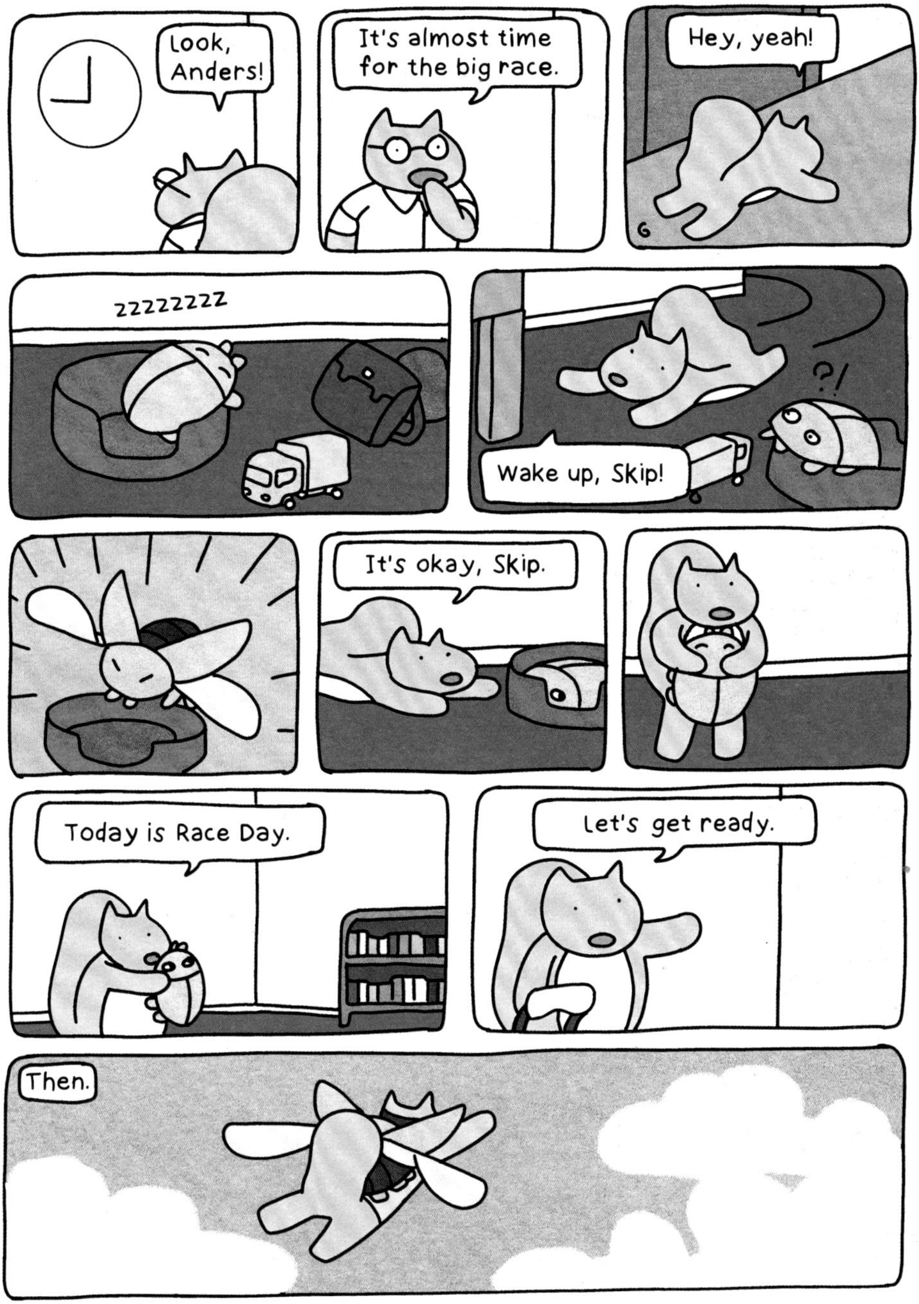
Look, Anders!
It's almost time for the big race.
Hey, yeah!
ZZZZZZZZ
Wake up, Skip!
?!
It's okay, Skip.
Today is Race Day.
Let's get ready.
Then.

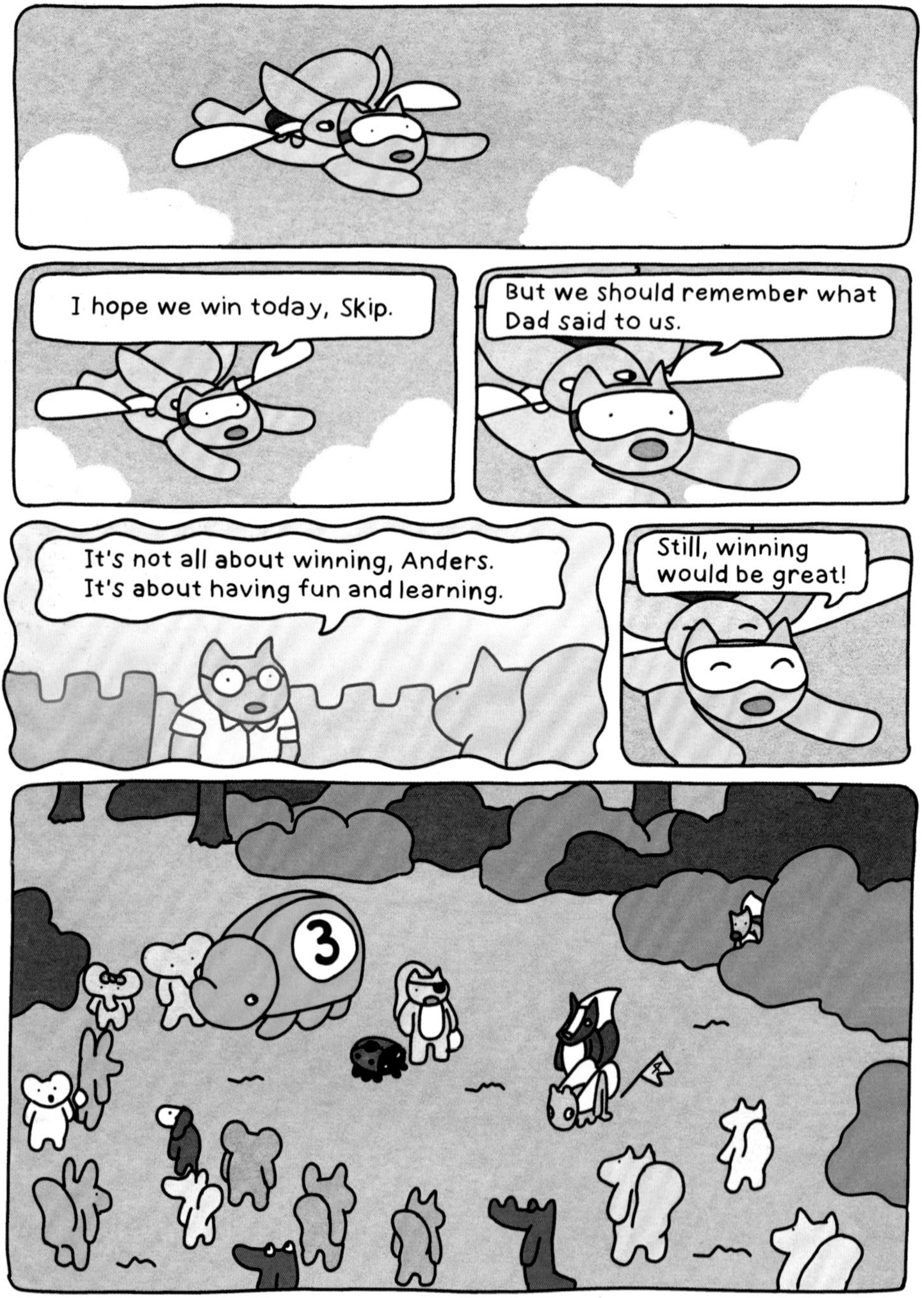
I hope we win today, Skip.
But we should remember what Dad said to us.
It's not all about winning, Anders. It's about having fun and learning.
Still, winning would be great!
3

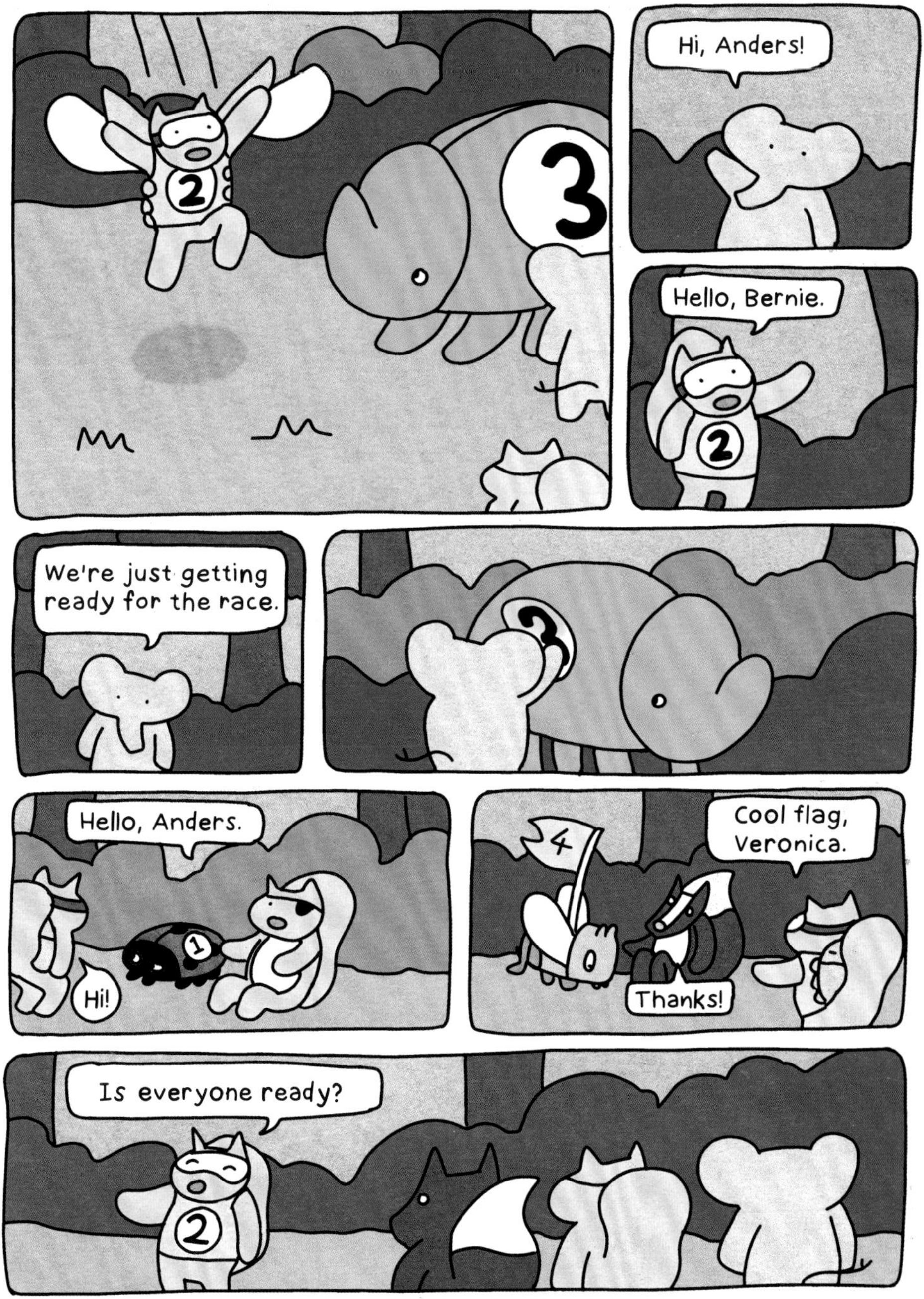
Hi, Anders!
Hello, Bernie.
We're just getting ready for the race.
Hello, Anders.
Hi!
Cool flag, Veronica.
Thanks!
Is everyone ready?

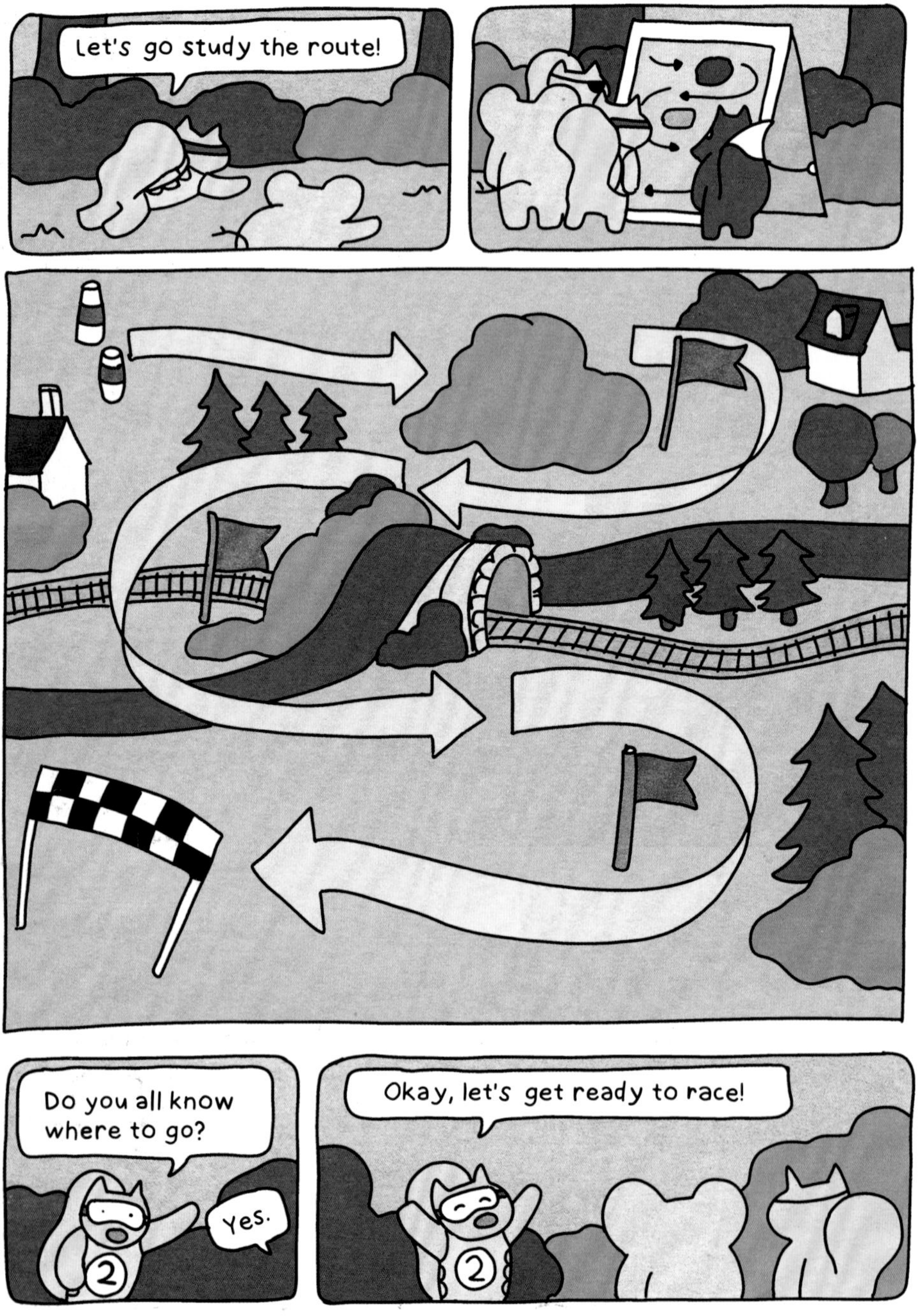
Let's go study the route!
Do you all know where to go?
Yes.
Okay, let's get ready to race!

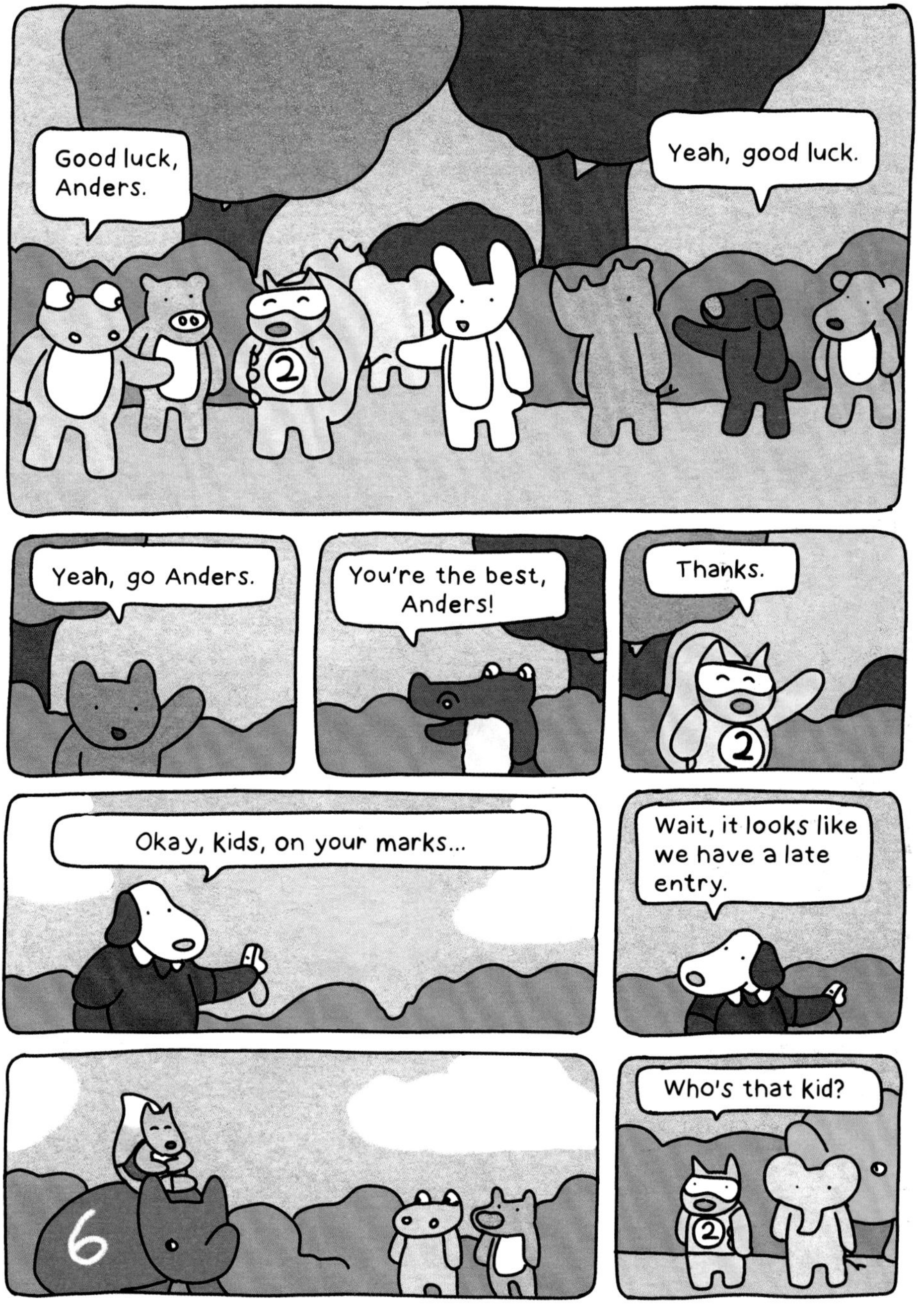
Good luck, Anders.
Yeah, good luck.
Yeah, go Anders.
You're the best, Anders!
Thanks.
Okay, kids, on your marks...
Wait, it looks like we have a late entry.
Who's that kid?

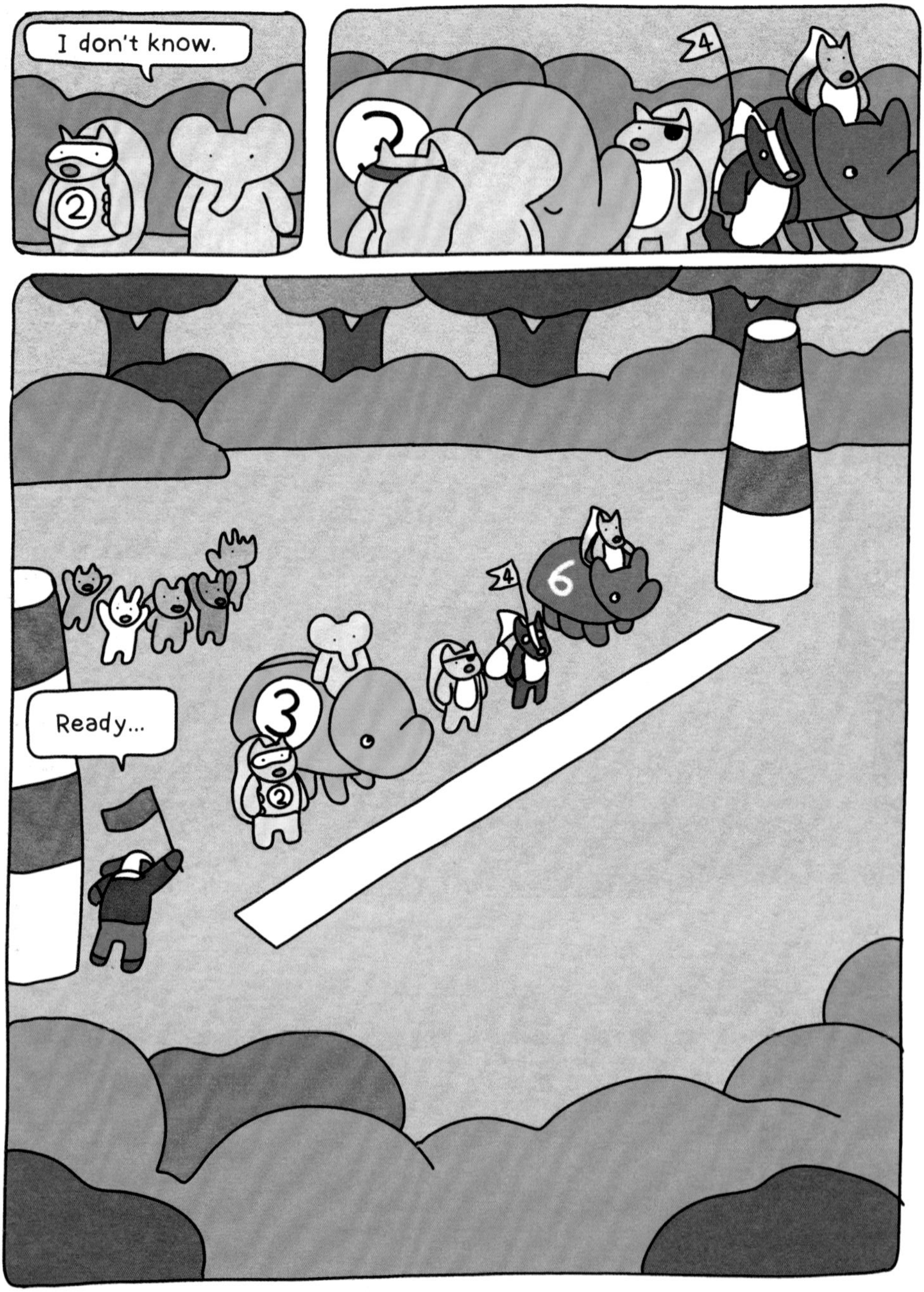
I don't know.
Ready...

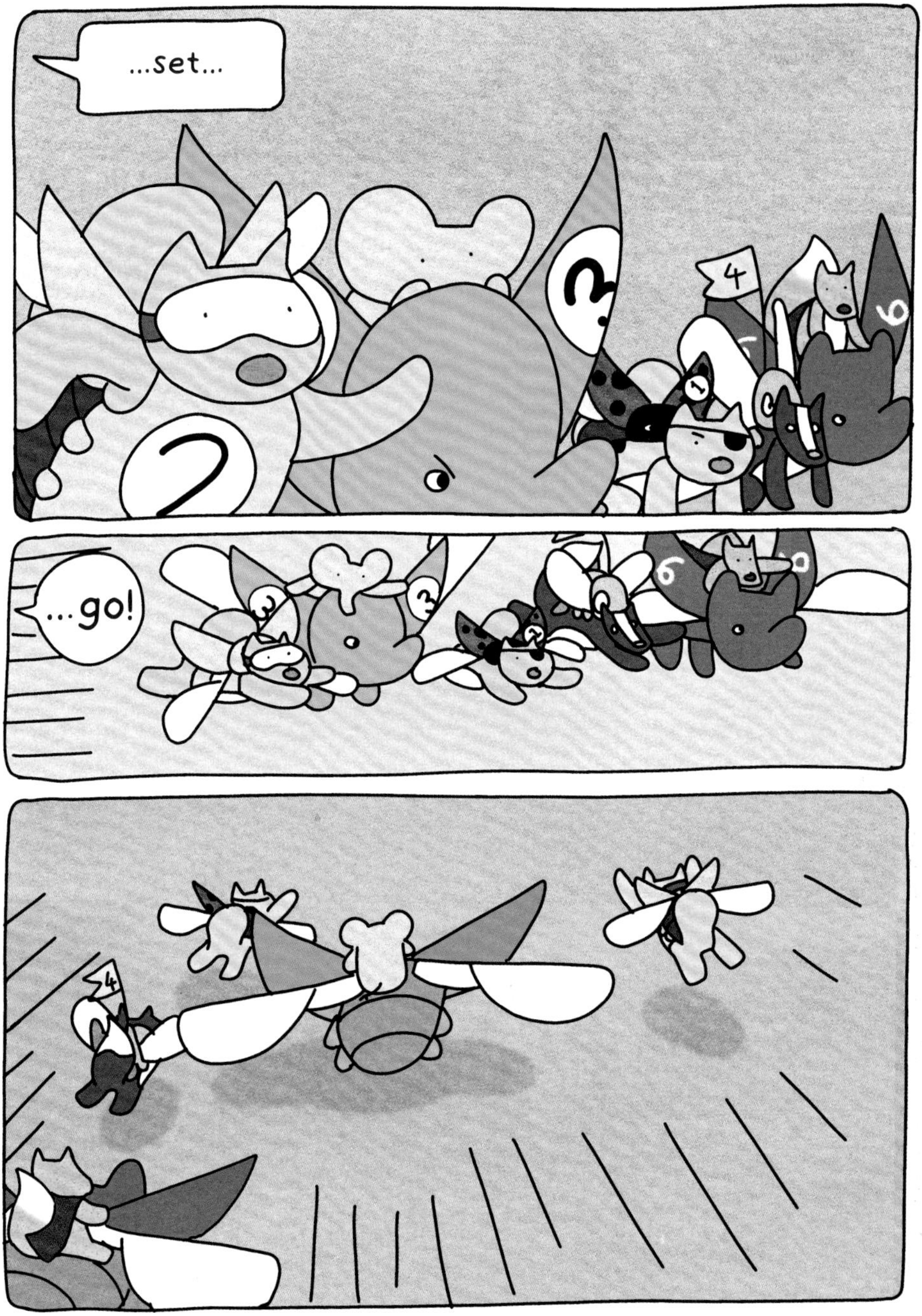
...set...
...go!

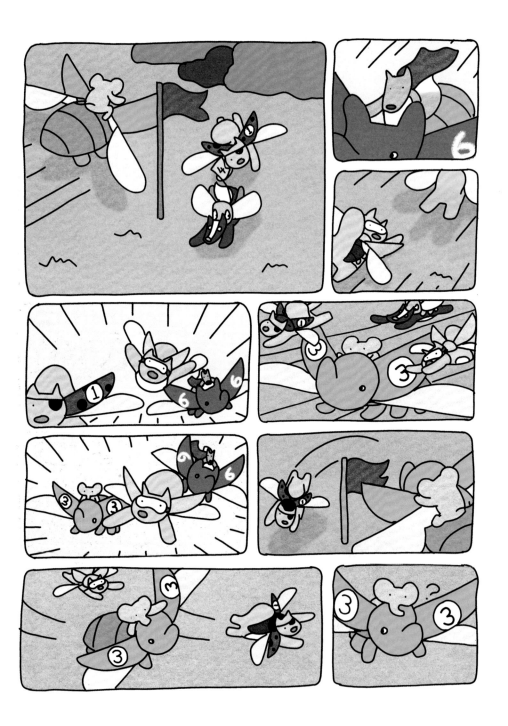

336

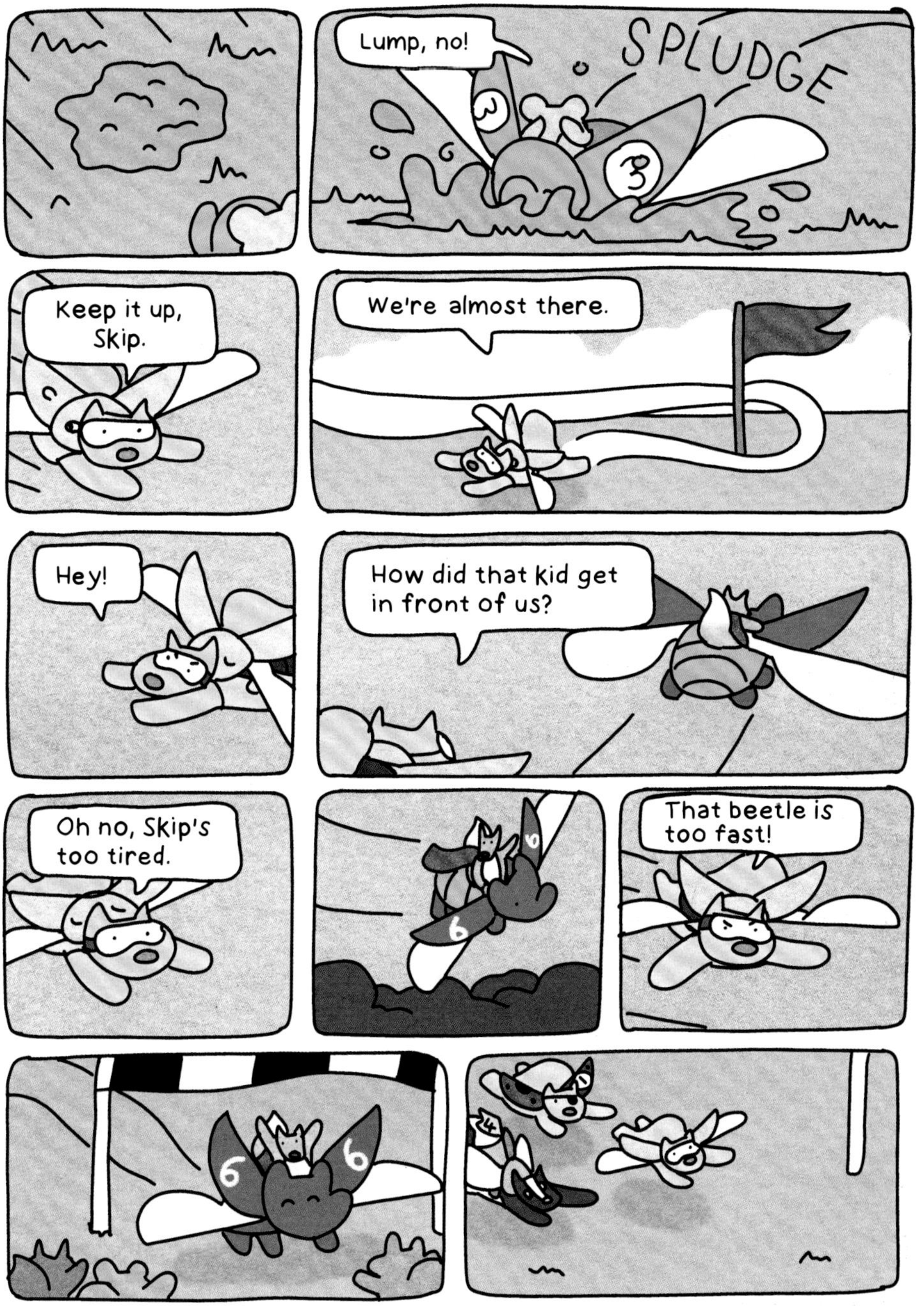
Lump, no!
SPLUDGE
Keep it up, Skip.
We're almost there.
Hey!
How did that kid get in front of us?
Oh no, Skip's too tired.
That beetle is too fast!

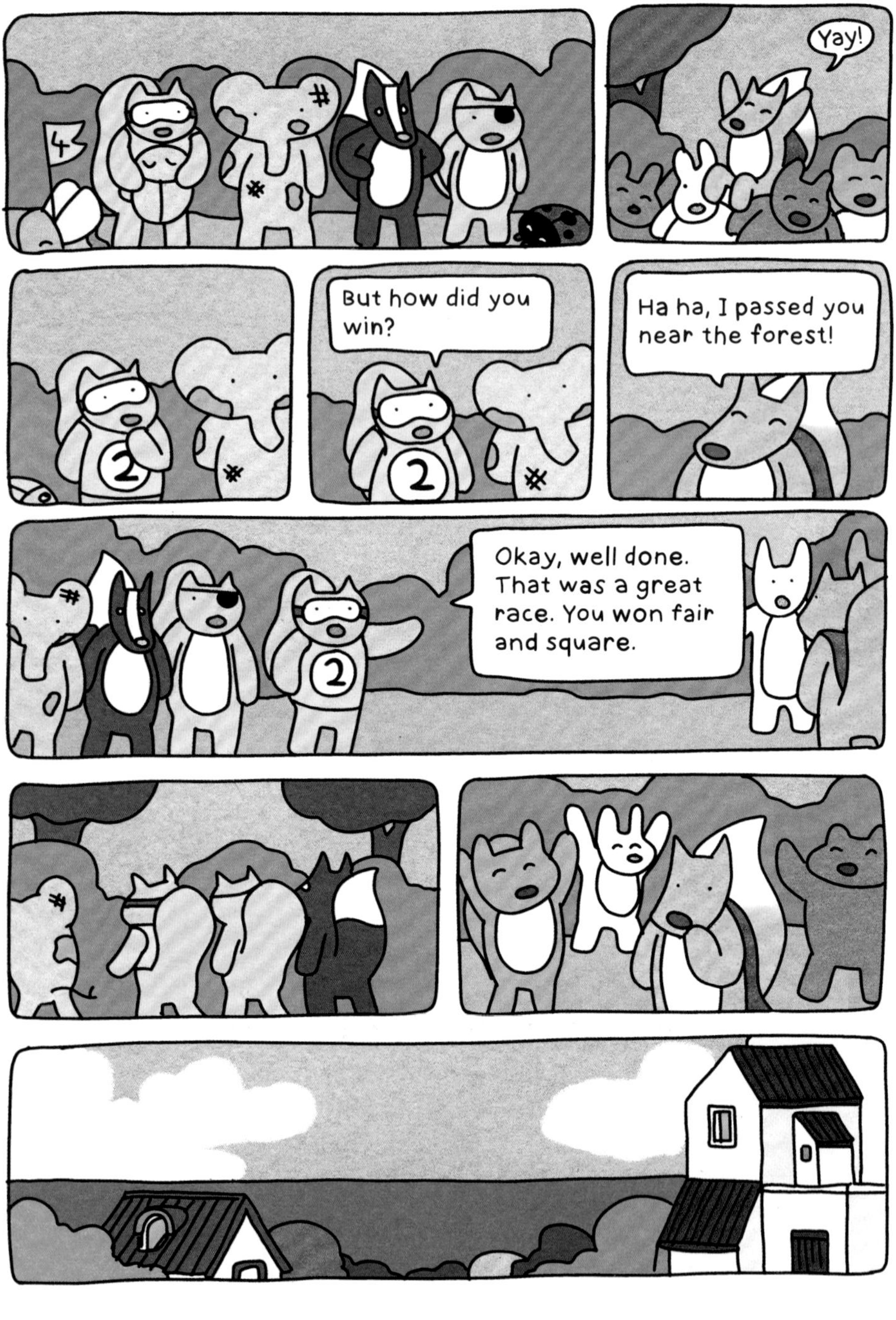
Yay!
But how did you win?
Ha ha, I passed you near the forest!
Okay, well done. That was a great race. You won fair and square.

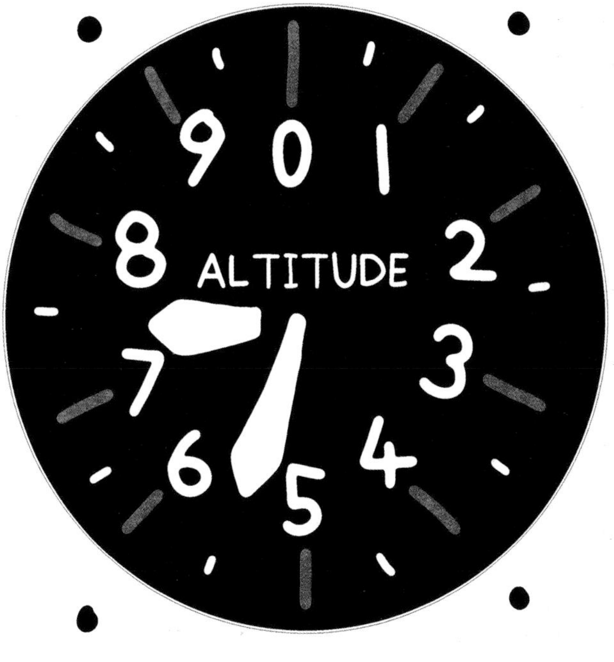
9 0 1
8 ALTITUDE 2
7 3
6 5 4

Chapter 2

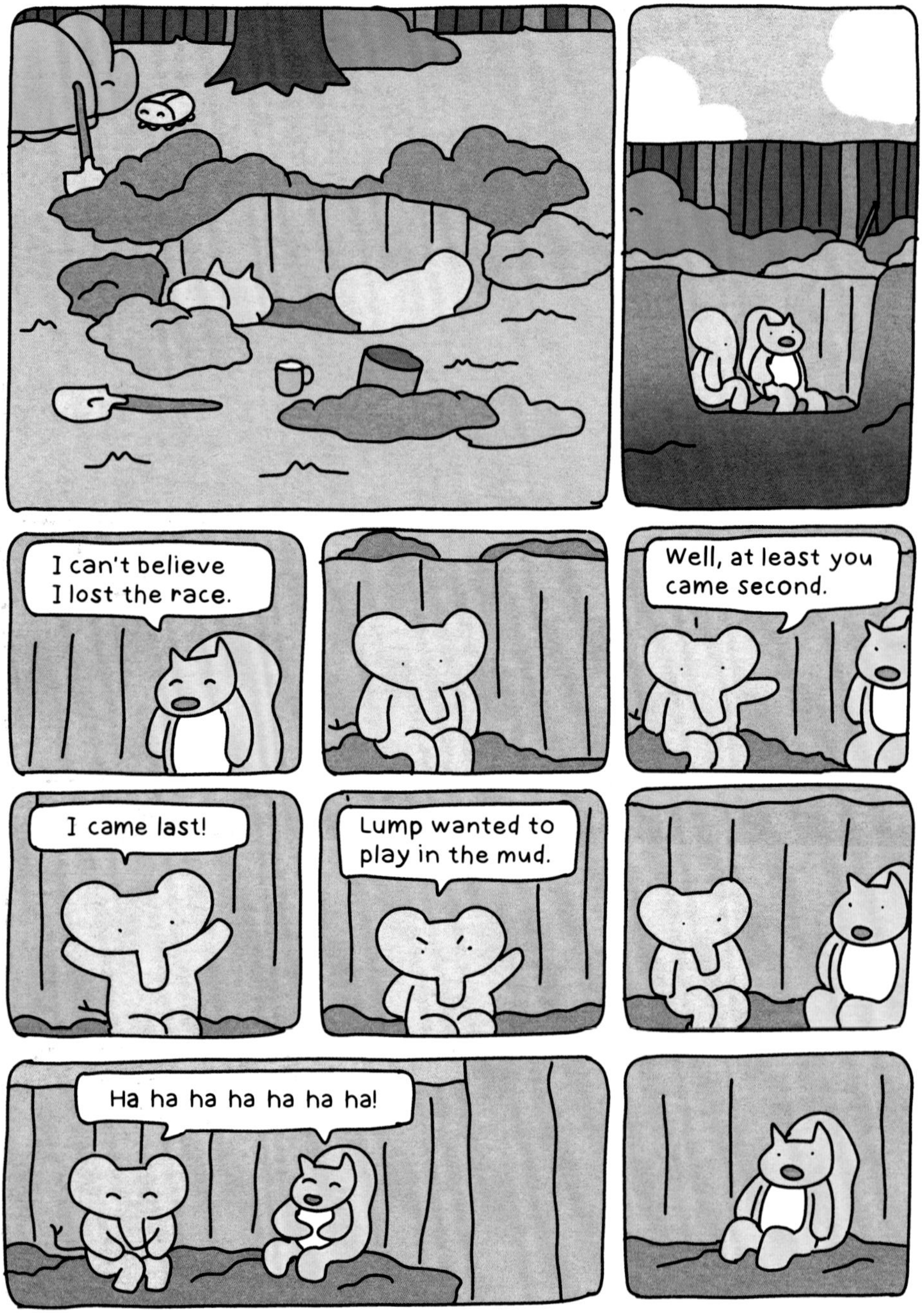
I can't believe
I lost the race.
Well, at least you
came second.
I came last!
Lump wanted to
play in the mud.
Ha ha ha ha ha ha ha!

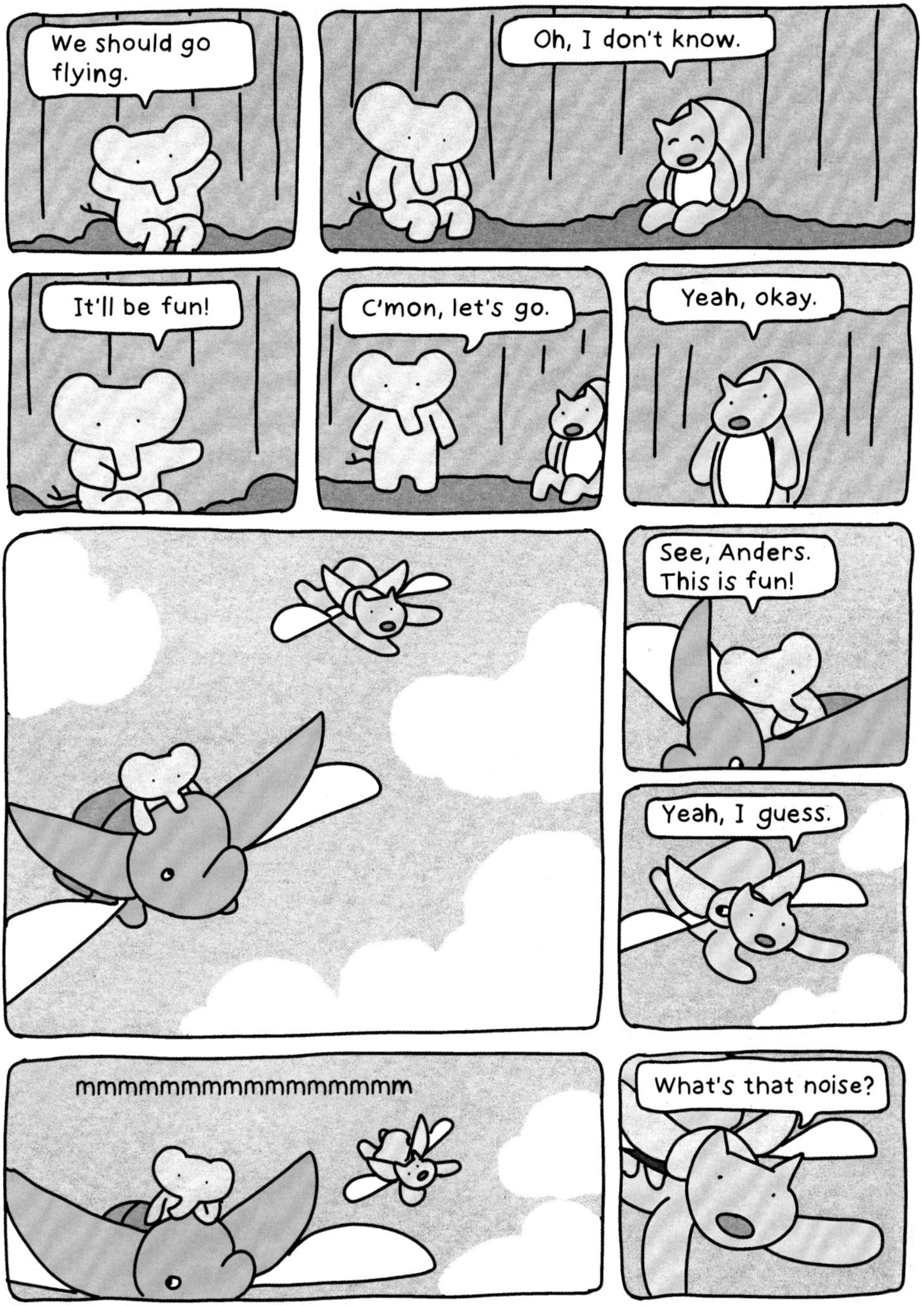
We should go flying.
Oh, I don't know.
It'll be fun!
C'mon, let's go.
Yeah, okay.
See, Anders. This is fun!
Yeah, I guess.
mmmmmmmmmmmmmmmmmm
What's that noise?

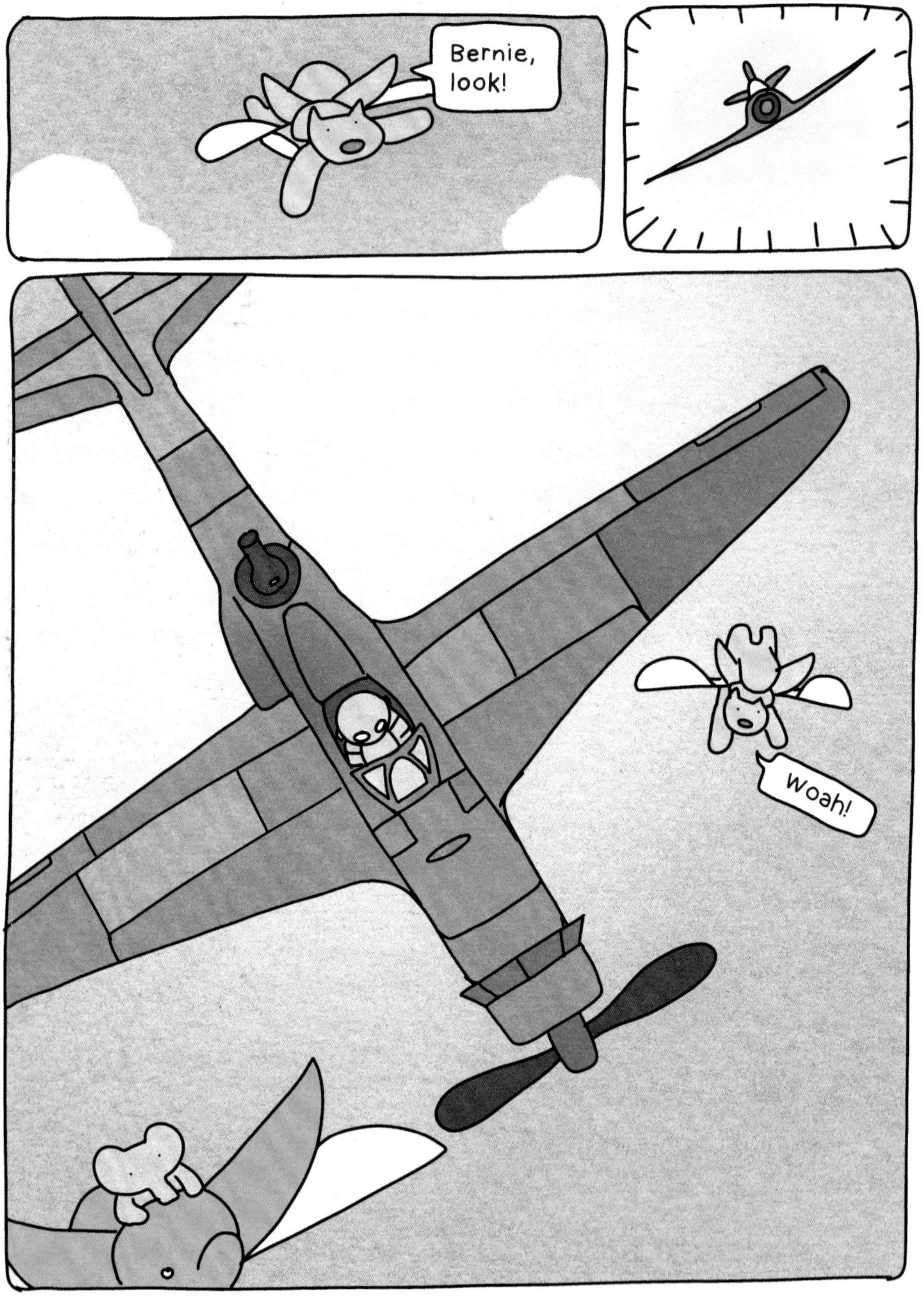
Bernie, look!
woah!

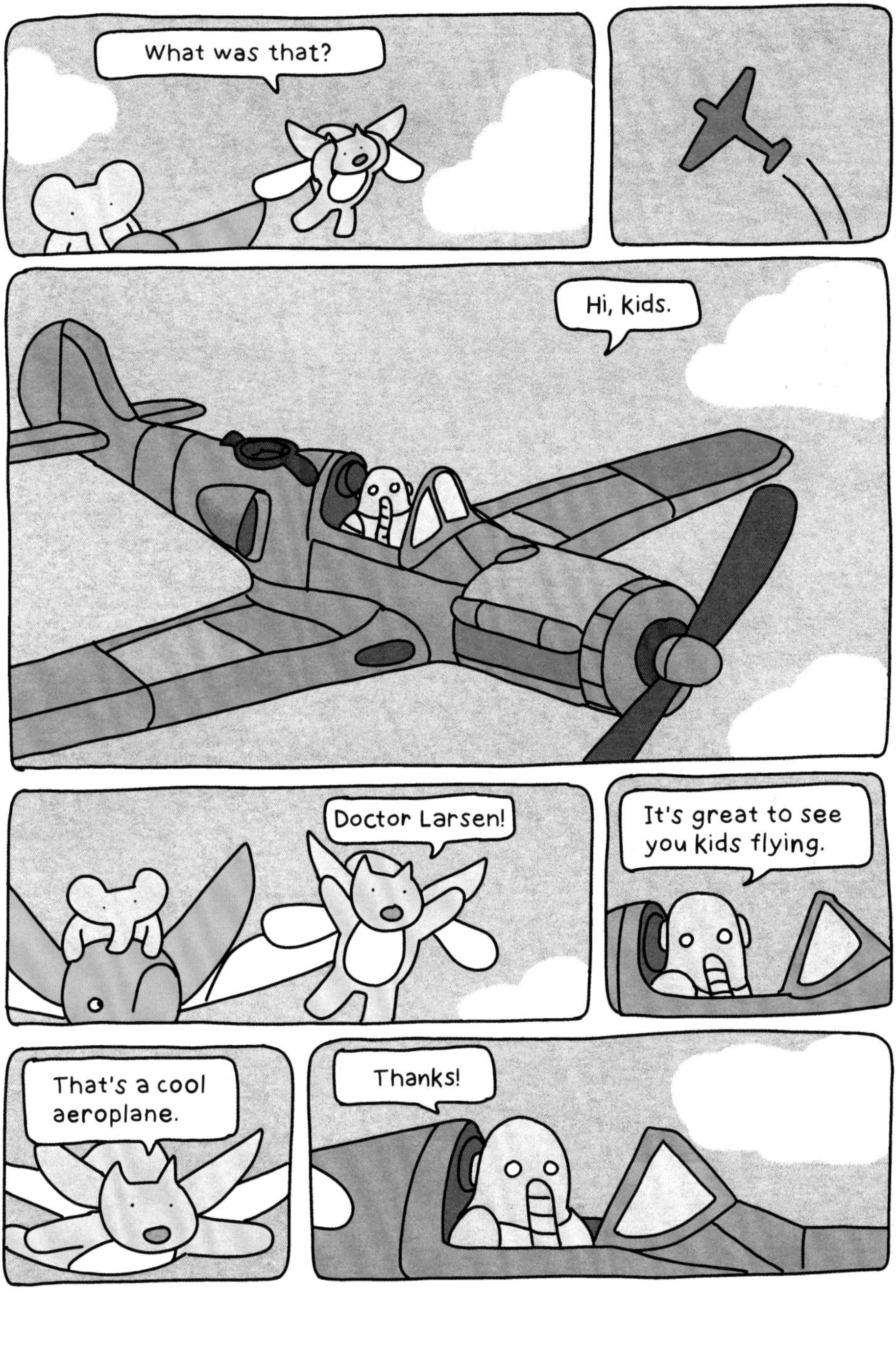

What was that?
Hi, kids.
Doctor Larsen!
It's great to see you kids flying.
That's a cool aeroplane.
Thanks!

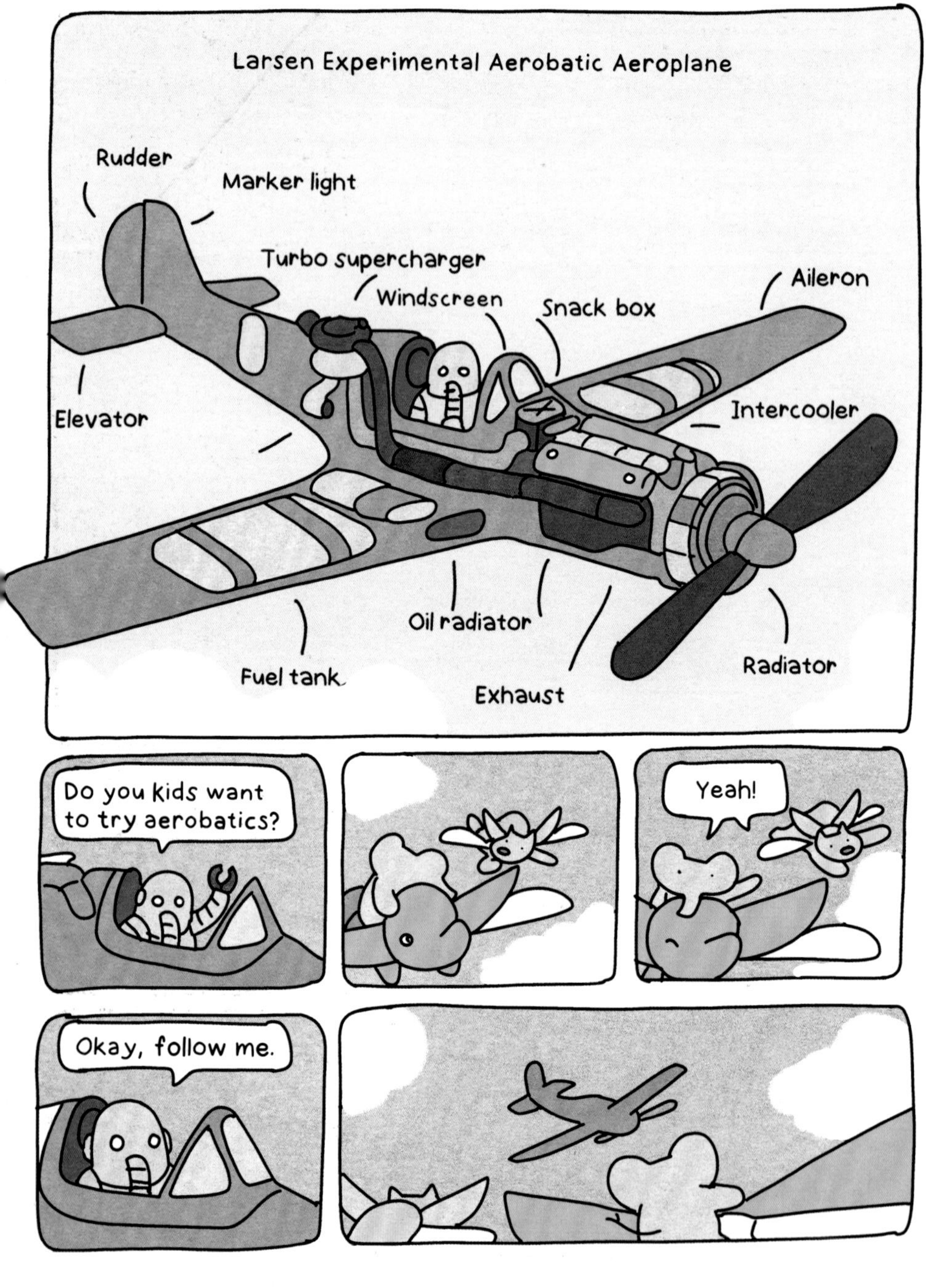
Larsen Experimental Aerobatic Aeroplane
Rudder
Marker light
Turbo supercharger
Windscreen
Snack box
Aileron
Elevator
Intercooler
Fuel tank
Oil radiator
Exhaust
Radiator
Do you kids want to try aerobatics?
Yeah!
Okay, follow me.

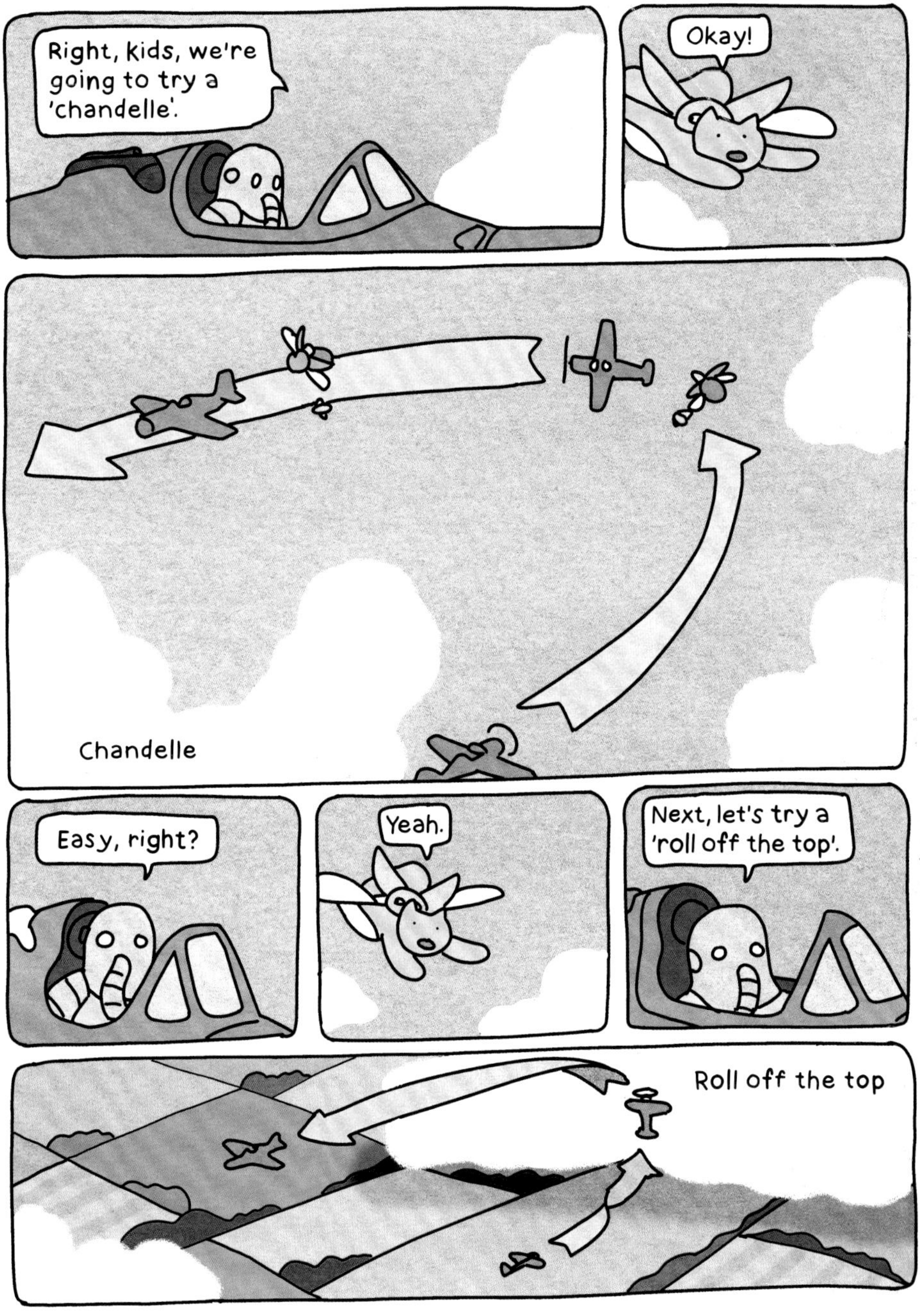
Right, kids, we're going to try a 'chandelle'.
Okay!
Chandelle
Easy, right?
Yeah.
Next, let's try a 'roll off the top'.
Roll off the top

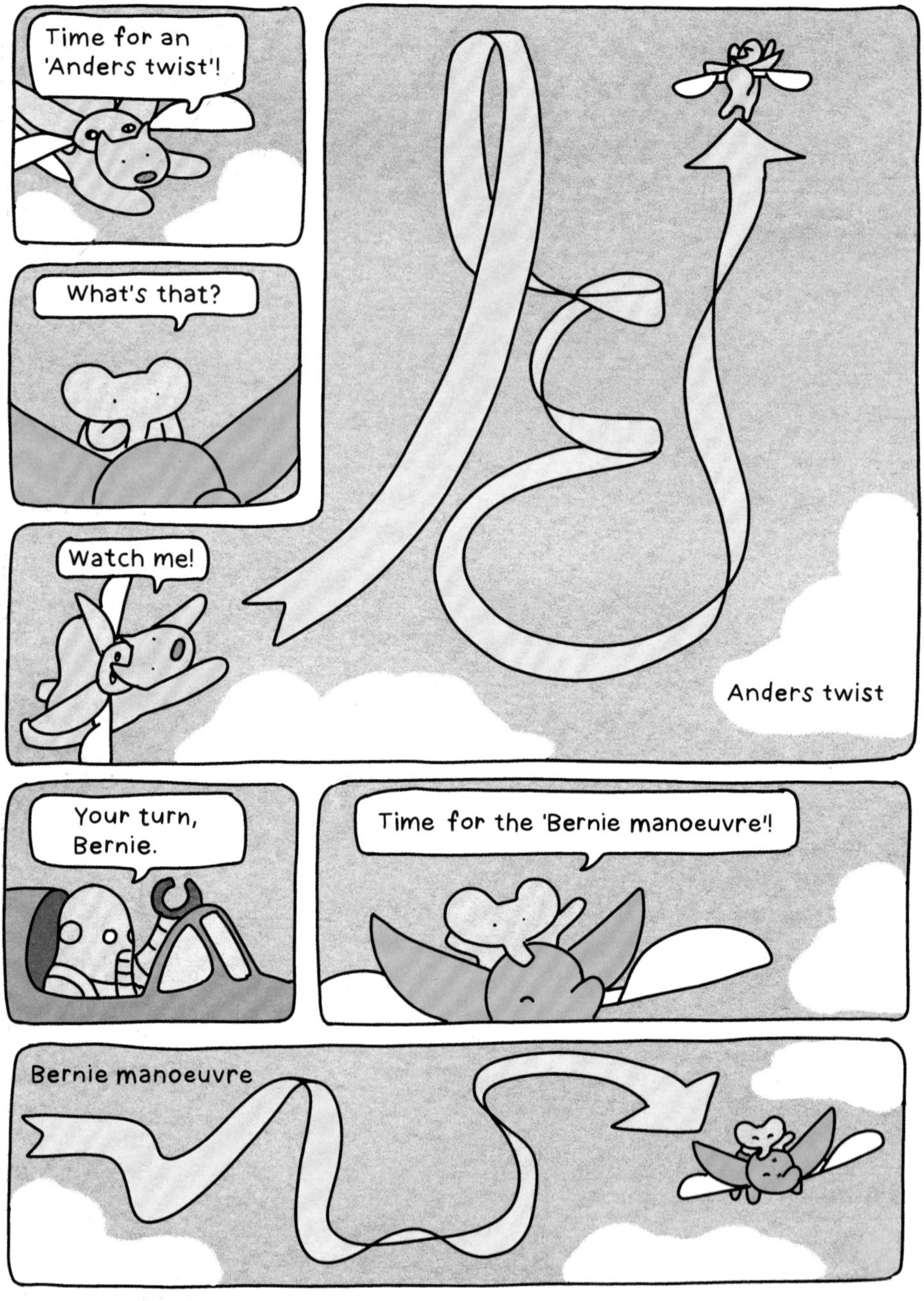
Time for an 'Anders twist'!
What's that?
Watch me!
Anders twist
Your turn, Bernie.
Time for the 'Bernie manoeuvre'!
Bernie manoeuvre

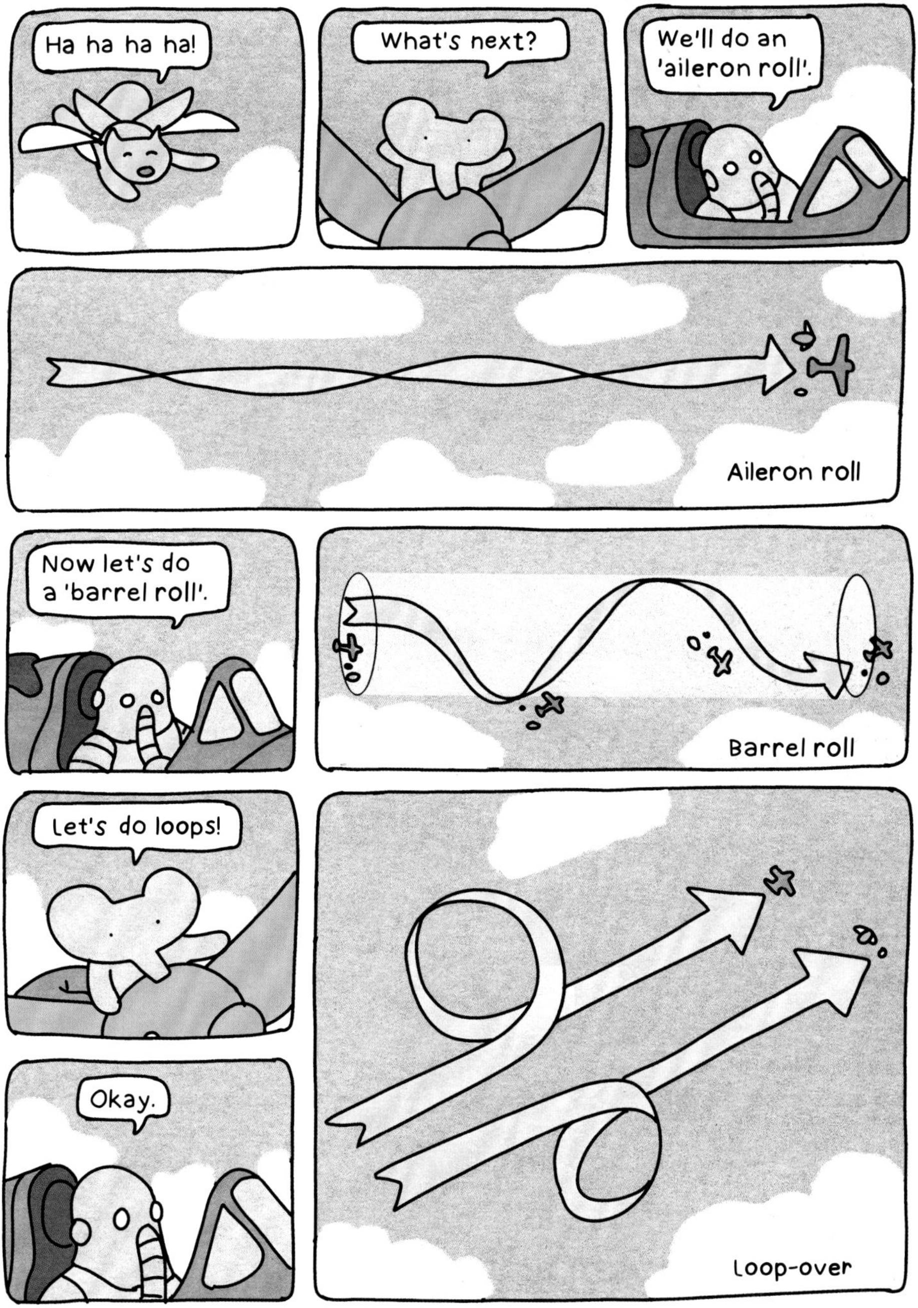
Ha ha ha ha!
What's next?
We'll do an 'aileron roll'.
Aileron roll
Now let's do a 'barrel roll'.
Barrel roll
Let's do loops!
Okay.
Loop-over

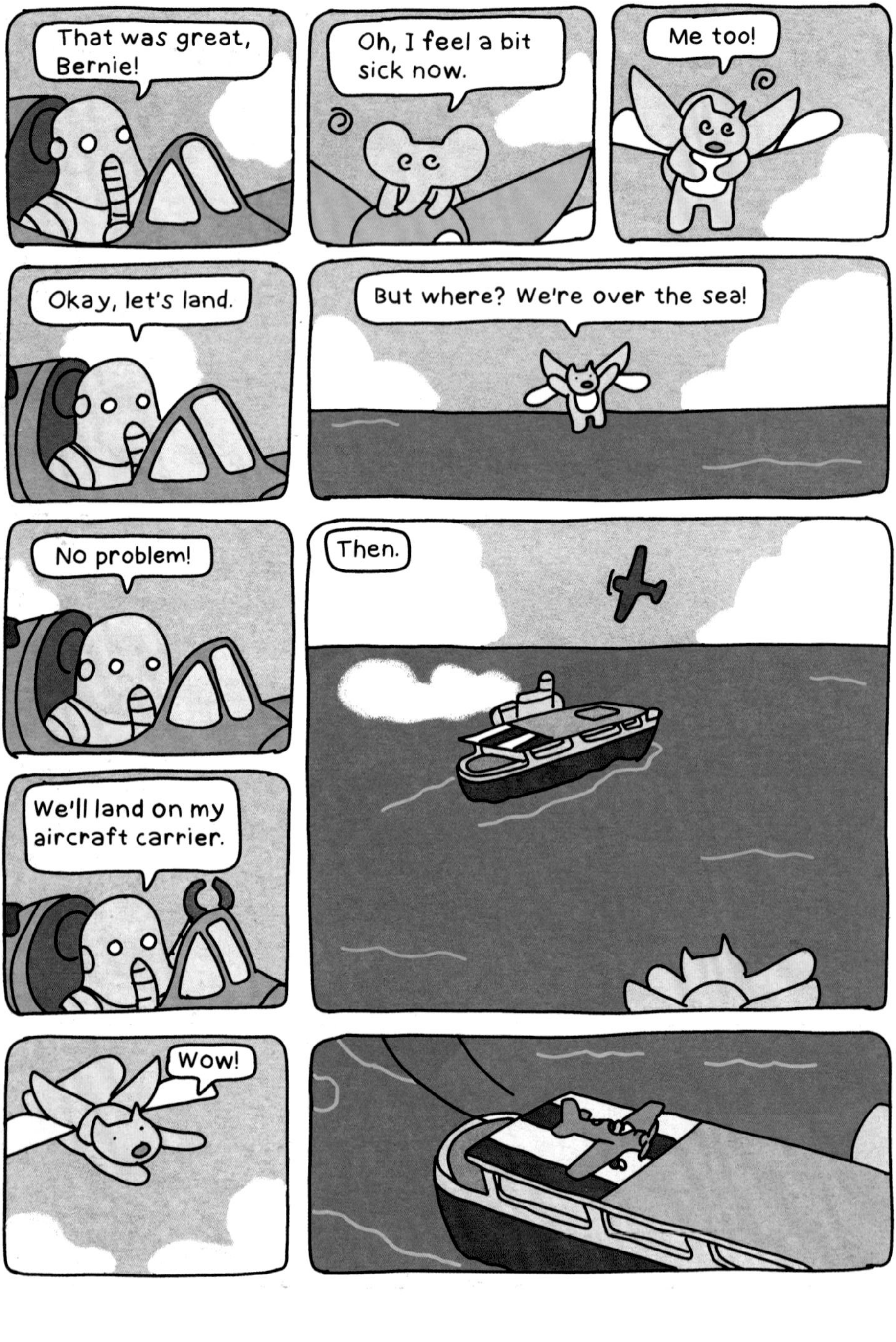

That was great, Bernie!
Oh, I feel a bit sick now.
Me too!
Okay, let's land.
But where? We're over the sea!
No problem!
Then.
We'll land on my aircraft carrier.
Wow!

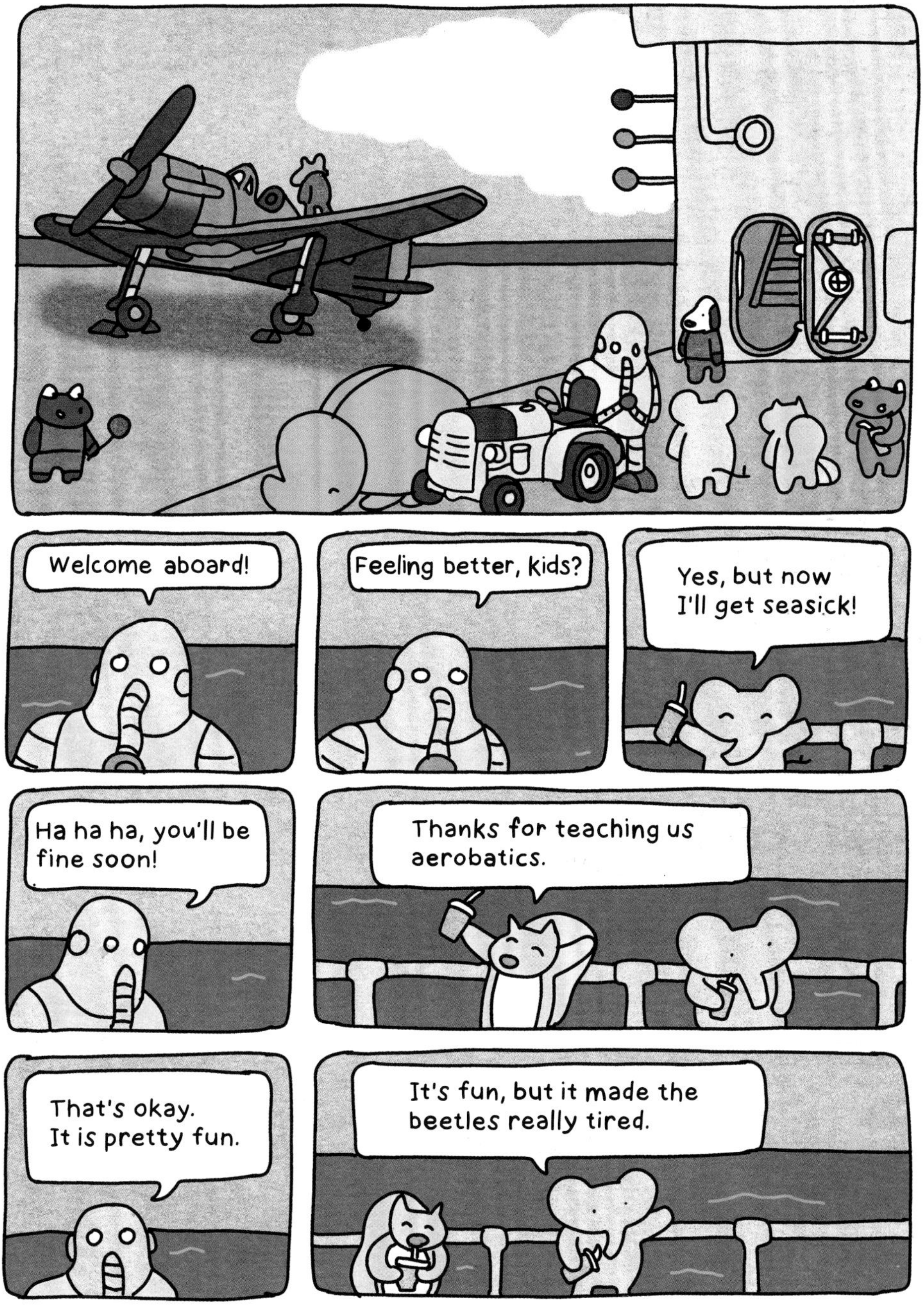
Welcome aboard!
Feeling better, kids?
Yes, but now I'll get seasick!
Ha ha ha, you'll be fine soon!
Thanks for teaching us aerobatics.
That's okay. It is pretty fun.
It's fun, but it made the beetles really tired.

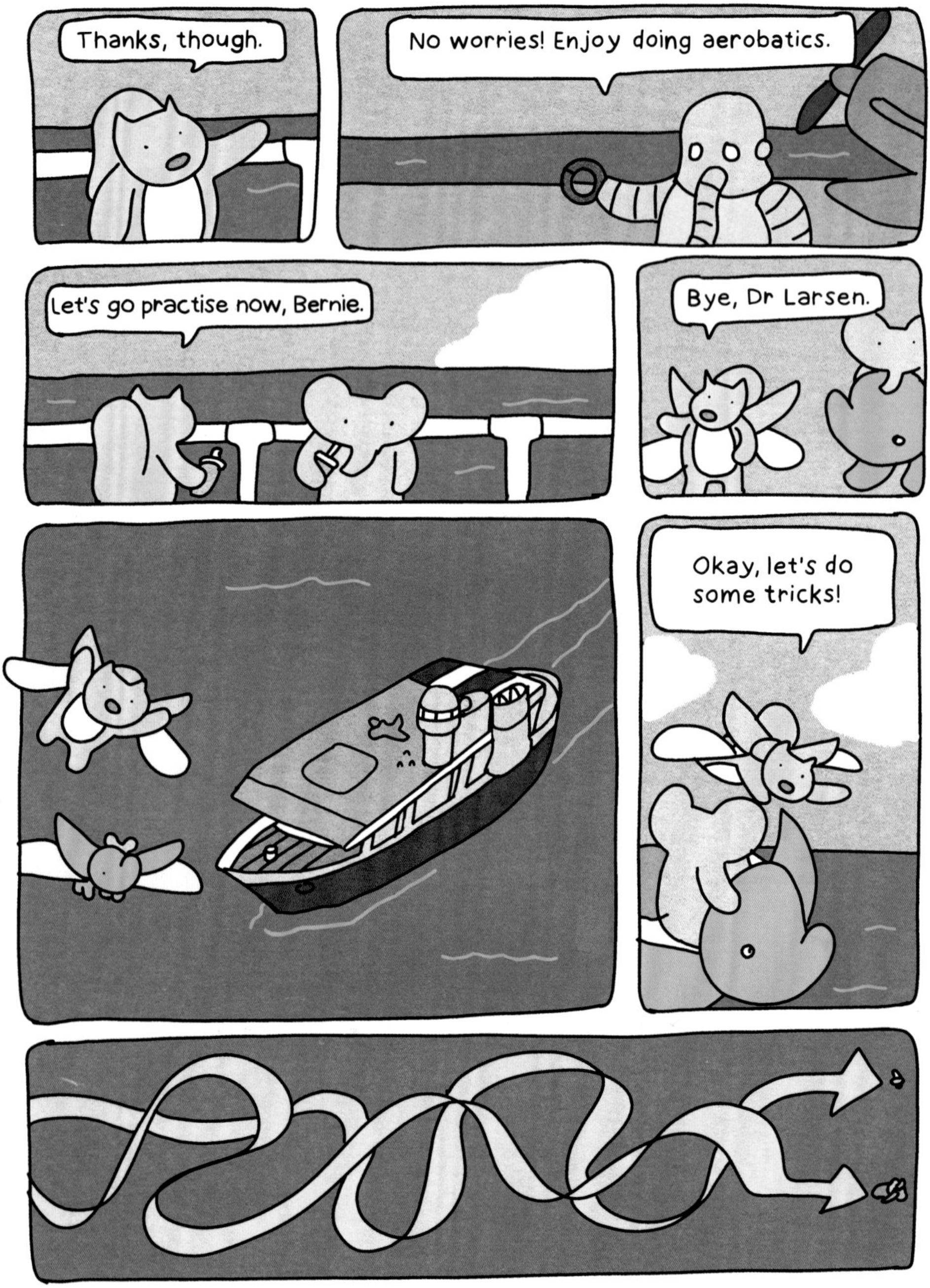
Thanks, though.
No worries! Enjoy doing aerobatics.
Let's go practise now, Bernie.
Bye, Dr Larsen.
Okay, let's do some tricks!

Chapter 3

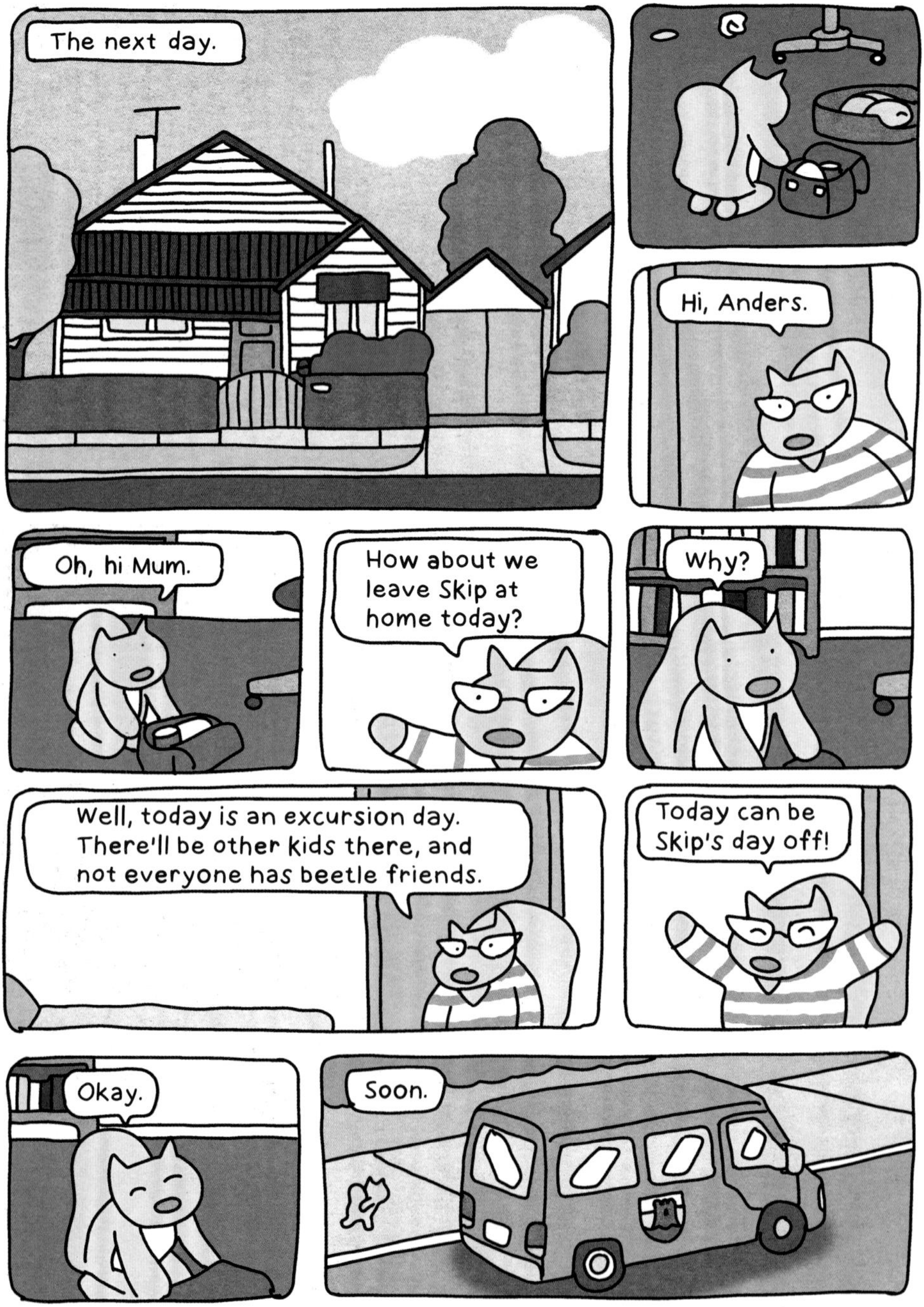

The next day.
Hi, Anders.
Oh, hi Mum.
How about we leave Skip at home today?
Why?
Well, today is an excursion day. There'll be other kids there, and not everyone has beetle friends.
Today can be Skip's day off!
Okay.
Soon.

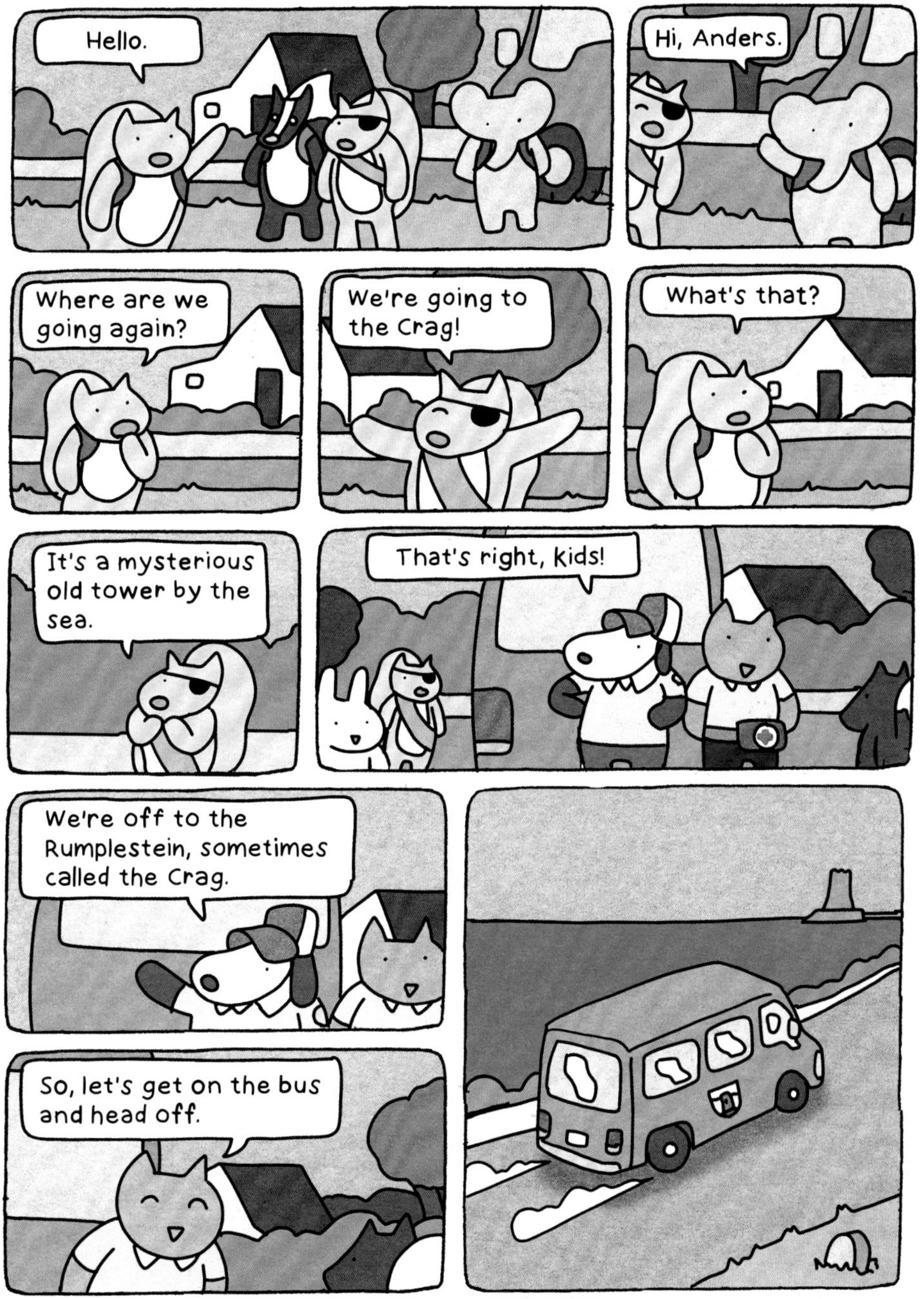
Hello.
Hi, Anders.
Where are we going again?
We're going to the Crag!
What's that?
It's a mysterious old tower by the sea.
That's right, kids!
We're off to the Rumplestein, sometimes called the Crag.
So, let's get on the bus and head off.

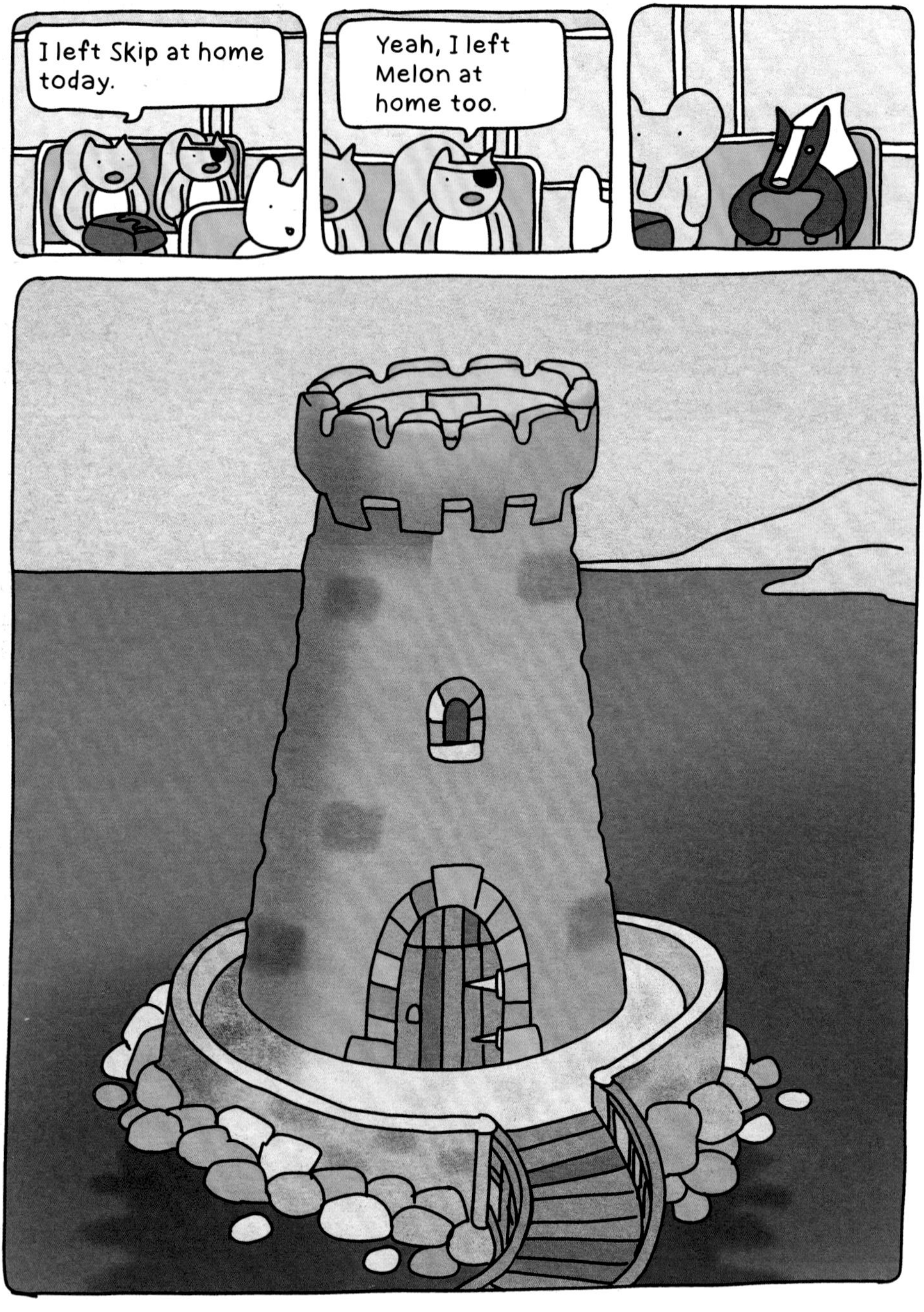
I left Skip at home today.
Yeah, I left Melon at home too.

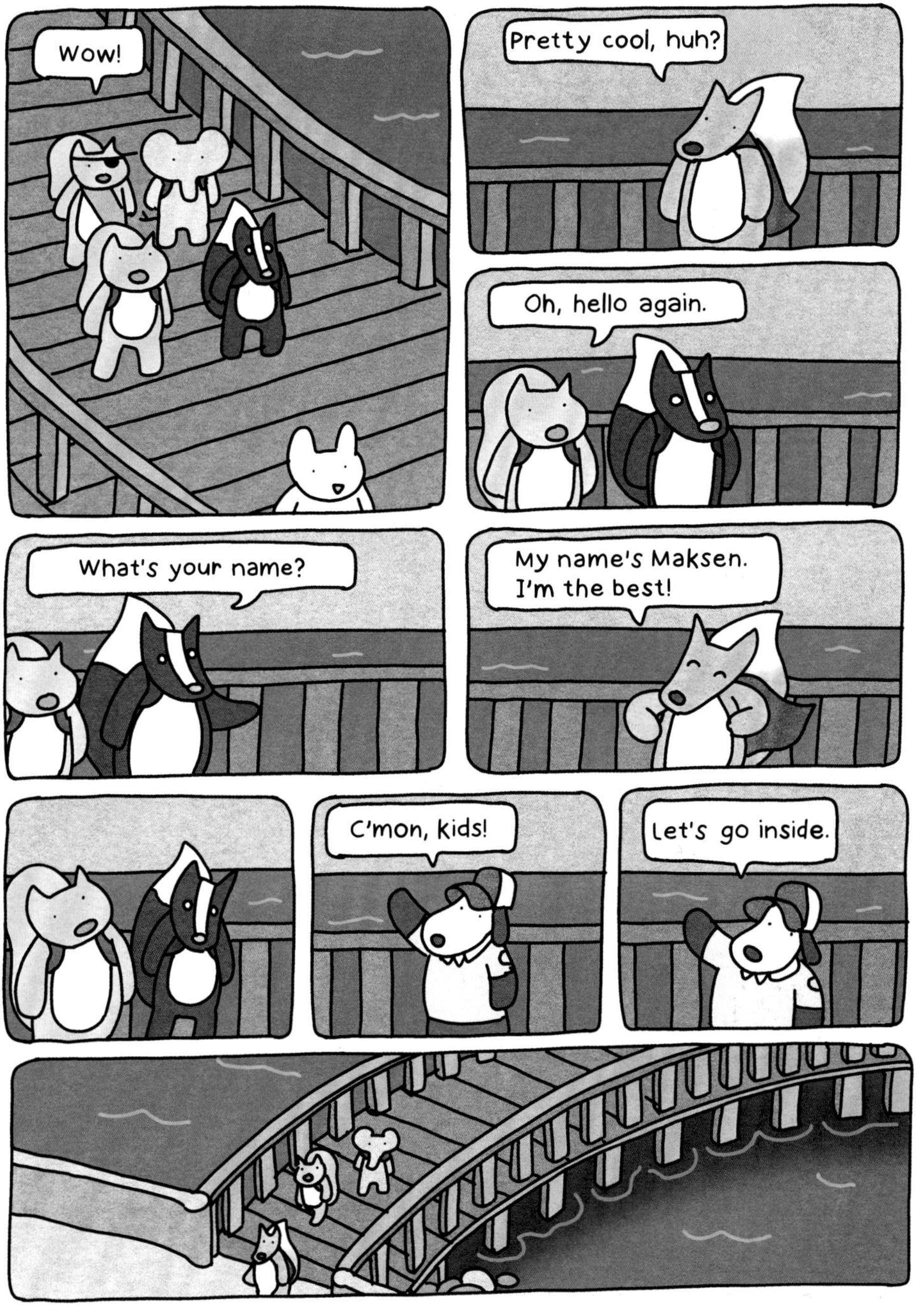
Wow!
Pretty cool, huh?
Oh, hello again.
What's your name?
My name's Maksen.
I'm the best!
C'mon, kids!
Let's go inside.

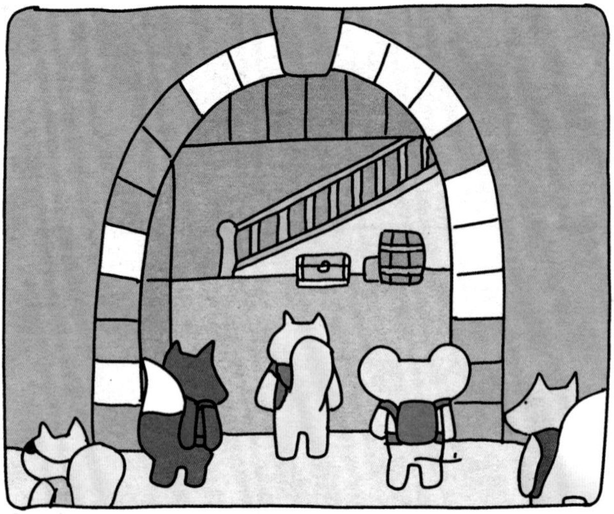

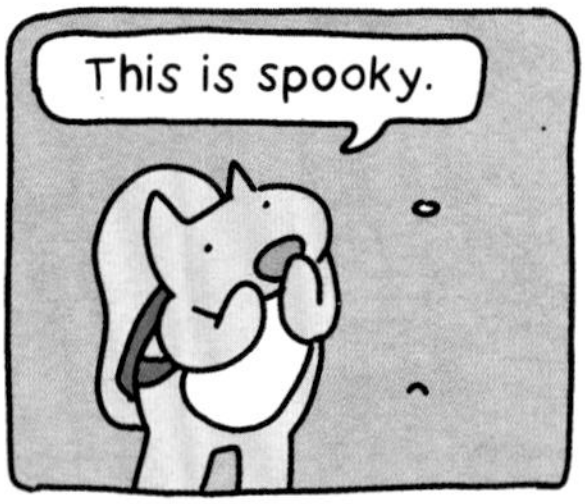
This is spooky.

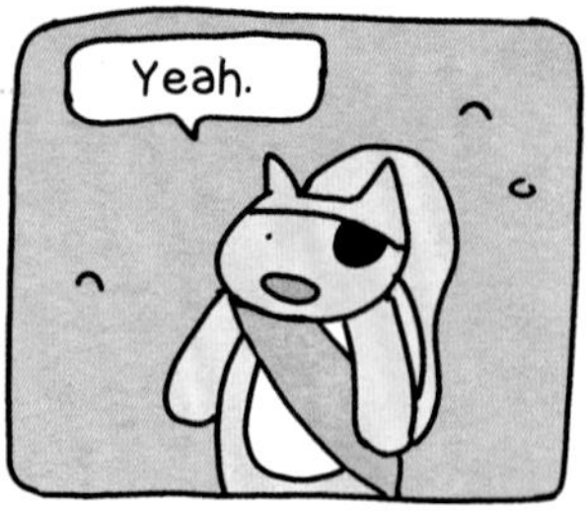
Yeah.

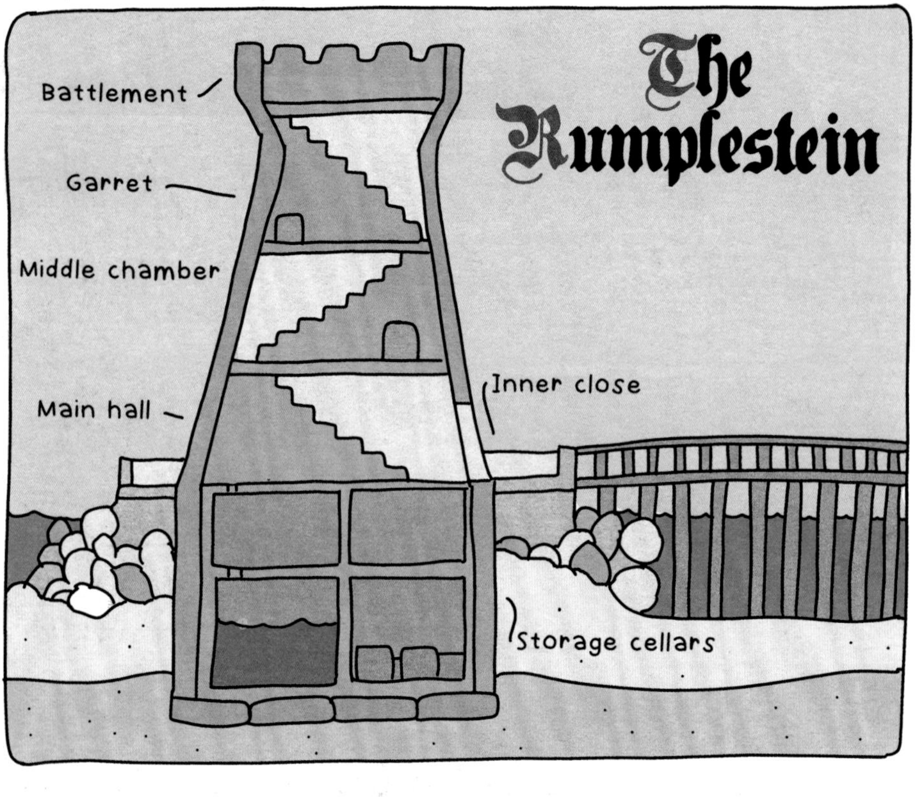
The Rumplestein
Battlement
Garret
Middle chamber
Main hall
Inner close
Storage cellars

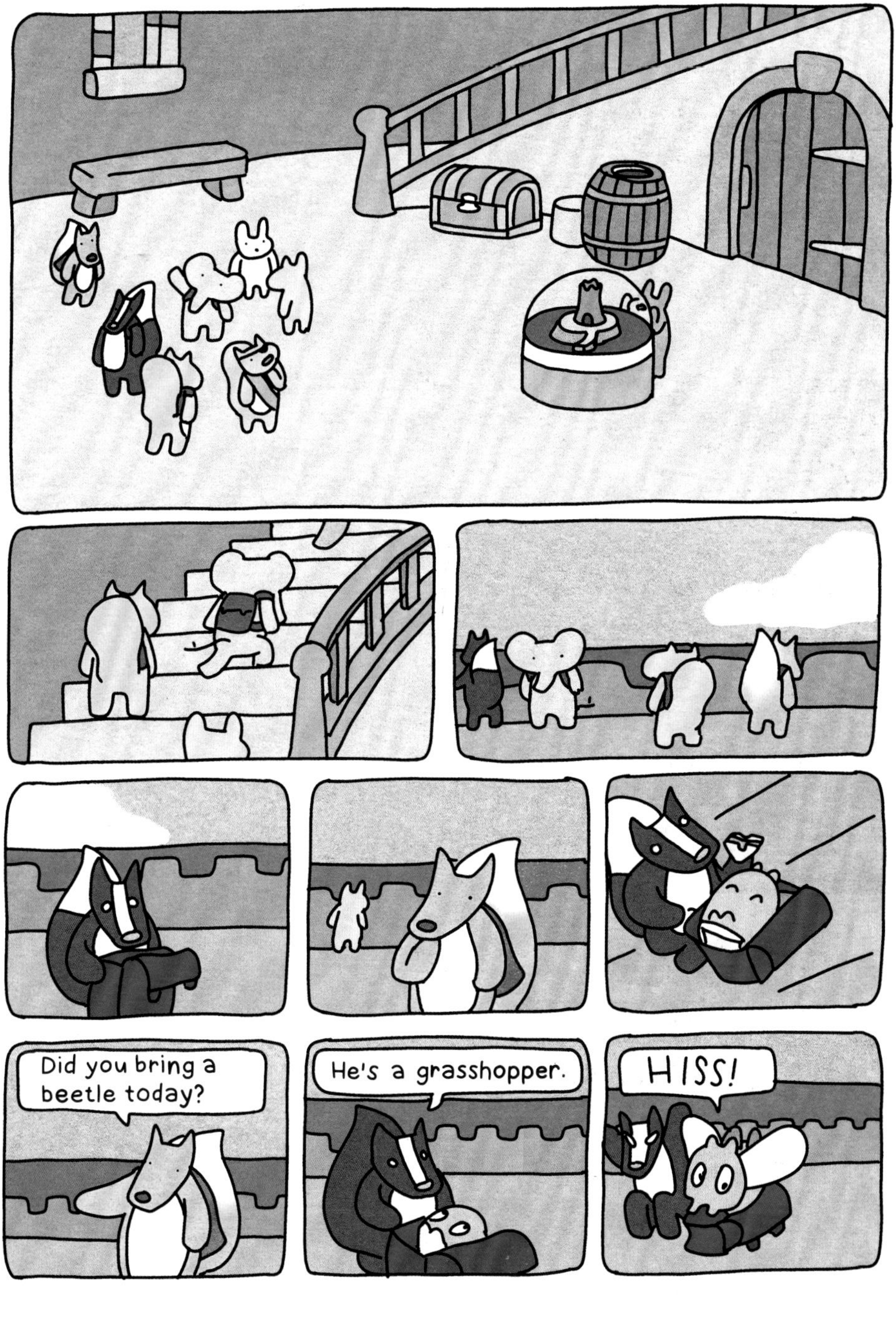

Did you bring a beetle today?
He's a grasshopper.
HISS!

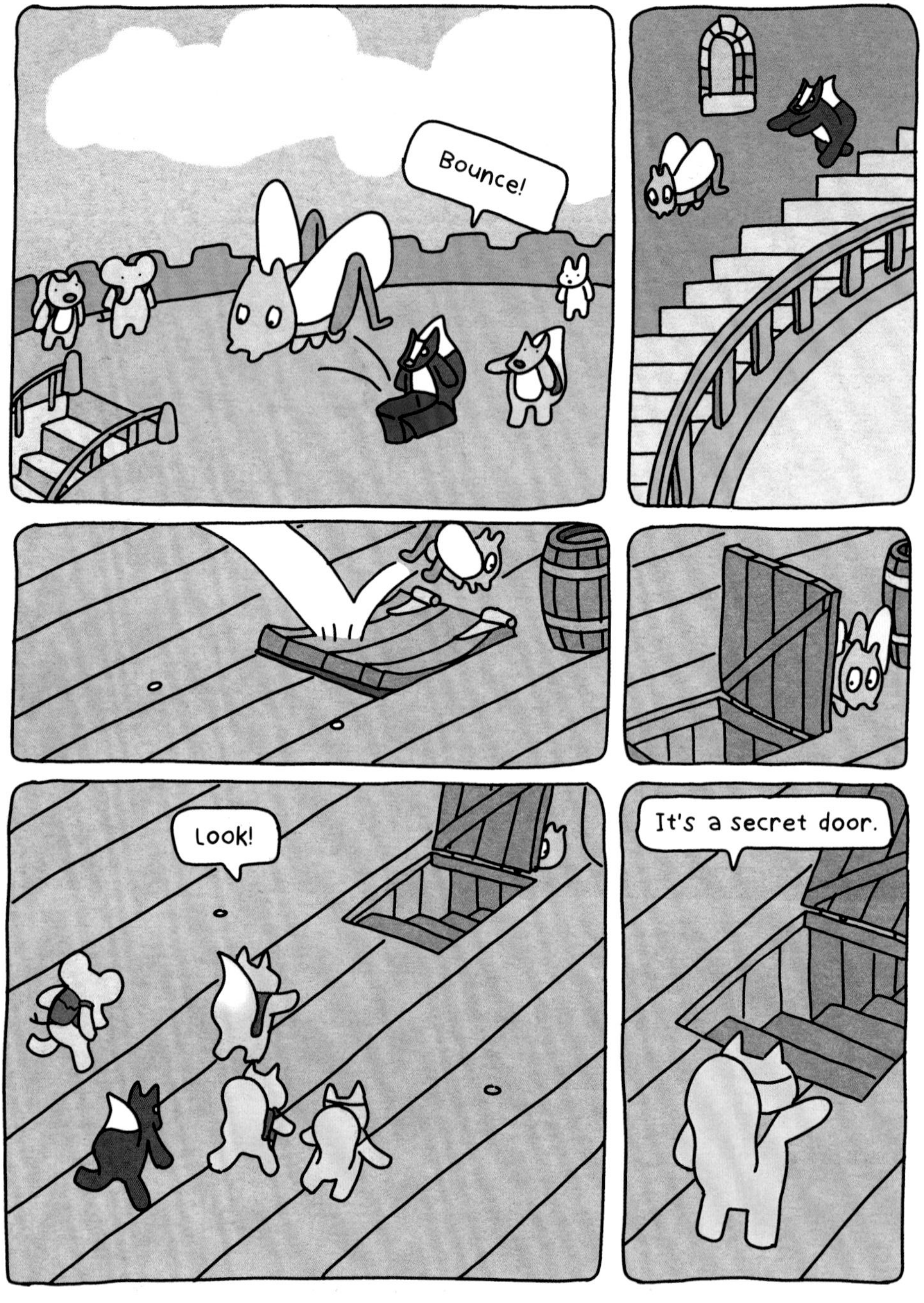
Bounce!
Look!
It's a secret door.

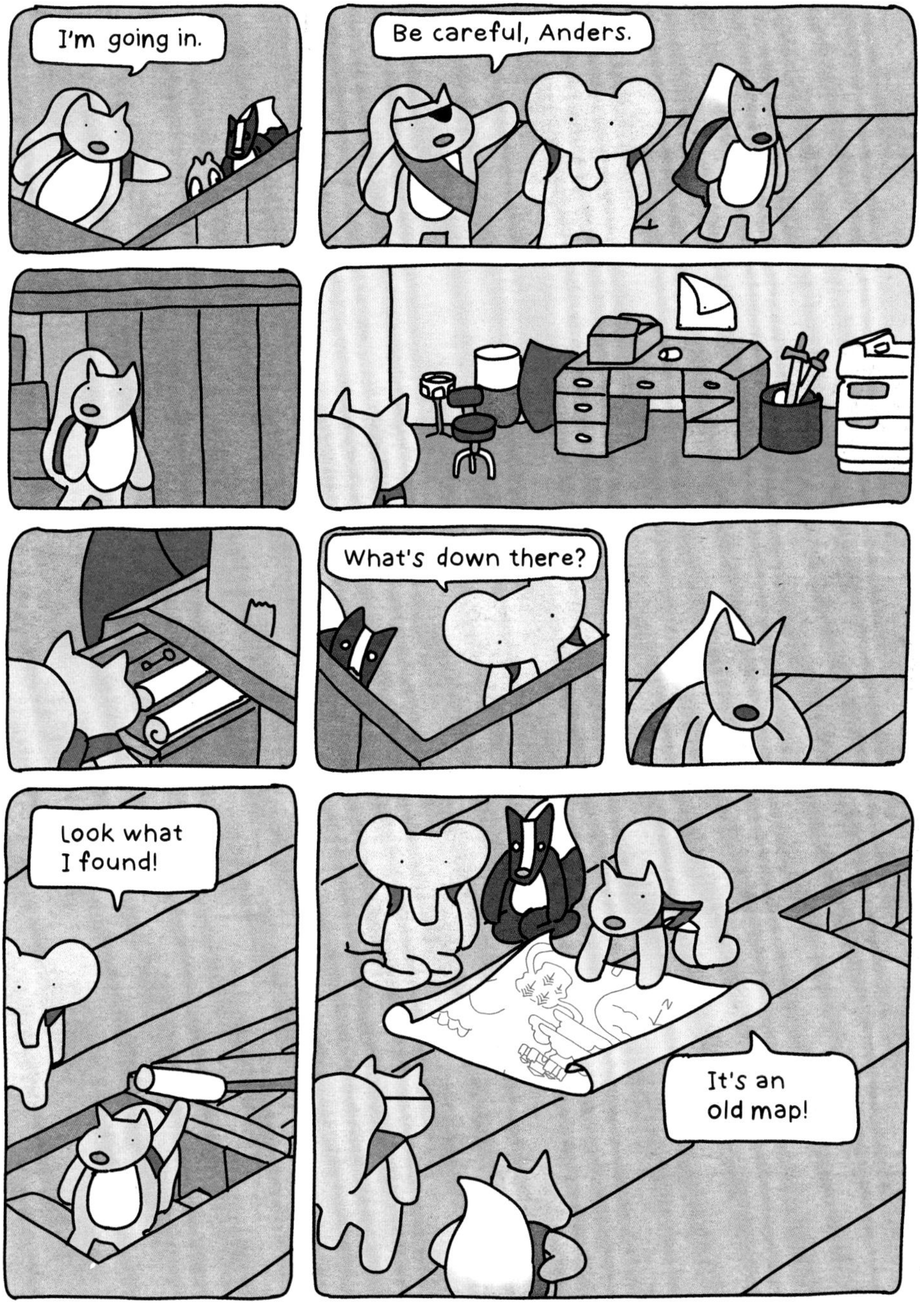
I'm going in.
Be careful, Anders.
What's down there?
Look what I found!
It's an old map!

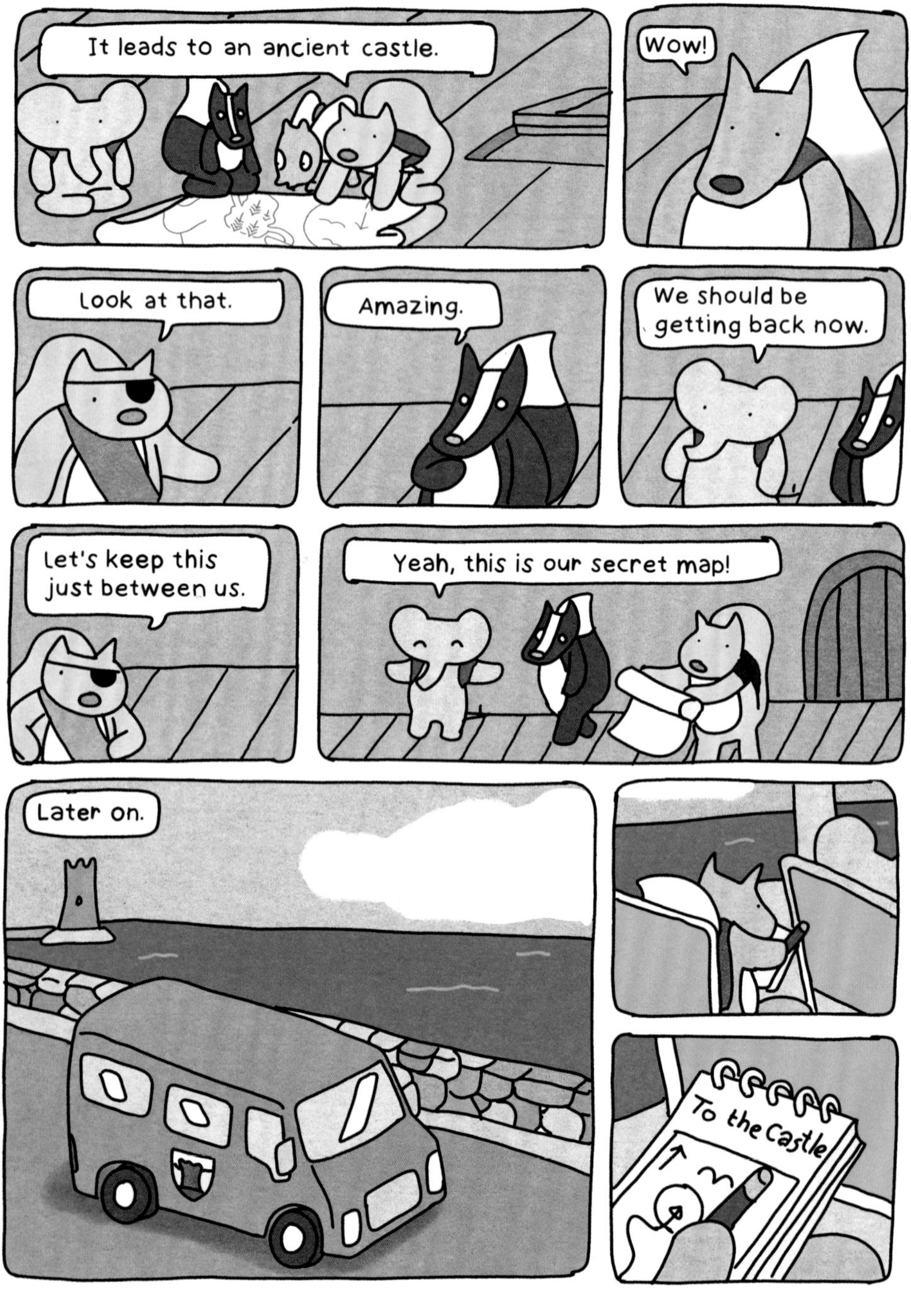
It leads to an ancient castle.
Wow!
Look at that.
Amazing.
We should be getting back now.
Let's keep this just between us.
Yeah, this is our secret map!
Later on.
To the Castle

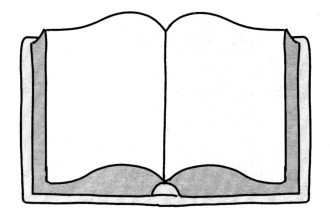

Chapter 4

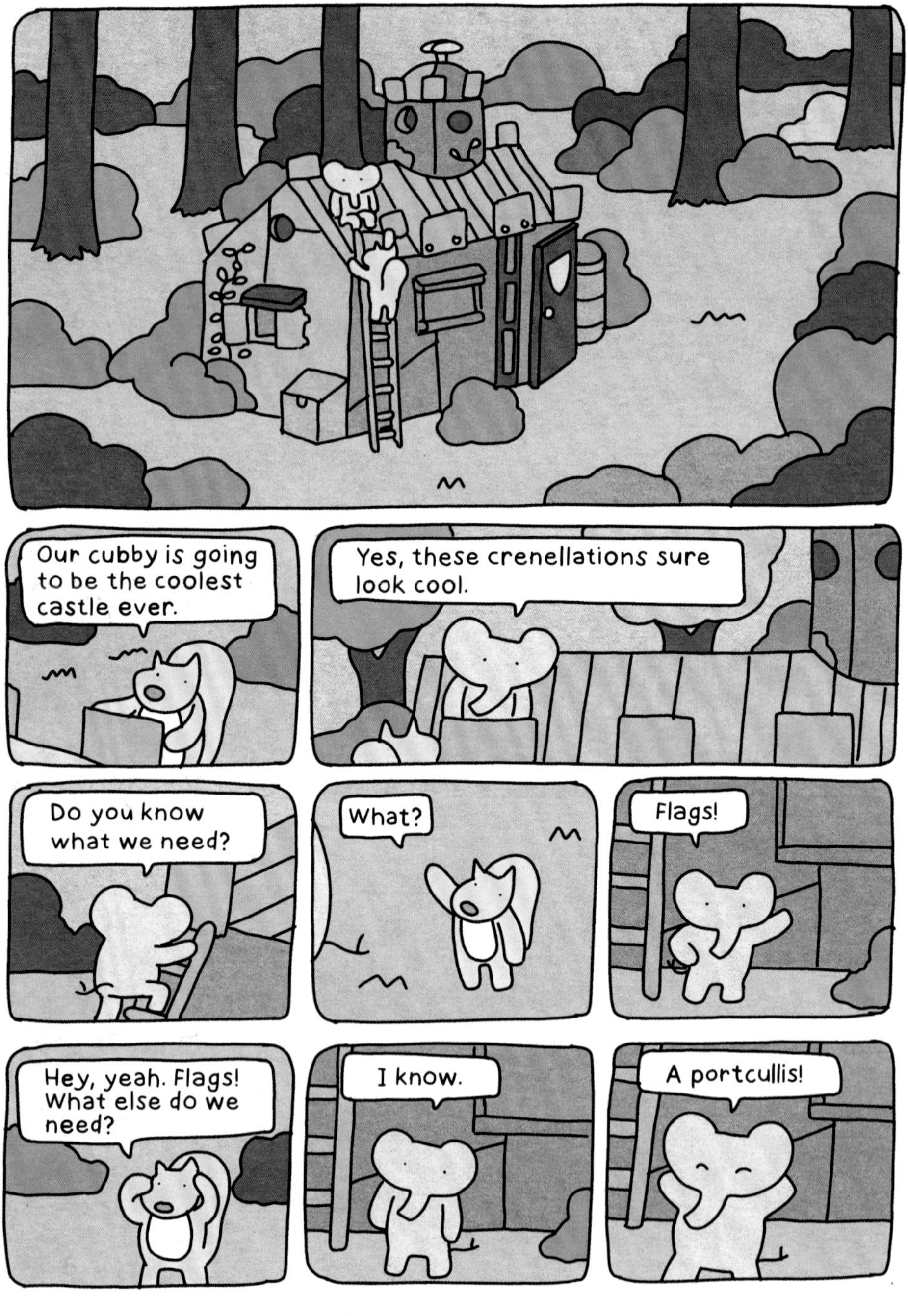
Our cubby is going to be the coolest castle ever.
Yes, these crenellations sure look cool.
Do you know what we need?
What?
Flags!
Hey, yeah. Flags! What else do we need?
I know.
A portcullis!

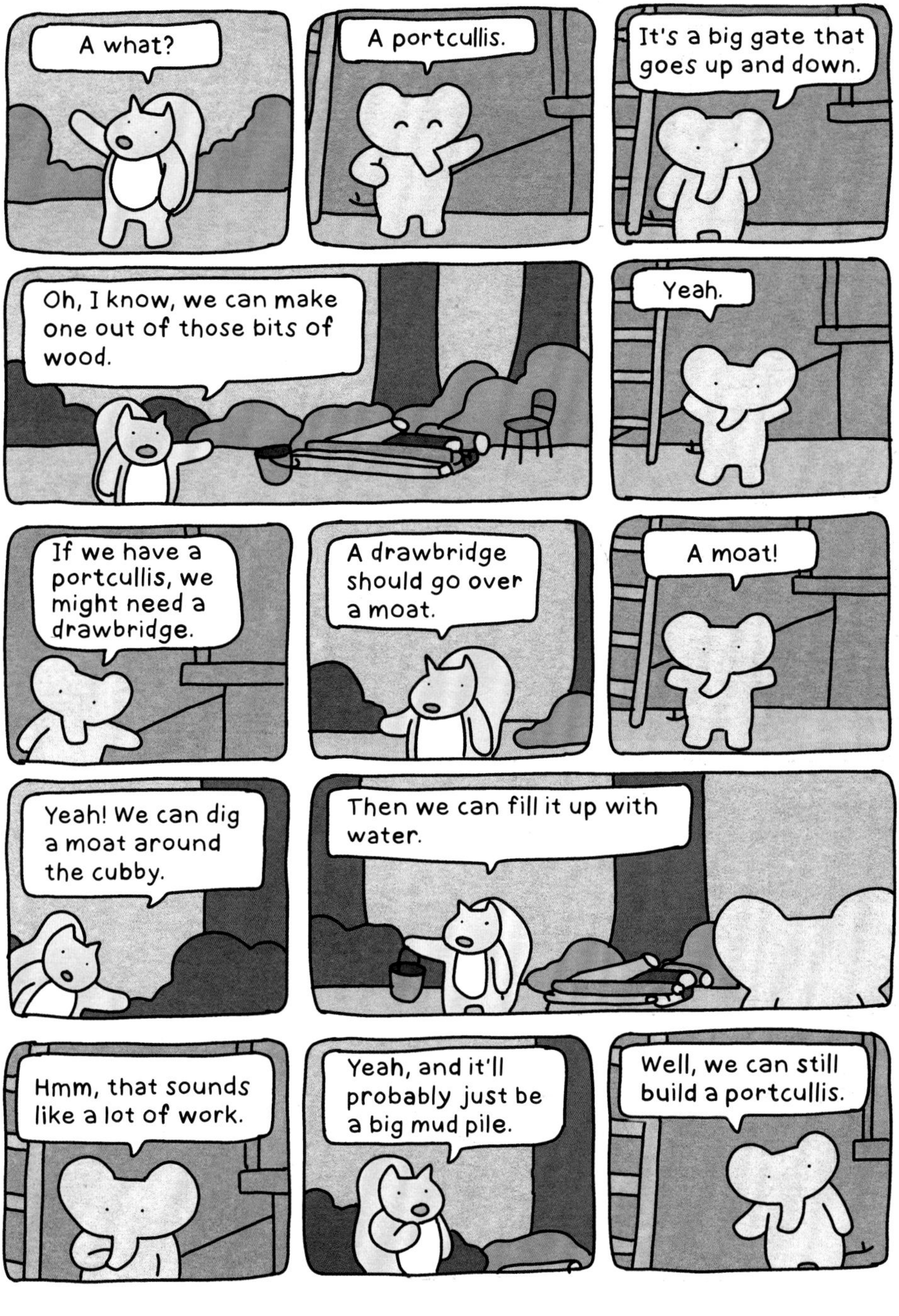
A what?
A portcullis.
It's a big gate that goes up and down.
Oh, I know, we can make one out of those bits of wood.
Yeah.
If we have a portcullis, we might need a drawbridge.
A drawbridge should go over a moat.
A moat!
Yeah! We can dig a moat around the cubby.
Then we can fill it up with water.
Hmm, that sounds like a lot of work.
Yeah, and it'll probably just be a big mud pile.
Well, we can still build a portcullis.

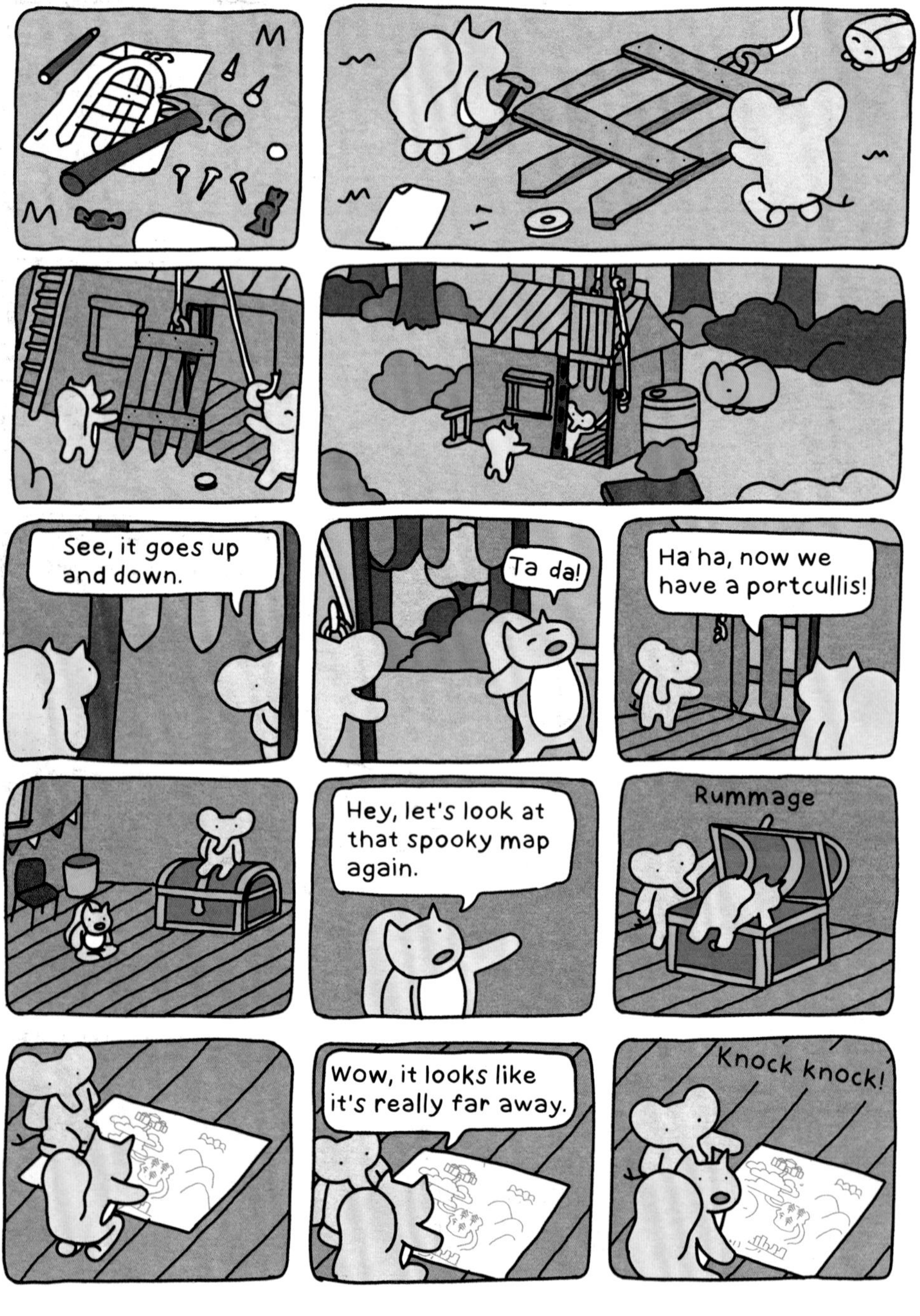
M
M
See, it goes up and down.
Ta da!
Ha ha, now we have a portcullis!
Hey, let's look at that spooky map again.
Rummage
Wow, it looks like it's really far away.
Knock knock!

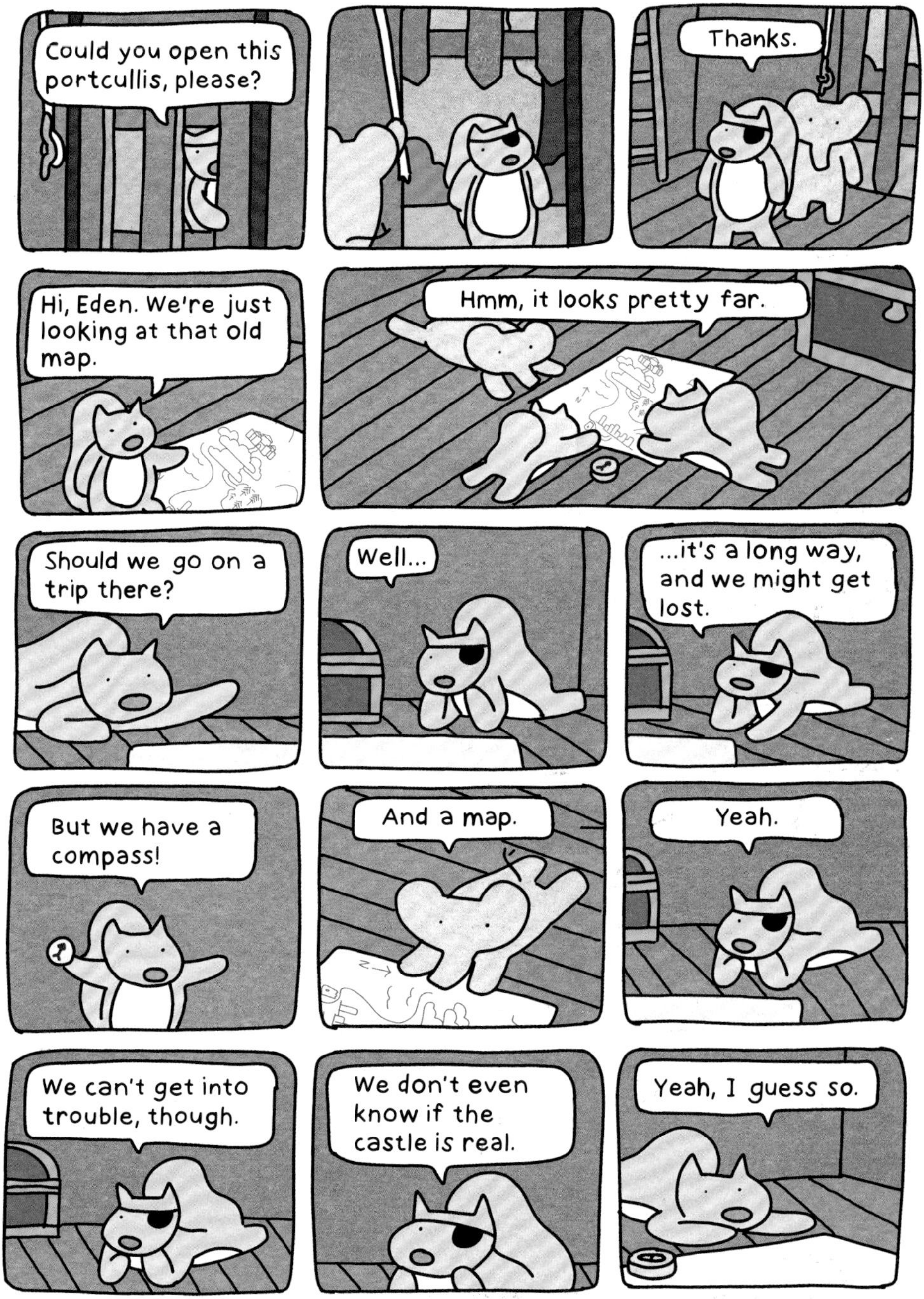
Could you open this portcullis, please?
Thanks.
Hi, Eden. We're just looking at that old map.
Hmm, it looks pretty far.
Should we go on a trip there?
Well...
...it's a long way, and we might get lost.
But we have a compass!
And a map.
Yeah.
We can't get into trouble, though.
We don't even know if the castle is real.
Yeah, I guess so.

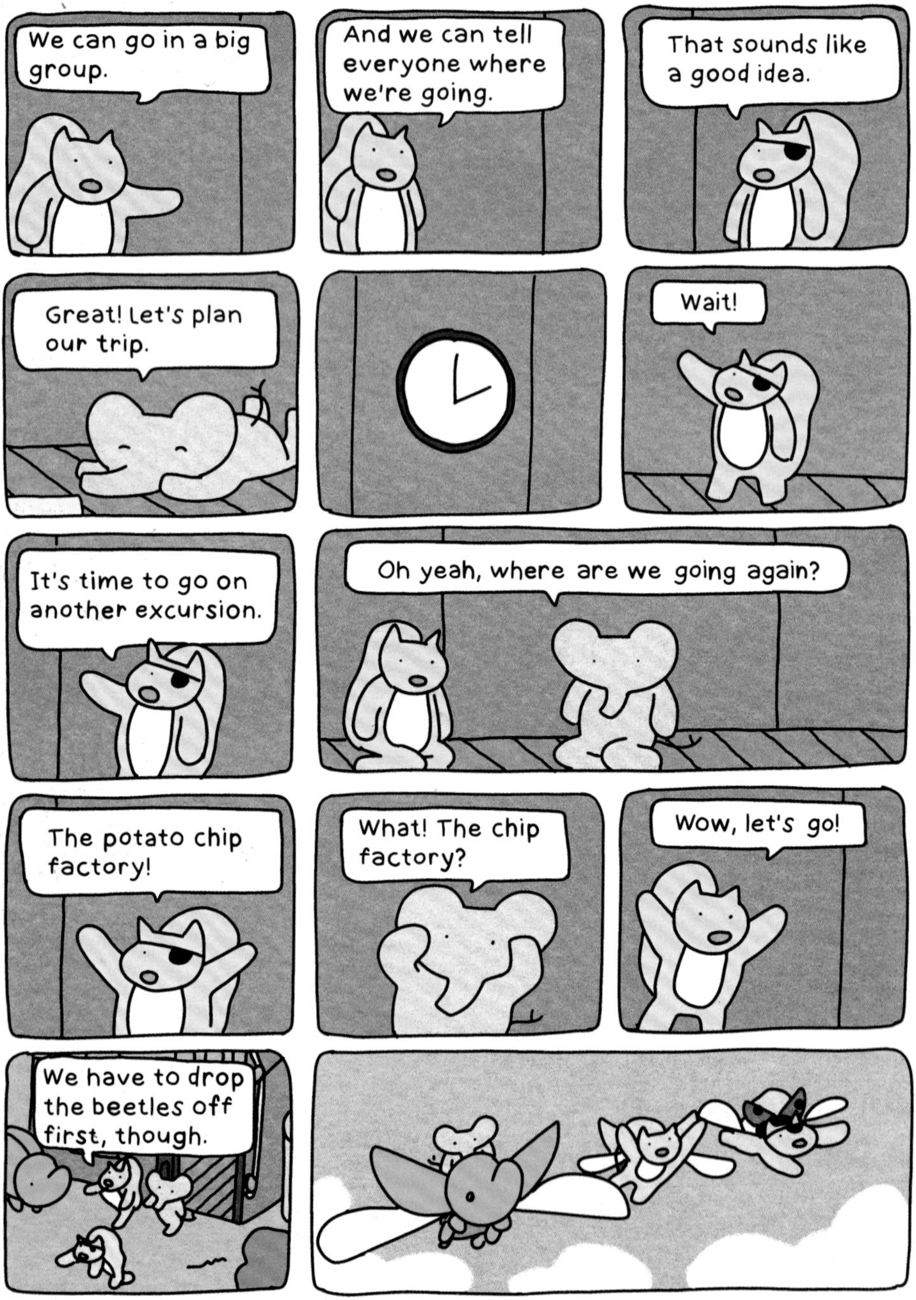
We can go in a big group.
And we can tell everyone where we're going.
That sounds like a good idea.
Great! Let's plan our trip.
Wait!
It's time to go on another excursion.
Oh yeah, where are we going again?
The potato chip factory!
What! The chip factory?
Wow, let's go!
We have to drop the beetles off first, though.

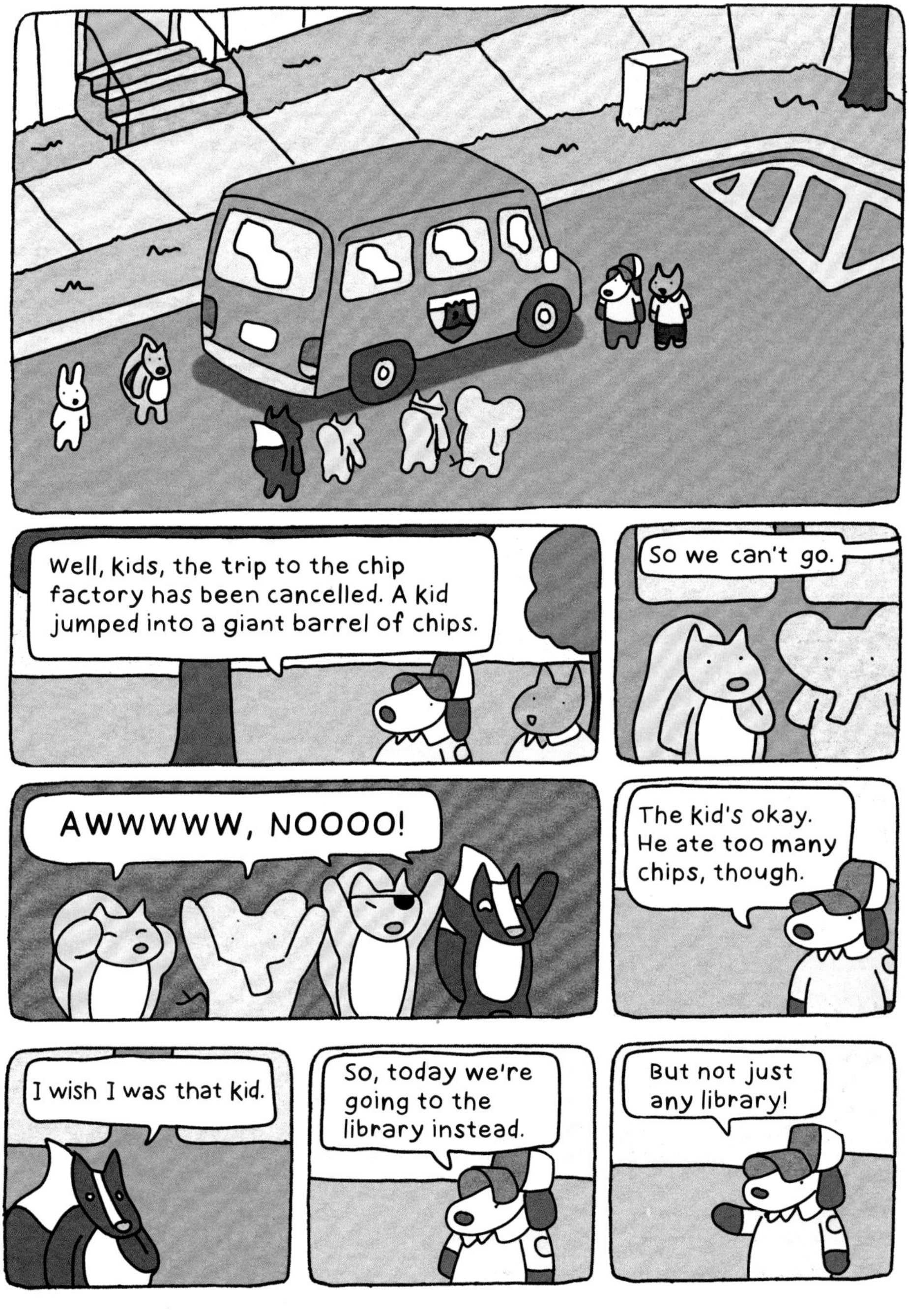
Well, kids, the trip to the chip factory has been cancelled. A kid jumped into a giant barrel of chips.
So we can't go.
AWWWWW, NOOOO!
The kid's okay. He ate too many chips, though.
I wish I was that kid.
So, today we're going to the library instead.
But not just any library!

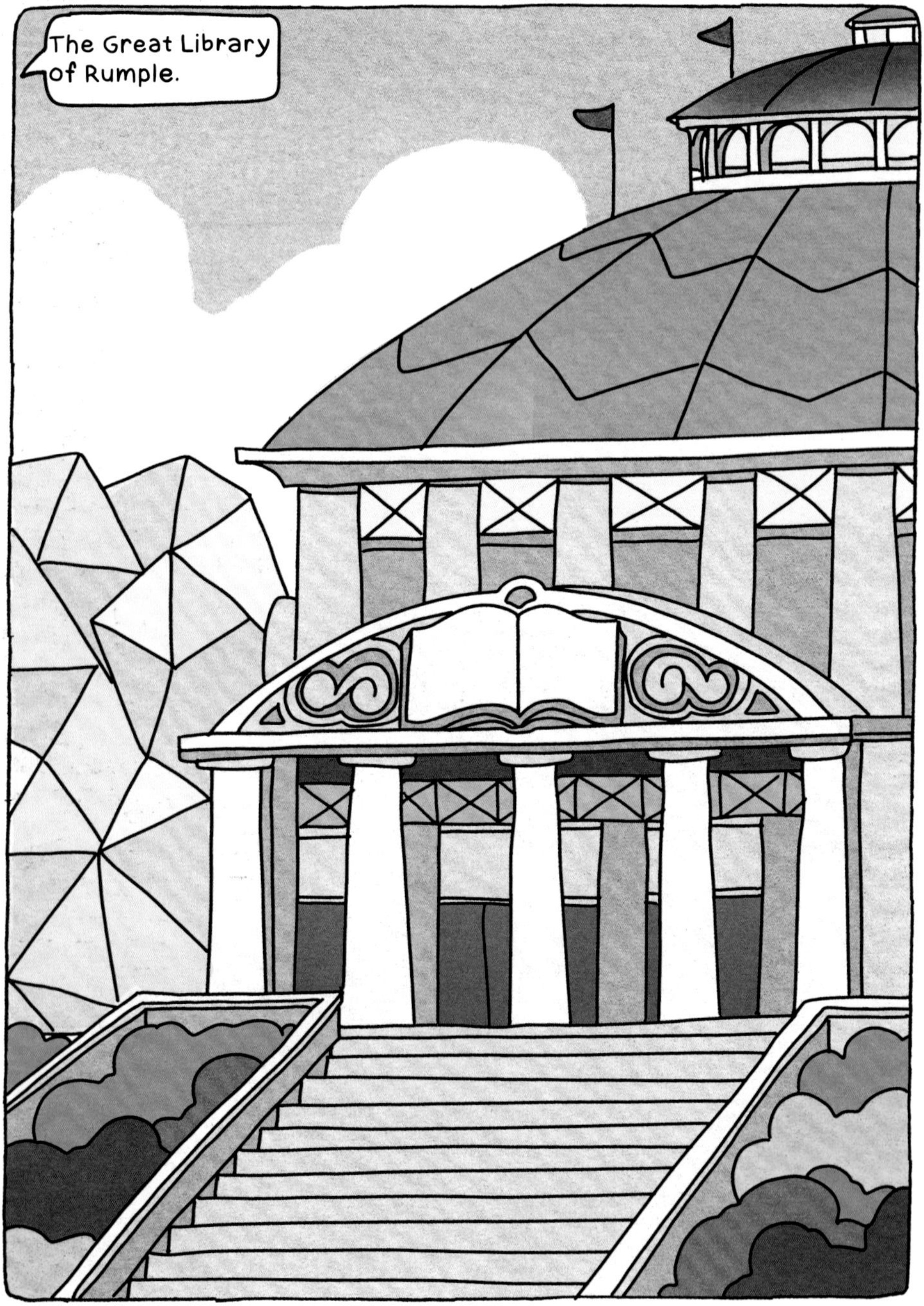
The Great Library of Rumple.

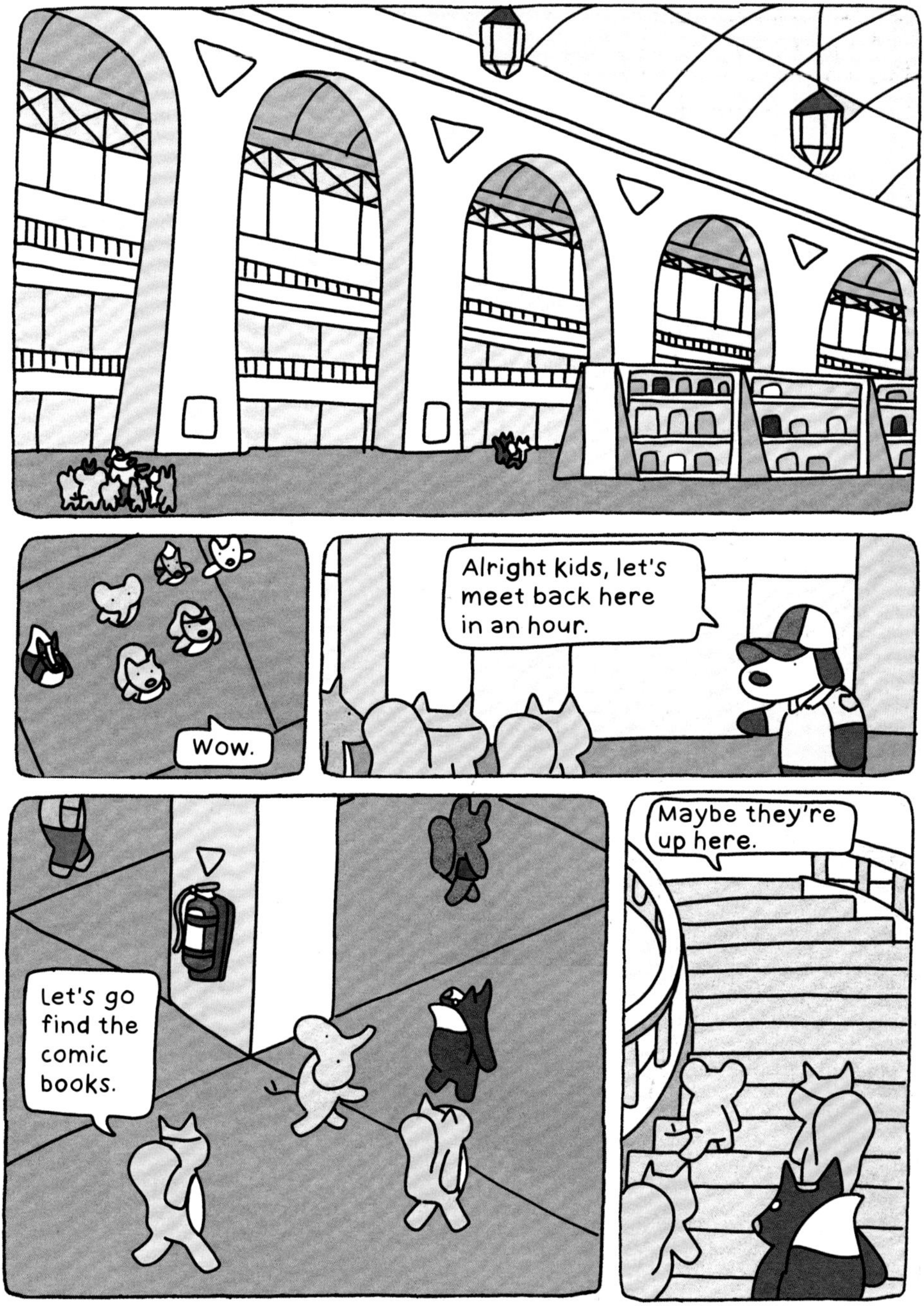
Wow.
Alright kids, let's meet back here in an hour.
Let's go find the comic books.
Maybe they're up here.

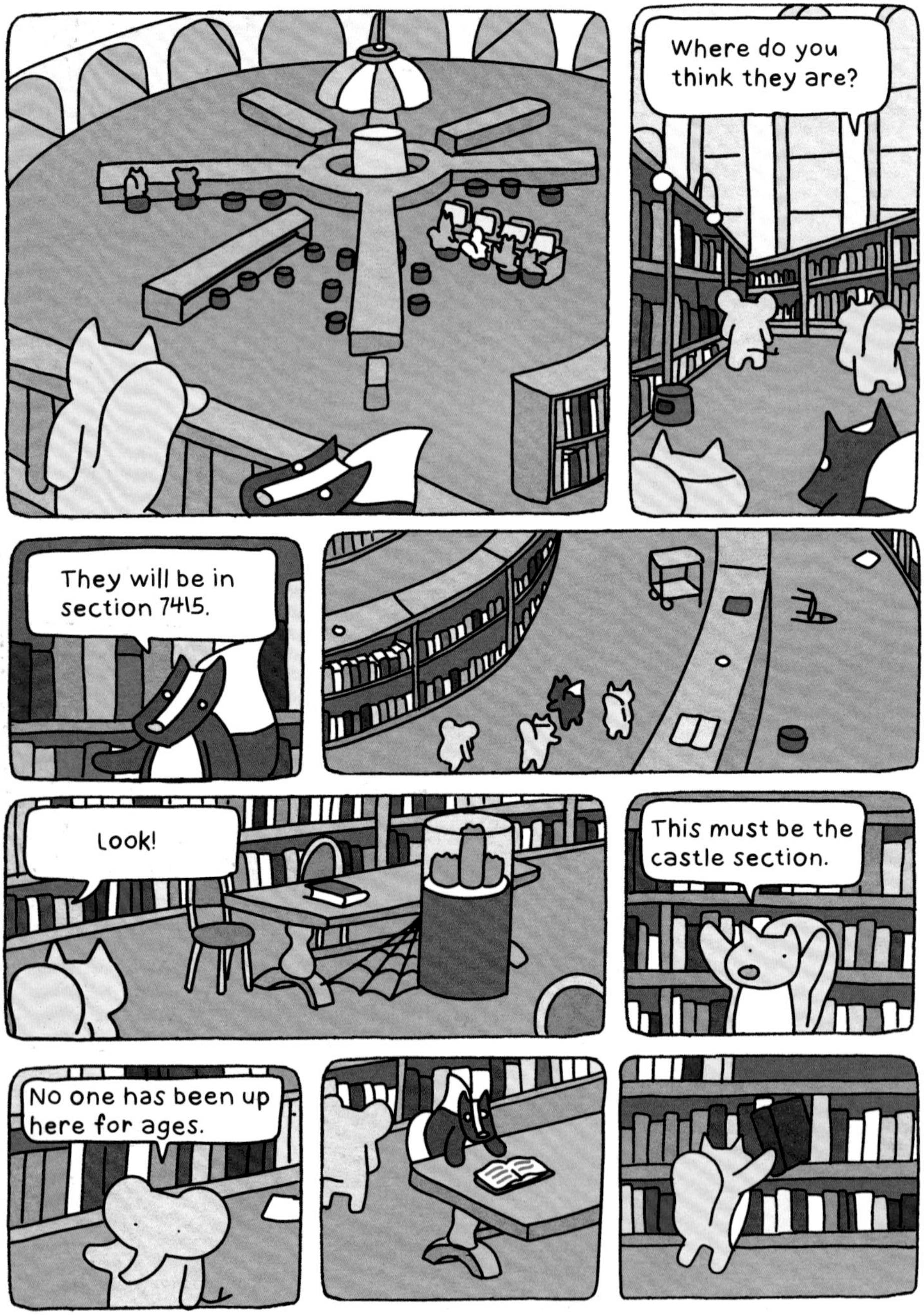
Where do you think they are?
They will be in section 7415.
Look!
This must be the castle section.
No one has been up here for ages.

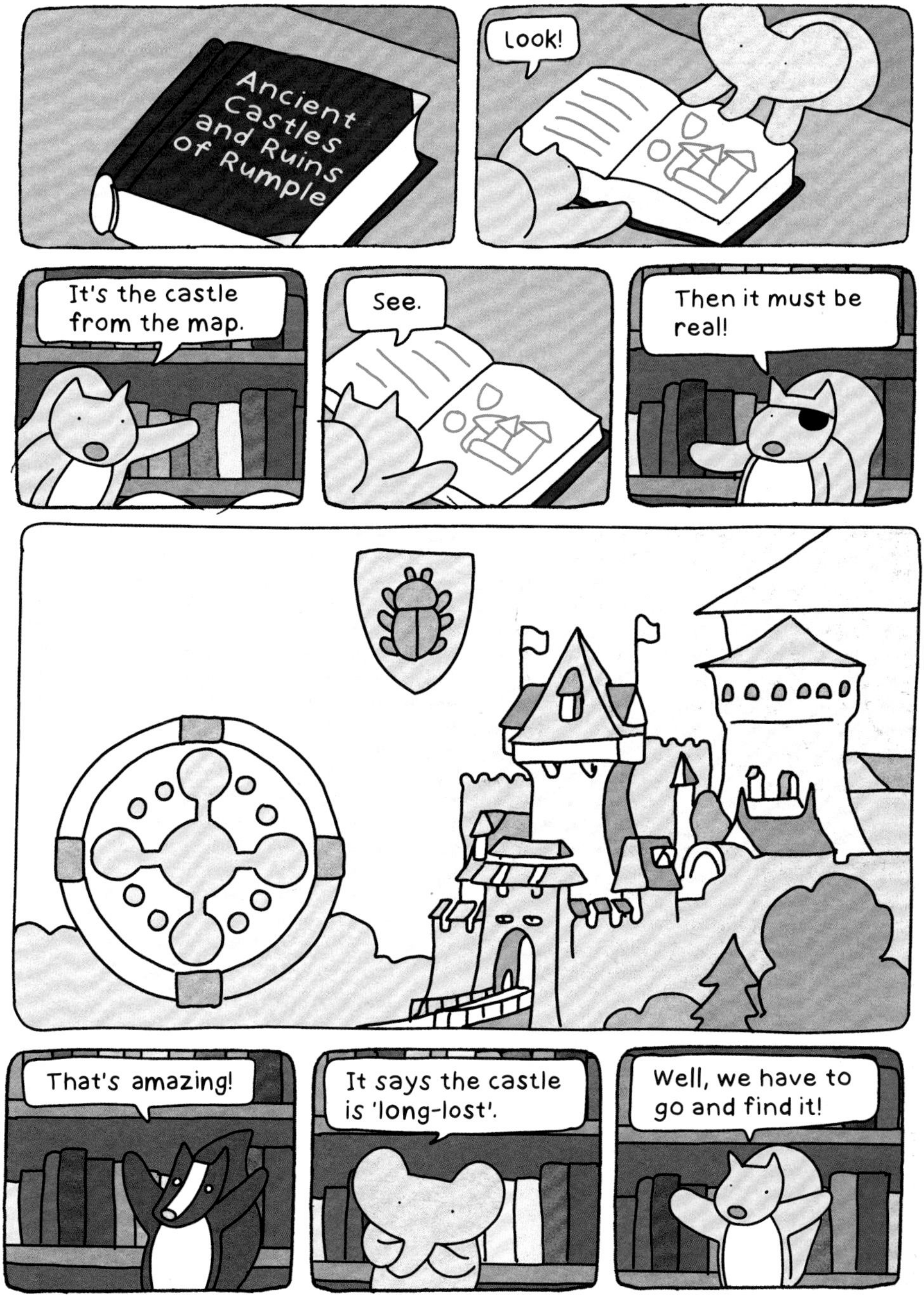
Ancient Castles and Ruins of Rumple
Look!
It's the castle from the map.
See.
Then it must be real!
That's amazing!
It *says* the castle is 'long-lost'.
Well, we have to go and find it!

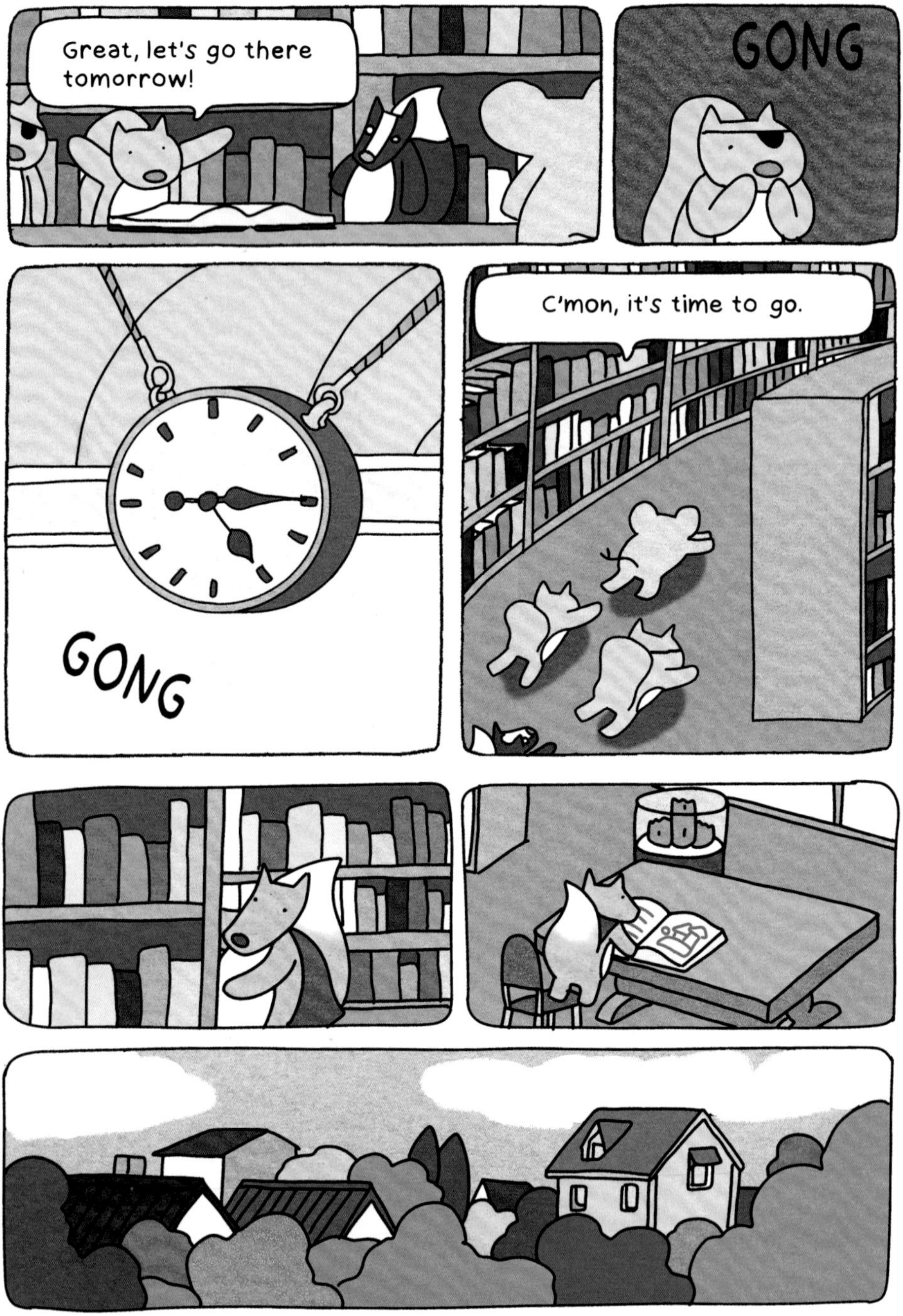
Great, let's go there tomorrow!
GONG
GONG
C'mon, it's time to go.

Chapter 5

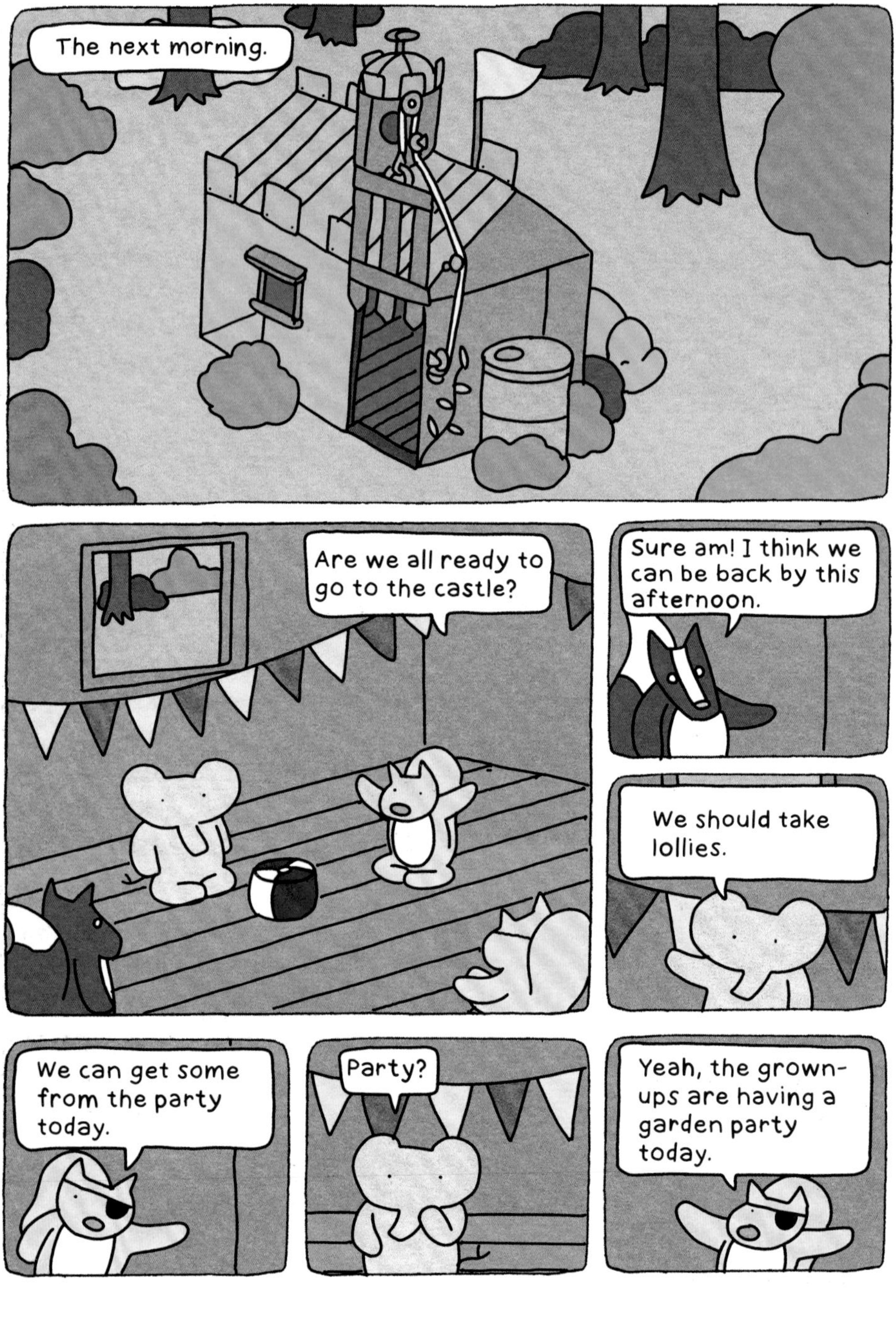
The next morning.
Are we all ready to go to the castle?
Sure am! I think we can be back by this afternoon.
We should take lollies.
We can get some from the party today.
Party?
Yeah, the grown-ups are having a garden party today.

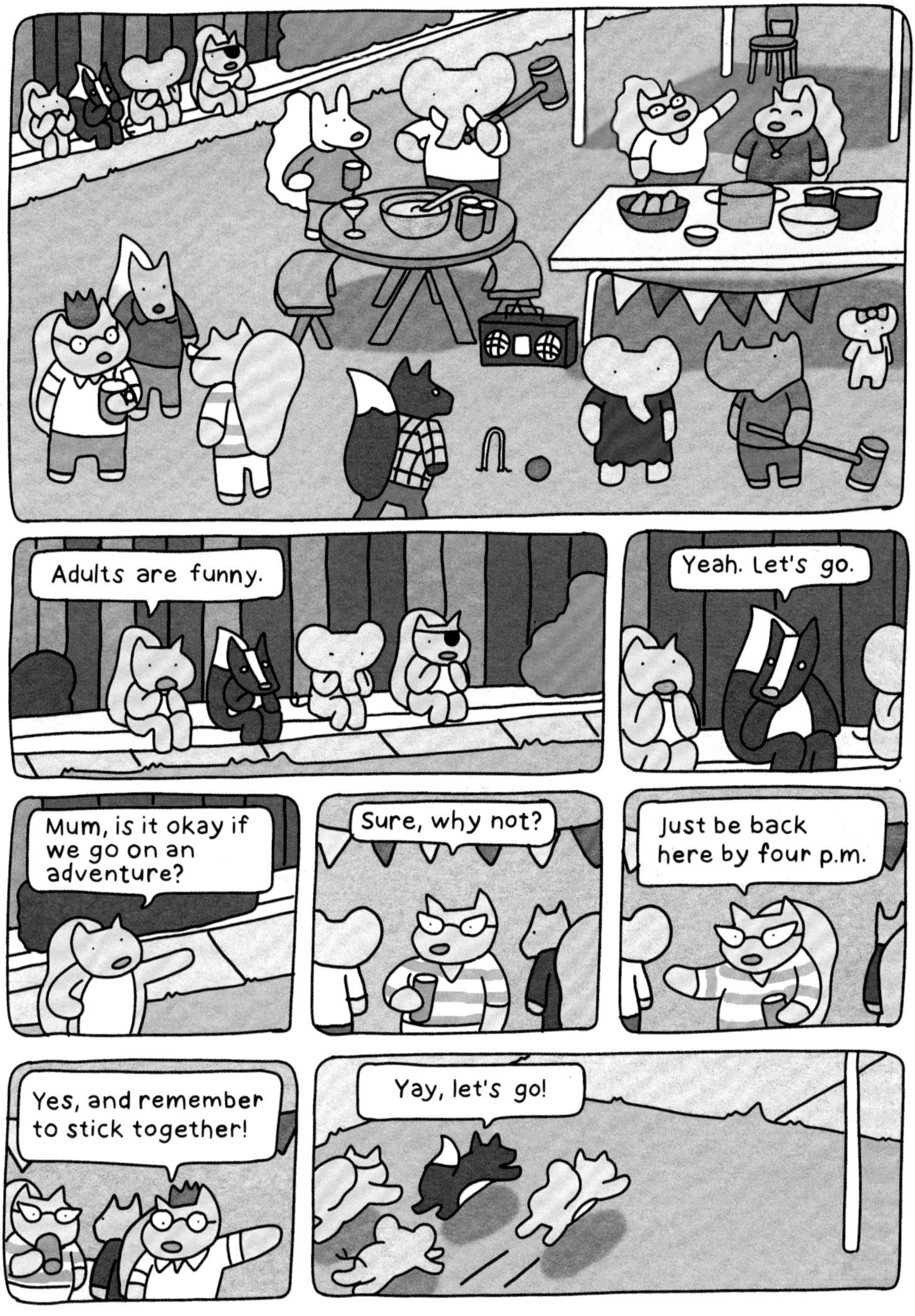
Adults are funny.
Yeah. Let's go.
Mum, is it okay if we go on an adventure?
Sure, why not?
Just be back here by four p.m.
Yes, and remember to stick together!
Yay, let's go!

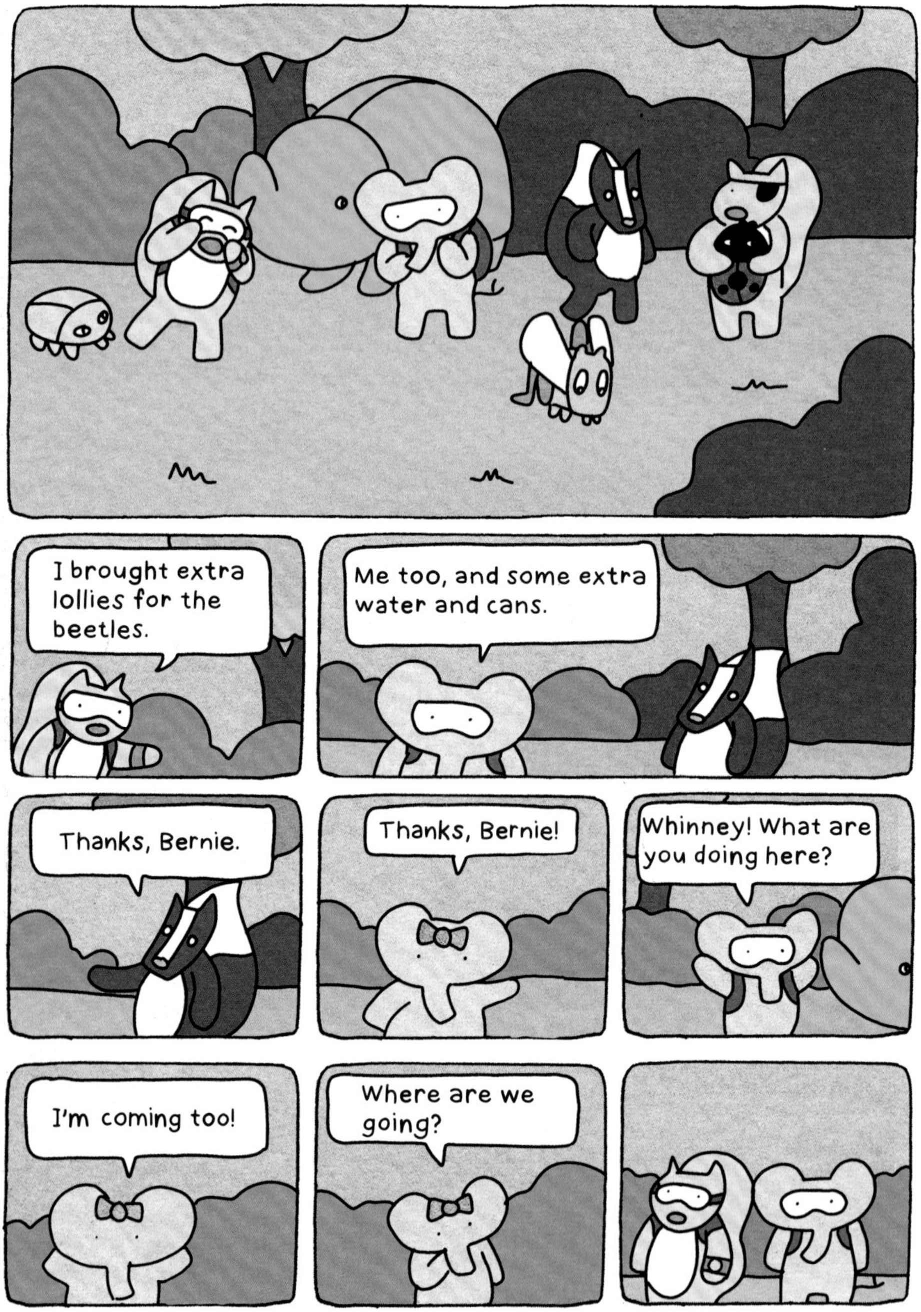
I brought extra lollies for the beetles.
Me too, and some extra water and cans.
Thanks, Bernie.
Thanks, Bernie!
Whinney! What are you doing here?
I'm coming too!
Where are we going?

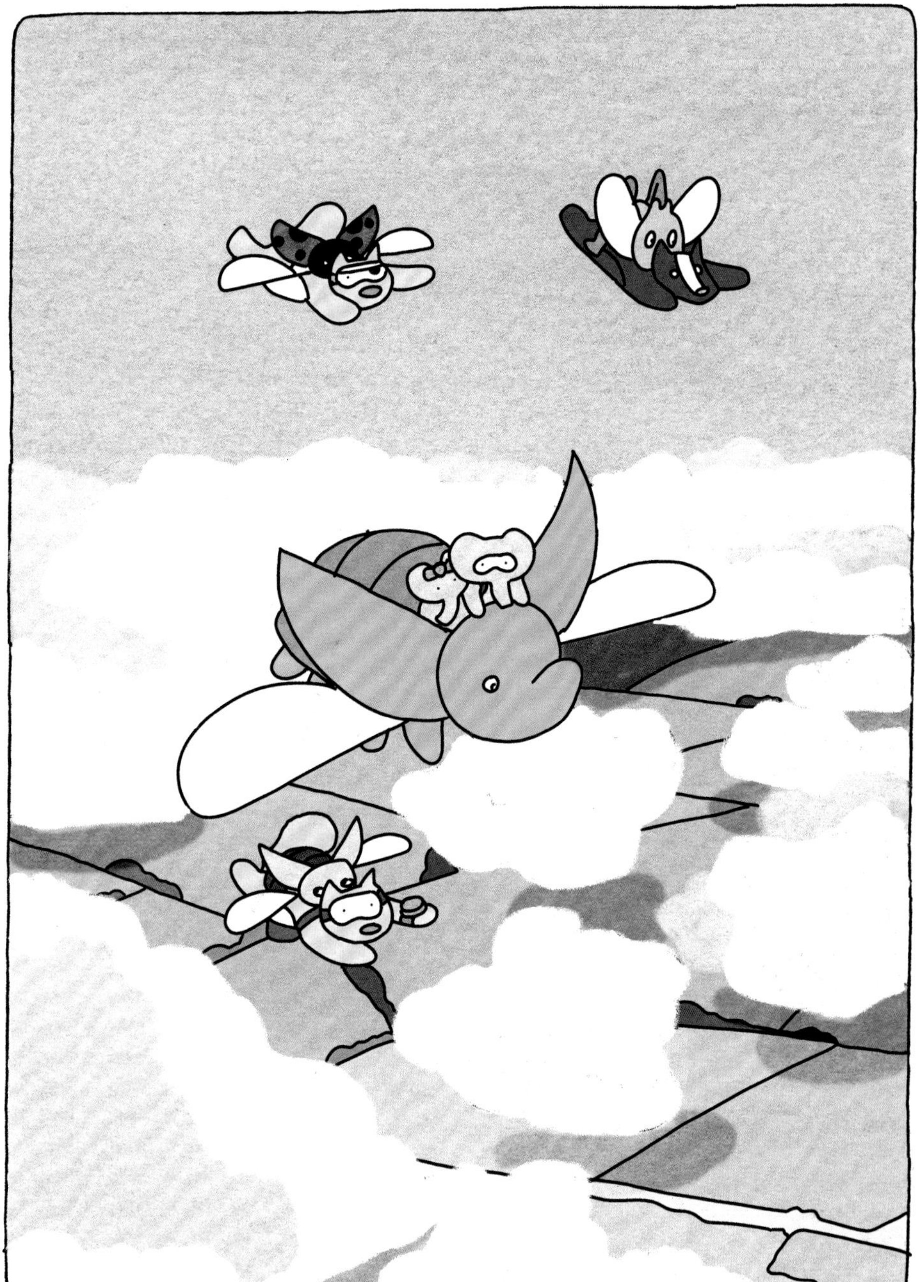

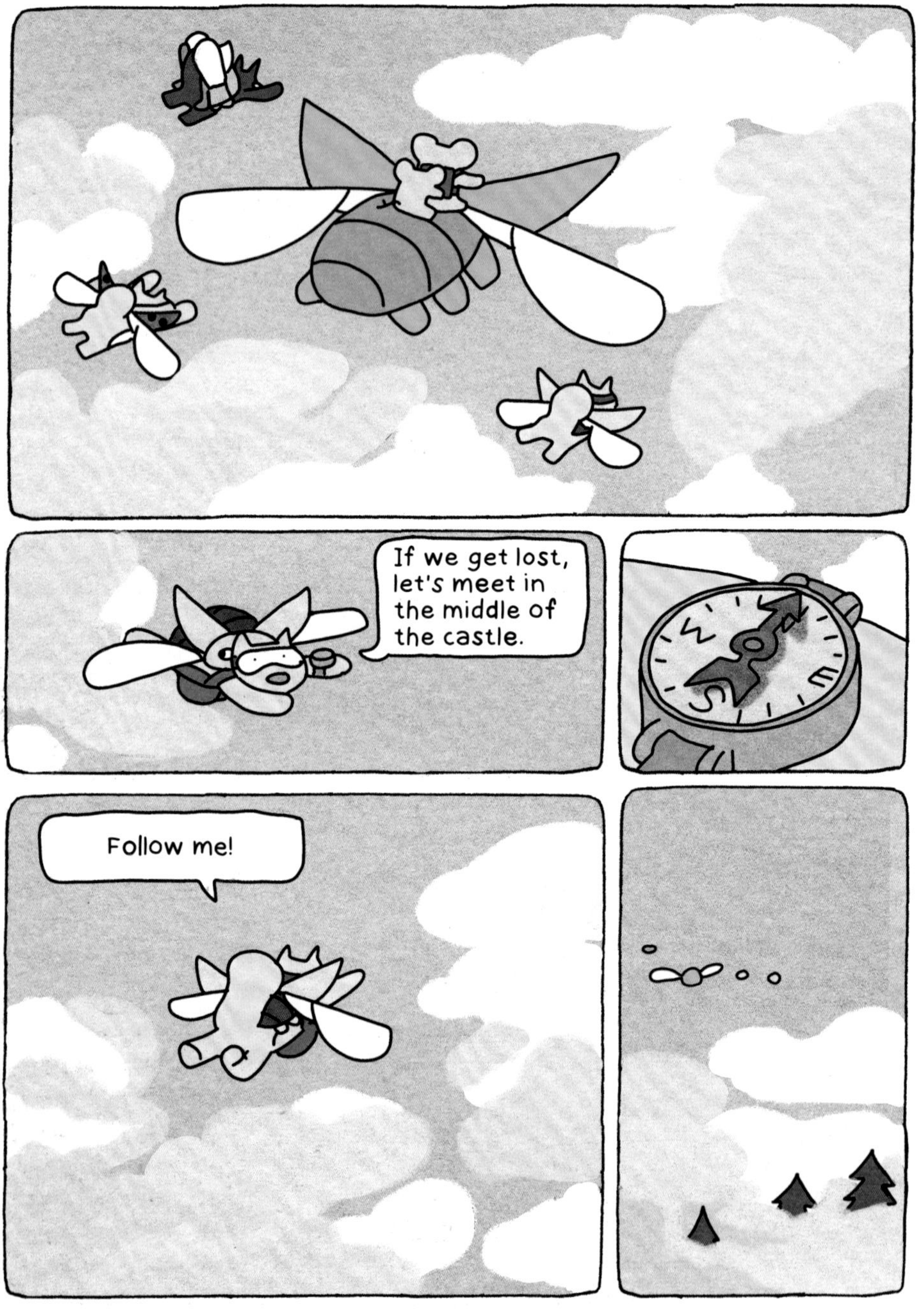
If we get lost, let's meet in the middle of the castle.
W
E
S
Follow me!

Look down there.

That must be the Foggy Forest!

We must be near the castle then.

I wonder what's down there.

It's a mystery.

It's getting foggy up here too.

It's getting hard to see!

Skip, can you light the way?

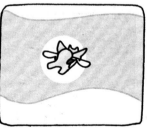

Stay together!

It's getting bumpy.

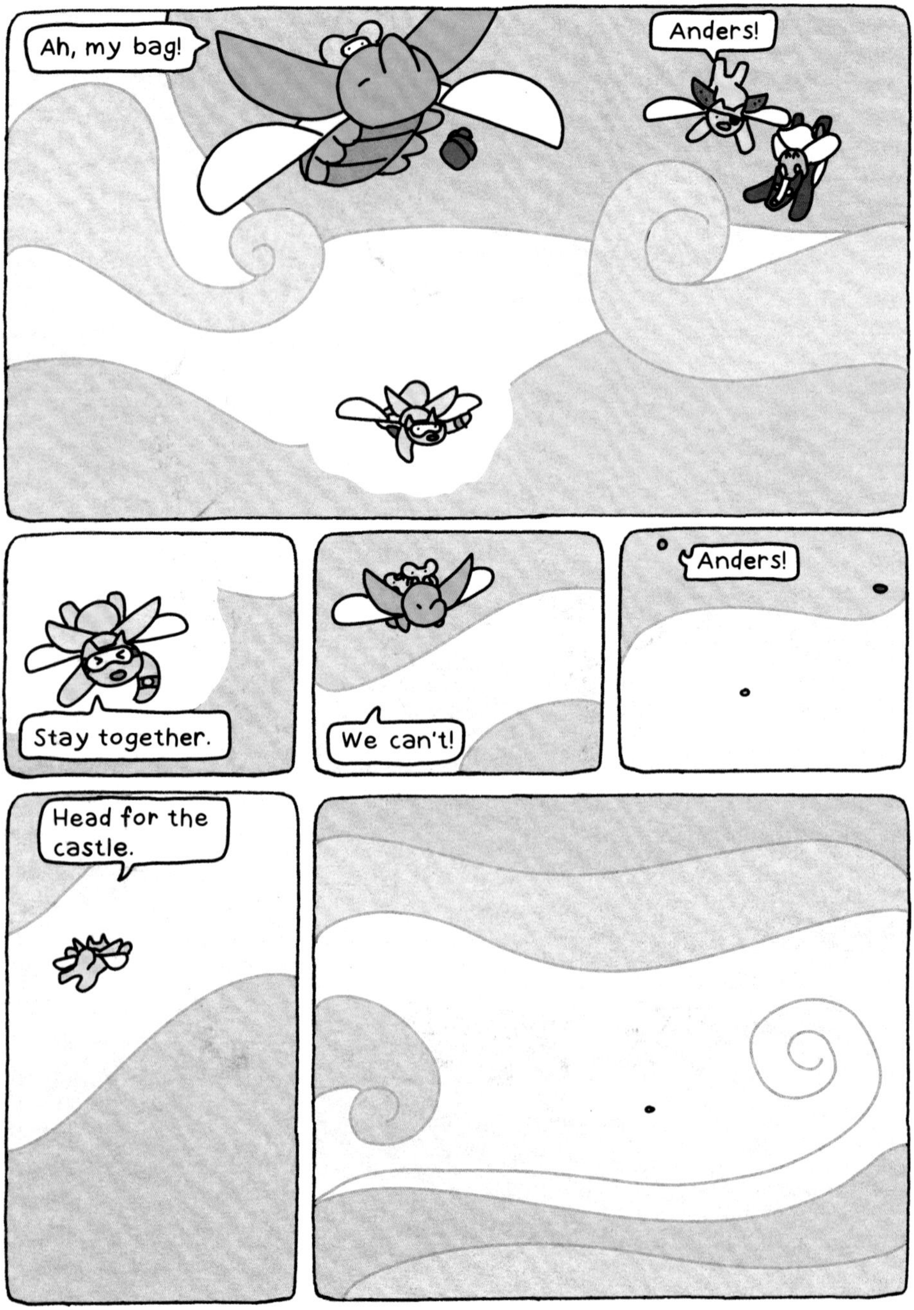
Ah, my bag!
Anders!
Stay together.
We can't!
Anders!
Head for the castle.

Chapter 6

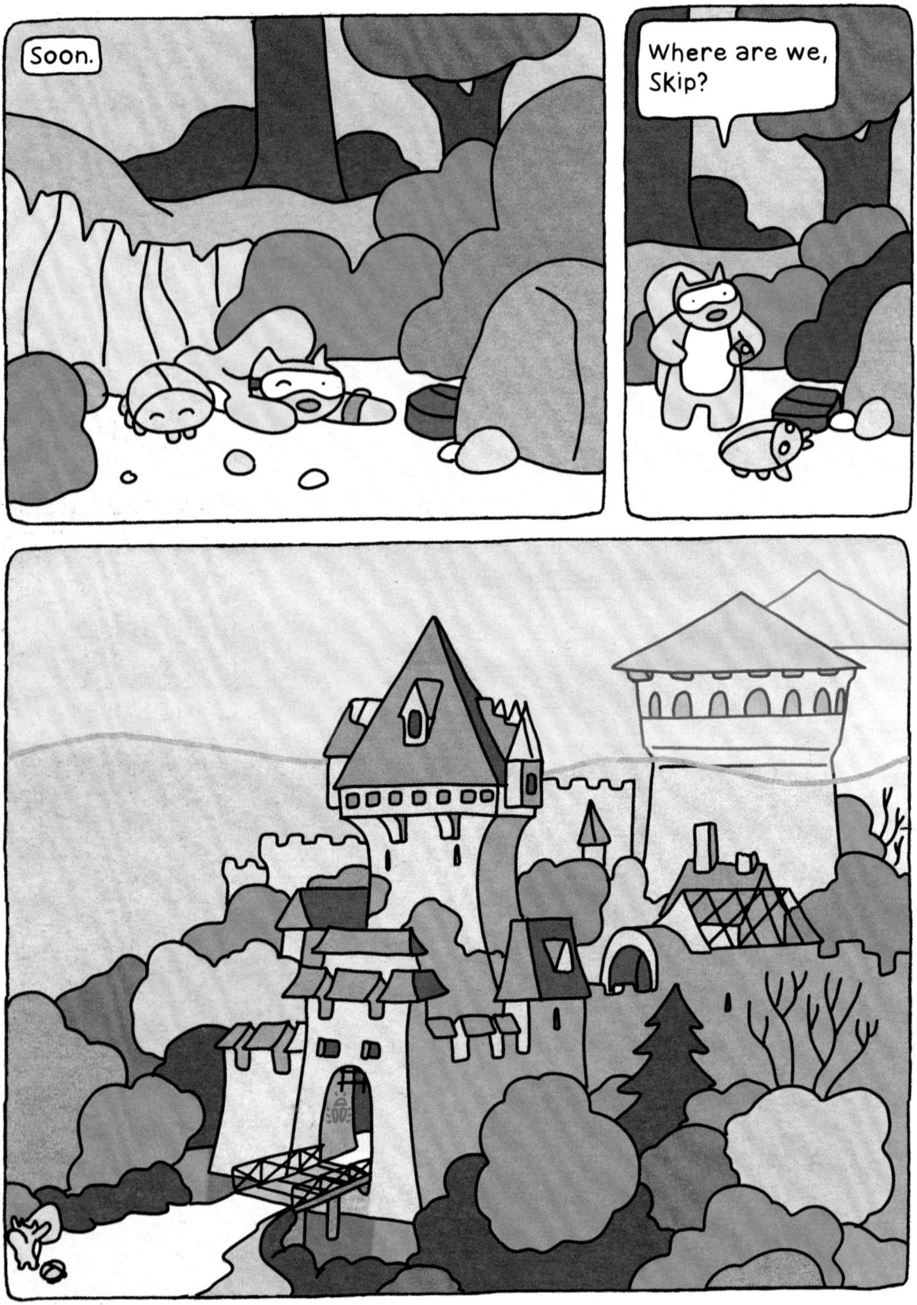
Soon.
Where are we, Skip?

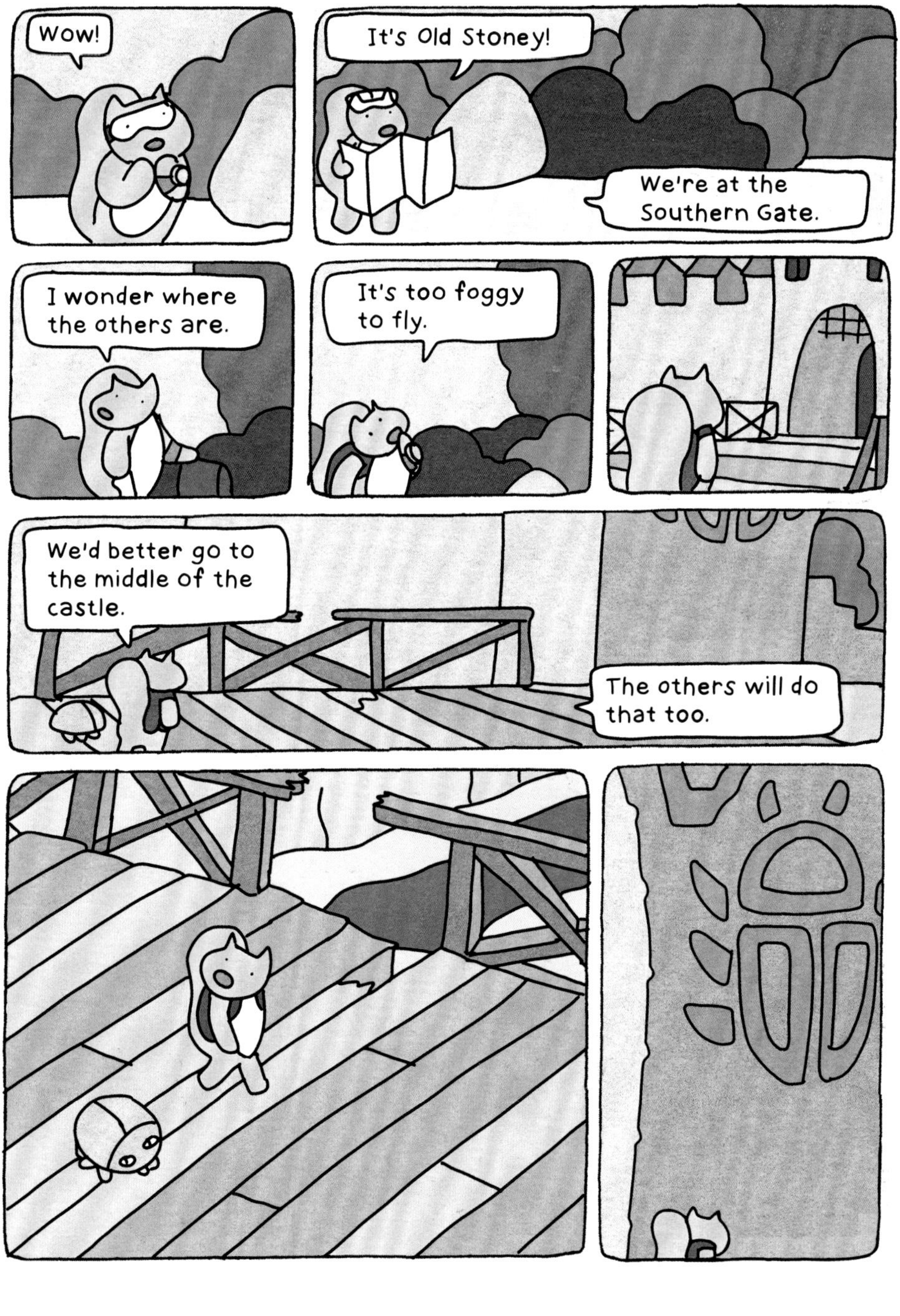
Wow!
It's Old Stoney!
We're at the Southern Gate.
I wonder where the others are.
It's too foggy to fly.
We'd better go to the middle of the castle.
The others will do that too.

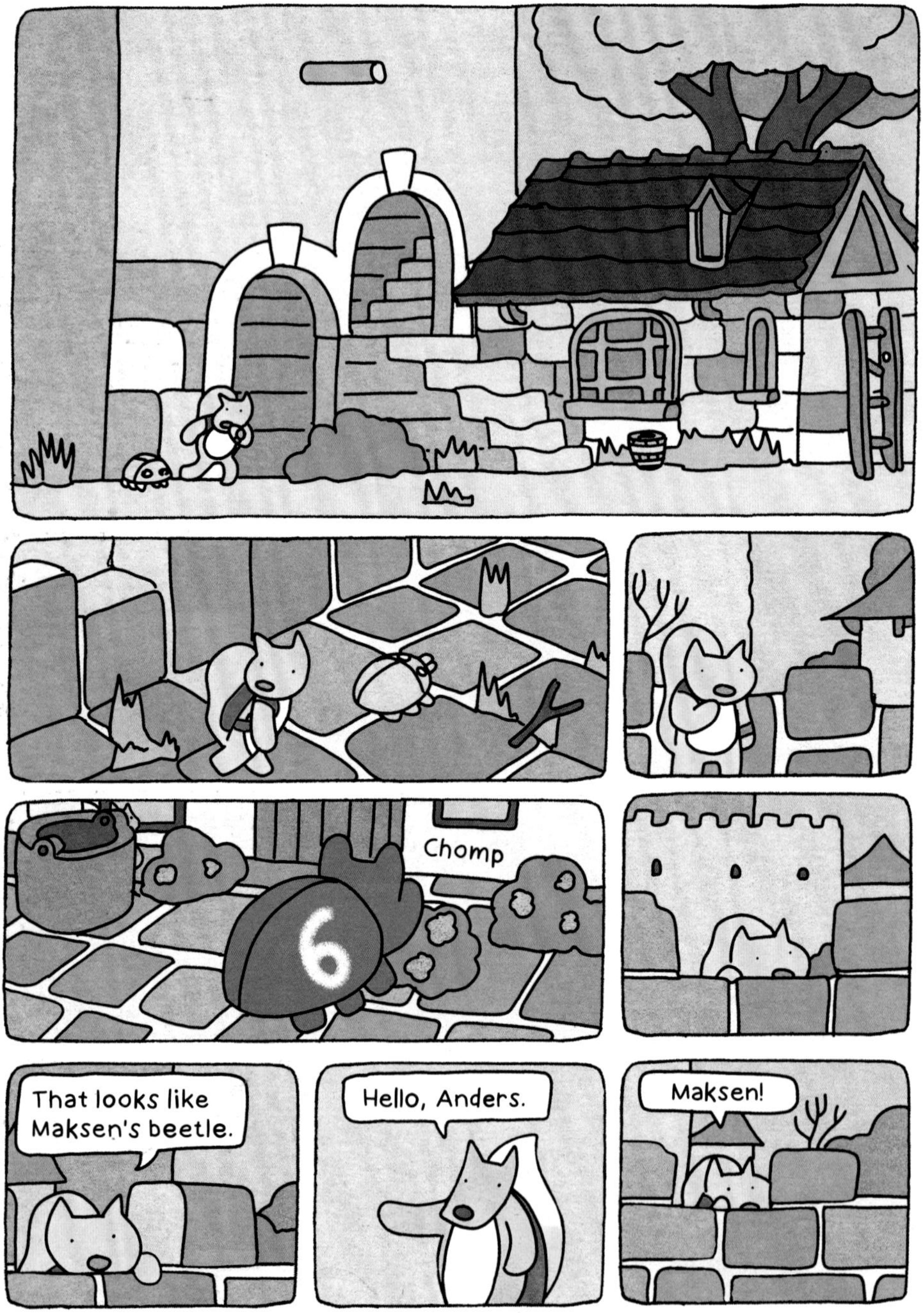
Chomp
That looks like Maksen's beetle.
Hello, Anders.
Maksen!

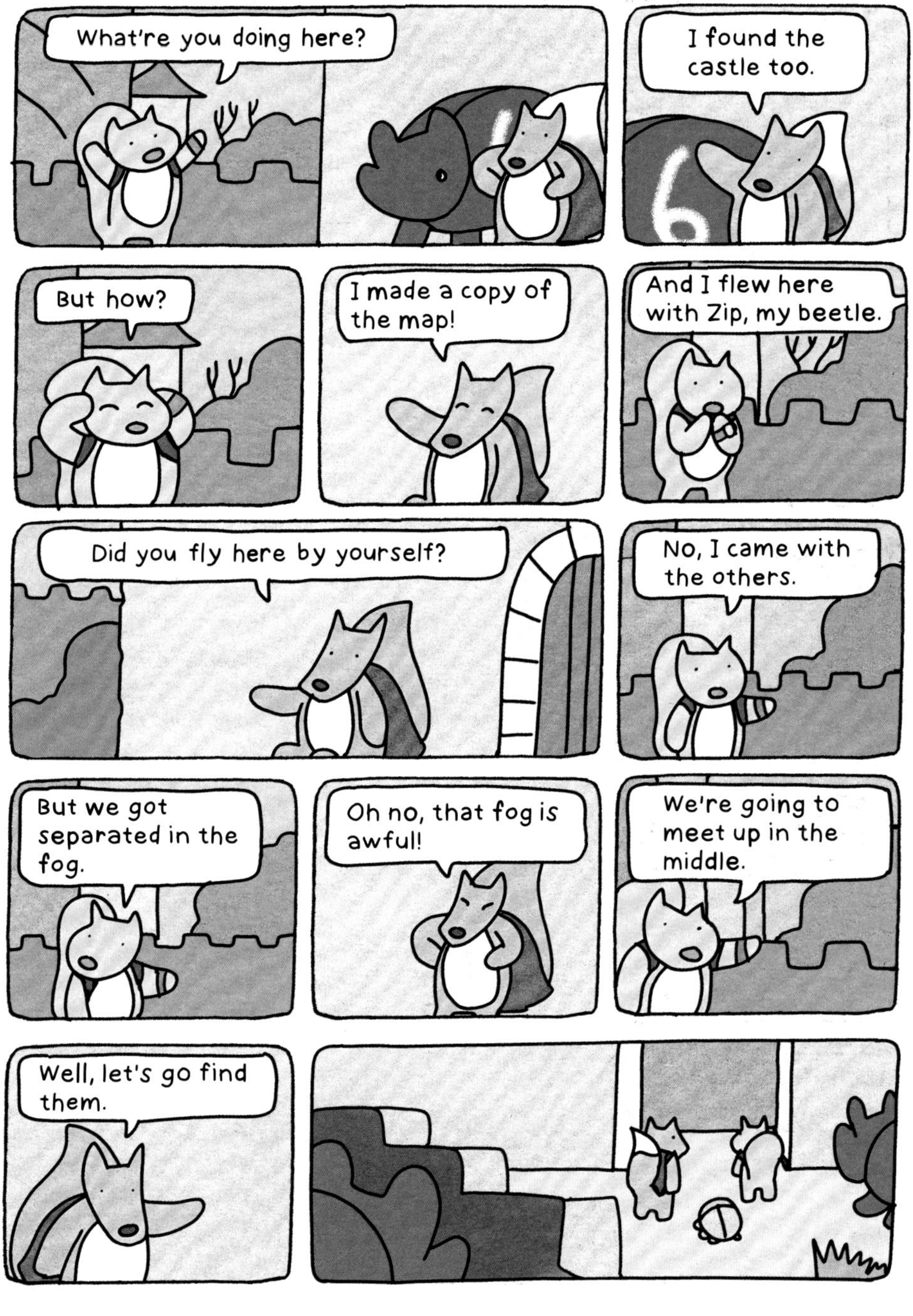
What're you doing here?
I found the castle too.
But how?
I made a copy of the map!
And I flew here with Zip, my beetle.
Did you fly here by yourself?
No, I came with the others.
But we got separated in the fog.
Oh no, that fog is awful!
We're going to meet up in the middle.
Well, let's go find them.

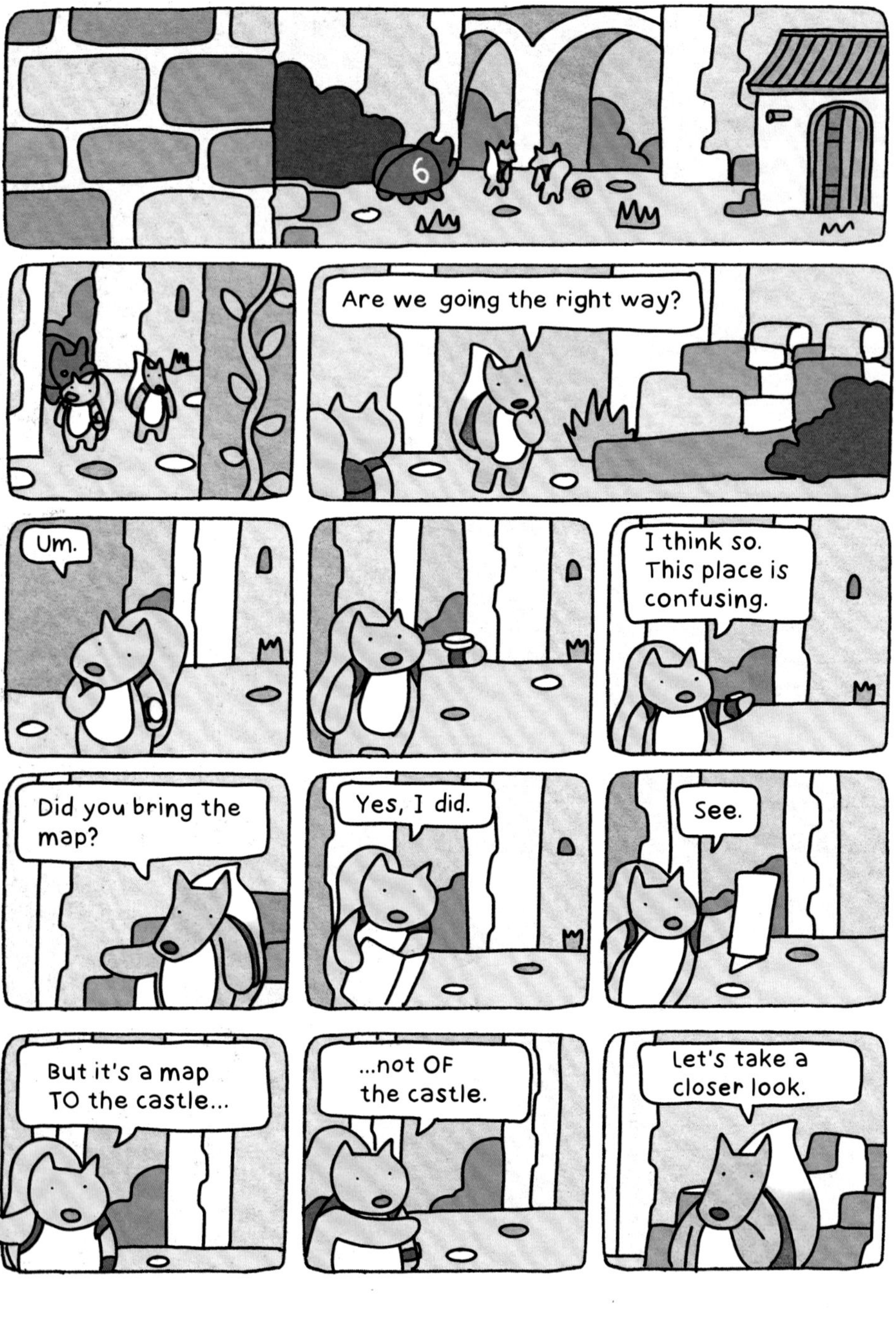
Are we going the right way?
Um.
I think so. This place is confusing.
Did you bring the map?
Yes, I did.
See.
But it's a map TO the castle...
...not OF the castle.
Let's take a closer look.

Hmmm.

What's on the other side?

Um, nothing.

Wait, look!

What?

There are two sheets here!

Swip

Woah!

There's another map here.

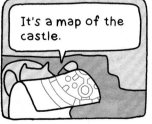

It's a map of the castle.

Amazing.

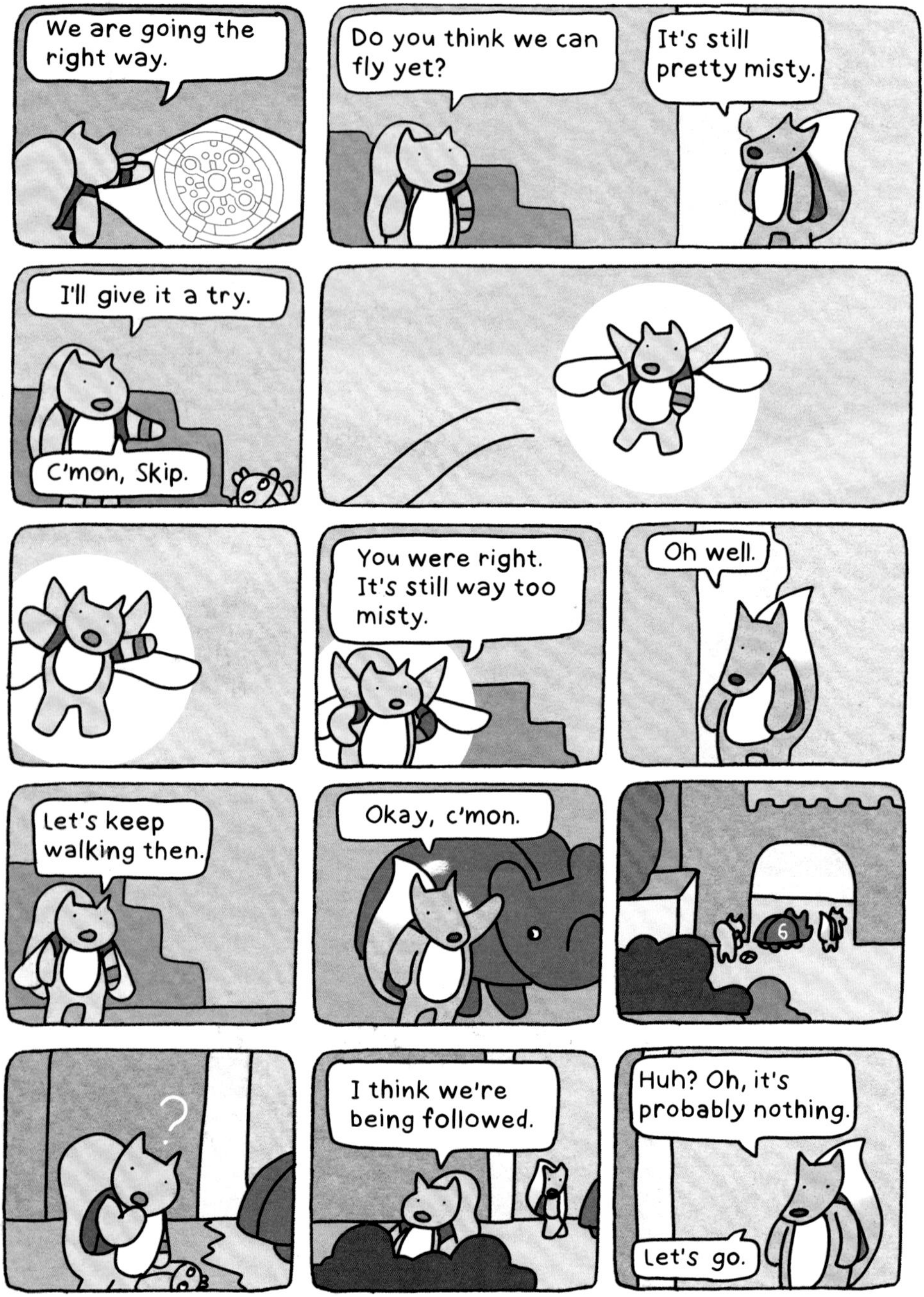
We are going the right way.
Do you think we can fly yet?
It's still pretty misty.
I'll give it a try.
C'mon, Skip.
You were right. It's still way too misty.
Oh well.
Let's keep walking then.
Okay, c'mon.
6
?
I think we're being followed.
Huh? Oh, it's probably nothing.
Let's go.

Chapter 7

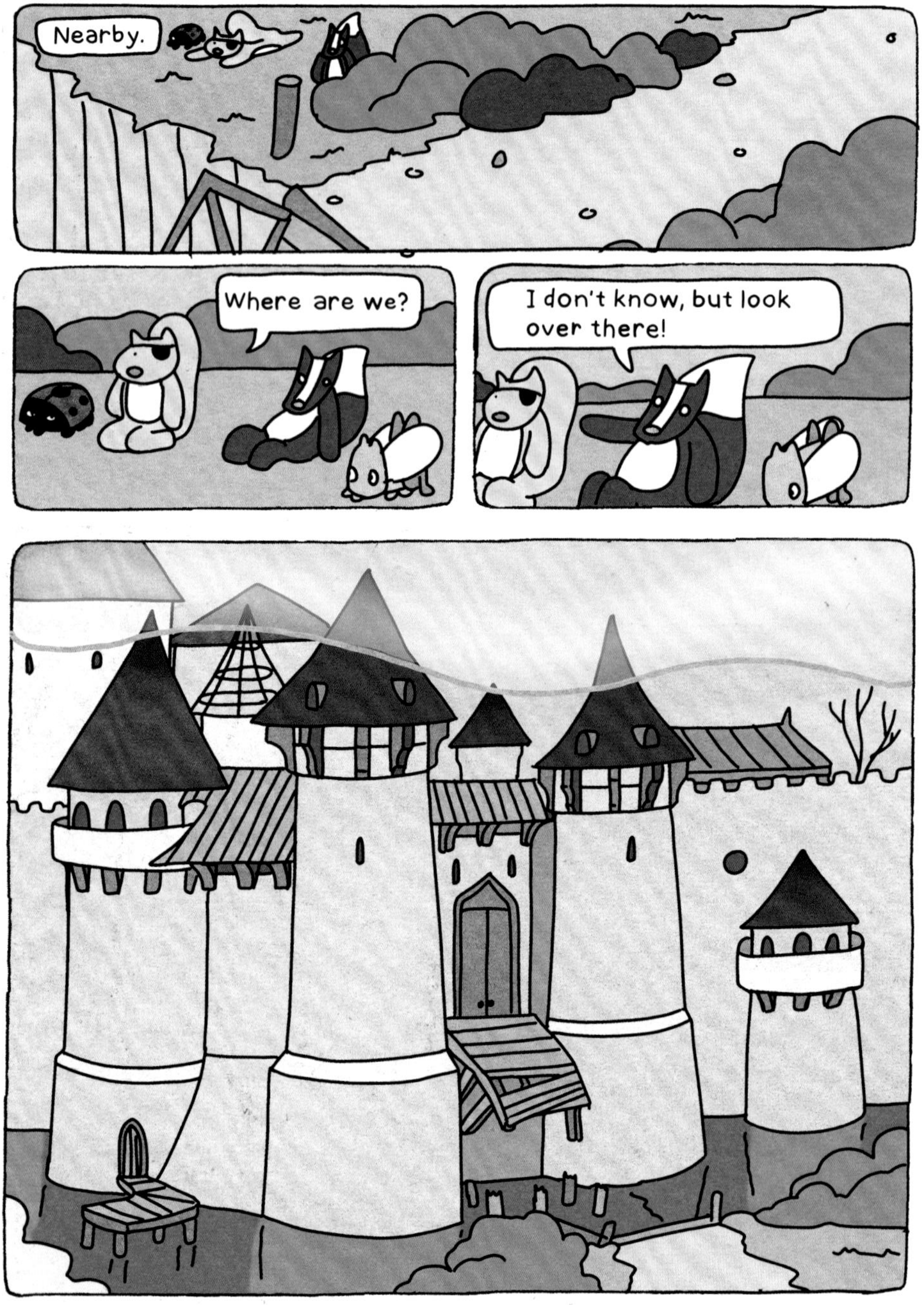
Nearby.
Where are we?
I don't know, but look over there!

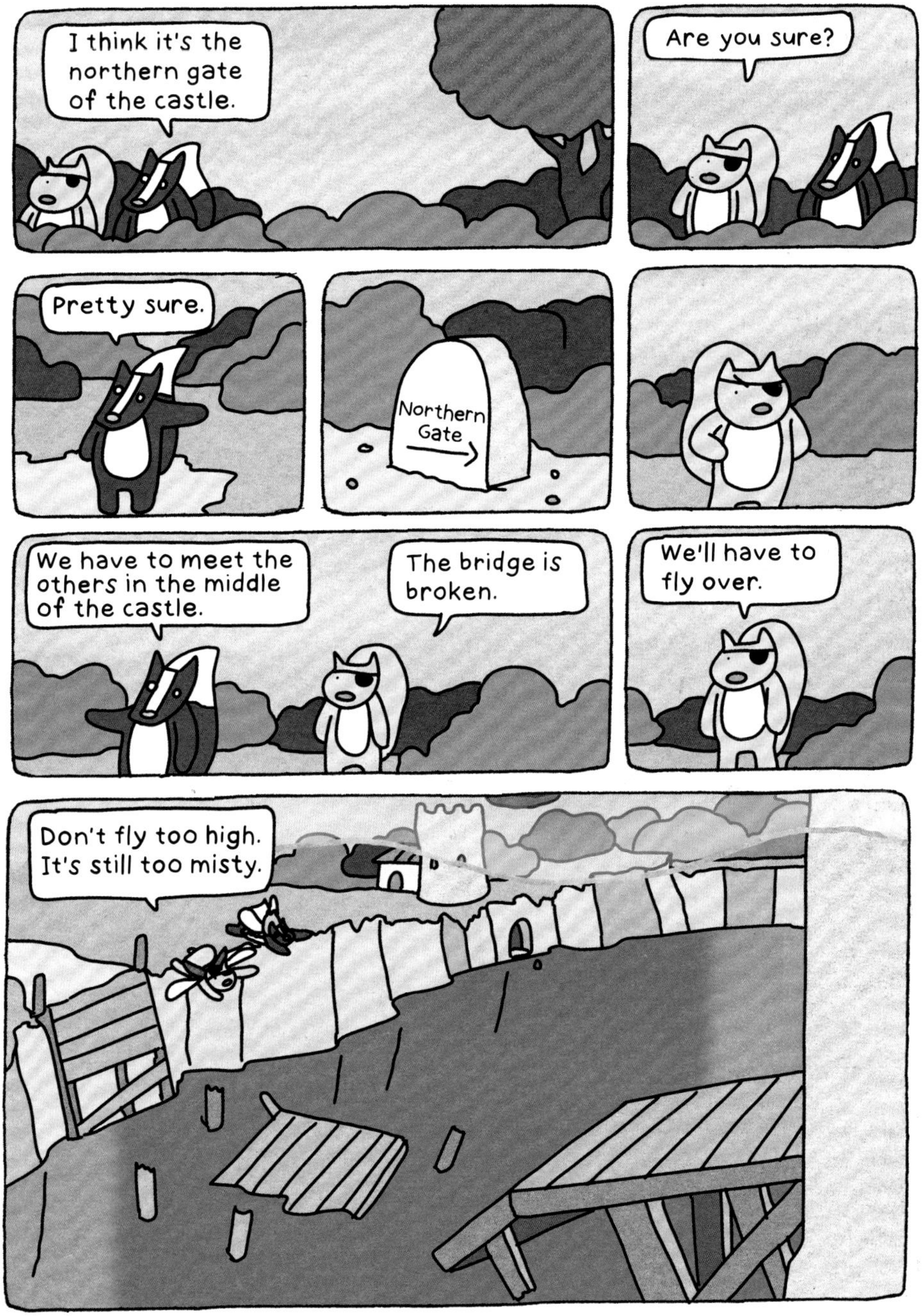
I think it's the northern gate of the castle.
Are you sure?
Pretty sure.
Northern Gate
We have to meet the others in the middle of the castle.
The bridge is broken.
We'll have to fly over.
Don't fly too high. It's still too misty.

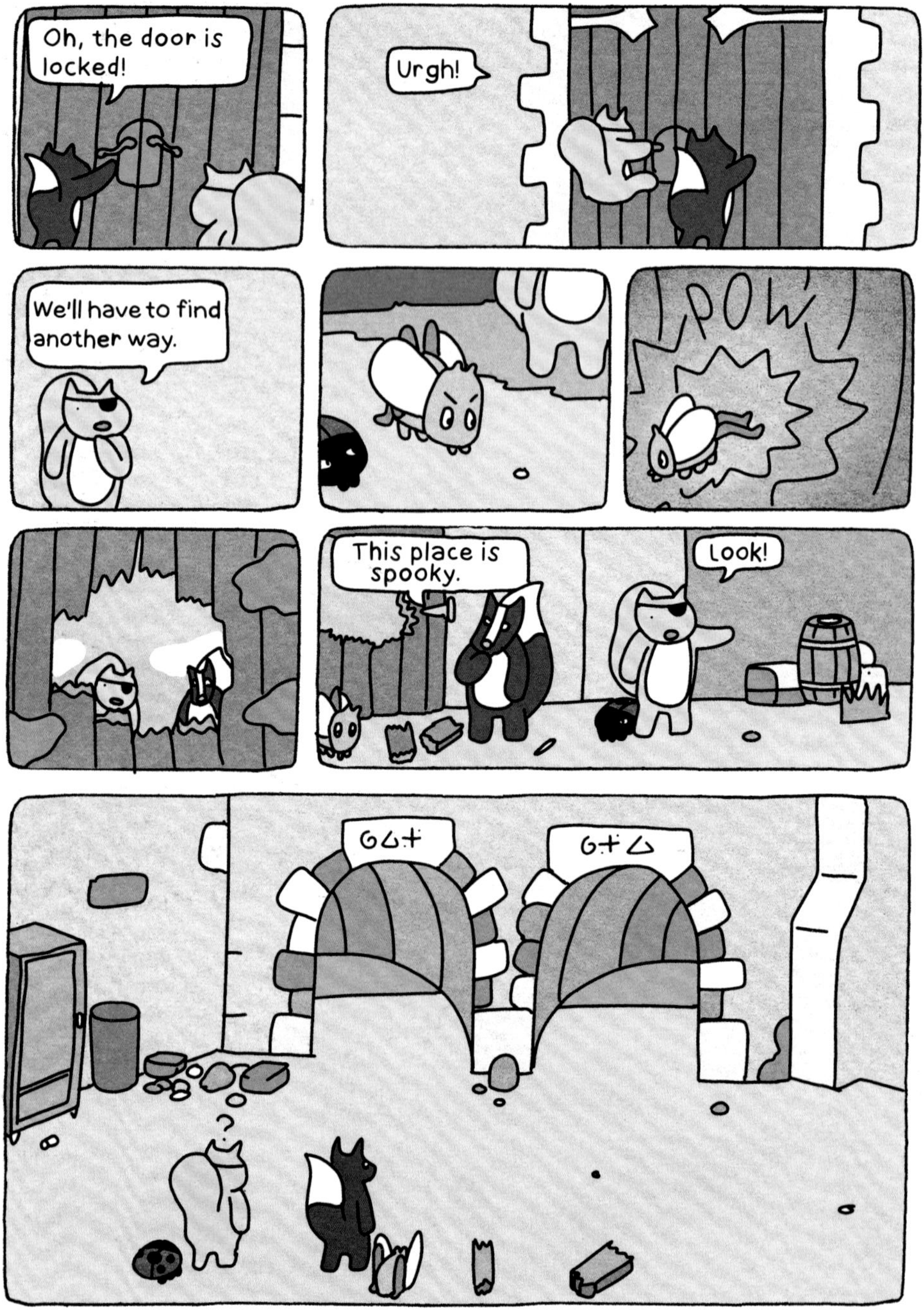
Oh, the door is locked!
Urgh!
We'll have to find another way.
POW
This place is spooky.
Look!

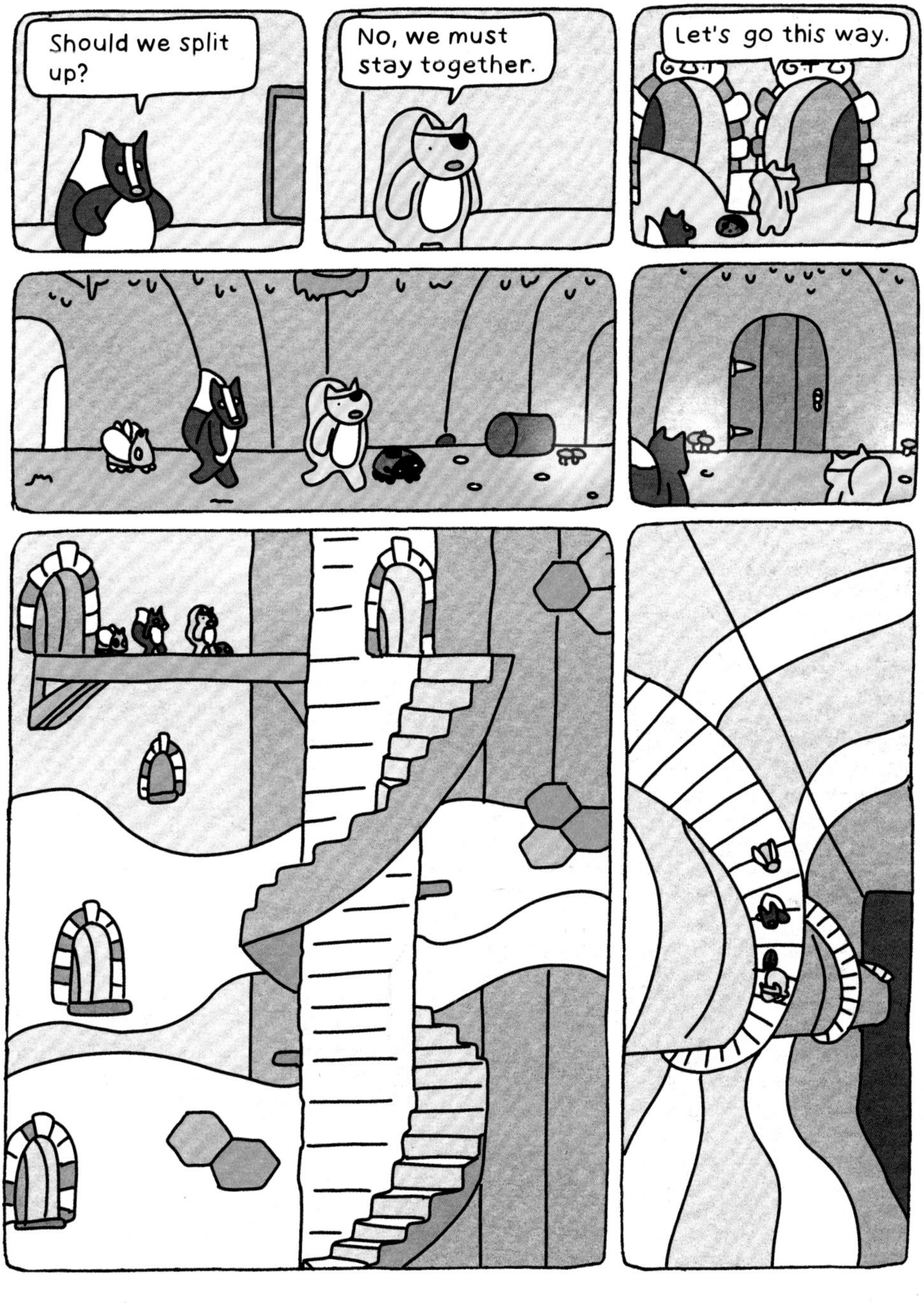
Should we split up?
No, we must stay together.
Let's go this way.

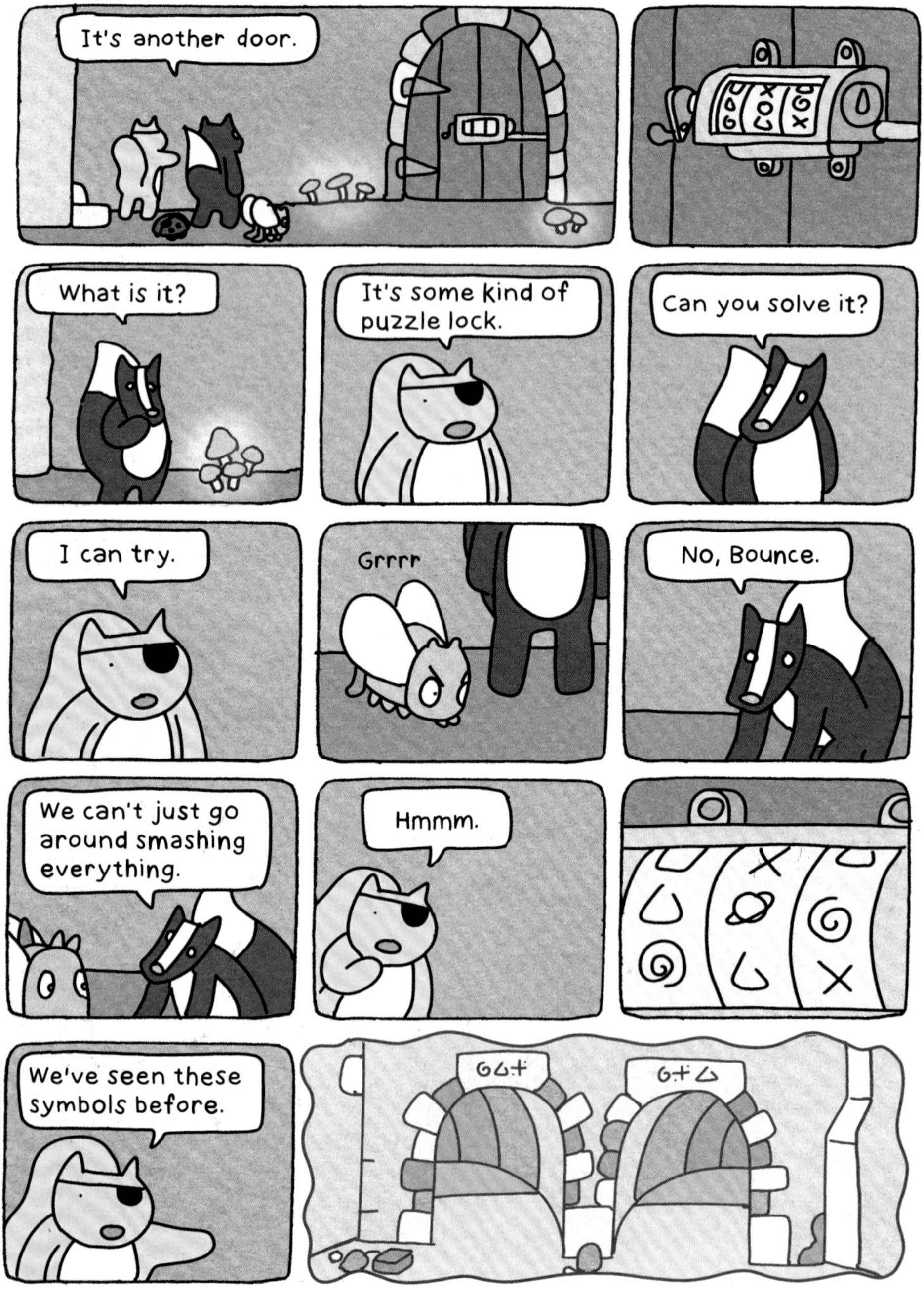

It's another door.
What is it?
It's some kind of puzzle lock.
Can you solve it?
I can try.
Grrrr
No, Bounce.
We can't just go around smashing everything.
Hmmm.
We've seen these symbols before.

Should we turn back then?

ZZZZZZZZZZZZZZZ

What's that noise?

ZZZZZZZZZZZZZZZ

Um.

ZZZZZZZ HISS!

Ah! Look out!

BZZZZ

Whump!

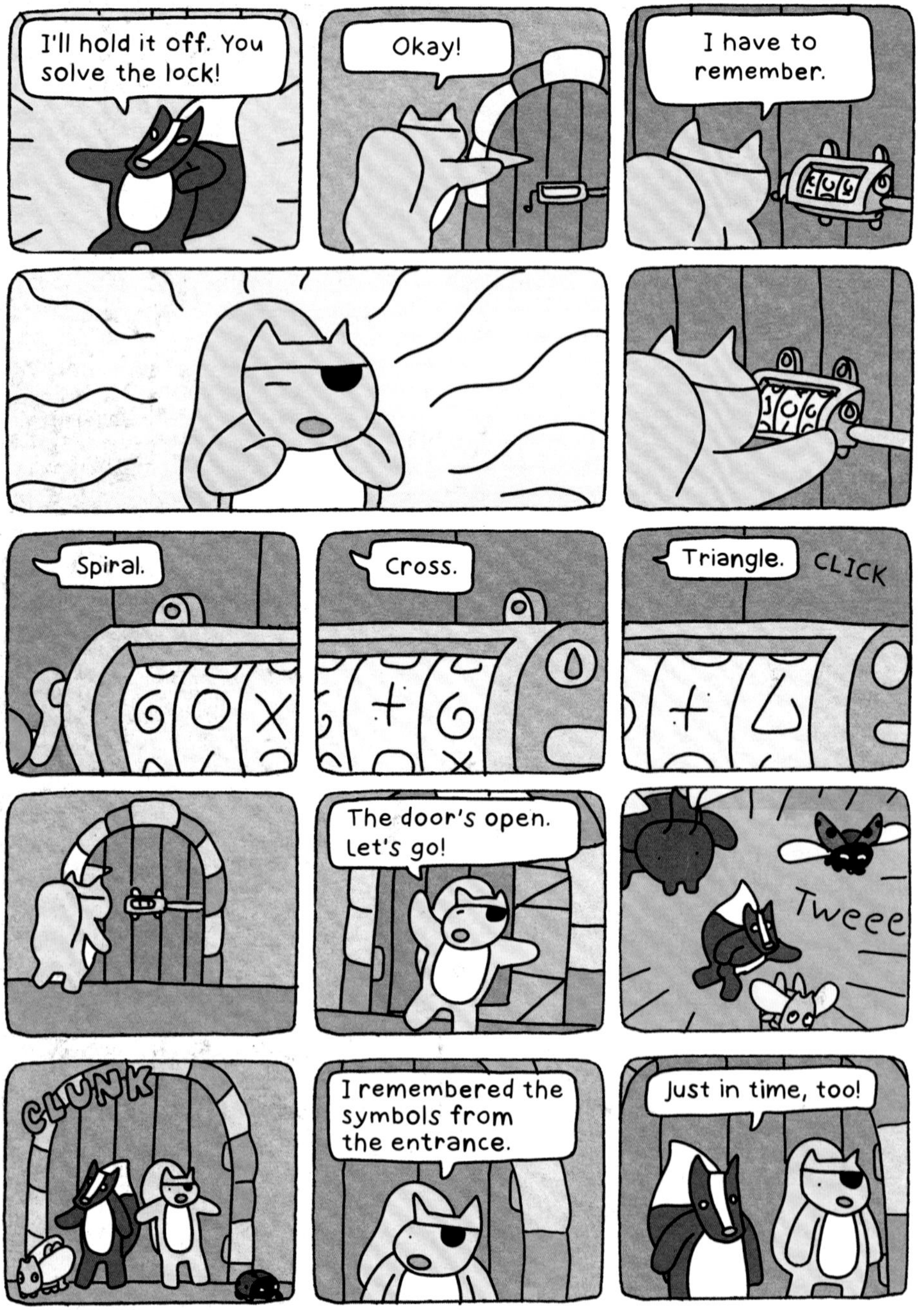
I'll hold it off. You solve the lock!
Okay!
I have to remember.
Spiral.
Cross.
Triangle.
CLICK
The door's open. Let's go!
Tweee
CLUNK
I remembered the symbols from the entrance.
Just in time, too!

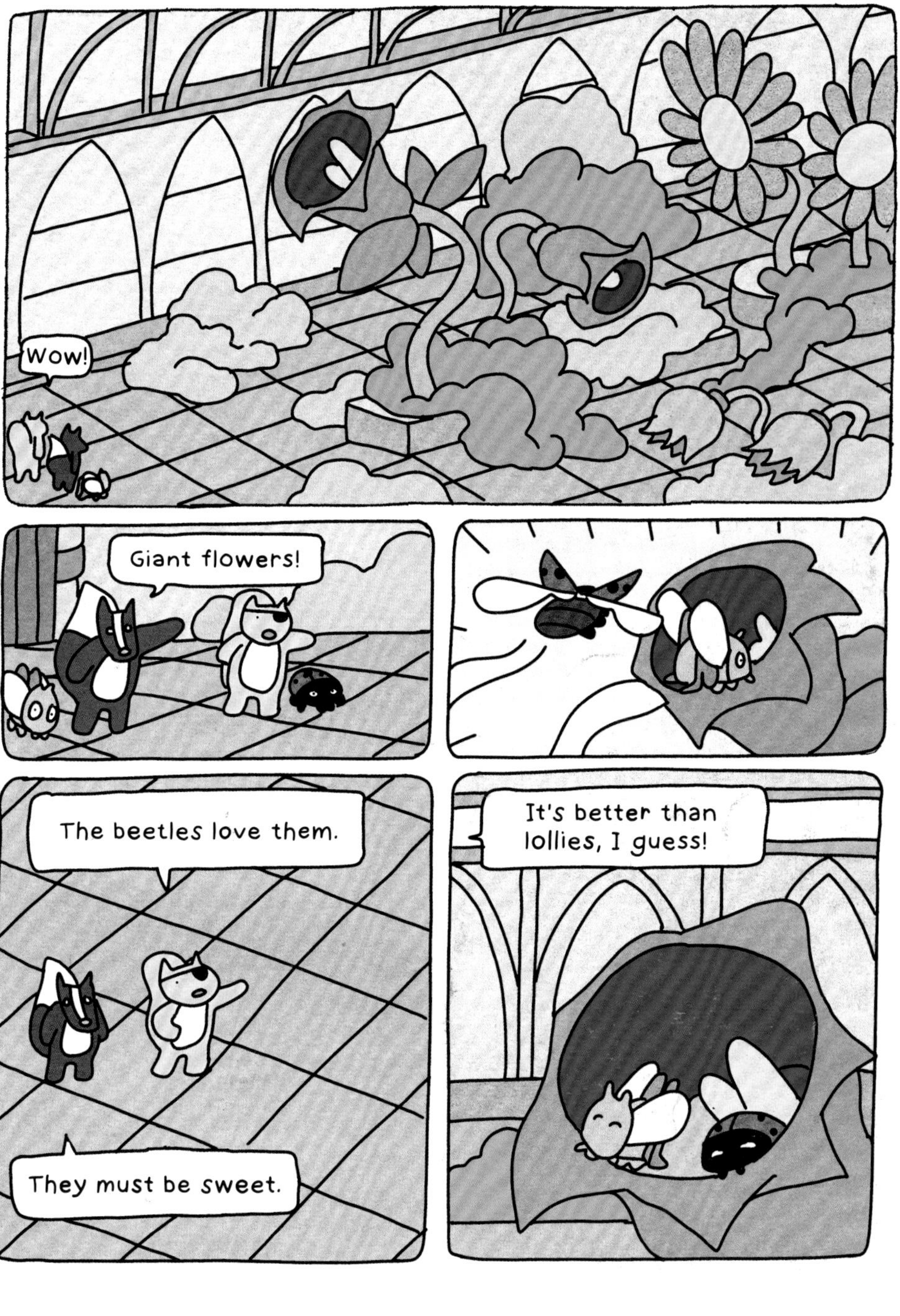
Wow!
Giant flowers!
The beetles love them.
They must be sweet.
It's better than lollies, I guess!

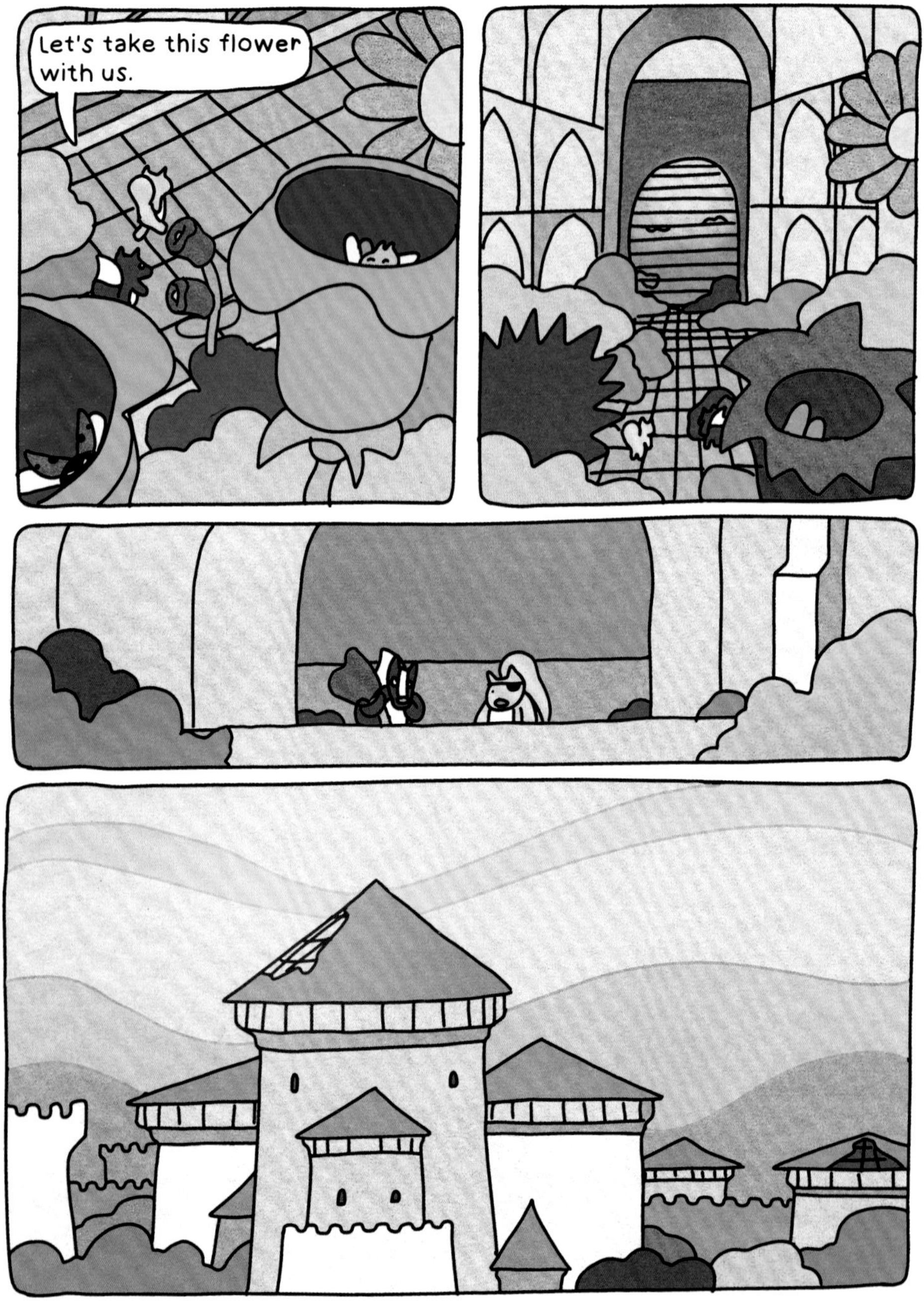
Let's take this flower with us.

Chapter 8

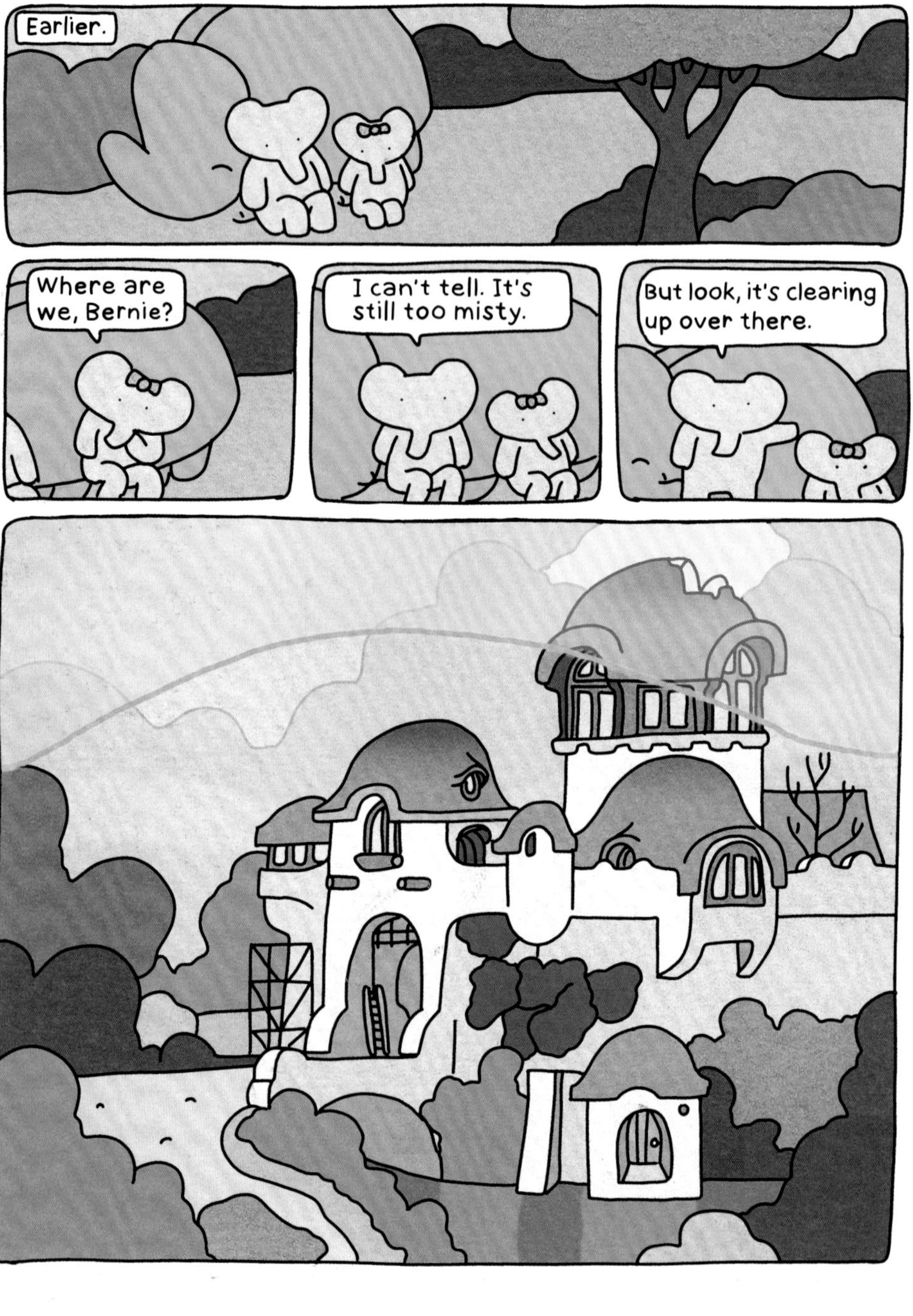
Earlier.
Where are we, Bernie?
I can't tell. It's still too misty.
But look, it's clearing up over there.

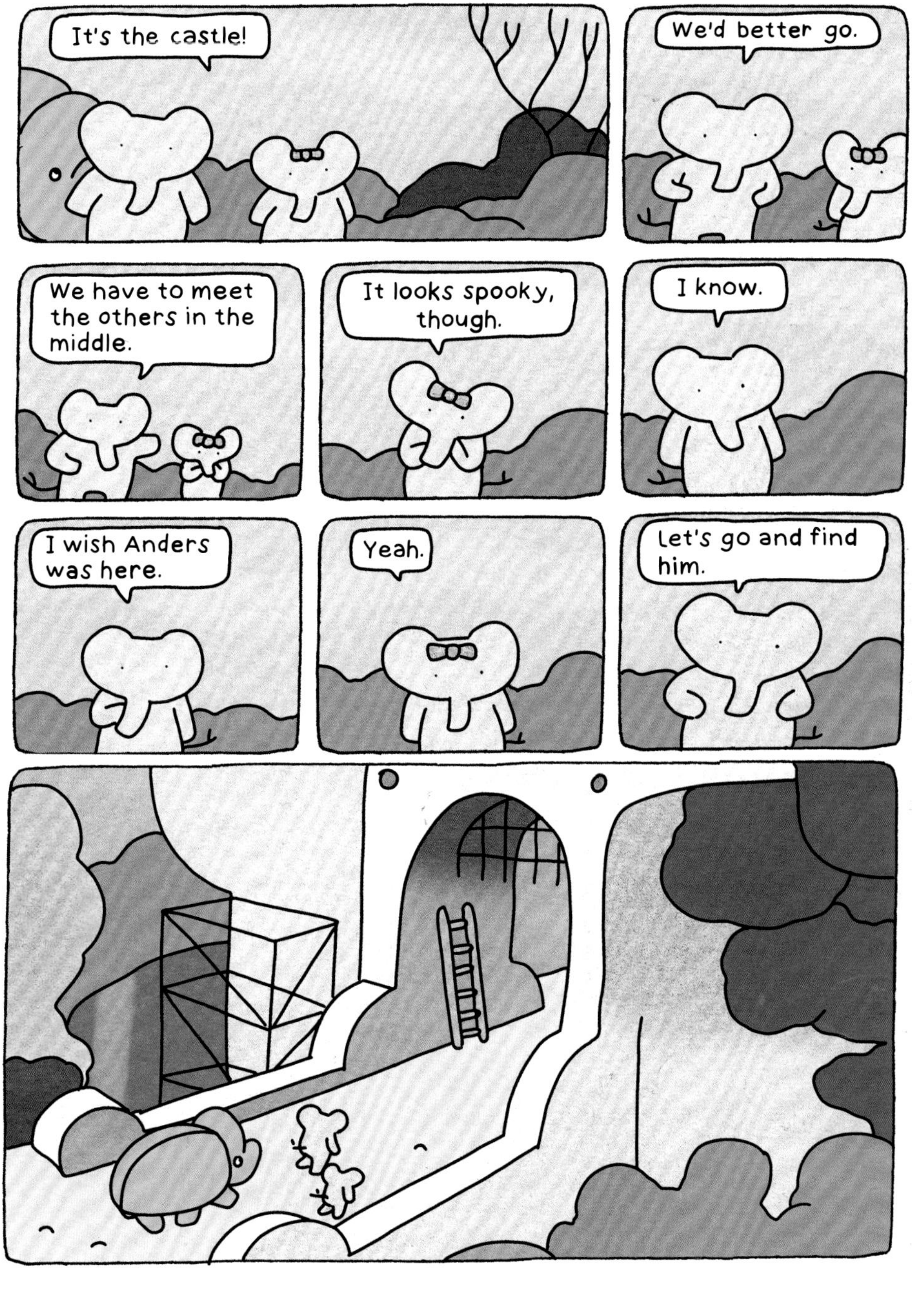
It's the castle!
We'd better go.
We have to meet the others in the middle.
It looks spooky, though.
I know.
I wish Anders was here.
Yeah.
Let's go and find him.

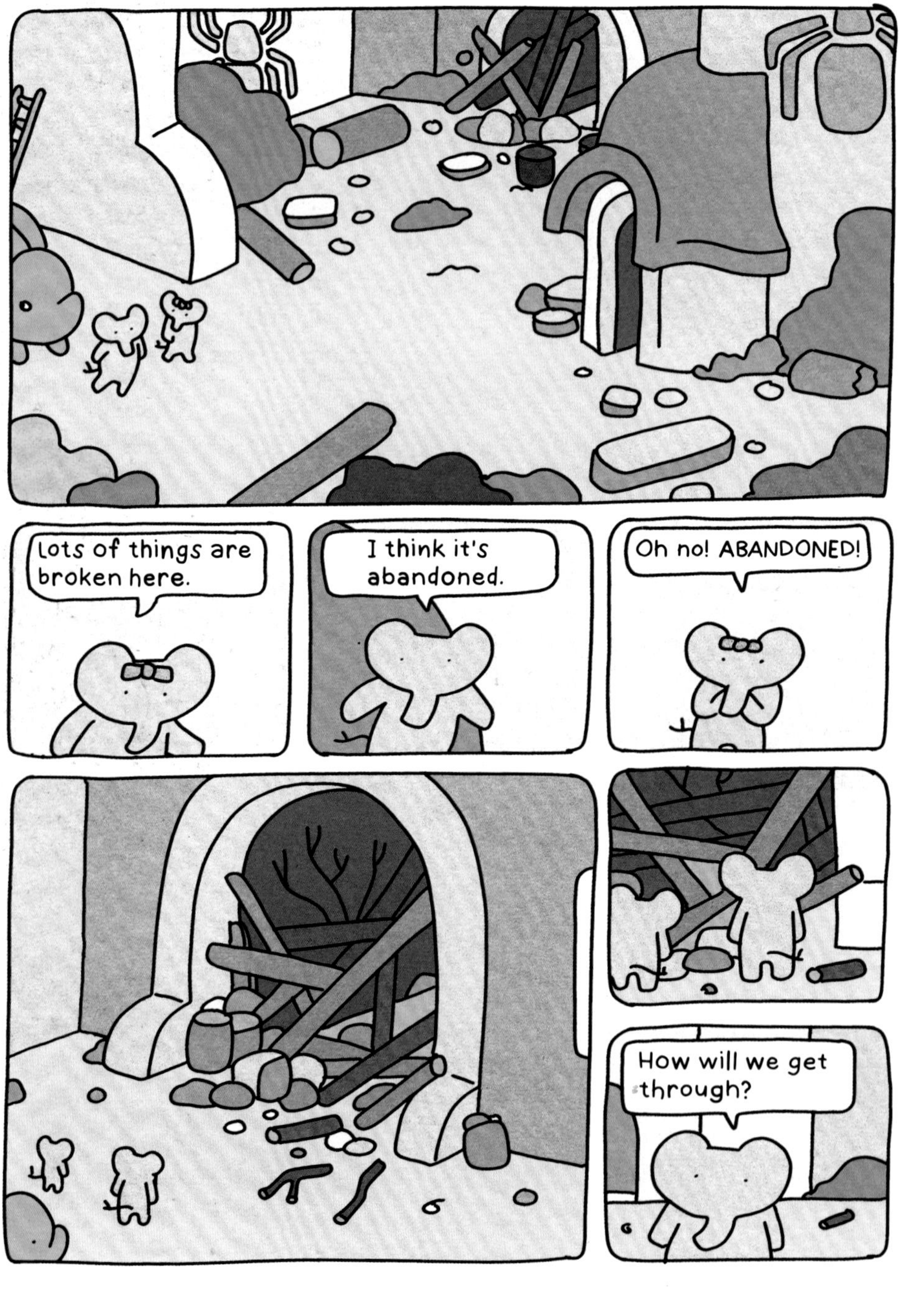
Lots of things are broken here.
I think it's abandoned.
Oh no! ABANDONED!
How will we get through?

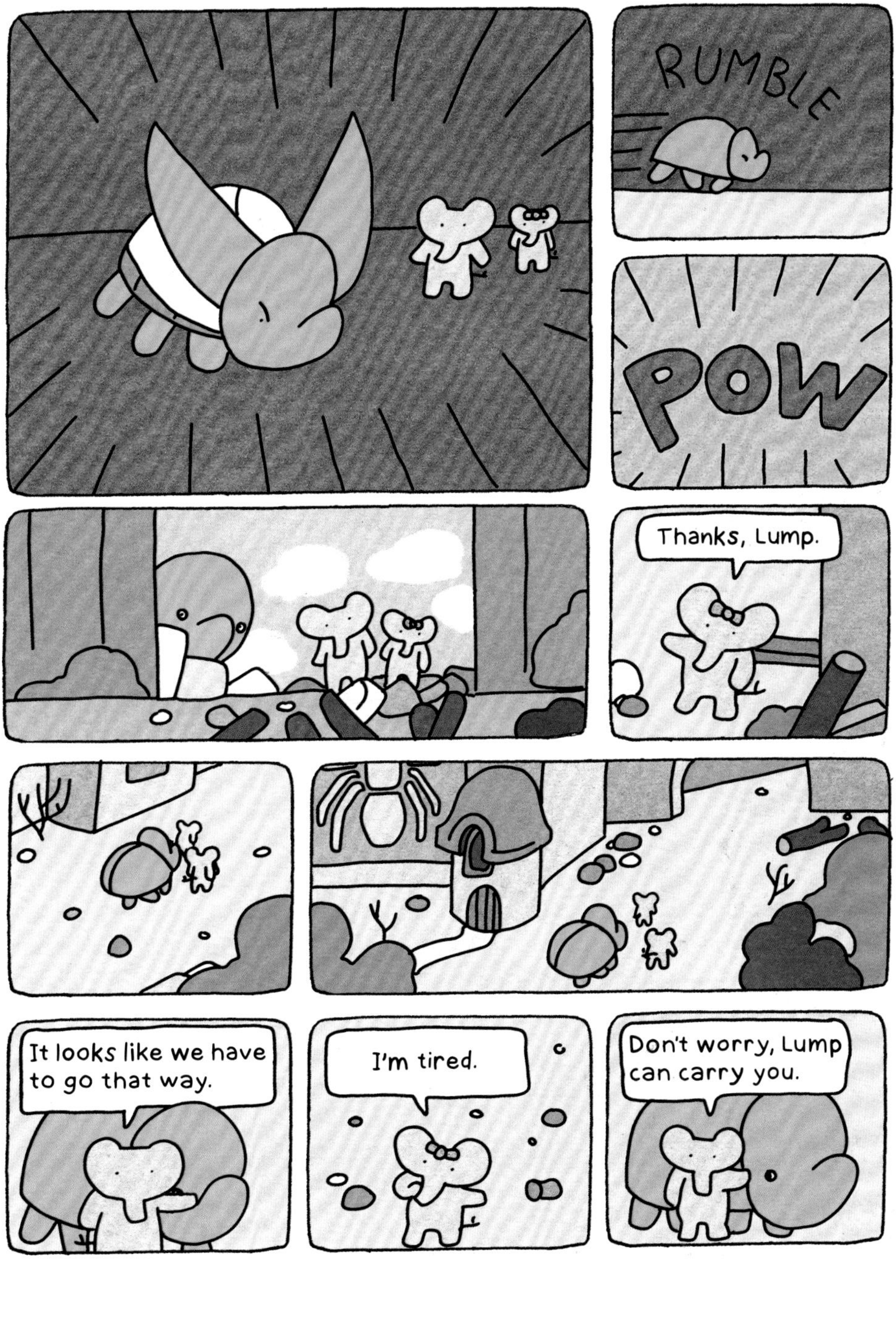
RUMBLE
POW
Thanks, Lump.
It looks like we have to go that way.
I'm tired.
Don't worry, Lump can carry you.

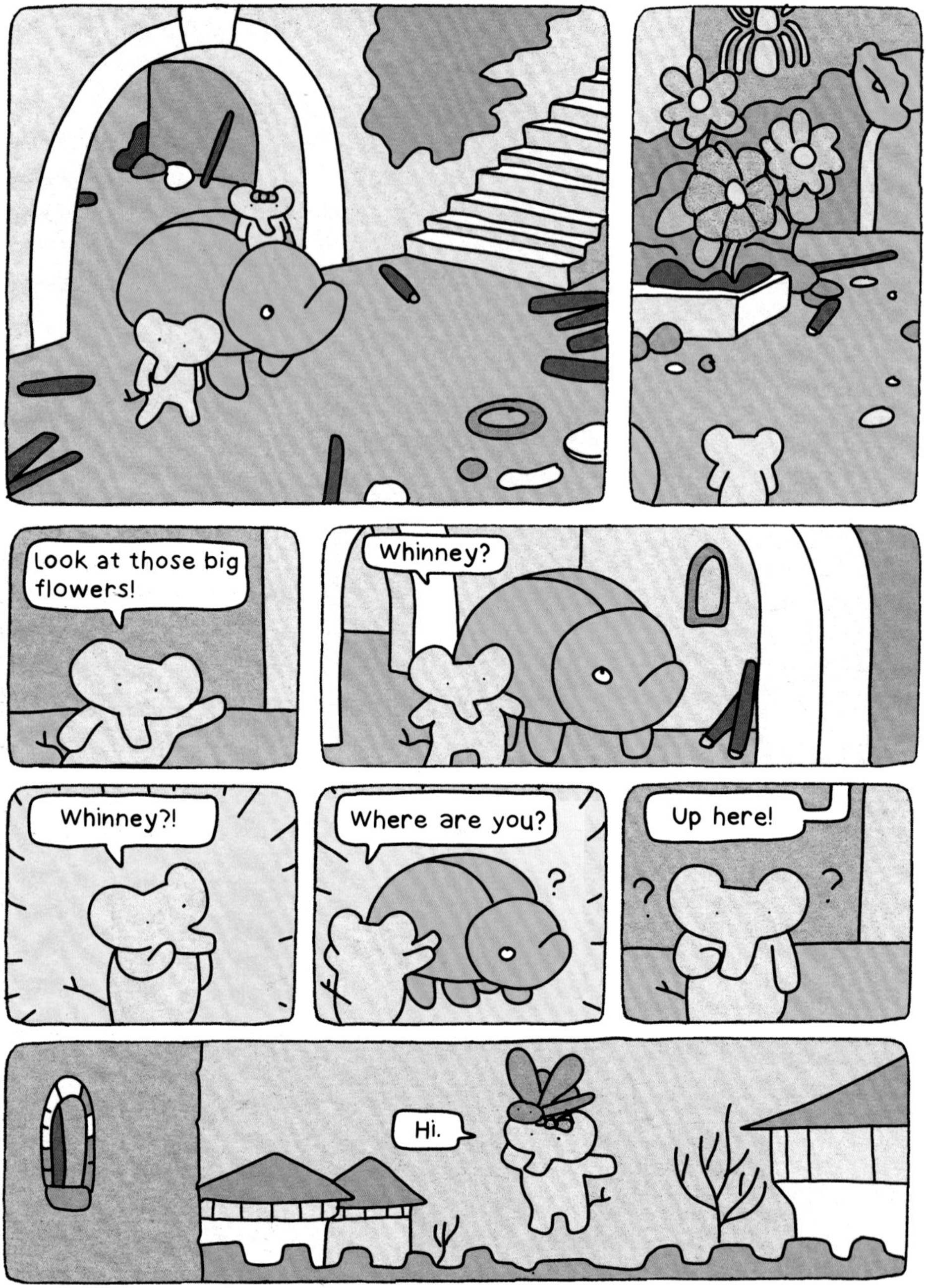
Look at those big flowers!
Whinney?
Whinney?!
Where are you?
?
? ?
Up here!
Hi.

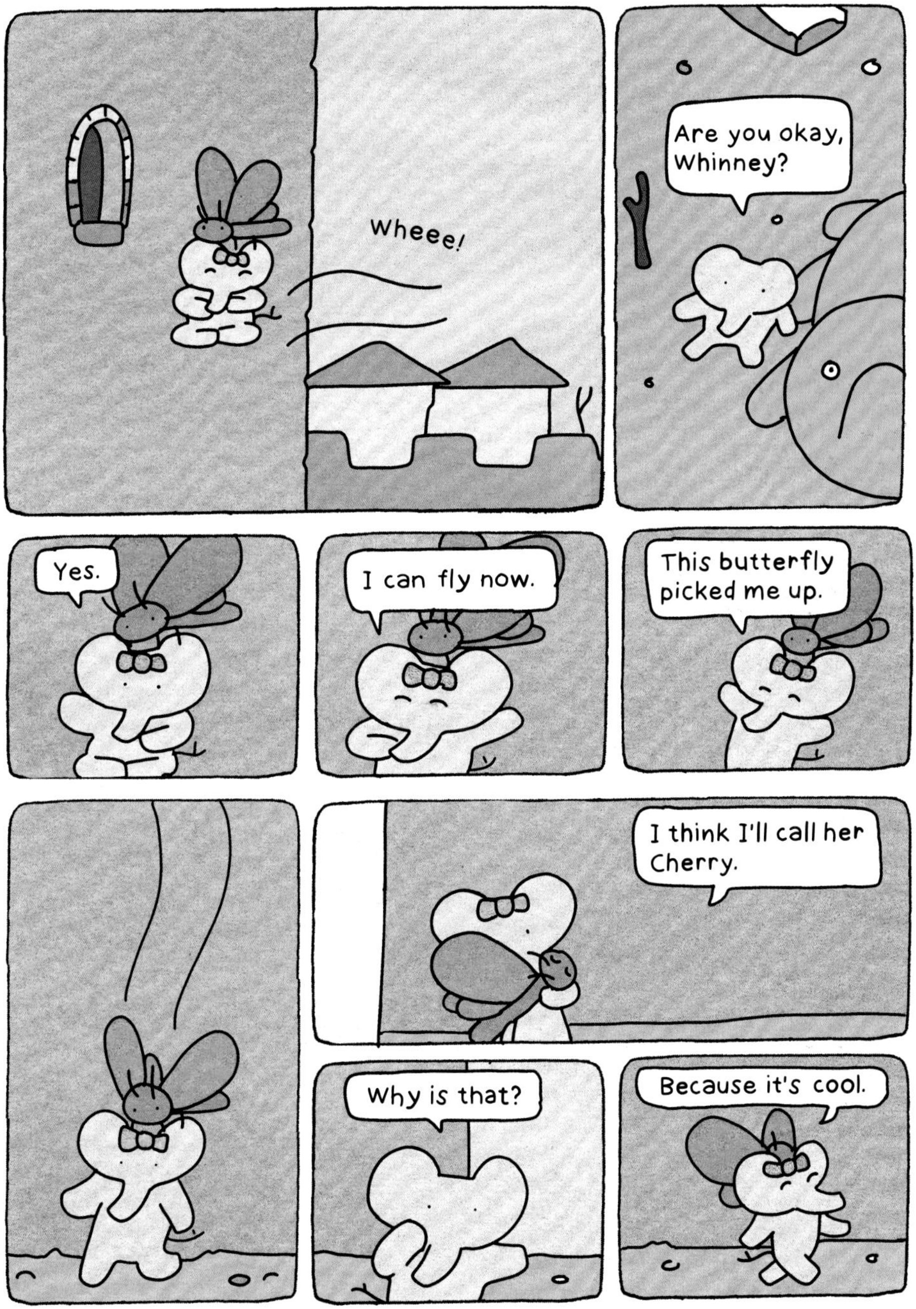
Wheee!
Are you okay, Whinney?
Yes.
I can fly now.
This butterfly picked me up.
I think I'll call her Cherry.
Why is that?
Because it's cool.

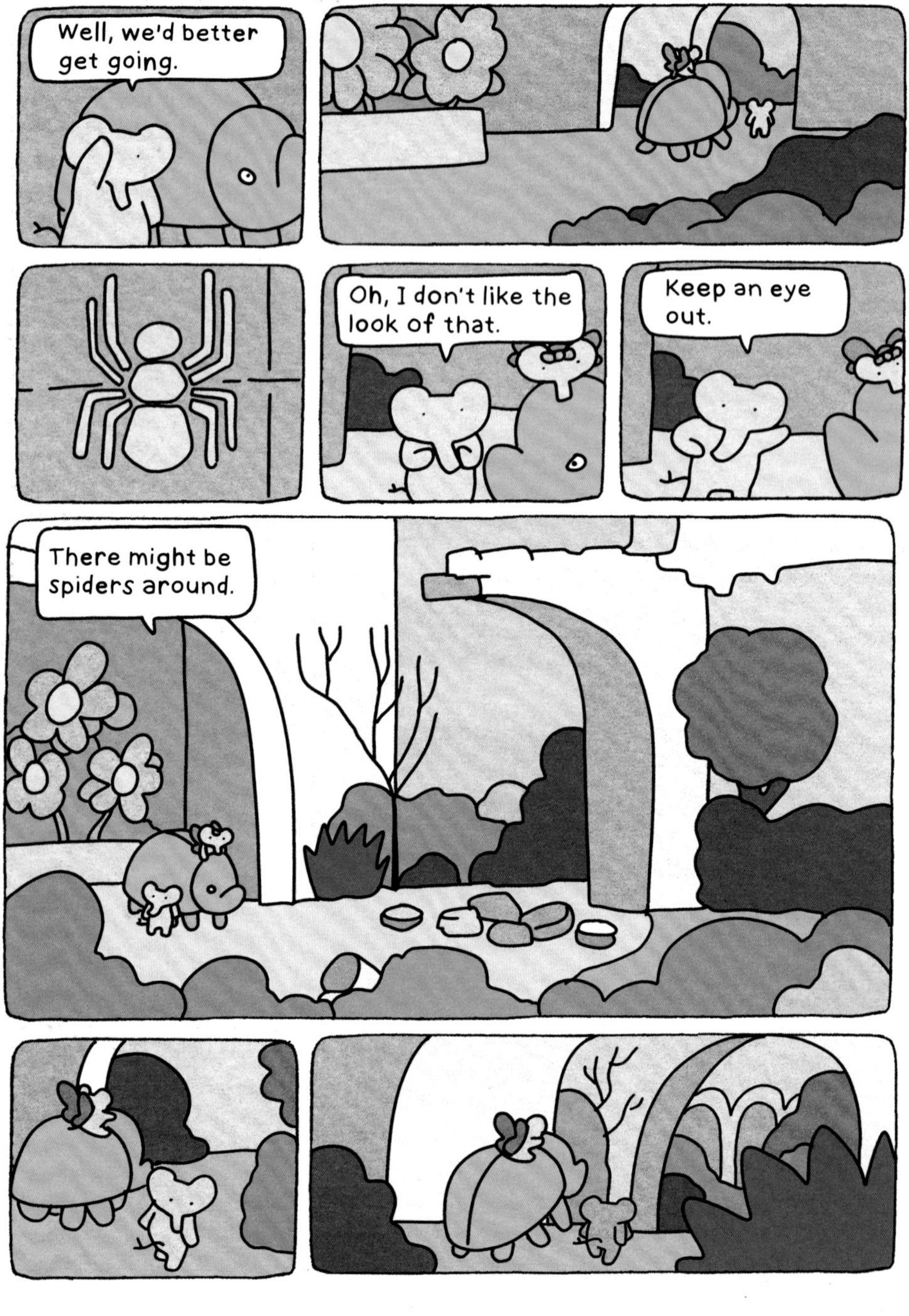
Well, we'd better get going.
Oh, I don't like the look of that.
Keep an eye out.
There might be spiders around.

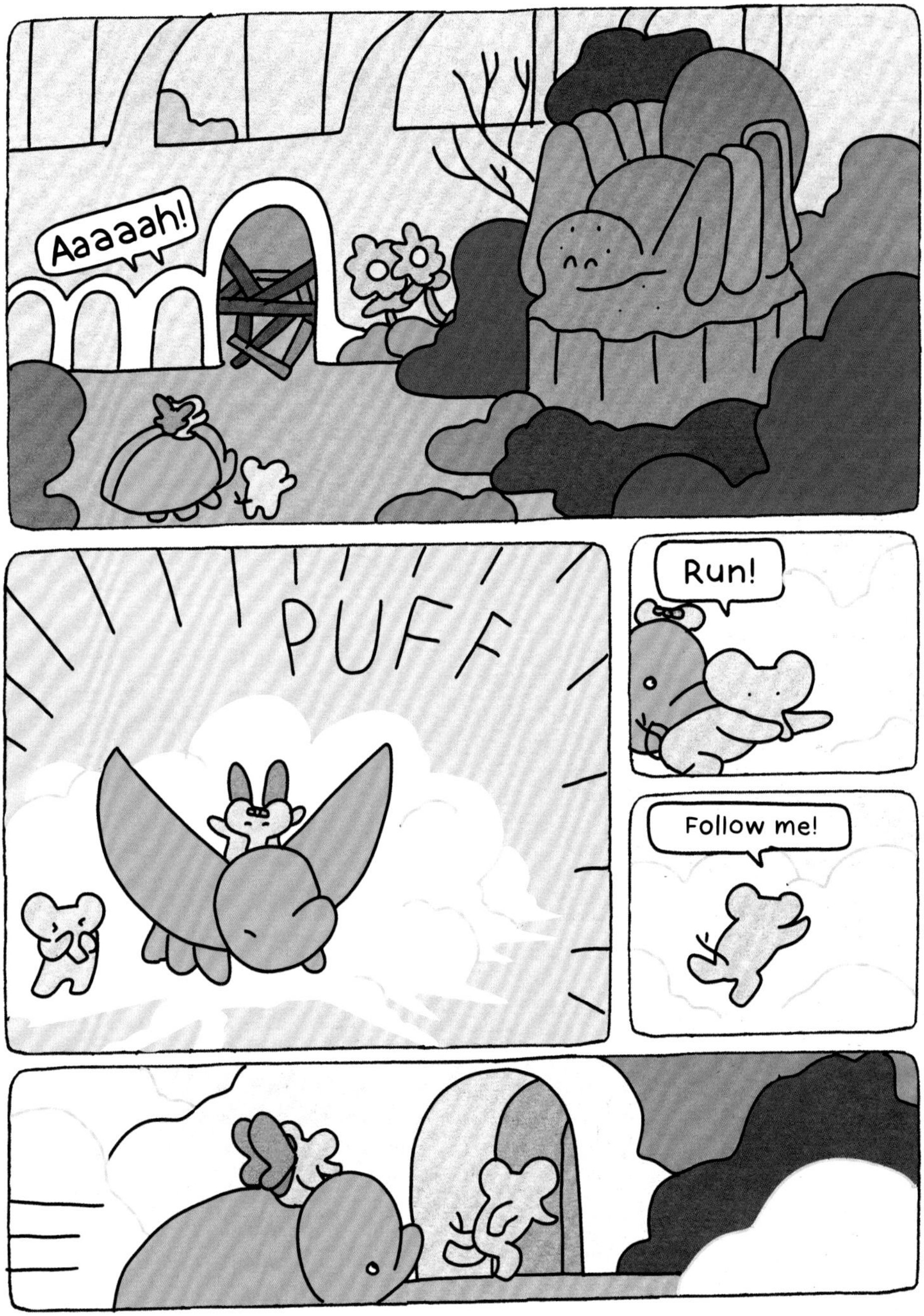
Aaaaah!
PUFF
Run!
Follow me!

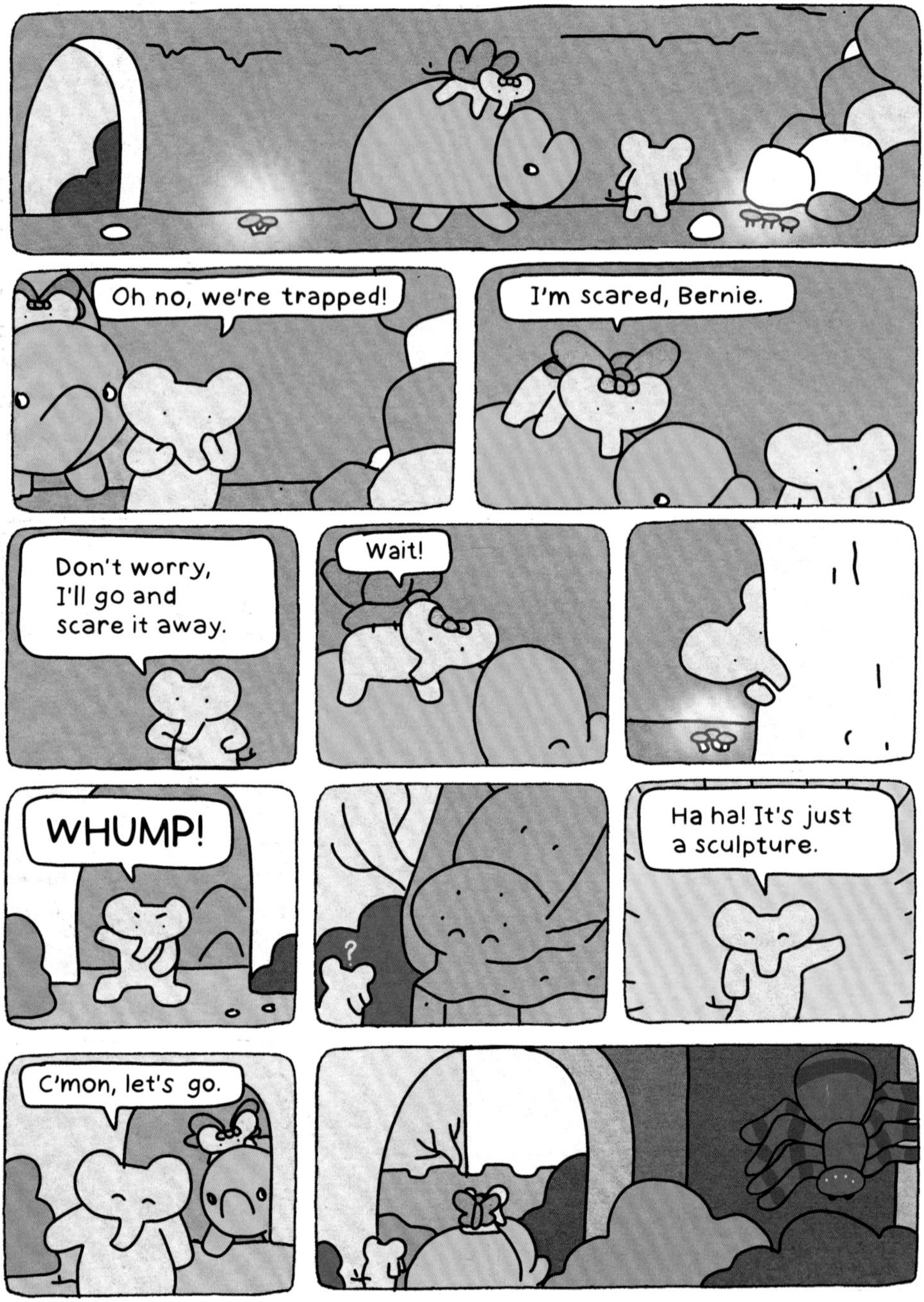
Oh no, we're trapped!
I'm scared, Bernie.
Don't worry, I'll go and scare it away.
Wait!
WHUMP!
Ha ha! It's just a sculpture.
C'mon, let's go.

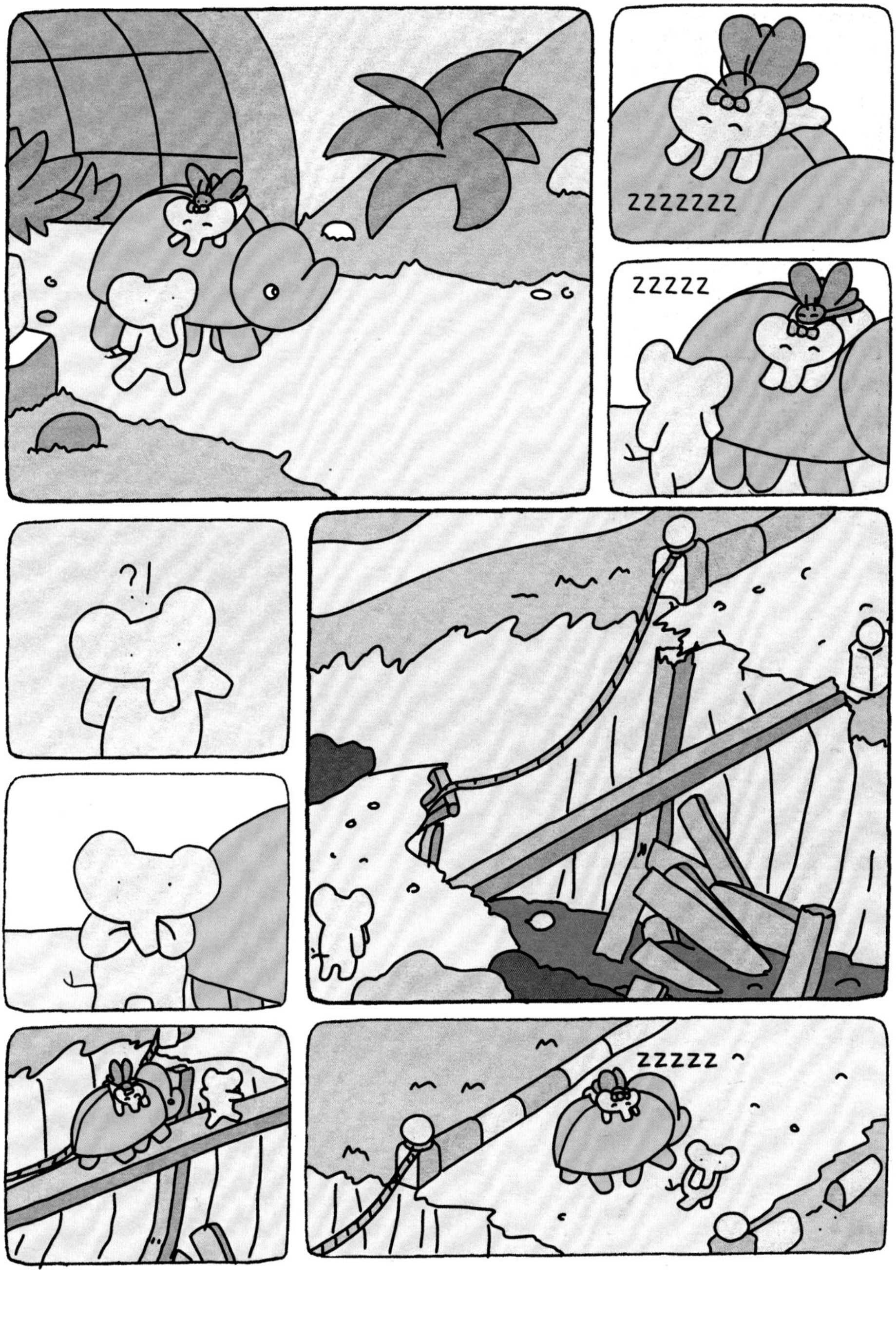
ZZZZZZZ
ZZZZZ
?!
ZZZZZ

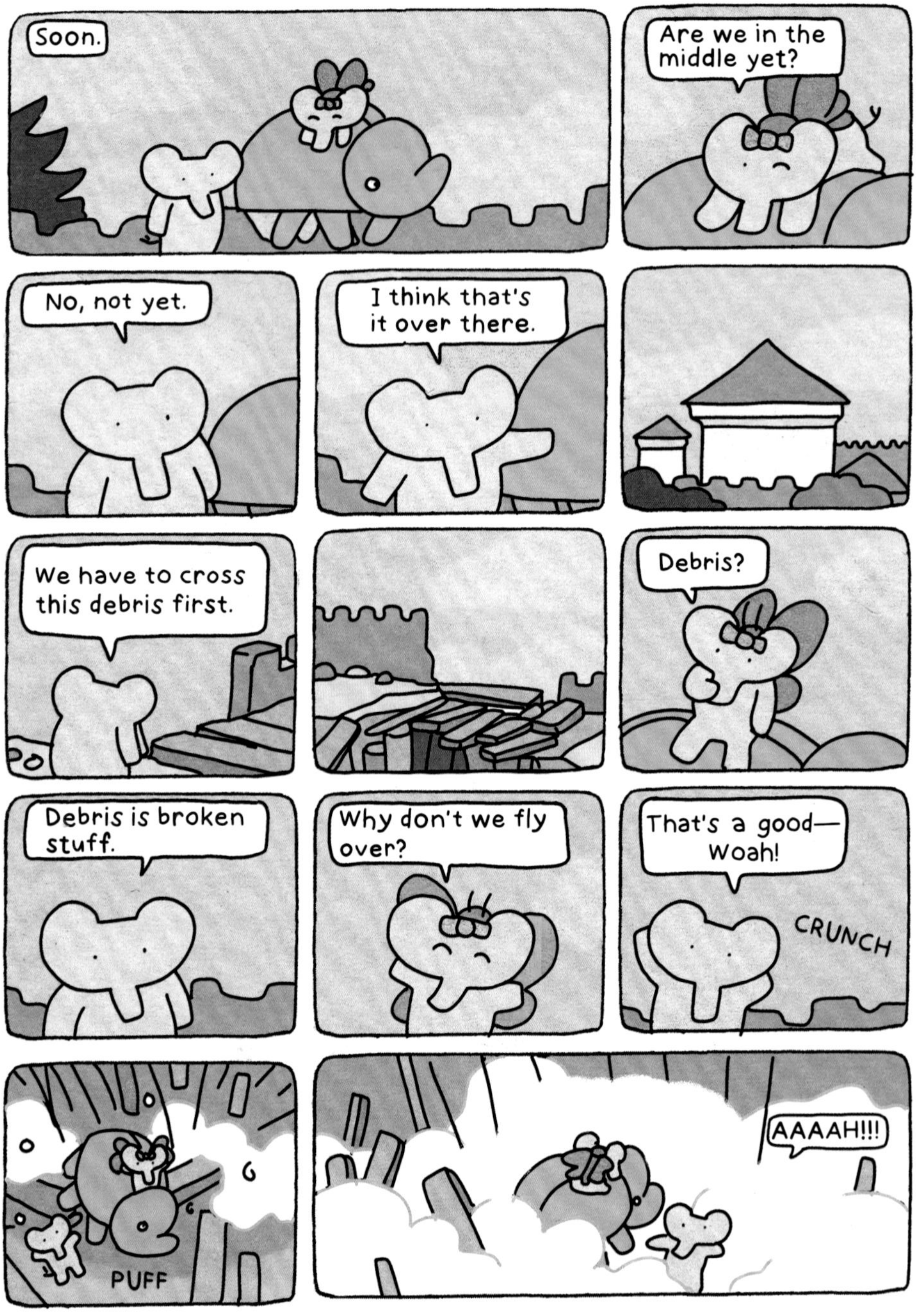
Soon.
Are we in the middle yet?
No, not yet.
I think that's it over there.
We have to cross this debris first.
Debris?
Debris is broken stuff.
Why don't we fly over?
That's a good— Woah!
CRUNCH
PUFF
AAAAH!!!

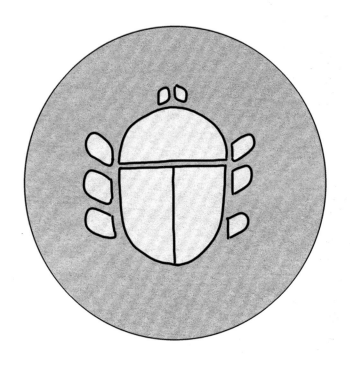

Chapter 9

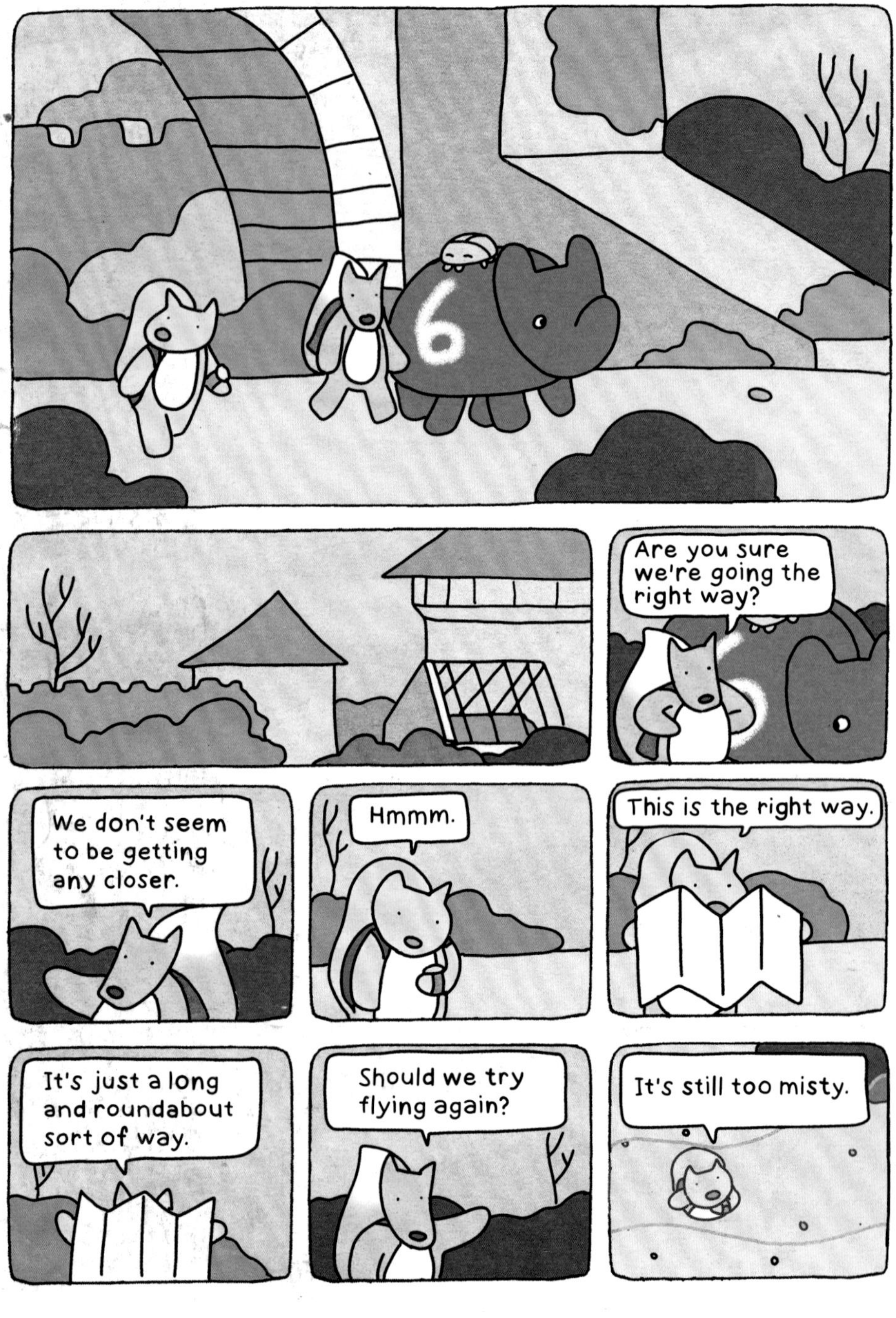
Are you sure we're going the right way?
We don't seem to be getting any closer.
Hmmm.
This is the right way.
It's just a long and roundabout sort of way.
Should we try flying again?
It's still too misty.

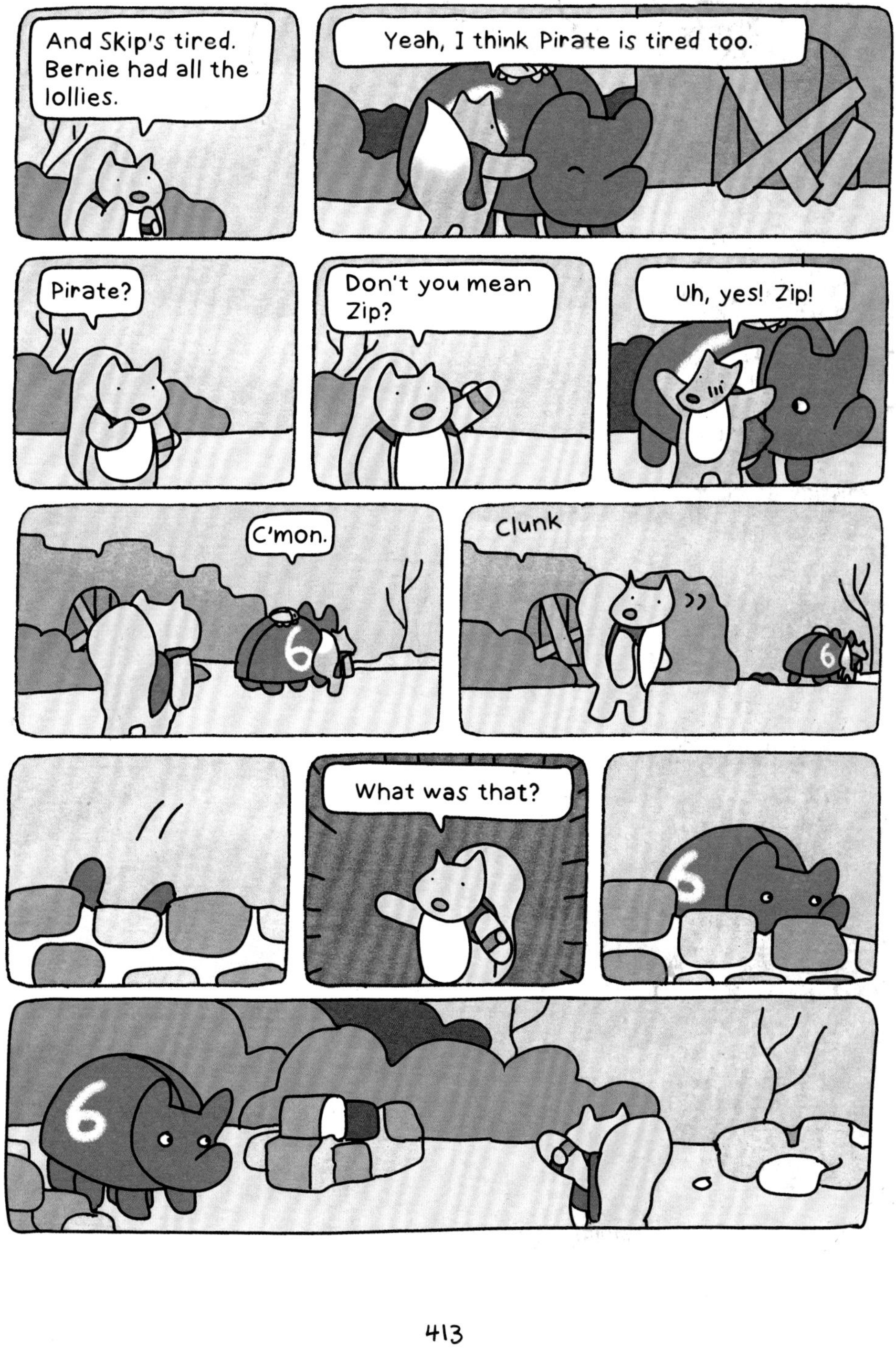
And Skip's tired. Bernie had all the lollies.
Yeah, I think Pirate is tired too.
Pirate?
Don't you mean Zip?
Uh, yes! Zip!
C'mon.
Clunk
What was that?

It's ANOTHER beetle!

Um...Anders?

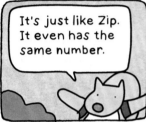

It's just like Zip. It even has the same number.

Um.

I have twin beetles.

This is Pirate.

And you've already met Zip.

I mixed up their names.

Hello, Pirate!

Ha, he can blow bubbles!

That's a cool power.

C'mon, let's go.

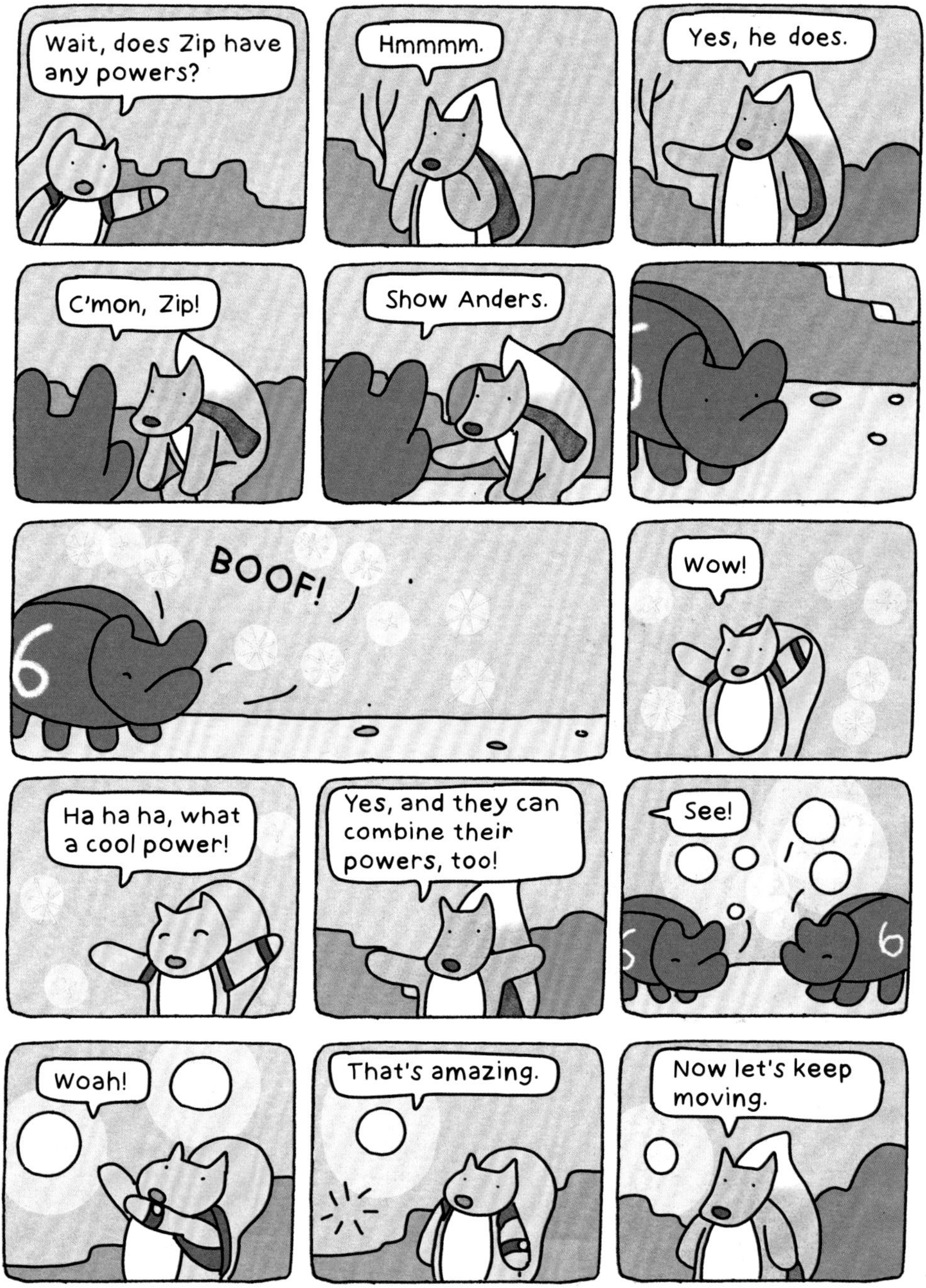

Wait, does Zip have any powers?
Hmmmm.
Yes, he does.
C'mon, Zip!
Show Anders.
BOOF!
Wow!
Ha ha ha, what a cool power!
Yes, and they can combine their powers, too!
See!
Woah!
That's amazing.
Now let's keep moving.

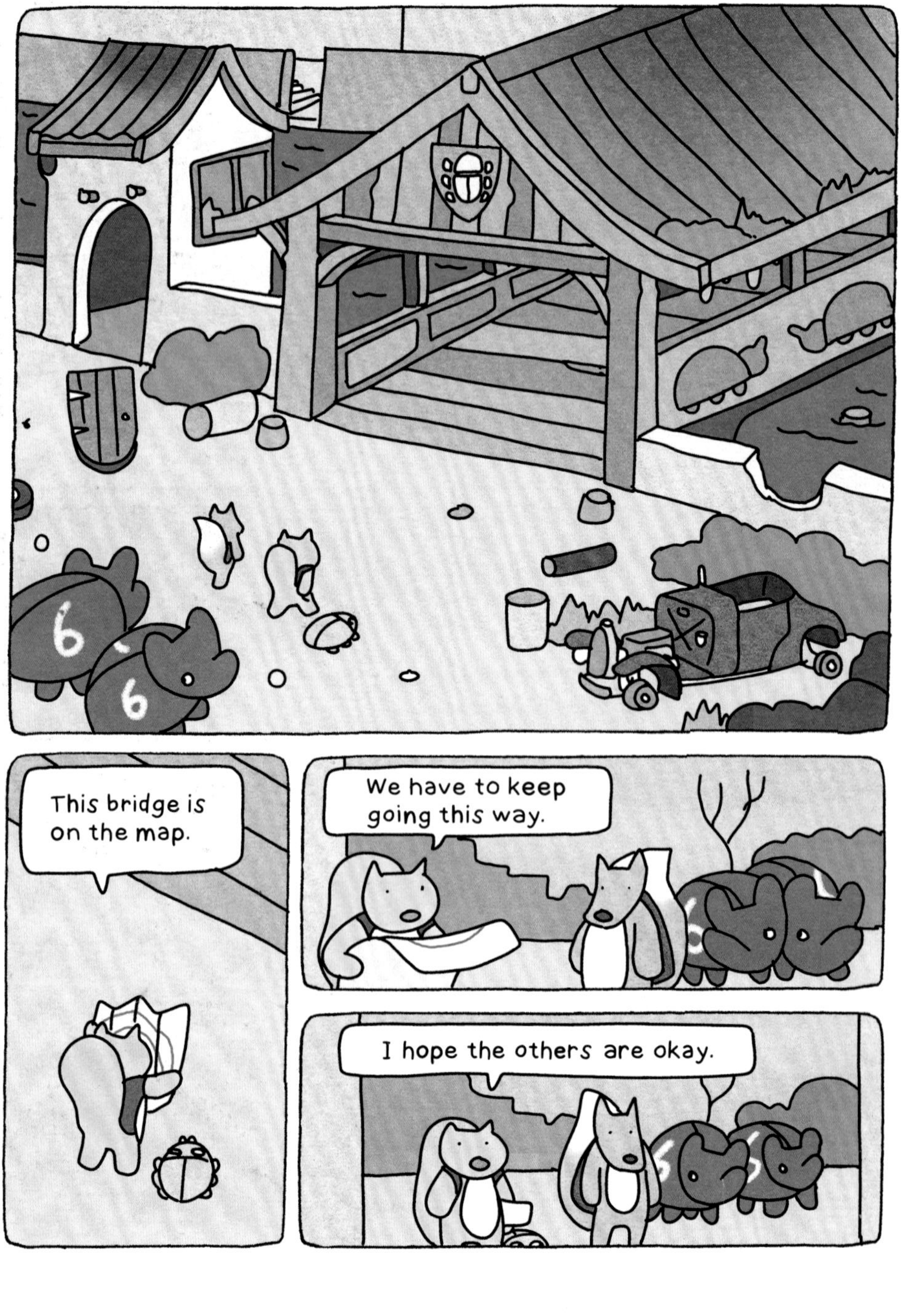
This bridge is on the map.
We have to keep going this way.
I hope the others are okay.

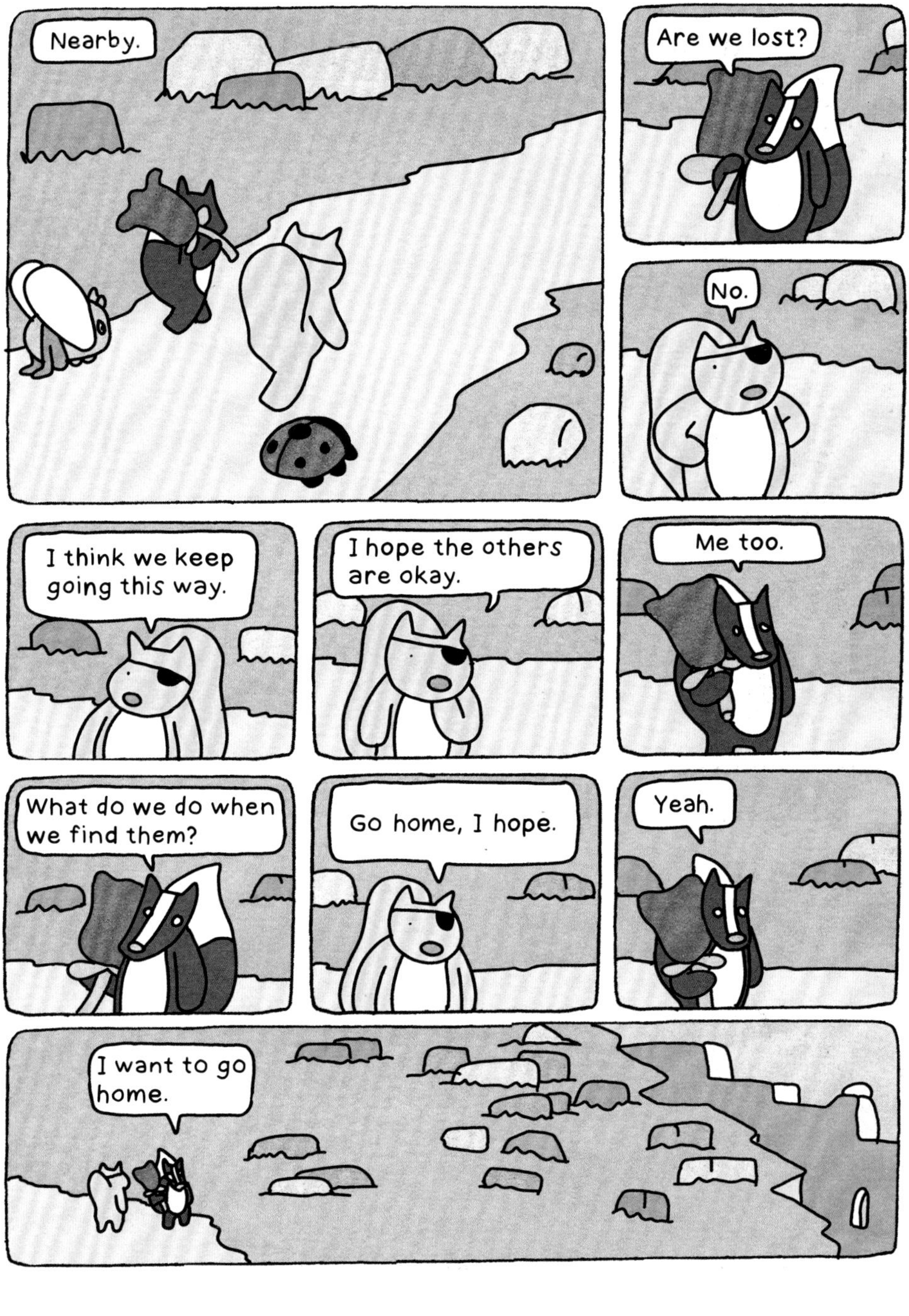
Nearby.
Are we lost?
No.
I think we keep going this way.
I hope the others are okay.
Me too.
What do we do when we find them?
Go home, I hope.
Yeah.
I want to go home.

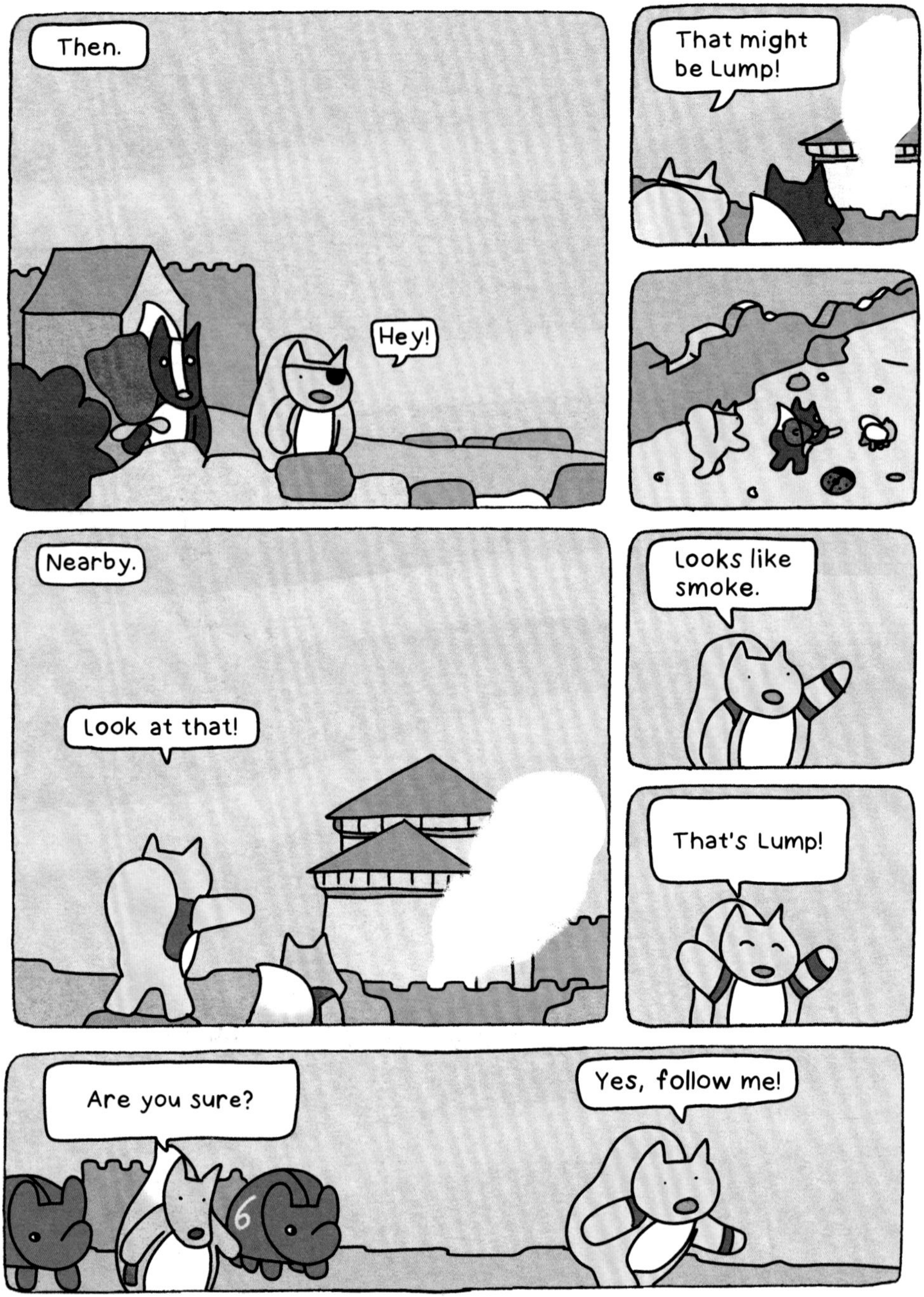
Then.
Hey!
That might be Lump!
Nearby.
Look at that!
Looks like smoke.
That's Lump!
Are you sure?
Yes, follow me!

Chapter 10

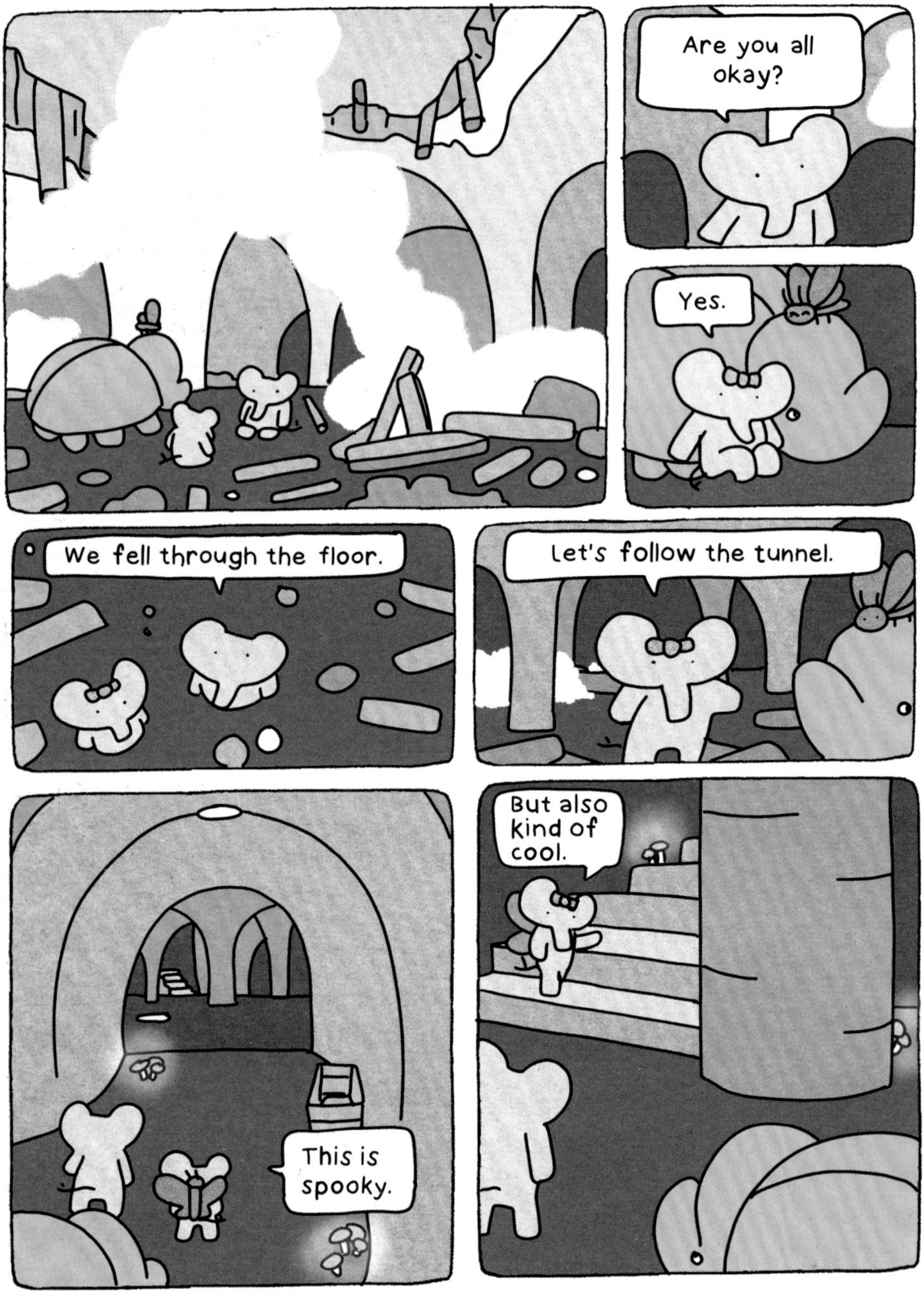
Are you all okay?
Yes.
We fell through the floor.
Let's follow the tunnel.
This is spooky.
But also kind of cool.

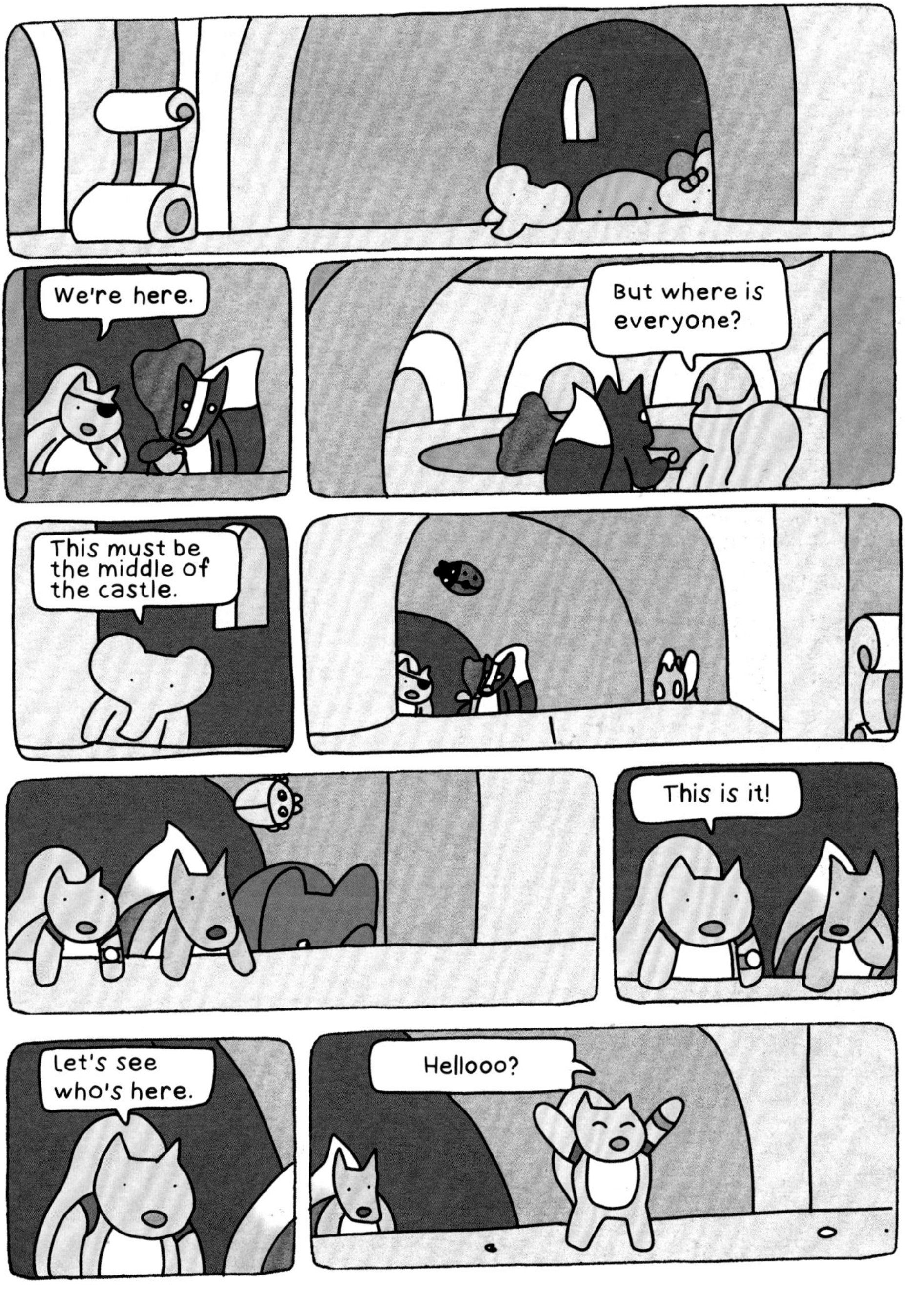
We're here.
But where is everyone?
This must be the middle of the castle.
This is it!
Let's see who's here.
Hellooo?

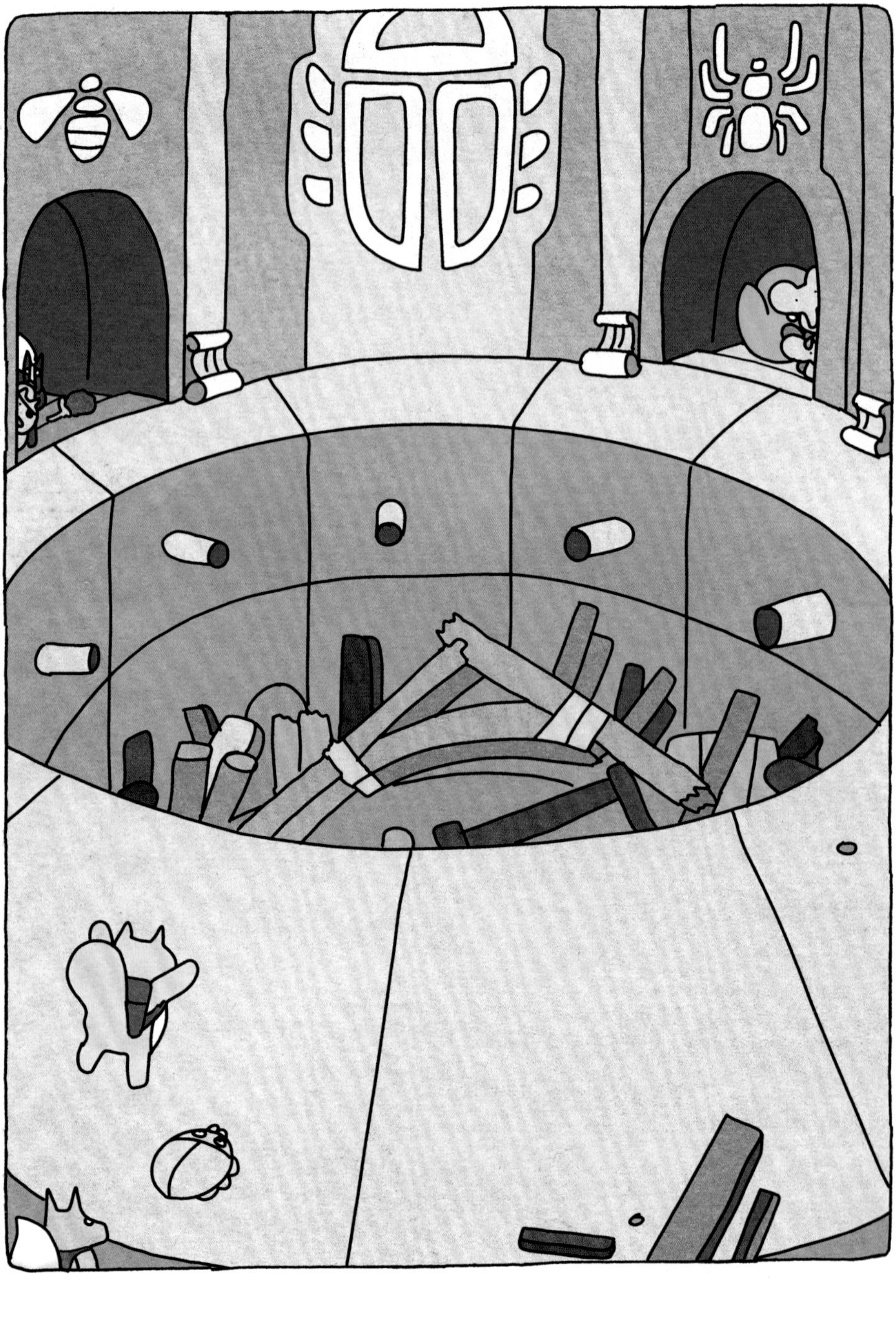

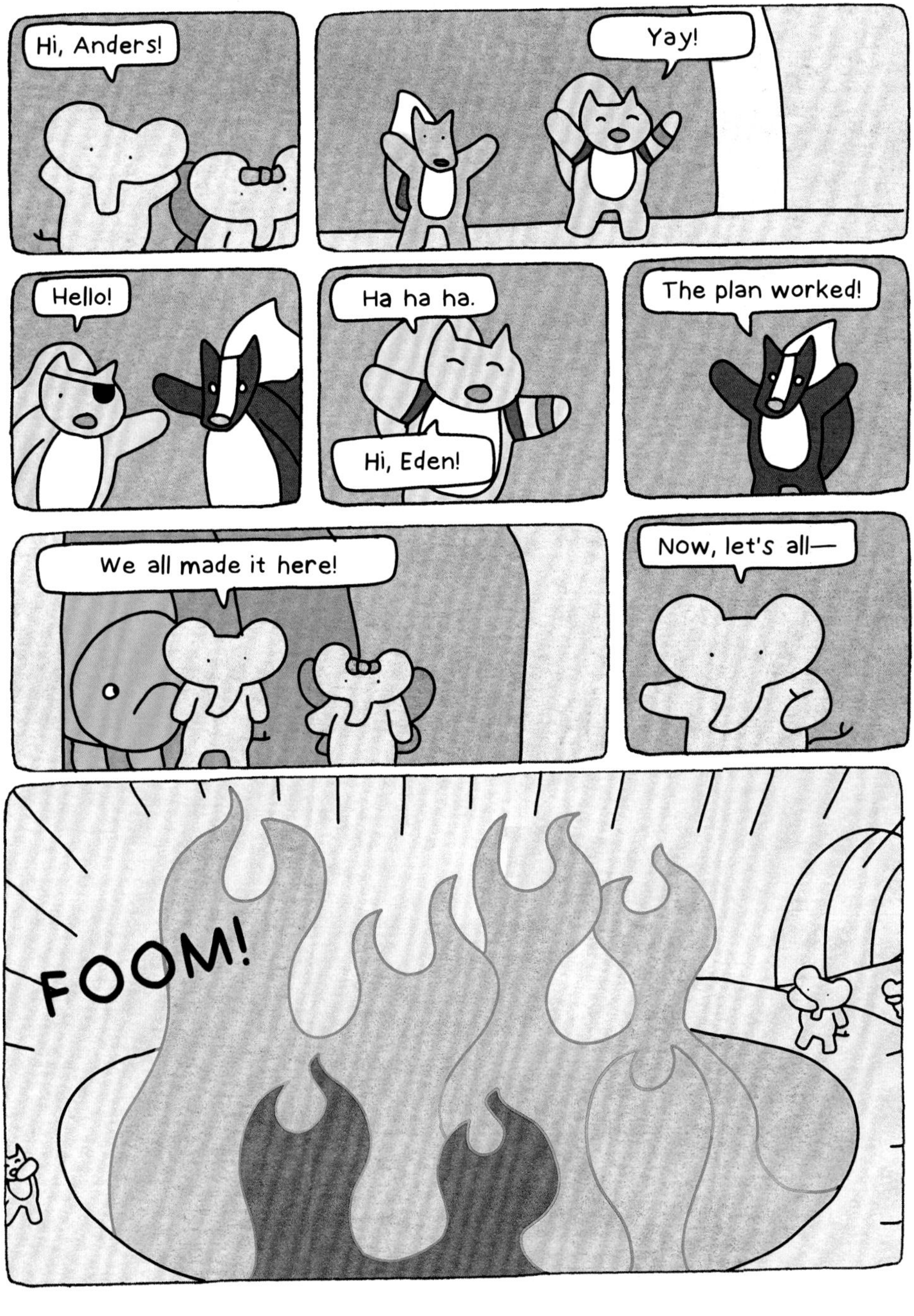
Hi, Anders!
Yay!
Hello!
Ha ha ha.
Hi, Eden!
The plan worked!
We all made it here!
Now, let's all—
FOOM!

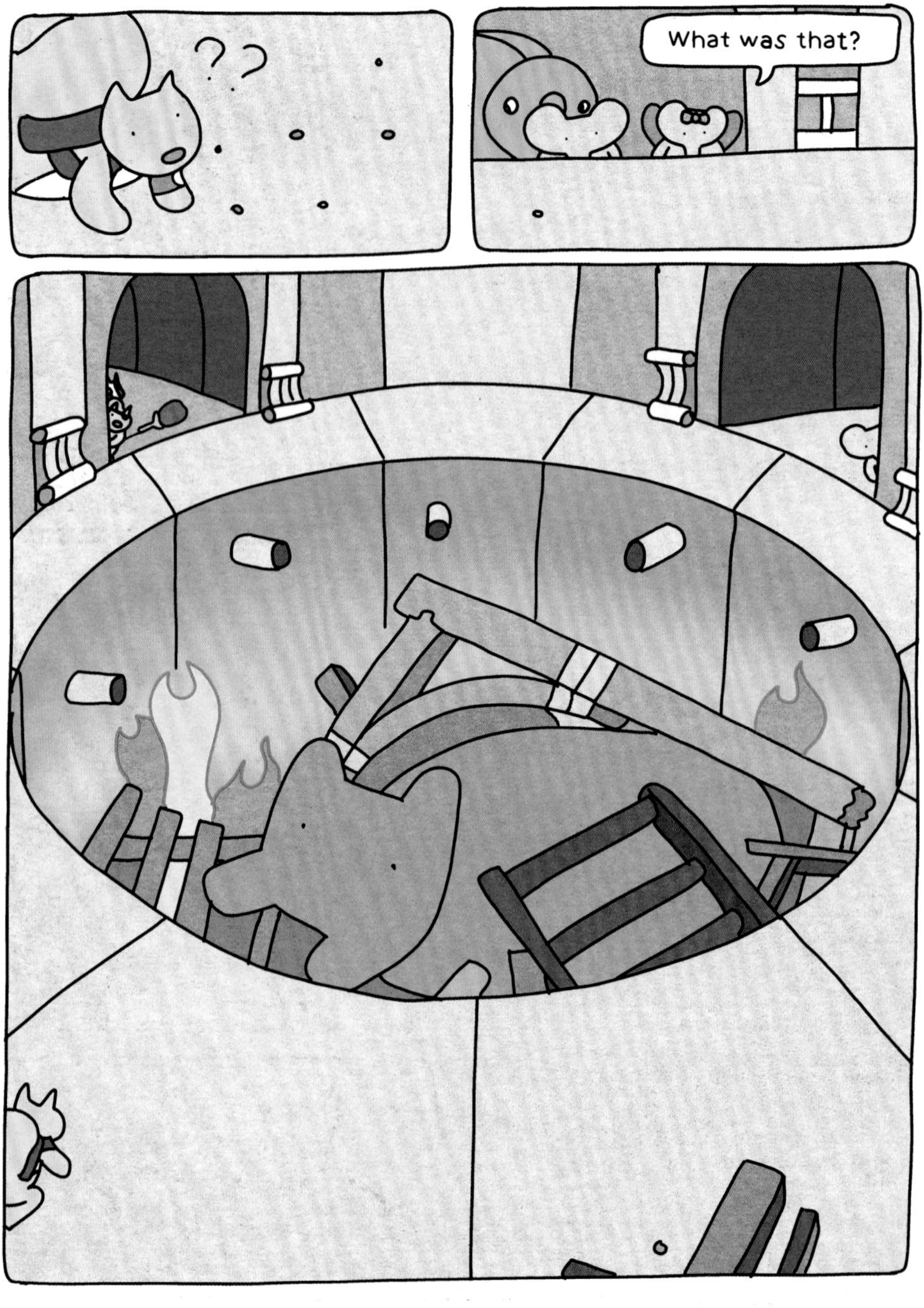
??
What was that?

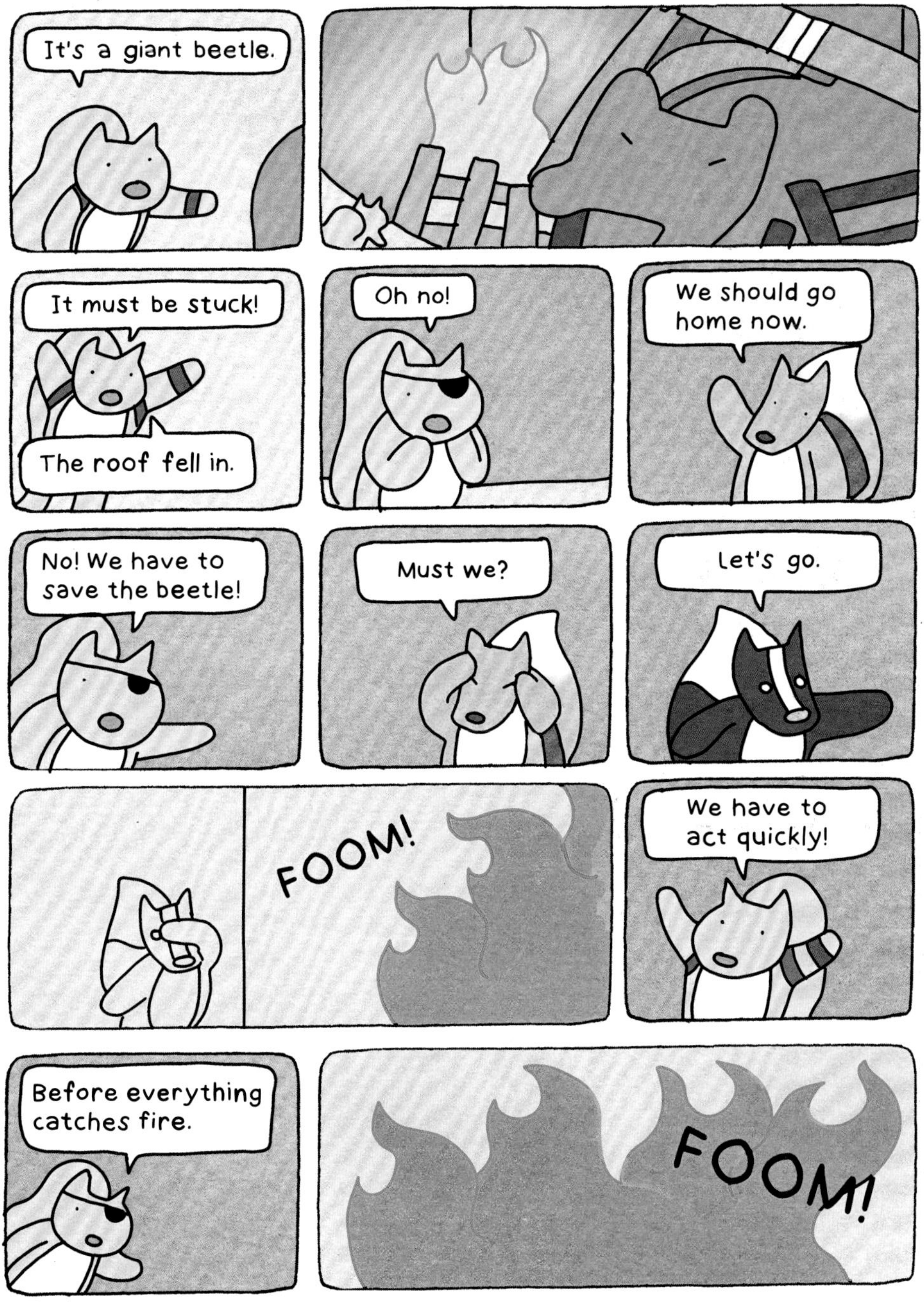
It's a giant beetle.
It must be stuck!
The roof fell in.
Oh no!
We should go home now.
No! We have to save the beetle!
Must we?
Let's go.
FOOM!
We have to act quickly!
Before everything catches fire.
FOOM!

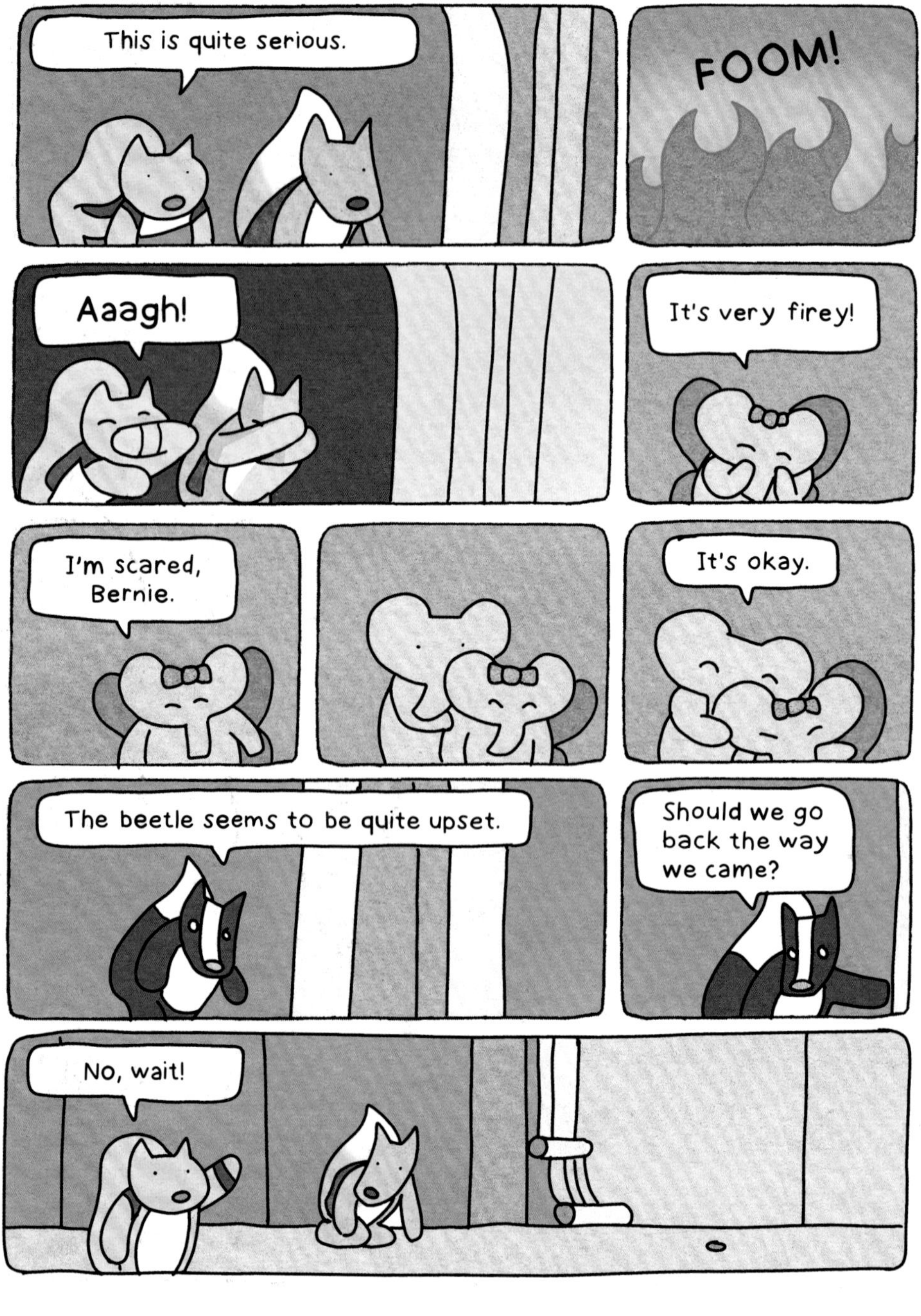
This is quite serious.
FOOM!
Aaagh!
It's very firey!
I'm scared, Bernie.
It's okay.
The beetle seems to be quite upset.
Should we go back the way we came?
No, wait!

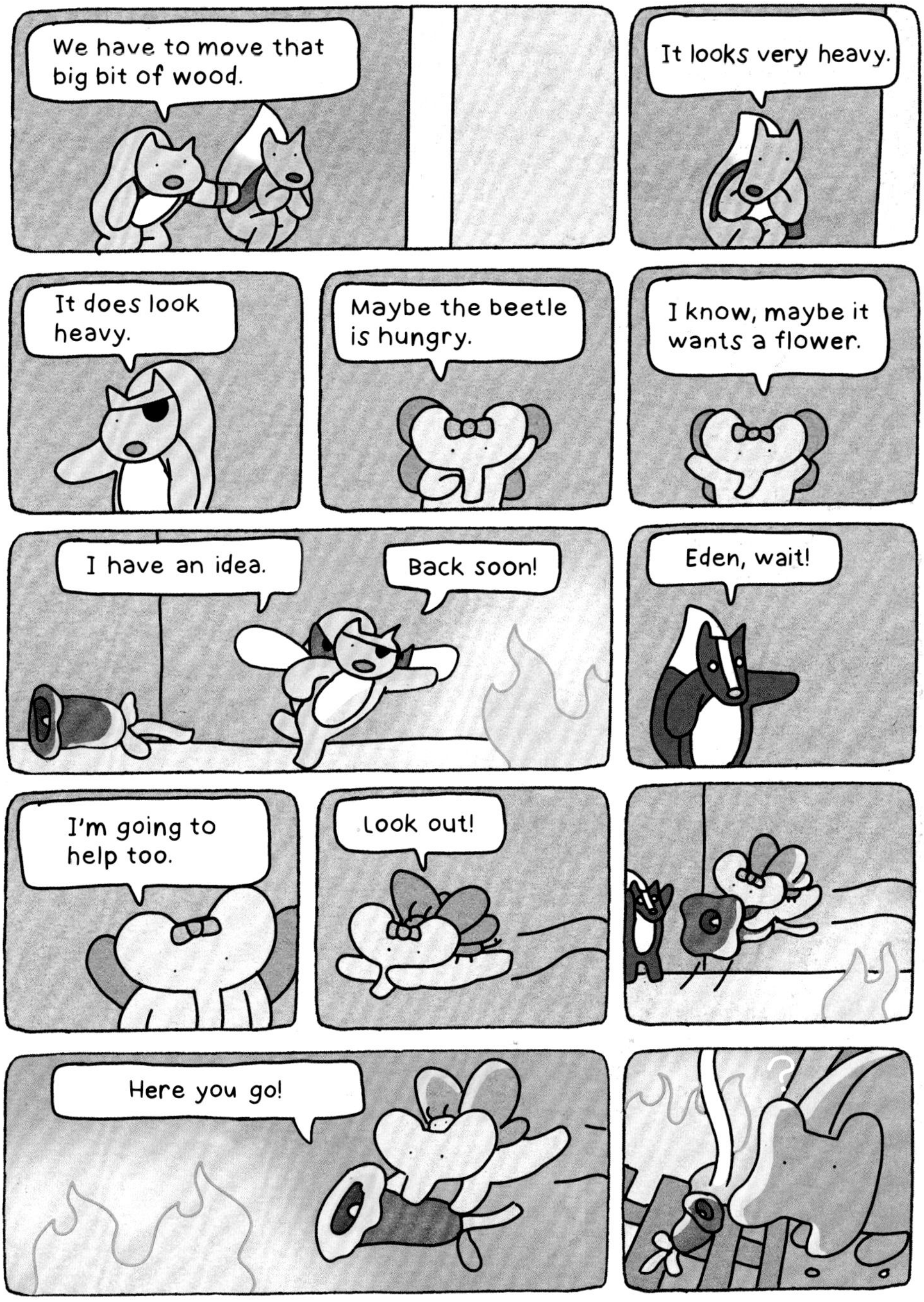
We have to move that big bit of wood.
It looks very heavy.
It does look heavy.
Maybe the beetle is hungry.
I know, maybe it wants a flower.
I have an idea.
Back soon!
Eden, wait!
I'm going to help too.
Look out!
Here you go!

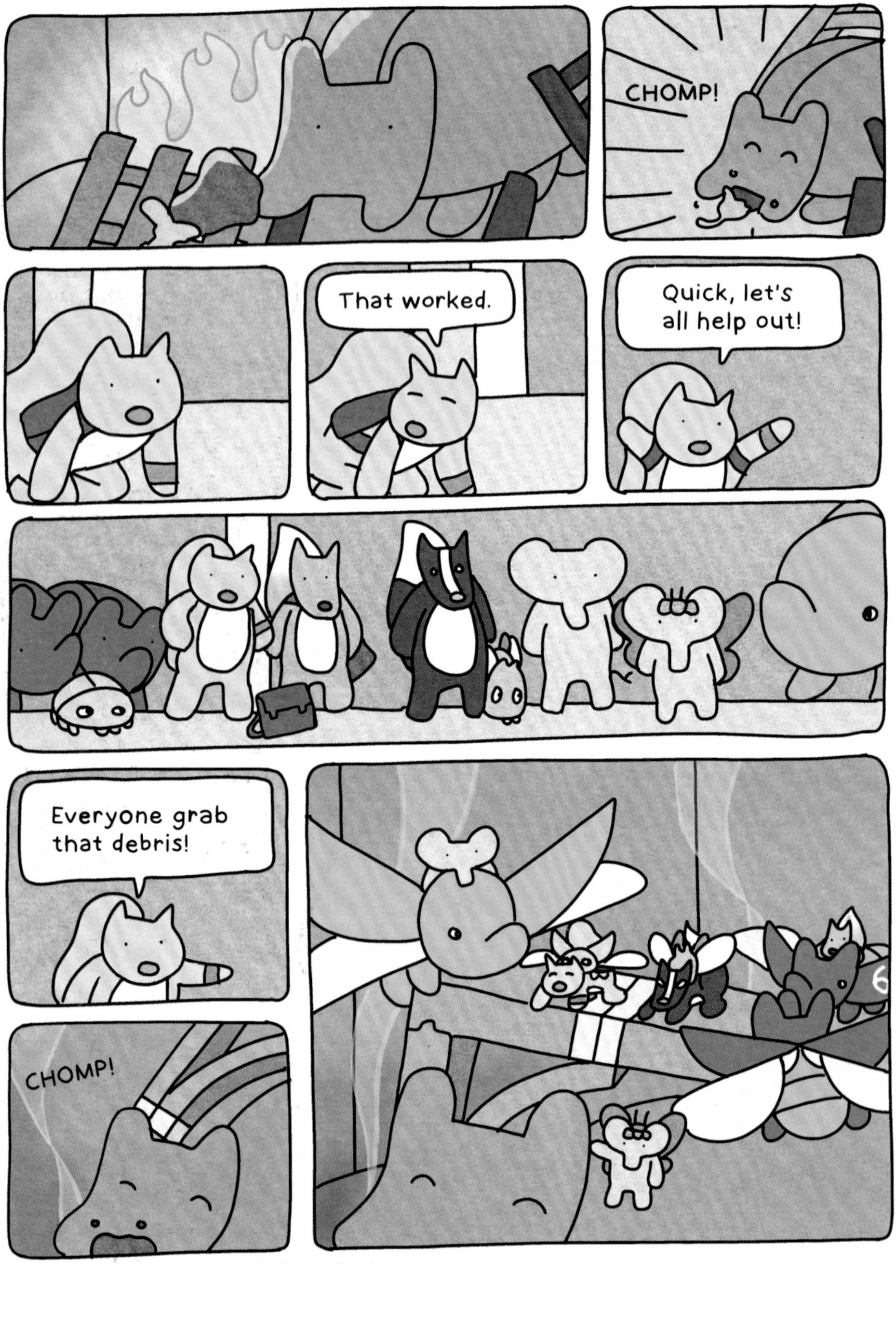
CHOMP!
That worked.
Quick, let's all help out!
Everyone grab that debris!
CHOMP!

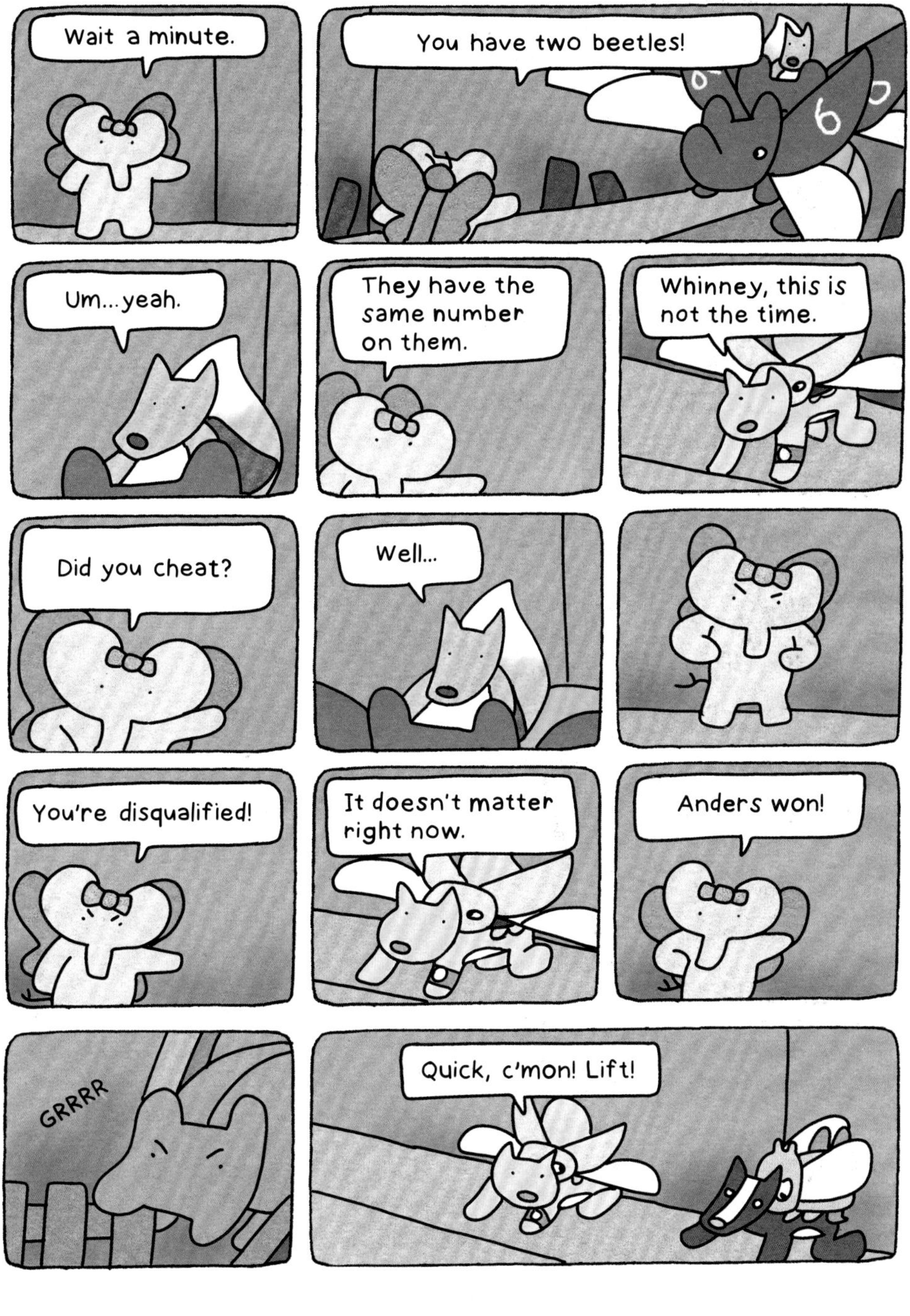
Wait a minute.
You have two beetles!
6
Um...yeah.
They have the same number on them.
Whinney, this is not the time.
Did you cheat?
Well...
You're disqualified!
It doesn't matter right now.
Anders won!
GRRRR
Quick, c'mon! Lift!

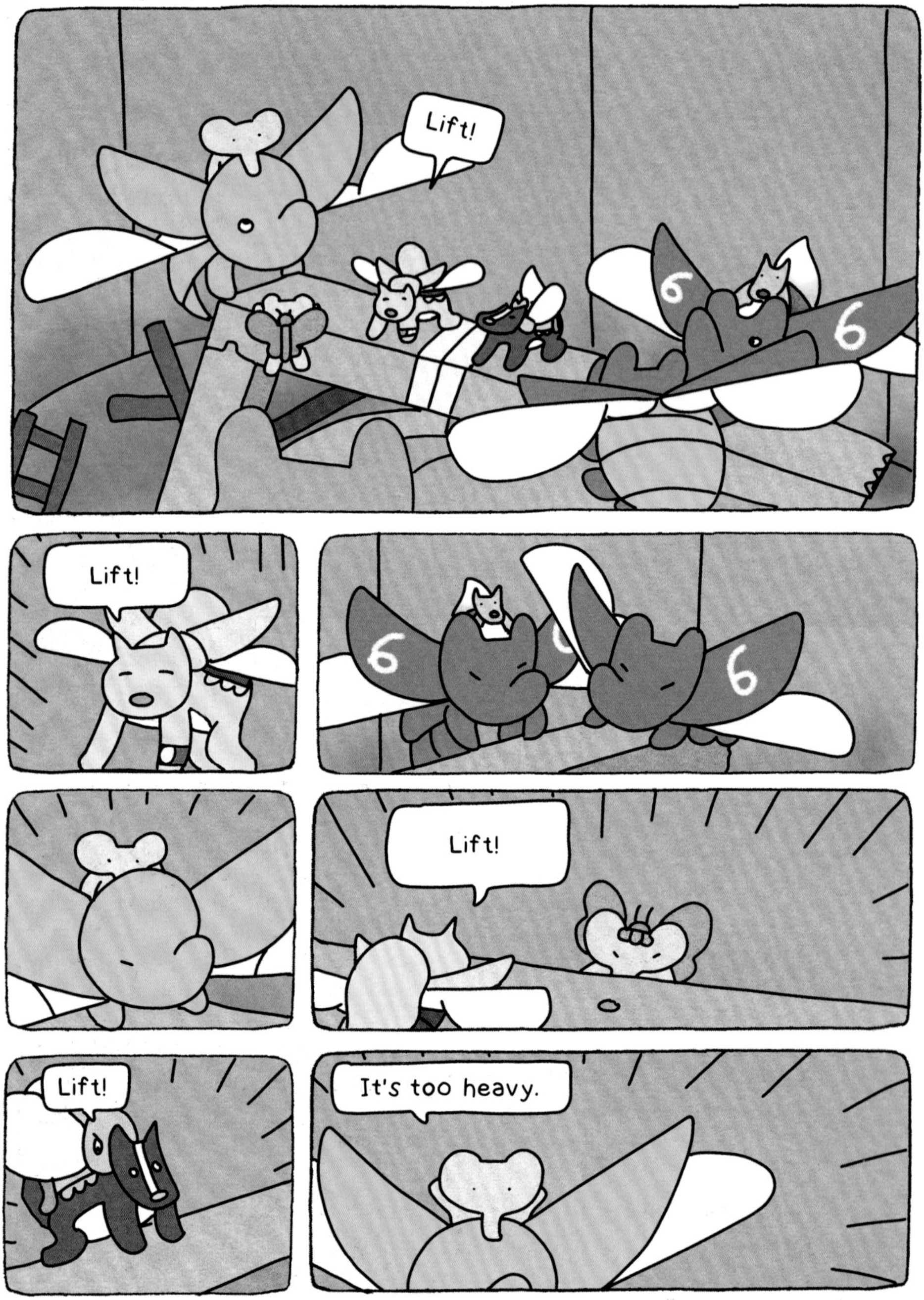
Lift!
Lift!
Lift!
Lift!
It's too heavy.

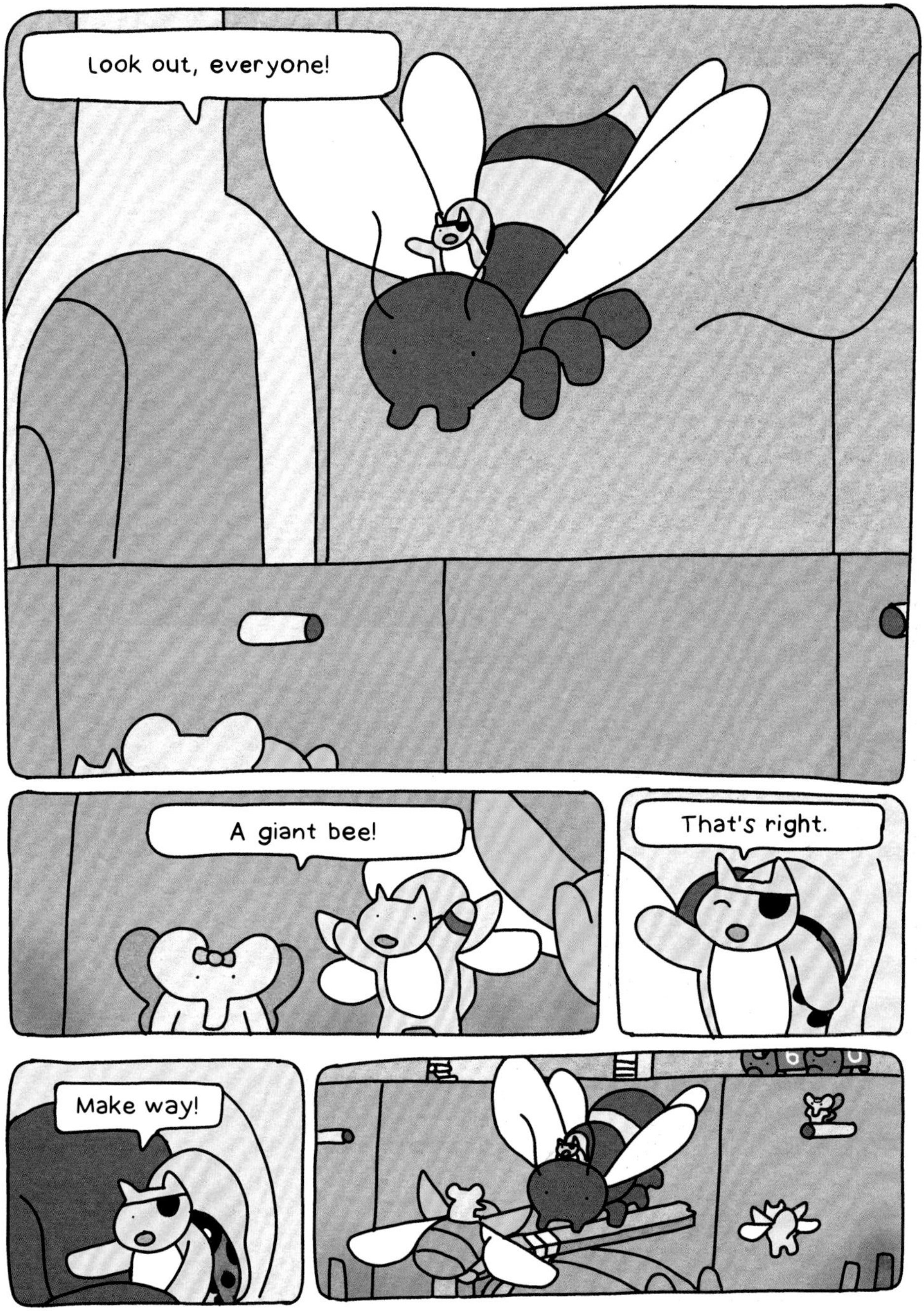
Look out, everyone!
A giant bee!
That's right.
Make way!

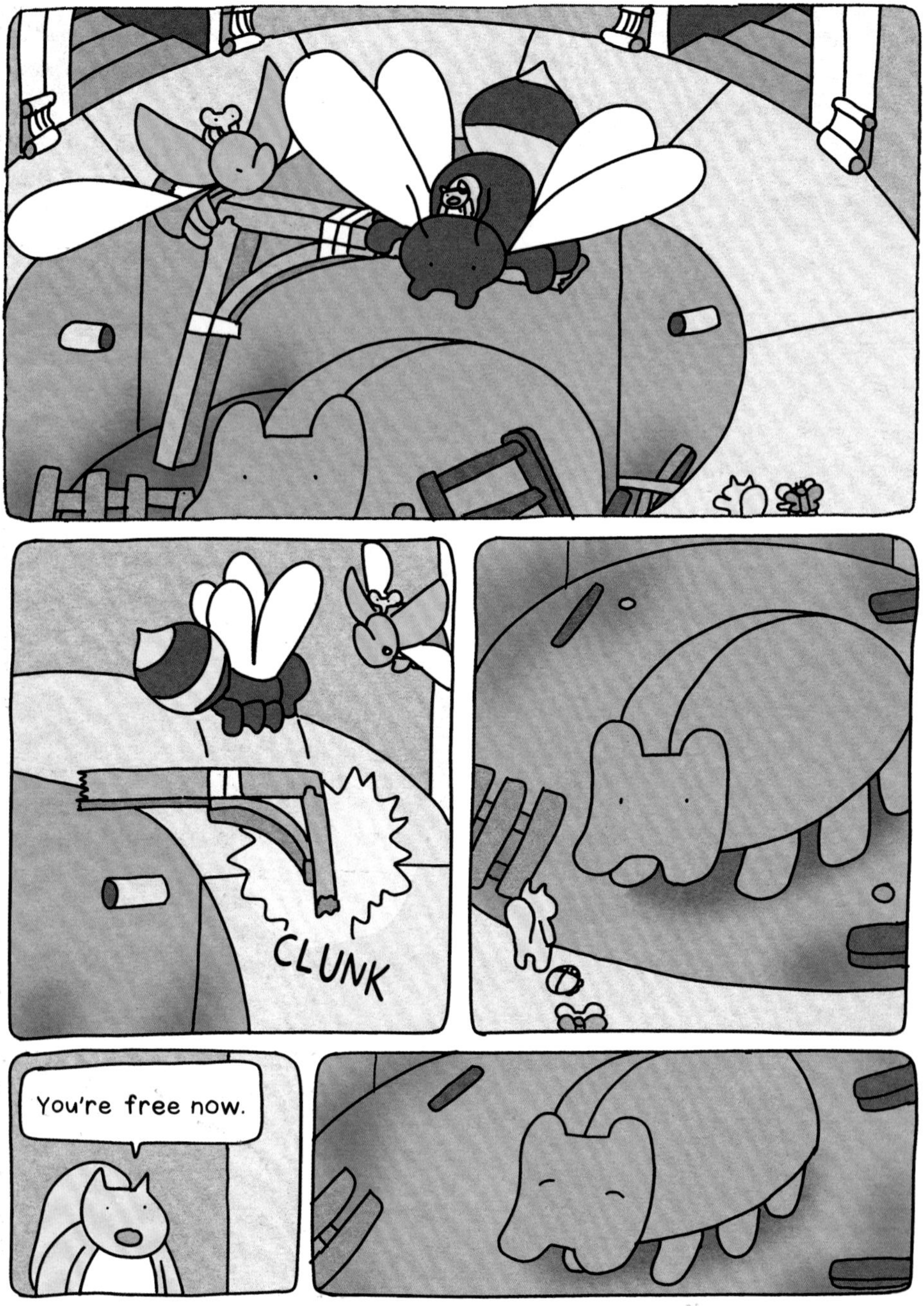
CLUNK
You're free now.

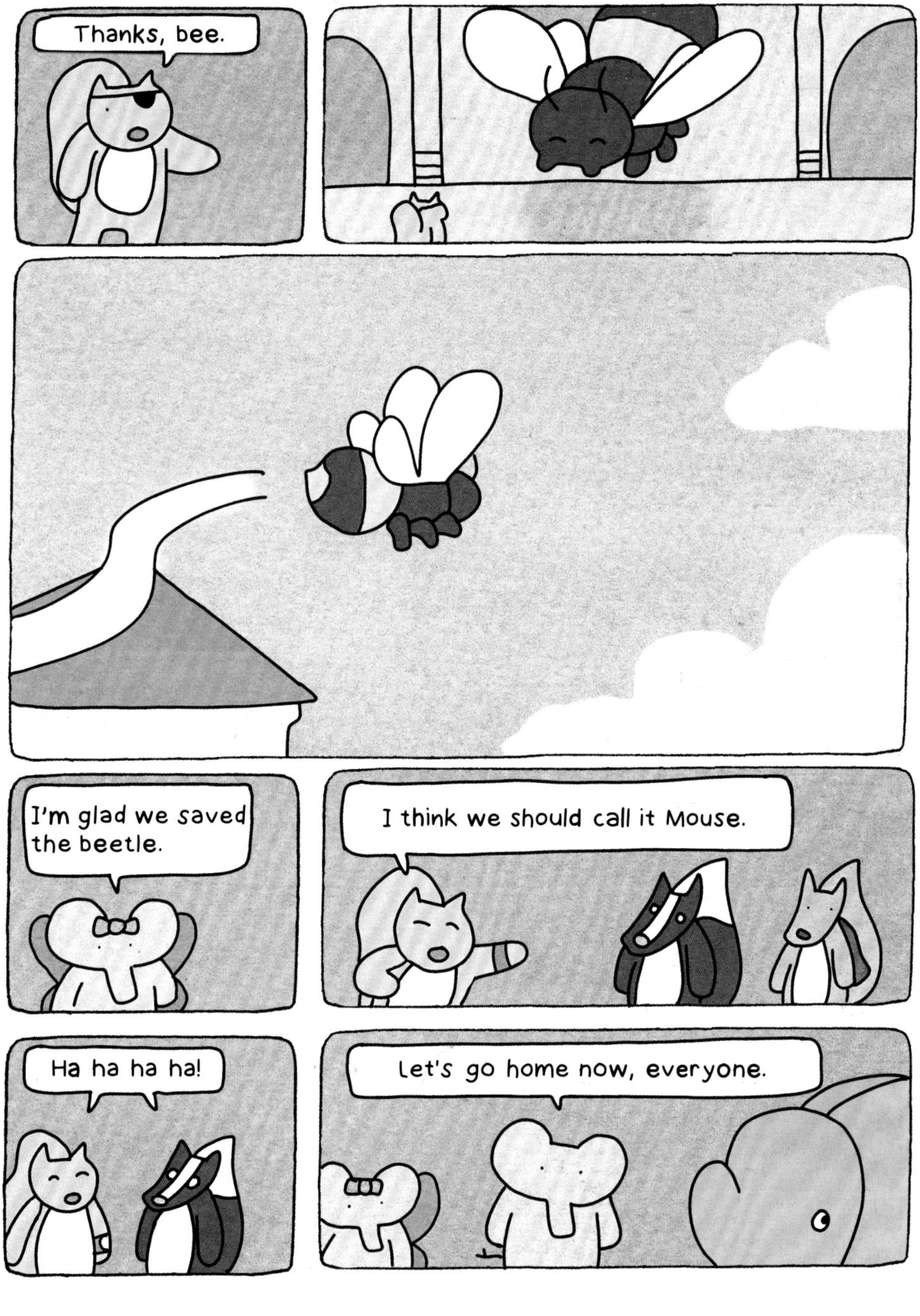
Thanks, bee.
I'm glad we saved the beetle.
I think we should call it Mouse.
Ha ha ha ha!
Let's go home now, everyone.

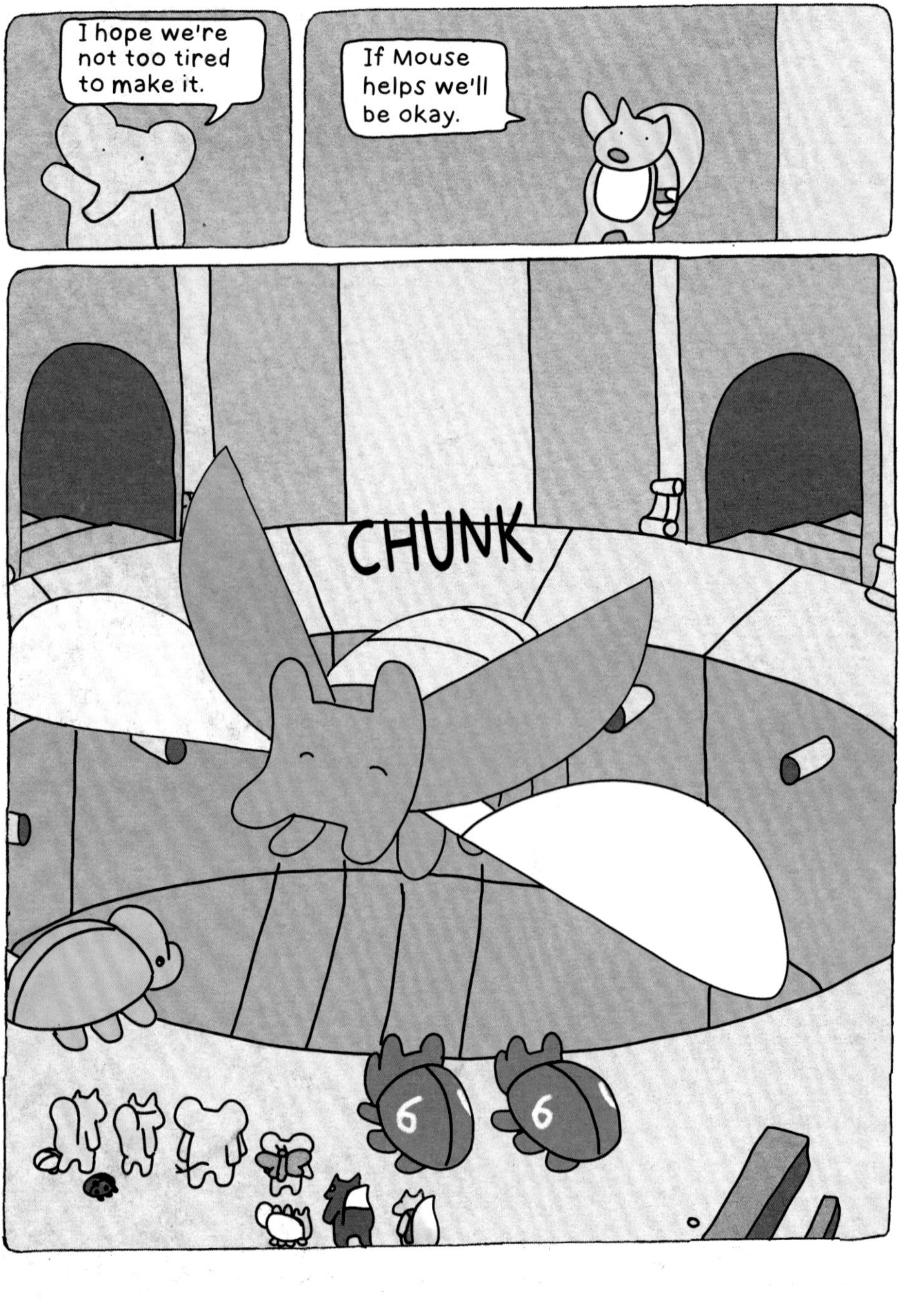
I hope we're not too tired to make it.
If Mouse helps we'll be okay.
CHUNK

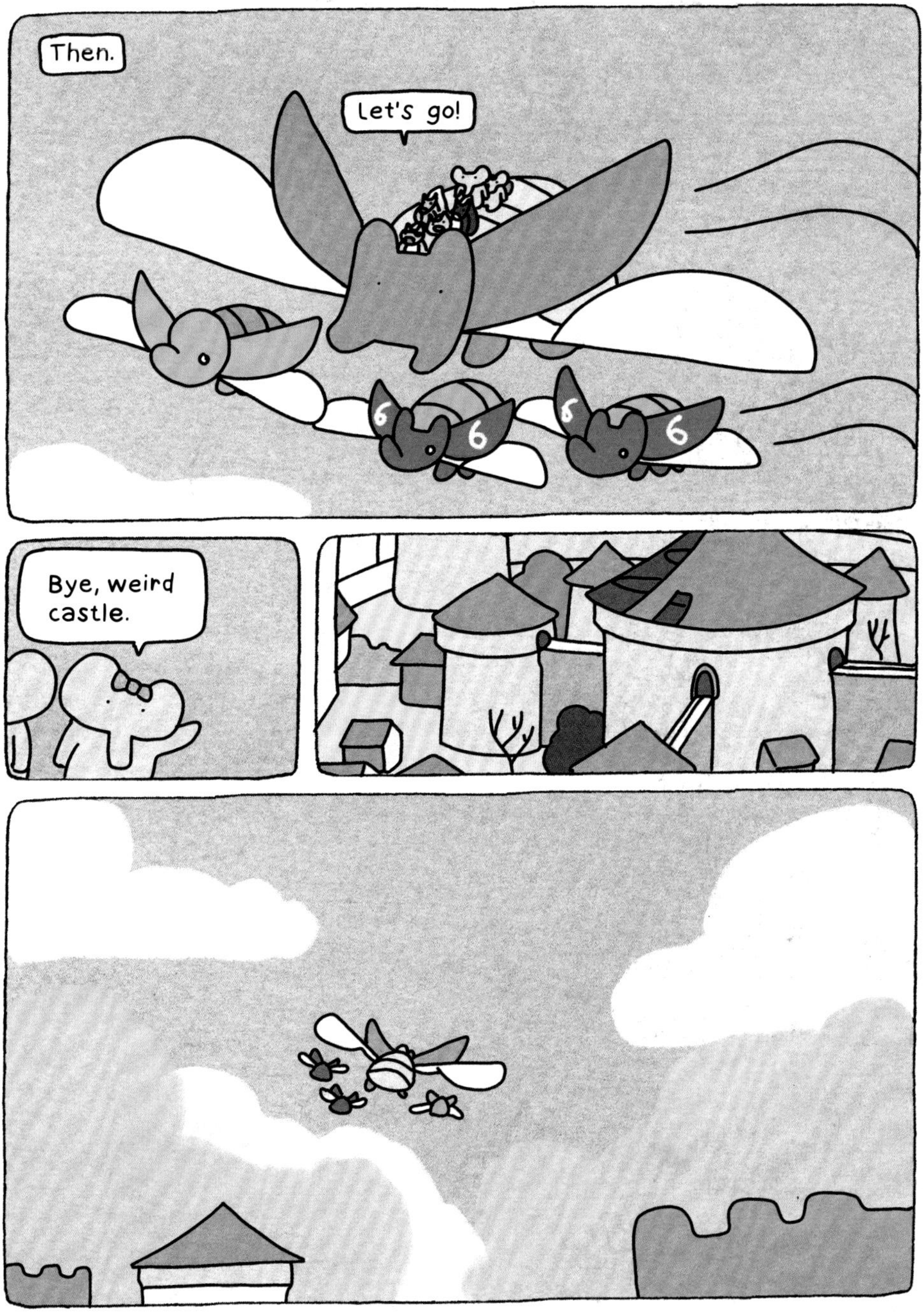
Then.
Let's go!
6
6
6
6
Bye, weird castle.

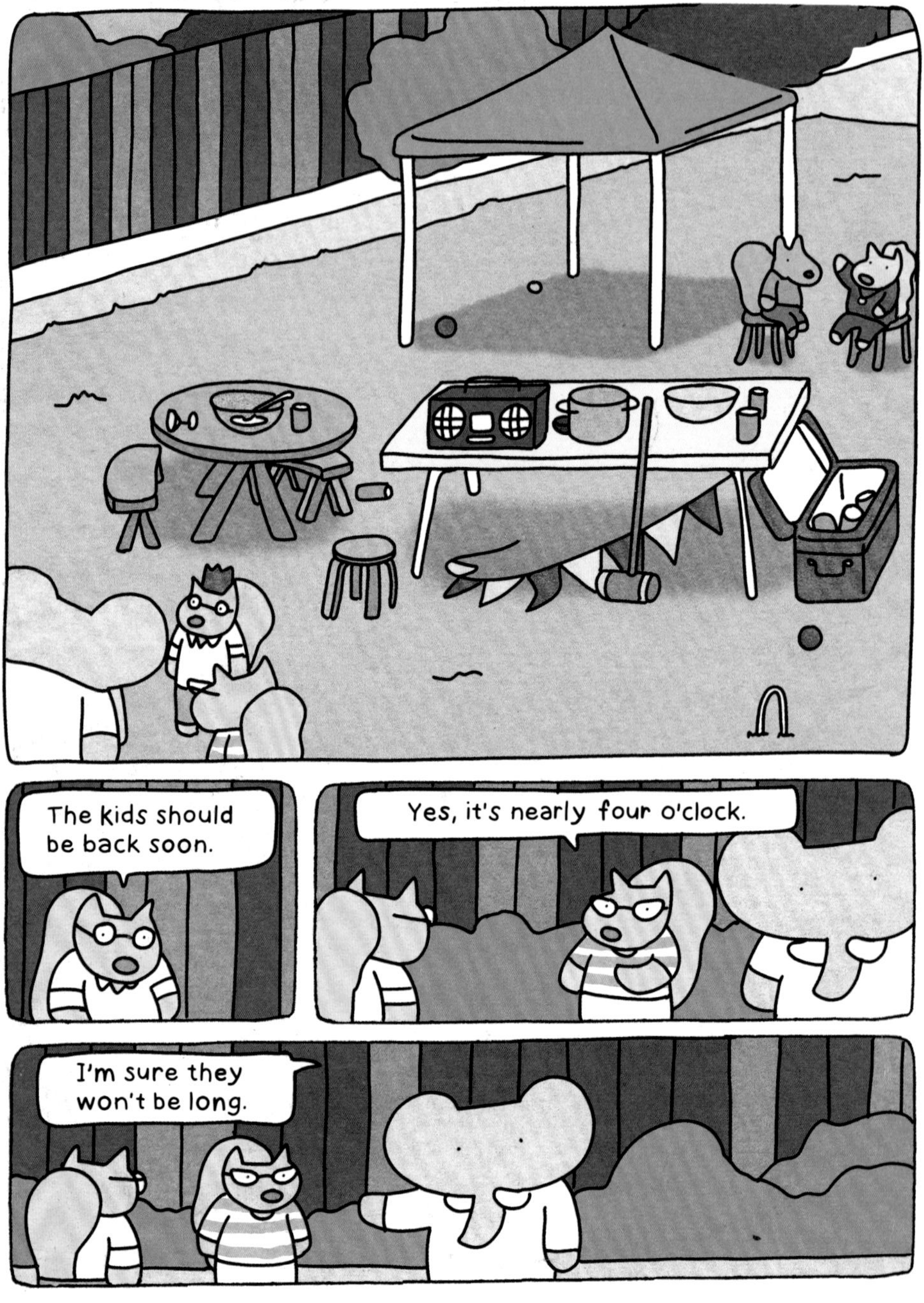
The kids should be back soon.
Yes, it's nearly four o'clock.
I'm sure they won't be long.

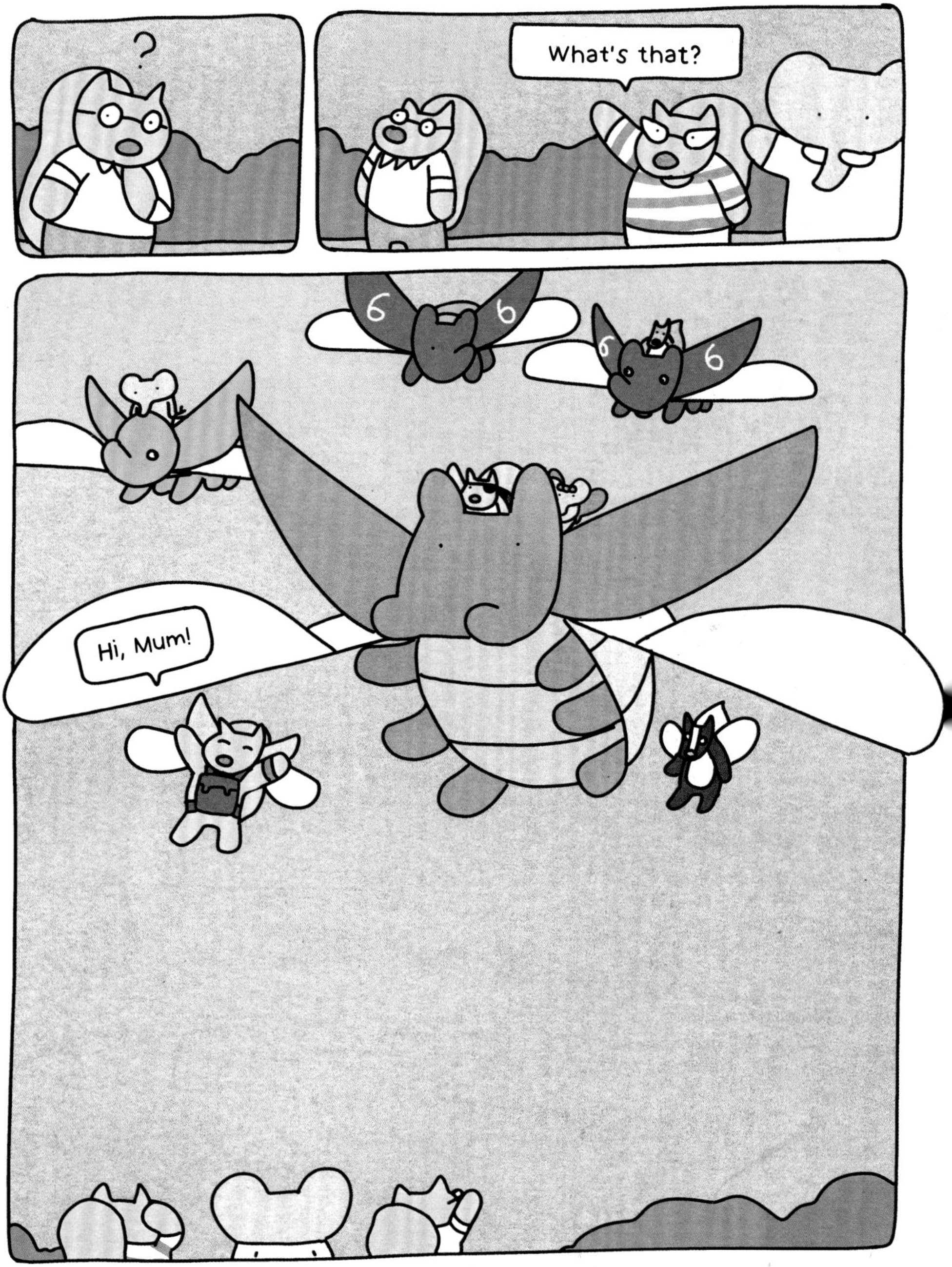
?
What's that?
6
6
6
6
Hi, Mum!

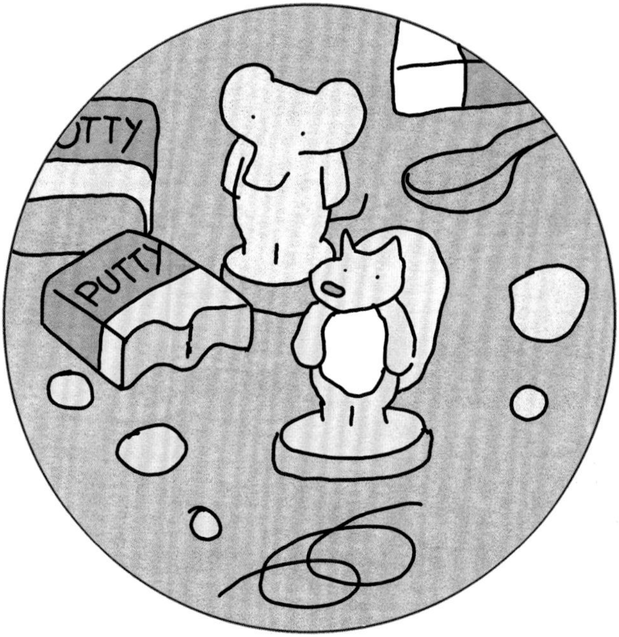
PUTTY
PUTTY

Chapter 11

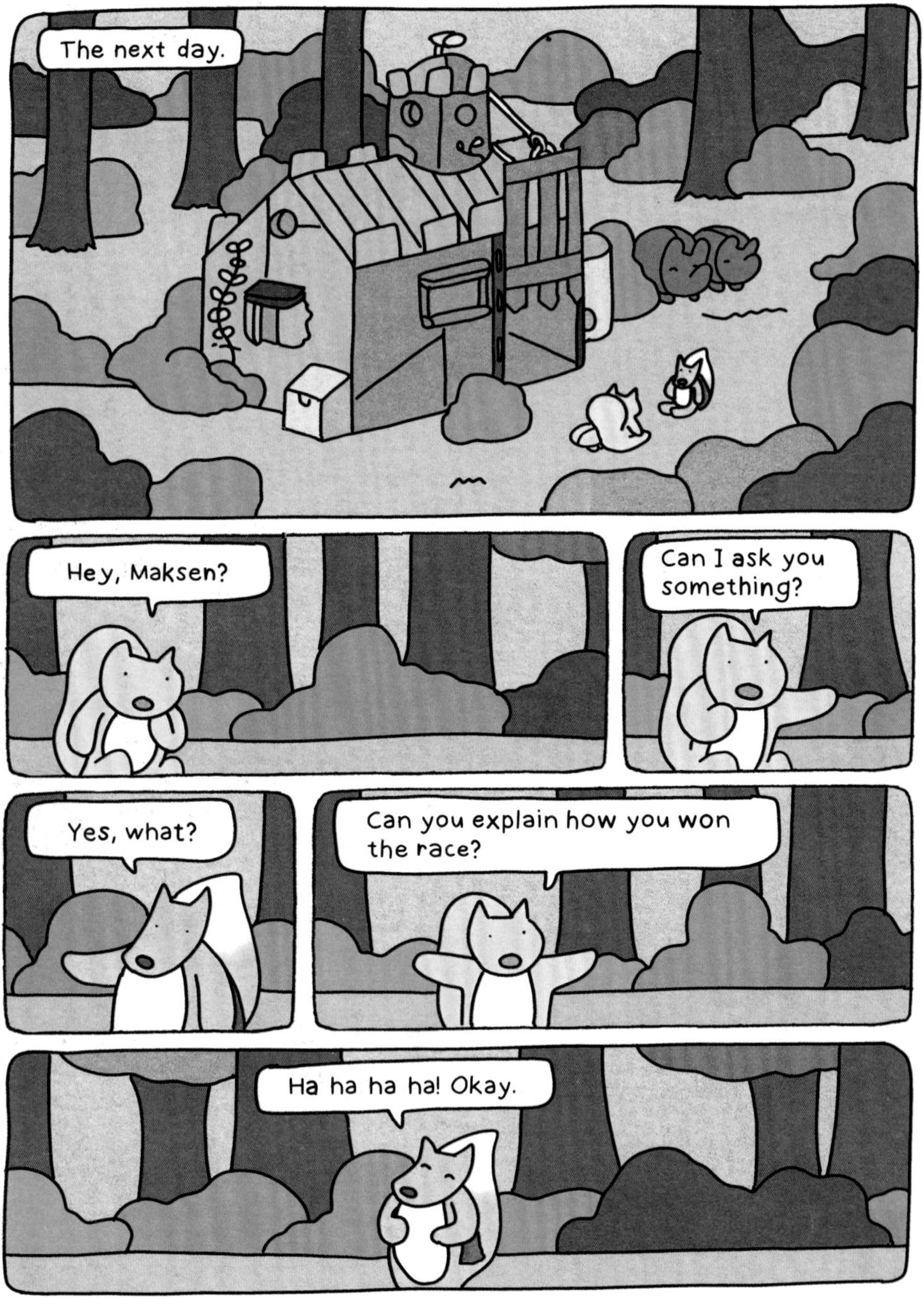
The next day.
Hey, Maksen?
Can I ask you something?
Yes, what?
Can you explain how you won the race?
Ha ha ha ha! Okay.

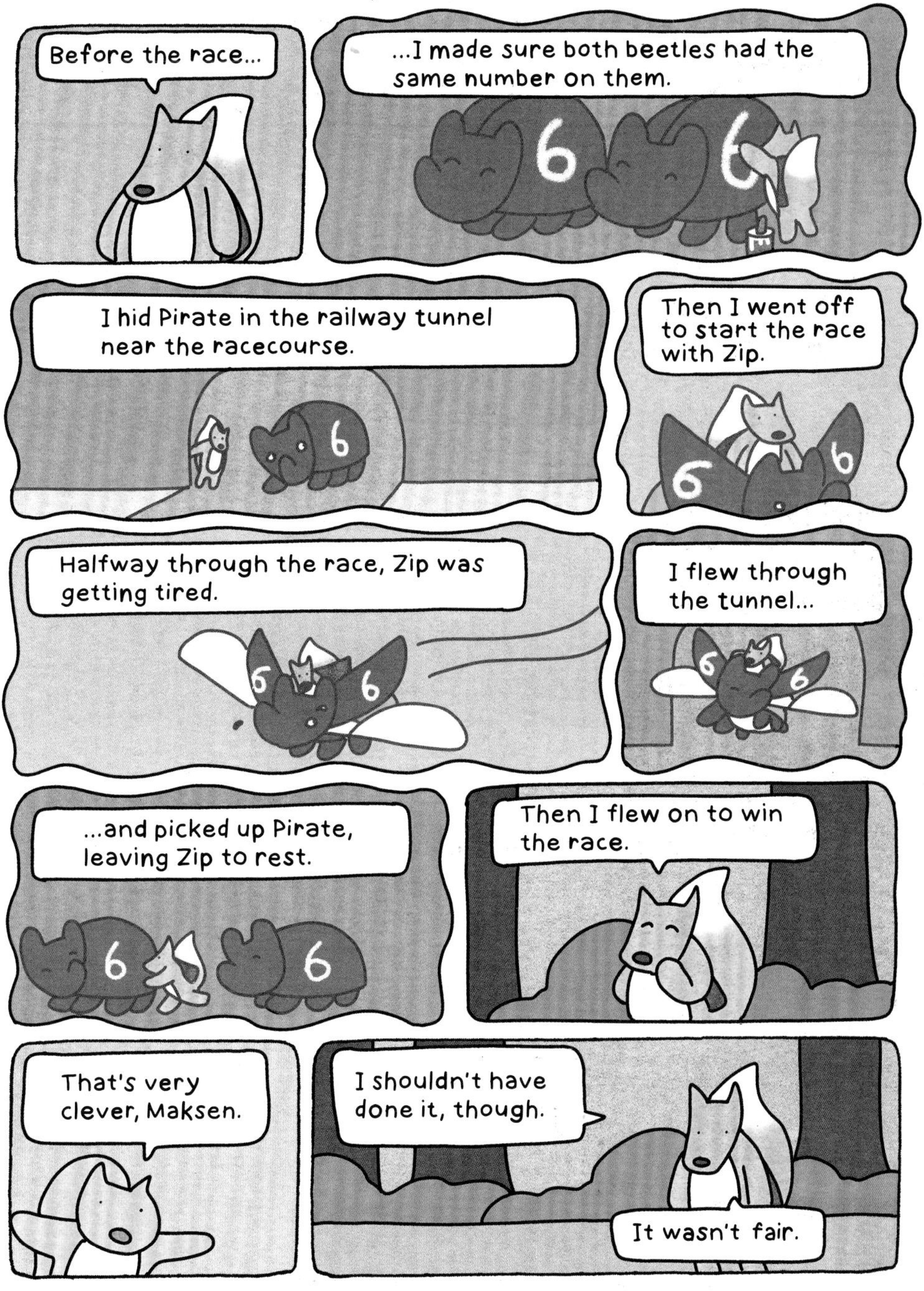

Before the race...
...I made sure both beetles had the same number on them.
6
6
I hid Pirate in the railway tunnel near the racecourse.
6
Then I went off to start the race with Zip.
6
6
Halfway through the race, Zip was getting tired.
6
6
I flew through the tunnel...
6
6
...and picked up Pirate, leaving Zip to rest.
6
6
Then I flew on to win the race.
That's very clever, Maksen.
I shouldn't have done it, though.
It wasn't fair.

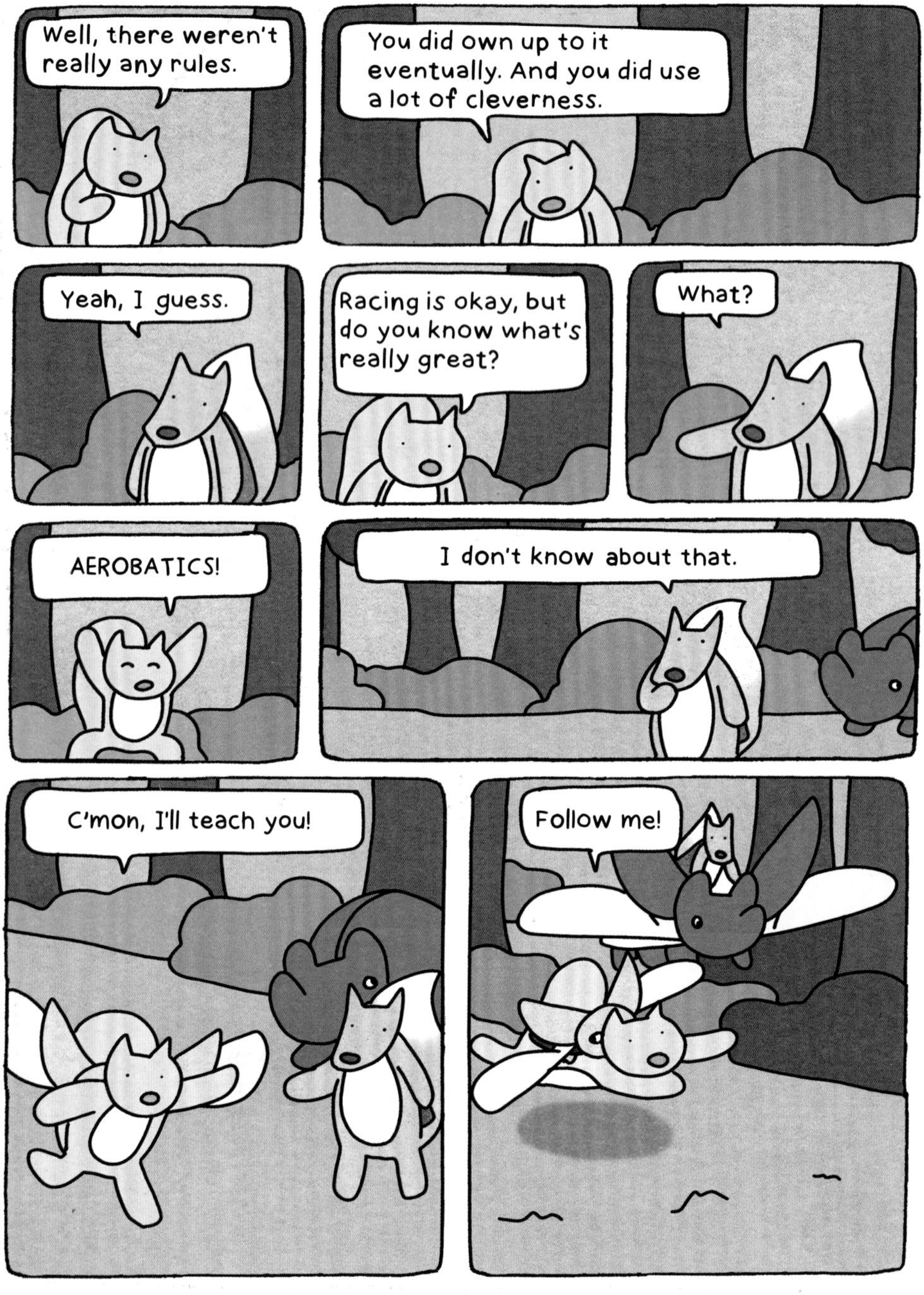
Well, there weren't really any rules.
You did own up to it eventually. And you did use a lot of cleverness.
Yeah, I guess.
Racing is okay, but do you know what's really great?
What?
AEROBATICS!
I don't know about that.
C'mon, I'll teach you!
Follow me!

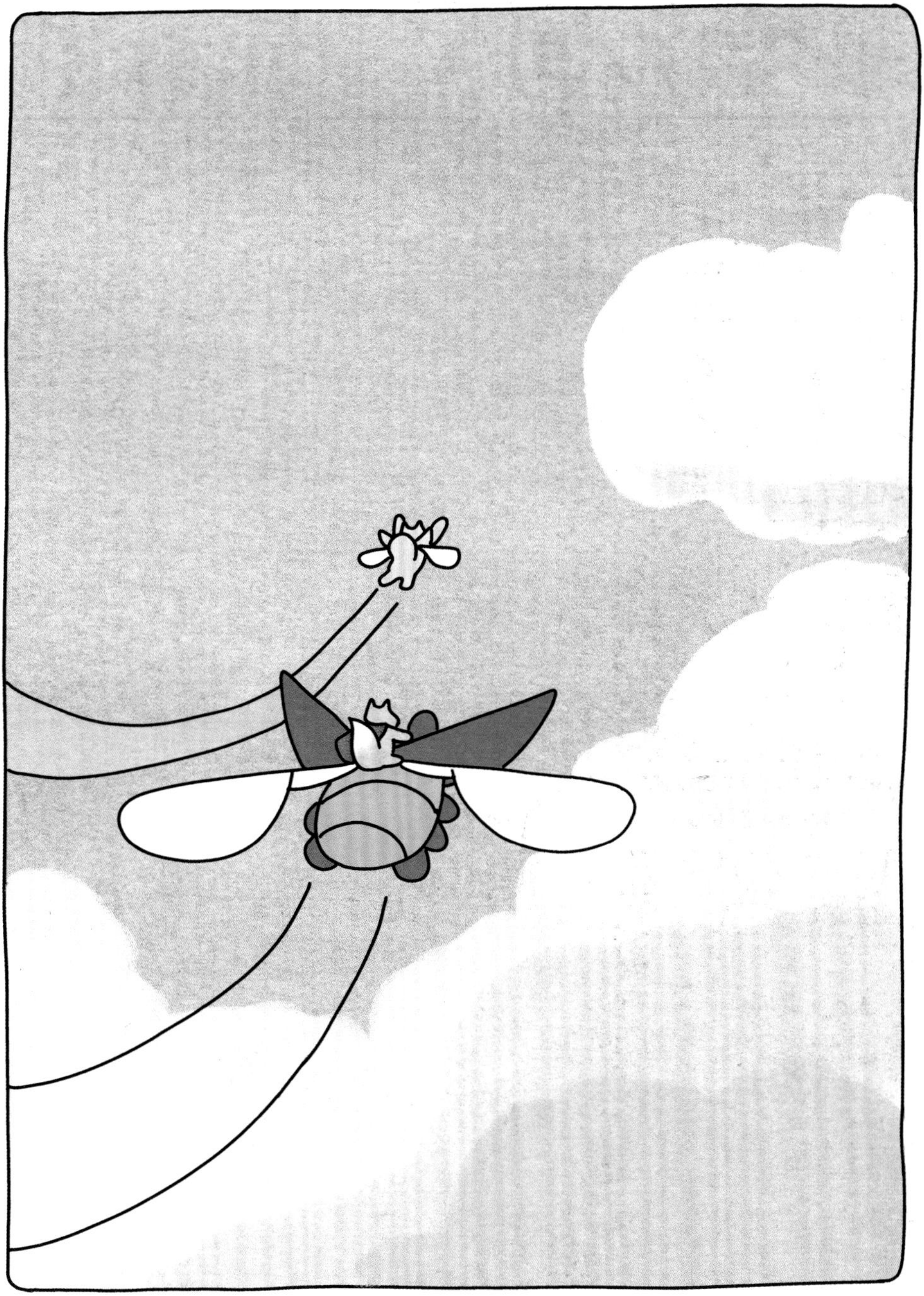

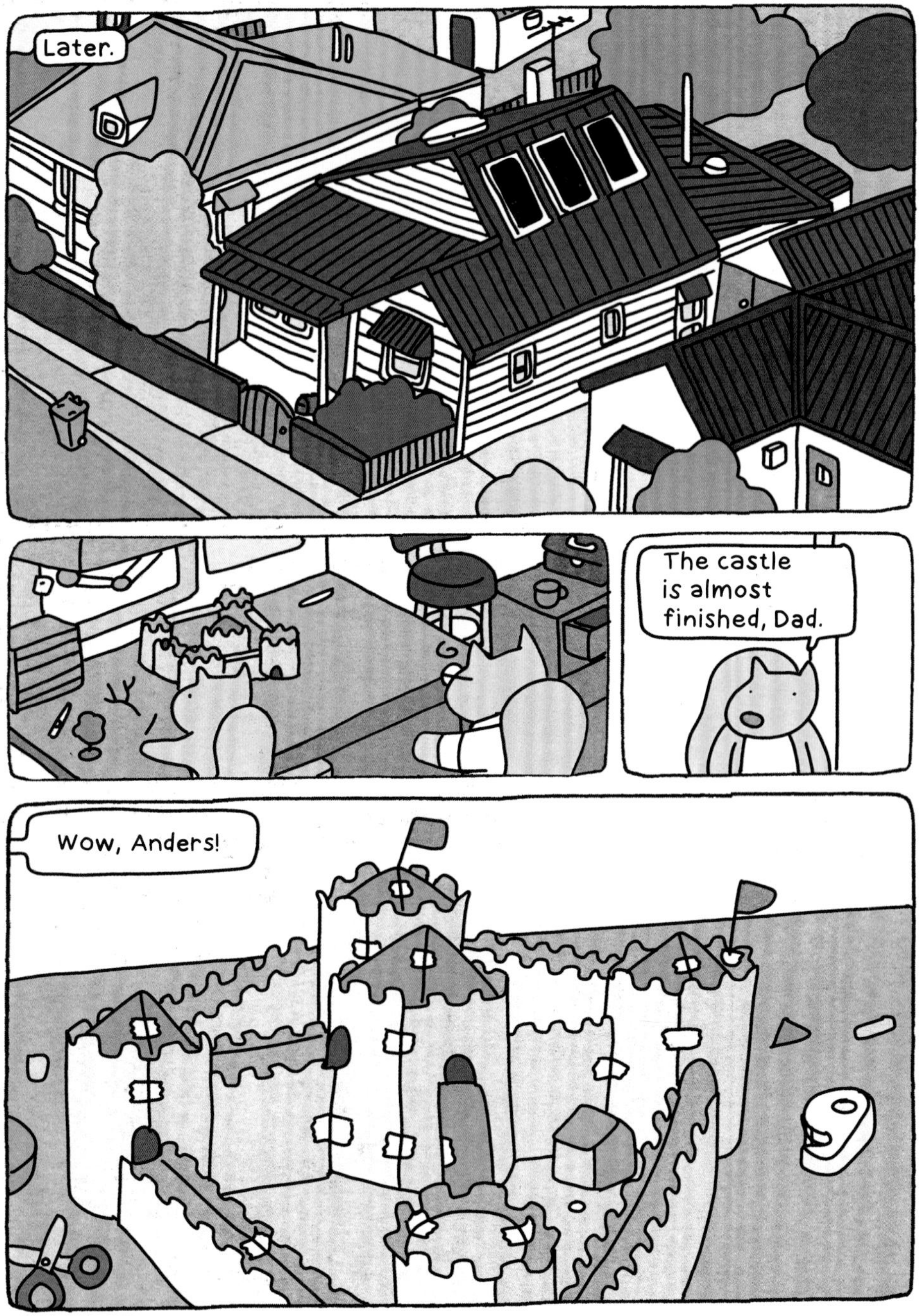
Later.
The castle is almost finished, Dad.
Wow, Anders!

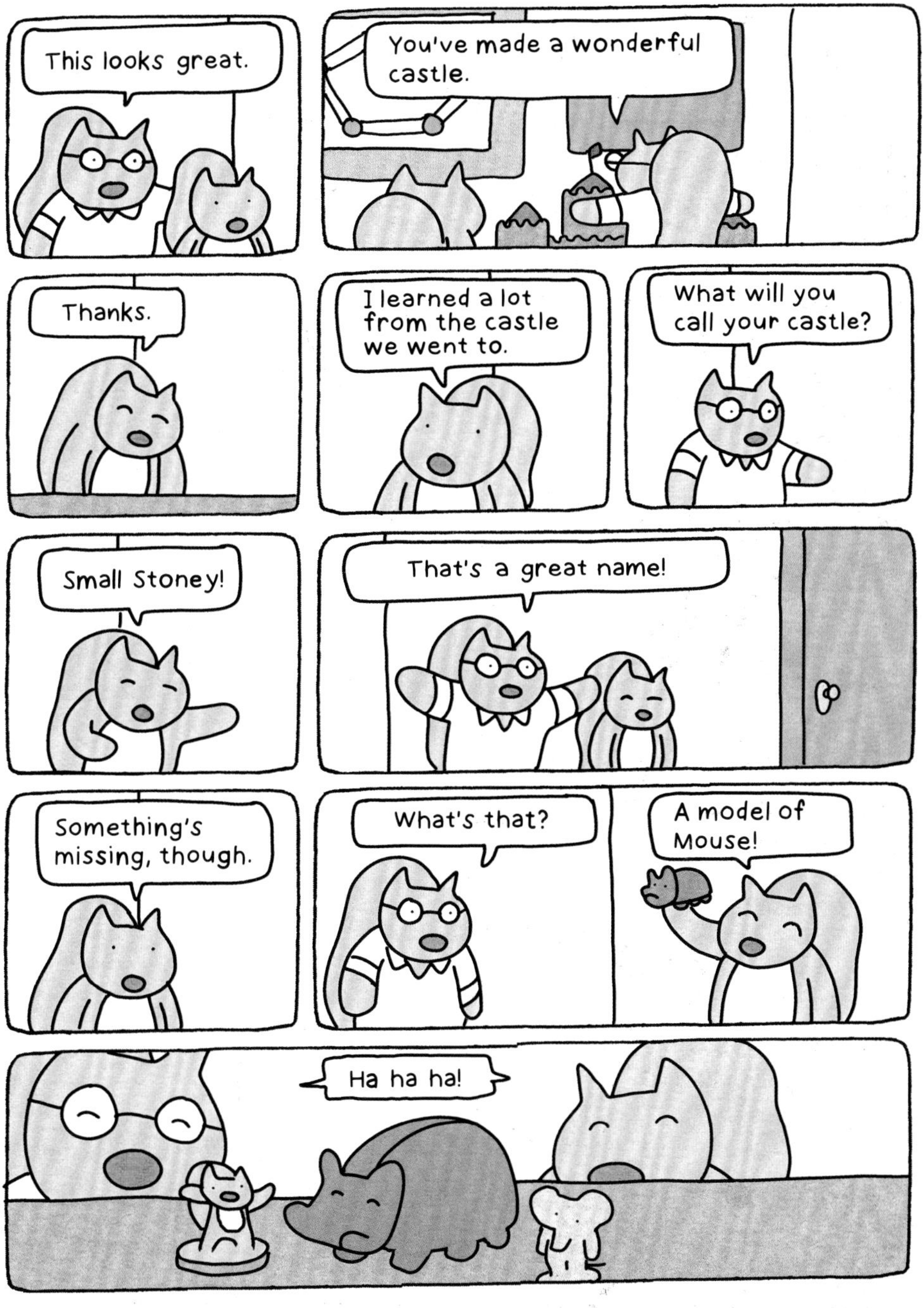
This looks great.
You've made a wonderful castle.
Thanks.
I learned a lot from the castle we went to.
What will you call your castle?
Small Stoney!
That's a great name!
Something's missing, though.
What's that?
A model of Mouse!
Ha ha ha!

Acknowledgements

Thanks to Erica Wagner, Elise Jones and
Sandra Nobes. Special thanks to Charlotte Watson.

About the Author

GREGORY MACKAY has been making comics since school.
He enjoys drawing and watercolour painting. He likes drawing
aeroplanes and machines, as well as building models and painting
pictures. Both *Anders and the Comet* and *Anders and the Volcano*,
his first books for children, have also been published in France,
and have been shortlisted for the Angoulême Festival, the most
prestigious comics awards in Europe, acknowledging the best
comics published across the world. *Anders and the Comet* was
also the winner of Australia's Silver Ledger Award, and in
2018 Gregory undertook a six-month Australia Council
for the Arts residency at the Keesing Studio at the
Cité Internationale des Arts in Paris.